The Counterfeiter's Daughter

A Sherlock Holmes Adventure

By

E.V. Blackwell

Published in the United States by Grey River Publications

Boise, Idaho

Copyright © 2017 E.V. Blackwell

The Counterfeiter's Daughter

A Sherlock Holmes Adventure

First Edition, June 2018

Library of Congress Number: TXu 2-064-983

ISBN: 978-1-7323978-0-4

CHAPTER 1

New Soil

Channel Dock - Calais 1884

Fine droplets beaded on the polished lid of the coffin, collecting until the surface could hold no more. They formed a rivulet and streamed down over the lip of the lid and across the polished brass nameplate. The young woman's black gloved hand reached out and gently wiped the moisture from the nameplate, her fingers slowly moving over the engraving. *Condensation, simple condensation; no doubt caused by the temperature difference between the inside of the coffin and the falling outside temperature. One of the strange truths of life; water could offer salvation or destruction - it was purely situational.* Her fingers traveled to the lip of the lid, checking the fit. A deep sigh escaped her lips as she lowered her head slightly, a few wisps of auburn hair falling from beneath her black bonnet. The seal seemed tight. She prayed that it was — not that she believed in prayer — purely a figure of speech. She just wanted her to be warm and safe, free from the bone-chilling damp that she had hated so much. "Next year," she recalled her saying, "Next year ma petite, you and I will be in Granada this time of year. Paris in Spring of course, but not in Winter." But the cold, grey damp that was winter in France was upon them, and the harsh reality was that Granada would never happen.

Thunder rumbled across the sky as dark clouds continued to amass over the channel. What had started as an occasional sprinkle of rain was now a steady patter, sending passengers waiting for the Rob Roy to dock scurrying for cover - umbrellas blossoming. She, however, remained in place - motionless next to the wagon that held her mother's coffin, oblivious to the rain.

"Child, come away before you catch your death," exclaimed the stout, older woman dressed in simple and worn mourning attire. Opening her umbrella, she hurried forward and gently pulled the younger woman, also attired in mourning but of finer quality, under the overhang of the ferry station. The older woman's grey blue eyes were kind and filled with compassion. Reaching out, she stroked the younger woman's cheek comfortingly.

"Edwina...you must understand, we only have your interests at heart. Your mother would have wanted..."

A flash of indignation sparked in the younger woman's weary, emerald eyes. Edwina Violette Schraeder Pennington stared at her aunt in disbelief, biting her lower lip as she struggled to temper her irritation.

"My mother... my mother would not want to be buried in a country she loathed...taken away from those she loved. How can you do this? Your own sister..."

"Edwina... child..."

"I'm not a child anymore Auntie Liesel," interrupted her niece, eyes red-rimmed and defiant. She tugged impatiently at the black satin ribbon under her chin, aggravated by the stiffness of her new bonnet. Edwina disliked wearing most head coverings, especially bonnets - preferring to wear her hair loose or tied back with a simple ribbon, but her aunt had insisted, citing the need for modesty on such a solemn occasion. England, her aunt warned her, was a country obsessed with propriety - it would not serve to make the wrong impression or come across as flippant. Edwina was painfully aware of the gravity of the situation but was at a loss to understand why she couldn't mourn her mother wearing something more comfortable like a black veil or straw boater.

"No... 'tis true... no longer a child," sighed the older woman dismally. Noting her niece's annoyance with the bonnet, she couldn't help but smile; there was so much of her sister in this child.

"Sometimes Edwina, we must make sacrifices. It's time to take your proper place in the world," she advised sagely, gently adjusting the ribbon under her chin.

The girl turned her head away and stared morosely out into the rain, and though her eyes threatened tears, Liesel Baecker knew her niece was determined not to let them flow. The child was resolute (cold and unfeeling her husband would say) that she would remain in control of her emotions and be strong. But Liesel Baecker knew her niece well enough to see through the stony mask; inside, the girl's heart was breaking. With a deep sigh, Liesel Baecker cast a mournful look at her sister's coffin resting on the dock, waiting to be loaded onto the ferry. She wiped vainly at the corners of her eyes for unlike her niece, she was barely able to contain her grief. *Patience ... you must have patience*, she reminded herself. Edwina's world had been upended by the tragic death of her mother; indeed, it had come as a shock to all concerned. It was true that her sister Katerina, usually so ebullient, had lately begun to suffer from debilitating bouts of melancholy - taking to her bed at a moment's whim. It wasn't the first time she had suffered so. After the loss of her young son and subsequent abandonment by her husband, she had spent nearly four months in her bed ... scarcely eating or leaving her room, barely speaking. But that had been many years prior, and after a period of mourning, she had seemed to rebound with new energy and enthusiasm, taking to the road in the warm summer months to travel about from city to city with her daughter, sharing a renewed zeal for life's adventures. A warm smile of remembrance touched the older woman's lips; they had truly been a sight to see . . . gypsies - the two of them more like sisters than mother and daughter. Katerina, even though well into her forties, was as enchanting and beautiful as ever, always the actress. The charmer of men...the social butterfly; and her daughter Edwina, who had inherited the beauty and strength of her mother if not her charm and skill with men. But what Edwina lacked in social graces and feminine wiles, she more than made up for in sheer intelligence, strength of character and bravura. They'd been so close, Katerina and her daughter, and truth be told, Liesel Baecker admitted to a certain amount of envy for she and her sister had never shared the same depth of bond. Katerina's impulsive and often wild nature had intimidated her. Edwina, however, seemed incapable of being intimidated; headstrong and fiercely independent, she was more than equal to her mother. She was used to moving freely between Vienna, where her university studies had occupied her, and Paris where her mother kept apartments. Unfortunately, it was now quite apparent that Katerina lacked her daughter's fortitude and resilience - a fact she had diligently concealed.

The Christmas holidays had been so lovely - mother and daughter spending time with Liesel and her husband at the farm in Salzburg. Katerina had exhibited not a hint of discontent or sadness then, only joy as she excitedly related how she was in discussion with Monsieur Robert Planquette, the renowned director of the Théâtre des Nouveautés on the boulevard des Italiens. He was launching a restaging of his 3-act operetta, La Cantinière and had been impressed with her audition for the lead. She had been ecstatic and confident at the prospect of returning to the stage. Even though she was now in the latter part of middle-age, Katerina was still a flawless beauty and talented chanteuse, and as always, the enchantress of men. Her return to the stage seemed a foregone conclusion. She had even begun to restrict her consumption of wine and had all but given up the taking of Absinthe - so devoted was she to the task of preparing for her stage return. In fact, the only nostrum she allowed herself was the taking of Laudanum in her bedtime tea to soothe her nerves and aid her sleep. So, Mother and daughter returned to Paris just prior to the New Year and life had resumed as usual; Katerina throwing herself back into preparations for La Cantinière and Edwina returning to her friends and studies at the Sorbonne. It had all seemed so promising until the morning of December 27th, when Madame Levan, the elderly and oft annoyed occupant in the flat below, returned from visiting her cousins in the country to find her ceiling ruined and water steadily dripping through the weakened plaster onto her dining room table. Seething and barely able to contain her indignation, (it wasn't the first time the silly "actress" upstairs had overflowed the bathtub), she strode up the central staircase determined to make her feelings known. Her anger only increased as the carpeting soaked through her best shoes as she approached the door to the flat. After pounding on the door for some fifteen minutes with her walking stick and getting no response, she angrily descended the stairs and sent the neighbor's boy for the landlord, retiring to her dining room to brood and stare sullenly at her waterlogged ceiling as she waited.

Monsieur Clouvet, portly, round-faced, and suffering from a well-earned hangover, was desperately trying to sleep in and ignored the knocking at his front door at first. However, when it didn't abate after 20 minutes, he reluctantly pulled on his worn robe and peered out the glass panel in his front door. On seeing the small boy and recognizing him as one of his tenant's brood from the flats at Rue St. Benoit, he groaned aloud and reluctantly opened the door. Twenty minutes passed and then he gave up on trying to follow the child's disjointed story; something about water (he was only 6 after all). He pulled on his work clothes, thinking it was once again a fractured pipe under the second-floor bath, and grudgingly agreed to leave the warmth of his flat. Of course, there was no rush, and he allowed himself a stop at the Café de Flore for a quick Café Crème. By the time he arrived, the water had spread steadily across the entirety of the ceiling and was seeping down the walls. After turning off the water main and resigning himself to a long and tiresome task, he took his tools and slowly climbed the entry staircase. Halfway up, he was confounded and alarmed to find not only the carpet on the second-floor balcony to be waterlogged, but the top flight of stairs itself. His trepidation increased, water oozing up through the carpet into his shoes as he approached the Schrader's apartment. He knocked on the door and waited, but there was no reply. After knocking for quite some time, Monsieur Clouvet, who by now was thoroughly unsettled, used his master key to enter the apartment. Five minutes later he emerged, his round-face the color of pastry dough and dazedly sent for the police. There was no broken pipe...only the overflow from the bathtub where Katerina Schraeder had floated for three days. She had apparently drowned after drifting off and slipping under the water; a bottle of laudanum sat on the edge of the tub - a half-empty glass of wine overturned on the floor. It was an end no one had foreseen.

The rain finally slowed to a slight drizzle, and Edwina watched distractedly as they began to load her belongings and her mother's coffin onto the ferry. She turned to her aunt and shook her head, her eyes taking on a plaintive expression as she broke the deep silence between them.

"I don't understand... why this? To send me away... send her away... to a strange country... to a father I haven't seen since I was 9. This husband who left her when she needed him most - left us. How can this be for the best? I don't know him Auntie Liesel. I don't know London. What of my studies? I was set to graduate soon; there is so much more to learn." Edwina's voice trailed off as the older woman reached out and hugged her reassuringly.

"Life is more than books child...you're 23 now. I was married and had 4 children at your age. Time for you to settle down. Your father has sent for you, and despite what you think, he is a good man Edwina. He loves you... he loved your mother..."

"Loved?" snorted Edwina with an air of disbelief. "That man abandoned her... us... after... after... Julian..." Her voice wavered slightly and then faltered - her eyes growing darkly veiled as she thought of her brother. In a flash, the painful image rose to the surface; little Julian, barely 6, cold, wet, and lifeless on the shore of Lake Fuschl. She bit her lip and forced the memory out of her mind.

"What kind of "husband" does that?" she muttered.

4

Her aunt's expression grew solemn as she took her niece's hands in hers, pressing them in an attempt to comfort her.

"Grief affects us in different ways Edwina. There's more to this than you know child - you mustn't judge him. It was such a difficult time for everyone. I loved my sister dearly, but she was not the easiest person to live with and there are things that happened between your mother and father that...well... just suffice to say all is not what it seemed. It's time for you to forgive the injuries of the past - real and imagined. Your father needs you, and whether you realize it or not, you need him."

"But why can't I stay here or go back to Vienna to finish my studies?"

"And then what Edwina?"

"I'll find a position... in Vienna or Paris.... perhaps teaching or research assistant at University... I'll take over mother's apartments and..."

Aunt Liesel managed a sad smile - the child just didn't understand.

"To live on your own? Your reputation will be ruined for certain child. A proper young lady would never take apartments on her own."

"Mother lived on her own," Edwina protested fiercely, her cheeks flushing brightly at the suggestion that she was somehow not capable of taking care of herself.

A frown darkened the older woman's face as she searched for the appropriate words to convey her feelings. Her sister's choice of a bohemian lifestyle had long been a source of heartache for the family. How could she convey, to this impressionable and adventurous young woman, that reputation and appearance were paramount in her future success as a wife and mother? The reckless choices one made in youth always came back to haunt the elder years; her sister was a prime example.

"Your mother, in choosing to be an actress, adopted a certain lifestyle and sacrificed her reputation in many ways," she said with a melancholy sigh. "Although, I will concede that she enjoyed success, ultimately you see what befell her – the unfortunate result. That, my dear child, will not happen to you. Your father and I will make certain of it. You will go to London and be a good daughter to your father. He will look after you, and when the time is right, he will arrange a suitable marriage. You'll learn to be a good wife and a good mother."

A look, somewhat akin to horror contorted Edwina's face. "But what if I don't want that Auntie? What if I want more?"

The older woman shook her head in resignation as she once again refastened the ribbon on her niece's bonnet.

"More? What more could you possibly want Edwina? Don't be silly child. All this book learning has muddled your brain. It's a man's world Edwina, leave the "more" to them. It's what they are suited for. Our purpose here is to be their helpmate - the Scriptures tell us so. The sooner you accept this, the easier it will be. No man wants a wife that is cleverer than he."

It was at that point that Edwina finally realized the argument was futile. She loved her Aunt Liesel dearly, but once the subject of Scriptures was brought up, she knew she would never be able to persuade her. Her aunt and uncle were simple, hard-working, god-fearing country folk. They would never understand her thirst for knowledge or independence. Although they were considerably relieved that she exhibited no desire to follow in her mother's footsteps and take to the stage, they had decided her studies, her passion for knowledge, was almost as detrimental and plainly an exercise in frivolity. They had no comprehension of her quest for knowledge, viewing it only as a tactic to delay accepting the responsibilities of a mature woman; a suitable marriage, children and managing a household. A world where men and women would stand toe to toe, making decisions jointly and on an equal basis, was inconceivable and frightening to them; for Edwina however, it was what she longed for most. Change was in the air. Women were beginning to find their voice, their courage. Organizations were springing to life and gaining momentum all over continental Europe, spurred on by the bravery of Mrs. Pankhurst and her sisters in London. Despite being the origin of the movement, England, however, seemed frozen in place. In the words of her aunt, "a man's world"; a circumstance that added to her ever-growing list of apprehensions regarding her soon-to-be new home.

Two short blasts of the Rob Roy's whistle reminded the onlookers that the ferry would soon be leaving. With a bleak expression, Edwina turned her attention toward the dock, watching the passengers slowly traverse the gangplank. Aunt Liesel sighed sadly and wiped at her eyes. She reached out and took Edwina's hands in hers.

"Patience child... be strong. Do this for your mother - she would be so proud of you."

The stoic mask slipped a bit as Edwina's eyes brimmed with tears, but none fell as she compressed her lips and took a deep breath forcing herself to remain in control. The older woman's face suffused with compassion and dismay; such resolve and stoicism in one so young couldn't be healthy. Reaching out, she hugged her niece lovingly and deposited a maternal kiss on her forehead.

"Think of this as just one more adventure Edwina," she soothed. As she spoke, she reached down into her portmanteau and withdrew a small walnut and ebony Japanese trick box.

"This is for you, dearest..."

Edwina's eyes flickered in recognition and surprise as she reached out and carefully took the box, her fingers gently caressing the polished surface of the lid. A myriad of alternating ebony and ivory inlays decorated the lid in an intricate sliding pattern of geometric shapes and designs; all arranged so carefully that only the correct alignment would unlock the box.

"Mothers'... I haven't seen it in months," she murmured, smiling slightly as she remembered the many happy hours she had spent as a child unlocking the patterns on the box. The process itself often providing more pleasure than the actual treasure hidden inside.

"She asked me to keep it for her. I don't know why, but she insisted." Her aunt shrugged. "I was only to give it to you should something happen."

With a small sigh, Edwina carefully placed the box in her tapestry valise all the while wondering why her mother had felt the need to hide the box. While pondering the implications of this and what the box could contain, her aunt reached into her pocket and pulled out one more item, carefully wrapped in an immaculate white handkerchief.

"This also... Edwina."

Once more, Edwina felt a lump rising in her throat as she took the object and began to unwrap it, the familiar shape taking form. Her mother's lapel watch; a simple silver pocket watch on a bow shaped pin, adorned with two small, but splendid emeralds in the center of the bow. It had been a cherished piece, which her mother had worn daily - no matter the occasion or dress required. A frown furrowed her brow as she thought on this and she looked to her Aunt questioningly.

"Auntie - how is this here? Did this not make it onto Mr. Bertram's list?" she asked, with some suspicion.

Immediately after her mother's death, the Pennington's solicitor, Mr. Geoffrey H. Bertram of London, had arrived to take inventory and control of Katerina's possessions for later distribution according to first, the marriage laws (Katerina and Wilfred Pennington had never legally divorced) and secondly, her will. In accordance with the marriage laws, only items given before Katerina's death could remain in the recipient's possession - in her death, all of her property and possessions were inventoried, locked up and transferred to her husband for distribution or disposal as he saw fit. There was no requirement for him to honor the wishes of his late wife as her property was now his.

Aunt Liesel met her gaze and managed a small, though slightly embarrassed smile.

"Such a little thing... so easy to get lost... missed," she explained tentatively and with such an air of chagrin that Edwina realized with much amazement that her aunt, this woman who was the model of all that was honest and forthright, had taken the watch and hidden it away from the solicitor.

"Your mother would want you to have this... as God is in the Heavens I know this. I don't need a law to tell me this. Take it and honor your mother." The old woman's voice was strong and confident as she spoke; with a tender smile, she reached out and grasped her niece's fingers, curling them tightly around the pocket watch.

Edwina's fingers trembled a bit as she carefully opened the case of the pocket watch to reveal the inner compartment. It contained a miniature photograph of her mother holding her brother by the hand; a photograph which had been taken only 3 months prior to his death. Unable to contain her emotions any longer, she dissolved into tears and collapsed into her aunt's arms, weeping. The older woman looked relieved - *finally, a show of emotion* - and let her cry for a few moments. Upon releasing her, she pinned the watch to her shawl.

"It's ok child...the time to weep is now. As time passes, you'll be able to remember her without weeping. Remember the good things - forgive the bad.

Be kind... be patient... and give your father a chance to be your father. But never forget... your mother loved you and you are her daughter through and through. "

The Rob Roy's whistle sounded one last time, and with a wistful expression, she took her niece by the hand and holding on tightly, began to walk her towards the gangplank.

"Your Aunt Gretchen..." began Aunt Liesel in explanation.

"Gretchen?" Edwina interrupted, frowning at the unfamiliarity of the name.

"Aunt Gretchen... your father's sister. she manages his household, she will meet you at the dock and accompany..."

"Won't my father be there?" Edwina exclaimed, incredulous.

A look of regret clouded the older woman's face as she shook her head, choosing her words carefully to try to soothe her niece.

"Your father... he is, according to Mr. Bertram, an extremely busy man and..."

"Of course, he is!" snorted Edwina disdainfully, her eyes flashing once more. She pulled on her gloves against the chill of the dock and stared up the gangplank at the waiting ferry.

"Give him a chance Edwina," pleaded her Aunt, pushing back a few errant wisps from under her niece's bonnet, "You owe that to yourself and your mother."

Edwina stared up at the sky watching as the grey darkness continued to mass overhead. After a moment, she seemed to come to a decision and with a deep sigh, turned to her aunt.

"Yes... of course Auntie," she sighed in resignation, leaning in to hug her aunt. After depositing a heartfelt kiss and thanking her aunt for all she had done, she picked up her valise and with an air of steadfast resolve, made her way up the gangplank. At the top, she suddenly paused and turned back to her Aunt, a bright, fierce little smile lighting her face.

"I'll give him a chance Auntie. I do promise ... but it will be on my terms," she announced staunchly and with that, she smiled once again and disappeared into the crowds on the deck of the ferry.

Liesel Baecker stood on the dock, a slight, almost proud smile brightening her face as she watched the Rob Roy move away from the dock and out into the channel. She watched it until it had all but virtually disappeared on the horizon and then headed back to the small farm wagon. Time to head back to Salzburg. She had a long journey ahead of her, as did Edwina. But as she thought of her niece, a sense of admiration and pride swelled in her breast overshadowing her maternal instinct to fret. Edwina was well on her way in the world...and of course... she would do so on her own terms; it couldn't be any other way. She was, after all, her sister's daughter.

»»««

Arrival at Dover

8

The meager sunlight that had managed to filter through the grayness of the sky was already beginning to fade by the time the Rob Roy pulled into the dock at Dover. Edwina closed her sketchbook and peered restlessly out the tiny porthole in the passenger saloon at the approaching white cliffs, uttering an audible sigh of relief. She had retreated to the cramped compartment, along with most of the passengers, after the weather had taken a nasty turn. At first, she had tried to be sociable, attempting to engage her fellow shipmates in polite conversation but had been coldly rebuffed. Oh, there had been a few warm smiles and a furtive nod or two from the gentlemen, but they also ignored her once their accompanying ladies noticed their attentions had wandered. The women were particularly aloof, regarding her suspiciously and were, on more than one occasion, blatantly contemptuous and disapproving in their glances; literally nudging their escorts away from her as if she carried a plague of some sort. It was a mystery she couldn't fathom. How could one woman, simply dressed in mourning attire, elicit the ire and resentment of the female occupants of the salon solely by her presence? In the end, she gave up trying to understand it and withdrew to a small bench in the corner by a porthole, busying herself sketching. The English were a rude lot she concluded. No wonder her mother had loathed the country. Hopefully her father's family would be more welcoming.

The loud clang of the gangplank being dropped into place signaled that they were docked at last. Eager to be free of the stuffy confines of the passenger saloon, Edwina gathered up her valise and quickly followed the steady stream of passengers out of the ship and down the gangplank. She filled her lungs with the cold, damp air, bonnet in hand - hair streaming out behind her and frowned, scanning the crowd on the pier. How in the devil was she going to recognize her aunt? The pier was lined with wagons and carriages waiting for passengers, and she had no idea what to look for or even what her Aunt Gretchen looked like. She didn't have long to wonder, however, for as she stepped onto the pier, a portly woman clothed in black, gray hair pulled tightly into a severe bun that was covered with an even tighter bonnet, marched towards her. Behind her, trailed a frail looking girl of about 16 in a maid's uniform and two liverymen. It was evident before she even spoke, this was Aunt Gretchen. Judging by the bright flush of her face and furrow of her brow, she was less than pleased.

"What manner of wickedness is this?! Have you no shame child?"

Edwina gaped at her - too astonished to reply, confused by the woman's anger. A disturbing trend seemed to be emerging.

"Your hat child, where is it?" hissed the woman abruptly as she grabbed Edwina's valise and began to rummage through it.

"My hat? I don't ... understand. It was giving me a headache Madame, so I removed it," she replied warily. There it was again ... obvious anger, and she'd barely stepped off the ferry. What could it possibly be?

The old woman grunted at her in obvious disapproval all the while still searching her valise. On finding the bonnet, she murmured an earnest, "Praise God," and proceeded to jam the hat onto her niece's head, drawing the ribbons

9

tight under her chin.

"No time to pin you - this will have to do for now. At least you are covered. Gracious . . . the very idea... swanning about uncovered ... hair all undone - in the presence of gentlemen mind you and your mother not even in the ground yet."

"Madame, I meant no offense," she stammered in embarrassment.

What? Her hair? Could this possibly be the reason for all the hard stares she had encountered on the ferry? It seemed ludicrous. Clearly a cultural difference - perhaps if she explained.

"In Paris, we have no such custom Madame. I do apologize," Edwina offered sincerely, hoping that the explanation would soothe any ruffled sensibilities. Despite her feelings about having to leave her home and studies, she didn't wish to cause anyone distress - and certainly, not on the first day.

Mrs. Gretchen Pennington stiffened and proudly drew herself up to all her 5 foot 4 inches. She peered up at her niece, who towered over her by almost three inches, with icy, haughty brown eyes that reflected her open disdain.

"You are in England now - a decent country, not France nor Austria. In addition, I am not a "Madam". I am your Aunt Gretchen and you will address me as Aunt Gretchen or at the very least, Mrs. Pennington. Do you understand? Now, let me look at you for it seems to me that you are entirely the wrong shape."

Edwina could only stare at her aunt - too stunned by the harshness of her words to offer a reply. She meekly allowed herself to be pulled forward towards the carriage stand, which was now illumined by the gas lamps overhead.

Mrs. Pennington's mouth compressed, her lips drawn so tightly as to lose all color; she studied the girl in the flickering light.

"I can see your ankles child. Only women of ill repute show their ankles. Is that what you are then? Will you shame your father so?"

Edwina's cheeks suffused with chagrin and rising annoyance. She took a deep breath, a tightness in her chest as she struggled to maintain her composure. This country was stuck firmly in the past; her worst fears were coming true.

"A shortened skirt allows me to walk swiftly and confidently Aunt Gretchen. It's quite in fashion on the continent. Quite frankly, I fail to see how the sight of the top of my boots or shoes makes me immoral or could lead to the fall of civilization as we know it," she sighed, trying to temper the exasperation she felt. Surely if she remained calm and unemotional, she could reason with the woman.

The sound of the slap echoed across the dock, startling the liverymen and the young maid who were loading her baggage onto a cart. They paused to glance nervously in her direction and then quickly returned to their work, avoiding any further looks. Edwina dazedly raised her hand to her cheek, gingerly touching it - a swell of anger rising up from within. Her eyes flashed fiercely, and she clenched her fists tightly at her sides, fighting her first impulse which was to return the slap, march back down the dock and purchase

10

passage on the next return ferry to France. But as she glared at her Aunt, reality slowly crept in. She had only a few francs in her valise - certainly not enough to purchase her passage. All her money was now under the control of Mr. Bertram and her father - who would dole it out as they saw fit. One of the things she treasured most, her independence, was slowly being stripped from her. She took several slow deep breaths - forcing herself to calm down. Now was not the time to overreact, she needed to think and study the situation - with a clear and focused mind. She only hoped that her father would be more reasonable. So, for now, she remained silent and kept her eyes fixed on the ground, brooding darkly about her current situation.

Mrs. Pennington somberly studied the girl and then perceiving that she had regained control, allowed a small, self-righteous smile - her anger somewhat soothed by her niece's retreat into silence.

"That's much better. Well, I can certainly see that I have been sent a mighty task before me. As a good Christian, it is my duty to accept this - daunting as it may be. I place my trust in the Lord — with his gracious blessings, much prayer and righteous discipline — I will mold you into a proper lady. Tomorrow, we begin with your appearance and manners ... you are surely lacking decorum in both. To be expected, I suppose. What my dear brother was thinking — to take up with an actress — I shall never understand. Now, don't just stand there, all slack-jawed and moony child. Get inside the carriage - the day is fading, and we have far to go. Hanna will help you with your valise."

Having no more to say, Mrs. Pennington gave her a firm nudge towards the waiting carriage and then strode off towards the wagon to supervise the loading of the baggage and coffin.

"Come inside then Miss, it's frightfully cold now the day has gone. I'll carry your bag for you – go on and climb in."

The voice, young and timidly sweet, called her back to the present and Edwina, turned to find the young maid smiling up at her. The sight of a truly friendly face warmed her heart, and she managed a smile.

"Yes - it is getting cold, but I'll carry the bag. It's awfully heavy, too many books I'm afraid," she explained, hefting the heavy bag as she followed the girl towards the carriage. "Your name is Hanna, isn't it?"

The girl, who couldn't have been more than 16, was as slender as a reed and looked as if the next stiff breeze would snap her in two. A slight pout darkened the girl's face as she glanced nervously towards the wagon where Mrs. Pennington was still supervising the loading of the baggage.

"Yes Miss, Hanna, and it's all right Miss - about the bag being heavy. I don't mind," she whispered. "Please, Mrs. Pennington will be right cross if she sees me slacking."

The obvious fear in the young maid's voice gave her pause and remembering the slap she had been greeted with, Edwina's expression darkened with anxiety. Her cheek still stung a bit from the blow and she was family; she could only imagine how those in service might fare.

"Of course, I understand, but at least let me lighten it a bit," she replied

11

quietly. With a sly, conspiratorial smile, she reached into the valise and withdrew several large books, setting them carefully on the empty seat as she climbed into the carriage. Hanna grinned up at her, and with a muffled grunt, lifted the slightly less heavy bag into the carriage and then plopped down into a seat across from her. She watched, eyes bright with curiosity as Edwina picked up one of the large books and began to leaf through it.

"All these book Miss... you've read them? Are you at school then?"

Edwina's face lit up with happiness as she cradled the book against her and leaned forward, flushed with excitement as she began to explain.

"Yes, nearly finished. I've been dividing my time between studies in Vienna and Paris."

"So - Miss ... you speak French and German too?" Hanna gazed up at her - doe eyes wide with amazement for she'd never met a woman who was at university let alone who could speak so many languages.

Edwina laughed brightly and nodded. "Of course. I was born in Vienna, but Mother and I spend a lot of time in Paris. She has..."

She abruptly broke off, her face dissolving into darkness. She kept forgetting, using the present tense. Compressing her lips, she took a deep breath and averted her eyes, a look of distraction upon her face as she continued her story.

"I... meant... She... she had apartments..." Her voice faltered, and she fell silent once more - struggling to push back the grief that threatened to overwhelm her. "I'm sorry... please forgive me," she murmured after a moment, looking away lest anyone see the tears brimming in her eyes.

Hanna's face suffused with understanding and with nary a thought, she reached out and tightly grasped Edwina's hands - pressing them reassuringly.

"You go ahead and cry Miss. Sometime, it's just what's needed, especially now. You lost your mum, no one's going to think the less of you for weeping on that."

The girl's sincere expression of compassion surprised and comforted her. Edwina wiped quickly at her eyes and then managed a slight smile, regaining her composure - grateful that she had found at least one considerate soul.

"Thank you, Hanna. So, yes... German of course and French. English... and a smattering of Russian. Great grandmother is from St. Petersburg."

"Russian!" the girl exclaimed, clapping her hands together in utter delight and much relieved to see her mistress' grief fading. "The greengrocer, Old Peter, I think he may just be Russian. He comes by with that old cart of his every other day or so and sometimes when he gets all worked up, he starts going off a mile a minute and Cook and I can hardly make out a word. Cook, now she says he's trying to put one over on us - well, I don't know about that Miss, but it sure would help to understand him better. Do you think you could help Miss?"

"Of course," Edwina reassured with a quick smile. Glancing briefly out the carriage window, she checked to see that her aunt was still occupied with the baggage and then leaned forward.

"Now tell me Hanna, is Mrs. Pennington always so cross? I've hardly

12

arrived, and already I've set her off."

A cautious look crossed the girl's face, and her face settled into a slight frown as she thought how best to answer the question. She pursed her lips, about to reply when the carriage door abruptly opened, Mrs. Pennington's dour face appearing in the doorway.

"What are you two about now?"

The two girls froze; Edwina recovering first. She smiled earnestly up at Mrs. Pennington and held up the book on her lap.

"I was only showing Hanna my books Aunt Gretchen."

Her aunt regarded her warily, cautious of this sudden mild turn, and took the book from her, frowning as she struggled to pronounce the title. Beitrage zur Phytogenesis. She looked up, the furrow in her brow deepening.

"What manner of nonsense is this?"

"Principles of Phytogenesis ... Matthias Schleiden," exclaimed Edwina, words tumbling out - a soft flush of excitement lighting her face. "Clinical observations in Botany - the cellular structure of plants and microscopic organisms. It's what I'm studying Aunt Gretchen - and Chemistry of course. I love Chemistry - discovering the very essence of life - the building blocks within us - all around us and ..."

"Be still child!" barked her Aunt in such a harsh manner that the young maid shrank back against the seat and clasped her hands together, eyes fixed firmly on the floor.

The older woman's face was red with anger and leaning forward, she snatched the book from Edwina's hands. "How dare you?" she hissed, her eyes burning in outrage. "The essence of life is God child - not this ridiculous drivel. I suppose next you'll be spouting Mr. Darwin's wickedness. I won't have it. Your father and I will be having a talk. I'll not stand by and watch you waste your life on this heresy. You want to learn and study - that's all well and good, but it's time you took on useful endeavours such as needlepoint or learning to run a household. Now, hand me the bag. I want to see what other foolishness is inside."

With great reluctance, Edwina nudged the valise with her foot towards her aunt and watched with a sinking heart as the woman rifled through her belongings. A deep frown creased Mrs. Pennington's face as she sifted through the contents of the bag, muttering under her breath as she scrutinized each item. With a grunt of disapproval and self-righteous shake of her head, she pulled out a book and held it up - her suspicions confirmed. On the Origin of the Species, Charles Darwin. Edwina sighed heavily and sank back against the seat; she knew what was to come.

"You are truly a godless child," announced Mrs. Pennington with an expression of disdain as she tossed the book back into the bag. "But no matter, I joyfully accept the task – 'tis my Christian duty, and as God is my witness, I will soon set you straight." Upon having nothing further to say on the matter, she reached into the pocket of her voluminous skirt and withdrew the small, red Book of Common Prayer, which she always carried and from which she began to read aloud.

"O Lord, open thou our lips."

Immediately, the young maid Hanna, who had remained silent up to this point, cast a furtive, apologetic look in Edwina's direction and then bowed her head, meekly answering:

"And our mouth shall shew forth thy praise. "

They continued in this manner until they had worked their way through all the verses of the Evening Prayer. Edwina listened to them, suppressing a slight smile. Praying for her soul no doubt. With an air of resignation, she settled back against the seat and closed her eyes - the trials of the day beginning to overtake her. Silence at this point seemed the best course of action. Exhausted, not only from the long journey but also from sparring with her aunt, she soon drifted off to sleep - lulled by the monotonous drone of the Evensong and the clatter of hooves on the road as the carriage steadily progressed towards London.

»»««

Fern Hall, Hampstead - London

"Miss ... Miss ... time to wake up. We're home now."

The gentle pressure on her arm shook her awake and with a somewhat confused expression, Edwina opened her eyes. She slowly raised up in the carriage seat and stared blankly at the young woman in the maid's uniform - trying to work out who this person was hovering over her, where she was and for what reason.

"Home?" she repeated dully, her brain still shrouded in the fog of the disturbing dream. Faces, first Julian's and then her Mother's, blurred and then merged in the rippling waters of Lake Fuschl, slowly dissipating like smoke. She closed her eyes briefly, banishing the image from her mind.

Anxiety flickered across Hanna's face as she peered closely into the face of her mistress.

"Yes Miss... Home... Fern Hall. You all right then Miss? You look a bit peaky."

Understanding slowly filtered across Edwina's face as her memory returned, and she sighed heavily in resignation. *England - so... this was home now... Fern Hall.* Unsure what to expect, she leaned forward to look out the carriage window into the deepening twilight. The carriage had drawn to a stop in front of a 3-story, brick Georgian manor; the horses pawing restlessly at the edge of a wide, grass lawn. Nine-pane, white sash-windows lined the facade of the first two floors in perfect symmetry while grey capped dormer windows peeked out from the gambrel roof. It brought a smile to her lips; it was beautiful, perfectly balanced and much larger than she had expected. She slowly climbed from the carriage unable to take her eyes from the entrance of the house which was lined with stately black poplars. Candlelight glowed softly in several of the front facing windows.

"It's so grand..." she murmured softly as she moved forward, slowly

14

surveying the area. Although the light was fading, she could still make out the shape of several outbuildings; one obviously, a barn or stable of some sort, and another which seemed to be of glass - perhaps a small greenhouse. To the back of the greenhouse lay a grove of apple trees, and in the quiet of the evening, the gurgle of a hidden fountain could be heard.

"I thought my father was in the printing trade... an engraver?" she queried, her voice betraying her bewilderment.

"Oh yes Miss... he is... best in London!" proclaimed Hanna proudly. "It's the family house you know... been here quite a while according to Cook. Your father's only recently taken it on – was a bit of a sorry mess before. Run of bad luck with the money the elder Penningtons had." The young girl paused, looking about to see if Mrs. Pennington was within earshot, and then smiled secretly as she leaned forward.

"Cook ... well she says that Old Man Pennington had quite a drink and gambling habit, nearly lost the house before he died" she whispered. "But that's all changed now with Master Pennington being so successful in the business. He's taken it on, fixing it up – still some rooms at the back all closed up but won't be long before they're all done up proper. He's even had gas lines run in for the lights and kitchen, though Mrs. Pennington, well... she turns it off in the night as she says it's dangerous and wasteful. She's quite..." Hanna paused – an intense look of concentration on her face as she grappled for a word less harsh than miserly. "Thrifty!" she exclaimed brightly after a moment. *Always best to put your best face forward ... that's what Cook always told her.*

"Turns the gas off at night?" Edwina echoed in amazement, suppressing a laugh. *Thrifty was far too kind a word.* What a strange thing to invest money in modern conveniences and then not use them? Gretchen Pennington was definitely out of step with modern times; a relic, and seemingly intent on dragging those around her back into the past. *Well – she could try. Clearly one more item to add to the growing list she intended to discuss with her father.*

"Oh, yes Miss ... that's why you see candlelight in the windows now ... gas is off – so that means no hot meals or baths until morning. Of course, if you want Miss, I can heat some water on the kitchen hearth and bring it up to you," she suggested quickly, not wanting to displease her mistress, though it was evident from her reluctant smile that the thought of lugging pails of heated water up the stairs was less than pleasant.

"You there! Edwina! Both of you!"

Both girls startled at the harsh voice of Mrs. Pennington. They'd almost forgotten about her as she had set out to supervise the unloading of the coffin and the luggage as soon as the carriage had come to a stop. With a nervous expression, Hanna scrambled to grab the valise and a few light pieces of luggage from the inside of the carriage. Edwina compressed her lips – once again pushing back a surge of irritation and turned to face her Aunt who was rapidly approaching from the service entrance, gesturing vehemently in their direction.

"What nonsense! Idling about in the night air... not a care in the world!

Fancy yourself the Queen, do you? Inside now before you catch your death. I'll not waste a farthing on a Doctor, mind you. Hanna will show you to your room. Step lively now!" And with nothing further to say, Mrs. Pennington vanished around the side of the house to finish supervising the unloading.

Edwina sighed heavily and reluctantly followed Hanna toward the front entrance, her eyes now fixed on the elegant carriage that sat just to the front of their hansom. It was a stately Brougham, coal-black in color and adorned with finely polished brass lamps. A uniformed liveryman stood at attention tending the horses, and as she passed by, tipped his top hat politely. She nodded in return and once past, turned to Hanna with a quizzical look.

"Father's?"

Once again, she was struck by the dichotomy of her father's merchant status and his apparent wealth.

"Oh no Miss... that would be your father's business associate. Come along – we best move on else we risk another scolding. I'll show you to your room... a lovely one it is – right at the top of the stairs and to the left. You've a pretty view of the rose garden, not that you can see it now mind you."

Edwina slowly followed Hanna inside, her eyes scanning the room which was lit in the soft glow provided by several tall candle stands that lined the vestibule. Making her way toward the central staircase, she suddenly drew to a halt in front of the fireplace. She lifted her eyes, staring in disbelief – hanging above the mantle was a portrait of her mother. It was, in fact, the same portrait as was in her lapel watch; her mother holding little Julian by the hand.

"Such a beautiful lady Miss... you two could be sisters," murmured Hanna with a sympathetic expression. "And the little boy?"

Edwina's face darkened, a sad smile touching her lips. "My brother... Julian..."

"Your brother... he's a podgy little one!" laughed Hanna brightly. "And where is he now... back in France? Will he be joining us soon?" she asked curiously, rather surprised that no one had ever mentioned the little tyke. Granted, she was new in the employ of the Penningtons (having been in service with them just two months), but it seemed odd that no one spoke about the little boy. In fact, there seemed to be a general reluctance to speak about the family history. *The problems of the gentry. Well, she'd likely never have to worry about that.*

Edwina paused, averting her eyes; for a moment, she said nothing. Clasping her hands in front of her, she sighed mournfully and then shrugged slightly.

"He's dead," she murmured in a dull, hollow voice, "Drowned ... just three months after this portrait."

A look of horror crossed the young maid's face. "Oh miss... I'm so sorry... no one breathed a word... I swear," she stammered, utterly distraught.

"It's all right... you didn't know," soothed Edwina, forcing a smile in an attempt to reassure the poor girl. "It happened long ago... so... to my room then... I've quite a bit of unpacking to do." And without waiting for the maid to reply, she headed up the stairs.

»»««

Reunion - Fern Hall, Hampstead, London

"Extraordinary!" murmured the Professor, his deep-set eyes glittering oddly as he gazed out the window, watching the two girls make their way down the path to the entrance. As they disappeared from view, he let the curtain fall back into place and turned from the window, sipping his claret, a pensive expression on his face. Settling at the card table, he drummed the table impatiently and waited for his partner. Flashes of light danced across the mahogany tabletop as the flickering candlelight glinted off the platinum signet ring he wore on his left little finger, the initials JM elegantly inscribed into the oval, onyx mount.

"Pardon?" puffed Wilfred Pennington, out of breath and panting as he emerged from an alcove tucked behind the bookcase. "What is?" he asked curiously, staggering under the weight of several heavy ledgers. He groaned slightly in exertion and deposited them with a loud thunk onto the table, wiping the sweat from his brow with a pocket square as he attempted to catch his breath. Settling into a chair opposite the Professor, he watched nervously as the gaunt man began to examine them.

"Edwina... the resemblance is quite remarkable," announced the Professor, scrutinizing the columns of figures. "So much like her mother... not a hint of you, fortunately for her!" he added, chuckling dryly. He looked up from the ledger and studied the little man carefully, his lips curling in slight disdain. The passing years had not been kind to Wilfred Pennington; his girth and roundness had expanded at the same rate as his hair, always sparse, had diminished leaving him with a thinning, unruly fringe of white that rimmed his glistening dome. The Professor, on the other hand, had changed very little, the only difference being that his hair and goatee, once a deep, rich brown, were now peppered with grey.

Wilfred uttered a nervous laugh at the insult and fidgeted, rubbing his palms together. They had been friends, if that was the appropriate term, for many years now and still he felt a certain amount of unease in his companion's presence. In fact, the unease seemed to increase the longer he was in acquaintance with the Professor. Upon reflection, however, a little discomfort seemed a small price to pay for the good fortune their partnership had delivered, despite its precarious and often dubious nature.

"I remember her being an exceptionally tall child; lovely hair, the same as dear Katia," Wilfred explained, a sweet, rueful smile touching his lips as he thought of his late wife. "I can only imagine how she must be now..." The smile began to fade as he moved further back into his memory, replaced by an expression of deep sadness; he sighed, shaking his head as he stared down at his hands. "Stubborn like her mother as well I recall, even as a child. Poor little Julian, always tagging along - running after her... seeking her approval...

17

desperate to keep up." He broke off abruptly, a look of utter desolation clouding his face as he thought back to that dreadful day at the lake; Julian had been trying to keep up that day.

The Professor arched his brow and leaned back in his chair, scanning Wilfred's face as he continued to sip his claret.

"Blame her... still? After all this time?"

He finished his drink and leaned forward, his eyes cold and hard, a cruel smirk darkening his face. "Hardly seems fair, my dear fellow. She was only nine after all; the boy couldn't keep up ... too weak... a tragic miscalculation. Perhaps, if he had been more like his mother – well, I'll say no more."

Wilfred shook his head vehemently, his expression a mixture of remorse and anguish.

"I blame only myself, James!" he exclaimed, his eyes glistening with wetness. "Edwina was too young. We should have been watching. She couldn't have known... didn't understand."

James Moriarity rested his chin in his palm, gazing intensely into the glowing embers of the hearth. A secret smile curled his mouth as he thought back on that day. He'd been on the shore having gone for a walk, watching from the edge of the forest trail that ran along the lake; closer and with an unobstructed view than Katia and Wilfred, who had been picnicking further up the embankment. The smile on his face deepened as he recalled his conversation with little Edwina as she and her brother had splashed in the shallow waters. She'd pouted and sulked, tugging irritably at her braids, her pretty face flushed with anger as she complained about her "bothersome" little brother, who, by her account, could do no wrong in the eyes of her parents. She was a precocious little thing, eagerly showing off for him by identifying various plants and insects, making observations about the lake; all the while trying to ignore little Julian who followed her about like a pup. Not long after their conversation had ended, the children had gone swimming. Edwina, with long, powerful strokes set out for the platform in the center of the lake as Julian splashed along behind her, struggling to keep up. So as he considered, just how much had Edwina understood that day, he came to the inevitable conclusion... everything.

"How do you find it, James? Everything to your satisfaction?"

Wilfred Pennington cleared his throat a bit nervously and cast a furtive glance at his pocket watch. The hour was growing late; he had yet to welcome Edwina or pay his respects to his late wife, who was now resting quietly in the small chapel that lay to the back of the apple grove.

The Professor slowly smiled and closed the ledgers, pushing them back towards his partner.

"Yes, dear fellow – all in order as usual. Production moving along nicely I see. Let's keep this pace; best not to move too swiftly, wouldn't want to call attention. There've been some rumblings out in Clerkenwell."

A look of alarm crossed Pennington's face; his usual ruddy complexion now pale and tense.

"Rumblings! How so?" he exclaimed.

The Professor sighed wearily and waved his hand dismissively; the little man was practically quivering in anxiety.

"Nothing to panic over. As long as you keep your head, all will be well. The boys out in Clerkenwell got a little greedy and decided to speed up production – flooded a few of the local banks in a short period. Rather vexing... attracted attention, and now the Yard is sniffing about. Had to cease operations for the time being – until the furor dies down. Damn nuisance!"

"The Yard!" echoed Pennington, wringing his hands tensely. "Bloody Hell" he murmured.

The Professor snorted a bit and shrugged. "Bah! ... Morons! ... One step removed from the village idiot. Don't worry about them... but be forewarned – they might call Holmes in."

"Holmes!!" cried Pennington, now truly alarmed and visibly sweating. "But we've had no issues here – surely he'll only look to Clerkenwell."

The Professor chuckled dryly and shook his head, rather amused by his partner's near state of panic at the very mention of the Consulting Detective. He smiled darkly, his eyes like two bottomless pools, devoid of any light as he reflected on the possibility.

"It is his method... to collect all data, no matter how insignificant or unrelated it may appear at first glance. Fortunately, he seems distracted at the moment – may not even accept the consultation. Calm yourself. I have every confidence that should he decide to poke about, you will find a way of diverting his attention or convincing him that he is on the wrong track."

Wilfred Pennington nodded tentatively, though his eyes reflected his doubt. He swallowed dryly and forced a smile, trying to conceal the depth of his apprehension.

The Professor snickered a bit, not fooled in the least, and grinned at him – a hint of contempt in his expression.

"Now that's settled. I'd like to see a specimen – if you please. Just a little quality check, and then I'll take my leave of you."

"Yes... Yes of course... right away," murmured the little man as he sprang from the chair and scurried back around the bookcase. A few moments passed and after much whirring and clicking (no doubt the safe), he emerged carrying several uncut sheets of pound banknotes. He handed them over to the Professor, holding his breath as he watched the gaunt man withdraw a pound banknote from the pocket of his waist-coat; he laid the banknote next to the uncut sheet on the table.

"Yes... this is fine... quite fine," murmured the Professor, running his bony fingers over the first uncut sheet and then the authentic pound note. "The texture is almost indistinguishable." He withdrew a silver framed monocle from his vest, fitted it to his left eye and held both the banknote and sheet up to the candlelight, a satisfied smile on his lips. "The color is remarkably true. Well done old friend! DaVinci would be impressed!"

Wilfred sighed audibly in relief.

"New process," he explained proudly. "The hemp fibers in the paper react perfectly with the indigo compound and..."

"Yes... Yes..." interrupted the Professor, waving his hand dismissively. "I'll leave the mysteries of the process to you." He smiled after a moment and then nodded his head in acknowledgement to the little man. "Well done! Follow my lead dear fellow and our partnership will only continue to grow. Now, I must be on my way... my travel commences in the morning," he explained as he took up his top hat and fastened his coat, making his way toward the library exit.

Wilfred Pennington rose also, following him to the door, a look of disappointment on his face.

"Oh... you are travelling then?"

"Yes... I leave for Venice. Matters of business and a visit with an old friend. Something amiss?"

"No... No," assured Pennington quickly, uneasy at the sudden tone of suspicion in the Professor's voice. He paused for a moment and then with a melancholy expression, explained, "I just thought perhaps... well, there will be a service for Katia tomorrow; very small, private... just family. I thought you might attend... you have known her almost as long as I."

For a fleeting moment, something close to compassion crossed James Moriarity's face as he thought back over the passing years. He was quiet for a moment and then sighed, shaking his head.

"My condolences on your loss, Wilfred. Katia was a remarkable woman, and despite your estrangement from her, I understand that she was still quite dear to you. Upon my return, I will of course, pay my respects. As you know, I take no stock in Christian ritual, but if it gives you comfort, feel free to offer up a prayer or whatever is customary in my name. I will leave instructions with my secretary. In the interim, should you need to contact me, I can be reached by telegraph. Again, my secretary has the information." Upon reaching the door, he paused and while buttoning his gloves, turned back to Wilfred, a contemplative expression on his face.

"How old is Edwina now?"

Pennington looked slightly startled. "She will be 24 come Spring."

"Ahhh... no doubt you'll present her this season," replied the Professor with a quick grin.

The little man looked flustered and rather surprised. "In light of current circumstances – it had not occurred to me."

The Professor arched his brow and nodded sagely, moving down the hall with such long strides that Pennington had to scramble to keep up with him.

"Of course, to be expected, but I would not delay too long dear friend. She will soon be past her prime and that would truly be a waste. After all, one unmarried woman in a household is enough." He chuckled sarcastically, obviously referring to Pennington's sister Gretchen. "As a matter of note, my old friend Augustus' son, Sebastian, will be returning to London in the next few months. Distinguished himself at Charasiab under Major-General Roberts; excellent marksman, Eton and Oxford educated... ambitious... proved invaluable in the advance upon Kabul. I am considering taking him on; his skills would prove useful. With your permission, I would like to suggest that he call upon you with regard to Edwina, after a suitable period of mourning of course. He's attained the rank of Colonel. Seems to me, quite a suitable match."

"Well... yes, of course!" exclaimed Wilfred, absolutely delighted at the prospect of having a decorated military man as a son-in-law. "Please inform him that I will welcome his interest. Four weeks should be suitable for general inquiry."

"Splendid! I'll send word to Colonel Moran of your acceptance. Well then old friend – I must be off. Again – my condolences. Remember, with regard to Holmes, remain calm and genial but not overly obliging lest you arouse suspicion. Contact my secretary should you need to get in touch."

A moment later, the Professor had vanished out the door. Wilfred Pennington stood at the open door, just inside the entryway, watching as the Brougham disappeared down the lane. He remained motionless for quite some time, staring out into the darkness, listening to the sounds of night all around him, and thinking on all that had come to pass in recent months. From inside the house, he could just make out the soft chime of the clock in the parlor as it announced half past nine. With a heavy sigh, he turned back inside, shutting the door behind him. Taking a deep breath, he mentally prepared as he slowly climbed the stairs towards Edwina's room. Time to make amends; welcome and offer comfort to his daughter. It was a reunion long overdue.

»»«««

Atonement - Fern Hall, Hampstead, London

At the sound of the knock, Edwina paused in the unpacking of her mother's trunk and glanced toward the door expectantly. Hanna had set out earlier to see what she could scrounge in the larder as neither of them had eaten since early morning.

"Come in Hanna... I've left it unlatched."

There was a moment of silence and then another soft knock, followed by a muffled utterance of her name. The door, however, remained closed. Edwina frowned; the voice was hesitant and low... certainly not the voice of the young maid. Pulling her robe close around her, she rose from the bed and went to the door. She pulled it open quickly to find a short, round little man with bleary eyes, a balding dome and a nervous smile. He pursed his lips as if to speak, but there was no sound and seemed only capable of nodding apologetically in her direction as he offered a tray of cold milk, cheese and bread.

"Oh... hello," she murmured slowly, somewhat surprised that he had finally decided to tear himself away from his business matters. She paused, carefully choosing her words and then awkwardly added, "Father." He was much the same as she remembered him; round and short but with much less hair.

Wilfred Pennington gaped at her, again unable to find his voice; this time not so much from anxiety as sheer amazement. The Professor had been right –

the resemblance to his late wife was astounding and a little unnerving. It was as if he had stepped back in time, and his dear Katia stood before him; vibrant, beautiful and radiant; the brightest star in the heavens.

"Is this for me?" she asked quietly, struggling to maintain an air of icy indifference as she reached out to take the tray. Inside her emotions were in chaos; a volatile mixture of bitter resentment, anger and grief that threatened to boil over as she stared at this man who had abandoned her and her mother so many years before.

He forced a smile and nodded. "Yes... I... I..." he sputtered for a moment, fumbling for words and then abruptly fell into silence.

Edwina stared at him – puzzled; her determination to remain aloof beginning to waver as the little man's face contorted in anguish and remorse. She stood up a little straighter and folded her arms tightly against her, trying to quell the doubt welling from within.

"Forgive me... please," he suddenly blubbered, tears streaming freely down his flushed face. "I know I failed both you and your mother. I know there is nothing I can say to erase that pain or to change my actions, but you must believe this Edwina; I never stopped loving you or your mother and I will regret my cowardice until the day I leave this earth."

Edwina swallowed hard, attempting to push back the lump she felt rising in her throat. Despite her best efforts, she felt her determination weakening. She unfolded her arms and fixed her eyes on him, her lips pressed tightly together – her jaw firm and unyielding.

"Then why did you leave us... when we needed you most?" she asked abruptly, though her bitterness was rapidly being replaced by weary sadness. She averted her eyes for a moment – feeling overwhelmed, and before he could offer a reply, in a broken, guilt-ridden voice, blurted: "I'm so sorry Father – about Julian. You must believe me... I didn't know — I really tried — but I couldn't reach him. I didn't mean for it to happen..." And then in an instant, her resolve had vanished, and she dissolved into tears, sobbing disconsolately.

A look of horror crossed Wilfred's face and without hesitation, he threw his arms around his daughter and pulled her close, hugging her tightly – offering comfort and reassurance.

"Of course, it wasn't your fault. You were a child dear – no one blames you," he soothed, gently cradling her head against his shoulder, wiping at her tears. He let her cry for a few moments more and then managed an encouraging smile. "What fault there is, is mine Edwina. What happened that day — it changed me — broke me, and although it wasn't the sole reason I left, it contributed. Still it was a cowardly act; I hope that one day, you will find it in your heart to forgive me."

The words, so sincerely spoken, seemed to have a calming effect. Wiping at her eyes, Edwina gently untangled herself from his arms and stepped away, reflecting on his words and now wondering if she had spent the last fourteen years of her life harboring animosity toward a man who didn't deserve it.

Relief flooded Wilfred's face, and he nodded towards the tray on the table. "Now, dry your eyes dear... eat a little something and then get some rest. Tomorrow morning there will be a small service for your mother. I was unable to find a Roman cleric, but the Vicar has agreed to say a few words and I don't think your mother will mind so much. Before I leave, is there anything I can do for you – anything you need?"

Her tears finally dried, Edwina took a deep breath and composed herself. She sniffled a bit and then nodding towards her now, half-empty valise, replied, "My books... Mrs. Pennington, she took my books — almost all of them — and my sketches."

"Your books? What kind of books?"

"Textbooks – from my studies... Schleiden and Darwin ... "

He groaned aloud, a look of doubt clouding his face. "I shall do my best but do not hold out too much hope. My sister is a devout woman, and she has little patience for anything scientific. I may have better luck with the sketches — she is not too averse to art — depending of course on the subject matter."

She nodded that she understood; warmed by the fact that he would at least try on her behalf. After he had left, she settled onto the bed, nibbling at a piece of bread and reflecting on all that had happened. It was all so much to consider and not wanting to think on it anymore, she blew out the candles and crawled into bed, waiting restlessly for sleep to overtake her.

CHAPTER 2

Celebration

January 6, 1884 - Baker Street

"Perhaps I should have used gold thread ..."

A hint of doubt crossed Mary Morstan's delicate features as she withdrew a small box from her beaded bag and rested it in her lap. She removed the ribbon and parchment wrapping, taking care not to tear them, and lifted out three white silk pocket squares and royal purple velvet tobacco pouch. As she inspected the items, her lace-gloved fingers carefully checked the stitching on the elegant monogram on each item; WSSH looked impressive in fine, black thread, but she now questioned her choice of thread color. She sighed a bit and looked to the young man seated across from her in the hansom, hidden behind the latest edition of the Times. He offered no reply, seemingly not hearing her. A slight look of annoyance darkened her face and she leaned forward, reaching out to lightly nudge him. Perhaps he hadn't heard her over the clatter of the horses' hooves as the hansom made its way down Marylebone towards Baker Street.

"John... what do you think then?" she asked, her voice a little louder.

Again, there was no response; just the whisper of the newspaper pages as they were turned. Mary compressed her lips tightly, a slight flush coloring her cheeks as her irritation increased. She thought for a moment, considering how best to get his attention and then announced in as serious a voice as she could muster.

"John... it pains me greatly, but I'm afraid I've bad news. I've decided to run away with him tonight after Caroline's party."

With an air of nonchalance, she adjusted the white ribbons that trimmed the flowing sleeves of her rose silk gown and waited – a small smile playing on her lips.

Silence fell once again – no response. Mary's smile faded replaced by a frown as her frustration increased. Her expression grew resolute... time to up the game.

"Of course, this means our engagement is broken and no doubt the end of your friendship. Can't be helped – I am sorry, but considering the circumstances... it seems to me the best course of action. You see, I'm carrying his child and he's offered to do what's proper. I will, however, not be returning the ring."

The pages continued to turn but at last there was a response, though not one she had expected.

"Sounds perfectly delightful dear! Splendid idea... you always know best in these situations," murmured the man absently, nodding his head as he continued to read the news from abroad. "Bloody heathens..." he growled, "Rumblings in the Sudan again. I supposed they'll be sending Gordon back over there; he'll soon set them straight!"

A small shriek of exasperation escaped her lips, piercing the relative quiet of the afternoon and Dr. John Watson startled, dropped his newspaper.

"Are you all right dear?" he exclaimed, wincing at the sound, his warm brown eyes fraught with concern as he leaned towards his fiancé.

In response, she exhaled and sharply rapped his knee with her purse.

"John Hamish Watson, you've not heard a word I've said! How dare you sit there and pretend to listen!"

Her cornflower blue eyes blazed with indignation.

She fixed him with a reproachful look, her head shaking so vigorously a few golden curls spilled from under her hat. The little stuffed wren, sitting in the midst of a nest of plum feathers and silk roses, bobbed about so precariously that it looked as if it would take flight at any moment or at the very least, tumble to the ground. John Watson's heart surged with love, and despite his best efforts, a tender smile of amusement curled his mouth. Fortunately for him, it was hidden by the impressive mustache that adorned his upper lip.

"Nonsense!" he soothed, "I've heard every word." He flashed his most charming smile and reached out to pat her hand. In truth, he hadn't heard a word, but he wasn't too concerned. After all, it was probably just the usual chatter about Lady Caroline's party or something else in a similar vein.

"Oh really?" she chuckled, leaning back in her seat – a look of utter disbelief on her face. "Tell me then, which part did you enjoy the most?"

Uncertainty clouded his handsome face, the mustache drooping a bit as he struggled for an answer. He laughed a little nervously and smiled, smoothing back his sandy hair.

"Why all of it dear... all perfectly delightful."

She burst into giddy laughter, covering her mouth with her gloved hands. John Watson looked on uneasily, fidgeting in his seat as he began to sense that he had just made a serious misstep. Worn out from laughing, Mary sighed softly and leaned forward, a sparkle of mischief in her eyes as she took his hand and pressed it lovingly.

"So glad to hear dear. What a relief! Perhaps we shall name the child after you. It seems only fitting. We can all sit down and discuss it tonight!"

"What!" he sputtered, his eyes wide with horror. "Mary... what are you saying? Have you gone mad!"

"The expression on your face... priceless!" she giggled in delight. "I can't wait to tell him. I'm sure he'll find it highly entertaining!"

John Watson stared at her, still somewhat dumbfounded and then uttered a deep sigh of relief, realization finally sinking in that it had all been a prank. He leaned back in his seat and shook his head.

"For heaven's sake Mary, you nearly gave me a heart attack!"

She shrugged, not a trace of apology in her expression.

"Serves you right you know, ignoring me so. You could at least wait until we're married to stop listening, like every other dreadful man in this city does to his poor wife!" she noted with some acrimony.

John Watson raised his eyes, looking into the face of this woman, a woman he loved and treasured above all else in the world, and was overcome with a deep sense of shame. His expression reflected his distress and leaning forward, he reached out and took her hands in his, pressing them tightly.

"You've every right to reprimand me... I've been a thoughtless fool. Forgive me... please," he pleaded, his voice sincere and filled with remorse.

Mary's heart melted; with a sigh of resignation, she smiled in forgiveness and leaned across, depositing a quick but tender kiss on his cheek.

"Lucky for you John Watson, I am in a forgiving mood today."

She flashed a smile at him and rose, quickly moving across the carriage to settle next to him. She closed her eyes, a look of deep contentment on her face as she rested her head on his shoulder, absently listening to the sounds of the carriage wheels on the cobblestones. She was quiet for a few moments and then opened her eyes, gazing up at him soberly.

"You're very distracted these past few days... even Mother and Father noticed. Something's troubling you. What is it John? May I help? "

Once more, a look of dismay clouded John's face. They had just returned from visiting her parents in Hertford where he had finally summoned the courage to ask her father for her hand in marriage. Much to his great relief, the elder gentleman, a highly respected and recently retired senior captain of the Indian campaigns, had found him suitable and given his blessing; no doubt in part owing to their shared history of military service. Although the week spent with them had been pleasant enough, and he was jubilant at the prospect of planning the future with his beloved Mary, he had begun to experience an overarching sense of melancholy which was strongest in moments of solitude. His life was about to change, in the most wonderful and welcome of ways and yet, he worried about those he would leave behind and how they would be affected; namely his best friend and flatmate of some four years now, Mr. Sherlock Holmes.

As if reading his thoughts, she gazed up at him and squeezed his hand in reassurance.

"Nothing has to change John, only our living arrangements. I don't seek to replace him in your affections. I know how much you value his company and the work; I would never attempt to part the two of you. Besides," she added playfully, "I expect once the novelty of the first few months of marriage has worn off, I'll be grateful for the opportunity to have you out of my hair."

He stared at her in surprise, and then after a pause, began to laugh. "Quite so!" he replied, with a nod of agreement and warm smile.

The extent of her patience and understanding of his friendship with his peculiar and often difficult flatmate, never ceased to amaze him. Sherlock Holmes was brilliant, steadfast in his devotion to his craft, and at times, the most charming of men; but he was also subject to wild swings of temperament, often within the same day. When taken by darkness, he became adversarial, dismissive and manipulative with friend and foe alike. He showed no mercy based on gender either, as could be attested to by their poor, beleaguered landlady, Mrs. Hudson. These episodes and their unpredictability had resulted in a condition of social isolation for the detective, which Watson had long suspected was the plan. Holmes seemed to relish this self-imposed exile, showing little inclination to engage socially for the sheer pleasure of companionship. If he was out and about, there was always some purpose behind it, even if it was solely for the collection of information which he would store away in the recesses of his mind for use at some later date. Holmes' reclusive nature and eccentricities had not only dampened a few of Watson's other friendships, but also resulted in more than a few ruined romances. At least, that had been the case until he had met Mary Morstan; she was different - taking it all in stride with a good sense of humor and limitless patience. He supposed the patience arose from her profession as a nurse and advocate for the down-trodden; if she could work amongst the unfortunates of White Chapel, she could certainly deal with Sherlock Holmes. With the passage of time and her quiet persistence, she even seemed to have earned a modicum of respect from Holmes which was quite a victory. Holmes, although always gentlemanly and mannered in the presence of ladies, expressed little desire to engage socially with the fairer sex, branding romantic "entanglements" as he called them, a colossal waste of his energy and time. That wasn't to say that he was averse or immune to the charms of women; he was a vigorous man in the full bloom of youth. When he was no longer able to redirect his baser instincts, and being of a practical bent of mind, he sidestepped the issue of relationships entirely by taking his pleasure in Limehouse; a practice that both worried and saddened the Doctor.

The hansom turned onto Baker street and slowed, falling in behind a steady stream of carriages as they inched their way up the stately row of Georgian terrace houses. The streets and sidewalks were crowded; it was Sunday afternoon and the weather was surprisingly mild for January. Many of the residents were getting ready to head out to visit relatives or were taking an afternoon stroll, intent on enjoying this rare glimpse of Spring. As the carriage continued to slow even further, a look of frustration crossed John's face. He peered out the window, watching as leisurely walkers on the sidewalk were outpacing the carriage; at this rate, they might arrive at 221B by sunset. Seeing his frustration, Mary smiled quickly and rapped on the ceiling to get the driver's attention.

"Pull over, please!!" she instructed. Turning to John, she grasped his hand as the hansom pulled to a stop at the corner of Marylebone Road and Baker Street.

"Let's walk John! It's a perfectly lovely day and you can tell me all about it..." she announced brightly and without waiting for him to reply, threw open the door and hopped down from the carriage, pulling him along. Watson grumbled a bit at first, a little annoyed that she had taken the lead but soon fell into step at her side, taking her arm in his. He moved to the outside, shielding her from the street and set a measured pace, beaming proudly as they headed towards 221B.

"So, tell me – what's troubling you? Has he spiraled into one of his black moods again?"

"Yes," he murmured, "darkest I've seen in quite a while. According to Mrs. Hudson, he didn't leave the flat the entire week I was gone, barely taking tea. God knows when he's had a proper meal."

Mary's eyes crinkled sympathetically, a sweet smile on her lips. Poor John... such a mother hen at times. Although the age difference between the two men was just four years, John often seemed to take on the mantle of older brother; given Holmes' unpredictable and sometimes reckless behavior, it was easy to see why.

"Well, I wouldn't worry so," she soothed, pressing his arm. "Isn't that always the way with him? First, he's up and dashing about like a madman and then he's in the doldrums... just his nature I suppose. Mind you, I don't know how you manage it – it would drive me round the bend. He's always moody between cases – you've said so yourself. And he had a bit of a let down on the last one, didn't he? Those missing paintings at the National Gallery – the case he couldn't solve. He always gets a bit down in the mouth when he can't solve one."

"Yes... that's part of it no doubt... but it's more than that," he explained, a frown darkening his face. "He grows more restless and malcontent with each passing day and what little joy his victories bring him, is fleeting at best. I can't predict his moods anymore Mary and that truly worries me. Old habits beckon."

Mary's face clouded at this and she tightened her hold on John's arm, offering comfort. Although John had never directly spoke of Holmes' use of mind altering substances, it was rumored that the detective would binge in periods of boredom and frustration, alternating between opiates and stimulants – depending on his frame of mind. Inevitably, he'd disappear for days into the bowels of Limehouse to take his pleasures and emerged on more than one occasion, battered and bruised as if he'd been brawling.

"Is he still going on about this supposed underground association – this ring of criminals led by a mysterious mastermind?" she asked curiously, a look of doubt in her eyes.

Watson sighed in resignation and nodded.

"Constantly. It has become his obsession I'm afraid. Down at the Yard, there've been some mutterings that he's finally cracked. Even Lestrade has raised doubts. And if that isn't enough, Mrs. Hudson tells me another letter arrived this week."

"A letter?" interrupted Mary, a look of alarm on her face. "From her?" she added hesitantly.

They had paused on the corner, just three blocks down from 221B.

Watson's face darkened as he nodded again, a hint of anger lighting his eyes.

"Well, she didn't open it; not after the ruckus he raised last time. She swears the handwriting is identical, it was posted in Milan and the envelope reeks of perfume. Not long after its arrival, his mood took a turn for the worse."

Mary's eyes clouded with dismay. The Woman, Irene Adler, bad news indeed. According to John, she was the only woman to have ever outwitted Sherlock Holmes and more troubling, also the only woman to have ever breached the detective's tightly controlled, emotionally constrained world. She didn't exactly know the details of what had occurred or was occurring between the detective and the retired opera singer, as John was reluctant to discuss such delicate matters with her, but she knew in her heart that it wasn't healthy. This woman — the woman — had a strange, almost magical hold over Holmes. Whenever the woman found herself in a difficult situation, usually involving another's husband, she needed only to send a letter or telegram and off he went to straighten out the mess. It seemed not to matter what he was in the midst of; when the woman beckoned, Holmes answered the call. Last time, it had been to suppress her particularly scandalous affair with a senior member of the Italian government. At the time, as she was married to an elderly Count from Turin. Holmes succeeded in convincing the nobleman that she, the woman, was the innocent victim of malicious rumours spread by a jealous, former housekeeper, with whom the Count had once had a dalliance. With her husband's blessing, the woman had gone to the island of Mykonos to calm her frazzled nerves; Holmes had accompanied her to "ensure her safety." He had remained with her at the sun-drenched villa for nearly a month, eventually returning to London relaxed, brown as a nut and almost content. Thereafter, life returned to normal with only occasional correspondence between the two; whatever it was or had been, seemed to have run its course – or so they thought.

The news was splashed across the society pages of the Times in two separate entries just two weeks apart. The first, the death announcement of the Conte Orcini of Turin; heart-attack it seemed. He had been 81 – not surprising really. The second concerned the engagement of his widow to a wealthy Bostonian. Upon seeing the news, Holmes uttered not a word, but never again mentioned her by name. The small photograph of her that he had kept in an obscure corner of the mantle disappeared into the bottom of the roll top desk, covered by their correspondence which in turn was buried under a mountain of case notes. John had expressed great relief, believing that she was finally gone from their lives and so it had seemed, until the letter arrived.

"What could she possibly want? Nine months on!" Mary exclaimed. "Besides, isn't she married now?"

Watson laughed slightly and shook his head. Marriage vows never seemed to pose a problem for The Woman, and Holmes was often openly dismissive of society's current moral constructs. 'Monogamy,' he insisted, 'is unnatural and scientifically unsound, created by politicians and clergy to control the masses. ' Still, he was worried. Holmes seemed affected this time around –vulnerable.

"Husband number two if my memory serves me correctly. She changes partners as freely as I do shirt collars. God only knows what she wants now. She's a menace – first class predator if I ever saw one."

Sensing the depth of his anxiety, Mary moved in closer and tightened her hold on his arm, squeezing it affectionately as they moved closer to 221B. They were a little less than a block down now and if she squinted and looked up at just the right angle, she could make out the polished brass door knocker.

So, do you think... he loved her then?" she asked hesitantly. She'd met Miss Adler only once and had taken an instant disliking to her; but who was she to judge? She hated the thought of anyone being the victim of a broken love affair, no matter how foolish or ill-advised.

"Loved?" scoffed Watson with a disdainful smile. "I wouldn't call it that. Neither one of them even knows the meaning of the word. He keeps his feelings locked away and she has no capacity for it – what little heart she has is made of stone. Whatever they shared was of a more..." he paused hesitating, choosing his words, "...carnal nature," he sighed, giving up on trying to be delicate. "Still, it obviously affected him. She outplayed him. I think he has finally realized that she used him, and that it was her intention all along. So now, in the light of this revelation, he no longer has a taste for the game."

"Poor dear man..." she sighed sympathetically. She drew to a stop and wrapped her arms around him and hugged him lovingly.

Watson returned the embrace though his face reddened; still not used to open displays of affection though it was now permitted. She laughed a bit at his discomfort and beamed up at him as they continued, now only three doors down from 221B.

"Well then..." she began brightly, "tonight is just what he needs! It's going to be a marvelous party. Caroline has something quite special planned and ..."

A sharp blast shattered the quiet followed by the tinkling of glass as the parlor windows of 221B blew out, raining shards of glass down onto the panicked passersby below. John instinctively threw himself over Mary, pushing her into the shelter of a nearby doorway. The air filled with the acrid odors of sulphur, cordite and smouldering fabric. He cautiously lifted his head and seeing that it had indeed come from his flat, drained of all color, staggering out to the sidewalk – gaping at the thick black smoke that billowed from the blackened and burst windows.

"Oh Christ!!" he cried out. "He's finally done it!"

He clutched at his head, staring in horrified disbelief – unable to move at first. Mary slowly lifted her head, uncovering her eyes and cried out in terror. She moved as if to join him, but he stopped her, pushing her back into the doorway.

"Stay here!" he commanded and then was gone, breaking into a run, his heart pounding wildly – knowing in his heart that the scene would be grim. The front door loomed in sight and as he sprang toward it, a scraping sounded from above as what was left of the window sash was thrown up. More glass showered down and the air filled with the sound of hoarse, violent coughing. Watson froze, staring up, incredulous as a wiry young man covered in soot, leaned out of the window in his scorched and tattered shirt sleeves. He ran a hand through his tousled raven locks, shaking out soot and embers, grinning gleefully like a complete madman.

"Not to worry!! No need to panic!" he called out in an oddly cheerful manner to the pedestrians below. "Just a little mishap... now off you go." Spying a couple of rag-tag boys, part of his network of urchins who roamed the streets collecting information for him, he reached into his pocket and threw down a couple of shillings.

"A guinea to the boy who gets to the fire brigade first and prevents them from coming!" The man laughed a bit, watching as the boys dove for the coins and then scattered, all scampering off down Baker Street in the general direction of the firehouse.

"You... You... bloody imbecile!!" sputtered the Doctor, his face contorted with a mixture of rage and genuine relief.

At the sound of Watson's angry outburst, the man turned around and glanced down, grinning broadly. He wiped at his sooty face and waved, leaning down over the window sill.

"Watson – why hello! No need to shout so... I think the residents of Baker Street have had their fill of noise for the day. Come up! Come Up!"

Seething, Watson pushed through the front door only to be enveloped in a cloud of black smoke as it drifted down from the second floor. Struggling to catch his breath, he stormed up the stairs, taking them in twos and burst through the door to the flat; there would be a reckoning.

"Ahh... there you are... come in... come in! I've just made the most fantastic discovery! Take a seat while I explain... oh and leave the door ajar... it's a bit smokey in here," announced Holmes excitedly, interrupting him before he could utter a word.

Holmes was tall, thin and pale, and at first glance, might be mistaken for frail until one noticed his toned, sinewy arms and lean build sculpted by years of fencing and Asian martial arts. He paced the floor, moving with a quiet, feline grace, his long, elegant fingers fluttering in nervous agitation as he spoke; the pupils of his piercing eyes constricted to pinpoints in icy pools of blue-grey. Watson surveyed the shattered remnants of test tubes, charred worktable and what may have once been a microscope, with a look of disbelief and fear.

"Have you completely lost your mind?" he exclaimed, eyes now fixed on a smouldering crater in Mrs. Hudson's Oriental rug. "Is it your intention to blow all of Baker Street to Kingdom come along with yourself?"

Holmes burst out laughing and shook his head, brushing futilely at the soot on his shirt.

"No.! Course not! Little mishap... apologies. A few too many drops of silver fulminate..." As he spoke, he frowned a bit and quickly stamped out a few embers in the carpet. Once he was sure it was out, he dragged a wingchair — one surprisingly intact — over the blackened hole and plopped down onto the arm apparently satisfied with his solution.

"There... all taken care of... No need to fret... doubt she'll even notice," he assured him with a quick grin, though the edges of the scorched ring were still clearly visible under the chair.

Watson could only stare at him – speechless as he slowly surveyed the parlor. Luckily, most of the damage was confined to the worktable, the drapes and the windows. The lack of glass was proving to be beneficial as most of the smoke had now dissipated out the shattered windows.

"Oh my god... Mr. Holmes are you all right?"

Light footsteps sounded in the hall as a frantic Mary Morstan darted into the room, her eyes wide with alarm. She ran past Watson with barely a glance, straight to Holmes, and proceeded to wipe at his face with her handkerchief. The edges of Watson's mustache drooped again as a slow frown spread across his face.

"You're hurt!" she exclaimed anxiously, gently dabbing at a gash on the detective's forehead.

"For God's sake Mary... it's just a scratch! Damn fool's luck continues to hold," grumbled the Doctor, more than a little annoyed at the attention being paid to his flatmate.

Holmes' eyes crinkled in amusement, noting Watson's irritation and detecting more than a hint of jealousy. He smiled reassuringly up at Mary and gently pushed her hand away.

"John's right... mustn't fuss... but I thank you for your concern. You are, Miss Morstan, a true angel of mercy... and a lovely one at that."

She blushed, a faint smile creeping across her lips, undeniably flattered by the compliment, always surprised at how charming and unexpectedly kind he could be at times. She peered more closely at the wound on his forehead. The bleeding had all but stopped but still – she looked unconvinced.

"There might be glass..." she protested, looking to Watson for support. "Perhaps your tweezers John..." The Doctor, however, only shrugged and looked away still rather irritated.

"Bah... nonsense," Holmes laughed. He ran his fingers over his face, checking his eyebrows and eyelids and broke into a wide smile. "This time... I even managed to keep my eyebrows." He suddenly paused, an intense look of concentration on his face as he leaned forward, sniffing, eyes scanning the lace collar of her dress.

"Lavender... lovely... yours... and traces of..." he paused, sniffed again – his smile widening, a wicked gleam in his eye.

"Bay rum.... sandalwood and clove... hah old fellow... I'd know that scent anywhere! Obviously, a very successful engagement weekend."

Mary started a bit, blushing intensely as he plucked a few sandy bristles from her collar. He held them up, studying them in the light. Mustache hairs, no doubt about it.

"Successful indeed... and very close... perhaps much closer than Miss Morstan's parents would approve," he remarked slyly.

"Bloody hell man... mind your manners!" hissed Watson sharply, crossing the room to stand by Mary's side. She looked utterly mortified, cheeks bright crimson and eyes focused on the floor. Watson wound his arm protectively about her shoulder.

Holmes sighed in exasperation and shook his head in bewilderment.

"I don't know why you're so out of sorts! I applaud you and Miss Morstan's decision to buck these ridiculous conventions. Sheer nonsense — only a fool would buy a carriage without taking it for a whirl round the block."

A small squawk of dismay escaped from Mary's lips and Watson bristled with anger. He compressed his lips until they were colorless, fists clenched at his side.

"There's been no whirling ... No whirling!" he protested vehemently, using every ounce of strength and determination he possessed to remain in control.

Holmes, however, seemed not to hear or care, already having moved on. He suddenly clapped his hands together, remembering that he had news to tell them. Dashing over to the worktable, he began to sift through the rubble – frantically searching. Finally, he uttered a sigh of relief and joyfully held up two pieces of canvas, both slightly singed and approximately the same size – 4 x 4. The only difference seemed to be their color; one was a dingy off-white, the other a mottled, reddish brown.

Watson's frown deepened as he regarded the cloth suspiciously, his eyes flickering first over the stain and then Holmes. He could just make out the outline of a bandage under the sleeve of his shirt, just below his left shoulder. Madman...

"That's blood?" murmured Mary uneasily. "Not... human, though?" she added hopefully.

"Yes... blood... and of course, it's human. That's the point! Now observe, I soaked both of these in blood, then this one in bleach. Mixed a compound of nitrogen, hydrogen, oxygen and carbon with hydrogen peroxide - sprayed it on and then..."

"But how?" interrupted Mary, "where did you get so much? It's not like hospitals or morgues just pass it out... I don't understa..."

She abruptly broke off – a look of horror spreading across her face as it came to her that it was his own blood. She looked nervously to John, a growing sense of unease enveloping her. Everything about the situation was unsettling – from the explosion to Holmes' manic behavior; she had expected to find him in the throes of depression yet here he was acting excited and almost cheerful.

"Troglodytes troglodytes!" Holmes exclaimed abruptly, eyes now fixed on her hat, chemistry forgotten for the moment. He moved swiftly across the room and snatched the hat from her head. He paced the floor restlessly, studying it – a pensive look darkening his face.

"The common wren. Such a splendid little fellow – or well... he was... before he ended up stuffed and fixed to your hat. They're quite beneficial you know. Keep the insect population at bay. Shame really ... I do wonder what you ladies will do when you've exhausted all our feathered friends for your silly hats? Suppose you'll move on. Small woodland mammals perhaps? I suggest rodents... wharf rats. London can certainly spare a few of those."

The words just tumbled out at lightning speed, without pause and all the while he continued to pace. Mary Morstan retreated towards John, a helpless and worried look on her face; his mania seemed to be increasing. Watson, who up to this point, had largely remained silent, finally reached the limits of his patience.

"Enough!" he commanded loudly; then in a much gentler voice, turned to Mary, advising, "Think we could all use a nice cuppa. Go on down and make us some, won't you dear? Go on now... Mrs. Hudson won't mind you using her kitchen."

She pursed her lips, ready to protest, but the Doctor smiled reassuringly and gave her a gentle, but firm nudge toward the door.

"Do as I say dear... Sherlock and I have some matters to settle and he does need to get ready now doesn't he? Can't go to Lady Caroline's in his current state, now can he? Run along dear... I'll have Earl Grey – herbal for Mr. Holmes... he certainly doesn't need any more stimulants." He took her by the arm and walked her to the door. Reaching into his pocket, he took out a few coins and a pound and pressed them into her palm.

"Make the tea but allow us an hour. Send one of the boys to Lady Caroline's with a note explaining that we are running a bit late. "

She hesitated a moment, looking anxiously back towards the parlor where Holmes had returned to the worktable, sifting through the shattered tubes and equipment – her presence all but forgotten it seemed.

"Will he be all right?" she whispered. "Is he... " she hesitated, not even wanting to voice the words.

"...Under the influence?" finished Watson, a look of utter frustration on his face. "Completely. Either that or he's stark raving mad."

Watson sighed heavily and cast a despairing glance in his flatmate's direction. "I suspect, a little of both. Now go on and I promise, when you come back up in one hour he'll be fit in his mind and presentable." Leaning over, he kissed her reassuringly on the forehead and with a confident smile, continued to nudge her towards the door. He waited until the flat door had completely closed, listening to the sounds of her steps receding down the stairs. Satisfied that she was well out of earshot, he narrowed his eyes, no longer bothering to disguise his anger and sprang towards the worktable. In one swift motion, he grabbed Holmes by his left forearm and yanked up his sleeve, confirming his suspicions. A small pattern of needle pricks tattooed the area just below the crease of his elbow; some so old they had almost disappeared, others fresh – slightly red and raised, obviously just a few hours old.

"How dare you subject her to this! Worry her so!"

Holmes arched his brow, somewhat surprised at his friend's ill-humor.

"She's a nurse. She works in the East End. I would expect this is fairly commonplace for her," he retorted with a dismissive shrug.

"You want to push that poison into your veins that's your affair, but you have no right to subject her to this! Which is it this time?" pressed Watson harshly, still holding onto his forearm.

For the first time that afternoon, Holmes' face registered anger. It was only a flash, however, quickly replaced by an icy glare and sullen grin. He pulled his arm free from Watson and rolled his sleeve back down.

"You know my methods... you've seen my behavior. Can you not make a deduction?" he mocked.

"Cocaine then... how much?"

"What does it matter? As you said, 'None of your affair."

Flushed with anger, Watson reached out and grabbed Holmes' wrist, index and middle finger searching for a pulse. The anger on his face soon dissolved into alarm as he tried to count the beats.

"Christ... I can't count them! One day your heart is going to burst! Perhaps then you'll be satisfied." Giving up, he released his wrist and pressed his fingers to the bottom portion of Holmes' neck, just to the side of his windpipe.

Laughing, Holmes pulled away, a wry grin curling his lips, though he spoke with the utmost seriousness.

"Well, in the words of Aeschylus, 'Call no man happy till he is dead."

At these words, Watson's expression grew increasingly troubled.

"There's nothing humorous in those words... why do you say that?"

Holmes offered no reply and only shrugged, retreating to the worktable to sift through his broken equipment.

"I can't help you if you won't tell me what's wrong? I want to help."

"Your assistance is not required Doctor... I'm quite fine," Holmes insisted in a quiet but firm voice, though he took care to avoid eye contact.

A pained look of disbelief crossed Watson's face. He shook his head, more distressed than angry.

"Watching you like this – spiraling downwards... is almost unbearable."

A heavy silence fell between them, breached only by the sounds of broken bits of metal and glass scrabbling over the surface of the worktable as Holmes continued to sort through the debris – head lowered, mouth drawn and tight. At last, he heaved a deep sigh and spoke.

"John... look," he began somberly, "if I've upset Miss Morstan, or you for that matter, please accept my humble apologies. It was never my intent." He paused for a moment, as if gathering his thoughts and then continued, his expression drawn and distant as if he was burdened by some great darkness.

"Now... I've things to do and judging by your dress, you're headed to a social engagement – so I say – let's call a truce and each one get on with what's needed."

John groaned in defeat and moved to stand before him at the table. He was exhausted, and the evening had barely begun.

"It's a party... at Lady Caroline's... and it's for you, Holmes. Lady Caroline and Mary have been planning this for weeks," he explained, trying to be patient.

"For me? Why on earth would it be for me?" chuckled Holmes with a quick smile, a bemused look on his face.

"Do you not know what day it is?" groaned John in utter exasperation.

"Of course, I do... January 6," snapped the detective, clearly irritated at the ridiculous nature of the question. A moment passed; he seemed briefly puzzled. As the significance finally sunk in, a look of weary acceptance filtered across his face.

"Bloody Hell... January 6th already," murmured Holmes wistfully. *January 6th... his birthday... 30th in fact.* "So soon. Seems like I just had one."

"They come once a year dear fellow, like it or not," chuckled Watson, brightening a bit.

"Don't suppose I can beg off?"

Watson began to laugh and shook his head.

"Do you really want to risk the wrath of both Mary and Lady Caroline? Besides, Lady   Caroline's been very generous with us. If I remember correctly, did she not fund the replacement of your equipment the last time you had a little mishap? Perhaps you should take that into consideration."

Holmes slowly nodded, acknowledging that it was so. Lady Caroline and her husband had been loyal supporters; often relieving financial stress in the slow periods between cases. He thought for a moment, face drawn in quiet concentration and then shrugged in resignation.

"Well then, I best go make myself presentable," he announced, with a general air of reluctance. Forcing a smile, he disappeared down the hall to clean up and dress for the celebration.

»»«

Reflection

The night was still, heavy with almost no moon. Holmes gazed out across the ever-deepening shadows of the formal gardens, somber and reflective as he perched upon the stone rail. He leaned forward into the darkness – listening, his lips pulling into a faint smile. Almost nothing. Incredible... just the muted warble and clicks of the nightjars. Yet, here he was... in the very center of London — heart of the city — mere blocks from the hustle and bustle; an island of tranquility floating in a sea of abject poverty that filled the streets with every manner of misery, degradation and depravity. The beating heart of London pulsed deeply within him. The beat, however, was irregular... diseased... corrupt. For most men, this would have caused great despair, but he was not most men; he welcomed the disease. It stimulated him and was, in his mind, the reason for his existence. Without the disease, the case, the puzzle, he was just another man. Granted, cleverer than most. He had spent his entire life thus far honing his powers of reason and perception, eschewing the normal relationships that young men pursued – all in the name of excelling at the game. The game was everything. As a result, he isolated himself; a

36

necessity to ensure his mind remained unbiased and guided by pure, cold reason instead of sentiment; interactions with few exceptions were shallow and fleeting. He had been successful maintaining this regimen all these years, but on this 6th day in the 30th year of his life, he was keenly aware of a deepening sense of emptiness. Over the past two years, he had begun to question his life course. Was it possible he had miscalculated? John Watson, the only man he allowed himself to call 'friend', had always insisted that life was truly about relationships and the quality of personal interactions; not how clever you were or the puzzles you solved. The two men had spent many hours at Baker Street locked in lively debate over this very issue and he had always dismissed his good friend with a laugh and shrug, but now he wondered. What if Watson was right? And if he was, didn't it follow that he had made himself irrelevant? Holmes had been mostly successful in suppressing these feelings of doubt, focusing on the cases, submerging himself in the science until her letter arrived. It came without warning after 9 months of nary a word save for the simultaneous death and engagement announcements in the society pages of the Times: *Contessa Irene Orchini nee Adler, widow of the late Conte Emilio Orchini of Turin, betrothed to George Wesley Astor of Beacon Hill, Boston; a spring nuptial is anticipated.* Her letter, of course, was another plea for a favor. That's how it always began, and up to this point, he had always rallied to the cause. He had been well compensated in more ways than one. Mykonos had been immensely satisfying. They had made an agreement; they would be casual lovers – bound only by mutual desire as long as it lasted and not society's conventions. It had seemed the perfect solution; neither one of them sought anything serious or an attachment. This was no love affair and yet, when the letter had arrived asking – demanding — his help, with not even a mention of why there had been scant contact for nine months or why she couldn't have at the very least dropped a short telegram mentioning her impending marriage, he had experienced an unexpected surge of resentment and hurt. How easily she dismissed him – as easily as the men she married and then discarded. The error had been solely his; he'd forgotten the rules and grown attached – allowing her to play him for a fool. The woman was simply better at the game. The weaker sex... indeed!

The sounds of the party drifted out across the terrace as the French doors opened and then closed, calling him back to the present. Such sober musings he decided were best left to the comfort of his wingchair and a fine glass of claret and as he pushed the thoughts from his mind, he took a deep breath, filling his lungs with the soothing fragrance of lilacs and gardenia. He lit another cigarette, turning back around to look upon the glow that emanated from the French doors of Bexly Manor. A warm smile curled his lips as he removed the monogrammed tobacco pouch from his pocket and turned it over in his hands, studying the meticulous stitching. John Watson had done well for himself. Mary Morstan was not only kind and compassionate, but also lovely and well-connected and that connection was proving quite useful. Her aunt, Lady Caroline Montague, was one of the most powerful women in

37

London. She was a bored, middle-aged socialite locked in a loveless marriage to a fading earl. The Earl, some 30 years her senior, often could not remember the day and time or comprehend that he was not still engaged in the Anglo-Afghan war. So, with nothing but time and money on her hands and possessed with an insatiable appetite for gossip, she threw parties, hosted young ladies' seasons and generally meddled. Fortuitously, she'd taken a shine to Holmes, having read every story John Watson had published in the Strand. Although he detested most social engagements, Holmes had instinctively known that social connections were vital to his collection of information, so he had carefully cultivated her amity. Watson, on his part, had firmly insisted that the family's status had nothing to do with his decision to become engaged so quickly, having known Mary for less than half a year. Holmes knew a well-made marriage could only boost his friend's standing in the medical community. Who was he to begrudge him – Watson had been a steadfast and loyal friend these past four years, having mostly borne his foul moods and difficult nature with patience and good humor. He would miss him to be sure, but only wished him well. With a shrug, he finished his cigarette and took up the silver and black cane that Watson had given him as a present. Grasping the silver handle, he gave it a quick twist and pulled up, his eyes lighting with delight as the cane sheath fell back to reveal the silver shaft of a sword. Brilliant!

"Ah hah! There you are! Hiding out I see." Watson's cheerful voice rang out in greeting as he crossed the stone terrace.

"Not very well apparently," chuckled Holmes wryly.

Watson laughed and took his place next to Holmes, leaning back against the balcony rail. He watched with great satisfaction as his friend continued to examine the sword cane; he was obviously pleased with his gift. Taking care to maintain a degree of nonchalance, Watson fixed his trained eye on his friend, experiencing a surge of relief. Much better, the mania caused by the narcotic seemed to have passed. Holmes' pupils were now almost normal and the slight tremor in his hand had all but vanished. However, all this attention to his physical condition did not go unnoticed by Holmes.

"Would you care to take my pulse Doctor?"

It was not so much voiced as breathed out with resigned weariness.

Watson bristled a bit. *Damn ... was there nothing the man didn't notice?*

"It is my duty as a doctor to monitor your state... and as a friend," he replied defensively. "I see you are better now and I am much relieved."

"Better?" Holmes' mouth curled derisively as he met his friend's gaze. "By better I take it you mean sober? If so, then yes... I am currently 'better' — so, rest easy dear friend — I expect I shall remain "better" throughout this little social ordeal. I wouldn't want to alarm our gracious hostess nor the ladies." The sharp edge of bitterness in his voice was unmistakable.

Watson drew himself up; his expression firm and resolute. "You judge me wrongly. You see this as meddling, passing moral judgement. But I tell you, my primary concern is your state of health... and the state of your mind."

"My mind !!" Holmes snorted, eyes suddenly ablaze. He compressed his lips tightly and Watson could see that he was struggling to contain his indignation. After a moment, a pensive look washed over his face, anger dissolving into an expression of somber melancholy. Reaching into his pocket, he withdrew his cigarette case and averted his eyes, seemingly focused on choosing the best cigarette.

"I assure you John, I am fine... as is my mind." The sharpness in tone had disappeared, replaced by a deep weariness. He lit a cigarette, inhaling deeply.

"You are not fine. I know you well enough to see you are deeply troubled," murmured Watson in protest. He was silent for a few moments and then let out a sigh of deep exasperation.

"That bloody harpy... this is her doing. I rue the day we ever set eyes on her. You should have let her rot in jail."

Surprise flashed briefly across Holmes' face. Such raw vitriol from Watson was uncharacteristic especially when directed at the fairer sex, but he offered no comment, remaining silent as he studied him through a haze of smoke.

"She came to me for help. How could I turn her away? Besides... that was years ago," he offered after a brief pause, breaking the silence.

"And this is how she repays you – treating you like her personal lackey. What now man? After all these months. What new predicament has she gotten herself into that you're supposed to fix? And don't tell me there's nothing because I saw the letter jackknifed to the wall!"

Holmes' eyes grew veiled - cautious. "Reading my correspondence again Doctor or did our dear landlady do the honors?"

Watson laughed bitterly, shaking his head. "I didn't have to read it. I recognized the handwriting and her damn French perfume. It doesn't take Sherlock Bloody Holmes to realize that the contents disturbed you, judging by the way you drove the blade into the wall – right up to the hilt."

Holmes arched his brow in surprise and then managed a slight smile, clapping his hands slowly. "Bravo old man – your deductive skills have vastly improved. You'll make a good detective one day."

Watson ignored the taunt, a look of mild desperation on his face. "For God's sake man – she's playing you... using you. She has no heart."

"The same has been said of me," muttered Holmes. "We used each other."

Watson's eyes grew disbelieving. "The people who know you, truly know that's not true. Please, at least consider my words or I fear that she will ruin you... or worse."

The earnestness of Watson's words touched him, though it was difficult to admit such things. After a moment of silence, Holmes let out a heavy sigh and managed a weak smile.

"It's Boston... some nonsense with husband to be number three," he admitted with a bleak smile. "What kind of trouble - I am not sure - I didn't bother to read any further."

"Will you go then?" pressed Watson gently, though his eyes reflected his fear.

Holmes was silent for a moment and then shrugged. "I have not reached a decision yet. I will, however, take your words under advisement."

A glimmer of hope washed over Watson's face. He breathed a little easier, his spirits lifting at the revelation that Holmes had not yet made up his mind.

"I pray that you will... serious consideration."

Holmes rolled his eyes a bit and exhaled in mild exasperation.

"I told you I would! Bloody hell! You're like an old dog with a bone. Poor Miss Morstan. I wonder if she realizes what a complete nag you are at times. I tell you, at times like these, I count the days."

Watson looked momentarily offended but then noting the slight grin on Holmes' face, he relaxed – a slow smile lighting his face.

"Well, your date with freedom has not yet been determined. Miss Morstan and I have not yet set a date. Now, your festivities are about to resume, and the ladies were wondering where you'd gone off to. I've been sent to retrieve you. Miss Clara in particular noticed your absence; she's quite taken with you. Not to mention the fact that Lady Caroline is anxious to reveal your final birthday surprise – a very special treat she has assured us!"

"Ahh God, more surprises. I can barely contain myself," groaned Holmes dismally, with a slight shake of his head. "This, I may never forgive you for Watson," he moaned though his eyes were alight with mischief.

Watson smiled in embarrassment. Holmes detested surprises, a fact he was well aware of.

"To be honest old man, I had no idea. Something the ladies concocted without my knowledge. Miss Clara is Lady's Caroline's niece. Just turned 21; inexperienced and ready to start her season. Lady Caroline is obviously looking to ease her gradually into the social circuit and views you as a secure first escort. You should take it as a compliment that she trusts you with her niece."

Holmes burst into laughter, always amazed at how easily Watson was led by the women in his life.

"Safe? Of course, she's safe. But who, dear friend, will protect me?" he chuckled. "One woman's machinations are annoying... two is worrisome... but three dear friend... three is a Shakespearean tragedy. I seem to recall something about a cauldron and three crones. "

"You've nothing to fear from such a shy, young woman," sighed Watson with some weariness, struggling to ignore the remark about the crones. "You don't find her attractive?"

"Humph....Pretty enough I suppose – but certainly a case of the light being on but no one at home. Not to mention the fact that those ringlets dangling about her face are extremely annoying – like springs bobbing about."

Watson sighed, shaking his head." Who are we to question women's fashion? And women don't need to be clever – it's not in their nature. That's why we're here... to protect them, provide for them and think for them."

"Is that so?" remarked Holmes, suppressing a smile.

Watson sighed patiently, as if he was teaching a lesson to a small child.

"Look, it's obvious you know very little about women. Sometimes, it's just best to let them go on believing that they are in control. Less fuss that way."

"Interesting," mused Holmes, thinking it best not to get into this argument. "But these things are of no concern to me John. You seem quite capable of carrying the mantle of the patriarchy without my assistance and I gladly leave you to it."

"All I am saying is that the less clever the woman, the easier they are to handle. Miss Clara is a perfectly lovely girl. She'll be starting her season soon. I know she's a little dim and perhaps a bit timid..."

"Timid?" sputtered Holmes, choking back a laugh. "That timid young woman has been nudging my foot and grasping my knee under the table for most of the evening. That, my dear Watson is desperation, not shyness."

Watson looked astonished at first and then deeply embarrassed. "Bloody hell! Well, I'm sorry about that. I must confess, I would have never suspected. I don't know what has gotten into these young women nowadays. All this fuss and bother about getting the vote and equal rights. Sheer nonsense! Next thing you know they'll be wanting to sit in Parliament. Can you imagine... women in positions of power? Where on earth do they get these ideas?!"

"You do remember a Queen named Victoria… a woman… in power?" snickered Holmes.

"That's different – power by inheritance and tradition. Besides, we all know that Parliament and the Minister are the true forces behind the monarchy. I just don't understand that's all. Women in my father's time knew their place. There was none of this nonsense."

Holmes sighed in resignation and smiled. *Good old Watson... mind forever planted in the 18th century.*

"You haven't expressed these views to Miss Morstan by any chance, have you?"

John Watson's face turned the color of vine-ripened tomatoes and he sputtered, obviously flustered.

"Well... no... not in so many words," he murmured, looking rather anxious.

A sly look entered Holmes' eyes and he nodded in approval.

"Good... good. I suggest you keep it that way... that is of course, providing that you wish to survive until your wedding day."

"Watson stared at him for a moment, not quite sure whether he was serious or joking. Catching his look of doubt, Holmes flashed a devilish grin and finished his cigarette.

"Rest easy. I'll make sure Mrs. Hudson delays renting out your room just in case. Now, shall we? The fray beckons. No sense putting it off any longer."

Refastening his jacket, he took a deep breath and strode quickly across the terrace towards the French doors, without waiting for Watson. Watson stared after him for a moment and then hurried to catch up.

»»««

Prophecy

"There you are... naughty boy!"

They pounced on him as foxes on hens as he entered the drawing room. Lady Caroline, slightly out of breath from dashing across the room, readjusted the lace on her neckline and smiled, swatting him playfully with her fan. Miss Clara, pretty face flushed pink in excitement, ringlets bobbing followed closely at her heels. She beamed wistfully up at Holmes, fanning herself but thankfully remained silent, unlike Lady Montague.

"You can't give me the slip young man. Not a man born, just ask the Earl, he tried once!" teased the older woman. She caught his arm firmly and drew him further into the room.

Holmes let out a sigh of resignation and forced a smile, glancing warily in the Earl's direction. The poor man was sitting in a wing-chair tucked in the corner, carrying on an animated conversation with an empty sofa. *Bloody Hell, surely there were other avenues of escape other than dementia?*

Following his glance, Lady Caroline's face settled into a worried frown on taking note of the confused state of her husband. *Not again. Why did it always seem to happen when she was entertaining? Time for an early evening – she would not have a scene like the last time.*

"Well, maybe not at the moment. He does seem a bit... preoccupied," she laughed, attempting to make light of the situation. "Bekins! Bekins, where are you?" she called out with some impatience. Immediately, a sober-faced butler appeared, his eyes already fixed on the Earl. Bekins knew exactly what to do. Thankfully, her ladyship was taking preemptive action while the Earl was still manageable. He was getting too old to be chasing the Earl out from under tables, cupboards and ladies' skirts.

"It's time for his lordship's bath and tuck-in. See to it and don't forget his special milk," she scolded. "The Earl is an absolute terror without his milk," she explained to her guests, looking mildly embarrassed.

Bekins nodded looking suitably apologetic. Although it hadn't really been his fault, this time he'd see to it that his lordship received the proper dosage of laudanum to keep him down and out. A moment later, he had the elderly Earl by the arm and was gently leading him out the door; the Earl, still engrossed in his imaginary conversation, continued to babble as they made their way down the hall.

Lady Caroline sighed audibly in relief as the door shut after them, her mood brightening considerably. She turned her attention back to the guest of honor and seized Holmes' arm once again, pulling him forward. She paused just before the door to the library, released his arm and turned to face all assembled, a secretive smile lighting her face.

"Now here's the fun part!" she exclaimed, clapping her hands together. "I've something very special but I need you all to wait right here; especially you my dear boy. Clara dear, I need for you to take good care of dear Mr. Holmes and when I give the word, bring him into the library but not before!"

"Of course, Auntie. I'll take very good care of him... promise," breathed the girl, starry eyes fixed upon Holmes as she latched onto his arm, holding fast.

Holmes suppressed a weary smile, glancing down at the girl pressed so tightly against him that he could feel every breath she took. She met his gaze and blushed though made no attempt to move away.

"I've no doubt you will," chuckled Lady Caroline with a sly smile. She quickly disappeared into the library, pulling the door closed behind her. Moments later, she re-emerged and stood in the now darkened doorway to the library, beckoning for them to come forward and follow her into the darkness. Giggling excitedly, Clara Barclay tightened her gloved fingers around Holmes' arm and led him into the darkened room.

"Mister Holmes, I can't tell you how excited I am for you," she cooed, her gloved fingers sliding along the sleeve of his jacket. "I can barely contain myself."

"Please try," he sighed, trying to ignore her as best he could. It was proving to be a difficult task, however, as she had a vise-like hold on his arm. The slightest movement away from her caused her fingers to grip him more tightly. For one so petite, barely five foot three and possibly 100 pounds including her seven pounds of petticoats and bustle, she was incredibly strong. He looked down at her gloved hand on his arm and frowned, wondering if there would be bruises. *A lioness lying in wait for her prey. Smaller than the male but inherently more dangerous .... ruthless... the female of the species .... the perfect predator.*

Clara giggled again, resting her cheek against his shoulder, taking advantage of the darkness of the room to move in even closer.

"You are ever so witty," she sighed, nestling close. "A clever man like you – man of the world... so much you could teach me. Dear Mr. Holmes, you'd find me the most compliant and willing of pupils. I'd be ever so grateful." She lifted her gaze, her lips pulling into a suggestive pout and fluttered her eyelashes.

Holmes stared at her for a moment, overcome with a surge of disdain – the meaning of her words not lost on him. *Lioness. No... on second thought... more like a spider spinning a web... black widow, and a rather voracious one.* He met her gaze steadily and then smiled politely but coolly. With a slight shake of his head, he shifted his shoulder ever so carefully out from under her cheek and then removed her hand from his arm. He had to proceed cautiously – she was after all the niece of one of his most reliable supporters.

"I am quite sure Miss Barclay, that whatever you lack in formal education will be arranged for you by your Aunt."

Clara's smile and dreamy gaze began to dissolve into a frown as her eyes took on a look of puzzled irritation. *This should be working. Why wasn't it working? She'd spent a considerable amount of time that afternoon in front of the mirror practicing her most alluring pout; devoted extra attention to her hair ensuring that the curls fell at just the right angle around her face and taken great care that her face and neck were the perfect shade of porcelain. Perhaps she hadn't laced tight enough... It couldn't possibly be that, could it?*

She could scarcely breathe as it was. Her frown deepened as she pondered all the possible reasons why she was failing.

Holmes continued, his voice taking on a barely concealed tone of sarcasm.

"As for anything else you think you may require, well, you are about to begin your season and being of a moderately attractive nature Miss Barclay, I expect there will be any number of young and willing swains eager to accommodate you in your quest for... knowledge."

Clara flushed bright crimson and uttered an odd little panting noise as if she couldn't quite catch her breath. She stared at him, lips parted, speechless, mortified. Holmes paid her no mind however, the matter was settled as far as he was concerned.

"Ahh... there's Lady Caroline now. Best not keep her waiting," he remarked with a deliberate air of detachment and then moved off, leaving the girl standing alone in the middle of the darkened hallway. Clara remained frozen in place for a moment, staring after him – too dumbfounded to even comment and then slunk off to the side, her delicate cheeks burning in shame and indignation.

Once clear of the hall, Holmes paused for a moment, waiting for his eyes to adjust to the darkness of the room as it was lit by only a few candles. In the center of the room stood a small table, draped in black linen, a single candle in the center of it, two chairs tucked on each side. There were a few chairs set to the side of the room by the wall for the other guests, now occupied by Watson, Miss Morstan and a very sullen Clara Barclay, who fanned herself rapidly, and pouted. Holmes sighed and turned his attention back to the center of the room. A look of vexation flickered across his face as he studied the scene. This didn't bode well; it bore all the earmarks of a séance or some other mode of spiritualism and he had scant patience for such charlatanism. As the evening progressed, his resolve to be of good humor steadily eroded. *Another seemingly endless social ordeal.* He cast a sharp glance in Watson's direction, trying to catch his eye and convey in no uncertain terms by his expression, that this would be the last such celebration he would endure, patron or not. But the edges of the room were still shrouded in shadow and he gave up, realizing that the good doctor most likely could not see him nor would he notice, being too busy chattering with Miss Morstan.

Once again, the library door opened and then closed, this time followed by the rustle of fabric and clinking of metal. *Jewelry ... bracelets – cheap trinkets judging by the tinny sound of the metal.* He wrinkled his nose distastefully as the air filled with the overpowering scent of patchouli and clove. Two figures stood in the darkness near the door — one was definitely Lady Caroline — the other, another woman who appeared short, rotund and obviously the source of the cloying odor. Holmes suppressed a groan. He knew what was to come now. Romani – not a séance but almost as annoying. Lady Caroline stepped forward into the dim light, eyes bright with excitement and drew him closer to the table. Once she had him positioned by the chair, she stepped back and gestured theatrically towards the shadows.

44

"It is with great love and excitement that I present a very special treat in honor of our beloved guest. From the mists of the Carpathian Mountains... the all-knowing and wise... Madame Rada Stoyanova."

A flurry of applause sounded from the guest seats as a stout woman draped in garish scarves and brightly colored skirts stepped into the light, cheap bangles and earrings clanking. A shock of unnaturally orange hair straggled out from under a head scarf of red and black silk covered with gold sequins. She waved eagerly and smiled, her attention on the seated guests – proclaiming her thanks and greetings in a heavily accented voice. Ready to begin, she clasped her ringed fingers together and whirled around to greet the guest of honor. As her eyes fell upon him, she froze ... a look of disbelief and dread overtaking her.

"Mister Holmes ... it's you ..." she croaked, her Romani accent suddenly overcome by a heavy dose of East London.

A low chuckle of amusement rumbled from his throat as Holmes settled into a chair at the table. *Well... well... the evening had just taken an unexpected and interesting turn.* He leaned forward, a sarcastic smile on his lips.

"Dora Miller ... as I live and breathe. The costume's serviceable but your accent could use some work ... patchouli is a bit overdone."

The poor woman turned white as a sheet and collapsed into the opposite chair. She wrung her hands in great agitation and leaned forward, keeping her voice to a whisper.

"I ain't done nothin' wrong Mr. Holmes ... swear on me gran's grave ... got mouths to feed." She cast a nervous glance in the direction of Lady Caroline and then turned back to Holmes, a desperate plea in her eyes.

"Just a bit of harmless fun ... these fine ladies... they do fancy a bit of the cards and tea leaves. Please Mr. Holmes... please... it's been rough with Nate up in Pentonville. Me youngest is just a tot. It's honest work Mr. Holmes...no harm in it is there?"

"Honest?" Holmes arched his brow and snorted contemptuously.

Dora Miller turned even more pale and offered a weak smile.

"More or less..." she murmured nervously. "These fine ladies fancy my readings for their parties. I provide them a bit of fun and they pay me for my service. Please Mr. Holmes... just trying to survive best I can."

Lips curling into a smile of disbelief, Holmes leaned back in his chair, one leg crossed casually over the other. *Really? Attempting to rouse feelings of guilt and pity simply because he had been responsible for putting Nate her husband (Natty Nate as he was commonly known for the battered bowler he always wore) in Pentonville for a string of house breakings. Ridiculous woman.* He pursed his lips, ready to admonish but paused as Lady Caroline cautiously approached.

"Is something amiss?" she ventured tentatively, anxiety clouding her face as she looked first to Holmes and then to Madame Stoyanova.

Holmes glanced up and met his patron's troubled gaze as indeed now all eyes were fixed on him and Madame Stoyanova. He remained silent for a moment and then slowly smiled as reassuringly as possible.

"Not at all dear lady," he soothed. "Madame and I are just getting acquainted. As a matter of fact, I do believe "Madame" is preparing to grace me with her predictions for my future. Isn't that right Madame?" he suggested slyly. A hint of a dark smirk curled his mouth as he leveled his gazed on the flustered "Romani" and extended his right hand, palm upright.

"Dominant first correct Madame?" he queried, his voice like frost on a window pane.

Dora Miller took a deep breath and smiled nervously, bobbing her head that it was so, too shaken to voice a reply. She took his outstretched hand and focused on the lines that transected his palm, waiting for her nerve to return. Satisfied that all was in order, Lady Caroline smiled in relief and returned to her seat, eager for the reading to begin.

"Thought so," Holmes chuckled and leaned back in his chair. He closed his eyes and sighed in weary surrender. "Well then Madame .... I eagerly await your prophecy."

And so, it was that Madame Stoyanova, more correctly known as Dora Miller of East London, with husband locked away in Pentonville for burglary by the very man who now sat before her, composed her ragged nerves and began her reading - aware of all eyes on her, particularly Holmes. She didn't quite understand why he had seemingly given her a pass and not exposed her but was exceptionally grateful. She took his hand gently and studied the palm, her rough fingers tracing the lines on his palm - a serious expression on her face - for although there wasn't a true Romani in her family, her gran had taught her a bit about palms.

"I see before me... a man of great intelligence... clever, strong, confident," she began, her voice strong and certain, once more taking on a heavy accent. The others leaned forward, straining to hear every word while Holmes remained still, head resting against the back of the chair, the faintest trace of a sardonic grin on his lips as he listened, eyes closed.

"You will achieve great things Mr. Holmes... but will also suffer great loss... there is darkness growing. I see... a woman... most untrustworthy."

At this pronouncement, Watson grunted in self-satisfaction, grumbled a bit, and was promptly rewarded by a sharp rap to his knee and a warning frown from Mary Morstan. Holmes however remained silent, though the grin on his face had increased. *Troublesome woman? Certainly not a revelation.*

Dora Miller frowned, staring at the line that ran the length of his palm, his lifeline – it was broken into three distinct and uneven sections.

"A woman," she repeated. She continued to stare at the lines, her frown increasing as she concentrated. "No... Two... No... three women Mr. Holmes... Three," she corrected.

At this, Holmes' eyes flickered open and he uttered a little snort, a look of obvious irritation on his face. Dora Miller ignored the look however and continued.

"First is passing. Fading fast... best gone... coldness...lies... trickery." She shook her head, a disagreeable look on her face. Re-positioning his hand

46

in hers, she moved onto the second section, her face growing more calm and relaxed.

"Second to come Mr. Holmes ... brave... clever... warm.... but darkness also... buried deep ... secrets and pain... great pain..." Dora Miller paused, a growing look of confusion and wariness on her face. A moment passed and then a look of hope brightened her face.

"But I also see happiness... together..."

At this pronouncement, a look of doubt crinkled Holmes' brow and he chuckled, shaking his head. She continued however, looking once more to his palm.

"It's unclear ... but they are mixed... something red... reddish... and bright green... like emeralds... strong devotion but also fire... heat... so many flames... a sacrifice Mr. Holmes... great misfortune... but..."

Her voice faltered and then died, a look somewhat close to complete distress crossing her face which was suddenly pale and tight, a slight sheen of perspiration on her forehead. She released his hand and inhaled deeply, as if she couldn't catch her breath looking shaken as she tried to regain her composure. The others looked on in surprise and Holmes in amused disbelief. She averted her eyes and clasped her hands together in an attempt to quell their shaking.

"No more on this. I can see nothing," she mumbled evasively, keeping her eyes fixed on the table. She fell into an uneasy silence and remained that way for quite some time until Lady Caroline, forgetting Madame Stoyanova's instruction for the participants to remain quiet, leaned forward restlessly in her seat.

"But what of the third Madame? You mentioned three!" she pressed urgently.

Dora Miller gave a little sigh of resignation and once more took Holmes' hand in hers, knowing she had to finish the reading. She focused on the third segment of his lifeline, her brow knit in puzzlement.

"Third... much like the second.... loving heart but wounded... she is stronger... she'll risk everything. I see a connection but many years away... I don't understand. More than a lifetime away and yet ... I see you Mr. Holmes as you are today, but everything around you is... strange... makes no sense. After... there is nothing." She quickly released his hand and sat back in her chair, an uneasy expression on her face. She didn't want to see any more – what she had seen was troubling enough.

The room grew silent as all eyes remained fixed on Madame Stoyanova, waiting expectantly for her to continue – uncertain whether Madame was finished or if more was to come. Holmes was silent for a moment as well, and then slowly sat up straighter in the chair. He leaned towards her, head tilted a bit and smiled disdainfully.

"Well, Dora... quite a yarn you've spun. Mildly entertaining if not somewhat predictable. Anything else? Perhaps you'll see more in the cards? Bit of Tarot then? I'm game if you are," he taunted quietly, his voice dripping with sarcasm. "We wouldn't want to give Lady Montague less than full value for her fee, would we?"

"No. No of course Mr. Holmes," stuttered Dora Miller in a nervous whisper. "I'll gladly do readings for the dear Lady and her guests. But, please sir, no more for you... please," she begged, her eyes wide with dread. Holmes suppressed a grin and rose from his chair. *Bloody hell! Did she actually believe the nonsense she spouted?*

"Well then," he chuckled wryly, "give them your best show. As for me, I prefer the element of surprise in what lies ahead ... makes for a more stimulating existence." With a slight nod, he turned as if he intended to exit the room and then paused, turning to face Lady Caroline and her guests, a sparkle of mischief in his eyes.

"Madame has completed her reading ... a round of applause if you please! Now, as I am feeling rather enlightened, please excuse my brief absence as I repair to the terrace to indulge in some tobacco and ponder her sage words. She will be delighted to perform readings for those who desire it, so please step forward."

The air filled with enthusiastic applause and as Lady Caroline and her guests surged forward, Holmes momentarily paused as he began to walk past Dora Miller on his way out to the terrace. He leaned in close to her ear, a slight smile but his eyes cold and sober.

"Word to the wise Dora," he whispered, "Lady Caroline is a dear friend of mine. As you leave tonight, be very certain that only your paraphernalia and negotiated fee accompanies you. I'd be extremely displeased to discover any of the dear lady's fine goods in Covent Garden."

The flustered woman managed a dry swallow and quick nod of acknowledgement. Satisfied, Holmes flashed a charming smile in her direction and then vanished out the terrace doors.

Limehouse

"Careful now, you'll muss my hair!"

Mary Morstan glanced up, attempting her most stern expression as John's fingers gently slipped into the silkiness of her hair, tugging ... playing gently with the strands that dangled along her neck. He ignored the look, not fooled in the least, and with eyes that radiated unwavering devotion, pulled her close.

"Not all I'd like to muss," he murmured softly, nestling her head against his vest, the tip of his chin resting lightly on the crown of her head.

He contemplated his good fortune, a contented smile played on his lips as he listened to the soft clop of the horse hooves as the hansom cab progressed towards Baker Street. Despite the day's troublesome start, it had turned out to be quite pleasant after all; all due to Mary of course. He could always count on Mary to provide a silver lining. Overcome with tenderness, he leaned forward, pressing his lips gently to her ear, whispering sweet endearments.

"Shh... Behave..." she giggled suddenly, her face turning pink though her eyes glowed with the warmth of love. Keeping her voice to a whisper, she cast a quick glance at the sleeping man slumped in the seat across from them, black silk top hat pulled low over his eyes, cane lightly resting against his knees. The faintest trace of a smile was still evident on his lips though by the gentle rise and fall of his waistcoat, she concluded he was fast asleep. Satisfied that they could safely indulge in an intimate moment, she reached her gloved hands up towards John and laced them around his neck, smiling in welcome as he bent forward to deliver a deep and loving kiss.

"I can barely stand until we are married," murmured Watson ardently as he removed his lips from hers, his hands tenderly cradling her face.

"Neither can I. At least then I won't be subjected to these mawkish displays. "

The comment, delivered with more than a trace of peevishness, rumbled across the aisle. They both froze and slowly turned to face Holmes, who, though still slouched across the seat, peered out at them from under the brim of the top hat, his mouth curled in faint disapproval.

John sat up quickly, primly against the back of the seat as Mary did the same, an embarrassed smile lighting her face. She hastily smoothed her shawl; her fingers trembling a bit as she quickly refastened her collar. Compressing her lips, she looked uncertainly from one man to the other. She wasn't a prude, but her parents were quite sensitive to gossip; a flippant remark that fell upon the wrong ears could prove disastrous not only in her personal, but also her professional life.

"Mary and I were just discussing..." protested Watson from beneath his mustache, his face a mixture of chagrin and irritation.

"Hmmm... Is that what they're calling it these days?"

"For God's sake Holmes," sputtered Watson, "please be discreet. If Mary's family... her reputation..."

49

"Oh, do relax Watson. Your clumsy attempts at seduction are scarcely worth noticing. One would be hard pressed to call you Casanova," interrupted Holmes with a sly chuckle. "In any case, I shall remain as mute as the Three Wise Monkeys, though why you insisted on my sharing a cab with you when you obviously wanted privacy, is a mystery for the ages. Do think it through next time."

Mary laughed a bit, visibly relieved, and managed a smile, smoothing back a few errant curls as she explained.

"Well, seemed silly to go separately seeing as how John and I were going for a ride in Regents. It's on the way to Baker Street. We thought you were asleep."

"Yes - nearly impossible, what with all the cooing and sighing."

A squawk of surprise escaped from her lips and she covered her mouth, face crimson with embarrassment.

Holmes laughed and flashed a charming grin.

"Not you Mary dear," he reassured as he removed his hat, absently turning it around in his hands, fingers sliding along the brim. "Watson, you really must learn to contain yourself... all those noises... dreadfully annoying."

She stared at him dumbfounded and then burst into hearty laughter much to Watson's obvious irritation and chagrin. Impulsively, she reached out across the aisle and grasped Holmes' hand, pressing it with great affection.

"Sherlock Holmes, you wicked man! There are times when I could just ..."

The words abruptly died in her throat and she coughed lightly, blushing... regretting her impulsiveness. She quickly released his hand and averted her eyes as she silently castigated herself. *What a foolish ...hurtful and possibly dangerous thing for her to say.* John Watson was the love of her life, the man she knew she was destined to be with, the only one that she could even imaging sharing her life with and having children. Yet, she had to admit, there were times when she was around Holmes that she experienced an intoxicating rush of excitement and stimulation that fluttered about most disturbingly in the very core of her being.

Holmes' eyes scanned her expression; he arched his brow and then smiled oddly, as if he had read her innermost thoughts.

"Yes... Well... Some things are best left unsaid," he remarked soberly, "and unexplored."

With a weak smile, Mary leaned her head against John's arm but remained silent, her fingers gently interlacing with his, giving comfort. Watson, though initially vexed by their playful banter, had offered no comment throughout their exchange. Once more reassured of his place in her heart, he visibly relaxed. Truthfully, he never really doubted it. Despite his misgivings about some of Holmes' character flaws, he realized this was one trust he would never violate between them; it was all just wordplay, undoubtedly for the sole purpose of provoking a reaction.

Holmes sighed a bit, realizing the tease had run its course. Reaching into his pocket, he withdrew a fine chain from which was suspended a handsome silver pocket watch. He clicked it open and studied the works, his face taking on a pensive expression. After a moment of consideration, he seemed to come to a decision, and with a firm click, closed the watch and pocketed it. Using his cane, he rapped sharply on the ceiling of the cab. As the hansom pulled to the curb, a mild look of alarm crossed Watson's face.

"What are you doing? We've still several blocks to go," he protested.

"Change of plans. I've decided," Holmes announced with a secretive smile as he leaned towards the door, grasping the handle.

"Decided what?"

"I require more..."

"More ... More what?" groaned Watson in exasperation.

"Celebration!" laughed Holmes. He repositioned his top hat and straightened his lapels. "My birthday after all. Do try to keep up John."

Watson stared at him, puzzled at first as the cab rolled to a stop and Holmes began to climb out. He peered out into the dark streets. In the distance, he could hear the faint but unmistakable noise from the docks. His expression grew troubled as he recognized their general location near the West India Docks - trouble indeed.

"Wait, we're not far from Baker. We'll go back to the flat. Open that bottle of claret ...perhaps some cards," he urged, leaning forward towards the door. Mary, who had been idly listening to their conversation, suddenly looked to John, alarmed by his obvious unease.

Holmes smiled in weary understanding but shook his head, his mind made up.

"Claret? Not really what I have in mind. Besides, you promised Miss Morstan a whirl through Regent's, and there's a lovely moon tonight – shame to waste it. I wouldn't want her to be cross with you, especially on my account. If you leave now, you'll have plenty of time to enjoy the park and still get her back to Lady Caroline's at a respectable hour."

"But where are you going? " Mary pressed anxiously. "Everything is closed now."

Holmes laughed heartily and leaned on the cab door. "Not quite. I know a place or two," he remarked cagily, an odd light in his eyes.

Watson blanched as comprehension sank in. He stepped quickly from the carriage, his face overcome with concern.

"This is ill-advised.... in light of recent circumstances."

"Circumstances," snorted Holmes, "which are none of your concern. "

"I really must protest," Watson asserted, his voice growing more agitated with each passing moment.

"Your protest and concern are noted Doctor," he replied with a melancholy smile. "Now ... I suggest you two make haste towards Regents and make the most of what's left of your evening. As for me, more celebration beckons. A pleasant good night to you both and many thanks for your lovely gifts!"

So, with a slight tip of his hat and a teasing wink towards Mary, Holmes fastened his evening coat and headed off down the alley, humming absently as he disappeared into a swirl of thickening mist. Watson watched him leave in silence, anxiety etched on his face. When the figure had all but vanished, he uttered a deep sigh of defeat and climbed slowly back into the carriage, his face drawn with worry.

Disturbed by his obvious distress, Mary settled next to him and grasped his hand.

"We should go after him quickly before we lose sight!"

"No," he murmured resignedly, "Doesn't matter. I know where he's going." He took both of her hands in his and pressed them tenderly, as much for his own comfort as hers.

Mary frowned, puzzled at his inaction for it was plain to see how distressing the situation was to him.

"Well let's go then... quickly!" she exclaimed, reaching up to rap on the ceiling to alert the driver.

He caught her hand gently but firmly and shook his head, holding onto her shoulders, a sadness in his eyes that made her even more anxious.

"No, not there... Best to leave it."

"What are you talking about?" she protested in growing frustration. "It's apparent you're worried. "

"He's gone to Limehouse," he exclaimed with some sharpness, exasperated by her exhibition of stubbornness.

Limehouse. The very word sparked a feeling of dread within her, for although she provided care and solace to the wretched of Whitechapel at London Hospital, the opium dens and denizens of Limehouse were in a class all their own. She drew herself up however and put on a brave face.

"Do you forget where I spend my days?" she reminded, her expression firm and calm as she met his gaze levelly.

"Make no mistake, I don't like the idea of you being at the London either, but I tolerate it for now... at least until we are married," declared Watson with an equally firm expression. Then, in a much gentler voice, he continued, "Limehouse is not a place for a woman ... any decent woman, and I will never take you there."

"But he's your friend," she protested softly. "I'll wait in the cab."

"No, not even then," he declared firmly. Then, seeing that she was still worried, he took both her hands in his and pressed them tenderly.

"Best to not interfere," he sighed resignedly. "When he gets this way, he won't be deterred – it'll only provoke him. He'll get it out of his system; get back on track; back to the work. You'll see... it'll be all right."

Realizing it was no use to argue any further, Mary shrugged in surrender and leaned her head against his arm, enjoying the comfort of his closeness. She nestled closer, her eyes filled with sadness.

"He needs someone. So alone..." she murmured. She closed her eyes, listening to the sound of the carriage as it moved off along towards the park.

Watson smiled and tenderly deposited a kiss on her forehead, holding her close. *Her heart is too kind*, he thought .... hence her weakness for strays and the wretched; though admittedly, an admirable quality for a nurse.

"Silly sentiment, that's what he'll say. Remember, cold pure reason is what he seeks. He's said it a thousand times," he reminded.

Mary smiled softly and looked up at him, shaking her head in disagreement.

"Just because he denies it doesn't mean it's not true. He needs someone!" she repeated, not in the least dissuaded. "Someone true and loving"

"Perhaps," he admitted in resignation, deciding it was best to concede this argument. "But don't we all?" His voice was tinged with weariness as he was rather tired of discussing his flat mate.

They lapsed into silence, arms wound lovingly around each other, each lost in their own thoughts as the cab entered the park, pulling onto the outer circle at a steady pace. A pale sliver of moonlight peeked through the shade in the hansom as they moved along towards the fountains and gardens that ringed the inner circle. John raised the shade, gazing up at the moon and then settled happily beside her, pulling her close as the cab pulled to a stop next to a three-tiered fountain. They sat quietly in the moonlit compartment, holding onto each other - listening to the soft splashing of the fountain. Smiling joyfully, his eyes alight with love, John leaned forward for a kiss.

"She said three… "

A groan escaped from Watson as he paused just inches from her lips. "What?"

Mary sat up a little more in the seat and nodded, a look of concentration furrowing her brow as she tried to work it out.

"Three... the old gypsy... She said three," she explained, apparently unaware of the thwarted kiss. "Now, the first is obviously Adler. She did say untrustworthy and that's being kind. But the second, who is the second? And what of the third? She also mentioned a third ... and what did she mean by all that nonsense about a lifetime and ...?"

She suddenly uttered a gasp and then a soft giggle of delight as her words were quickly muffled by a deeply passionate kiss. Properly silenced, she melted into his embrace, her head sinking down onto his chest. She smiled contentedly, her eyes partially closed enjoying the moment.

"I'll be quiet now," she whispered with a half-smile, snuggling even closer.

"That's my girl!" chuckled Watson in utter relief and together, arms wrapped around each other, they sank back into the seat to enjoy each other's company and counted their blessings, knowing in their hearts that the biggest blessing of all - was each other.

CHAPTER 3

A Chance Encounter

Aftermath   Baker Street - January 7, 1884 around 8 a.m.

He had just crossed Marylebone Road, stepping up onto the curb and heading up Baker when a loud clatter sounded from behind. Jarred from his reverie, Watson pivoted, quickly jumping out of the path of the Black Maria as it rumbled to a stop at the curb, the horse team pawing and dancing about restlessly.

"Halloo! Dr. Watson! Pleasant morning!" called out a cheery voice.

Shading his eyes against the first meager rays of sun, Watson glanced up towards the driver's perch of the police wagon to find a sallow faced man, short in stature and rather weaselly in appearance, seated next to the bobby at the reins.

"Ahh... Inspector, pleasant morning indeed!" he replied, suppressing a slight smile as the little man brushed off his extremely bold-patterned suit. *Plaid was all the rage these days... unfortunately.* Inspector G. Lestrade, the senior most man on the Met's squad of 25 detectives, scrambled down from the police wagon, smiled broadly and proudly dusted off his new suit. He was, in the words of Holmes, "the best of a sorry lot", which, depending on your point of view, was either a back-handed compliment or an insult. Knowing Holmes, Watson strongly suspected the latter. There was no disputing the man's enthusiasm for his profession. His methods and the ensuing results, however, were often as questionable and disastrous as his fashion sense. Perhaps sensing this, Lestrade had often come to rely upon Holmes for assistance, which was more often than not grudgingly given.

"Busy morning?" Watson inquired solicitously, glancing curiously towards the prisoner compartment at the back of the wagon. The sounds of soft weeping and murmuring drifted out from the small barred window. As he listened, Watson's expression darkened with dismay for the sounds were unmistakably feminine. Peering in through the bars, he was surprised to find four women, ranging in age from seventeen to middle-aged, shackled arms linked and holding onto each other for comfort. Their clothes were of good quality, appearance clean and respectable; obviously, women of good standing. The youngest was sobbing her heart out, face pressed against the shoulder of a stern-faced dowager in black mourning who glared balefully out

54

at him. Watson's handsome face clouded with concern; what could these ladies possibly have done to deserve such treatment? He was about to question Lestrade on this when he noticed them, the distinct green, white and purple sash of the suffragette; Votes for Women stood out in bold black letters on the white silk. They all wore them he realized, a look of weary irritation darkening his face.

"Bit of trouble then... Early risers?" he sighed. He thanked the Heavens every day that Mary was of a sensible and practical nature, not given to challenging what God had intended as the natural order of things; the man as head of the household, the woman his supportive but compliant helpmate. He had not a doubt that once they were married she would give up her duties at St. Mary's.

Lestrade chuckled merrily and nodded towards the back.

"Nothing we couldn't handle! Caught them mucking about in Regent's ... marching ... carrying on ...waving their banners. Damned nuisance they are ... disturbing the fine folks in the area. All this rubbish. I tell you, what's needed here is a firm hand. Votes for women indeed," he scoffed.

"Disturbing times indeed," commiserated the doctor with a rueful smile. "Well then, I must be off. We've that business today out at Fern Hall as you requested."

"Ahh, capital! " exclaimed Lestrade, his face lighting up at the confirmation that Holmes would indeed assist his investigation. "As a matter of fact, I was on my way over to Baker with a few items for Holmes. Bit of information I thought he might find useful, but then this happened. Chief Superintendent is in this morning, so I best be heading in to take care of processing this lot – he's a stickler. Look, I'd be very grateful if you would pass this on to Holmes, and please express my regret that we weren't able to confer," he explained, looking bitterly disappointed at the lost opportunity to chat with Holmes; something he was always eager for much to Holmes' irritation. Reaching inside his jacket, he withdrew a thick envelope crammed with bits of paper and thrust it into Watson's hands.

"You let me know if you be needing anything else. I'd handle it myself, if it weren't for Chief Superintendent. He's got us right busy as bees."

Watson chuckled a bit, watching as Lestrade climbed back up onto the wagon, for he knew the truth was that Lestrade was not so much busy as stumped. He let it pass however and gave a pleasant wave as the Black Maria headed off for the station. He opened the envelope and scanned the first sheet as he headed off down Baker, his brow furrowed in concentration. Lately, there had been a surge in counterfeiting in the city and outlying areas. Nothing particularly unusual in that save for the exceptional quality of the notes being passed. As he studied the file, he experienced a surge of relief; there was nothing better than an engaging puzzle to set his errant flatmate back on course. These feelings of optimism didn't last long however, for on approaching the entry to 221B, he discovered their landlady Mrs. Hudson, a portly and generally good-natured woman, on her knees by the open front door, sweeping up bits of glass and broken wood, muttering agitatedly to herself. The fan-shaped glass panel above the door was broken and a large piece of brick lay along with the debris just inside the doorway on the hall floor. Black scuff marks from a boot marred the finish of the front door where the thieves had obviously climbed up onto the side rail, broken the window and then shimmied inside.

"Oh dear, Mrs. Hudson, are you all right?" he exclaimed anxiously as he helped her to her feet. "Did you see the scoundrels? Did they take much?" He peered down the block to see if he could catch sight of a bobby on patrol, all the while his mind reeling, wondering where Holmes had been and why he hadn't intervened. Surely, he would have heard the commotion.

Margaret Hudson wiped her hands on her apron and let out an exasperated sigh as she pushed a few wayward strands of greying hair back into her bun. She folded her arms tightly across her chest and nodded, more than a hint of anger in her hazel eyes.

"Heard and saw 'em all right! 5 o'clock in the bloody morning .... singing and carrying on enough to wake the dead. Starts pounding on the door. Scared me half witless. Nearly jumped out of me skin," she explained, her voice growing increasingly tense and sharp.

Watson stared at her not quite sure he understood, though a hint of suspicion began to gnaw at him.

"Lost my keys! Open up dear lady!" she continued. "Just kept shouting it over and over, pounding the door and laughing like a madman. By the time I got me robe on and out the door, he'd already done the deed – chucked a brick through and climbed in. Found him on the stairs, hands and knees - crawling up blind drunk and reeking of Limehouse."

Comprehension sank in; a look of utter disillusionment on Watson's face as he thought over all she had been subjected to during their tenancy.

"I'm so sorry," he began earnestly, reaching out to take her hands in his. "Dear Mrs. Hudson, I know this is difficult but…"

"Worst tenant in London!" she blurted, interrupting him, her face still crimson with anger. "I don't know how much more I can take. If I had any sense, I'd send him packing...."

Watson's face suffused with compassion and he nodded in understanding. "No one would fault you. You've been more than patient," he sighed with a sad smile as he continued to pat her hand reassuringly.

"Bad enough with all the nasty smells from his experiments. Then he nearly blows us all to kingdom come. Ruins my furniture, my best Oriental. Me gran left that to me. Playing his bloody violin at all hours… now this. You tell him for me John Watson.... It's all going on his rent… the windows, the table, my oriental, the door," she ranted, her agitation growing until she was visibly shaking. Then, when she could absolutely stand it no longer, she burst into tears, burying her face in her hands.

"I just don't know what he'll do," she sobbed, her anger dissolving into motherly concern, "once you've gone. "

"He'll be all right dear ... he always is," he soothed, wishing he was as certain as he sounded. "Just a rough patch… you'll see."

With a gentle smile, he offered her his handkerchief and patted her shoulder while she dried her eyes and attempted to regain her composure. He waited until she had calmed down and then gave her hand a soothing squeeze.

"I know it's a lot to ask, but can you find it in your heart to forgive once more?" he asked gently, "I'll talk to him."

Her nerves restored, Margaret Hudson dabbed briefly at her eyes and after brief consideration, managed a forgiving smile.

"You'll be missed John Watson," she murmured, her expression tinged with sadness, "and not just by me." Watson smiled fondly and nodded.

"I'll count on you to remind him of it. Now, don't you worry dear lady, I'll set this straight," he vowed and with a determined expression, turned to head up the stairs. A gentle tug at his coat made him pause for a moment, and he turned to find Mrs. Hudson, a slight smile on her face.

"You give him bloody hell," she advised firmly though a hint of a smile now touched her face, "and these." Watson looked down and arched his brow in surprise as she held out a set of keys on a sturdy ring. *She really had forgiven him. She rarely gave out more keys when lost.*

As if reading his mind, she managed a chuckle and shrugged in resignation, once more taking up her broom to continue sweeping. "Silly sod. Didn't lose them at all. Bill Wiggins found them out in the gutter. Must have dropped them when he was stumbling about." She paused briefly, a surprisingly kind and warm smile on her lips.

"I'll be up right soon as I finish clearing this nightmare... bring some tea...and tarts... the raspberry ones he loves so much. I'm sure he'll be needing a cuppa. " With the matter now settled and mostly forgiven, and having nothing more to say, she nodded to herself and returned to her sweeping.

Watson shook his head slightly, always amazed at how quickly she forgave him once she had vented her anger. Pocketing the keys, he hurried up the stairs wondering just what he would find and if he could also be as forgiving.

The door to the flat was slightly ajar, small splinters of wood littering the carpeting, the metal strike plate bent back. This didn't bode well. Holmes had obviously been in no shape to pick the lock as he usually did when he couldn't find his keys. Steeling himself, Watson cautiously pushed the door open and stepped inside. Immediately, the cloying odor of joss sticks and sickly sweet, pungent smell of opium overwhelmed him, driving him back, bringing him to a halt; the unmistakable reek of Limehouse. Once you had smelled it, you would never forget it; it clung to your clothes - an unwelcome reminder of a reckless night. Thanks to Mary, it had been a long time since he had experienced that stench firsthand. It took a few moments for his lungs to adjust to the odor. Once he could breathe easier, he continued his progress into the flat. The room was shrouded in darkness; the remnants of the curtains still drawn over the boarded-up windows. Frowning, he felt along the wall near the entry and flipped up the toggle for the gas. After a few seconds, a soft, greenish light began to glow from the gas pendant lamp that hung over the center of the room. Now able to at least discern the outlines of furniture, he went to the lamp, adjusted the flow of gas into the center mantle and waited as the light slowly began to brighten. Impatient, he carefully picked his way across the room, uncomfortably aware of the unknown objects his feet kicked along the floor and tugged open the tattered curtains. Not satisfied with the meager light that filtered in, he grit his teeth in determination and pried off one of the boards that covered the shattered window. Immediately, he was rewarded with a waft of fresh, brisk air and a flood of light. He turned back around to survey the room and groaned in disgust. The room was an explosion of upended chairs, books and papers strewn about, drawers gaping open, cushions on the floor, the beloved violin tossed to the side. Holmes, though immaculate and precise in his dress and manner, was an avowed pack-rat whose method of organizing his numerous files and case notes seemed to consist of piling them in stacks around the flat or cramming them randomly into drawers. In fact, he had on more than one occasion berated poor Mrs. Hudson for her good-hearted attempt to clean and organize. This, however, this was utter chaos and spoke not only of great intoxication but also desperate and sudden rage. Watson took a deep breath, his emotions a boiling cauldron of despair and bitterness as he turned, eyes fixed on the closed bedroom door.

"Holmes!!!" he bellowed, in a voice that was not such much an irate command as a verbal challenge. He strode towards the bedroom door, fists clenched at his side, his voice shattering the eerie stillness of the room. There was no answer, only the unnaturally loud tick of the clock on the mantle.

"Bloody hell man, you've gone too fa..." The words abruptly died in his throat as his eyes fell upon the crumpled form face down on the settee, legs splayed and dangling, his face ghostly white and half-buried under a cushion.

"Holmes..." he cried out again, though this time with a sense of alarm and urgency. Watson rushed forward and dropped to his knees, face drawn with worry as he gently lifted the unconscious man to a sitting position, fingers quickly checking for a pulse. Thankfully, he found one though it was abnormally slow. More worrisome was the clamminess of his skin and slight rolling back of the eyes. He shook him vigorously, calling his name once more but still there was no response. Watson's heart sank – the classic signs of opiate-induced stupor. Leaning forward, he pressed his ear to the detective's chest and listened. After what seemed like an eternity, he could just make out faint breath sounds and the slow, suppressed beat of his heart. Not dead... yet. Now to wake him. With an expression that reflected a mixture of relief and sheer frustration, he scanned the room. What he needed was something to jolt him awake...something that would break through his stupor and... His eyes fell upon the pitcher on the side table. *Perfect.* After propping Holmes up in the corner of the settee, Watson grabbed the pitcher and disappeared down the hall. Moments later, he re-emerged with the pitcher filled to the brim and then dumped its frigid contents unceremoniously onto the unconscious man's head. Immediately, Holmes' sputtered to life ... eyes fully open .... gasping and shivering at the icy greeting.

"Are you completely mad?" squawked the indignant and thoroughly drenched detective.

"Exactly my question to you," snapped Watson caustically as he made his way carefully across the debris-strewn floor and set the empty pitcher on the roll-top desk. Though keeping his attention focused on Holmes, he quietly slid open the center desk drawer where Holmes kept the black leather Morocco case; the case that held his most troublesome vice. He needed an answer to one more question.

"I was sleeping," protested Holmes petulantly as he attempted to stand and straighten his disheveled clothes. His legs, however, were not in a cooperative mood and a moment later, still somewhat disoriented, he gave up and sank back down onto the settee, pale and breathing unevenly.

"You were in a stupor...senseless," stated Watson bluntly, a grim look on his face. He surreptitiously lifted the lid of the leather case; the vial of cocaine and the syringe were still firmly nestled in their velvet lined slots. Still not convinced, he righted the vial just enough to where he could study the level. The level hadn't changed; a wave of relief and gratitude enveloped him. Well, at least that was one thing he needn't be concerned with.

"Ridiculous," snorted Holmes, ready to argue, "I was merely...."

"You were comatose," bellowed Watson abruptly, his face flushed with sudden anger. "I could barely find a pulse... your heartbeat so slow I missed it the first time. Face down ... unresponsive ..." he added after a moment, his voice taking on a distressed tone as the anger slowly faded.

Effectively silenced, at least for the moment, Holmes pursed his lips as if he wanted to protest but could think of nothing appropriate to say. He frowned and ran his long fingers through his hair, a look of absorption on his face. After a moment, he gazed up at Watson and managed a wan smile.

"Bradycardia," he began, his voice rather scholarly though a twinkle of mischief shone in his eyes.

"What?"

"Bradycardia...abnormally slow heart rate. Usually less than 60 beats p.."

"I know what it is you idiot!" Watson swore in frustration, "I'm a doctor! Remember?"

Holmes shrugged, a wry smile lighting his face. "Of course. I must say your bedside manner leaves much to be desired Doctor!" he taunted, his smile broadening as he once more attempted to rise to his feet. This time he was successful and with a mild look of vexation, slowly traversed the room, surveying the chaos he had wrought, righting overturned chairs.

"The point is, you bloody imbecile, you could have died..." blurted Watson with such acrimony that Holmes visibly startled, pausing in his work. He remained with his back to the Doctor, however, silently waiting for him to finish for he could sense that Watson had more to say.

"...or was that your intention all along?" finished Watson somberly, the harshness fading, replaced by an air of disheartenment.

The air was still, thick with silence as neither man spoke again. Finally, after what seemed like an eternity, Holmes broke the silence though he remained with his back to Watson as if he couldn't bear to meet his gaze.

"Perhaps," he admitted in a voice that was just shy of a whisper, "Perhaps

I did overindulge ... a bit. "

Watson sighed audibly, shaking his head in defeat. Holmes would never confirm or deny his suspicion – the conversation was pointless.

"Go wash the stench off of you," he groaned, "and dress ... we have an interview at Fern Hall this afternoon or did you forget?"

Holmes turned slightly and shrugged. "Lestrade. That simpleton! Of course, I remembered... the forged banknotes," he sighed, his lips curling disdainfully. He cast a final glance around the room as if he was searching for something and then ambled off down the hall.

"Cup of tea would be lovely." The words, delivered with a fair amount of sarcasm, drifted down the hall in his wake as he disappeared.

Watson bristled at the tone and with a resigned sigh, once more set about trying to straighten the room, all the while grumbling to himself. It was while he was in the process of gathering up the empty bottle of brandy that lay at the foot of the settee that he caught sight of it, a small scrap ... blackened around the edges, slightly burned. It lay at the edge of the hearth which was filled with a considerable amount of ash; ash he didn't recall being there the previous evening. Curious, he picked it up, recognizing the texture of what had once been a photograph. With a wary glance down the hall, he paused and listened; the sounds of running water confirmed that he was alone and he relaxed a bit, gently brushing the soot from the scrap. As the soot fell away, remnants of the image came into view. The soft curve of her shoulder wrapped in the finest silk, the slyness of her smile, which promised neither love nor fidelity but beckoned all the same, an exquisitely sculpted cheek. There wasn't much left, barely a fragment, but enough for him to recognize the woman all the same. His eyes drifted to the desk, catching sight of the bottom drawer which had been open all along only he hadn't noticed. The drawer where Holmes had deposited her image along with every scrap of their correspondence, burying them under case files. The drawer was now empty; the files tossed haphazardly onto the floor and the letter which had been jack-knifed to the wall was also absent, no doubt among the ashes with the rest of the lot. And as he pondered this, reflecting on all that had transpired within a few short days, a trace of a smile, a relieved smile, began to tug at his lips. He supposed he should feel sad; some regret for the loss that Holmes had experienced, but in truth, he felt only a surge of gratitude and joy. This poison, this cancerous rot that had loomed over his friend's life, diverting his focus, sapping his energies, bleeding his intellect was finally vanquished. He stared at the only remainder and then smiled as he reached into his pocket and withdrew a match. The match flared to life and with a smile of deep satisfaction, Watson touched the match to the scrap and tossed it into the hearth. As he watched the flames spark and then devour the scrap, his smile widened.

"Good riddance," he murmured. The woman was no more.

»»«

Grendel Strikes

January 7, 1884 Early morning - Fern Hall - Hampstead, London

Beads of perspiration dotted Wilfred Pennington's brow as he threaded his way through the rows of hemp plants that filled the center of the greenhouse. He wiped at his brow with a pocket square, loosening his collar, his face tight with anxiety. The air was warm and heavy with moisture, but it was more than the humidity generated by the thick panes of glass and dense foliage that made the little man sweat. He was worried; the plants were failing, and he didn't understand why. What had just two weeks prior been a healthy and thriving experimental strain of the crop was now wilted and turning yellow, the tall stalks bending low to the ground, no longer able to support the weight of their leaves. He carefully examined the plants and studied the log that he had started when the Professor had suggested he try the new strain of seeds he had brought back from Russia. Nothing had changed that he could see; the fertilization and watering regimen all meticulously noted; temperature strictly controlled and noted. He slowly closed the log and returned it to the drawer in the potting worktable; it didn't make sense. With a troubled sigh, he wiped at his forehead and then removed his spectacles, carefully polishing them. The Professor would not be pleased. Hemp was the key ingredient, vital for their success. This new strain was supposed to be stronger and faster growing. It had seemed so promising. He couldn't imagine what had gone awry. Perhaps he could enlist Edwina's assistance. He seemed to have a vague recollection that her university studies had somehow involved plants and she'd been champing at the bit for something to occupy herself with that didn't involve needlepoint or learning the correct placement of seating cards at high tea. It was a possibility, though he had to admit to some apprehension at the notion of involving her, even if it was in an indirect manner. Pennington remained motionless for quite some time, staring blankly down the rows of plants as he considered his options, until the peal of Christ Church's bells drifted up from Hampstead Village and roused him from his stupor. He fumbled for his pocket watch and on seeing the time, grew even more anxious; he had a meeting to prepare for – a most important one. Pushing all thoughts of his failing crop from his mind, he scurried from the greenhouse, muttering to himself.

A whiff of acrid smoke assailed his nose as he neared the back entrance of the house. Squinting in bewilderment, he slowed to a trot as his eyes followed a plume of white smoke drifting lazily up into the air. As he rounded the edge of the garden path, the back entrance to the kitchen came fully into view and he drew to a halt as he came upon George McTavish, head liveryman and faithful employee of some thirty years and his young nephew Tom. They were bent over a large pit dug into the earth from which bright orange flames would erupt every now and then sending sparks and ash into the air. Curious as to what they could possibly be burning so early in the morning, he hurried forward, his mouth twitching nervously. On catching

61

sight of him, McTavish and his nephew paused and removed their caps to pay their respects.

"Morning Guvnor... Pleasant day," greeted the elder liveryman.

"Yes, Yes," muttered Pennington distractedly, moving closer to peer into the pit.   "What the devil are you burning so early in..."

The words died in his throat as his eyes fell upon the contents of the pit. His face drained of all color; his head snapped up and fixed on McTavish.

"Have you taken leave of your senses?!"

A look of surprise crossed the elder liveryman's face.

"Beggin' your pardon sir. Mrs. Pennington it was... brought these this morn," mumbled the man. "Said best get on with it ... no sense keeping such rubbish round. She was right firm about it ... so Tom an me set right to it."

Pennington stared numbly into the pit, unable to find his voice as he watched the flames lick at the books, greedily devouring them with a soft crackle and pop. *Incredibly cruel ... even for his sister.*

A look of unease crossed the face of the elder McTavish; he cast an anxious look at his nephew who was fiddling with his cap.

"We ain't done wrong 'ave we sir? Mrs. Pennington, she told us best finish before young miss was up and about. "

Pennington said nothing for a few moments, lost in thought. *Of all the days for this to happen.* He glanced down; a few books remained by the edge of the pit along with part of Edwina's sketchbook. He picked up the sketchbook and flipped through it. *Perhaps he should rescue these. She was so proud of them, especially the figure work; all those sketches of Michelangelo's David. Shame really, she was quite good.* Pennington smiled regretfully; that was definitely dear Katia's influence. She'd had a particular passion for Florence; in fact, they'd honeymooned there. A look of sadness darkened the little man's eyes as he remembered; heady days spent exploring the museums and galleries, nights at the theatre followed by bouts of passionate coupling. *To be that young again ...*

"Sir ... should we stop then?"

He startled a bit and glanced up. McTavish and his nephew were staring at him ... waiting.

"No, carry on," he sighed in defeat, slowly setting the sketchbook back onto the condemned pile of books. There were just too many things to worry about; he didn't have the time or energy to battle his sister on this. "I suppose my sister knows best in these matters. But for God's sake man ... be quick!" he urged. He glanced nervously up at the house; thankfully, the bedroom curtains were still drawn. With one last woeful look towards the pit, he hurried off towards the house.

»»««

Edwina awoke with a dull throbbing in her temples and a feeling of general malaise; she hadn't slept well. Truth be told, she hadn't had a decent night's sleep since arriving in England. Stirring restlessly, she rolled over on the pillow to face the window and then sat up, wondering why the devil she felt so warm. The air in the room was thick and unbearably stifling despite having purposely left the window cracked open. She pulled her lace morning robe over her light cotton gown and padded to the window, rubbing the sleep from her eyes. As she drew back the curtains, her lips compressed; the window was not only closed but locked tightly. Her frown increased; she distinctly remembered leaving the window open. The thought of someone creeping about her room while she slept was somewhat unnerving. *No doubt the work of her Aunt. Damn bloody English ... afraid of a little fresh air.* Muttering under her breath, she unlocked the window and shoved the frame upwards, leaning out to breathe in the crisp morning air whereupon she was immediately rewarded with a waft of acrid smoke. Struggling to contain her coughing, she covered her mouth and leaned further out the window, noticing the small plume of smoke drifting across the garden from the area at the back kitchen. Disgusted, she slammed the window down. *Ridiculous ...only the English would burn their garbage right outside their door and first thing in the morning.* Frustrated, she paced the room and then knelt down by her mother's trunk. Perhaps a little sketching indoors until the smoke cleared; besides she wanted to avoid her aunt if at all possible. She set aside the latest issue of the Illustrated London News (which she had devoured from cover to cover in one evening) from the top and lifted the lid, stretching far inside to gather up her pencils and a few sheets of paper. Now, what to sketch? She supposed she could do a few more plant studies, but she was getting rather bored with drawing inanimate objects. What she really wanted was to continue her figure studies. She smiled slightly remembering how her mother, through her various contacts in the theatre and art world, had been able to secure her place in a few live model drawing classes with a prominent professor at the Ecole des Beaux-Arts in Paris. It had been an exhilarating addition to her university studies just to be able to tread in the footsteps of the many great masters who had walked the halls was an honor, not to mention the fact that the live model had been quite handsome (*not a David but close*). Once she had summoned the courage to speak to him (shortly after her seventeenth birthday), she'd been extremely disappointed to discover a vacuous and shallow boy (*man only by virtue of his physical age*). The art professor, however, was intelligent, charming, twenty years her senior and seemed to take an interest in her. A fact Edwina recalled with some irony, which caused her mother enough discomfort to end her participation in the classes although oddly, not enough to keep her mother from having supper with the man himself on several occasions. Edwina sighed softly in resignation, a wistful smile on her lips. It had always been so; perhaps she should stick to what she was best at, inanimate objects. *Plants it is then... time for Schleiden.* Rising quickly, she crossed the room, heading towards the bookcase.

»»««

"So, how's young Miss? Settling in is she?"

Hanna smiled brightly at Cook, watching as the older woman rolled out the dough for the next day's bread. She sipped her tea contentedly as she perched on a stool at the edge of the kitchen table. It was lovely and peaceful this time of the morning.

"I think so. Yes. Maybe a bit off still. She has terrible dreams sometimes... but better. " A slight frown creased the young maid's brow as she leaned forward, lowering her voice to a whisper, more out of habit than necessity.

" I know I shouldn't say," she began hesitantly, "but she'd get on much better if Mrs. Pennington..."

"Ahh, that old bat," laughed the older woman interrupting her. "She's a right piece of it. Good Christian she is ... holiest of the holy," she added with a disdainful snort. "Even got old McTavish shaking in his boots. "Cook paused a moment and then shrugged as if considering whether she had said too much.

"She'll be all right your Miss. She's bricky... clever... Once she accepts some things can't be changed, why it'll be peaceful as the churchyard day after the Reckoning ..."

A bloodcurdling shriek split the tranquility.

Startled, Hanna dropped her cup and stared at cook, eyes wide with fear as she scrambled off her stool and ran to the door. Both women looked at each other in surprise and cautiously opened the door, just a sliver as they peered out into the hall. A string of angry expletives in German sounded from above and was soon followed by the sound of bare feet pounding down the stairs. Edwina, still clad only in her nightclothes, hair wild, eyes fiercely bright, flew down the staircase. On catching sight of them, she jolted to a stop at the bottom.

"Where is she?!" she cried out, her face the color of pastry dough save for her crimson cheeks. She swiveled frenziedly, scanning the hall.

Dumbstruck, Cook and Hanna gaped at her, unable to find their voices. The silence only served to increase Edwina's rage and shaking visibly, she strode across the room towards them.

"Where is she? That shrew! Old witch! Tell me! Speak!!"

"Ch ... Church... Miss..." Hanna managed to stammer, wringing her hands agitatedly, "and ... and maybe the village after."

"Church! She'd best pray hard. She'll need more than her God when I'm finished with her!"

The words were spat out with such contempt that even Cook, a woman of a particularly unflappable disposition (she'd been in service long enough to learn to ignore emotional outbursts) was taken aback. She watched warily as the girl continued to pace like a caged animal.

"She's taken them again. Taken them all... even my sketches! Why? Why?" wailed Edwina, more to herself than anyone in the room, her anger slowly changing over to bitter despair.

Shaken by the girl's distress, Hanna and Cook could only murmur a few vague words of comfort in an attempt to calm her.

The soft click of a latch being drawn sounded from the library and all eyes glanced up expectantly as the door opened just enough for Wilfred Pennington to poke his head out and see what all the commotion was about. As his eyes fell upon Edwina, he drained of all color for he knew immediately. Without a word, he flashed a nervous, apologetic smile and hastily retreated into the library, pulling the door shut after him. He was, unfortunately, a split second too slow as Edwina grabbed hold of the door and burst in after him.

"Where are they? Do you know? Tell me. She had no right!" she pressed, her eyes fixed and resolute as she slowly advanced.

Pennington backed up until he could go no further as the desk barred his progress, wiping quickly at the sudden perspiration that drenched his forehead. His daughter's anger had mostly diminished, a fact he was most grateful for, though he could tell she was nonetheless determined. He'd seen that same firm set of the jaw and fierce resolution in his wife many times before; it was not to be discounted.

"Now Edwina dear, I'm sorry, but I'm really quite busy," he mumbled anxiously, "but I'm sure we can replace most ..."

"Replace?" Edwina drew to a halt and stared at him, narrowing her eyes suspiciously. "What do you mean replace?" she asked sharply. "Why would they need to be replaced?"

Pennington swallowed dryly, realizing too late he had said more than needed.

She suddenly froze, a look of horror clouding her face. *The smoke... the smoke by the kitchen ... Surely not ... even she wouldn't... would she?* But one look at her father's face was all the confirmation that she needed; she stared at him speechless.

"I'm sorry dearest. Truly. I didn't know. And when I saw, well it was too late," he stammered in weak apology.

Edwina's eyes, now more despairing than angry, locked on his; she shook her head in disbelief.

"You knew... You knew how much my books, my drawings meant yet you did nothing,"

"I never imagined she'd," he whimpered, "not till I saw the smoke," Pennington stuttered defensively in a bumbling attempt to placate her. He continued to wipe at his forehead and impulsively blurted, "She means well..." It was another foolish miscalculation on his part.

"Means well?" she snorted disdainfully, "she means to run my life as she does yours... as she does this house. Well that, father dear, will never happen. She may think this is finished but you tell her for me it's only just begun," she pledged with such vehemence that Pennington involuntarily shrank back a little further.

Edwina pursed her lips as if she had something else to say but then seemingly reconsidered. She took a deep breath, struggling to regain her composure and studied her father's face, attempting to divine what it could possibly have been that her mother ever saw in him. That was not to say that he was without merit; he was obviously a kind and gentle soul, exceedingly loyal to family and friends. It was his weak nature however, the absolute spinelessness that he exhibited that bothered her the most. It was a quality that she found distasteful in both the sexes, but particularly in men. Or perhaps, as her Uncle Karl suggested, her heart just beat a little colder than most of her sex. With a melancholy smile, she shrugged slightly as if in surrender and left the room, heading up the staircase without another word.

Pennington followed her to the door, watching in uneasy silence as she ascended the stairs, torn between wanting to go after her and plead his case or retreat to the solace of his study and leave matters as they stood. He was a great source of disappointment to her, of that he had no doubt, but he detested confrontation. The sharp click of her bedroom door settled the matter for him. He sighed, admittedly relieved that the incident was tabled at least for the moment and returned to the library to prepare.

Twenty minutes later, he was once again distracted by the muffled sounds of a disturbance outside from the direction of the stable. Rubbing his eyes wearily, he set down his ledgers and crossed to the window. Edwina, now dressed in black jodhpurs (the outer riding skirt conspicuously absent), tall, fitted Spanish boots and a short black jacket with black velvet lapels, stood in the door to the stable gesturing animatedly as she talked with McTavish. Although he couldn't hear the conversation, he suspected that the older man was trying to dissuade her from riding. She'd been quite vocal all week of her desire to take the bay stallion out for a run and visibly exasperated with their insistence that she must wait until her saddle was properly finished. Pennington himself didn't ride and had primarily purchased the horse as an investment. As a result, the only saddle that existed was the one used by the grooms to exercise the horse. He had commissioned a proper sidesaddle for his daughter, despite her protests and pledge that she would never use it, but it had yet to be fitted. Pennington watched with an air of surrender as true to her word, Edwina disappeared into the stable and a few moments later emerged astride the bay, reins held confidently in one hand as she walked him out into the yard. The elder McTavish also seemed resigned to losing the battle as he carefully checked the bridle and saddle, adjusting the length of the stirrups. After a preliminary walk around the yard to warm up the horse and clearly satisfied, she thanked the liveryman and then trotted off at an easy pace, adjusting her position as horse and rider grew accustomed to each other. As Pennington watched her disappear from view, the thought that he should go after her flashed across his mind. She was unaccustomed to the horse and the area, having scarcely left the grounds since her arrival and his sister, who was due back shortly, would surely be displeased by her abrupt departure. All valid arguments, all reasonable concerns. He paused, a frown darkening his face as he oscillated between leaving well enough alone and sending McTavish out to retrieve her. Ahh... but there it was – blessed silence, something that seemed in short supply these days and he did have important business matters looming that he had yet to prepare. His oscillation vanished;

Edwina would be fine – she was quite a skilled rider. Perhaps it was just what was needed, a day out in the fresh air to clear away the anger and hurt of the morning's events. Besides, what possible trouble could she get into out on the heath.

By the time Edwina reached the edge of Fern Hall's grounds, the bay had settled into a comfortable canter. As they moved out through the gate and into the lane, Edwina's smile widened in anticipation. It was deserted, not a soul in sight. She took a deep breath as she leaned forward and eagerly nudged the horse into a gallop, giving the bay his head as they thundered up Frognal Rise. Golder's Hill loomed in the distance – time for a little fun.

Happenstance

"Is that a tart?"

Watson glanced up from his notes and sniffed the air suspiciously.

"Pardon?" came the muffled query from behind the latest copy of the London Illustrated News.

"A tart ... Raspberry tart?" exclaimed Watson crossly as the smell of Mrs. Hudson's freshly baked tarts filled the cab of the Clarence carriage.

Holmes paused in mid-bite and smiled archly as he peered over the top of the newspaper.

"As always, your powers of perception never cease to amaze." He tossed aside the London Illustrated News and brushed a few crumbs from his grey frock coat.

Watson bristled, lowering his notes.

"Thought they were finished with breakfast ... She said there were no more."

Holmes shrugged, a smug little smile playing on his lips.

"For you perhaps."

"Bloody hell!" huffed the Doctor, more than a little put out, for despite all her moaning and complaining about Holmes being the "worst tenant in London," Mrs. Hudson clearly doted on him.

"Well, if it makes you feel better," sighed Holmes in a half-hearted attempt to mollify the Doctor's resentment, "she slipped them into my pocket along with a bill for damages. She's going to increase our rent it seems." He shrugged once more as if it hardly mattered at all and reached into his pocket, withdrawing a linen napkin which contained the tarts in question.

"Tart?" he offered with exaggerated courtesy, holding out the napkin to Watson.

Still grumbling a bit, Watson nonetheless took one and in between bites, studied his friend carefully. Despite all that had occurred the previous night, Holmes looked surprisingly refreshed and dapper; the man's powers of recuperation were simply astounding. His eyes scanned the detective; a slight frown formed as they settled on the bruising across his right knuckle.

"Our rent?" Watson mumbled distractedly, his mouth full of raspberry tart, his mind on the bruising. *Perhaps it occurred when he broke through the entry door.*

"Yes, ours," asserted Holmes with a sly grin.

"Ha! You mean yours, " he insisted sharply, snapping back to reality.

"Of course it's ours, we're flatmates," reminded Holmes with icy patience.

"I'm not the one who tossed a brick through the glass and broke the lock," protested Watson indignantly.

"Minor discrepancy. As I said, flatmates. "

"Not for long," grumbled Watson, carefully wiping the crumbs from his mustache.

"I count the days," came the swift and acerbic reply.

Watson's head snapped up a bit. The two men stared long and hard at each other and then burst into laughter. No matter how much they squabbled, they would miss each other's company, whether they admitted it or not. When the laughter had subsided, Holmes sighed a bit and shook his head slightly, now focused on Watson's journal.

"What are you writing?"

"I'm making notes. "

"I can see that. On what precisely?" Holmes pressed, a mischievous gleam in his eyes.

"On the case."

"We've barely started, how could you possibly be making notes?"

"I'm making notes on Lestrade's notes. He's provided a bit of background if you care to read," offered Watson, holding forth a stack of documents.

"Rubbish," scoffed Holmes, narrowing his eyes as he cast a cursory glance at the nearly illegible scrawl.

"He's compiled a rather extensive list," Watson protested, "some very interesting information."

"Prefer to conduct my own investigation thanks!" snickered Holmes with an air of condescension. "That way, I'm guaranteed only the truly important data has been collected."

"I find his notes most useful," countered Watson, "particularly when I go to write up the case."

"I see, helps you in your fabrication, does it?"

"How do you mean?" sputtered Watson defensively.

Holmes nodded towards the Illustrated News, his mouth curling disdainfully.

"I've just finished your latest, *The Case of the Missing Lynx*. Quite a tale you've spun."

"You didn't like it?" Watson's voice betrayed his disappointment.

Holmes smiled tightly and steepled his hands beneath his chin.

"There was no rooftop chase."

"Slight embellishment. Poetic license," protested Watson with a weak smile.

"No rooftop chase," Holmes repeated emphatically, "No fearsome battle with a savage beast. Oh, and perhaps most important of all, the lynx was not a lynx at all, but a rather large, overfed, ill-tempered house-cat named Oscar; a fact which is conspicuously absent from your account."

Watson chuckled a bit, looking slightly embarrassed.

"It was a rather boring case, so I spruced it up a bit for the reader's enjoyment."

"A bit? It has almost no basis in reality!"

Watson shrugged a bit, trying to remain patient as he explained.

"The readers want to be entertained Holmes... feel like they're along for the adventure. The paper's already been in touch; they want more. The public loves reading about your adventures."

"But they're not my adventures when you make them up! That's not writing up the case, that's creating fiction!" exclaimed Holmes as he threw up his hands in exasperation.

Watson sighed deeply and leaned forward across the aisle, not ready to give in on this argument.

"Look, I do understand, but let's be honest about this. The last few cases haven't been very exciting. Just where do you think our clients come from? People read the stories and some of those people are bound to have problems; problems that need solving. They read about you, see how brilliant you are and realize that you're the man for the job. No one is going to hire the world's only consulting detective if they think he spends his time searching for some old woman's missing cat."

"But there was no rooftop chase!" reiterated Holmes, his voice rising in agitation. He paused a moment and then took a deep breath, struggling to regain his composure. "Besides," he added in a much calmer voice, as he smiled through clenched teeth, "she was a very wealthy old woman and the cat was exceptionally clever."

Watson shrugged and pursed his lips, ready to remind him that it was still a cat when the carriage abruptly jolted to a full stop. Watson was thrown forward a bit and struggled back into his seat with Holmes' help.

"What the devil!" he cried indignantly, brushing at his suit.

"Are you all right?" inquired Holmes, suppressing a slight smile.

Watson nodded that he was fine and peered out the window, staring in bewilderment at the road in front of them. Finchley Road was the major passage from the city to the outlying areas and estates that radiated out towards Hampstead Village and the heath. The road was always full of carriages in both directions, but now there was nothing coming towards them and their lane was at a standstill with hansoms stopped and waiting as far as the eye could see.

"Road must be blocked," murmured Holmes as he climbed from the carriage. All around them, passengers were peering out from their carriages and grumbling; most of the men climbing out while the women remained inside. Turning up his collar at the chill of the morning, Holmes followed the small stream of men as they headed up the road to discover the source of the blockage.

"Accident?" suggested Watson as he fell in step beside him. It wouldn't be the first time a carriage or cart had gone into the ditch.

"Hmmm... Perhaps."

Holmes continued, scanning the surrounding area as they threaded their way through the crowds of the curious. He quickened his pace. Watson scrambled to catch up. He suddenly paused and then turned to face Watson, a sarcastic smile lighting his face.

"Or maybe it's your missing lynx. "

Without waiting for Watson's reaction, he turned back to the road and set out, calling over his shoulder as he disappeared into the crowd, "Come along

Watson. Time for a little investigation."

Muttering darkly, Watson hurried after him.

»»«««

*Heaven. Pure heaven or what she supposed heaven would be like if she
believed in heaven. Perhaps bliss was a better word.*

Edwina sighed contentedly and lifted her head from the makeshift pillow
she had made of her jacket. She slowly sat up and tilted her face to the sun,
enjoying its surprising warmth as she lounged on the rise of Golders Hill. The
day had warmed up nicely, the morning's chill vanishing as the sun rose in the
sky. The bay grazed tranquilly nearby, under the shade of a row of ancient
oaks that marked the border of a large estate house on the crest of the hill. She
would have loved to ride to the summit to get an unobstructed view of London
and Hampstead, but the estate stood in the way. It was surrounded by a thick
stone wall as far as the eye could see; not a problem really – she could easily
climb over by scaling one of the many surrounding trees and dropping down
inside. She smiled, laughing a little. It would be trespassing of course. The
estate was large enough to where she could probably get away with it if she
didn't venture too close to the manor house. It was tempting. Though on
further consideration, she decided that perhaps she had caused her father
enough strife for the morning without adding to it by aggravating his
neighbors. Not to mention the fact that there was bound to be more trouble
when Grendel (the nickname she'd settled on for Aunt Gretchen) returned
from the village. No matter, the view was perfectly lovely from her current
vantage point.

Shading her eyes against the sun, she peered down the expanse of the
grassy slope dotted with snowdrops and heather, absently watching the line of
hansom cabs, carriages and wagons of all sorts make their way down Finchley
Road. She'd spent the better part of the morning just watching and listening to
London's inhabitants pass. It was so quiet up on the hill that she could hear
the soft rumble of the carriage wheels as they rolled up the hard packed and
rutted lane; so quiet that she could even hear an occasional call out as the
drivers urged their horse teams on toward the rise. So, it was quite noticeable
when all noise abruptly ceased. Puzzled by the sudden silence, Edwina slowly
rose to her feet, gazing down toward the road. It had all stopped – no
movement at all. The entire lane going up towards the rise had come to a
complete halt, and there was not a carriage to be seen approaching from the
opposite direction. Some of the carriage passengers were beginning to climb
down, moving slowly up the lane. A small flutter of apprehension filled her.
The road must be completely blocked; something dreadful had occurred.
Without a second thought, she grabbed her jacket, pulling it on as she
scrambled up towards the treeline. She untied the bay, mounting hastily,
hoping fervently that it wasn't too late to help. Moments later, the bay
thundered down Golder's Hill, racing towards the long line of idle carriages.

"That's a bruise. "

"Hmm?" Holmes continued to move forward, threading his way down the long line of carriages.

"The knuckles on your right hand, they're bruised. How'd it happen?" pressed Watson, quickening his pace to keep up.

There was a pause and then a soft chuckle. Holmes cast a sideways glance at him and grinned.

"Slight disagreement."

Watson frowned.

"Disagreement regarding?"

"Sportsmanship...specifically lack thereof."

Watson groaned aloud, his mustache drooping in disapproval.

"Cards again?" he sighed, "were you cheating?"

Holmes stopped dead in his tracks to turn and glare at him.

"I don't need to cheat!" he growled, eyes fierce and indignant.

"No, you don't," agreed Watson, "but were you?"

Holmes offered no reply but flashed a tight warning smile as he walked off, heading further down the lane.

"Ah hah! Counting then!" declared Watson knowingly, as they continued to thread their way through the idle carriages. Soon, the lane began to narrow and curve sharply, the undergrowth on either side thickening.

"Counting is not cheating," hissed Holmes over his shoulder, "Counting is…" He suddenly froze; his entire body stiffening as he abruptly stopped and whipped around, his eyes scanning the road behind them, just beyond the curve.

Watson stared at him puzzled. "What?"

"Quiet!" commanded Holmes as he held up his hand, his eyes focused on the road behind Watson. There was a sound, but he couldn't quite discern what it was yet.

"What? Why?" protested Watson, growing more irritated by the moment.

"Don't you hear it?"

"Hear what? What are you on about?" No sooner had he spoken the words, Watson also drew to a halt. He turned to look down the road behind him. . . listening. He could hear it now, something... though he wasn't quite sure what; a sound, heavy and rhythmic, growing louder and louder with each passing moment.

"What is that?" he murmured absently, moving a few paces towards the sound which continued to increase in volume and cadence. He stood in the center of the lane, staring down towards the bend in the road as if transfixed.

Holmes' eyes widened in alarm as he recognized the cadence. Hoofbeats. Hoofbeats on hard-packed soil; the hoofbeats of a galloping horse as it bore down on them.

"John! Look Out!"

Without a moment's hesitation, he launched himself at Watson tackling him to the ground. Both men crashed noisily into the hedgerow just as a massive bay stallion about 18 hands high careened around the bend, the rider bent low and tight. The horse never paused; the rider either unaware of their presence or indifferent. Moments later, both rider and horse were just a blur, swerving recklessly around the hansoms as it vanished down the road, heading towards the blockage.

"Bloody Hell!!" exploded Watson, brushing leaves and twigs from his clothes as he scrambled to his feet with Holmes' help.

"Are you all right then?" asked Holmes, peering into his friend's face in a moment of unguarded concern.

"Insanity!! What manner of madman!" he bellowed, more than a little indignant at having nearly been trampled and in one of his better suits no less.

"Madwoman," corrected Holmes with a bit of a smile, genuinely relieved upon realizing that only Watson's pride had been injured.

"What?" snorted the Doctor, still brushing at his clothes.

"It was a woman," Holmes continued nonchalantly, straightening the cuffs on his coat.

"A woman? How could you tell?" sputtered Watson incredulously.

Holmes choked back a laugh and smiled.

"If I need to explain that to you Doctor."

"You know what I mean," sighed Watson in exasperation. "It was all just a blur... flash of black on an exceedingly large horse." Fully recovered from the ordeal, he once more fell into step beside Holmes as they continued forward, carefully picking their way. The road had become increasingly uneven and marked with deep ruts and rocks.

"As always John, you see but you do not observe," sighed Holmes wearily. "Young. I'd say mid-twenties, slim, auburn haired." He paused a moment, a slight smile curling his mouth. "Quite comely actually. I'm surprised you didn't notice."

"The horse seemed more important at the time," grumbled the Doctor. "How the devil was she riding? And was she wearing trousers?"

"Astride," chuckled Holmes. "Two legs. One on each side and yes those were jodhpurs."

"Shameful." Watson's face darkened with disapproval.

"Entirely logical and practical," argued Holmes. "I'd like to see you try to maneuver a galloping horse in a skirt and riding sidesaddle, Doctor."

"Well, it's all just nonsense," Watson grumbled with growing irritation. "Unacceptable behavior. And where the devil did she get off to?"

"Haven't the faintest," chuckled Holmes. "Let's find out, shall we?"

The road began to straighten as they completed rounding the bend, the woods on either side thinning. A small clearing loomed up ahead where passengers from the stranded hansoms had begun to congregate. Their voices, harsh and agitated, drifted back through the woods. Holmes increased his pace, glancing down, eyes scanning. Little bits of splintered wood littered the ground along with scattered produce; apples, a few onions, lettuce and a couple of oranges.

"It's the old Russian," he murmured as he reached down and snatched an orange. "He's cracked an axle, probably lost a wheel."

"How could you know it's the Russian?" asked Watson, his disbelief evident. London was teeming with fruit and vegetable peddlers. Their dilapidated carts and overworked horses were as common as the manure they left behind in their wake.

Holmes scrutinized the orange, rotated it with his fingers and then raised it to his nose, inhaling deeply. Satisfied, he picked up another and deposited them into the pockets of his coat.

"Blood oranges. These are from Sicily. He's the only one that carries them," he explained with a quick grin. "Off we go. Best get up there. From the sound of this crowd, things are about to get ugly," he urged. He quickened his pace, weaving his way into the middle of the crowd. Watson stared after him for a moment, still processing the deduction and then scrambled after him.

As they threaded their way towards the front, Watson became aware that Holmes was correct on both accounts. Small groups of men, primarily disgruntled passengers and a few drivers milled about, their voices no longer whispers as they angrily discussed how best to remove the obstacle from their path. The obstacle, as Holmes had surmised, was indeed the old Russian peddler and his cart. The cart lay overturned in the center of the road, the rear left axle shattered, the wheel up against a tree. The man's unfortunate draft horse lay in the road on its side, panting, terrified and helpless, tangled in the reins and harness. The young woman, who only moments before had nearly run them down, was kneeling in the dirt with her back to the crowd. With one hand, she stroked the fallen horse's muzzle in an attempt to calm him while she gently pressed the old man's hand with the other. He bled from a gash in his forehead and babbled incoherently in Russian, looking fearfully at the crowd.

"What do you say lads?" cried out an angry voice from the mob. "Let's grab the chains and drag the beast from the road. "

A raucous chorus of approval sounded from the crowd; the young woman, however, remained in place as she gently bound the old peddler's wound with her handkerchief. She comforted him in Russian, her voice soft, warm and soothing.

"So, she's Russian!" exclaimed Watson in amazement, trying to suppress his unease as he and Holmes continued to push their way forward. It was getting more difficult as the crowd had begun to close ranks as it surged forward towards the Old Russian and his horse. The tension in the air was palpable.

Holmes looked warily around at the crowd. "No. Austrian. Viennese to be exact. Though her vocal inflection and accent indicate she has spent considerable time in Paris."

"But she's speaking Russian," protested Watson, watching the crowd around them uneasily.

"Not her native language, but most likely has family ties near St.

Petersburg. Now tell me, do you have your pistol with you?" Holmes was now at the front, eyes scanning the crowd.

"Well yes," replied Watson hesitantly, "but surely you're not going to just shoot the beast?" His hand slipped into his pocket as he spoke and rested on his service revolver. He had learned early on in his association with Holmes it was always best to be prepared.

Holmes laughed a bit and shook his head. "Actually, I was thinking of it more for protection. Come along."

"What... Where?"

"To offer assistance of course. I'll see to the horse, you tend to the injured peddler."

"But you dislike horses!" exclaimed Watson incredulously. His words however fell on empty air as Holmes had vanished into the mob.

»»««

"Enough of this!! Out of the road you ridiculous woman!"

A young man, blonde with a pencil mustache, tall but slight of build and somewhat nasal voice, stepped forward into the road, angrily advancing. In his right hand, he brandished a buggy whip which he had taken from one of the carriages.

Edwina bristled, cheeks flushing in anger as she rose to her feet and turned to face the malcontent; she studied him carefully. Despite the threat of the whip, she found it hard to feel intimidated. Although taller than herself, she noted with some amusement, he had an almost wasp-like waist; much more than herself. The "proper shape" that Grendel was always carrying on about, corseted perhaps. She had heard of such things as ridiculous as it seemed. Despite the time of day, he still wore elegant evening attire which was rumpled and creased as if he'd slept in them; his eyes were dull, bloodshot and his hair unkempt. The small purple bruise along his jawline, peeking through stubble, hinted at trouble the night before. Conventionally handsome some would find him she supposed, though his features were far too delicate for her tastes – almost pretty. A faint smile tugged at her lips. A dandy, no doubt about it, on his way home from a night on the town; no threat at all. With a brief, dismissive look in his direction, she ignored him and once more knelt next to the horse, her fingers gently gliding over the animal as she checked for injury.

Laughter and catcalls erupted from the crowd. Humiliated, the young man's face reddened in fury as he strode forward, whip raised in the air.

"Impudent minx! Out of my way or this horse won't be the only creature to feel the lash!"

Edwina scrambled to her feet, so angry and indignant she could scarcely keep from shaking. She lunged forward to meet the threat.

"Try if you must! I doubt you'll succeed," she hissed, eyes fierce and resolute as she reached out and grabbed onto the whip.

Another chorus of catcalls and jeers burst forth from the mob as several of the drivers began to lay odds on who was most likely to triumph.

Shocked by her defiance, the young man began to sputter incoherently and tugged furiously at the whip, attempting to regain control.

"Let go witch! I'll give you a lesson in manners you won't soon forget!" he squawked, surprised at her strength as they continued to tussle.

"For God's sake Percy," sighed a blasé voice from the shadows, "put the whip down lest you hurt yourself. If anyone requires a lesson in manners, it's you and I shall be more than happy to oblige."

"Christ, you again."

Percival Isaiah Gilchrist took a step back, still holding the whip and smiled anxiously as a tall, wiry man impeccably dressed in a dark grey frock coat and matching trousers stepped forward into the clearing. Edwina compressed her lips, watching the scene unfold, utterly transfixed. Though physically only slightly taller, the stranger towered over the dandy. There was a quiet, almost feline grace about him which spoke of great confidence and a serious nature. He seemed a man who didn't suffer fools gladly. It was also clear from the interaction that these men were acquainted, though perhaps not amicably.

"Yes, me again," chuckled the stranger in a low rumble of a voice that betrayed no anger but menaced all the same. He held out his hand and smiled. It was a simple gesture but coercive nonetheless. Percy Gilchrist uttered a nervous laugh and held out the whip. Edwina noted that his hand appeared to tremble a bit.

"Just offering assistance in clearing the road," he stammered, backing up a few paces more though the stranger remained stationary. A second man, shorter in stature and bearing an impressive mustache, stepped into the clearing. He said not a word but scanned the crowd warily, his right hand tucked in the pocket of his tweed jacket. After a moment, he turned to the tall stranger but said nothing, as if waiting for instructions.

"Assistance? Is that so?" chuckled the stranger, his voice laden with skepticism. He tossed the whip to one side and methodically brushed the dirt from his hands, his impenetrable eyes fixed on Gilchrist. He sighed after a moment and then shrugged, murmuring, "Run along now Percy lest you soil your hands. We all know how distressing that would be to you."

Needing no further encouragement, Percy Gilchrist smiled weakly and without another word, backed as quickly and unobtrusively as possible from the clearing. The mob reacted with a loud round of jeers and taunts. As he disappeared into the woods, the two men exchanged looks and then burst into hearty laughter. The confrontation resolved, the shorter of the two had now turned his attention to a bruise on his companion's right knuckle; a bruise she soon realized that appeared a perfect match for the bruise on the malcontent's chin.

"How much does he owe you then?" sighed the man with the mustache.

"Enough," chuckled the stranger with a sly smile as he flexed his fist.

They continued to chat for a few moments, apparently having forgotten her presence. As she listened to them, Edwina began to frown; it wasn't that

76

she was ungrateful, but she didn't want them to think that she had needed rescue. For reasons that she herself didn't quite understand, it seemed of the utmost importance that she impress this upon them. She cleared her throat and stood up a little straighter. Best to set things straight.

"Gentlemen, although I appreciate your kindness, rest assured, I had the situation well in hand," she proclaimed with the utmost confidence.

At the sound of her voice, both men turned around to face her. The shorter of the two frowned, looking mildly irritated as if she was indeed ungrateful; his companion only smiled, his attention now focused solely on her.

"Yes, I'm sure you did. Percy is only a threat to himself, especially when suffering the aftermath of a lost evening."

He moved a little closer to her, his eyes grave and assessing, taking in every detail of her appearance and expression.

"You see, I must confess," he continued solemnly, "my motives are not altogether altruistic. I am en route to a very important meeting for which I must not be late. I offer assistance in the hopes of expediting a resolution. My colleague is a doctor, he will tend to your Russian friend, I will assist you with the horse." And without waiting for her to reply, he turned towards the old peddler and explained the situation to him in seamless Russian. The old peddler nodded that he understood and smiled gratefully as the doctor looked after him.

All the while he spoke, Holmes continued to advance until he stood directly in front of her. She was tall and lithe, more than was fashionable in London, possessing a more natural shape than the exaggerated hourglass figure that the ladies seemed to favor. Her clothing was of fine quality, well fitted but not the current fashion and certainly foreign made. Her only jewelry was a simple lapel watch; silver, on a bow-shaped ribbon, adorned by two small but fine emeralds; more than likely a family heirloom. She was luminous; alabaster skin, free of any traces of makeup; a few light freckles dotted the bridge of her nose and cheeks as if she had been out in the sun without a hat. He couldn't help but smile; it was something a proper lady of London would never allow to happen. They feared the sun almost as much as they feared spinsterhood. Emerald eyes, lively and bright with curiosity, peered up at him; her auburn tresses gleamed in the sun, uncovered and loosely tied back with a black velvet ribbon. The breeze caught the faint scent of lilies of the valley; he inhaled deeply. Ingenuous. Quite charming.

Edwina, not usually one to be at a loss for words, awkwardly found herself in that very state. The words, a witty rejoinder, a few pointed barbs regarding the rudeness of the English, which had been on the very tip of her tongue had simply vanished. It happened in an instant; the moment his eyes, so impossibly blue and mesmerizing, locked onto hers, the moment he reassured the old peddler in flawless Russian. The free flow of thought in her mind simply ground to a halt. It was as if he was inside her head, slowly peeling back the layers like an onion, divining her every thought. She fumbled for words, unable to break away from his gaze and much to her embarrassment, felt herself blushing like a lovelorn schoolgirl.

"Have we met?" she managed to stammer after an awkward silence as she followed him back over to where the horse lay in the road. She breathed a little easier noting that his companion was carefully tending to the Russian peddler. She glanced furtively up at him as she knelt by the horse, stroking his muzzle. There was something vaguely familiar about this man, though she was certain that they had never met before. She would have remembered; there was nothing ordinary about this gentleman.

He began to laugh as he crouched in the dirt with her beside the horse and smiled.

"In a manner of speaking, I suppose you could call it that, if nearly being trampled in the road counts."

A look of dismay clouded her face.

"Was that you? In the road... thrashing about in the hedgerow? I thought it was a woodchuck or badger!" she gasped.

"Quite understandable," he chuckled. "It's his bloody mustache. I've told him time and again, but he never listens."

Edwina gaped at him for a moment and then burst into laughter, her apprehension all but a memory. The sound brought a smile to his lips; it was an honest laugh, hearty and unrestrained for a woman. The fine ladies of the gentry seemed to have lost the ability to laugh as they fretted about how common they might appear; the most they could manage was usually an annoying, pretentious giggle.

"I'm so sorry," she began earnestly, having once more regained her composure. "I wasn't expecting anyone to be standing in the middle of the road. Your friend is very lucky."

Holmes narrowed his eyes, studying her carefully. "How do you know he's my friend?"

A look of surprise filtered across her face. What an odd thing to ask. She met his gaze, her eyes searching for an answer.

"Well... I don't know for certain, but you seem close. You took a risk pushing him out of the road; you acted without hesitation. And it seems to me, that he has tremendous respect for you. He waits on your instruction." She paused for a moment and then averted her eyes as if she now regretted her words.

"If I've spoken out of turn, please accept my apology. A serious failing of mine ... as others have pointed out."

"No. No. It's fine... just fine," he quickly assured, not altogether sure why he felt vaguely troubled at the sudden downturn in her mood. He flashed a quick smile. "You're quite perceptive."

A look of absolute joy lit her face. "Really?"

Holmes nodded and was about to reply when Watson's voice interrupted him.

"Any progress then? We do have pressing business."

They looked up to find the Doctor standing near the upturned cart, watching them with impatience and curiosity.

"Well then, I suppose we should get on with it," Holmes sighed with a slight smile. "But you'll have to direct me on how to assist as I know very little about horses."

Edwina arched her brow; a statement she found hard to believe, but she said nothing and nodded that she understood. With a confidence that astonished all who watched, she directed Holmes to hold the horse's bridle to keep him still while she carefully reached under the horse to unhook his belly straps. It was a risky procedure; the horse was a large Percheron and if spooked, could easily have crushed her. Holmes watched her with a growing sense of admiration as she skillfully unbuckled the quarter and back straps from around his legs, crawling about the underside of the massive beast with not a trace of fear. Once all the straps had been released, she gently eased the harness and padded collar from about his neck. After checking him over once more for injury and a few moments of reassuring whispers and comforting pats, she slowly coaxed the giant to his feet.

A cry of relief sounded from the crowd as she slowly walked the horse to the side of the lane. In the meantime, the Doctor and a few of the carriage drivers righted the cart and pushed it out of the way. The show now over, the obstacle removed, the crowd began to dissipate, drifting back towards their waiting carriages. The old Russian hugged her gratefully and then carefully mounted the Percheron. Edwina spoke quietly to him in Russian and then turned back to the two men.

"He'll be all right now; the horse also. He'll leave the cart here and come back for it tomorrow. I'll ride with him to the village just to make sure." She grinned happily and wiped at a bit of dust on her cheek. There was a brief silence and then with a warm smile, Edwina extended her ungloved hand – first to the Doctor and then to Holmes.

"I wanted to thank you both for all of your assistance. I couldn't have done it without you Mr. …. Mr. …" She broke off, a frown creasing her brow. "I'm sorry, I just realized I didn't catch your names. "

Watson politely shook her hand, though it was plain to see he was disturbed by her lack of gloves. He pursed his lips, about to introduce himself when Holmes suddenly laughed and shot him a warning glance. He took her hand and firmly shook it, a playful expression in his eyes.

"No. You didn't. They weren't offered, nor did we catch yours."

She started in surprise and then began to laugh, a look of disbelief on her face as she realized that he wasn't about to share that information. With a shake of her head, she smiled and met his gaze directly.

"Ahh, men of mystery. Well then, turnabout's fair play. I enjoy a puzzle as much as anyone else!" she chuckled gamely. Grabbing the reins of her horse, she swung agilely into the saddle, turning to face them.

"Many thanks again for your kindness gentlemen. Perhaps we shall meet again." As she spoke, she reached down and patted her horse's neck, though her eyes were focused on Holmes. Their eyes met and for a brief moment, his eyes warmed as he smiled up at her.

"Auf Wiedersehen Fräulein. Es war ein Vergnügen. Ich freue mich auf sie." Goodbye Mademoiselle. It has been a pleasure. I look forward to it.

Her face lit with surprise and delight. How could he have possibly known?

"Auf Wiedersehen mein mysteriösen Freund." Goodbye my mysterious friend. She raised her hand, waved and then a moment later turned the horse around and trotted off, the Old Russian following close behind. Holmes watched her disappear into the distance and then turned, heading back towards the clarence without another word. Watson followed, his face creased in thought as they climbed back into the carriage.

"Strange young woman," he mused, glancing at Holmes for a reaction. His friend had once more retreated behind the London Illustrated News, glancing every now and then at his pocket watch. The clarence started forward once more, slowly falling into line behind the other carriages as they progressed down the road.

The paper rustled as Holmes paused in the midst of turning the page.

"Yes," he murmured quietly, eyes still focused on the page. "Refreshing, wasn't she?
"

»)««

The Interview - Fern Hall - January 7, 1884 Early Afternoon

"Refresh my memory."

"What?"

"Remind me ... Pennington's profession?" mused Holmes, peering out through the windows of the Clarence as it rolled through the granite gate columns of Fern Hall. His face darkened with reflection as he surveyed the wide expanse of lawn, gardens and outbuildings they passed on the way towards the manor house. He noted a stable, small maze and what looked like it could be a greenhouse. *Lovely estate...very old.*

"If you had bothered to read Lestrade's notes," Watson grumbled, with a curt nod towards the papers spread out on the seat.

Holmes arched his brow and grinned. "If I had," he muttered acidly, "what need would I have for you?"

Watson bristled; despite their many years together, he was still occasionally offended even though he realized it was just his companion's nature. He managed a smile after a moment and inhaled deeply, wondering how Holmes would amuse himself when he wasn't available to torment on a regular basis.

"Printing trade," he explained evenly as he sifted through Lestrade's notes. "Mostly adverts for shops, fine stationery, society notices, calling cards. Your cards as a matter of fact. Several prominent clients ... well-respected; has a block of warehouses and presses down off Fleet street."

"Interesting. Even so, a bit grand for a tradesman successful though he may be." Watson knit his brow in thought. "Family estate, according to the records. Not uncommon for families to lose their status over time; money troubles and such. Some heirs eventually take on a trade to make ends meet. Pennington's ambitious ... determined to restore the family name. No harm in that, is there?"

Holmes was silent for a moment, lost in thought. "Remains to be seen," he murmured after a moment and then abruptly reached up and rapped on the ceiling, commanding the driver to stop. The carriage rolled to a stop, adjacent to a newly replanted hedge maze. They were still quite a distance from the manor house; the outlines of a few outbuildings could be seen in the distance. Alongside the maze, a series of small paths branched out, surrounded by tall, wildflower plantings on either side which afforded them some privacy and seclusion. Various paths veered off towards what looked like a greenhouse that fronted an orchard, others toward a stable and paddock and eventually the back of the house; still another seemed to head off towards the splash and gurgle of a hidden fountain.

"What are you doing?" cried Watson, watching in astonishment as Holmes abruptly scrambled from the carriage. Utterly bewildered, he climbed out after him. "Are you mad?" he cried out in disbelief as Holmes paid the driver and sent him off, leaving them by the maze. They were a long way from London; he'd assumed that the cab would wait on them as customary while they conducted their interview. But now, here they were, quite a distance from the main house with no arranged transport back into town. True, cabs traveled the main road routinely, but they would have to send for one when finished; it could be a substantial wait. Watson frowned and glanced at his watch; a delay he hadn't counted on.

"I'd arranged to take Mary to supper," he warned irritably as he followed Holmes along the path, dodging sprigs of flowering shrubs and small saplings. "I mustn't be late." It wouldn't be the first time that he had been late for an engagement due to his companion's whims and utter disregard for the commitments of others.

"My, my," chuckled Holmes, "barely one month engaged and setting your calendar already." Up ahead, the outline of a stable loomed and a murmur of voices, stable-hands more than likely, could be heard. He immediately veered away from the sound, taking a path that skirted around the back of the buildings.

Watson bristled at the implication as he hurried to keep up.

"We both agreed on the time and date, that's what betrothed, mature people do. They discuss and commit, but I wouldn't expect you to understand this given your viewpoint on these matters and how little you care."

Holmes stopped abruptly and turned to face him, and for a brief instant, Watson thought he detected a bitter regret, just below the mask of icy indignation. The moment passed however as Holmes' face settled into the familiar smirk, his eyes veiled and distant.

"Don't worry Doctor, I promise you won't miss supper." He set off once more, moving at a brisk pace, but pausing briefly every now and then to examine the soil and plantings along the path.

"Where are we going?" groaned Watson, his impatience somewhat moderated by the feeling that he may have been sharper in tone than warranted.

"To the house," replied Holmes frostily, "we have an interview, remember? It's what I do. What I care about." And then, perhaps noting Watson's troubled expression, his demeanor softened, and he managed a rueful smile.

"We all have our talents John. As a physician, your capacity to empathize is an asset. It's also your nature, and I suspect, you couldn't be much different no matter how hard you tried. As for me, I ferret out information; solve puzzles often of the most heinous nature. To allow myself that luxury; to allow emotion to taint the cold logic my profession demands, is a disservice to those who engage my services and to my nature. I am who I am... as I must be, unpleasant as that is at times."

"And what of moderation Holmes? Can you not find a balance?" protested Watson, his face drawn with sincere concern. "You're not a machine despite your best efforts."

The two men exchanged looks and then Holmes shrugged, his lips pulling into a sarcastic smile. "One must always strive for perfection Watson, no matter how elusive." And with that he darted off, disappearing into the thick foliage.

Muttering under his breath, Watson surrendered the battle and hurried after him. The day had warmed up considerably and he contemplated loosening his collar, at least for the moment despite how coarse it might seem. Holmes, for his part never seemed to be bothered by changes in weather, or if he was, he never let on. Had he truly mastered "mind over matter" as he so often insisted; Watson wasn't sure. Or was it just that he felt the warmth less due to his lean frame? Either way, Watson was uncomfortable and disgruntled; he'd had about enough of the great outdoors.

"The main entrance is the other way," Watson grumbled as he caught up with him. Giving in, he unbuttoned his collar and jacket, sighing in some relief.

"Yes, I know," chuckled Holmes. "I find the back way round much more interesting. You never know what you will find. Besides, we're a bit early and it's a lovely day for a walk. The exercise will do you good; you're looking a bit thicker in the middle lately."

"Been exercising all morning thank you very much," growled Watson. At this rate, he was going to need a wash up and fresh suit before supper; something he hadn't anticipated. Then, just as quickly as he had been moving along, Holmes suddenly stopped in mid-stride. He held up his hand, signaling for Watson to also stop and stood in the center of the path, sniffing the air, his eyes bright and eager. They were not far from the back of the house now; from what Watson could see, it looked like the entrance to the kitchen.

"Smell that? Someone's been busy," noted Holmes as he slowly moved forward toward the area of the odor.

"So what," sighed Watson in exasperation. "We're in the country, Holmes. People burn their kitchen rubbish all the time."

Holmes shook his head in disagreement and continued to move forward with great caution. "Not trash at all," he murmured as he continued to sniff the air like a champion bloodhound. "Smells of leather... paper. "

They came upon a small clearing, in the center of which was a fire pit; a pile of ash still smoldered. The area around the pit was deserted. Holmes stepped forward and crouched down, pulling on his leather gloves. As he began to sift through the still warm mounds of ash and debris, his face clouded in mild surprise. With the utmost care, he carefully lifted out the blackened fragment of a book spine. There wasn't enough left of it to discern a title or even identify the type of book. However, upon closer examination of the contents of the pit, it became quite clear that it wasn't an isolated discard. The charred debris of the fire pit were all that remained of someone's collection. Holmes sighed a bit and stood up, brushing the ash from his gloves.

"Never a good sign," he muttered to no one in particular.

Watson frowned, not quite sure he understood. "How so? Just a few books someone discarded. I fail to see what this has to do with anything."

Holmes stared down into the pit, obviously still distracted. "You may be right... perhaps nothing at all... perhaps the beginning..."

"Beginning of what?" sputtered Watson, by this point totally exasperated by his friend's habit of speaking in half-riddles. Holmes, however, never offered an answer as he was once again on the move, his attention now drawn by a fluttering of white in the weeds just beyond the fire pit. Bending low, he reached into the tall grasses and moments later, retrieved a few ragged sheets; pages that had escaped the fire. As he studied them, a look of profound cynicism clouded his face. He held them out to Watson as confirmation of his previous declaration.

"Never a good sign..." he reiterated.

Watson furrowed his brow, staring down at the pages. One appeared to be an index page of some sort, of what he couldn't tell as it was written in German; the other, a title page but from a different book, as it was written in English. He peered closer at the blackened page, straining to decipher the words, many of which had been burned away.

ON TH   OR GI O SPEC

OR   PR SE   ATION OF FAV RED RACES IN HE STRU LE OR IFE.

y Cha s D win, M.A.,

Fel ow T e   Ryal, Geological, Linaea   Etc, Soci es;

LONDON:

J N MUR   Y, AL MARLE STRE

1859

Watson grew quiet, lips moving wordlessly as he tried to piece the fragments together. After what seemed like an eternity, a look of understanding flashed across his face and he looked up in surprise.

"On the Origin of the Species!" he exclaimed. "Bloody Hell. Darwin. Well... not fond of science it would seem. "

Holmes nodded, lips curled scornfully. "Apparently."

"Hardly a crime," suggested Watson with a shrug of indifference. Although a man of medicine and science himself, he wasn't quite ready to leap on the evolution bandwagon as others in his field.

Holmes shot him a withering look. "In your opinion, Doctor."

Ignoring the reproach, Watson turned his attention to the page written in German. "And this one?"

Holmes studied the page; a look of pained recognition darkening his expression.

"Schleiden, German botanist" he announced, "Brilliant man. Revolutionary theories on the cellular structure of plants. This is one of his tomes, often used as a text at University." He took the pages back and with the utmost care, tucked them away inside the inner pocket of his coat.

"But why would a printer have a scholarly text on plants? Do you think it has to do with the bank notes?" pressed Watson, his face creased with concentration.

Holmes was silent for a moment and then shrugged. "Unknown, " he announced with a quick and eager smile. "Dangerous to speculate. Not enough data yet to draw a proper conclusion. Let's go find out, shall we?" A moment later, he had once again set off. This time, however, much to Watson's surprise, he turned completely around and headed back down the path towards the front of the house. Watson noticed with some irritation that the back entrance was now was less than thirty feet away. Groaning in resignation, he hurried after him. There were just some things he would never understand.

»»«««

"There's been a death ... recent," Holmes noted with a troubled frown as they approached the main entrance. A large, laurel wreath, wrapped in black ribbon and crepe, hung in the center of the door. The wreath was still fresh; the ribbons showing little sign of weathering.

Watson stared at the wreath, looking flustered and uncomfortable. "Lestrade's notes never mentioned," he sputtered, fumbling for an explanation.

"As I said, rubbish!" growled Holmes curtly, cutting him off before he could elaborate further.

Effectively silenced, Watson managed an apologetic wince and averted his gaze, too mortified to look his friend in the eye. It was a major piece of information to have been missed. Holmes had every right to be irritated.

Perhaps sensing that he had been too harsh in his reaction or maybe out of the realization that he needed to regain the cold detachment required for a successful interview, Holmes' expression softened.

"Well, perhaps now you understand why I distrust his methods. No real harm done I suppose," he sighed bleakly. There was an awkward pause, during which time Watson continued to stare down at the ground. Then, with a sly smile and an edge of sarcasm, Holmes quipped, "Though if it's

84

Pennington who is dead, it might make for a difficult interview."

Watson looked up and slowly smiled, relieved that Holmes' disapproval was fading.

"If that's the case," vowed Watson earnestly, "I'll thrash Lestrade myself."

"Quite so," chuckled Holmes in agreement. "Well then, shall we?" Straightening his lapels, he turned back to the door and extended his gloved hand to ring the bell. He had no sooner barely touched it when the door swung open. A dour-faced woman, lean and dressed in mourning attire stood on the threshold and glared balefully at them.

"Good afternoon Madame," began Holmes graciously as he proffered his business card. "Your employer, Mr. Pennington, is expecting us. Sherlock Holmes and Dr. Wa..."

"I know who you are!" she hissed, interrupting his greeting. "That yarder Lestrade was about earlier in the week, said to expect you," she added sullenly as she pulled the card from his fingertips. "The nerve of that man, all of you, bothering my brother so and at such a time as this. Have you no respect?"

A look of guilt crossed Watson's face and he quickly removed his hat, nodding that he understood her anger. Perhaps sensing that Watson was about to apologize, Holmes stepped forward to cut him off. Although still smiling, his eyes had now taken on a cold hardness; he slowly removed his gloves and slipped them into his pocket.

"We understand, Madame, that this is an inconvenience; the timing is unfortunate," he remarked in a quiet but deliberate manner, "but we are here on official business, and your brother did graciously offer his assistance. So, that being said, wouldn't it be prudent to invite us in so we may conduct our business without further delay and thus allow you to resume your grieving?"

A flush of red crept across the woman's pinched countenance, and her mouth twitched visibly as if she were about to speak. She regarded them with icy hostility, and it seemed as if she would continue to deny them entrance. The moment passed however and with a curt nod, she stepped aside and motioned for them to enter. Once inside, she ushered them into the vestibule and directed them to follow her. Their footsteps echoed hollowly off the marble as they made their way down the long hall past tall wrought iron candle stands and tall, heavy medieval chairs that looked anything but comfortable. As they approached a large central staircase, she veered off to the right and directed them into a small, candle-lit drawing room. A very grand house indeed, mused Holmes, for a printer.

"You can wait in here while I fetch my brother," she announced coldly. "I'll send Hanna in with tea." With an expression that made it quite clear that they were unwelcome, she turned and silently left, heading back down the hall.

"Charming," chuckled Holmes as he began to explore the room, picking up and examining various books and objects that were scattered about on tabletops and shelves. He was like a child in a toy shop at Christmas; eager to touch and explore all that was laid out before him.

Watson began to laugh, nodding in agreement as he settled onto the settee that faced the fireplace.

"Do you think it's wise to drink the tea? I've felt more welcome at Old Bailey." He had barely gotten the words out when his gaze settled on the portrait over the mantle. With an expression of disbelief, he slowly rose from the sofa and crossed the room for a closer look.

"Bloody Hell," he murmured incredulously, unable to take his eyes from the portrait. "it's her."

"Who?" muttered Holmes, his back still to the fireplace as he poked about the opposite end of the room.

"Your mysterious rider," breathed Watson. "What an odd coincidence."

By this point, Holmes had turned around to see what Watson was carrying on about. As he approached the fireplace and his eyes fell upon the painting of a woman and a small boy, a look of astonishment filtered across his face.

"Incredible," murmured Watson, still transfixed by the portrait, "and the boy, what do you think? Son? Brother?"

Holmes scrutinized the portrait, his eyes intense and focused as he took in all the details. He smiled slightly after a moment and shook his head.

"It's not her," he concluded.

"What? No. Of course it is. Has to be! Look at her." argued Watson.

Holmes' smile widened. "No, it's not," he insisted. "I agree that the resemblance on first glance is extraordinary, but there are noticeable differences ...variations in hair tint and bone structure. The lips, for example, are thinner, the curves more pronounced. In addition, the style of dress in this portrait is at least 10 years past – Parisian. Unquestionably, they are closely related. Older sister perhaps but given the age difference, more likely mother."

"And the little boy?" pressed Watson, his curiosity piqued by the growing mystery.

Holmes stepped up to the mantle, so close that he could almost distinguish the individual brush strokes on the portrait. He stared at the figures, how their hands were clasped together, the woman's steady gaze upon the child and then smiled somewhat somberly. There was a definite air of melancholy in the portrait; a sense of great loss.

"Son," he said simply as his eyes drifted down to the mantle over the fire, surveying the objects.

"Son?" repeated Watson, face drawn with concentration. "And where do you think he is?"

Holmes' gaze had finally come to rest on a small arrangement of violets in a dark vase, black ribbon interwoven; in the center of which burned a black votive candle. On a silver tray, next to the arrangement lay a few elegantly inscribed cards with a black border. He picked one up and with a solemn expression, handed it to Watson.

"Unknown, but we know where the mother is."

Watson glanced down at the card; his expression crumbled with sadness as he read.

In Affectionate Remembrance
Beloved Wife and Mother, Katerina Schraeder
Pennington, who tragically departed this world on the
27th day of December 1884
Paris, France
The heavens burn brighter because of you.

He was about to comment when the door swung open and a frail, fresh-faced maid of about sixteen staggered in, laboring under the weight of a heavy silver tea service. Watson sprang to her aid and quickly took the tray, setting it down in front of the sofa. She thanked him gratefully then blushed shyly as she backed up a bit, unaccustomed to the kind attentions of such a handsome, older gentleman as the Doctor.

"You're very kind sir. Please enjoy and if you should need a bit more, there's a pull on the other side of the fireplace – give a ring. Mr. Pennington asks your indulgence for a few minutes more; he'll be with you shortly," she announced, still keeping her eyes averted and after attempting an awkward curtsy, backed out of the room closing the door behind her.

Holmes frowned slightly, impatient to begin the interview as he settled into a wingchair. Leaning back, he crossed his legs casually, fingertips drumming absently on the arm of the chair as his eyes settled on the portrait. Watson settled onto the sofa and glanced at his pocket watch; half past 12:00. His eyes drifted to the tea service and settled on the covered tray, he became aware of a distinct rumbling from his stomach. Holmes heard it also and glanced over at him, unable to keep from smiling.

"Well, go on then," he sighed with a slight shake of his head.

Watson shrugged and reaching out, lifted the dome off to reveal a tray of fresh scones with pots of fresh jam and clotted cream. The buttery smell filled the air with a delicious richness.

"Be a shame to waste. Impolite," he justified with a guilty smile as he began to fill his plate. Laughing, Holmes nodded not so much in agreement as surrender. He settled back with a cup of tea to wait, there being no other recourse.

»»«««

Wilfred Pennington stood motionless in front of the drawing-room door, lips pressed tightly together as he once again polished his spectacles. When he had finally removed all the imaginary dust, he slowly replaced them on the bridge of his nose, face pinched in deep concentration as he struggled to recall the Professor's words of caution. To wait any longer would be imprudent. Steadying his nerve, he drew a deep breath and pushed open the doors, affecting his most cordial expression.

"Gentlemen, thank you for your patience. The travails of modern business, I'm afraid; my time is scarcely my own anymore. Now, how can I be of service to you?" The little man's smile was polite and obliging; his demeanor almost jovial.

Holmes and Watson rose to their feet and crossed the room, each one shaking his hand in greeting. It was in the midst of this greeting that Holmes did a curious thing. Bewildered, Watson watched as he moved across the room and deliberately positioned himself under the portrait of Pennington's departed wife and the little boy. Forced to look upon the portrait, Pennington's smile began to fade, his mouth twitching noticeably.

"Words cannot express our gratitude sir," Holmes began, his tone taking on an air of quiet sincerity and somberness that caused Watson's face to settle into a frown. "That at such a troubling time as this, you are able to lift yourself out of your grief and offer assistance. You are most generous. Our deepest condolences upon the loss of your wife." It was a consummate performance, and although Watson felt compelled to nod in commiseration, the knowledge that it was just that — a performance — filled him with a deep sense of displeasure. Holmes was a master of manipulation; one of his most effective and ignoble talents.

The desired effect was achieved; Pennington was clearly unnerved. He shifted uncomfortably and turned away from the portrait, his face anguished and vacant.

"Dear Katia," he mumbled vaguely, "Who could have foreseen? My poor girl's so lost without her."

"Long illness?" prodded Holmes gently, his expression the embodiment of compassion and concern.

Pennington shook his head, still lost in the haze of his misery, the need for caution all but forgotten. He stared into the fireplace, watching the flames flicker and dance, lost in a thousand memories.

"Drowned ... an accident. How cruel is fate I ask you, to be so cursed again?"

Again? Holmes arched his brow, his curiosity thoroughly provoked at the use of the word. He narrowed his eyes, his expression losing some of its empathy as he prepared to follow up. It was not to be however, as the chiming of the clock on the mantle announced the hour of one. The spell was broken and Pennington shook himself, slowly coming out of his fog. A look of anxiety filtered across his face and he forced a smile, wondering if he had said too much.

"But forgive me for rambling so. We are all very busy men," he laughed, a little too lightheartedly. "Now, the Inspector seems to believe I can be of assistance ...something about paper. If you please, this way." Having recovered his composure, Pennington headed quickly across the room towards a double set of doors, leading them quickly into his library, never once looking back at the portrait. He settled into a massive wooden chair behind an equally imposing desk, an obvious attempt to regain control of the meeting. Unimpressed, Holmes slowly smiled as he sat across from him. Dwarfed by the chair, Pennington for all his efforts had only succeeded in making himself seem that much smaller.

"What can you tell me about these Mr. Pennington?"

The little man compressed his lips and readjusted his glasses, peering down at the two, one-pound notes that were laid on the desk before him.

"They're pound notes Mr. Holmes, I'm afraid I don't understand," he hedged, a nervous little smile on his face.

"The paper Mr. Pennington, tell me about the paper. Only one of them is authentic. This one," Holmes explained as he slid the note on his left forward, "is forged."

"Remarkable!" exclaimed Pennington, his eyes wide open in what he hoped was a convincing display of surprise. "They seem identical." Reaching into his desk, he withdrew a small loupe which he affixed to his glasses and examined the note. As his fingers carefully slid over the paper, it was difficult for him not to feel a swell of pride; it was after all his best work. Ever mindful of the Professor's words, he suppressed the urge to smile too much and finished with his examination, removed the loupe and laid the note back on the desk.

"Extraordinary work... the ink, the paper. Nearly impossible to distinguish between the two Mr. Holmes."

"Yes, I concur, obviously, the work of a skilled craftsman. Precisely why we've come to you Mr. Pennington, for your expertise. I need you to tell me all that you can about this paper, the ink, the printing process. How complicated would it be? What amount of manpower would be necessary?" Holmes leaned back in his chair, fingers neatly steepled under his chin as he studied the little man shrewdly.

"Why of course Mr. Holmes! Anything to aid you in the quest for justice," he effused, secretly proud that London's esteemed detective had come to him for counsel. "It may take some time to gather the information; I wouldn't want to miss anything," he advised with a chuckle, leaning back in his chair, looking almost relaxed.

"Of course, Mr. Pennington. I certainly understand attention to detail. In the meantime, however, I'll start with your samples."

"Samples? I don't quite understand." Pennington's smile began to crack, a look of apprehension crossing his face.

"Samples of all your stock – specialty, newspaper, card stock ... All," asserted Holmes with a slight grin.

"All my... All?"

"Yes of course Mr. Pennington, all. I'm collecting a complete set from the area printers; you're next on the list," Holmes explained patiently. "There's something very special that the paper of these two notes share; chemical analysis should shed light on it. However, any analysis using an incomplete sampling would invalidate the results. I'd be forced to start all over again, an inconvenient waste of my time. We wouldn't want that to happen would we Mr. Pennington?" The smile on Holmes' face widened, his eyes grew a little colder.

Pennington turned noticeably pale and shook his head. "No, of course not Mr. Holmes. I wouldn't want to inconvenience you," he stammered, his fingers fluttering nervously as he readjusted his glasses. "It will take some time, to collect them from the shop. I'll gladly send them over to Baker Street when ready."

"Oh, don't trouble yourself Mr. Pennington. I'll come around to your shop by the end of the week. 85 Fleet Street, is it? Shall we say Friday around two? That way, you can give me the grand tour."

Pennington pursed his lips to speak, but no sound came. He managed a weak smile of resignation while his mind raced frantically as he tried to recall just how far along they were in the process for the next batch.

"That isn't a problem is it Mr. Pennington?" inquired Holmes with a deceptively amiable smile.

"Of course not Mr. Holmes. Friday should be fine, just fine … plenty of time. I'll make sure everything is arra..."

A barrage of sounds, angry female voices and the slam of the outer drawing-room door, silenced poor Pennington mid-sentence. The reverberation was so severe that it shook the library door and rattled the china in the serving tray. Stunned, the little man stood up behind the desk. With a face the color of putty, he stared at the closed doors, motionless, his mouth agape but no sound coming forth. Holmes and Watson exchanged baffled looks as the voices intensified. They were now just outside the closed library doors, the words spewing forth so furiously and viciously that the argument was nearly unintelligible. The voices however were immediately recognizable as the elder, stern-faced woman who had grudgingly allowed them in and the young woman from the road with the Parisian accent.

Flustered and as if in a daze, Pennington stumbled out from behind the desk, eyes fixed apprehensively on the door.

"I'm so sorry gentleman, please excuse me, I... " he stammered, his shame evident as he scurried towards the door.

Snatches of argument, incomplete phrases – heated words seeped through the closed door, filling the air with venom.

"Harlot... ungrateful Jezebel!" brayed the hoarse voice of the older woman. More words followed, unintelligible but clearly a command.

Pennington paled, fumbled for words and cleared his throat a bit.

"My sister's impatient..." He hesitated at the door, as if afraid to open it.

"Miserable busybody...you've no right!" The volatile words flew back in response along with what sounded like china, which shattered against the door.

Pennington jumped at the sound and uttered an awkward laugh, his eyes fixed anxiously on the door.

"Edwina my daughter, she's excitable sometimes," he stammered.

A heavy thud against the door interrupted him, followed by a slap so fearsome that as it echoed through the room, all three men flinched. There was a moment of silence followed by the muffled sounds of footsteps scrambling up the stairs. Drained of all color, Pennington raced from the room without further explanation, leaving the door slightly ajar. Watson watched in anxious disapproval as Holmes sidled up to the door to listen in. Pennington stood in the hall, visibly agitated as he attempted to reason with his sister; his daughter was nowhere to be seen.

"Holmes, enough!" protested Watson in a hoarse whisper. "For God's sake man ...some consideration, I beg you." Watson was mortified. He thoroughly understood the need for careful observation and surveillance to ferret out information, but to eavesdrop on personal family matters in the midst of such grief and turmoil seemed unconscionable.

"Quiet! I can't hear," hissed Holmes sharply as he peered through the crack in the door, listening intently. Despite his efforts, he was unable to discern most of the conversation. However, what little he heard left no doubt in his mind that Pennington was at odds with his sister with regard to his daughter. Whatever success and respect the man enjoyed in his business ventures apparently didn't carry through at home where his life seemed controlled by the whims of the women in his household and the strife between them. Holmes almost felt compassion for the man as he watched him plead with is sister ... almost.

Gretchen Pennington, unmoved by her brother's pleas for patience and understanding, stood at the foot of the stairs and regarded him with icy disdain.

"As you seem reluctant or incapable of taking her in hand, I will. Support me Wilfred or step aside. I won't allow our good name to be disgraced, not again. Either she learns to obey, or she'll be sent away. There are institutions that will teach her some manners." Finished with her brother, Gretchen Pennington turned away from him. Removing a large white box from the hall table, she thrust it into the arms of the young maid Hanna, who seemed to perpetually hover in the shadows awaiting instructions.

"Take this to your mistress and tell her it is to be worn at tea – no excuses. Madame Stafford is expected tomorrow for a final fitting," she instructed sternly and with one last warning glance in her brother's direction, she turned and then vanished down the hall. Pennington remained mute as he watched her leave, his head slightly bowed, the very picture of a browbeaten man.

"That's another battle in the making," chuckled Holmes as he watched the maid struggle up the stairs. The box she carried bore the name of a well-known London corsetiere.

"What?"

Watson frowned at him in confusion, waiting on an explanation as he had not seen the box. He would have to wait a little longer however, as Pennington decided to let the matter rest. Turning abruptly, he wiped at his brow with a pocket square and composed himself, heading back towards the library. Startled, both Holmes and Watson hurried back to their seats; as the door opened and Pennington slowly entered, they both rose to their feet as if they had never left them. Pennington, Holmes noted, looked distracted and miserable, his mind obviously still on his family troubles.

"Gentlemen, I do apologize," murmured the little man absently. He shook himself, drawing a deep breath in an attempt to regain his composure. "Now, where were we?" he asked, forcing a half-hearted smile but still avoiding eye contact with Holmes. Watson leaned back in his chair expectantly. This would be the moment that Holmes would pounce; catching the subjects of his queries off-balance was his specialty. So, he was particularly bewildered when Holmes rose from his chair and with a genial smile towards the little man, extended his hand and bid him farewell.

"I've nothing further at the moment Mr. Pennington, we won't take up any more of your time. You've been most generous, thank you again for your assistance. We'll stop by your shop Friday for the samples. Again, my deepest condolences on your loss. Now, as our cab seems to have deserted us, would you be so kind as to send one of your boys out to hail one from the road? It's such a lovely day that Dr. Watson and I will wait out back in your splendid little garden."

"Garden?" mumbled Pennington, more than a little perplexed by the abrupt end to the interview.

"Yes, out back by the fountain. I swear I spotted some lovely specimens of Convallaria Majalis, Lily of the Valley to laymen. Quite a favorite of mine. You don't mind, do you?"

Pennington felt an uneasy lurch in his gut. The idea of Holmes poking about unsupervised rattled him, particularly as the greenhouse was quite near the fountain garden.

"If you prefer, we will wait elsewhere," intoned Holmes politely, though his cold smile conveyed that it was a most unsatisfactory alternative.

"No... no, of course not Mr. Holmes," he stammered quickly, smiling as pleasantly as he could muster. "Please, feel free to enjoy the gardens as you wish. I'll send young Tom to fetch you when the cab arrives." He pushed back his feelings of dread; what else could he do? To deny Holmes would seem suspicious; besides, he doubted that Holmes would be so bold as to break into a locked greenhouse in the middle of the day.

"Splendid! Well, off we go then. Once again Mr. Pennington, my condolences. Please don't trouble yourself, no need to show us out, I remember the path. Good day sir. I'll be in touch."

Moments later, they had vanished out the doors and down the hall, leaving the little man standing outside the library, staring numbly at their retreating figures. On hearing the reassuring sound of the front door closing after them, he heaved a deep sigh of relief. Grateful that the interview was finally over, Pennington retreated into the solace of his library and closed the doors, reflecting on how best to proceed.

>>«<

Proper Introductions

"Lovely ... Simply lovely... What have we here?" mused Holmes, grinning in delight as he strolled down the path past the fountain. Every few moments he would stop to inspect plants, crushing leaves and buds in his long fingers, watching drops of sap slowly ooze out, inhaling the fragrance.

"Convallaria Majalis ... Nerium Oleander ... Atropa Belladonna... Ah hah.. Brilliant... our old friend Digitalis Purpurea."

Watson arched his brow in surprise, recognizing a few of the names. "Oleander... Foxglove. Christ, they're all poisons. Bit suspicious eh?"

Holmes shrugged, carefully wiping the plant sap off his hands with his handkerchief.

"Not necessarily. Mustn't jump to conclusions. There are a multitude of lovely flowering plants which happen to be poisonous. More common than you think. What I find more interesting is that someone's been tending this garden quite recently with great skill and affection."

A thought occurred to Watson, and he looked up with an expression of confidence. "Of course – the owner of the book...by the German... Schladen."

"Schleiden," corrected Holmes, quite pleased that Watson had made the deduction. "Yes, of course. Logical, a university text on botany – a student would have such skills."

"Pennington?" posed the Doctor.

"Doubtful," chuckled Holmes.

"The old woman then, his sister – of course!" exclaimed the Doctor with great confidence.

Holmes frowned and shook his head in dismissal.

"Hardly, seems more the type to have a gardener than garden herself. Besides, I suspect she had a hand in the burning of the books. She has something of the air of a religious zealot about her – not a fan of science. She wouldn't expend her time and energy on tending these plants.

"Well, who then?" exclaimed Watson, mildly exasperated.

"Unknown at the moment," replied Holmes with an easy grin. "Let's find out, shall we?" So once again, he bounded off down the path out of the main garden and past the fountain without waiting for Watson.

"Where are we going now?" grumbled Watson with some irritation as he scrambled to catch up. "We're supposed to wait by the fountain. Besides, I fail to see what any of this has to do with the banknotes."

"Humor me," chuckled Holmes with a slight grin.

"Do I ever have a choice?" muttered Watson under his breath. Holmes only smiled and forged on ahead, glancing back over his shoulder briefly.

"Relax Doctor, it will be awhile before the cab arrives. In the meantime, I need data," he advised, abruptly veering off onto a shaded path that ran along the side of the house.

A small screen of trees on the edge of the path afforded some privacy from the rest of the garden. Holmes increased his speed, though now and then he would glance up at the house, scanning the windows. He drew to a halt in the middle of the path, so suddenly that Watson, who had been hurrying to catch up, nearly ran into him. Before Watson could utter a word of protest, Holmes held up his hand to silence him, commanding him to listen. Holmes continued to edge along the ivy-covered wall, listening. Drifting out from somewhere above them, the two female voices they had heard engaged in battle out in the hall were arguing once more. This time, however, the argument was short lived as the sound of a door being slammed announced the end of the battle. There was a moment of silence and then a clear, Parisian accented voice cried out:

"Are you mad? Your Hell will freeze over before I subject myself to this medieval instrument of torture!" The declaration was delivered ferociously and punctuated by the sound of a door slamming once again.

"Poor man," murmured Watson, "I don't envy his situation." His words fell on empty air however as Holmes had once more moved off; a glimpse of his coat disappearing around the corner of the building. Cursing softly under his mustache, Watson shook his head in surrender and trudged off after him.

»»«««

Hanna choked back a giggle and covered her mouth, nodding in agreement. Although she wasn't one to make light of such dissension, she couldn't help but laugh at her mistress' wit.

"And my father?" asked Edwina, her mood quite subdued as she entered her room. She shrugged out of her jacket, draping it over the back of a chair and sank onto the edge of the bed, her slim booted legs stretched out before her. Her eyes drifted restlessly to the large box that Hanna had struggled with, which now lay on the bed. With a resigned sigh, she lifted the lid, fingers absently toying with the tissue inside.

"Back into the library Miss, his appointment," replied the young maid as she hung up the riding jacket. Spying the lapel watch, she carefully removed it from the jacket and handed it to her mistress.

Edwina pinned the watch to her blouse and glanced up in surprise.

"Appointment? Business?"

"Oh yes Miss, I believe so. Two fine gentlemen. They took tea in the drawing room before meeting with sir."

Edwina's mind spun back to the tea tray in the drawing room, the one from which she had snatched a cup to fling at Grendel. The two cups in the tray had been soiled, one still containing a remnant of tea. Her face darkened in chagrin; uttering a low groan of dismay, she lowered her face into the palms of her hands.

"Christ, I'm such an idiot."

What had she done? It wasn't that she intentionally set out to create dissension, she just wanted to be free to choose how to live her life. But to cause her father such distress and embarrassment was truly shameful. Whatever his failings or weakness, he was providing for her; something she was still unable to do for herself, despite all her protestations about independence. She hadn't a tuppence to call her own, only what he slipped to her when Grendel wasn't looking.

"I'm sorry Hanna, truly," she murmured after a moment as she lifted her head up. "I've caused such a ruckus. You must think me terribly ungrateful."

Hanna, who had been fussing about the room, tidying up while she listened to her mistress, paused by the window, a reflective yet uncertain look on her face.

94

"No Miss. Not ungrateful but..." She paused as if she were afraid to continue and turned back to the window, busying herself with tying back the curtains. With the curtains now secure, she lifted the sash, opening the window fully to circulate the air in the room.

Edwina smiled, realizing that Hanna wanted to speak her mind but was nervous. She leaned forward, curious to hear her thoughts. She was a bright little thing, whom she suspected was held back mostly by the limits of her low birth and lack of education.

"Go on then, speak freely, I won't be angry," she urged reassuringly.

Hanna met her eyes and then took a deep breath, nodding that she indeed did wish to offer her opinion. She chose her words carefully.

"It just seems Miss, that maybe if you didn't go against the grain so," she offered with a sweet smile as she went to the basin stand in the corner and poured water from the pitcher onto a soft cloth.

"You think I should change my opinions to keep the peace?" interrupted Edwina, her eyes sparking a bit.

"No, no Miss," Hanna stammered a bit anxiously. "But maybe not be so quick to argue. Cook always says, 'Flies go to honey more than vinegar' or some such like that," she soothed as she rung out the excess water from the cloth and handed it to her mistress.

Edwina chuckled a bit; not the exact quote but close enough ... she understood the gist of it. She furrowed her brow and stood up, pacing a bit as she pondered the girl's words. It was true that being openly combative hadn't gained her anything other than a slap. As her fingers lightly touched the side of her face which was still a bit tender, she winced and wondered if perhaps Hanna was right. She pressed the damp cloth to the side of her face, grateful for the cool relief it offered.

"Perhaps... definitely something to consider. One should choose their battles wisely," she mused as she handed the cloth back to Hanna. Her attention turned back to the box on the bed and with a wry smile, she bent over it and peeled back the wrapping.

"This, however, I find it difficult to compromise on. Bloody Hell, how does one breathe in this?" she gasped in disbelief as she lifted an elegant but rigid, white satin corset from the box. Her eyes widened as she tried and then lost count of the myriad straps and laces that dangled down from the back. It seemed incredibly small in size. No wonder genteel ladies were prone to fainting.

"Barbaric! A perfect instrument of torture," she murmured, turning it over in her hands. After a moment of study, she seemed to reach a decision and managed a slight grin.

"Well, as I said, choose one's battles, and this is one I choose not to cede," she chuckled. With a dismissive shake of her head, she pitched the garment back towards the bed. Whether it was due to her being too aggressive in her throw or her aim just being off, the result was the same. The corset took flight and both girls watched in astonishment as it missed its mark and sailed out the window, unimpeded by a lack of curtains. For a moment, there was no sound, only a stunned silence and then they burst into laughter, Edwina's laugh being the heartiest.

Needing no instructions, Hanna flew from the room, down the stairs and out the door to search. Edwina, still trying to regain her composure, crossed to the window and leaned out, peering out into the garden. A better finale she couldn't have asked for.

>>«<

"Holmes, I must protest. This spying is most improper," groused Watson as he followed the detective through the undergrowth, pausing every now and then to glance nervously over his shoulder. Thankfully, they were still undiscovered. Hopefully, it would remain that way. Now, if he could only convince his flatmate of the impropriety of the situation. Skulking about near a young woman's window indeed! What would his dear Mary think?

"Yes, yes - noted," murmured Holmes in weary dismissal. He continued to creep forward along the wall, all the while listening to the murmur of feminine voices above which increased in volume as they drew closer. Upon reaching the optimal vantage point, he drew to a halt and gazed up towards the window, a peculiar light in his eyes as he watched the shadows of the women moving about the room. After a moment, his attention wandered to the wall directly underneath the window, noting the ivy; it appeared fairly sturdy. On closer inspection, he detected a splash of white underneath; his smile widened ... trellis.

"If we are found here," whispered Watson with great agitation, "it could be ruinous. Not only to you but to..."

"Well, if you'd stop making so much noise," hissed Holmes curtly. Watson bristled, feeling a slow surge of anger welling from within. Holmes' capacity for selfishness and disregard for convention still astounded him. He pursed his lips ready to retort when a rustle sounded from above; a disturbance in the air. Both men stopped and looked up, squinting against the now strong sun.

"What the Dev..." Watson had no chance to finish however as the swishing grew louder, the object now directly overhead and falling rapidly.

Holmes reacted without hesitation, snatching it from the air before it hit the ground. As his fingers closed around the smooth fabric of the object, he stared at it and then burst into laughter. He held it up for Watson to see.

"Dear God. Is that a... a...?" Watson was so aghast, he couldn't even force the word out.

"Yes indeed," chuckled Holmes, "I believe the word you're struggling with is corset."

Watson blanched, fumbling. "Great Scott man, put on your gloves. Or at the very least use your handkerchief! You can't just handle it with bare flesh."

"Why not?" argued Holmes with a roll of his eyes. " Just a bit of satin Doctor, some boning, metal busks, lace. Quite lovely, exceptional craftsmanship," he commented, lips curling into a slight smile as he inspected

96

the garment.

"It's indecent!" croaked his companion, apprehension and embarrassment increasing with each passing moment.

"Do take a breath, Doctor," Holmes sighed. "It's not as if the woman was inside it." Noting Watson's great discomfort, he snickered a bit and shook his head. "I worry about you Watson, are you sure you're ready for matrimony?"

"You go too far Holmes, such liberties cannot..." muttered the Doctor under his breath, very much disturbed by Holmes' lack of concern for propriety.

Light but hurried footfalls and a rustle of fabric caught him mid-scold. Both men turned around just as the young maid that had brought them tea earlier appeared around the bend in the path. On seeing them, she froze in surprise and blushed, wringing her hands nervously. When she had recovered from her shock at finding them on the path, she composed herself enough to manage a small curtsy and bowed her head.

"Beg pardon sirs, but you wouldn't happen to have seen...?" She hesitated, the words dying in her throat and she blushed again, looking nervously from one man to the other as she struggled for a delicate way to finish the question.

"Seen, Miss?" pressed Holmes with a sly smile as his eyes latched onto hers. "Have you misplaced something?"

Watson frowned at him, puzzled by his question and then realized that the missing garment in question was no longer in sight. His annoyance increased when he noticed that Holmes was holding his frock coat closed rather awkwardly, one hand tucked inside as if he were hiding something. It wasn't hard to guess what that might be.

The girl lowered her eyes, unnerved by Holmes' penetrating gaze and took a few steps back.

"Excuse me sirs," she stammered after a moment, "it must have gone elsewhere." And quick as a flash, she gave them an awkward little nod and then turned on heel, fleeing back down the path.

"What are you about? Why didn't you give it to her?" grumbled Watson impatiently.

Holmes only smiled and replied, "I prefer the personal touch. Besides, it would be a shame to squander such an opportune moment."

"Opportune for what?" cried Watson in alarm.

"An introduction Doctor," laughed Holmes over his shoulder. "Time for a proper one! Coming?"

Horrified, Watson watched in disbelief as Holmes left the relative safety of the undergrowth and stepped out into the open. He strode purposefully towards the ivy-covered trellis under the window, where moments earlier they had watched Pennington's daughter lean out, calling to her maid. The window was still open but now empty, the girl having disappeared back inside. Watson scrambled after Holmes, catching up with him just as he grabbed onto the rungs of the trellis and began to climb.

Edwina paced restlessly, debating whether she should climb down into the garden and join Hanna in the search or wait until she returned. There was the distinct possibility that they would duplicate each other's search, a genuine waste of time. More worrisome was the fact that she didn't know whether her aunt had returned, and the prospect of that encounter filled her with a sense of dread. In the midst of her deliberation, a soft scrabble sounded, just outside below the window. She frowned a bit at first and then began to grin. Hanna, she thought excitedly and with an eager smile, ran to the window.

"Bloody hell, about time," she laughed as she leaned out over the ledge, "did you find...?"

She froze and uttered a sharp gasp of alarm; it wasn't Hanna at all. "Who the devil are you? What do you want?" she cried, her stomach twisting in a mixture of alarm and outrage as a tall, lean man with dark hair in a dapper frock coat climbed the trellis toward her. Her eyes darted around the room and then settled on the silver candlestick on the nightstand. As she reached for it, the man chuckled softly and lifted his head, a sparkle of mischief in his piercing blue eyes.

"If you could see your way to not bludgeoning me, I'd be exceedingly grateful. Hello again." His voice was cool and effortless, without a trace of worry.

She stared at him, dumbfounded as recognition settled in. Christ, the man from the road, the only one who had offered assistance. Her arm, as if on its own, slowly lowered the candlestick while her stomach continued to flutter a bit, but this time not from fear.

"It's you," she murmured, leaning against the window jamb as if in a daze. "But how? Why are you here?"

He smiled charmingly and with a shrug, leaned forward on the trellis, holding on lightly with one hand. "You did predict this morning, that we would meet again," he said casually. "So, here I am, though admittedly, sooner than anticipated."

She smiled at this, albeit somewhat tentatively as he reached the top of the trellis. His eyes were impossibly blue, infinite and radiated profound intelligence. As she gazed into them, she found herself sinking down onto the ledge, back against the window frame.

"I don't understand," she murmured, finding it difficult to break eye contact. To say that she found him attractive was an understatement; striking being a more apt description.

"It's a rather long story," he sighed with a wry smile. "Tedious even. I fear it would bore you. Suffice to say, I am here with a purpose – primarily, to return your property."

"My property!"

Edwina's face darkened in bewilderment, watching as he reached inside his coat. All confusion soon vanished, however, replaced first by astonishment and then a tinge of discomfort as he produced the corset and offered it to her with a bit of a flourish.

"I presume this belongs to you. How did you call it? Ah yes, a medieval instrument of torture," he quipped with a roguish smile. "Strange days are upon us it seems. The most extraordinary objects fall from the sky."

Despite her embarrassment, she couldn't help but laugh a bit as she reached out to take the corset. "I suppose I should thank you," she sighed with obvious reluctance. "I am apparently the wrong shape; at least according to Grendel." A look of bitter disillusionment clouded her face as she tossed the corset inside onto the bed.

"Grendel, clever," he chuckled, deftly appraising, and deeming her a most unlikely Beowulf. "I assure you, your Aunt Gretchen is quite mistaken."

She blushed slightly though her lips pulled into a grateful smile. Leaning back against the sill, she drew her booted feet up under her on the sill and studied him quietly. Once again, she was filled with a strange sense of familiarity; that she knew this man or knew of him and not just from the events of that morning. She racked her brain, searching for an answer and in the process, was suddenly struck by another troubling notion. She cocked her head to the side a bit and frowned, leaning forward slightly.

"How did you know I was referring to my Aunt? How could you possibly know what was said? I…"

She stopped, mid-sentence as her mind reeled back to the argument with Grendel outside the library. The soiled teacups … there had been two in the tray in the drawing room just outside the closed library doors. She blanched, her eyes widening in dismay; father's business appointment … they had heard every disgraceful word.

"Christ! It was you in the library. Father's meeting," she groaned, thoroughly mortified. "You must think me terribly ill-mannered. I meant no disrespect. I'm not ordinarily so uncivil despite appearances to the contrary." Her tone was sincere, and Holmes watched curiously as she rubbed her forehead for a moment and then tucked back a few errant locks of auburn hair, adjusting the black velvet band. It was such a simple gesture, yet he felt oddly moved by it.

"You do seem to have a flair for confrontation," he chuckled. "But, no harm done," he soothed, a faint smile tugging at his lips. "The meeting had run its course. Please don't concern yourself over it."

A look of genuine relief brightened her face and she smiled warmly.

"Was my father of help to you? Is there anything I can do Mr. … Mr. ….?" She abruptly stopped and although her brow crinkled a bit, she began to laugh. "I'm afraid I still don't know your name … Mr.?"

Holmes smiled, lips pursed ready to comply but lost the opportunity as the sharp crunch of gravel below the trellis announced Watson's return.

"Holmes! " Watson hissed insistently, looking flushed and irritable, "The hansom is here. We really must…"

Edwina looked startled and stared at the man on the trellis. As comprehension sank in, she drained of all color.

"Holmes? Oh. Christ!" she exclaimed in disbelief, gaping at him. "Not…

the Holmes?"

"I'm afraid so," he chuckled resignedly and with a slight smile, extended his hand.

"I see my reputation precedes me. William Sherlock Scott Holmes, at your service Miss Schraeder. Or do you prefer Pennington? Oh, and lest I forget, the disapproving man at the bottom of the trellis scowling up at us is my colleague, Dr. John Watson."

And there it was, the answer to the question that had plagued her - but one she hadn't expected. *Incredible ...the great Detective himself. The man was nearly a legend.* She had spent countless hours at university pouring over his case studies, discussing his reasoning process, reading his monographs and now here he was ... in the flesh. She bit her lower lip and drew herself up, determined to regain her composure. The last thing she wanted was for him to dismiss her as some fawning schoolgirl.

"Edwina," she murmured, taking his offered hand, hoping that her own wasn't trembling noticeably. "Schraeder, if you please," was all she could manage at first. She studied his face and managed a warm smile. He was much younger than expected and certainly more handsome than any accounts had portrayed him.

Holmes pressed her hand and smiled, once more noting that despite her momentary awkwardness and obvious surprise, her grip was firm and confident, her eyes bright and curious. She met his gaze levelly; most unusual for a woman.

"It's such an honor to meet you Mr. Holmes," she said earnestly, breaking the silence. "I've followed your work. It's brilliant. Your monographs are astounding."

"Monographs!" echoed Holmes with a grin, "You've read some of them?" he exclaimed with a great deal of satisfaction and cast a smug look in Watson's direction. Watson snorted a bit, looking disgruntled and dubious. He could barely make it through one of Holmes' tedious technical papers, he sincerely doubted a woman could have any understanding of the technical issues outlined within them.

"Not some, Mr. Holmes, all!" she asserted with an amiable laugh. "Or at least all I could get my hands on. I particularly enjoyed the one on distinguishing between the types of cigar and cigarette ash. The one on perfumes is extraordinary. Regarding your thoughts on blood spatter and spray patterns, I was wondering if..." Abruptly, her voice faltered and died out as a look of utter dismay drained the color from her face. The change in her mood was so acute he was caught off-guard; his eyes grew pensive as he watched her mood spiral and darken, a slight frown creasing his brow.

"Of course, that's all changed now," she murmured mournfully as her head drooped forward, eyes cast downwards.

"How so Miss Schraeder?" he prodded gently, though he anticipated where the conversation was headed. He cocked his head slightly and leaned forward a bit.

Edwina shrugged and lifted her head slowly as if she were weighted

100

down by a great burden.

"They're gone. She burned them. Everything. My books, case studies, your monographs," she explained tersely, her mounting frustration and anger evident. "Even my sketches," she added with a bitter laugh. "I'd been compiling them from our travels. We, that is Mother and I, visited so many galleries and museums on our travels. So many wondrous things. Michelangelo's David. Winged Victory. Venus de Milo, all my figure studies. "Her mood continued to darken, emerald eyes now distant and mournful though they remained free of tears, an ember of resentment smouldering just under the surface.

"She wants to erase all traces of my mother. All traces of who I am. Mold me into something I am not nor wish to be," she muttered, sullen and bitter.

Holmes was quiet for a moment and then smiled, his words sober yet unexpectedly comforting.

"I'm not a man given to sentiment Miss Schraeder. These are all just objects - the things we fill our lives with - immaterial nonsense - such a loss would mean little to me. I am however, a keen judge of character and I see in you a strength of character that does not need these objects to retain your sense of self. Your aunt has misjudged you as I suspect many do. You will prevail - of that I have no doubt."

The solemnity and sincerity of his words took her by surprise. Though she didn't really know this man, she knew his reputation. Although polite and charming at times, as a man of science, he was not prone to demonstrations of empathy or warmth. Such an uncharacteristic display elicited a surge of gratitude that coursed warmly through her. Struggling to contain the urge to reach out and embrace him in gratitude, Edwina's face lit up with joy and she smiled.

"You are most kind Mr. Holmes. I shall endeavour to live up to your expectations."

His eyes darkened for a moment, his expression sage and thoughtful.

"The only expectations that are important are those you set for yourself, Miss Schraeder. In the words of the great Lao Tzu, 'Care about what other people think and you will always be their prisoner.' These are words I have used to set my own path."

Edwina lifted her gaze to his, her expression reflective as she contemplated his words.

Of course," he added with a wry grin and chuckle, "I am often reminded by the good Doctor that I am painfully inept with social convention - so perhaps my words should be taken with a healthy dose of skepticism. Grain of salt if you will."

Her face lit up, the dark traces of self-doubt vanishing as a warm smile crinkled the corners of her eyes.

"That's better," he murmured, undeniably pleased by the brightening of her mood. His eyes grew contemplative for a moment. He reached inside his coat and withdrew two scorched and blackened pages. They fluttered a bit in the breeze as he held them out to her.

"I retrieved these near the fire pit," he said simply, eyes fixed on her.

Edwina arched her brow quizzically as she reached out to take them.

There was silence for a moment during which he detected a strong undercurrent of emotion bubbling up within her. As she gently brushed at the ash on the pages, the smile began to fade from her face and her eyes grew pained and damp as she recognized the pages.

"Not much left grant you - still, perhaps some small comfort," he offered quietly. He paused briefly, choosing his words with great care and then added, "Forgive my inconsideration Miss Schraeder. I've neglected to offer my sympathies on the loss of your mother. If I can be of any assistance in your time of need, do not hesitate."

At his words, spoken so kindly that he surprised even himself, Edwina raised her eyes to his and managed a small but sincere smile of gratitude.

"Thank you," she murmured softly and reaching out, impulsively pressed his forearm warmly with both of her hands. "Treasured gifts from mother. Her eyes were still slightly misty though she forced a small, brave smile.

Holmes drew back a bit, surprised and a little disquieted by the emotional intensity of her reaction. His lips drew into an uneasy smile, his eyes drifting down to where her fingers still rested softly on his forearm and he was uncomfortably aware of the growing warmth of his skin beneath the sleeve where her hand lay. He shifted a bit, she was close and although he found it rather unsettling, he felt inexplicably reluctant to move away. The breeze lifted her hair slightly, filling the air with the delicate, fresh scent of lilies of the valley and as he gazed into her face, he couldn't help but smile. Extraordinary – her eyes were the color of emeralds and her perfume mirrored her perfectly; sweet but not cloying, warm but not heavy, light but memorable. Genuine and lovely. Distracting to say the least.

"Holmes," interrupted an impatient voice from below. "The hansom... how much longer man?"

His reverie broken, Holmes furrowed his brow slightly and cast a warning frown in Watson's direction to silence him. He leaned back slightly on the trellis, noting the shadow of disappointment in her eyes as her fingers slipped from his forearm.

"It seems I am summoned," he explained with a shrug and genial grin.

Edwina nodded that she understood and settled back once more on the window sill, back pressed against the frame. She breathed slowly and deeply, and he could see that she was struggling to regain control over her emotions.

"I hope my father was of assistance to you. A new case I presume?" she asked, her eyes growing bright with curiosity as she once more regained her composure.

"A general inquiry. Your father has expertise which may prove invaluable," he explained glibly.

"Anything I can do Mr. Holmes, please don't hesitate," she offered. "It would be an honor," she added, eyes warm and earnest.

A slight smile curled his lips and he nodded. "Noted Miss Schraeder. Now, I must be off. Watson's patience is wearing thin and I wouldn't want to draw the wrath of your ..." He paused a moment, chuckling to himself quietly, "Aunt... Grendel," he added with a mischievous grin.

Her laughter was immediate and genuine, filling the air with warmth and good cheer. As Edwina's face glowed with the joy of a shared secret, his own smile widened. He nodded, moved as if to start descending and then paused, a thoughtful expression creasing his brow. Reaching inside his coat, he withdrew a calling card and finely engraved silver mechanical pencil. He began to write on the back of the card, swiftly and with great precision. On completion, he handed it to her and once more began to descend. She looked at the card, front and back and then glanced to him, somewhat puzzled. The engraved side bore his name and the celebrated address of 221B Baker Street, the blank side, two brief lines:

Hatchards - 187 Piccadilly
Josiah Fleming, Managing Agent

She leaned forward, out over the sill, her hair flowing loose from the velvet band as she watched him descend.

"I don't understand." She looked down in bewilderment.

Holmes reached the bottom of the trellis and grinned up at her, brushing a bit of paint and grit from his hands.

"Finest book seller in London. Should be able to assist you in replacing some of your books. Ask for Fleming, show him the card, let him know I recommended you. As for the lost monographs, well I've a mountain of them collecting dust on the shelves. You, Miss Schraeder, may be the only other person to have ever read them, or even cared to, other than myself. If you find yourself the in the area of Baker, feel free to come around. I'm certain I can spare a few." Then, with a flash of a smile and a slight nod, he bid her a genial "Good Day Miss Schraeder," and vanished down the path.

The effect on her mood was immediate and her face lit with unabashed joy and gratitude.

"Good Day Mr. Holmes. Thank you," she called out after him and then settled back onto the sill, drawing her knees up, head resting against the window frame. She looked at the card again and smiled, thinking that she might very well be in the area of Baker in the near future. Closing her eyes, she slipped the card into the right front pocket of her blouse and angled her face up to catch the remaining rays of the sun. Perhaps England wasn't as much the wasteland as she had feared.

»»««

"About bloody time," grumbled Watson irritably, glancing at his pocket watch as Holmes entered the hansom and settled into his seat.

"Patience Doctor. You'll meet your supper engagement. Plenty of time to spare. "

Watson scowled a bit and shook his head, watching as Holmes began to scribble a few notes in a small, leather-bound notebook.

"What was all that about?"

103

"What was what about?" murmured Holmes, continuing to write, never lifting his eyes from the notebook.

"All that...chitchat?"

Holmes paused in his writing and arched his brow, leaning back against the quilted upholstery.

"You believe me to be insincere," he commented with a sly grin.

Watson choked back a laugh and cleared his throat.

"You're not exactly known for idle conversation or geniality...certainly not without a valid reason. Is there a reason Holmes? What do you suspect?"

Holmes grinned and laughed a bit, shaking his head.

"Suspect? What could I possibly suspect at this stage?" He narrowed his eyes and leaned forward, rubbing his hands together, his eyes dark and brooding. "You're too engrossed in your own fiction Doctor. I fear your mind has become muddled."

"No, no. You know what I mean," exclaimed Watson in exasperation, bristling at the reproach. "Her father then ... do you suspect him?"

Holmes arched his brow slightly and then shrugged. "We've just begun. Too soon to draw conclusions. At this point, everyone and no one is a suspect, Doctor. You know my methods."

"But the girl," protested Watson, not ready to concede the argument. "Why all the chatter? You spent more time with her than you did interviewing her father."

A brief silence fell between them and as he waited for the answer. It seemed to Watson that Holmes looked noticeably irritated. It passed quickly however, as the detective fixed his gaze upon him and smiled rather fiercely.

"I was collecting data. It's what I do old fellow, isn't it?" he reminded pointedly with more than a trace of sarcasm. And the matter being settled, at least in his own mind, Holmes shut his notebook and leaned back with eyes closed to consider all that had transpired that day.

For a few precious moments, the silence was punctuated only by the clatter of hooves on the cobblestones as the hansom headed back towards London. Watson frowned a bit and then withdrew the Times from under his jacket, slowly turning the pages, his face drawn with skepticism.

"Lovely brown eyes though," Watson commented after a short pause with deliberate nonchalance. "Quite complimentary with her golden hair."

"As ever you fail to observe," came the swift yet equally casual correction from across the cab. Holmes never opened his eyes though a hint of a smile played on his lips. "Her eyes are quite green... vivid... the color of emeralds... her hair auburn...and lustrous."

The detail of Holmes' response caught Watson off-guard, his face settling into a curious frown as he pondered his friend's remarks. Holmes' attention to detail and precision in his descriptions was legendary but this seemed beyond that to him. In fact, it struck him as almost poetic, but he held his tongue, sensing correctly that the detective was in no mood for further discussion. With a sigh of resignation, Watson let the matter go and glanced out the window. As familiar landmarks rolled by signaling their return to the outskirts

104

of London, his lips settled into a smile of relief. Upon glancing down at his pocket watch, his smile widened even more ... plenty of time – just as promised.

»»««

Welcome to London
A Fortuitous Connection

Saturday morning - Fern Hall

"Perhaps this isn't such a good idea. We should wait dear until your Aunt feels better. Cook and Hanna can manage the errands on their own as they've done many times before."

Wilfred Pennington's face was drawn with indecision as he leaned against the door of the Clarence, eyes fixed on some distant point beyond the gates of Fern Hall. He felt a vague sense of unease and he wasn't altogether sure why. His sister, who was rarely ill — having the constitution of a horse — had taken to her bed three times in the past week, afflicted with weakness, nausea and little appetite. He had considered sending for a doctor, but had delayed as she always seemed to rally just before he was called out. Besides, her symptoms seemed mild enough, nothing terribly serious, just enough to keep her close to her room and subdued. Pennington managed a reluctant smile. In all honesty, he had to admit that the resulting peace and quiet was a welcome change. A light, gentle pressure on his arm called him back to the present and he turned around and peered into the carriage, where his daughter met his gaze with a warm and comforting smile.

"You mustn't worry so father. Grend..." Edwina stopped abruptly, correcting herself with a faint grin, "Aunt Gretchen will be right as rain soon. I'm sure of it. Just needs to rest."

Pennington felt a sudden surge of affection as he looked upon his daughter; he was so proud of her – still so headstrong and independent yet she had lately been making an extra effort to be more accommodating. With the unexpected onset of his sister's infirmity, Edwina had proven to be a source of comfort and encouragement, even taking tea into his sister and sitting with her. The kindness of her actions touched him deeply and gave him hope that she was indeed settling into her new life. He reached out and took her hand in his, squeezing it fondly.

"I'm sure she will, but perhaps you should wait. I'm almost certain to have some free time shortly. London can be such a labyrinth," he hedged, his voice tinged with concern. "You shouldn't be alone, you need a proper escort."

Edwina took a deep breath and compressed her lips, struggling to contain her growing irritation. She smiled as sweetly and convincingly as she could, all the while fighting the urge to let out a shriek of exasperation.

"But I won't be alone," she protested. "I'll be with Cook and Hanna and Vienna and Paris are hardly what could be called rustic. Mother didn't raise me as some bumpkin father, I do have a wit or two about me. I managed to cross the channel on my own, surely I can navigate London with their help.

Pennington winced a bit at the slight reproach in her voice, mulling it over. Well, it was true that she wouldn't be on her own and she was a singularly clever girl. He peered into the coach, scrutinizing the faces of Cook, Hanna and his daughter. Trusted servants ... trusted daughter. His resolve began to weaken – how could it not? Just to look at her; demurely attired in mourning, a modest black walking skirt and tightly buttoned matching jacket. He noted with some relief that the skirt flowed well over the top of her boots and her hair was pinned up under a black boater with a satin band. Her only jewelry, the ever-present heirloom watch, pinned to her jacket. The epitome of a sensible, modest young woman.

"Father, please, I won't let you down," she murmured, her voice earnest and almost pleading.

That was all it took. Pennington heaved a great sigh of resignation and nodded. How could he turn her down? She seemed to have the same sway over him as her mother had. With a small smile, he leaned into the carriage and gave his daughter a peck on the cheek, bidding her a pleasant afternoon. A few moments later, the carriage was rumbling out past the gates and turning into the lane. He watched it go for quite some time and then turned, heading back towards the house, his mind already moving onto his work. Besides, what could possibly go amiss?

As the carriage cleared the end of the lane and pulled onto the main road heading into the city, Edwina exhaled in relief and unbuttoned her jacket. Grinning with anticipation and delight, she unpinned her hair from under her boater, shaking it loose. She leaned over in her seat grasping the hem of her skirt.

"Well I had my doubts for a moment," she chuckled. She lifted the hem of her skirt to reveal a border of red lace on the underside into which were sewn a series of hook and eye loops. As Cook watched in astonished disapproval, Edwina rolled the hem up and fastened it to where the bottom of the skirt just grazed the top of her boots. Ignoring the look, Edwina smoothed her skirt and leaned forward, her eyes bright and eager.

"Now, here's the plan..." she instructed with a confident smile, fixing her gaze upon the two servants. Several miles and 5 shillings later (3 for Cook - she had taken extra convincing and 2 for Hanna, who had balked at the offer of any money at all) the scheme was laid out. Satisfied, Edwina settled back in her seat and gazed out the window, mentally reviewing the itinerary she had set for herself and humming contentedly as she watched the buildings of London draw near. First stop, Hatchards on Piccadilly and after that - well, perhaps a stroll around Regent's Park and the surrounding area.

»»«««

A shaft of meagre winter sunlight peeked in through the half-drawn shade and Watson rolled over, groaning a bit. He reluctantly opened his eyes, blinking

106

dazedly as he looked about the room. For a few moments, he procrastinated, not quite ready to leave the warm sanctuary of the blankets. Realizing that it was no use, he surrendered to the inevitable and sat up on the edge of his narrow bed, reaching for his pocket watch. As his eyes adjusted to the light in the room and he noted the time, a look of surprise crossed his face. Dear God, half past nine already and he still felt as if he had just crawled into bed. Pulling on his trousers and braces, he stretched wearily still exhausted from the night before. It had been a horrendous accident; collisions between the railway and horse drawn transports were becoming more prevalent. By some small miracle, no one had been killed - horses included though the injuries sustained had been numerous and severe. Shaking his head, he poured water into a basin and washed up. Damned nuisance this modernization; too many unhappy meetings of the old and the new. Lathering his face for a shave, he peered into the mirror wondering if they were all just rushing blindly into the future. Out with the old, in with the new and consequences be damned... that seemed to be the order of the day. Tradition, decency and morality all seemed in jeopardy in the rush to embrace all that was modern; a way of life was being lost. It was here that he differed most sharply from his flatmate. Holmes often accused him of fogeyism, mocking him for his reverence of traditional values and roles. It was true he supposed, maybe he was antiquated in his outlook but at least in his father's time, men and women had a clear idea of their role and place in society. But he had long ago given up on trying to convert Holmes to his point of view; it was a losing proposition. Lifting the straight razor, he peered into the mirror preparing to make the first pass but was suddenly halted by the grating rasp of a violin bow being dragged harshly across the strings. The discordant yowl made him wince and he waited for silence to fall before he attempted to make a pass with the razor. He had nearly completed the shave when a succession of screeches once more shattered the tranquility of the morning. Distracted, his hand faltered and he swore softly under his breath as a few drops of scarlet speckled the porcelain basin. It was all the more frustrating as Holmes in actuality was an accomplished violinist, when he chose to play the instrument. Often, particularly when he was vexed or stymied in the midst of a case, he would torture the instrument (and those within hearing distance), claiming that it helped him focus. Suffering from a lack of sleep and general frustration, Watson grabbed a towel, dabbing at the nick just below his right earlobe and strode out into the hall, determined to remind his flatmate of what it meant to be a good neighbour. As he approached, the door to the flat opened. He was met in the hall by a very perturbed Mrs. Hudson. She muttered under her breath as she struggled to carry a tray of dishes from the previous night. Forgetting his grievance for the moment, he rushed forward to help her balance the tray noting that not one morsel of dinner had been touched – only the tea had been consumed.

"Bless you," she whispered gratefully, giving his arm a warm squeeze as he carried the tray downstairs into the kitchen. "I don't know why I even bother... no breakfast or dinner for the past two days... tea... just tea for me....

that's all he says," she complained with a shake of her head. " I tell you Dr. if he doesn't manage to poison or blow himself up, surely he'll starve to death."

Another jarring screech drifted out from 221B causing both to cringe. Compressing his lips in mounting annoyance, Watson set the tray down on the sideboard, remarking, "Dear lady, if he doesn't give it a rest, either of those options are charitable compared to what comes to mind."

A broad smile creased her face and she joined him in laughter, knowing in her heart that the good Doctor was being facetious.

"He's been at it most of the morning," she advised with a disapproving nod. "I'm surprised you slept through it 'till now. Between that blasted noise and the nasty chemicals, it's enough to make a body lose their wits. He's in a right mood today; barely grunted at me when I came in with his breakfast. Had two callers this morning and wouldn't even see them."

"He refused to see potential clients?" he remarked incredulously. Watson's frown deepened. Although it wasn't unusual for Holmes to decide not to take a case, it was out of the ordinary for him to do so without even interviewing the caller. At the very least, he would sit in his chair and stare up at the ceiling looking bored out of his mind as he listened – even if the eventual outcome was a shrug and dismissive, "Away with you – not interested."

"Oh yes," she replied quickly. "Bloody cross about it too. Said he didn't have time to waste on nonsense. Can you imagine? Making such a statement and not even the courtesy to come down and meet the callers. But that's what he did ... had me send them off without so much as a pleased to meet you." Mrs. Hudson frowned and sniffed the air somewhat self-righteously. "I made excuses for him of course. Two fine gentlemen they were. German, I think. Such fancy dress and manners... very grand. They left their cards and some papers relating to their case. I promised them I'd make sure he reviewed them. You'll see that he does won't you Doctor? You have a better way with him than me," she wheedled, her smile suddenly warm and motherly. "And remind him won't you... that he still owes the cost of the repair to the windows," she added with some accusation and placed the packet in his hands.

"Well... I ... Yes... I suppose I could try," he sputtered, staring down at the papers.

"Bless my soul! I knew I could count on you. Now off you go. I've got work to do. His "lordship" is waiting on another pot of tea; mustn't keep him waiting eh?" She gave him a quick nudge towards the stairs and then with a merry chuckle, bustled off to the kitchen.

Watson looked down once more at the packet in his hands and then with a sigh, trudged resignedly back up the stairs. He had barely taken hold of the doorknob when it began to turn in his hand. The door jerked open and Holmes abruptly appeared in the opening, grey silk dressing gown thrown loosely over a rumpled white shirt and grey striped silk pyjama bottoms, eyes wide and almost feverish. He was pale, disheveled, frenetic and barefoot; there was no doubt in the Doctor's mind that he hadn't slept since he last saw him – nearly two days prior.

"Watson... there you are! Well, where is it then?"

"Where is what?" asked Watson, watching in bemusement as Holmes pivoted, peering suspiciously at the packet of documents in his hands.

"My tea of course... Isn't that why you're here?" he replied sharply, obviously annoyed that he even had to ask.

"Have you forgotten I live here? And no, I don't have your tea, but there are these documents – a possible case." Watson held them out, a hopeful expression on his face. To this, Holmes only narrowed his eyes and exhaled in exasperation as he strode past the Doctor to the bannister. He barely gave the documents a second glance.

"Bah! What use then?" he growled as he grasped onto the rail and leaned over, peering down the stairs.

"Missus Hudson!!... the tea! Now would be perfect!" he bellowed. Without waiting for a reply, he turned on heel and stormed back into the flat. Watson followed and upon opening the door, drew back a bit, gagging as his nose was assailed by the harsh odour of chemicals and shag tobacco. An array of flasks and beakers filled with liquids of various hues, bubbled away on the work table, flanked by two new, state of the art microscopes which replaced the ones damaged in the mishap. He picked his way carefully across the room, the center of which was still blocked by the packing crates they had arrived in the previous weekend; straw littered the floor and Mrs. Hudson's Oriental rug. Watson grunted a bit; Lady Caroline had come through as always for her favourite.

"Still the straw on the floor? Haven't straightened yet?" he groused testily.

Holmes snorted a bit, unfazed by Watson's not so subtle attempt to shame him into tidying up and settled onto a stool behind a microscope, eye pressed to the lens.

"As you like. I 've no objection as long as you're quiet. Mind you, I am working," he reminded in a chilly voice.

Watson bristled; not only was the room in disarray, it positively reeked of foul chemicals. A thick haze hung in the air, making him pause for breath. Beakers of varying shapes and sizes were scattered about the table, all were filled with precisely cut cubes of paper soaking in unknown solutions. All were in differing stages of liquefaction and without a doubt, the source of the foul odor. Holding his breath, Watson crossed to the window, still holding onto the documents. He set them down on the edge of the worktable as he passed and crossed quickly to the window, pulling back the heavy drapes and sliding up the sash. A welcome waft of cool air filled the room; he filled his lungs and sighed in relief.

"Ahhh... fresh air and sunlight ... how novel! Now we can all breathe thanks to the new windows which our dear landlady has once more reminded is still owed."

"Peevish today, aren't we?" murmured Holmes, ignoring the remark about the window, as he continued to hover intently over the microscope. He removed one slide, quickly replacing it with another and readjusted the focus, never once lifting his head. "Perhaps you should have slept in and given us all a rest," he added dryly, his fingers tapping impatiently at the base of the microscope.

Watson snorted a bit. "Capital idea. Unfortunately, I have the misfortune of an inconsiderate flatmate."

Holmes arched his brow and finally looked up; a tight smile on his lips. "Not a fan of music then?"

"That wasn't music," snorted the Doctor with a pointed laugh.

Holmes' expression darkened, his lips curling bitterly.

"Well, how fortunate you'll soon be rid of 'him'. Though I predict you'll soon find you traded one form of misery for another."

A look of surprise crossed Watson's face. Sharp words, even for Holmes, who for all his sarcasm, had never once voiced an ill word toward Mary Morstan, no matter how veiled. But he held his tongue – considering the words. On closer reflection, the barb seemed not so much aimed at her as a general grumble of disillusionment. He wondered if Holmes was still experiencing a sense of loss and isolation. Not a trace of the woman remained in the flat nor was she ever mentioned. It was as if she had never existed. Holmes still visited Limehouse on occasion, though it seemed to render him less satisfaction and contentment as time passed. All these questions crowded his thoughts, but Watson never had the opportunity to raise them however, for the next moment the detective suddenly uttered a fierce cry of exasperation, wrenched the slide out from under the scope and flung it against the wall. It shattered into slivers, solution trickling down the wall.

"What is it?!!!" Holmes exclaimed heatedly, "What have I missed?!" He pushed away from the table, nearly overturning the stool and began to pace agitatedly. His grey silk dressing gown flapped wildly out behind him, as if the very garment itself was struggling to keep pace.

"I don't understand," mumbled Watson, unnerved by Holmes distress. His eyes drifted to the locked roll top where he had last seen the Moroccan case and he wondered if he should check the levels.

"Of course you don't," he hissed. "The key, man... the common link... I cannot find it! and yet, it must be here but somehow I have missed it!" Swearing under his breath, he began to rifle through the samples on the table. Unable to find what he needed, he ran his hands though his hair, tugging ferociously as if he could extract the answer by sheer force. Giving up, he strode over to the mantle and grabbed the silver cigarette case, flipping it open. Empty - his agitation increased and with a grim expression, he reached into the coal scuttle searching for the frayed Persian Slipper where he stored his rolling papers and a reserve stash of fine Turkish blend. But much to his growing exasperation, this was also empty. It had been a long sleepless night fueled by tobacco and other stimulants and now he was completely without. He collapsed into his chair, hands entangled in his tousled locks. "This won't do! Won't do at all," he mumbled.

Watson was tempted to smile at the melodrama as it unfolded but gave in to pity. Holmes' ego was fragile when it came to failure. One of the great tragedies of his genius was that he allowed himself even less forgiveness for the occasional error than he did others; any failure, no matter how small or insignificant, was a great source of personal distress.

"Perhaps a nice pipe. I've some lovely cherry blend," suggested Watson kindly.

"Ughh. Dreadful stuff, " snorted Holmes. "How do you smoke that foul weed? No. The solution is clear. I know what is needed."

"It is?" ventured Watson with some hesitation and a modicum of dread.

Holmes abruptly stood and with a sudden grin, grabbed Watson's hat and coat from the corner rack and flung them at him.

"Of course, you'll simply have to go to the tobacconist. Do be careful and get the correct blend this time. The last lot was disappointing. "

"But... Mary..." protested Watson in vain, as he found himself, hat now jammed on his head, coat over his arms, being propelled out the door towards the staircase. Despite his annoyance, he had to admit to being relieved that the craving this time was focused on a lesser vice.

"What about her?" sighed Holmes wearily, rolling his eyes.

Watson's face flushed, and he stopped abruptly at the top of the stairs, brushing angrily at his frock coat.

"I am to meet her at London Hospital at half past one and take her to tea. I will not be late," he groused resentfully.

"Well, then you'd best be off," Holmes growled with a sarcastic smile. Watson stared at him, momentarily speechless, and then tramped noisily down the stairs, attempting to contain his fury. He had almost reached the front door when Holmes leaned over the bannister.

"And don't forget to remind Mrs. Hudson about my tea!"

Watson froze, his face now the color of summer tomatoes and turned around, glaring up the stairs. Words however escaped him and without even the smallest sound, he lowered his head and then stormed out the front door, slamming it after him. The man was insufferable... unfathomable. He disappeared down the street, hat clamped tightly on his head against a growing breeze, now focused on his new task, intent on completing it as swiftly as possible.

Holmes' face suffused with amusement at the slam of the door and he shrugged. Shaking his head, he headed back into the flat to wait.

"Man grows more irascible by the moment," he muttered.

Holmes cast a final glance at the samples soaking in the glass evaporation dishes and sighed ... still not ready. Scanning the worktable, his gaze settled on the packet of papers that Watson had left. He recognized it immediately as the documents Mrs. Hudson's "fine German gentlemen" had left. Giving in, he gathered them up and settled into his wingchair. Might as well he supposed — no tea or tobacco yet — he had to find something to occupy his mind while he waited. His eyes dilated, drifting momentarily to the locked roll top. Unconsciously, he licked his lips, his thoughts turning dark for a moment. But it was only for a moment and with a sigh of resignation, he settled farther back into the chair and began to read.

"Which book would that be again Miss?" squawked the red-headed clerk, scarcely more than 13. He stared at her nervously for a moment and then averted his gaze, his eyes drifting downwards. As they settled on the tops of her boots, peeking out from under the hem of her skirt, his eyes widened; he blushed furiously on catching the briefest glimpse of her grey stockinged ankles. He turned his attention to the worn floorboards and fixed on the fissures filled with dust and grit as he fiddled uncomfortably with the buttons on his ill-fitting vest; a child in man's clothes.

Edwina groaned a bit in exasperation and forced a smile, trying to remain patient; he was still a child after all. Her eyes clouded for a moment; probably the same age as Julian would have been and seemingly just as timid.

"Up on the top left... Charles Darwin..." she instructed with as much kindness as she could muster, pointing to the book.

He stared at her for a moment and then the book, as if trying to decide what to do.

"Is there a problem?" The edge of impatience in her voice was now unmistakable. He hesitated, his face now almost the color of his hair.

"I... I'm not certain Miss... it may not be for sale."

Edwina frowned and fixed her gaze steadily upon him.

"It either is or isn't. Are you not a bookseller? Why would you display a book that is not for sale?"

The clerk laughed nervously, fingers still working the buttons. He had nearly twisted the top two off the vest; they dangled, held on by just a few threads.

"I shall have to check with Mr. Fleming Miss.... Please... Wait..." he sputtered and then scurried off into the backroom.

Sighing in resignation, Edwina glanced at her watch; she would give him the consideration of a few moments and then slowly moved along the narrow aisles, browsing the overflowing shelves. Amazing collection – Hatchards was living up to its reputation as one of the finest booksellers. Pity they didn't seem motivated to make a sale. After a few moments, the curtains to the stock room parted and a tall thin man with a perpetual frown and thinning red hair came forward. He approached quickly, his face creased with disapproval as he looked behind her for the rest of her party or some form of chaperone.

"I'm Josiah Fleming... Proprietor... I'm told there is a party interested in the Darwin book. I should like to speak directly with them."

The patience that she had been struggling to maintain began to slip.

"You are Mr. Fleming. I am that party." She forced a little smile, teeth pressed against the underside of her lips.

"What? Impossible!" he huffed looking more than a little put out. He was a busy man with little time to waste on such nonsense.

A slow flush spread over her cheeks, nevertheless, she smiled again, suppressing her irritation.

"Yet sir, as I am the only one here, not so impossible."

The sarcasm in her voice took him by surprise and he drew himself up, brows knit as he peered closer at her. Hmmm... shortened skirt ... hair unpinned ...shameless... insolent. He'd seen her type before, the ones causing all the fuss in the city lately, like a plague, slowly spreading throughout London.

"And what need would you have of such a book? Where is your guardian? How are you here Miss?"

Edwina drew a deep breath, focusing her energy on maintaining control.

"I intend to read the book sir... and as for a guardian, I am more than capable of looking after myself."

"You?" he snorted dubiously. "Even if you understood it. what use of it to you? Not to mention unsuitable." The matter settled, he waved his hands dismissively and started to turn away.

"Unsuitable?" "It's science! " she burst out, losing patience.

"Precisely... Unsuitable!"

She let out an indignant gasp and parted her lips but was unable to find the words to protest. Josiah Fleming looked impatiently at his pocket watch and then shrugged, nodding towards the shop door.

"On your way Miss... I've no time for such nonsense."

Edwina trembled in anger, using every ounce of her willpower to maintain control. She adjusted her jacket and reached into her tapestry bag, her eyes smoldering, smile tight and contemptuous.

"And I have no time for small minded men," she intoned curtly. "I came here sir because your shop was personally recommended to me by a well-respected gentleman. You can be certain that when I see him again, I will inform him of the warmth and courtesy of your welcome."

Josiah Fleming paused in mid-stride, his hand on the curtain to the back room. He let the curtain fall and then turned, fixing her with a skeptical glare.

"And what gentleman could that possibly be?"

Edwina smiled a little smugly and held out the signed calling card.

"Mr. Sherlock Holmes - perhaps you've heard of him."

"I don't believe you," he snorted, a look of surprise and amusement on his pinched face. He took the card and studied the signature; his frown deepened, it seemed authentic. Suspicion clouded his face.

"How did you come by this? What manner of trickery ... or should I say... thievery?"

The accusation stunned her for a few moments and she could only gape at him, her shoulders quivering in bitter indignation. He turned the card over, giving it another glance and then offered it back to her.

"You best clear out Miss, " he warned tersely, "Your kind isn't welcome here. Go on now before I lose patience and call in the constable."

The words left her short of breath, cheeks crimson with heat. Eyes ablaze with fury and shame, she ripped the card from his hand.

"Keep your damn books. I hope they rot alongside you," she hissed venomously. After a few choice words in French, Edwina stormed from the

113

shop, slamming the door after her. It wasn't until she reached Fulbourne Street, near the bottom of Whitechapel Road that she realized her cheeks were wet; her resolve to remain strong and not show weakness had obviously crumbled. She was furious and more than that -- mortified. It was one thing to face disapproval because of her dress and outspokenness, she was used to that; what stung her the most, gnawed at her soul, was the accusation that she couldn't possibly know Sherlock Holmes and had come by his card through duplicity. Wiping at her eyes, she took a deep breath and removed her hat, using the satin ribbon from the brim to tie her hair back from her face. She compressed her lips, smiling grimly, she would have no kind words for Mr. Josiah Fleming when she saw Mr. Holmes again. Ahhh.... Mr. Holmes. At the very thought, the smile on her lips softened, most of the melancholy lifting from her face, as she considered that eventuality, for earlier in the day she had determined it was a question of when rather than if.

Thus, with her head filled with fanciful musings and schemes, she wandered aimlessly up the road, weaving in and out of the throngs that filled the streets. One thing was unmistakable, it certainly wasn't the best of areas. The narrow street was clogged with peddlers, horse carts, unwashed tradesmen and the ever-present drunken mariners who loitered dangerously near alleys, regarding her with a leer. She gave them a wide berth and smiled determinedly, ignoring the icy stares and vulgar catcalls as she passed. Some forty-five minutes later, she grudgingly conceded that she had absolutely no idea where she was or where she was headed for that matter. A small sanctuary of green loomed up ahead at the corner; she carefully crossed the muddy street and made her way towards it, coming to settle on the low stone wall that surrounded a small park whose grounds had seen better days. Still, it was more pleasant than the street and provided a chance to rest her feet. After sitting for a few moments, she became aware of the sounds of music, a brass band to be precise, led by the rhythmic boom of the bass drum. Craning her neck, she peered curiously down the street. A mass of women, young and old alike, arms linked and all wearing the green, white and purple sash of the National Society of Women's Suffrage rounded the corner. As they neared the entrance to the park, she experienced a surge of excitement and leapt to her feet. A young woman, barely out of her teens, broke from the ranks and approached her ... face bright and eyes burning with the enthusiasm and hope of a zealot.

"Votes for Women Now," she chirped as she thrust a handbill into Edwina's hands. "Come and listen Sister. It's time to take our rightful place."

Edwina scanned the list of speakers ... Millicent Fawcett, Emmeline Pankhurst, Emily Davies ... The list was impressive. Needing no further encouragement, she smiled resolutely and fell in step behind them along with a swell of like-minded people and the curious. Within a very short time, the small park was filled to capacity. As the speakers took to the tiny, impromptu podium, Edwina moved in closer straining to hear, the disappointment of the morning beginning to fade.

114

Mary Morstan sat on the cold, stone bench under the portico of London Hospital, waiting patiently; as patiently as she could manage. The amiable smile on her face belied her growing irritation as she tucked a few errant golden curls up under the crisp white nurse's cap. The breeze had grown stronger and colder, now coming off the docks. She pulled her cloak closer around her against the sudden chill. That promised tea would be heaven right now. With a weary sigh and one more glance at her watch, she rose from her seat and walked to the top of the stairs, pausing underneath the brick archway to peer out towards the noisy street. Colleagues streamed past calling out cheerful greetings which she returned with her usual warmth and geniality while deep within, her anger simmered. Where the Devil was he? He'd promised to be on time no matter what. She loved John with all her heart and soul but sometimes she wondered how a man who had served so honorably and heroically in the wars could allow himself to be so put upon. As she had often reminded him, Holmes was a but a man, flesh and bone same as him. Admittedly, cleverer than most, but truly a deity only in his own mind. She suspected that most of John's reluctance to assert himself came not from cowardice or intimidation, but from a deep and abiding respect and loyalty for the detective. By the same token, she sensed that despite Holmes' outwardly aloof and cynical nature, he was equally fond of the Doctor, though he would never admit to such sentimentality. They were like siblings who squabbled incessantly yet would brave the fires of hell to render aid to the other. Their bond was steel; tempered by years of adventure and adversity and she had no desire to weaken that bond. The thought had crossed her mind, usually after a mild quarrel, that she hoped John never had to choose between her and Holmes, for she wasn't always confident of what the outcome would be.

So, with her mind clouded with such thoughts, she turned away from the main entrance and walked slowly towards the stairs near the south end of the portico which overlooked Fulbourne Street. Gazing out in the direction of the small park square at the end of the street, she frowned a bit as her ears detected the sounds of some sort of commotion; it was growing louder. There'd been talk all morning on the ward of another rally by the National Society of Women's Suffrage. The handbills and posters were plastered all over the city. She hoped it would be peaceful. The last rally at Victoria Square had ended in a veritable riot. The newspapers of course, had a field day vilifying the suffragettes. She had her doubts; every story had two sides, of that she was convinced. She felt a sense of admiration for the suffragettes, although she was always circumspect in her conversations with John out of respect for his views. Not all women wanted marriage or were fortunate enough to be as lucky as she. She had even, out of curiosity, briefly considered asking John if they could stop by the square on the way to tea and listen to some of the speakers. However, upon further reflection and knowing John's mindset on such matters, she relinquished the idea. There were some things that the good Doctor wasn't ready to accept yet, though he was considered progressive in his views by his medical colleagues. Thankfully, he hadn't even mentioned her leaving work upon their marriage (though he wasn't very keen on her working in the East End). A tender smile curled her lips as she moved back from the stairs and leaned lightly against one of the columns to get a better view; no matter, soon she would have a lifetime to convince him of the error of his ways.

»»«««

It happened in a flash, so quickly Edwina wasn't sure quite what had happened. Mrs. Pankhurst had been speaking, valiantly ignoring the jeers and catcalls from the edges of the square where a group of rough looking men had gathered. Women of all ages stood in the center transfixed – listening intently to her words, arms linked in a show of solidarity. From the outer fringes of the crowd, a rock was hurled forward. It struck one of the waiting speakers squarely on the forehead and dropped her to the ground. Chaos erupted. The peaceful crowd disintegrating into a seething mass of confusion and panic. Ruffians from the fringe rushed in while some of the more valiant suffragettes rushed forward to meet them and engage while others tried to flee. The sounds of panic and confusion filled the square along with the whistles and clanging bells of the Black Maria as the Yarders surged in, truncheons at the ready to restore peace. Not wanting to end up in the back of a police wagon nor the business end of a truncheon, Edwina fled the park, all the while aware of the sound of pursuing yarders at her heels. As she rounded the corner of the square, she caught sight of a massive building with a long, covered portico. Lifting her skirt even higher, she put on an extra burst of speed and darted down the street, recklessly weaving in and out of the crowds. She kept her eyes fixed on the granite stairs that led to the shaded colonnade. Lungs nearly bursting, she scrambled up the stairs and darted down the long corridor, eyes wildly searching for cover. A door opened off to the side as a group of doctors emerged to take some air. She lowered her head and made a beeline for it. She had nearly reached it when a young nurse wrapped in a light gray cloak stepped out from behind one of the columns. They collided, and it was only by some small miracle that they managed to stay on their feet.

"Christ! So sorry! Are you all right?" Edwina exclaimed quickly and with a sheepish smile, reached out to steady the young woman. As she spoke, her eyes scanned the hallway; the door had closed eliminating her escape route. She looked anxiously out to the street and beyond as the sounds of the disturbance in the square grew closer. Whitechapel street was beginning to fill with constables and police wagons as they continued to round up all those who had fled the square. She needed to disappear and quickly.

The young nurse straightened her cap. Despite the smile on her face, Edwina sensed she was more than a little irritated.

"You should take more care, you'll hurt someone," scolded the nurse, who though only slightly older than herself, sounded rather maternal.

"Yes… yes... sorry again," replied Edwina quickly, her eyes still focused

116

on the chaotic street. She hardly had time for another lecture.

The nurse studied the young woman curiously and with a fair amount of caution, noting her odd accent, modern style of dress and forward demeanor. The good Doctor was correct; the world was changing right before their very eyes, though she held out more hope at the prospect.

A shadow fell across the hall as a pair of constables began to mount the stairs at the end of the south portico, their hobnail boots clicking sharply on the hall floor. Trying to contain the feeling of panic that threatened to overwhelm her, Edwina turned to the nurse with a plaintive expression.

"Your cloak... quickly," she whispered urgently.

The nurse stared at her in alarm and took a step back, suddenly uneasy. She watched in bewilderment as the woman unrolled the hem of her skirt, produced a small black boater from her tapestry bag and began to pile her auburn locks onto her head. She was a flurry of frenetic but precise movements. When finished, she quickly covered her hair with the hat and once more turned to her, her eyes dilated with distressed excitement.

"Please... help me," she begged once more, her voice simultaneously plaintive and insistent.

It was at that moment that the circumstances of the situation — the young woman's dress and bold manner, the disturbance in the street — coalesced in an epiphany.

"You're one of them," Mary Morstan blurted in surprise and awe. "A suffragette. "She took a closer look at the young woman, noting her unpowdered face and natural shape. She 'd never met a suffragette before though she'd seen their marches through London and followed their struggles in the papers. Being of a curious nature, she had on more than one occasion expressed an interest to the good Doctor in attending one of their rallies, with his accompaniment of course. It was a request that was gently but unequivocally rejected. She had been disappointed of course but had accepted his decision. But now, by some odd stroke of fate, there was one right before her very eyes.

Edwina was caught off guard by the announcement, though her eyes never left the hall behind the nurse as she answered.

"What? I'm not... Well... not specifically... though I wholeheartedly agree with their position. Not much of a joiner I'm afraid."

The sound of the heavy boots echoed down the hallway as the yarders grew closer and with a look of utter desperation, Edwina turned back to the nurse and reached out to her.

"Please...I'd really hate to spend the rest of my day incarcerated."

Following her gaze, Mary Morstan nodded that she understood and quickly removed her cloak, helping the woman fasten it around her. Once that was completed, the two ladies settled on a bench in plain sight, engaging in conversation as though old friends. Edwina firmly believed that the best hiding places were often in plain sight. The yarders approached, glanced at them briefly and then satisfied, tipped their hats and continued down the hall. Once they had passed, Edwina let out a sigh of relief.

"Thank you," she said, with a warm and grateful smile as she handed back the cloak. "I really didn't fancy spending the afternoon locked up or trying to think of an excuse for my Aunt. She'd never believe me – the old busybody." She paused in her ramble on seeing her companion's look of confusion. "Sorry, forgive my lack of manners. I'm Edwina by the way. Edwina Schraeder but my friends call me Eddy. Feel free to if you like, you certainly qualify." And with a bright smile and slight laugh, the woman removed the hat from her head and stuck out her hand in greeting.

Mary Morstan took note of her ungloved hand and smiled tentatively, though she gently shook her hand.

"Mary Elizabeth Morstan. Pleased to meet you Miss Schraeder is it?"

"Edwina at the very least please," she insisted with a slight shake of her head. "Everyone is so damn proper here; even when they're being horrible. I've been thrown out of two shops today by very polite men. To be honest, it's really beginning to get on my nerves. One can only bear so much politeness."

At this, Mary burst into laughter though she quickly covered her mouth with her hands to soften the noise. She nodded in agreement and grinned at the young woman, feeling an instant affinity. She liked her frankness, it was unusual,   especially in a woman her age. To always be polite and never really say or express your true feelings was something that had been drummed into her head since an early age. She was beginning to tire of being regarded as a small child; seen and heard from as little as possible. Even the Doctor treated her that way sometimes; though on the whole, he allowed her to express herself more freely than most men – a fact she was most grateful for.

"Are you here on your own? Where is your chaperone?" she asked abruptly, forgetting her manners for the moment. She was fascinated by this young woman. Everything about her. Her strange accent, the way she dressed, her unpinned hair, how she didn't shade her face against the sun, the rolled-up hem on her skirt.

Edwina arched her brow in surprise at the outburst and smiled. An unexpected spark ... how delightful. She paused a moment, carefully considering her words.

"I will be five and twenty come Autumn," she began solemnly, meeting Mary Morstan's gaze. "I've just crossed the Channel on my own to lay my poor mother to rest in a country she didn't want to be in when she was alive let alone in death. I live with my father, a man whom I've had scant contact with since I was nine, his sister – my Aunt – despises me. My new country neither respects nor wants me. So, to that I say... I say... Where is your chaperone Miss Morstan? As for me, I do quite fine without one, thanks very much."

For a few moments, Mary sat in stunned silence, not quite sure what to say or if she should even say anything at all. It was a lot of information to process at one sitting. So much bitterness and yet, under the circumstances, quite understandable. After a pause, she drew a heavy sigh and reaching out, gently squeezed Edwina's ungloved hand to offer reassurance.

"I'm so sorry Miss Schraeder... for the loss of your mother and for all the ill-mannered louts who have made you feel so unwelcome. Not all Londoners are such. I hope that in time you will come to see that."

Edwina's face suffused with regret and groaning aloud, she rubbed her forehead anxiously.

"Bloody hell! I'm an idiot! It's a fault of mine to be sure. I either whine or scold; often both at the same time. I'm so sorry. What I meant to say is that I seem to do best on my own. I haven't the patience nor the desire for a minder. My aunt and father think differently of course, but so far, knock wood, I've been successful at outmaneuvering them. In fact," she added with a mischievous smile, "as far as they are concerned, at this very moment I am shopping in Covent Garden with cook and Hanna after spending the morning being fitted for a new wool cape."

"But what if they find out?" pressed Mary, her blue eyes wide with apprehension.

Edwina's face lit with a smile and she shrugged. "Cest la vie," she laughed. "I shall cross that bridge when I come to it and not a moment before. Life is too short don't you think?"

Mary began to laugh and nodded in agreement. The initial unease she had felt upon meeting this odd young woman had all but faded, replaced by a general sense of curiosity and exhilaration. She wasn't quite sure exactly what it was about her new companion that captivated her so – all she knew was that her presence somehow made her feel more hopeful and confident.

"So, you are French then?" she concluded somewhat uncertainly as her accent was a little different than most Parisiennes she had met. It would however very well explain the lack of head covering and unstructured shape. The French were always trying new things; they were quite adventurous. She frowned slightly, the Doctor would say that it was due to a lack of decorum and shame, not forward thinking.

"No, not exactly. Though I studied and lived in Paris for quite a while. Vienna is where I was born. I guess I'm a little of both. But what of you Mary Morstan? From where do you hail and your minder, where is he this fine gentleman?" she asked with a teasing grin.

Mary knit her brow in bewilderment. How on earth could she possibly know?

"Edinburgh... my father's family is from there and mother's from Cornwall. As for my minder, beg pardon, how did you know?"

Edwina began to laugh and shrugged. She reached out and lightly tapped the engagement ring on Mary's hand which although hidden by a pair of light grey gloves, was still quite distinguishable.

"A very recognizable shape. Congratulations. Your fiancé, is that who you were looking for when you were standing by the columns peering out? You seemed concerned. Is anything wrong?"

Mary hesitated a moment. It was indiscreet to divulge such personal information, but she somehow felt she could trust this woman.

"Well, no, I don't believe so. He promised to meet me here after my shift to take me to tea but he's late. "

"Late? How late?"

Mary frowned slightly and popped open the gold heart shaped locket around her neck, revealing a small pocket watch. Her frown deepened as she studied it.

"Close on two and a half hours now. I'm sure it's nothing. Most likely got caught up in something," she sighed with a resigned smile, though her eyes hinted at frustration.

"What? You've waited that long!" exclaimed Edwina in disbelief.

Mary smiled gently and leaned forward with a conspiratorial smile, unable to stop herself from expounding.

"He has this flatmate. Brilliant man but extraordinarily eccentric, arrogant, demanding, and sometimes John... well... he has difficulty saying no. "

"John?" Edwina repeated with a chuckle as she leaned forward, intrigued. So, the minder had a name after all. Thank goodness, she was beginning to think it was Doctor.

Mary Morstan blushed and compressed her lips, folding her hands primly in her lap as she spoke. She'd forgotten her manners, it was too easy to be relaxed around this young woman.

"Pardon. What I meant to say is my fiancé, the Doctor, well his flatmate, he can be very persuasive. I'm sure all is well, and he'll be here shortly."

"But how long will you wait?" interjected Edwina in disbelief. "Two hours is excessive. Perhaps he's forgotten. "

"Why, as long as I must I suppose. What choice do I have? It's not as though I can just head out on my own."

"Of course you can," chided Edwina. "You can and will do exactly that. It's decided. I shall come with you then you won't be alone, and your fine Doctor will have nothing to scold you about."

Mary looked unconvinced.

"I'm not sure that is a good idea," she hedged. "What if he shows up here just after we've left?"

"He's made you wait all this time? Well then, a dose of his own medicine won't kill him," she remarked pointedly. "Your time is just as valuable as his. Besides, if he's even the smallest amount of clever, he'll figure it out. But if it makes you feel better, perhaps you should leave word at Hospital Reception. Now, no more excuses. Come on then." And the matter being settled, Edwina rose from the bench and took the young nurse by the hand, lifting her up from her seat. Seeing that it was futile to argue, Mary gave in and slowly followed her towards the hospital entrance. After leaving a brief message at the reception, just in case the good Doctor did stop in, the two women set off down the street, heading towards Whitechapel Road. As they stepped out onto the busy sidewalk, Mary refastened her cap and adjusted her gloves, trying to look confident as she looked up the road.

"Well then, we'll just take a cab," she announced with forced brightness. She'd never set out on her own before; her stomach fluttered a bit at the prospect.

"How far?" pressed Edwina with a slight frown, recalling the thinness of

120

her purse. What Josiah Fleming had helped her save by not selling her the books had quickly been spent on a few bits and bobs from street vendors as she had explored the city.

"Not too far. Just a few blocks but I've walked the wards all day, I'd rather not walk," replied Mary as she scanned the street for a hansom.

"Hmmm... Noted," sighed Edwina, reluctant to admit that she didn't have the fare. While she was trying to think of a way to persuade her companion of the virtues of walking, the sharp clang of a bell caught her attention. As a horse drawn Omnibus came into view, her face erupted into a delighted smile.

"Will that get us to our destination?"

"Well yes, I believe so. But..." Mary chewed her lower lip in hesitation as she watched the two-level tram round the corner and move slowly up the street. It was crowded with tradesman and merchants. A small ball of anxiety stirred in the pit of her stomach. She'd never actually been on one. John had absolutely forbidden it, reminding her that no respectable woman would put herself in such a common vehicle. Edwina however had no such trepidation having spent most of her student days in Vienna and Paris hopping on and off trams.

"Come on then, stick close to me," she urged with a laugh. Grabbing tightly onto Mary's hand, she pulled her along forcing her to keep up. The Omnibus rarely ever came to a complete stop, moving at a slow, steady pace which allowed riders to hop on or off as they neared their destination. Realizing that she had no choice, Mary grasped her skirt, lifting the hem up to her ankles and took a deep breath, following Edwina's example. Reaching out, she grasped the outside rail of the car to pull herself up. With the help of Edwina and young man in a stained butcher's apron, she was lifted safely inside. With a giddy laugh and blushing nod of thanks, she soon found herself following Edwina as she headed further back into the crowded tram.

"Oh, what about our fares?" she asked curiously, reaching for her purse as they maneuvered through the car, bypassing the conductor for the moment.

"Later," advised Edwina with a sly grin as she continued to weave her way towards the back of the car. Finally, they settled into a window seat at the very back of the car close to the rear exit stair. Mary pulled her cloak tighter and rubbed her hands together quickly; it was quite chilly with the windows open, but she didn't mind the cold so much. She leaned forward, looking out the windows in wonder. How often she'd viewed these very streets through the windows of a hansom with John or walking on his arm, yet somehow, from her perch on the hard wooden bench of the tram, it all seemed fresh and exciting. Instinctively, she realized that it would be best to keep this to herself; the Doctor would be appalled at her riding the tram. By the same token, she had to admit that she was over the moon. Imagine, she was having a proper adventure.

"How far?" asked Edwina after a moment, watching warily as the conductor began to work his way down the aisle.

"Euston Road... 1 pence... Hampstead 3 pence... next corner... Marylebone, Baker and Regents Park... Six pence. "The conductor's voice rang out clear and loud over the clanging of the bell as the tram slowly rounded a corner and began to head down Euston Road. There was a short flurry of activity as passengers rose from their seats and squeezing by each other in the aisles, paid and then hopped off.

"Oh... Time for the fare then," murmured Mary with a smile of pure enjoyment as she reached into her purse and began to count out six coins.

"How far then?" repeated Edwina, a little more edge in her voice as she fidgeted a bit ... her eyes fixed on the conductor.

Mary frowned slightly, a puzzled look on her face. Her companion seemed suddenly tense, her eyes dark with concentration.

"Not far," she said slowly, "perhaps 3 more stops." She looked out the window, studying the passing buildings in order to get her bearings. A feeling of unease began to nag at her.

"Good," interrupted Edwina with a resolute grin, "let's... shall we?" And with no further explanation, she abruptly rose from her seat and taking hold of Mary's hand, pulled her to her feet and began to head for the back stairs.

"But we haven't paid." Mary stared at her in disbelief, even as she was being dragged towards exit.

"Shh... Not so loud," hissed Edwina, tightening her grip. Passengers were beginning to stare at them, obviously having overheard. The conductor meanwhile continued to advance.

"But it's not right... we mustn't!" protested Mary as they reached the back stairs. She reached out and grabbed onto the handrail, holding on defiantly even as Edwina stepped down onto the first step ready to hop off. There were principles at stake here.

"I haven't the fare... sorry," sighed Edwina with an apologetic frown. On seeing her companion's distressed expression, she truly did feel some regret.

"But... Why did we..." Mary stared at her in disbelief, mouth slightly agape.

"Have you enough for me then?" Edwina interrupted her again with some impatience. It really wasn't the time for long drawn out discussions on the whys and wherefores.

"Well... No..." Mary's expression grew even more troubled. "Surely if we explained ..."

The conductor was almost on them and Edwina choked back a laugh at the naivety of the nurse. With a resigned shrug, she moved down onto the first step, holding on to the outside handrail.

"Well, you may do so if you like, stay on then. As for me, well Miss Morstan, it's been grand." She smiled playfully and gave her a small wave as she prepared to hop off.   .

A look of utter horror crossed Mary's face as she realized that she was about to be left behind.

"Wait!!" she cried out in sudden alarm. "Don't leave me!!"

In the blink of an eye, she reached out and latched onto Edwina's hand as she moved to hop off. She really didn't want to experience the rest of the tram ride on her own and holding on as tightly as she could, they jumped from the tram as it slowed to turn onto Marylebone. As they landed solidly on the street, a shout of indignation and anger echoed after them. Edwina burst into laughter at the sight of the conductor shaking his fist in their direction. The merriment was short lived however for a moment later, the tram which almost never stopped, did just that, pausing further down Marylebone. Edwina's face crumbled as she watched in astonishment as the conductor hopped down off the tram and approached a constable who was standing post on the corner. He began to gesture animatedly and although she couldn't hear his words, she had a fair idea what the topic of conversation might be. His rant completed, the conductor simply turned and pointed them out.

"Oh, Bloody hell! Bugger if he didn't!" she swore in utter disbelief. The constable turned away from the conductor and fixed his sight on them. He reached for his whistle. The shrill sound pierced the air and Mary, jumped in alarm at the sound and turned to Edwina, a look of utter panic on her pale face.

"What now?" she wailed.

"Run!!" was all Edwina said and then took off.

Mary, needing no further encouragement, gathered her skirt and sprinted after her. For the first few moments, they ran blindly down Marylebone with Edwina setting the pace. It soon became apparent however that Mary was truly the one who knew where they were heading. Edwina slowed just enough to allow her to take over the lead. The sound of the police whistle continued to fill their ears as they darted down Marylebone and took a sharp right onto Baker; the constable was gaining. As the row of neat Georgian terrace houses loomed up ahead, Mary seemed to gain new incentive and put on an extra burst of speed. Gasping for breath, she made straightaway towards the fourth house in from the corner, sped up the sidewalk and barreled through the green wooden door which was thankfully unlocked. Edwina sped in blindly after her, more concerned with the pursuing yarder than noting the house they were entering. They slammed the door soundly after them, drew the double bolt tight and then collapsed in a breathless heap on the bottom step of the narrow staircase.

CHAPTER 4

Baker Street - 221B

The outer door slammed, reverberating through the flat, rattling the beakers on the table. The sound jarred Holmes momentarily out of his rumination. He'd been lounging in his wing chair, pouring over the documents that the German callers had left. His forehead furrowed in mild irritation as he glanced towards the flat door, listening. He thought about getting up to investigate but soon dismissed the idea. Most likely Watson returning from his task and obviously still out of sorts. Returning his attention to the documents, he wondered perhaps if he had been hasty in discounting the German callers. The documents were intriguing; they laid out a lurid tale of scandal involving a prominent member of the Austrian monarchy, an illicit love affair, a very displeased wife and missing emeralds. Cabochon emeralds to be precise ... very old ... quite rare and the bulk of them being uncut. The emeralds, which had been part of a wedding gift from husband to wife in the early days of their marriage, seemed to have vanished as had the mistress. The wayward sovereign now sought their recovery in the hopes of quashing the debacle and regaining the good graces of his wife. He leaned further back into the chair and stared up at the ceiling considering the possibilities. The fee was considerable and though he rarely took on a case based upon the promise of recompense, well, new equipment would be most welcome...a tesla coil came to mind.

An insistent pounding on the entry door, followed by a muffled shriek from somewhere downstairs, interrupted his reverie. What the devil was that? Could Mrs. Hudson have possibly gotten another dog after he worked so diligently to get rid of the first little rat faced mongrel? His face darkened at the possibility. Perhaps it was only the annoying parrot of Mrs. Turner's from next door. Mrs. Hudson sometimes looked after the dreadful creature. He certainly hoped that was the case, a visiting annoyance was preferable to a live in one. The pounding sounded once more on the outer door and with a groan of exasperation, he crossed to the window and raised the sash.

"Afternoon Constable. Is there a purpose to all this commotion?"

At the sound of the window opening, the young policeman who looked barely old enough to shave, looked up. On seeing it was the great detective himself, he attempted to seem as professional as possible and nodded his head towards the outer door.

"Ah... Mr. Holmes. Good day to you sir. Sorry to bother. Your entry door... it's bolted."

"Is it?" Holmes frowned a bit as he perched on the window sill and gazed down at the constable, noting the ill fit of his jacket and youth. Lestrade was cradle robbing it seemed... must be desperate.

"Oh yes sir. Shut tight."

"Well... what of it then?" he sighed, already bored by the policeman's tale and he'd scarcely begun. It was well known that he insisted on the outer door being left unlocked during daylight hours; easier access for potential clients. Perhaps Watson, in a fit of spite, had locked it on the way out. If so, he would have to have a word.

"Do you know if it's been locked all morning sir?"

"Constable, I'm in the midst of a delicate experiment If you could get to the heart of the matter, I'd be exceedingly grateful."

The young constable flushed in embarrassment. The dismissal in Holmes' voice was unmistakable. He nervously fiddled with the strap on his nightstick but took a deep breath, drawing himself up proudly.

"Beg pardon sir, but there's been some disturbance in the area."

"Disturbance?" At the word, Holmes arched his brow and leaned forward, a little more interested.

"Oh yes sir. Near riot in the square down by the hospital. All sorts of mischief... bloody running wild they are."

"They...?" Holmes smiled slightly and leaned forward, amused by the constable's earnestness and zeal for his task.

"Why them sir. You know, those women with their banners and all, marching about creating a ruckus. We've orders from Chief Inspector to round em up, restore the peace. Jenkins and I thought we saw two of em' heading up this way. Running to beat the devil. Dodged the fare on the trolley too. So, we'd be much obliged if you could check the hall. Just to make sure... if the door was unlocked before..."

The smile on Holmes' face dissolved into a smirk as he glanced down the street and noted Jenkins, the other yarder, making his way down the row of houses in the search for the miscreants. If only they'd devote themselves to the capture of actual criminals with the same intensity, perhaps there wouldn't have been another slashing in the east end. With a sigh of resignation, he turned his attention back to the constable.

"Well th, now that you've fully explained the situation, I'll come down straightaway and give the hall a thorough search," he replied, barely able to conceal his derision. "After all, it's only a short fall into anarchy eh?" he chuckled as he made his way out the door and towards the stairs.

The two women huddled at the bottom of the stairs, straining to hear the conversation, catching only snatches of the constable's words. Edwina could feel the young nurse trembling and squeezed her hand reassuringly though she placed her finger to her lips to warn her to remain silent. Up above, a door clicked softly, there was a rustle and slight creak at the top of the stair. Mary started in alarm, eyes wide with fear and emitted a sharp shriek.

125

"Quiet!" hissed Edwina sharply as she clamped her hand over the girl's mouth. The creak stopped replaced by a low rumble of laughter.

"What in the devil have we here?"

Both women scrambled hastily to their feet and turned to face their inquisitor. Mary, already pale and distressed, lowered her head on seeing Holmes, her cheeks burning with sudden shame.

"Mister Holmes... I..." was all she could stammer before she turned away once more to look anywhere but in his direction. Her hand tightened around Edwina's. She was mortified. Dear God, what would John think? He'd be so cross and perhaps even ashamed for her. She stared down at the carpeted hallway and tried to ignore the fact that Holmes wasn't even properly dressed.

Edwina was also at a loss for words though for quite different reasons. She gaped at him, red lips slightly parted, forming a half smile, eyes bright and sparkling with curiosity and disbelief. She recognized him instantly – at the first sound of his voice. It was unmistakable and sent a shiver of warmth through her. Incredible. She wondered at what strange confluence of events had occurred to once more place her in the presence of this great man. There was no mistaking that the man who stood before her, although barefoot, rumpled and clad only in dressing gown and pyjamas, was the same elegant gentleman she had met the previous week. Beneath the disheveled hair and two days' chin stubble, lurked the familiar wicked grin and impenetrable blue eyes that burned with fierce intelligence and acumen. A smile tugged at her lips as she racked her brain for something witty and memorable to say.

The sharp rap of the constable's nightstick on the outer door stole her chance and startled them.

"Mister Holmes, Are you all right sir? It's been quite a while."

The constable's voice was anxious and as he continued to bang on the door, Mary once more choked back a cry of fear. Edwina wrapped her arms around her tightly in an attempt to calm her nerves.

His curiosity piqued by the odd state of affairs occurring at the bottom of the stairs, Holmes turned his attention back to the two women. Mary was exceedingly pale and looked as if she might faint at the next sound while Pennington's daughter though agitated, seemed more vexed than fearful. He suspected that if anyone had an explanation it would be Edwina Schraeder.

"Upstairs, no questions. Close the door, stay back from the windows and do be quiet!" he growled as he padded down the stairs past them, heading for the door.

Needing no further urging, Edwina grabbed Mary's hand and pulled her quickly up the stairs and through the door to the flat. Inside, she quietly shut the door and pressed her ear against it, listening. But there wasn't much to hear as the constable, on seeing that the hall was indeed empty, had moved back outside. Unable to suppress her curiosity, she moved away from the door and turned, noting the large wooden packing crate in the center of the floor. The lid had been pried off, laying on one side and straw littered the Oriental carpet; the crate was empty. Intrigued, she stepped cautiously around it as she crossed to the window, pausing to admire the laboratory equipment that cluttered the long rectangular table that stood in front of the windows. Peeking out from behind the curtain, she watched the two men who stood chatting on the pavement below. Mary, horrified at such blatant disregard for Mr. Holmes' direction, struggled to her feet, breathing harshly.

"What are you doing? Please come away from there. He said we mustn't!" she pleaded. She continued to wheeze for a few moments and then sank unsteadily onto the sofa, trying to hide her distress as she attempted to regulate her breathing.

"Did he?" Edwina chuckled, her focus still on the pavement below as she strained to hear. "I must have missed that." But try as she might, she couldn't make out any of the conversation between the men and giving up, she shrugged slightly and spun back around, moving away from the window. She removed her jacket, depositing it on the back of the sofa and once more began to explore the room.

Incredible. It was everything she had imagined and more. Every detail was perfect from the overflowing bookshelves, writing desk littered with journals, magnifying lenses of varying sizes to the worktable crammed with laboratory equipment. As she continued her survey of the flat, her attention was once more drawn to the empty crate. It must have held laboratory supplies. She approached it again and began to walk in a circle, trying to work out what the contents had been. The crate was exceedingly large ... too large to have held just one item and as she glanced towards the lab table, a gleam of brightly polished brass caught her attention. The two items responsible for the gleam made her catch her breath. Her lips curled into a smile of intense admiration and a modicum of envy. She shook her head in amazement and approached, unable to take her eyes from them for in the center of the table stood two identical Powell and Lealand Number One microscopes. They were instruments of the finest caliber and magnification at a price too dear for most research facilities. She had only ever seen one at University and that had been from afar. The Department of Chemistry had acquired only one which the department chair jealously guarded and kept under lock and key. It was off limits to all students and most faculty. And here, there were two — brand new — within reach.

She sighed a bit and wondered if she dared to sneak a look into the lens. It would probably be her only opportunity. As she approached, fully intent on taking a look, she began to waver as she reconsidered. Fine equipment to men of science such as Holmes were as precious as love letters to romantic natured young women. To use without permission was a serious breach of etiquette. And though Edwina rarely fretted over such things, she had no desire to antagonize a man she regarded with the utmost respect. She cast a wistful glance at the scopes and then rejected the notion, deciding that she would just have to wait for the opportunity to present itself naturally or the appropriate moment to maneuver an opportunity. She moved away from the table, continuing her exploration of the flat and as her eyes took note of the scorched ring on the Oriental, she began to laugh. The pattern was unmistakable as she had experienced a few chemical mishaps at University. The room was a study in organized chaos and just being there filled her with pure joy; it was an unexpected gift and she silently thanked whatever force in the cosmos had allowed her this great privilege.

"So, your fiancé is Doctor John Watson, assistant to Sherlock Holmes," she murmured thoughtfully, still taken aback by the coincidence of the morning's events.

Mary half-rose from the sofa, still very pale, her blue eyes wide with anxiety. She compressed her lips at the use of the word "assistant", grateful that John hadn't been there to hear it. It didn't trouble her much, but the good Doctor would have been greatly annoyed at its use. Thankfully, the dreaded word "secretary" hadn't been uttered.

"You know of Mr. Holmes then?" she asked, fighting to control her wheezing.

"Doesn't everyone?" laughed Edwina with a slight shake of her head. "Though I scarcely imagined that nearly trampling them would lead to my standing in the middle of 221B." A look of immense pleasure lit her face as she crossed to the lab table and began to examine the equipment, fingers eagerly exploring each item save for the microscopes. "Perhaps my luck is changing."

Mary frowned in bewilderment. "Your conversation makes it sound as though you've met them."

It was Edwina's turn to be surprised. "Yes, of course. Twice in the same day as a matter of fact. Did he not tell you?" she exclaimed incredulously.

A look of indignation flashed across Mary's face at the revelation. Although it wasn't really a lie, the discovery that there were events John concealed from her was distressing. By no means did she expect that he share each and every detail of his day with her, but surely something as significant as nearly being trampled by a horse should have been mentioned at least in passing. She began to cough again, her shortness of breath aggravated by her agitation. Seeing her distress, Edwina looked up, regretting her quick tongue and lack of diplomacy.

"I'm sure it was purely an oversight. The Doctor speaks very fondly of you," she soothed with a warm smile. It was a bit of a lie as neither man had mentioned Miss Morstan at all. Though she was fairly certain that if they had spoken of her, it would have been only complimentary. Miss Morstan struck her that way; sweet, good-natured and unwaveringly devoted. All those wonderful qualities that men demanded in the objects of their affection and all qualities that she perhaps didn't possess – at least not in sufficient quantity. No matter, she decided after a moment's reflection, for it seemed to her that perhaps Miss Morstan was a tad too compliant, a trait she hoped never to be accused of.

Mary seemed to take some comfort in her words and managed a small smile of resignation. It wasn't as though she had much choice; a man could choose to share as much or as little as he cared, and it was her role to accept and make the best of it. She turned her attention back to her new companion; a slight look of alarm once again crossing her face as Edwina lifted a large beaker of solution and gave it a sniff, swirling the liquid about.

"Oh no, you mustn't touch. Stop! He's very particular about his things," she rasped. The tightness in her chest continued to increase.

"Of course he is," chuckled Edwina lightly with a grin and roll of her eyes. She set the beaker down onto the table and continued to poke about, thoroughly engrossed in her exploration of the flat.

The door abruptly swung open. At the sound both women looked up as Holmes strode in, coming to a stop in the center of the room.

"I expect you have an explanation of some sort," he remarked brusquely. He fixed them with a sober gaze, arms folded as he waited for a response.

"Of sorts," replied Edwina cagily, unable to suppress a smile. The man was positively rumpled and still radiated an undeniable charisma. Mary, however, was acutely mortified and holding onto the arm of the sofa, feebly pushed herself up.

"Mr. Holmes, words cannot express how sorry," she gasped as she struggled to remain standing. "It's all a terrible misunderstanding... I... we..." The words died in her throat as a surge of weakness overtook her, her knees beginning to buckle.

The irritation vanished from Holmes' face as he sprang forward and caught the poor woman by the shoulders. With an expression of concern, he lowered her onto the sofa with the utmost care.

"My dear Mary be still, calm," he soothed as he gently tucked a pillow under her head and lifted her feet onto the sofa. "All will be well. Concentrate on each breath," he counselled. Once he had her comfortably situated, he covered her with a chintz throw and turned to Edwina.

"Smelling salts! Quickly!" he barked.

"Me?" she sputtered defensively, surprised at his swing in temperament, "I've no use for them. I..."

She stopped in mid-sentence, realizing that he wasn't looking for an explanation but assistance. Without another word, she scrambled towards the lab table and began to rummage about. A moment later, she came forward with a bottle of ammonia and knelt next to him in front of the sofa.

"Will this do?" she asked tentatively, holding out the bottle.

His expression softened, and he nodded in approval as took the bottle and poured a small amount of the pungent liquid onto a handkerchief.

"I see you have some knowledge of chemistry," he commented as he waved the handkerchief under the unconscious woman's nose.

"Second favourite study after botany," whispered Edwina, her playful mood subdued by the abrupt turn of events. Feeling anxious and guilt-ridden, she sat back on her heels and quietly watched him administer the ammonia. After a few moments, the prone woman began to cough and opened her eyes, looking about in bewilderment. Edwina heaved a sigh of relief and gently adjusted the pillow under her head while Holmes went off to get some water.

"What happened?" Mary mumbled, her breathing still uneven. Edwina smiled comfortingly and gave her hand a squeeze, pursing her lips to explain.

"You fainted," he replied in a matter of fact tone and handed her a large glass of water. "Most likely due to overexertion and ribcage constriction. I suspect however, that being dragged through the streets of London didn't help," he added pointedly with a sharp glance in Edwina's direction.

"It was all a terrible misunderstanding," whispered Mary sorrowfully. She took the water gratefully and sipped it. "We didn't intend to deceive. The doctor was to take me to tea, but he never came. I waited and waited, and I didn't know what to do. So, when Miss Schraeder came along, she offered to accompany me. I've never been on the trolley before. We didn't... She didn't have the fare. I'm sure it was an oversight, not having the fare."

Holmes smiled reassuringly and pressed Mary's hand though his eyes drifted sideways towards Edwina, a hint of skepticism lighting them.

"I am certain you are blameless Miss Morstan," he soothed. "I haven't a doubt that leading half of Scotland Yard on a reckless and absurd chase through the streets of London over a trolley fare was the furthest thing from your mind. Rest now, use my room. It's dark and quiet in there and Mrs. Hudson's just changed the linens."

Mary's cheeks turned a light shade of pink at the suggestion and though it was from embarrassment, Holmes was grateful to see color return to her face.

"Oh, But I couldn't," she demurred, "it wouldn't be proper."

"Nonsense. I insist. Miss Schraeder will assist you. To ease your mind, use these throws to cover the linens. That way all possibility of contact is eliminated, and the argument of impropriety is negated. If you still feel uncomfortable, leave the door ajar. I shall remain out here with Miss Schraeder. You must rest and when John returns, he will see you home. I won't take no for an answer Mary. John would never forgive me for not looking after you." His smile, although warm and genuine was resolute.

Realizing that it was futile to argue, Mary uttered a small sigh and nodded in acceptance. She took Edwina's arm and with both of their assistance, slowly rose to her feet. On the way to the bedroom, she paused and turned slightly to Holmes, her face drawn with worry.

"You won't tell John about the trolley or the constable?"

Holmes' expression grew compassionate and he smiled, shaking his head.

"Not a word. Some adventures are best kept to oneself. Off you go now. "

By the time Edwina returned to the living room some 20 minutes later, Holmes had dressed. Gone were the pyjamas replaced by a pair of wrinkled gray trousers and equally wrinkled white shirt, which was loosely buttoned, the sleeve cuffs unfastened; he remained barefoot. He had once more donned the dressing gown though it was untied, the belt dangling down to the floor as he perched on a stool at the lab table. She grinned a bit wondering where on earth he had produced the clothes from, though as she scanned the cluttered room, she imagined he could conceal all sorts of things amid the mess.

"She's resting more comfortably," she assured with a bright smile. "Loosened her up a bit. Bloody Hell. No wonder she fainted, trussed up like a Christmas Goose. I'm amazed she ran as well as she did." She approached the lab table, watching him keenly as he hovered over the microscope.

"And you, of course, suffer from no such impediment. Still the "wrong" shape I see," he commented wryly, eyes still fixed on the slide.

"I enjoy being able to breathe," she advised with an easy laugh. The sound was bright and unapologetic, filling the room with warmth and Holmes found himself smiling. He lifted his gaze, watching closely as she sniffed one of the beakers and studied the dissolving paper. Extraordinary, most women shied away, disliking the strong odours or fearful of the chemicals themselves. It was evident however, from the ease and confidence with which she handled the beakers, that she was quite familiar with laboratory equipment and protocol. A rare find in the fairer sex. It was also apparent from the expression on her face as she handled the equipment that she had a passion for it. His smile increased; that, in and of itself made her most singular indeed.

Edwina moved closer, lingering opposite him. Her fingers carefully, reverentially, examined the various solution filled beakers. A tingle of excite coursed through her. Did she dare ask him if she could look through the microscope?

"You needn't have changed Mr. Holmes, not on my account. You looked so comfortable," she added wistfully. She lifted a beaker up to the light from the window, studying it intently. "When I was at University," she commented, "I practically lived in my gown and slippers, except for class, of course; that was frowned upon. Early morning, just before dawn or right after midnight, I'd wrap up in my robe and climb out onto the ledge of the dormer."

As he listened, he arched his brow and suppressed a chuckle as the mental image of her scrambling out onto the roof in her nightclothes flashed in his mind.

"Well, it's just about the perfect time then isn't it?" she sighed. "The skies are glorious. That faint glow... last or first bit of light... just at the edge of the horizon. Seemingly no end or beginning... and the stillness..." She paused unexpectedly, a shadow crossing her face and then averted her eyes which, up to this point, had been luminous, now clouded and obscure. The silence was brief but heavy and after a moment, she seemed to slump a bit and ran her fingers over the rough edge of the table, her eyes were still cast downwards. "The stillness is everything, isn't it?" she murmured.

"You can see everything then. Within and without, but mostly within – even if it's unwelcome."

The downturn in her mood was striking. The heaviness of her words caused him to furrow his brow, intrigued at what lay behind the unexpected shift in her disposition. She was still in mourning, so a certain amount of melancholy was to be expected – even required. But as he studied her face, now partially turned from him, a tinge of doubt nagged at him. It seemed that something deeper and more unsettling than the loss of her mother lay behind this descent into darkness.

Perceiving his unease, Edwina smiled wanly and shrugged as if in apology.

"Sorry. Rambling again. Bad habit. I only mean to say that... well... I take no offence at your appearance; not in the least."

Holmes met her gaze and found himself at a loss for words. Such a blatant attempt to dismiss her prior words of melancholy was deeply troubling. The fact that he was disturbed by this young woman's descent into misery even more so.

"I confess it was more for Miss Morstan's benefit. She is of a sensitive nature and appeared embarrassed. I didn't wish to add to her distress. She is quite genteel, a proper lady."

Edwina looked momentarily surprised and then frowned, her emerald eyes growing serious and mildly vexed.

"Which, of course, I am not," she acknowledged, in a voice that was disheartened. These words spoken by anyone else, would have been shrugged, even laughed off. The mere thought of his disapproval however, filled her with dismay.

He choked back a laugh, his first reaction; it was met with silence. He peered closely at her and frowned, comprehension setting in.

"That is by no means what I meant," he declared firmly, his eyes uncharacteristically apologetic. She managed a weak smile but seemed unconvinced. His frown increased, and he cocked his head slightly, to meet her gaze.

"Miss Schraeder," he began soberly, "you are something quite different. Beyond classification perhaps."

At these words spoken so earnestly, she lifted her head. Meeting his glance, she ventured a smile, her expression reflecting hope, her cheeks slightly flushed.

"I shall take that as a compliment Mr. Holmes. Thank you," she replied. She inhaled deeply, her eyes dark with reflection and then with a sudden grin, unexpectedly moved around the table. She nodded towards the microscope. "May I?" she asked politely but breezed past him, without waiting for his consent. Caught off guard by her boldness, Holmes stepped back slightly to allow her to pass. The scent of lilies of the valley tickled his nose as she stood in front of him and leaned over the microscope. Her unpinned hair slid over her shoulders as she peered through the lens. Strangely distracted, his eyes fixed on the black satin ribbon which was beginning to slip from her hair. It peeked through her auburn tresses and dangled haphazardly from the back of her neck, almost beckoning. She seemed not to notice. The fingers of his right hand twitched involuntarily, and he frowned, clenching his fist tightly by his side, resisting the urge to reach out and straighten it.

"These samples… all very fine paper…" she murmured, as she adjusted the focus on the microscope and examined the slide. "Is this from a case? The case you've consulted my father on?" A look of pure excitement flickered across her face.

Her sheer exuberance brought a smile to his lips, but he hesitated, reflecting on how best to respond to her question. There was the consideration that she was the daughter of a possible suspect. His inner voice, the one that diligently reminded him to remain detached and true to his quest, advised caution. Despite this, he felt strangely compelled to encourage her curiosity. Her enthusiasm was infectious, only serving to reinforce his own.

"Precisely," he acknowledged after a brief pause, "Though I am ashamed to confess that I find myself at an impasse."

"You? How so?" she blurted, astonished at such an admission.

Holmes chuckled to himself, undeniably flattered by her steadfast confidence in his abilities. "I have been examining these samples for hours on end. Adjusting the solutions... fine tuning my calculations. Yet despite my best efforts, I seem no closer to discovering the defining characteristic shared with the control." With a sigh of frustration, he ran a hand through his tousled hair.

Edwina lapsed into silence, her attention now focused on the puzzle at hand. Lost in thought, she compressed her lips and bent back over the microscope, studying and then changing out various slides. Upon reviewing each slide, she painstakingly jotted notes in the well-worn notebook that lay next to the microscope. Holmes watched her meticulous movements with a faint smile of approval; her protocol and attention to detail was impressive. When half of the hour had passed, she suddenly stood up and with an expression of glee, blurted:

"All identical except for the control. It has a dense fiber composition...sisal ... perhaps even hemp. "

His smile of anticipation crumbled; it was hardly a revelation. "Yes, of course. I know," he grumbled.

Edwina stared at him, rather astonished that he wasn't following. Poor man, he truly was fatigued.

"They're the same. All of them save for the control," she repeated with a patient smile, prodding him towards the solution.

"Yes, I said that before," he snapped, anger momentarily darkening his face. On seeing her startle at his outburst, he shrugged in slight apology and sank onto a stool at the table. Muttering, he began to sift through the slides, his face drawn with bitter disappointment.

"My dear Mr. Holmes, " she chided with a gentle and sympathetic smile, "the forest for the trees."

He stared at her blankly for a moment, bewildered and rather annoyed; he was not particularly in the mood for word games. Another moment of silence passed, the only sound was that of the clock on the mantle and then in a flash, his mind snapped into focus and he leaped to his feet.

"Idiot!" he exclaimed in self-reproach, "The forest for the trees," he echoed, staring at her in astonishment. He grabbed his notes, scanned them and then began to laugh at his own failure to piece it together. "Bloody Hell. I've been so distracted at finding only commonality in the samples, that I failed to realize the oddness of that very fact. The test is flawed," he groaned in exasperation.

"Not only flawed Mr. Holmes, but also invalid. You shall have to start over," she advised ruefully, her expression compassionate.

"Agreed," he sighed wearily, his eyes distant as he focused on some point beyond the room, "As I said, Idiot."

Edwina was well acquainted with the bitter disappointment of having well-laid plans go astray; a metaphor for her life up to this point. Sensing that he might need a moment of privacy, she rose from the stool and moved back into the parlour. Spying the overstuffed wing chair, she settled onto the seat and leaned back, propping her feet onto the ottoman that stood just off to the side. As her head sank back into the comfort of the padded back, she closed her eyes and smiled. The exotic scents of leather, clove and Turkish tobacco wafted up; his chair – there could be no doubt. It was in exactly the right spot; warmed gently by the sun and close enough to the window to catch a light, refreshing breeze. Her smiled widened as she settled in even deeper, stretching luxuriously. This was a chair in which to ponder all the puzzles and mysteries of life ... a chair she could easily drift off in.

The padded cushion of the ottoman gave way slightly under pressure and she opened her eyes, surprised to see him perched there, just off to the side by her feet.

"Well done Miss Schraeder," he remarked softly. "Your observations are spot on...you would prove quite a worthy assistant."

"I understand a vacancy is forthcoming. Shall I apply? " she teased with a playful laugh.

"I think you just have," he chuckled and met her gaze levelly, his eyes dark and penetrating.

Edwina began to laugh and then faltered a bit, experiencing a surge of warmth as he cocked his head to the side slightly and leaned in closer, observing her every move. Their eyes met and from that moment, all her uninhibited playfulness and bravura began to crumble. She fumbled for a clever response but found herself tongue tied and vainly hoped that her cheeks weren't too flushed. Unable to meet his gaze, she found herself inexplicably focused on his dressing gown and as if in a trance, reached out and tentatively grasped his sleeve, fingers sliding over the smooth fabric.

"So lovely. Silk?" she asked in a whisper of a voice, her eyes still averted. Despite her embarrassment, she seemed reluctant, perhaps unable to remove her hand.

A curious smile tugged at his lips as he watched her fingers caressing the fabric. They were trembling slightly, though she was making a concerted effort to conceal the fact. He made no effort to withdraw his arm; the sensation it produced was not unpleasant. Holmes leaned over a bit more, his eyes now level with hers and nodded.

"Gift from a former... acquaintance," he replied soberly, eyes fixed on hers.

"Former," she murmured to herself, her expression torn between relief and sympathy. Although he didn't offer anything more in the way of explanation, she had the feeling that he wasn't referring to Doctor Watson. "I'm very sorry," she offered quietly after a pause, her hand gently pressing his forearm to offer comfort. A vague sense of guilt washed over her, for she was admittedly grateful at his use of the word "former".

"No need," he replied with icy detachment, "I'm not prone to sentimentality; it was a convenience that ran its' course."

The sheer coldness of his words caught her by surprise and she slid her hand from his arm, not quite sure what to say at that or if she should say anything at all. Her cheeks burned with chagrin; he must think her a simpleton.

"I didn't mean to pry. I'm sorry," she murmured after a moment, feeling foolish and awkward.

Holmes studied her quietly for a few moments and then smiled, his eyes gradually warming. "You didn't," he reassured, "Apology unnecessary." "Now, where were we?" he remarked with a light clap of his hands. "Ah yes, the problem was paper," he reminded.

"Or lack thereof," she laughed, grateful that the subject and tone of the conversation had shifted. "I could help," she suggested, her enthusiasm bubbling over. "With the paper... the samples. What you need is a complete set. Father can easily provide that. As a matter of fact, I could..."

The door to the flat abruptly swung open and crashed into the wall with a thud. John Watson stormed in, red-faced and muttering irritably to himself as he crossed the room.

"Bloody nuisance. Four shops I've been to, four mind you. And now I'm very late... again. My poor Mary," he grumbled as he draped his coat over a chair and deposited a medium size parcel, wrapped in twine and brown paper, onto the table. It made a metallic clink which brought a smile of satisfaction to Holmes. The doctor removed his scarf, continuing his rant. "But what do you care? Because you absolutely require your precious Turkish." He pivoted as he spoke, turning to address Holmes directly and then froze, mouth agape, staring dumbfounded at the scene before him.

"Dear God. You again!" he squawked incredulously. It was confounding. How could this be? That girl, the brash, reckless one from the road who had nearly trampled them, Pennington's daughter. Yet here she was, lounging, seemingly without a care in Holmes' favourite chair – a chair he was still, even after five years, denied the pleasure of using. Equally disconcerting was the sight of Holmes, dressed but still barefoot and wrapped in his dressing gown, sitting casually on the ottoman. He seemed unconcerned with the loss of his chair, chatting easily with the girl, a sly little grin lighting his face.

Edwina glanced up at the Doctor and smiled tentatively. His displeasure at her presence wasn't difficult to discern.

"Hello again Doctor Watson. I hope the day finds you well," she greeted amiably, in an effort to soothe his ruffled temperament.

Other than a deep frown, Watson ignored her and turned to Holmes in exasperation. "If someone would care to enlighten me, I'd be very much obliged!" As his words echoed across the parlour, the door of Holmes' bedroom creaked opened and Mary Morstan appeared in the doorway, a chenille throw wrapped around her shoulders. Her hair was unpinned and disheveled as if she had been asleep.

"Has something happened? I heard shouting," she murmured, blearily rubbing her eyes.

The Doctor stared at her, his jaw dropping slightly., briefly at a loss for words. "Mary... What the blazes is going on?"

On seeing him, a look of profound embarrassment clouded her features and she self-consciously tightened the wrap around her.

"John, you're here at last" she murmured. "It's all so silly. I can explain," she added with a weak smile. Watson knit his brow, casting a wary glance first at Holmes and then Edwina.

"Yes, I insist," he remarked pointedly as he offered her his arm. With an apologetic smile in their direction, she stepped forward and took his arm, allowing him to lead her out into the hall for a private discussion. As the door closed, Edwina turned to Holmes, her eyes wide with disbelief.

"Bloody hell, is he always that way?" she murmured. Holmes snorted a bit and then shrugged.

"Grumpy? Cantankerous... Ill-tempered? On the whole, I'd say yes," he replied with a flash of a smile.

She burst into laughter and pursed her lips to comment when the door opened once more, and the couple reentered the room. Without a word, Mary, looking duly chastened, crossed the room to Holmes bedroom and disappeared inside. Watson remained silent also, standing erectly by the table, gazing at his pocket watch - clearing his throat every few seconds as he waited. Sensing that she was mostly to blame for this uncomfortable situation, Edwina scrambled up out of the wing chair and disappeared into the room after her. Holmes remained silent, a hint of disdain on his lips as he watched the scene play out; this was a well-travelled road. Taking the parcel from the table, he settled into his now vacant wing-chair and began to unwrap the tin. He laid the papers out on the ottoman, opened the tin and extracted a precise quantity of Turkish blend; his long slender fingers expertly rolled a cigarette.

"Your anger is misplaced Watson," he remarked in a quiet voice, "Miss Morstan is blameless in this."

Anger darkened Watson's face briefly and with a snort, he shook his head and met Holmes' gaze levelly.

"I know exactly who the culprits are," he replied pointedly. "I may lack exact knowledge of what occurred this morning, but I know this, it wasn't proper, and it wasn't something that she would have set about on her own. She needs to be stronger. Her heart is too kind; she is easily swayed."

"Swayed?" laughed Holmes derisively as he leaned back in his chair and lit a cigarette. "Is she not allowed to have a mind of her own? Is that what this is about? Control? For God's sake Watson, she had a bit of an adventure. Leave it. Probably the most excitement she's had in a while."

Watson's face turned crimson and it was only through extreme effort that he managed to keep his voice level.

"You, lecturing me?" he snorted. "A man whose only commitment is to his work. Whose only relationships other than myself, which is tenuous at the moment, involve either a needle or the exchange of money. This association is ill-advised. I don't know what you are about with all this but mark my words, this girl... this..."

"Hardly a girl," interrupted Holmes with a wry grin, leaning back to better enjoy the rant.

"Girl. Woman. What have you," sputtered Watson in frustration. "She's impudent, a troublemaker, doesn't know her place. I've a bad feeling about this Holmes. No good will come..."

The words died in his throat as the door to the bedroom swung open and the two women emerged, arms linked and talking quietly. Mary Morstan, her hair once more pinned, her tidy appearance restored, gave Edwina a gentle nudge and nod of encouragement. With a heavy sigh, Edwina stepped forward and although her expression mirrored reluctance, her sincerity was unquestionable.

"I'm so sorry Dr. Watson, for any distress I've caused. My only intention was to assist Miss Morstan, nothing more. I hope that you'll accept my apology." She compressed her lips and met his gaze, extending her hand. The room fell into silence as Watson frowned, weighing her words. As his silence continued, Mary's expression began to cloud over. She stepped close to him and gently pressed his arm, peering into his face with concern.

"John," she whispered so quietly to where only he could hear. "No harm was done... please... for me."

Gazing into her eyes, so gentle and full of love, his resolve crumbled. With a quiet sigh of resignation, he nodded slightly and turned to face Edwina.

"Apology accepted," he murmured in surrender, forcing a meagre smile as he gingerly took her ungloved hand and pressed it in forgiveness.

"Outstanding!" exclaimed Holmes gleefully as he sprang from his chair. "Nothing more satisfying than a truce. For a moment, I thought I should have to serve as a second, a situation of which our dear landlady would heartily disapprove." He turned to Edwina with a playful wink and came forward, puffing on his cigarette as he explained. "Mrs. Hudson takes great issue with the discharge of weapons indoors. Trust me, I speak from experience. Not to mention the fact that the pistols haven't been cleaned for ages and there's scarcely room to swing a dead cat let alone mark off twenty paces. "

Both women erupted into hearty laughter while Watson blanched, looking more than a little exasperated.

"Will you please just leave it," he pleaded, weary of the entire conversation.

Holmes paused in the midst of his manic rant and arched his brow, "Of course Doctor, as you wish," he replied with exaggerated courtesy and then fell into silence, settling back onto a stool by the microscope. Edwina hovered nearby, watching quietly.

"We must be getting on then," remarked Mary, grateful the disagreement had come to an end. "The Doctor is taking me to Criterion for tea and I think perhaps to Harrods after for a new hat." With a contented smile, she turned to them advising, "You are welcome to join us – both of you of course. And after dear, we will ensure that you are delivered safely to meet up with your attendants."

Edwina looked mildly surprised but hesitated. The thought of leaving Baker Street so early filled her with disappointment.

"How kind, but it's really quite early," she hedged, "and I've only just arrived. Besides..."

"Besides," interrupted Holmes with a confident grin, "Miss Schraeder will be taking tea with me. I've just discovered my appetite again. A plateful of Mrs. Hudson's scones are in order. Perhaps a proper breakfast also. Afterwards we have work. She's been very helpful with my analysis. Be forewarned old fellow, she's quite the assistant."

Watson frowned once more and shook his head. "Well, this hardly seems proper," he muttered and much to Edwina's surprise, Mary nodded in agreement, though her expression was sympathetic.

"I'm afraid he's right dear. To be here unaccompanied with Mr. Holmes, well... it might give the wrong impression. People will talk."

A look of frustration darkened Edwina's face. "I don't give a fig about that...let them. I trust Mr. Holmes and that's all that matters as far as I'm concerned."

"Well, there you have it, settled. No need to fret. I'll personally see to it that Miss Schraeder connects with her party within the time requirement," Holmes announced definitively. Watson shrugged in resignation and looked away, while Mary nodded that she understood.

"As long as you're sure," she sighed and with an expression of genuine warmth, crossed the room and hugged Edwina tightly. "I'm so glad to have met you," she whispered in her ear. "It really was quite thrilling," she added with a secretive smile. Moments later, they both disappeared down the stairs and Edwina lapsed into silence, a pensive look on her face.

"The Doctor disapproves of me," she concluded after a moment, with dismal certainty. She sank into a chair at the table, her face drawn with discontent. As much as she protested that it didn't matter, the truth was to a certain extent it did.

"Clearly," Holmes agreed with a convivial laugh. "But take heart, I often find myself in the same predicament. So, it seems then, that you are in good company." Lifted by his words, she looked up and smiled.

"The very best indeed," she laughed in agreement. "Now, about the paper Mr. Holmes," she began, leaning forward eagerly.

"Ah. yes, the paper, we shall get there presently, but first things first. Time for Tea," he announced. Crossing the room, he opened the door and stepped out onto the landing, bellowing for Mr. Hudson. Inside, Edwina reclaimed the wing chair and settled in, smiling contentedly as she listened to him call out instructions to his beleaguered landlady. Perhaps she had been hasty – London was proving to be quite exhilarating.

>>«<

DECISION

Watson grimaced, pausing on the stairs as he climbed towards the flat. He gripped the bannister until his knuckles turned white and waited for the tingle of pain in his left leg to pass. It always did, usually lasting only long enough to remind him of time spent at Maiwand, but even that was too long. Eventually, the pain subsided and taking a deep breath, he continued his climb. On reaching the landing, he noted that all was dark, no light evident from the crack beneath the door. He grunted in satisfaction as he took the key from his pocket. Perhaps Holmes had actually given in to the notion of sleep for once. What a novelty that would be. As his key turned in the lock, he hesitated for a moment before he pushed open the door. At least, that's what he hoped he would find. He stepped over the threshold into the flat.

The only light came from the glow of embers in the fireplace and Watson stopped for a moment, allowing his eyes to adjust to the darkness. Once he was able to make out the vague shapes of furniture, he carefully crossed to the sideboard that stood just to the left of the roll top desk. He debated whether he should turn on a side lamp but decided against it; best to let sleeping dogs lie. It had been a contentious afternoon. Mary had been surprisingly unyielding and assertive in her opinions and he had little doubt as to where that influence had come. He was in no mood for further sparring, he'd had his fill for the day. Reaching out with the utmost care, he smiled as his fingers made contact with the fine crystal decanter of claret. Still using just his sense of touch, he gently removed the stopper, pausing as the fine aroma filled his nose. Entirely deserved, he thought and then took a glass, turning towards the faint light of the fire as he poured.

"Pour one for me old friend, if you please."

He nearly dropped the glass and spun around towards the darkened comer of the room from where the voice had come.

"Christ, I'd thought you'd turned in," Watson sputtered in alarm, straining his eyes to pierce the darkness. Gradually, he began to discern the outline of Holmes, motionless in his chair, his face lit only by the dim glow of a cigarette. With a dutiful sigh, he poured another glass, gathered up his own and crossed the room. As he did, he glanced warily around the darkened room.

"She's not here," chuckled Holmes as he took the glass. "Delivered safely for the journey home some hours past." He stubbed out his cigarette in the pewter ashtray and sipped the claret slowly, watching as Watson moved his own chair closer.

"Well... good, as it is quite late," the Doctor muttered as he took his place opposite Holmes. "So then, how was your... tea?" he ventured cautiously, taking note that Holmes was now completely dressed and clean shaven.

"Enlightening," laughed Holmes with a cryptic smile, "and yours?" Watson knit his brow, his lips pulling into a frown.

"Enlightening, how so?" He shook his head and uttered a dismissive grunt. "Solved the case for you, has she?"

Holmes arched his brow at the sarcasm and grinned, leaning

back in his chair. "Not quite... but she's proving quite invaluable."

"How's that? What could she possibly have to offer? Just another woman who doesn't know her place. Mark my words Holmes, she's..."

"You don't find her clever?" interrupted Holmes with a wry smile.

Watson snorted, his lips twisting disdainfully and shook his head as he drained his glass.

"Clever! More crafty than clever I think. I can't say for certain why, but there's something off about her. Something hidden."

A shadow darkened Holmes' face briefly as he considered the Doctor's words. He shrugged after a moment, draining the last of his claret and set the empty glass on the side table. "Ahhh, well we all have secrets Watson, don't we?" he mused quietly, gazing up at the ceiling. "Women especially seem to have the most. They're inscrutable. I've never quite been able to fathom their thought process. And Edwina's had her share of misfortune... losing her..."

"Edwina?" blurted Watson abruptly, taken aback at the familiar use of her name.

"Her' s name's Edwina. Why so shocked? As I was saying, losing her mother so unexpectedly, exiled to live with a father she's had no contact with since she was ten – a terrible shock. He left the family not long after her brother drowned. She was there you know, in the lake when it happened.

"Dear God," muttered Watson, "how dreadful"

"They were swimming, having a contest to see who could swim the furthest. The goal was the swim platform towards the center of the lake. Edwina's a strong swimmer ... she'd been out to the platform several times already, so she knew she could make it and was egging him on ... teasing him. He couldn't keep up ... vanished before she could get to him. She blames herself. All nonsense of course. One can hardly hold a nine-year old child responsible."

"Bloody hell. She told you all this?" Watson murmured, greatly disturbed by the revelation. "Some tea indeed." He leaned forward, watching distractedly as Holmes retreated to his chair. His eyes dark with contemplation, he withdrew something from his pocket. It looked to be a piece of black satin or ribbon. It dangled loosely between his fingers for a moment and Watson frowned in puzzlement as Holmes began to absently wind it around his fingers. A look of surprise flickered across his face, recognition setting in. What in the blazes? Cat's Cradle? That's what it reminded him of – the child's game. Unable to bear the distraction any longer, he abruptly reached out and snatched it away. He held it up to the dim firelight for inspection.

"What the devil have you?" he exclaimed, "A hair ribbon?" He narrowed his eyes after a moment, surprise turning to suspicion. "Her ribbon. How have you come by this?"

Holmes' face registered puzzlement for a moment and then he began to chuckle, shaking his head at Watson's vague insinuation.

140

"Quite innocently I assure you," he sighed, taking the ribbon back, a faint smile lighting his face as his fingers slid gently over the satin. "I found it jammed down in the cushions. It must have slipped from her hair."

Watson considered his explanation for a moment and then slowly nodded, ultimately satisfied. "Yes, well. I'll be heading to the post office in the morning, give it here then, I'll tuck it in an envelope with the address and post it for you, " he offered as he reached out to take it.

Irritation flashed briefly across the Detective's face as he pulled the ribbon back, quickly followed by a sly smile. He shook his head and leaned back in the chair, draping the ribbon over the arm of the chair, his fingers resting firmly on top. "No need, I'll see to its' return."

"So, you expect to see her again?" murmured Watson, vaguely uneasy at the prospect.

Holmes met his gaze and then smiled, a peculiar light in his eyes. "No doubt. As I explained earlier, she's assisting me – procuring more samples. It's inevitable."

Watson stared at him for a moment, ready to continue the argument and then shrugged in defeat. "As you wish. Well then, I'm all in. It has been a long day. Good night Holmes," he sighed, rubbing his eyes wearily as he rose from the chair.

"Good night Watson. Before you retire, there is one thing."

Watson paused midway across the room and turned back around, a wary expression on his face as Holmes approached, a smile on his lips, a sheet of paper in his hand. Watson frowned, looking down at the paper which seemed to be a list of questions. "What's this then?" he asked, tentatively taking the document.

"A favor," coaxed Holmes with a charming smile. "Tomorrow morning, after you've gone to the post, I need you to visit our friends at the Austrian embassy. Interview them for me. Let them..."

Watson gaped at him, utterly astonished. "What! The emeralds. So, you'll take the case after all?"

"Of course, I'll take the case," laughed Holmes, "Why wouldn't I?"

"But the counterfeit notes, what about the notes?"

"What of them?" growled Holmes abruptly, cutting him off. "I'm more than capable of handling two cases at once."

"Yes, yes, of course, but I thought you weren't interested, "replied Watson somewhat defensively.

"Ah, well once again," sighed Holmes with a resigned shrug, "you've rushed to judgement before all the facts were in."

"Apparently so," murmured Watson in surrender, too tired to continue the debate. "As you wish." Bidding Holmes good night once again, he glanced down at the document and then pocketed it, making his way across the room. He had almost made it to the door when Holmes addressed him once more.

"Before you go, a question."

Watson paused, hand on the doorknob and drew a deep sigh. "Yes..."

"Does Lady Caroline still hold her afternoon teas?"

"Yes, of course. Fourth Friday of the month, why do you ask?"

Holmes smiled, ignoring the question for the moment. "And I assume I am still on her invitation list."

Watson frowned, bewildered. Holmes rarely attended the mixed socials, going only often enough to stay in Lady Caroline's good graces and when he felt the gossip that invariably ensued might prove useful.

"Yes, you know you are. She's always over the moon when you attend. What is this about then? Why the sudden interest?"

The slight edge in Watson's voice brought a smile to Holmes' lips.

"No reason," he chuckled slyly, "Good night then. Rest well. You've a very busy day ahead."

"And what about you?" groused the Doctor, bristling at the idea that he was doing all the legwork.

Holmes smiled craftily and shrugged. "Clay for bricks my friend..."

"Bricks... what?" Watson stared at him blankly.

"Impossible to lay a sound foundation without good bricks, good bricks require good clay."

Watson groaned in exasperation. Why couldn't the man just come out and say exactly what he meant. Surrendering to the futility of the situation, he disappeared out the door without a word, leaving Holmes to retreat once more to his wing chair to reflect on all that had occurred.

The embers in the fireplace continued to dim until they were merely a faint glow. 221B once more descended into darkness.

>>«

CLAY FOR BRICKS

A match flared, briefly illuminating the early morning shade beneath the massive yew tree. As the soft white silhouette of the grieving angel came into view, James Moriarty removed his top hat and ran a bony hand through his thinning hair. His eyes constricted as they settled on the epitaph carved in the polished granite: *Beloved wife and mother -forever in our hearts.* How touching. Mouth curling into a disdainful smirk, he lit a cigar and leaned back against the iron fence that enclosed the small churchyard, noting with some amusement that her grave lay just outside, on the unconsecrated side. Undoubtedly the work of Pennington's shrew of a sister. No self-respecting Anglican would allow a papist to be buried in hallowed ground. Ludicrous. If those pious fools would only stop and consider, they'd realize that the worms were nonsectarian. He took a deep drag on his cigar and stared at the monument, an ambiguous expression in his cold, brown eyes.

"Well my dear, so here we are. Far be it for me to say I told you so, but I did warn you. Then again, you never were much for listening. All this acrimony ... and what exactly did you accomplish? I'll find them. This is nothing more than a slight delay and all of this will have been for naught. I hope that Edwina has more sense than you."

He lapsed into silence, watching as a few rays of meagre sun managed to penetrate the gloom of the morning and dappled the surface of the granite. Finished with his cigar, he flicked the remnant over the fence into the churchyard. Reaching inside his coat, he moved closer, stopping just short of the headstone and withdrew a small crystal flask containing a green liquid. With a dark smile, he removed the cork, pausing to inhale the herbal licorice aroma and sprinkled the absinthe over the freshly turned earth. Saving the last few drops for himself, he raised the nearly empty flask in a mock toast and then downed the remnants. As he was replacing the flask in his pocket, a rustle sounded from behind him and he turned to find Wilfred Pennington hovering timidly at the edge of the fencing, a bewildered expression on his face. His arms overflowed with an enormous spray of white callas lilies and he shifted his weight from side to side, a nervous smile on his flushed face.

"Professor, I did not realize you had returned. I didn't see your carriage."

"It's just on the other side of the lane. I was on my way to the house when I realized I still hadn't paid my respects." Noting that Pennington's gaze was now fixed on the crystal flask, he chuckled and shook the now empty bottle.

"A small toast to dear Katia. If I had known you were on your way Wilfred, I would have saved a few drops of the Fairy for you."

"It was her favourite," sighed the little man wistfully as he knelt and tenderly arranged the flowers on the grave. His fingers lingered for a moment, caressing the monument.

The Professor's lips curled with slight disdain and he nodded, an almost amused expression in his eyes.

"Yes, well as I recall, we were all quite fond of it then, weren't we?"

Memories flooded back, threatening to overwhelm him and Pennington's face creased with sorrow as he struggled to his feet. He kept his eyes averted, ashamed at his loss of control, knowing it would be perceived as weakness.

"Those were grand days weren't they James? The three of us. Paris... Geneva... my God, the mischief we made... and Katia was right there with us, wasn't she? Not on the sidelines, but right in the midst of it all. In all my days, I'd never met a woman like her. Never dreamed it possible."

An odd light entered the Professor's eyes; he smiled tightly. "She was a most singular creature," he murmured, his expression guarded and bitter.

Silence descended, each man lost in his own thoughts, unbroken until the Professor fixed his somber gaze on Pennington.

"Come old friend, let's return to your study. We'll drink one more toast to the grandest of days and companions now absent and then leave it. The past is best left to the dead. We have business to attend to. I am eager to hear about the progress of our endeavours, how your daughter is adjusting to her new home and most of all, the details of your encounter with that meddler Holmes. Berlin was enlightening. I'll share with you news of our German friends and the opportunities they may offer."

"Yes, yes, of course," assured Pennington hastily. He could tell by the tone of the Professor's voice that the time for mawkish remembrances had finished. With one last mournful look at the grieving angel, he composed himself and brushed the loose soil from his trousers and scurried down the path after the Professor.

»»«<

A brilliant flash of white split the heavy grey sky, quickly followed by a low rumble of thunder. The air filled with the pungent odour of ozone. Holmes cast a wary eye upon the lowering wall of clouds that seemed to hang just above the British Museum; not a trace of the early morning sun, feeble as it had been, remained. He pulled his collar close, tucking his walking stick tightly under his arm as he hurried through the massive ornate gates towards the south entrance. The choice of walking stick over umbrella now seemed incredibly foolish; no matter, he'd be inside soon enough. He quickened his pace, taking the stairs two at a time. As always, his eyes travelled upwards to the Greek style pediment that hung above the stairs and colonnade. The sight of it always brought a bittersweet smile to his lips. He wondered how many of those who passed beneath the fifteen allegorical sculptures, aptly named The Progress of Civilization, ever stopped to consider their significance; man emerging from a rock using the pursuit and acquisition of knowledge to move towards enlightenment. He was doubtful they even noticed. The public seemed more interested in the latest artefacts and exotic acquisitions brought back from the ever-increasing expeditions. His mouth twisted slightly; perhaps pillage was more precise than expedition. It was wondrous to see the Rosetta Stone up close, but wouldn't it be even more inspiring to view it in its natural setting? And as far as the natural history elements, how many stuffed elephants and giraffes does a museum really need? Still, the museum had served him well all these years and as the first spatters of rain began to darken the stair, he decided to continue his musings indoors or at least under the shelter of the portico. As he reached the top of the stairs and began to pass between the two central columns, his eyes caught a glimpse of grey just off to the left, sticking out from behind the column. Puzzled, he paused on the stair and moved closer, noting first a black lace-up boot followed by a grey stockinged calf; it was a rather lovely one at that. Intrigued, his eyes followed the wool stocking all the way up to the knee, which was covered with a modest grey skirt, though the hem was slightly upturned and trimmed in red lace and eye hooks. A figure wrapped in a dark cloak, auburn hair partially covered with a small black boater was seated on the stairs, bent over a sketchpad, oblivious to everything other than what was on the paper. His smiled widened in

144

recognition. He cleared his throat lightly.

"My dear Miss Schraeder are you stalking me?"

The pencil between her fingers rasped to a stop and Edwina looked up, her eyes wide with astonishment. Surprise soon gave way to delight.

"I ask the same of you, Mr. Holmes," she countered with a laugh, her eyes crinkling warmly, "as I was here first!" Setting the pencil in her lap along with the sketchbook, she gently smoothed the folds of her skirt. Holmes noted that she left her hem upturned, the grey stockinged contours of her calves readily visible. It seemed to him though a natural act, one performed without deliberation or artifice, which made it all the more endearing.

"Well said," he chuckled with a wry smile. "But why are you here?" His eyes scanned her face and then moved to the sketchpad in her lap, curious as to what she was drawing. There were at least two sketches in progress. The top seemed to be series of line drawings of the surrounding building facades - competent if ordinary enough. It was the second drawing however, that piqued his interest. From what he could he make out, for it was mostly hidden under the first drawing, it seemed to be the outlines of a gentleman's trousers, legs extended as he sat in what appeared to be an overstuffed wing chair; he arched his brow and tried to get a better look. The smile on his face broadened in amusement; the pattern of that worn carpet, marred with a scorch mark looked suspiciously familiar.

"Why does anyone come to a museum?" she replied with a look of bewilderment. Noting his interest in her sketches, she suddenly blushed and quickly slid them inside her large tapestry bag. He began to laugh and shook his head, moving further under the shelter of the portico. The rain was beginning to intensify, little spatters moving their way up towards them, encroaching on the shelter offered by the column. He extended his arm politely and gently lifted her to her feet, drawing her further under the protection of the portico.

"What I mean," he began patiently, "is why are you out here in the elements instead of inside? There's no fee for the ticket so I don't expect the authorities will be involved," he added with a wicked grin.

Edwina managed a weak smile at his good-natured ribbing and shook her head. She sighed a bit and shrugged a look of mild exasperation clouding her face and though she remained soft-spoken, Holmes sensed her growing agitation and discontent.

"One would believe so," she murmured, her eyes unsettled and pensive, "and yet, I am denied entrance. The porter at the door informs me that I cannot enter without an escort, a proper escort, not one of my own sex. He gives no further explanation, just that I may not enter without a gentleman. I had hoped to visit the Pre-history room to view the skulls for my sketches but now..." Her voice trailed off and she averted her eyes. Holmes could see by the flush of her cheeks that she was struggling to maintain her composure. After a few moments, she uttered a deep sigh and turned back to face him, her eyes pained and full of disappointment.

"I don't understand this country Mr. Holmes, or what place I have in it."

"I'm afraid you are suffering the consequences Miss Schraeder, of a senseless act of vandalism. One week ago, two treasured paintings, nudes by a Spanish master, were damaged severely when a young woman dressed in the colors of a suffragette entered the gallery and threw acid on them. Until that incident, there had been no restrictions on entry. Unfair as it must seem, I'm certain you can see the reasoning behind it."

"So, I am punished because of one angry woman's outburst and lack of control?" she sputtered with sudden bitterness, no longer able to contain her resentment. "Perhaps if we were given our due, allowed our voice and not treated as something less than a simpleton, we wouldn't be forced to lash out to be heard."

The virulence of her words took him by surprise; it seemed out of character. He shrugged, acknowledging her sentiment but raised his hands in a somewhat defensive gesture.

"I'm not the enemy Miss Schraeder. In general, I have no issue with the Suffrage movement. I believe we should be judged not on the basis of our gender, but on the fitness of our minds. I do, however, take issue with wanton violence and this act was exactly that, wanton and   senseless. So, forgive me, but I beg to differ. Losing control, lashing out, does nothing to further one's cause. To be respected, one must show respect; one must earn it."

Edwina's lips quivered for a moment and at first, he thought she would retort, but instead the anger seemed to drain from her face, slowly replaced by regret and shame.

"I'm so sorry Mr. Holmes. Of all the people I have met here, you deserved that the least. You have treated me with nothing but respect. I had no right to speak to you in such an insulting manner. I let my emotions get the better of me and I truly regret it. If you could find it in your heart to ..." Her voice faded off for a moment and then averting her eyes, she spoke once more. "Your forgiveness would mean so much. You are the only one who really talks to me and listens without judging. I would hate to lose that," she explained earnestly and with a plaintive smile, lifted her gaze to his.

The sincerity of her words both surprised and unsettled him, and as his eyes met hers, he managed a somewhat cautious smile.

"Accepted Miss Schraeder. No harm done," he reassured. "Now, if you still wish to enter, I would be pleased to offer my services as an escort to the skull room, provided of course that you are willing to accompany me to the Reading Room for a little research."

Her face brightened instantly, a sparkle of curiosity in her eyes. "Research? What of Mr. Holmes?" she exclaimed eagerly.

He smiled slyly and shrugged, his eyes resting briefly on the antique lapel watch that was pinned to the collar of her cloak. "Emeralds Miss Schraeder. Know anything of them? The library here has quite an extensive research selection."

"Nothing much at all! Are you on another case Mr. Holmes?" Edwina's eyes sparkled with excitement.

"Perhaps," he chuckled, an odd light in his eyes as he studied the heirloom. He had noticed it before, of course, she was never without it. The two small emeralds that adorned the watch were lovely if not particularly spectacular. On second glance however, he noted the emeralds were quite old, possibly rare and cabochon rather than faceted. A tinge of suspicion gnawed at the corners of his mind; he did not believe in coincidence. It at least warranted closer examination.

"Well then, what first Miss Schraeder? Skulls or precious stones? Your choice."

She thought only for a moment before blurting out: "Bones before stones always, Mr. Holmes!"

"Splendid," he chuckled in agreement and offering her his arm, led her into the vestibule.

A few moments later, they had all but vanished down the hall, laughing and chatting in semi whispers like two school children on holiday while the porter on guard at the entrance looked on in disapproval.

»»«

"God save us," muttered Watson as he hurried up the walk, his head bowed against the driving rain. He pushed open the outer door to Baker Street and ducked inside as lightning crackled across the sky, momentarily washing everything out in a blinding flash of white. "If this keeps on, we'll be needing Noah to get us about." He removed his bowler, carefully shaking the water from it into Mrs. Hudson's prize rubber plant while the rain continued to pound relentlessly against the door. By God, he had not seen rain this fierce since the plains of Jaipur. Of course, back in those days, the monsoon rains were the least of his unit's worries. He hung up his greatcoat, taking care to ensure that the rainwater dripped onto the burlap matting that Mrs. Hudson had laid out to protect her floors. Scraping the mud off his boots, he noted the muddy footprints ascending the stairs toward the flat. He shook his head. Holmes... had to be ... he never was much for following Mrs. Hudson's rules. As he contemplated the footprints, he knit his brow in consideration noting that there were two distinct sets of varying size, one small and one large. As the sounds of laughter drifted down from 221B, his frown increased significantly. He recognized her voice immediately; the accent was unmistakable.

The kitchen door opened abruptly, and Mrs. Hudson backed out into the hall, laboring under the weight of a heavy tea tray. The tantalizing aroma of beef pasties, scones and jam wafted out into the hall. Watson's stomach rumbled, reminding him that the tasks Holmes' had set for him that day had allowed time for only a cup of tea, and it was well past his morning breakfast.

"Please, allow me dear lady," he offered solicitously. Unaware of his presence until he spoke, Margaret Hudson uttered a small shriek of alarm and whipped around to face the intruder, the tea tray tilting precariously. With a reassuring smile, he reached out and steadied it. On seeing it was only the Doctor, she heaved a sigh of relief, gratefully handing over the tray.

"Bless my soul John Watson, you gave me a fright. I didn't hear you come in... with the rain and all."

"My dear Mrs. Hudson, I am so sorry. Are you all right now? Let me help you then. Is this for Holmes and his..." He paused for a moment, fumbling for the appropriate word, "guest?"

She snorted a bit and made a face, shaking her head in maternal disapproval as she straightened the dishes on the tray. "Guest, client, well we don't really know what she is, do we then? Mind you, I'm pleased as punch that he's taken to being a bit more social. It's good to hear him laugh again but there's bound to be talk. I run a proper establishment and I tell you this John Watson, it just isn't proper. It wasn't back in my day and it isn't nowadays either. A lady, true and decent, would never keep company alone with a gentleman, especially in his flat. But she's up there, not a care in the world, chatting and carrying on like she's known the man for years." At this point, Mrs. Hudson's voice had dropped to a whisper, her cheeks blushing as she continued her explanation. "And mind you, not even proper dressed in little more than her knickers. Mark my words, no good will come of this. But the two of them are oblivious, not a thought about what people will think or say. Reputations will be ruined."

Watson stared at her in astonishment, not quite sure he had heard her correctly. "Knickers?" he blurted. How do you mean?" But instead of waiting for her reply, he dropped the tray onto the sideboard and bolted up the stairs. Dear God, had Holmes finally lost all sense of reason?

A look of annoyance darkened her face on realizing that she would have to carry the heavy tray after all. "So, I'll bring it up on my own then, shall I?" she called out in frustration up the stairs after him, but there was no one there to hear. Defeated, she shook her head and hefted the tray, carrying it back into the kitchen to warm the food and add one more pastie. *Pensioners and the married - they would be her first choice for tenants in the future... definitely no more bachelors.*

Edwina moved the wing chair closer to the fireplace and leaned towards the hearth, carefully drying her hair with a towel. Finished, she smiled gratefully and handed it to him, which he draped over the fire screen. He took up the poker and stirred the embers, his eyes pensive, fixed on some point just beyond the flames.

"Are you warm enough? Shall I put on another log?"

She smiled and shook her head, curling her bare toes as she waggled them at the flames. The warmth from the fireplace was heavenly.

"No need thank you, it's quite lovely," she sighed, adjusting the sash of his second-best silk dressing gown, which he had lent to her. "Almost worth the misstep.

With a secretive smile, she reached over and began to rummage in her tapestry bag, once more taking out the sketchpad and pencils she had been working with at the museum.

Taking care to keep her work hidden from him, she peered over the pad for a moment, a warm smile on her lips as she scanned his face and then began to sketch.

Holmes arched his brow and chuckled to himself as he turned his attention to the items of clothing draped over chairs near the hearth to dry. Three petticoats, a wool skirt, and a pair of grey stockings; he was grateful the rest of her clothing had remained dry as he was out of chairs. His eyes darkened as his fingers lingered on the stockings while straightening them.

"If you had allowed me to help you down from the cab, instead of jumping out like a lunatic," he chided in a soft growl, "you wouldn't be sitting here in your petticoats and my flat wouldn't resemble a Chinese laundry."

Edwina paused in her sketching and glanced up. "I almost made it ... a slight miscalculation."

"Slight?" he snickered. He settled on the footstool and made a tutting sound. "'You were showing off. If not for my quick reflexes, you might very well have been washed out to the Thames with the rest of the runoff. And, believe me, you wouldn't like that one bit. The drainage gets considerably foul the closer you get to the docks. Your petticoats would need more than a dry out... burning wouldn't be too far off the mark. Not to mention the scrub-up you'd require."

Edwina grinned, ignored the remark and rolled her eyes dismissively. Somewhat of an exaggeration she suspected; still, she was grateful, else she would have been soaked head to foot.

"These damn petticoats, always in the way. What possible reason can there be for seven petticoats in the first place? I bet my eyeteeth Holmes, there's some man behind these ridiculous fashions – no woman would dream up such burdensome clothing."

"Perhaps," he admitted ambiguously. "Though under the circumstances, the extra garments proved fortuitous."

She pouted, leaning back in the chair with an exaggerated sigh. "I suppose, but the simple truth remains that if not for them, I would have made it." Taking care to keep the sketchpad turned face down in her lap, she rested her feet on the footstool and closed her eyes, as if lost in thought. After a moment, she smiled with utter contentment and casually stretched her legs, enjoying the warmth from the fire.

Holmes glanced down at her bare legs and feet, which were now very close to him on the footstool, almost touching the fabric of his trousers. His mouth curved into a distracted smile. The shapely swell of her calves was just visible under the edge of her ivory petticoats; her skin was smooth and supple. She possessed the firm muscle tone of a woman who was used to being active, little time to waste on needlepoint or papier mâché. Her ankles were slim, the feet and toes pale and quite delicate. In fact, her feet were much smaller than he would have expected for a woman of her stature as she easily matched Watson in height. So, neither an Amazon nor the frail, retiring angel of the house as she was expected to be. Edwina Schraeder was her own woman, intelligent, strong, captivating; every bit as beguiling and seductive as The Woman, though she lacked that siren's malice and duplicity. He reminded himself that it was this, which made her all the more dangerous. The attraction he felt was powerful, more than he had anticipated it would be, more than he had experienced in quite a while. It was to be controlled at all costs; sentiment was a luxury he would not allow himself. On her part, it was increasingly clear that she was quite fond of his company. Fern Hall offered little in the way of mental stimulation and she had grown bored with nothing more than sketching and gardening to occupy her time. She craved intellectual discourse and it was quite apparent that she found it in her interaction with him. And most importantly, she sought his approval ... useful information to be sure.

There was silence for a moment. Edwina remained with eyes closed, head back against the chair. Holmes perched on the footstool, eyes focused in the general direction of her feet, an odd expression on his face.

"Well then," he murmured after a pause, "Have you something for me? Something you'd like to share. "

Her eyes fluttered opened and she found herself staring into two orbs of impenetrable blue. "Share? I'm afraid I don't understand," she mumbled in hushed voice. Unable to look away, she became aware of a flush of warmth spreading slowly throughout her. She groaned inwardly, dreading how red her cheeks must be.

His gaze remained fixed on her and then he suddenly grinned, a mischievous twinkle in his eyes. He leaned in a little closer.

"Share... yes... your drawings."

"Drawings..." she echoed, her thoughts still elsewhere. She inhaled a bit, noting the faint but pleasing scent of clove and ginger mixed with Persian tobacco. Unconsciously, her fingers drifted to the sash of her dressing gown, absently toying with the knot at her waist.

His eyes followed the movements of her fingers; his grin widened and he began to laugh.

"Yes of course, the sketches... the pad in your lap. What else then?"

Embarrassed, she could only manage a feeble smile. Her cheeks burned crimson as she listened to him continue his explanation – he must think her a fool.

"I assume they're of me – the oriental pattern is unmistakable as is the scorch mark which you have so meticulously reproduced. Additionally, you spent more than half the day staring at skulls – fixating on the zygomatic arch. So, you're having difficulty sketching cheekbones... mine in particular.

150

If you show them to me, I'll be more than happy to assist. I'm a fair hand at drawing... though it's been awhile." He grinned charmingly and extended his hand to take them.

She compressed her lips, her face mirroring her reluctance as she considered his offer. "I'm afraid they're not very good yet... need work," She held the sketchpad close, turned away from him.

"Well, how bad could they be? They can't be any worse than those dreadful ones in the Strand."

Indignation sparked in her eyes. "They're much better than those," she replied with some sharpness. "At least I haven't made you into a hawk nosed old man!"

"Ah... well all the more reason to get it right then," he chuckled. "I'd be delighted to help." And as he spoke, his eyes took on a strange glitter as they fixed on the sketch pad. It had come to him as he had watched her earlier in the day, as she drew so diligently in the skull room, that there was something peculiar about the texture of the paper she was working on. It seemed unusually fine and smooth, unlike any drawing papers he could recall. He needed a closer look but most of all, he needed to touch and examine it with his fingertips.

With a hesitant smile, Edwina began to extend the pad out towards him, that is until the door swung open and Watson, face creased with annoyance, strode in. Startled, she drew back her hand and much to Holmes' disappointment, quickly stashed the sketch pad and pencils back into her tapestry bag.

For a moment, Watson stood in the center of the room, speechless as he took in the sight before him. The atmosphere was tense, and Edwina stood, a sheepish smile on her lips.

"Dr. Watson, I suppose you're wondering,"

"Holmes... a word if you please... in private," announced the Doctor abruptly, interrupting her, as if she wasn't present.

"Can't it wait? We're about to take lunch. Join us if you wish. I'm sure Mrs. Hudson will be happy to add on one more plate."

"No. I will have my say now... but it would be best in private."

"Private?" repeated Holmes, a look of weary annoyance clouding his face. "Well, then as I said, surely it can wait."

Watson's habit of interrupting at crucial moments was quite exasperating.

Edwina spoke up, breaking the silence first.

"I think the Doctor is reluctant to speak in front of me as it concerns me," she said quietly, her expression troubled and dispirited. "And if that is the case," she continued, her voice growing stronger and resolute, "I ask that he speak openly. I much prefer to have such words said directly to me than behind my back."

Neither man said anything for a moment, both taken aback at her directness. A slight smile played on Holmes' face as he watched the scene

151

unfold. No need to intercede on her behalf at the moment, she seemed more than capable of holding her own. He could see by the look of unease on Watson's face that her bluntness had unsettled him. Her tenacity was a treat to watch.

Watson compressed his lips, his face slightly flushed as he struggled to control his irritation. He sighed deeply and began.

"Very well Madame - as you wish. I shall be brief."

Holmes choked back a laugh, suppressing a smile as he waved him on to continue. Watson narrowed his eyes warningly in response and then cleared his throat.

"In our brief acquaintance, it has become exceedingly clear that you care nothing for the opinion of others nor value your reputation. All well and good, you have made that choice - it is your prerogative, foolish as it may be. What concerns me is..."

"Bloody Hell Watson, not again with this," groaned Holmes in exasperation.

Watson silenced him with a scowl while Edwina stood motionless, listening, waiting for him to continue.

"What concerns me," repeated Watson forcefully, "is your unmitigated selfishness and lack of regard for the reputation of others. Did you not once even stop to consider how this would appear to the outside world? The very core of Mr. Holmes' profession depends on his integrity. Any hint of..."

"There's been no impropriety," Edwina cried out in protest, her face pale with alarm. "Mr.: Holmes has been nothing but a gentleman," she assured fervently, though Holmes detected a trace of wistfulness. "A very simple explanation – if you allow me."

"You owe him nothing Edwina," Holmes advised firmly, cutting her off. With a shake of his head, he turned to Watson, his lips compressed into a tight smile of suppressed fury. "You know me Watson, so you must know what you are saying is ludicrous. Once again, you've made the leap without the facts."

"That's what you've always failed to grasp," argued Watson, his voice beginning to rise in volume. "Society doesn't care about the facts old man. What is perceived as true will ruin you as easily as what is fact. Your image cannot sustain..."

"My image," hissed Holmes, "is a product of your fiction, not reality. I did not ask for this creation. I was perfectly..."

"Need I remind you that my "fiction" more than doubled your client list. My "fiction" has provided you with the means necessary to expand your knowledge, provided   you with the contacts to furnish your precious laboratory. Or have you forgotten that your most ardent supporter and patron is the aunt of my fiancée, whom I doubt you would have met if not for Miss Morstan and myself. And what of those moments of darkness, when there was no one there save for me – not even your brother, did you forget those as well?"

At these last words, Holmes seemed visibly shaken, the anger fading from his face, replaced by a bitter sense of regret as he turned away. An awkward silence descended, casting a pall over the room. Edwina fidgeted, greatly disturbed, glancing hesitantly at each man, unsure what to say or if she should even speak at all.

Holmes recovered first and with the most solemn of expressions, crossed the room to Watson and grasped his arm.

"A word then Doctor, in private," he urged with quiet firmness, nodding towards the hall. After a moment of consideration, the Doctor nodded in acquiescence and both men disappeared into the hall.

Edwina glanced briefly out towards the hall; they had left the door open partially. She watched them for a few moments, noting every gesture each man made, the brief nods in her   direction. Their voices were subdued; she could not discern any of their conversation.   It mattered not. With an anguished expression, she turned away and quickly began to gather her clothes. Holmes caught up with her just as she was heading into his room to dress, her arms full of clothes. He was alone, Watson having returned to his room.

"What are you doing?" His voice reflected surprise and a trace of annoyance.

"Please, I need to change," she sighed.

"Absurd, your clothes are still damp," he argued.

"Dry enough. I need to leave." She kept her eyes averted, her hand on the door. She didn't want him to see that she was struggling to maintain her composure.

"No," he insisted quietly, "you really don't."

Edwina paused, and clutching the clothes to her tightly, turned towards him though she could not bring herself to meet his gaze. She took a deep breath and shook her head, hoping that her voice was steadier than she felt inside.

"He's right. I've been incredibly selfish. I never even gave it a thought... your reputation. You've a standing in the community Mr. Holmes, and I wouldn't..." She broke off, biting her lip to suppress the surge of emotion that threatened to overtake her.

Holmes arched his brow and began to chuckle softly. He shook his head, a bittersweet smile on his lips. "You pose no threat to my reputation. You mustn't take it to heart. Watson means well but is a meddler all the same – much like your Aunt Grendel. I don't need a minder and neither do you. I've far darker deeds; if anything, those will be the ruin of me, not a perceived impropriety."

She lifted her gaze, still uncertain. "He cares for you greatly. I don't wish to be divisive.   True friendship is a gift that shouldn't be taken lightly."

"I agree," he replied with a peculiar smile. "Watson 's like an old mother hen. Not happy unless he's fussing. We'll sort it out, we always do, but that's between the two of us. You mustn't concern yourself with it." And as he spoke, he had slowly advanced, to where he stood mere inches away, his eyes locked on hers.

Edwina drew a deep breath, her mouth suddenly dry, her face flushed, unable to look away. "Still," she hedged, lowering her eyes to stay level with his shirt collar, "I... should leave."

Holmes' mouth curved into a smug grin. "But you won't," he chuckled and reaching out, took the clothes from her and laid them back on the chair. "What you will do is stay. Give me your hand, Eddy," he coaxed. "Come sit with me at the table. We haven't even had our lunch yet."

Edwina looked up, pure astonishment in her eyes. What had he said? What had he called her? Eddy... it was a name she hadn't heard in a long time – not since her mother had used it. Her eyes misted slightly as she searched his face for confirmation that she had heard   correctly.

"You don't mind do you... if I call you that?" He knew the question was superfluous, but he asked anyway. She nodded that it was perfectly fine and smiled a bit dazedly, reaching out to place her hand on his.

"Excellent," he announced with a charming smile. Grasping her hand with a firm gentleness, he led her over to the table and pulled out a chair, indicating that she should sit. "Now, Mrs. Hudson will be up shortly with our lunch. Afterwards, we'll see what we can do with your drawing. I have some thoughts regarding the composition. In the meantime, I insist that you tell me everything; we could scarcely talk at the museum. I want to know how you are getting on at Fern Hall, how's your delightful Aunt Grendel and your father, how is he adjusting to the change. I particularly want to hear how it is you are in London again. Has Grendel suddenly grown a heart, or has she had another one of her spells?" He arched his brow, regarding her shrewdly; he had begun to formulate a theory on these sudden spells her aunt was experiencing and the convenience of their occurrence.

Edwina began to laugh, the anxiety finally fading from her expression and nodded. "They come and go," she murmured, a rather cagey smile lighting her face. She settled at the table and propped her elbows upon it.

"I've a favor to ask," she asked, emboldened by his kindness, "before we begin."

"Ah... need I worry about the propriety of this request Eddy?" he teased. She laughed, her spirits thoroughly cheered by his good-humor.

"Not at all. It's just I was wondering... is there some other way I can address you?

Mr. Holmes... well, that seems ridiculously stuffy.

"Surprise flickered across his face and he seemed uncertain as if it had never occurred to him that she would ask such a question. After a moment, he shrugged in resignation.

"Well, I've been called many things," he laughed, "some I will not repeat.

Watson calls me Holmes, so for the time being, I think that will suffice... if you're agreeable."

"Holmes..." she repeated, knitting her brow as she mulled it over. It wasn't what she had expected or hoped for. Only slightly less formal without the Mr.

"It is my name," he reminded with a wry grin, sensing her disappointment. "Perhaps in time, that can be amended."

Her eyes sparkled with unabashed joy. "Until then," she laughed, "Holmes it is."

"Splendid!" he exclaimed, "Now, where were we... ahh yes, you were going to tell me all about Grendel and her sudden spells. And your father, did you mention something about a second shop? I thought I heard you say..."

Edwina leaned forward, only too eager to share the goings on and all the gossip from Fem Hall. Holmes listened attentively, offering appropriate interjections as needed. He did not need to coax, she spoke freely, without restraint, for that is what confidants do. And as he listened, his belief grew that the resolution to both of his cases was linked to this woman and might be closer than originally suspected.

»»«««

With a droll smile, he settled into the chair just outside the library to wait. Angry voices drifted out from the closed room. Pennington's voice was a mere squeak, muffled by the sheer vitriol of the women. After selecting a cigar from the humidor that Pennington kept on the drawing table in the comer, he clipped the end, lit it and returned to his seat; his eyes drifted towards the door. Shouldn't be long now. James Moriarity smiled in delight as he listened and rolled the smoke of the Partagas over his tongue.

The voices stopped abruptly, and the door banged open. Edwina flew from the room, cheeks flushed with anger, her eyes red and brimming. She paused for a moment, fists clenched by her side as she composed herself, unaware of the man seated in the corner. The door closed behind her and Gretchen Pennington's shrill voice once more filled the air. A look of pure hate contorted her delicate features as she listened.

"Bad news then?"

She froze. The voice was calm and quiet, but still made the hairs on the back of her neck prickle. Edwina forced a smile as she turned to face her father's business partner. Although he had never been anything other than polite, the very presence of this man set her nerves on edge.

"Professor, I didn't see you... I'm sorry." She averted her eyes from him, glancing uneasily towards the closed library door where the debate over her future was finally coming to a close. "Father will be out soon. You shouldn't have to wait much longer."

155

He began to laugh and shook his head. He stubbed out his cigar and rose from his chair, crossing the room to stand in front of her. He was uncomfortably close, and she stepped back automatically.

"But I wonder how much is left of the man, after she's chewed and spat him out. He has no backbone... never had," he sighed disdainfully with a nod towards the closed door. A peculiar smile twisted his mouth as he turned his attention back to her. "Fortunately, you take after your mother," he chuckled softly. "Dry your eyes then," he advised darkly as he offered her a pristine handkerchief, "you're made of much sterner stuff. You've been clever enough to circumvent the old shrew thus far – though I've noticed she's stopped taking the tea you've prepared."

Edwina stared at him, a tingle of fear travelling up her spine. "I... I don't know what you mean," she murmured, averting her eyes from his.

The Professor made a tutting sound and shook his head, a particularly unpleasant little smile twisting his mouth. "Come now, no need to fret," he intoned glibly, "I applaud your ingenuity; Convallaria Majalis was a brilliant choice – no long-term side effects if dosed properly. Too bad she wasn't as stupid as you presumed – or perhaps you should've increased the dose and just saved yourself future trouble."

Edwina's face drained of all color and she drew a sharp breath, too stunned for words. How could he have known? She looked down at the floor and made as if to leave until he unexpectedly grasped her arm, gently pulling her back. The slick coldness of his fingers made her skin crawl and she stepped back, though couldn't break free.

"Fear not," he whispered with a malicious smile, "Our little secret... now run along and be clever. I have faith in you dear... you will find a way. Survival of the fittest."

And just as suddenly, she was free and fled the room, his mocking laughter ringing in her ears.

CHAPTER 5

The Plot Thickens

221B Baker Street - Early Sunday morning, one week later

The volumes, heavy and cumbersome, crashed to the floor, rattling the china in the tea service. Watson, who had been dozing with one elbow propped on the table, woke so suddenly that he nearly fell from his chair. He rubbed his eyes and squinted blearily at Holmes, who was retrieving four of Pliny's volumes on Natural History from the floor.

"Rough night old fellow? Shouldn't you be at St. Stephen's with Miss Morstan praying or whatever it is you do there?" Holmes murmured with a smirk as he returned the volumes to their place on the side table. He marked his place in the section on gemology and closed the book. Watson shook himself, attempting to rid himself of the fog of sleep. When he had sat down for tea, it had been early and Holmes had been nowhere to be seen; still asleep he had assumed.

Somewhere between his second cup of tea and waiting for Mrs. Hudson to bring up breakfast, he must have drifted off. He grumbled and poured another cup, wincing at the sound his spoon made as he stirred in sugar.

"Bit under the weather," he muttered, gazing sheepishly into his cup. "I sent word, she'll understand." He was certain she would, as long as she didn't know the particulars behind his sudden affliction. One drink too many with members of his old unit — the Fifth Northumberland Fusiliers — had left him feeling foggy and out of sorts. Holmes began to laugh and settled into his chair. He glanced up with a wry grin as he once more leafed through Watson's notes from his interview at the Austrian embassy.

"How are Stamford and Shepperton these days? Three old friends reliving their regiment days. Between the three of you, I'll wager the Grenadier is now short of ale. He shook his head in mock disapproval. "Any other mischief you care to confess? I can be the sole of discretion," he chuckled sarcastically.

Watson bristled, glancing sharply in his direction. "There was no mischief... no impropriety... just friends sharing a laugh and a drink."

"Of course," replied Holmes snidely, "one mustn't jump to conclusions or accuse one of impropriety where none exists."

Watson sighed wearily; the allusion was not lost on him. "For God's sake man, how many more times must I apologize?" Holmes smiled crookedly.

"I haven't decided yet."

Watson compressed his lips tightly and then shrugged his mouth curling self-righteously beneath his moustache. "Still, it seems to me worth it. Delightfully quiet this past week, isn't it? Your disciple has been noticeably absent; perhaps my friend, you're not as charming as you believe."

Holmes paused and glanced up from his reading, a look of mild vexation darkening his face. He offered no comment, irritated by Watson's statement. It had been nearly a week and not a word from Edwina; he was more than a little disappointed and vaguely concerned. His mind raced, searching for a possible explanation, although he was fairly certain it had nothing to do with him "charm."

Brooding, he turned his attention back to Watson's notes; abruptly, he sat up. His entire body tensed, his face grew taut and pale. "Bloody hell! How could I have missed this?" he murmured, staring at the page before him. He looked to Watson and glared with unabashed acrimony.

"How could you not have pointed this out?" he accused tersely.

Watson knit his brow in confusion. "What?"

"This!" snarled Holmes with great exasperation as he shoved the notes toward Watson; his index finger tapped impatiently at the columns of names on the page. Watson groaned and studied the page. It contained a considerably long list of Franz Joseph's known mistresses and suspected lovers, and halfway down the first column, just two down from Irene Adler was the name Katerina Schraeder. He blanched, an expression of shock clouding his features.

"Dear God! Is that her mother? The dead actress?" he cried. Holmes did not reply but sprang to his feet and began to pace restlessly, his face drawn with concentration.

"It's not hard to conceive. She was well known in Vienna and Franz Joseph's penchant for ladies of the theatre is notorious. And there is that lapel watch... the stones are quite old and fine."

Watson shook his head in amazement and pursed his lips to question him further when a sharp rap, more of a kick really, sounded at the door.

"If one of you could get the door," pleaded the weary voice of Mrs. Hudson. As Watson opened the door, the poor woman, breathing hard and sweating slightly, staggered in carrying a tray not only laden with breakfast but also a small brown parcel. After depositing the tray on the dining room table, she paused long enough to catch her breath, then picked up the parcel, and waved it in Holmes' direction. Her face was pinched with annoyance as she extended her hand to him, palm up expectantly. He seemed not to notice and reached for the package eagerly; his face settled into a slight frown when she pulled it back, once more holding her hand out for payment.

"Three bob, if you please... sender was short on the fee."

Holmes smiled glibly and gave a nod in Watson's direction.

"Watson, pay the dear lady."

Watson sputtered indignantly while searching his pockets for coins as Holmes snatched the parcel from Mrs. Hudson. He tore off the string and outer paper, recognizing the handwriting on the label. Inside were two parcels, carefully wrapped. He tore open the thicker of the two, his face radiating delight. The paper samples... had to be, judging by the weight. His joy was short-lived however upon further examination of the sheets. There were only ten, and they were the ten he already possessed. Once again, the sampling was incomplete, and he was no closer to the truth then before. He threw the samples down onto the table in disgust and began to pace, his brow knit with frustration and disbelief. How could this be? She had given her word.

"So, all for naught," sighed the Doctor in commiseration. "Lestrade will be disappointed – he's been champing at the bit."

"I don't arrange my investigation to coincide with Lestrade's ambitions," Holmes snapped as he once more turned to the parcels on the table. Lips compressed bitterly, he reached for the second parcel and began to tear off the paper. An ivory note card, inscribed with a delicate hand, fluttered to the floor. With a sigh of resignation, he scooped it up and began to read; at the very least, he hoped it would contain an explanation. As he continued to read, his expression softened, sullen resentment giving way to mild surprise and concern. Upon finishing, he sank back into his chair, his brow furrowed in deep thought.

"This won't do," he murmured, pressing the note lightly to his chest. "Not at all."

"Do?" Watson shrugged at him, utterly baffled.

Holmes knit his brow, eyes dark with contemplation, and absently tapped the notecard on the edge of the chair; occasionally he would pause and touch the card to the tip of his chin.

"They're sending her away," he began, in a voice that was a mixture of incredulity and melancholy. "St. Mary Magdalene 's in Woolwich."

"God save them!" guffawed Watson, his face red with laughter. The very thought of the pious Anglican ladies of St. Mary's trying to instill a sense of decorum in Edwina Schraeder provided the best laugh he had experienced in quite some time. Holmes however, found no such amusement in the situation and fixed him with a withering look.

"For a Doctor, you are noticeably lacking in compassion," he growled as he rose from his chair and crossed to the window where he stood listlessly for some time, gazing out across Baker Street. Watson stared at him incredulous. Certainly, a case of the pot calling the kettle black. Still, he composed himself and murmured an apology, though he found himself wondering if Holmes' recent consideration for others was genuine or merely convenient. Holmes waved the apology off and returned to his chair though he didn't sit, standing stiffly behind it, one hand grasping the edge.

"Her father feels it is in her best interest, to prepare her ... improve her marriage prospects." His face contorted with disdain. "Her aunt has her hand in this...vile creature. "

"Well, with all due respect, perhaps it is for the best," offered Watson sincerely.   "Given her current demeanour, her prospects for marriage are non-existent. A pity ... she is pleasant enough in appearance and as you said yourself, clever. But this obstinacy and aversion to accepting her role – well, it's off putting at the very least. It's clear her father doesn't want to see her end up like his sister: unmarried, bitter and resentful. She needs disciplined guidance .... molding."

"Molding!" The word was spat out so forcefully that Watson flinched. "Molding ... by

that you mean breaking, that's what they'll do! Break her spirit... grind her down into some feeble-minded simpleton who will come to believe that her only purpose in life is to sit at home tending house, fretting over her appearance and waiting upon instruction from a husband who will control every aspect of her life, including her thoughts.   He will take everything...   intellect,   body,   spirit, autonomy... self-respect."

The sheer passion of Holmes' outburst left Watson at a loss for words. After a moment, the detective sighed and continued, his voice more controlled, eyes distant and veiled.

"And what will he give in return? A few children she may or may not have wanted. She will raise them mostly on her own for he will be too busy with his work... his club... his mistresses. She will have surrendered all to him and not even have the power to protest. There will be nothing left of that sharp wit – that spirited nature that you find so disagreeable. She'll become a shell, docile, empty and broken... and that Watson, I find unconscionable."

"Dear God man, you make it sound as if marriage is a prison," groaned Watson, still bewildered by Holmes' tirade. He was well aware the Detective held a dim view of the convention of marriage, but he had never before heard him speak so openly or fervently against it. It made him wonder if there was something in his past, his childhood of which he knew little, that had shaped his beliefs.

Holmes smiled darkly and shrugged, his fingers once more resting on the note card. "I mean no offense old friend. I realize that you will treat your beloved Mary with all the consideration and respect that she deserves. You will be an exceptional husband and father - of that I have no doubt. However, look around you, for the majority, especially a woman as singular and intelligent as Edwina, prison would be kinder. Holmes paused once more, this time to regain his composure and air of detachment.

"But, I digress, the point being that St Mary's in Woolwich is most inconvenient and would limit access. There is a second shop!" he exclaimed with great enthusiasm. Seeing Watson's look of astonishment, he smiled slyly – a little smugly. "She mentioned it in passing during tea – offered it freely along with other little morsels of information which may or may not prove useful; unfortunately, no details. I expect it is where I will find what I seek. I must gain access," he mused.

"So, you have settled on her father then," concluded Watson. Up to this point, Holmes had been evasive as to whether Pennington was his main suspect or merely one among many.

"At this juncture, all seems to point that way," Holmes admitted albeit with some reluctance.

"Well, Bloody hell man," grumbled Watson impatiently, "can we not just let Lestrade and his boys loose? A quick shake up... bring him in for an interrogation. The man's afraid of his own shadow Holmes – a bit of time in the Old Bailey with Lestrade and the boys and..."

"And... and..." snorted Holmes in annoyance, "I put little stock in a confession beaten out of a man. Watson, do you forget we have no proof as of yet, only supposition. If we move too soon, we risk everything. Have you considered the fact of the plates, for surely there are plates? How did he acquire them and from where? Perkins, Bacon & Company have reported no thefts in the last five years. Pennington didn't just clap his hands and make the plates materialize. And what of the second shop? Where is it? Or do you propose that we raid every warehouse and shed on the docks in London?"

Watson frowned, thoroughly bewildered. Holmes had a point – Perkins, Bacon & Company of Fleet Street was well respected and the sanctioned manufacturer of the plates the Crown Treasury used to print bank notes. Everything was strictly documented and regulated – a single missing plate would not go unnoticed, but no thefts had been reported.

"If we tip our hand," warned Holmes, "he will take the evidence and disappear with it down the rat hole. But there's more. Consider this. Does Pennington strike you as exceptionally intelligent? Is he a man who could plan and coordinate an operation as complex as this... interweave all the aspects and players?"

The question gave Watson pause and after some consideration, he shook his head that he also did not believe him capable. "So, who is behind this?"

"Ah... now you're thinking. Who indeed? Pennington doesn't list any business partners. His license has him as sole proprietor yet, Eddy mentioned an associate of her father's in passing. A rather unpleasant fellow who always seemed to be lurking about in the shadows. So why isn't he listed...why the deception? Even a silent partner should still have a record somewhere... and I can find no evidence of a partner."

Watson arched his brow, his interest piqued in more ways than one. Eddy? There it was again, the familiar use of a nickname by Holmes. Extremely unusual – a slip of the tongue perhaps. It made him wonder if Holmes had been forthright that the main focus was the resolution of the case. This time however, Watson held his tongue on the matter.

"Perhaps she's mistaken," he ventured after a moment. Holmes narrowed his eyes at him and waved the suggestion off; it seemed unlikely, she was too careful and exacting. Watson frowned deeply in concentration and then in sheer frustration suggested, "Or lying..." The reaction was immediate and volatile.

"Impossible!" hissed Holmes, obviously taking great offence, "Not to me. She has no reason." Watson once more found this odd but said nothing, mentally stashing it with all the other bits he had found curious in Holmes' temperament lately.

"Name?" he queried, chewing the edge of his mustache.

Holmes shook his head. "Unfortunately, no, only that he's called Professor"

"Professor?" echoed Watson with a half-smile, "Professor of what? Bit odd," he commented and then with a shrug added, "Maybe it's nothing at all."

Holmes frowned darkly, his disagreement apparent. "Or maybe it's everything," he countered sharply. "Nevertheless, we must proceed with all due caution."

"Yes, so it seems," grunted Watson peevishly. "Well, here we are again with more questions than we started and few answers in sight. Bloody annoying."

Holmes stared at him for a moment and then began to laugh, nodding in agreement as he crossed to the mantle and began to search for his cigarette case. Tobacco was what he needed now ... to concentrate and focus.

Cheered by the sound of the detective's laugh, Watson smiled and picked up the parcel that Holmes had not finished opening and apparently forgotten for the moment. "Well, maybe this will cheer you. You haven't even unwrapped it. Who knows, maybe the answer to all your questions is just inside," he joked as he removed the paper. As his eyes fell upon the sketch, they widened in amusement and wonder, and he began to chuckle. "Dear God, is this you?" he laughed as he held the sketch aloft. "Is this how she sees you... practically a deity...Byronesque even. "

"What? The sketch?" Holmes cried, "She finished it?" He pitched the cigarette into the fireplace and lunged towards Watson.

᠎   "Hmmph... cheekbones seem a bit exaggerated in my opinion and your hair. As if your ego needed any more..." Watson didn't finish but with a shake of his head, held the sketch up to get a better look.

"Give it here!"

"What? Calm yourself. I'm not saying it's not good just..."

"Dammit man, give it here!" bellowed Holmes, who much to Watson's astonishment, sprang forward and snatched the drawing from his hands. The moment the detective's fingers latched onto the sketch, his agitation ceased and he grew calm, an almost rapturous expression on his face. His smile began to widen as his fingers caressed the paper. Watson looked on nervously as if he was watching a descent into madness. Seeing the Doctor's concern, he smiled in understanding and then crossed to the desk, where he had stored various items and notes from the case. Still holding onto the sketch, he picked up a small box and crossed to the doctor. He handed the sketch back to him.

"Feel this... remember how it feels... keep the fingers of your right hand on it... and close your eyes."

"Close my what?"

"Do as I say Watson," he sighed, "close your eyes... right fingers on the sketch. Focus."

Warily, the Doctor complied. "So, now what?" he asked after a moment, his eyes still closed. *Bit childish ... like a ruddy parlor game.*

"Extend your left hand... but keep your right on the sketch... and with eyes closed, examine what I give you with your left hand." Holmes carefully presented an authentic bank note to where Watson could feel it but not discern exactly what it was.

As Watson made his examination, his face registered surprise. "Identical!" he cried.

Holmes smiled but neither confirmed or denied, reminding Watson to continue to keep his eyes closed. Once more, he removed a bank note but this time, he presented the counterfeit to the Doctor and instructed him to follow suit.

"Well, it's the same old man," grumbled the Doctor, rapidly tiring of the game. "All of them... identical."

"Hmm... so you think so do you?" chuckled the Detective with a knowing smile. "Open your eyes and tell me what you see!" Taking the sketch from the Watson, he laid it next to the banknotes on the table and waited.

Convinced that he was right, Watson grumbled a bit and opened his eyes. He stared at the three objects on the table, a look of abject bewilderment on his face which continued to grow, until he reached out and examined each one. As his fingers slid over each one, a look of astonishment furrowed his brow.

"The same... all of them... the paper and the notes," he cried excitedly, "even the counterfeit. But then... by God Holmes, you 've done it. Solved the case. "

"Not quite."

"Nonsense. Pennington's our man. Here it is, the sketch; the paper's the proof!"

"Yes, yes. the paper is part of the proof. Chemical analysis is needed but there's only this sheet and…"

"Balderdash," scoffed Watson, "Formality... shred the sketch! Soak it or whatever you need do to run your tests... and…" Watson abruptly stopped in mid-sentence and frowned, scanning the detective's face. He couldn't quite fathom why, but there seemed a sudden reluctance on the part of Holmes to acknowledge success. And he certainly was at a loss as to what appeared to be a decided aversion to using the sketch to complete his analysis, until comprehension sank in. The only way Holmes could properly use the sketch for analysis was to completely and utterly destroy it. And that reluctance to destroy the sketch, Dear God, dare he even think it – seemed sentimental?

"I suppose I could trim the edges of it a bit for analysis," murmured Holmes grudgingly, more to himself than anyone in particular. Once more, he took up the sketch and examined it, eyes dark and pensive. "Sufficient perhaps if I'm vigilant. On the other hand, if I wait for the other samples...well, gives me a bit of breathing room." He looked up at Watson and smiled somewhat sheepishly, as if he couldn't bear to acknowledge this sudden surge of emotion and attachment to Edwina's gift. An uncomfortable silence fell on the room for a few moments and Watson chewed the edge of his moustache as he reflected on all that occurred. After a while, he shrugged his shoulders, giving up for the moment.

"Well then ... what next?" he sighed, at a loss on how they should proceed.

Holmes did not answer at first, his mind still consumed in finding a solution he found palatable. Gradually, a sparkle of mischief returned to his eyes and he began to smile.

"What day is it?" he asked abruptly, as he raced to the mirror and began to check his appearance, straightening his waistcoat, scrutinizing his collar.

Watson stared at him. "Still Sunday."

"Capital!" he announced with sudden glee. He ran his fingers through his hair, fussing for a moment and then glanced at his pocket watch, nodding to himself. "If we don't delay, we'll catch them just as the game begins."

"Game? What?"

"Croquet!" he laughed, "come then – quickly!" He frowned slightly as he grabbed his frock coat, pulling it on. "Are you wearing that? I suppose it'll do, but do something with that moustache man... I believe I see last night's meal."

Watson, thoroughly embarrassed, swiped at his moustache but hesitated, at a loss as to what was happening. Nevertheless, he dutifully checked his appearance.

"I don't understand, Croquet?"

"Yes, Croquet. Every Sunday at Hertford Villa. Lady Montague."

"Lady Montague?" exclaimed Watson, "now I'm truly at a loss. What does Mary's aunt have to do with any of this?"

"Yes, yes, of course you are," laughed Holmes, "every Sunday she plays Croquet with Lord Aldenham. If we hurry, we'll catch them before they strike the first ball."

"Lord Aldenham, the Governor of the Bank of England!" exclaimed Watson in disbelief.

"Yes, the same, but he's not important. Lady Montague..."

"Not important," sputtered Watson, unable to follow the thread, "he's in charge of the Bank of England...the bank notes... is that why we're going?"

Holmes stared at him for a moment and then began to laugh, shaking his head.

"Oh no. Sheer coincidence. He's of no use. But Lady Montague, now she's the key."

"I am still at a loss."

"Naturally," chuckled Holmes with a smile, "but come then, quickly, and I'll explain it all on the way. I've the most brilliant plan... perhaps my best yet." And without waiting for Watson, he pulled on his gloves and dashed out the door and down the stairs to the street, where he set about hailing a hansom. Watson stared after him for a moment utterly at a loss as he tried to make some sense of what had just occurred. In the end, he gave up. As he pulled on his coat, he cast a mournful glance in the direction of breakfast which lay untouched on the dining table, then trudged after Holmes. Brilliant plan indeed!

»»«««

HOW TO BEHAVE: A POCKET GUIDE TO ETIQUETTE

Fern Hall - Wednesday, Mid-afternoon

Small beads of perspiration formed on the smooth surface of her forehead, collecting in the comers of her eyes and finally streaming down her flushed cheeks. Unable to stand it anymore, Edwina grunted wearily and paused in her attempt to dig out the weeds that seemed to have sprung up overnight. They threatened to choke her beloved Convallaria majalis and the violet monkshood she had planted just two weeks prior. She bit her lip, staring at the plants; they were thriving, growing stronger each day, taking hold. Her eyes blurred as she struggled to suppress the surge of bitterness that bubbled up inside. Who would tend them now? Who would care enough to nurture them after she had worked so hard to establish them... and herself? She threw the hand rake down in disgust; no one. They would be cast aside and abandoned as she. Swallowing hard, she clenched her fists, filled with self-loathing. It was her own fault; she had allowed herself to become hopeful, allowed herself to believe that despite her initial misgivings about her new home, she was making her mark, finding her way. She had been foolish, convinced that she had found a confidant; a kindred spirit with whom she could express her thoughts without fear of judgement, privy to her darkest thoughts and fears. Apparently, also untrue; she hadn't heard from Holmes, not a peep, since their afternoon at the museum. She picked up the rake and scratched listlessly at the earth. She didn't understand. It had been a glorious afternoon. She had never felt closer or enjoyed anyone's company as much as his, save for her mother. And there had been a spark of something that she couldn't quite put into

165

words. The sensation was almost euphoric; a soft, warm glow burning within that occurred whenever in his presence. She thought, mistakenly it now seemed, that he had experienced the same, or something akin to it. So why then had he not even acknowledged receipt of the sketch? Could it be he found it offensive in some way? He had been charming and encouraging – offering to help. She had graciously but firmly declined his offer, insisting that she would correct the sketch herself. At the time, he had seemed to accept her stubbornness with good humour. In all truth, she doubted something so insignificant as a sketch would trouble the man; it had to be something more. Edwina knit her brow in reflection, her face clouding over. Oh of course, there was another possibility and one that seemed more likely. The samples – she had promised him and had failed miserably. A feeling of despair stirred within. Her father had moved most of his stock to his second warehouse. On the surface, it seemed not much of a problem until Holmes had emphasized the need for confidentiality; not one word to her father must be uttered; he had been unequivocal. The Yard had sworn him to secrecy in the matter and he was bending the rules by even mentioning it to her. He had confided with some reluctance that he was at the mercy of her prudence. This revelation, of profound trust and vulnerability, filled her with warm contentment and a deep sense of determination; she would not let him down. Originally, it had not presented too much of a problem. She had already begun to formulate a plan, a nighttime excursion, one she intended to share with Holmes. It would be a lark; a brilliant adventure shared by two of the same mindset; kindred spirits under the stars. Perhaps the good Doctor would even deem it worthy of a mention in the Strand – indirectly of course. Impossible now of course, given her impending banishment to St. Mary Magdalene's. Woolwich seemed as remote and inaccessible to London as the far side of the moon. She compressed her lips tightly and sank the prongs of the rake deep into the earth; she wondered if she'd be allowed a garden.

The rustle of leaves along the path disturbed her dark meditation. Glancing up, she was surprised to find Hanna hurrying towards her. The girl's face was pale and nervous. Every now and then she would glance over her shoulder. In her hands, she carried a parcel, small but obviously with some weight judging by the way she carried it. Edwina waited until she caught her breath before she questioned her about it.

"For me," she cried eagerly, extending her hands. "What do you have then?

Hanna panted a bit and then managed a smile, relieved to see some of the clouds vanishing from her mistresses' face.

"Don't quite know Miss. I was at the market when a lad..."

"A lad? " Edwina frowned – it was not what she had expected to hear.

"Yes Miss... tattered little runt... couldn't be no more'n 8... come right up to me while I was looking at needles and asked if Miss Edwina was my Missus. I asked him why. I was a bit leery him being such a mess. He had a sack and inside of it was this. He said it was for you if you was my

Missus, but he wouldn't give it to me, not right away. Asked me some silly questions about the color of your hair and what was the color of the thread that hemmed your skirts. I was going to tell him to bugger off. Imagine askin such questions... cheeky... but then I thought well, maybe I should wait a bit. He kept saying that he was on a mission of the greatest importance and that he mustn't fail. A sovereign was dependent on it. Can you imagine? Big words like that from the likes of such a ragamuffin. So, I told him what he wanted to know. He thought about it and then handed this over, grinning like a fool. A moment later, he was gone."

"And he didn't say who gave it to him?" Edwina quickly dropped the hand rake and reached for the package, her eyes scanning the package for some tell-tale clue of its origin. A slight frown creased her brow; there was no address to be seen; blank except for the corner of the package which bore the stamp of Josiah Fleming. Fleming, her lips curled in annoyance - she remembered him. Still... unable to contain her curiousity, she tore at the string, dropping it to the ground.

"No Miss he wouldn't 't say," replied Hanna, a look of bewilderment on her face, "but he did say something odd; something I was to tell you... something important."

"What's that you have? Give it here child!"

The voice which could easily have curdled the freshest of milk sounded from behind. Both girls froze and looked up to find Gretchen Pennington striding down the garden path. Without waiting for a reply, she snatched the package out of Edwina's hands - pulling off the paper, discarding it on the path. In her hands she held two books, the titles of which the girls could not make out. She opened the first one, looking puzzled and suspicious, but not angry as she inspected.

Fear and anxiety washed over Edwina, she hadn't a clue as to what the package contained or who had sent it. Expecting the worst, she racked her brain furiously for an answer - it was Hanna however who recovered first.

"Books Mrs. from Mr. Fleming's shop – I picked them up for Miss."

"I can see that. I'm not blind," she growled sharply at the young girl. "How have you come by them?" She turned her hawk-like eyes towards Edwina.

"I ordered them some time ago," replied Edwina quickly, though she still couldn't see what they were. A lie of course. It didn't matter she supposed...they were bound to be problematic whatever they were.

A look of disbelief shadowed Gretchen Pennington's face and then she did something quite unexpected – she began to laugh. "You? Ordered these?" She frowned at Edwina suspiciously and turned the books to face her.

The Book of Household Management" by Isabella Beeton and *How to Behave: A Pocket Manual to Etiquette,* publisher - John S Marr & Sons, Glasgow. Edwina stared at the books - utterly at a loss for words. It made no sense at all. She licked her lips and forced a smile.

"I thought they would be useful at St. Mary's," she murmured with as much conviction as she could muster.

Gretchen Pennington frowned, her face mirroring disbelief and leafed through the books once again - unconvinced. However, she could find nothing and reluctantly returned the books.

"Yes, if you take them to heart. I've no doubt they will. Mind your clothes child, you're a mess. I've no patience for untidiness in my house. Supper is in an hour... it would behoove you to be prompt," she warned and having nothing more to say, turned on her heel and vanished back down the path.

Edwina waited until she had gone and then abruptly turned back to Hanna, a look of wild excitement in her eyes. She scrambled to her feet, still clutching the books and grabbed Hanna gently, giving her a shake.

"The boy... you said he had a message for me. Something important. Quickly now, speak!"

"Yes Miss, a moment please. I have to think," Hanna implored, a bit flustered. She closed her eyes tightly, trying to remember exactly the words.

"I'm sorry," sighed Edwina, forcing herself to calm down, "of course, in your own time."

The girl remained with her eyes closed for a moment and then began to smile as she spoke. "I remember now. It was quite curious. I don't understand it but here it is - the words exactly: 'When troubled or given a fright, a table of contents makes things right, by strong sun or lantern light."

"That's it?" Edwina stared at her not quite sure she understood, repeating the words to herself silently.

"Yes Miss, the boy's words exactly. Oh, and one more thing, he said, 'look to Beeton for help."

A look of pure astonishment filtered across Edwina's face as comprehension sunk in. Her face flushed with excitement. She grabbed The Book of Household Management and turned to the Table of Contents. Holding the book open to the page, she squinted as she held it up to the sun, which was still quite strong in the sky, turning it slightly every now and then so the page could absorb the rays. Little by little, as the page warmed, shiny spots began to glisten   illuminating certain words and letters. It was the most amazing thing she had ever seen and filled her heart with warmth and hope. She stared eagerly waiting for the entire message to materialize and then burst into laughter: *I suppose a note would have been quicker - but not as much fun. Take heart and be courageous - you have not been forgotten - help is near. Fond regards - H.*

Hanna looked at her in puzzlement because try as she might, she couldn't make out the words let alone the sentence.

"Good news Miss?"

Edwina stared at the book and smiled happily. She held the book close, a far away look in her eyes.

168

"The very best," she sighed. Help was on the way - but more important than that - he had not forgotten.

>»«<

THE INVITATION

FERN HALL - Thursday morning

Edwina stared at the closed library door, brow furrowed in exasperation as she listened. The morning had been reasonably peaceful until the arrival of the Post at half-past eight. One hour later, her father and Grendel had sequestered themselves in the library and commenced quarrelling; she had been summoned to wait. Sighing deeply and with arms folded, she began to pace in front of the door. What could they possibly be arguing about now? Her fate had already been decided. She was bound for St. Mary's. In fact, she was supposed to be upstairs at this very moment packing for the dreaded event. Of course, she'd spent the morning procrastinating, lounging on the windowsill, enjoying the early rays of the morning sun. To keep herself occupied, and mostly to avoid packing and thinking about her impending banishment, she poured over Mrs. Beeton's Book of Household Management. She was on the hunt for more hidden comments and hadn't been disappointed. Forty-seven comments thus far, a veritable treasure trove of Holmes' dry, acerbic wit, all penned neatly in the margins. So many in fact that it made her wonder if the detective lacked casework. Surely, he had better things to do with his time than offer a scathing discourse on Mrs. Beeton's cookery advice and the joys of domestic life; all apparently for her amusement. Not that she wasn't grateful; his notations were brilliant and greatly lifted her spirits. But they were more than just pointed and witty, they were astute. In the section on cooking fowl, Mrs. Beeton had lamented that domesticity had gravely eroded the moral character of the mallard. It had made him polygamous and unfaithful. The assertion that one should be concerned with the moral integrity of your dinner was absurd. And if that wasn't amusing enough, just after Mrs. Beeton's words, Holmes had written, "As with the mallard, so goes man; domestication – the scourge of us all." It had made her laugh so loud that she had frightened poor Hanna, who had been sitting quietly in the corner sewing. When she recovered her composure, she reread the comment and found herself deeply moved. Beyond the wit of the words was a hidden poignancy. For all his confidence and genius, she sensed shadows behind those impenetrable eyes. She wondered at the cause of those shadows, and if he would ever come to confide in her as she had in him.

The abrupt cessation of sound from the library woke her from her reverie and as the door flew open, she stepped back to make way. Grendel, face pinched and flushed crimson, paused in the open doorway and fixed her with a venomous look.

"Ungrateful child! You'll be the ruin of this family," she hissed, her entire frame vibrating with barely contained rage. She paused a moment, recovering some of her composure, anger now tempered with bitter indignation. "I have done all a good Christian woman could, but the wickedness of your soul is too strong. There's witchery here, but only I see it...your father is blind. No matter... my conscience is clear. I wash my hands of the matter and leave it in God's hands." With nothing more to say, she crossed herself and pushed past, slamming the library door behind her. Edwina watched her leave, dumbfounded. She didn't understand what had just occurred but judging from the expression on Grendel's face, it seemed her father may have won an argument. The possibility filled her with hope.

"Edwina dearest... please come in."

Her father's voice from the other side of the door hinted at a man on the brink of exhaustion, too drained to enjoy his small victory. As her hand reached for the knob, the sharp odour of cigar smoke assailed her and she hesitated, peering uneasily down the dim hall.

Apprehension fluttered within her. Not again, didn't he have a home of his own to haunt? She forced a smile, trying to conceal her unease, as the Professor stepped from the shadows.

"Let me be the first to congratulate you dear," he chuckled, his eyes cold but approving. "You've learned one of the most important rules of the game...the value of well-placed connections."

Edwina narrowed her eyes at him and shook her head, struggling to keep from choking on the vile smoke. "I don't know what you mean."

He began to laugh and smiled at her through the haze. "You'll see soon enough. A word of caution, connections are vital but be wary of motivation. All may not be as it seems. Remember, the best players in life, as in chess, are those who are in control. Only a fool plays the part of a pawn, and I would loathe to hear of you in that role."

Bewildered and troubled by his words, she gave him only a slight nod of acknowledgement and then escaped into the library. She shut the door quickly, resisting the urge to turn the lock and then settled at the table.

Pennington glanced up as his daughter sat down opposite him and then smiled. He took her hand in his and pressed it lovingly. "Have you packed yet dear?"

She shook her head, peering curiously into his face. He looked weary but also relieved – as if a great burden had been removed. She squeezed his hand in return, waiting for him to explain.

"Not yet," she murmured, and then with an impish smile, added, "I was rather hoping for a reprieve."

The little man's eyes lit up and he began to laugh – something he hadn't done in quite some time. He shook his head, eyes misting slightly in warm remembrance; so like his dear Katia. He squeezed her hand once more and then handed her an exquisite ivory note card of the finest paper. Edwina took the card eagerly, her heart skipping a bit in anticipation. She studied the flowing, elegant script and then frowned. The hand was unfamiliar, definitely not Holmes. She shrugged and then handed it back, more than a little disappointed.

"It seems your wish has been granted," he continued. "Quite extraordinary really. Lady Montague has..."

"Lady Montague?" she interrupted, "I don't know that name. Is she important?"

Pennington stared at her in disbelief for a moment and then began to laugh, charmed by her naivety.

"Only the second most important woman in England at the moment. Lady Montague is very influential. Her circle of acquaintances very select. It seems that you have come to her attention and she has extended an invi..."

"Attention? But I've never met the woman. I..." she interrupted once more, her brow furrowed in mild frustration.

Pennington scanned the invitation once more and then looked up. "It says here that you were referred by her niece ... a Miss Mary Morstan.

"Mary!" At the name, her eyes sparkled with sudden joy, her spirits lifting again. This had to be the handiwork of Holmes but where it was heading, she couldn't discern.

"Ahh, a name you know... good, good. Apparently, you made such an impression on the young lady that..." Pennington paused for a moment, a slight look of bewilderment clouding his face. "How did you meet her then?" he asked, overcome with curiosity. His daughter hadn't received any visitors, of that he was sure. Social calls were arranged through Gretchen and he was certain she hadn't permitted any.

The directness of the question startled her, but she recovered quickly and smiled. "At market, yes, with Hanna while shopping. Miss Morstan, she's lovely... a nurse at the Royal London... quite respectable."

"Ahh, a nurse... good then," he remarked, bobbing his head vigorously in approval.

"Well, as I was saying, you made such an impression on Miss Morstan that she has referred you to her aunt, Lady Montague. Lady Montague is one of London's most lauded socialites, her galas are the toast of the city. She is also a woman of great charity and kindness and she has extended an invitation to tea this..."

"Tea?" she blurted, biting her tongue in an attempt to conceal her astonishment. That was it? An invitation to tea? Of what bloody use could that possibly be?

"An invitation from Lady Montague is rare – to be envied. But this Edwina is so much more. She is a charitable woman not only involved in aiding those less fortunate, but also assisting in the proper education of young ladies. One of her greatest friends was Isabella Beeton, God rest her soul, and in tribute to her every year, she selects several young..."

"Beeton? The Mrs. Beeton?" she exclaimed, both shocked and amused to hear that name. Is that what this was all about? Surely there had to be more.

Pennington smiled patiently and leaned back in his chair, waiting for his daughter to regain her composure. When he was satisfied that he had her full attention, he once more squeezed her hand and continued his explanation.

"It's not just tea Edwina, it's an invitation to live at Bexley Manor and be one of a select few to attend private classes in the social graces. And when you are ready, you'll have your season. It's an opportunity for a proper marriage and a gracious life, something I could only dream of providing."

She nearly choked and found herself unable to speak at first, conflicted and unsure as to how she should feel. "So... not to St. Mary Magdalene's?" she ventured after a pause. That was good news but as for the rest...

He smiled and shook his head. "Not at all. London. not far from Regent's Park. "

As he spoke, hope sparked within as she began to finally understand what was going on. It was either the most brilliant of schemes or Holmes' idea of a joke; at the moment, she wasn't entirely sure which. Nevertheless, she rose from the table and threw her arms around her father, embracing him gratefully.

"I won't let you down... I promise."

"Of course you won't. I have faith in you," he sighed, wiping quickly at his eyes as he hugged her tightly.

A few moments later, she was scrambling up the stairs, two at a time, her face flushed with excitement, her eyes bright and luminous. She flung open the door to her room and burst in, exclaiming: "Well what are you waiting for? We've packing to do!"

Hanna gawked at her - unsure what to make of her mood. "So, we're still going then, to St. Mary's?"

Edwina burst into laughter and with a shake of her head, plopped down onto the bed. "Thankfully no... to London!"

"What's in London?"

"Lady Montague and some place called Bexley Manor."

Hanna's eyes grew wide as saucers.

"Oh Miss, that's so lovely. Lady Montague... she's quite famous and, begging your pardon, I hear her house is three times the size of Fem Hall. That's what Tom says; and they even have peacocks. But why Miss if you don't mind me asking?"

Edwina sighed a bit and then stood, turning to gaze out the window. After a moment, she shrugged and picked up Mrs. Beeton's Book, and much to Hanna's delight, placed it atop her head in attempt to balance it. It fell to the floor with a crash.

"Well, I can't say for certain," she replied with a mischievous grin, "but it seems their intention is to make a lady of me. "

Hanna began to giggle and then quickly covered her mouth. "Can they do that Miss?" she asked quietly, in all seriousness, when she had recovered her composure.

172

Edwina flashed a smile and shook her head. "Not if I can help it," she asserted with a heartfelt laugh and fell in beside her maid to help with the packing.

»»««

Pennington paused on the path back from the greenhouse and looked up towards the house, now shrouded in deepening shadow. His eyes settled on the glow from the windows of the second floor and as he listened to the sounds of their laughter, a melancholy smile touched his lips. How much his life had changed over the course of a few short months. When his dear Katia had died, and he had been approached by her sister regarding the care of his daughter, he had been more than a little apprehensive. He and his wife had been living apart for quite some time and his daughter was truly a stranger to him. But little by little over the past few months, she had wormed her way into his heart. The very prospect of her leaving, even temporarily, filled him with a great sadness. The gravel crunched beside him and he looked up, his face drawn with doubt.

"Have I made the right choice James? It's all so sudden. I still don't understand how any of this came about. And London is... well... London. Hardly the place for a woman on her own."

The Professor shrugged, rather amused by Pennington's fatherly concern. "You made the only choice Wilfred. Edwina's clever and more than capable, she'll manage just fine. She is destined for much greater things than St. Mary's."

"You believe so?" asked the little man, his face brightening with pride at the suggestion.

The Professor met his gaze steadily, impassively and said nothing at first, as he busied himself with clipping the end off another cigar. He lit it – the flame briefly illuminating the most peculiar of smiles.

"Oh yes, " he chuckled, "it's inevitable." He glanced briefly up at the window and then down at Pennington, a slight curl of disdain briefly visible at the comer of his mouth. He smiled once more and then clapped Pennington firmly on the shoulder, nudging him along.

"You mustn't worry," he soothed as they headed back towards the house, "she'll be well cared for at Lady Montague's and not without monitoring."

Pennington drew to a halt and looked up in surprise. "How's that then? At Lady Montague's we have..."

"Nothing you should concern yourself with. Let's just say Lady Montague's social circle is select but diverse. Invitations to her teas are prized."

"You then?" blurted the little man, both surprised and somewhat amused. Though in truth, he shouldn't have been. The Professor was no stranger to social circles and drifted in and out of them seamlessly, often

173

without notice.

"No, not this time," he chuckled, "someone Edwina may find more agreeable. But enough of this, we've business to discuss," he announced firmly and once more nudged Pennington along the path to the house. "As I was saying earlier, we must always be mindful   of our long-term goals. The time has come to move the operation abroad."

Pennington stopped so abruptly that he nearly lost his balance. "What? But, but why?" he sputtered, flushed and short of breath. "When we've been having so much success spreading out little by little on a daily basis."

The Professor smiled, always amused by his Pennington 's reaction to change. He was a creature of habit, entirely predictable – boring. The slightest ripple in the status quo seemed to send him into paroxysms of anxiety. It was at the very least a most aggravating trait but now he had come to view it for what it really was – a liability. And liabilities would always need to be dealt with... but not just yet. He smiled smoothly, coldly and once more, clapped the man on his shoulder.

"Did you really believe that this was all my friend? Something so paltry? Insignificant? The world my friend is ripe for the picking. After all these years, surely you know me better. Cheer up then. I've set our goals much higher. This was always going to be just a little exercise, and now that our friends in Berlin... "

"Germany..." murmured Pennington with a look of utter dread. "They say there might be war."

A slight sheen of sweat began to bead on his upper lip. The papers were full of rumblings of political unrest in the region. The Triple Alliance between Germany, Austria-Hungary and Italy was just two years old but already there were signs of cracks in the treaty. It was even rumored that Bismarck 's own party, perhaps even the man himself, was behind the growing dissent.

Professor James Moriarity took a long draw on his cigar, a look of immense satisfaction and pleasure on his face as he rolled the smoke over his tongue. He exhaled and then smiled, with an icy slyness that chilled Pennington to the bone.

"Yes, well, if all goes as planned... Come along then..."

»»«««

WELCOME TO LONDON – REVISITED

Bexley Manor, Friday Afternoon

It wasn't at all what she had expected.

The small caravan, led by the Clarence carriage, clattered noisily through the ornate iron gates that graced seemingly the only opening in the imposing ivy-covered walls. Towering black poplars lined both sides of the lane. Edwina leaned forward, peering out the window, utterly transfixed as they wound their way towards a distant vision of what looked very much like an old country castle. Up above the tree line, she could vaguely discern pale colored stone turrets. Not an unusual site if you were in the Viennese countryside, but this was the very heart of London, a stone's throw from Regent's Park and Baker Street. As they grew closer, she realized that it wasn't so much a medieval castle as a manor house plagued by an odd mixture of assorted architectural styles. The roof was primarily gothic; turrets of stone along the front, each wing of the house capped by a tower of pale colored stone, complete with stained glass windows which sparkled in the afternoon sunlight. Conversely, the entrance of the house consisted of a long, covered portico fronted by marble stairs and a Greek-style colonnade. The memory of the museum steps where she had encountered Holmes on a rainy afternoon not so long ago flashed in her mind; it brought a wistful smile to her lips. Formal gardens, reminiscent of Versailles, graced the front of the house. These in turn were surrounded by a large grassy meadow that stretched out on both sides towards a dark wooded area. The woods turned back towards the ivy walls that enclosed the estate. Eccentric, to say the least, though the word bizarre also came to mind.

"Well... not exactly what I envisioned," Edwina admitted with a shrug as she glanced back at Hanna, who seemed equally perplexed at the changing landscape.

Hanna smiled tentatively. "Beg pardon Miss. I don't think I've ever seen anything like it."

"Bit of a hodgepodge, isn't it?" she laughed, nodding in agreement as she sat back in her seat. "Still, it's home for a while... and not St. Mary's, for which I am exceedingly grateful." She smiled pensively and gazed out again, looking up at the roofline. "I think I might fancy a tower room. What do you think Hanna? Shall I be Rapunzel? Though my hair isn't really long eno... Oh...! Where are we going now?" she exclaimed as the carriage jolted abruptly, veering off to the left. Curious, she leaned forward once more, resting her elbows on the ledge of the window as she peered out. She craned her neck to look back behind the carriage and realized that they were now moving away from the main house and towards the woods.

"Curioser and curiouser," she mumbled under her breath with a grin, feeling very much like Alice in her Adventures. A shimmer in the air up ahead caught her attention and another slight turn in the lane revealed two ponds, one slightly larger than the other, on opposite sides of the path. The larger of the two was covered in white water lilies and ringed by several follies including a towering black obelisk, a circle of ancient stones and an open sided, domed temple. The smaller pond was more of a marsh, shallow water edged by reeds and tall grasses.

They continued to skirt the pond with its follies until the carriage turned once more towards the woods. Just past the edge of the pond, the Clarence rolled to a stop in front of the most charming if ordinary looking stone cottage, complete with thatched roof. The wheels had barely ceased to turn before Edwina was scrambling out, eyes bright with anticipation. The green timbered door, framed by an abundant spray of wisteria, creaked open. Much to her delight, out stepped Mary Morstan, her delicate features radiating joy. She threw open her arms in welcome and both women embraced as long, lost sisters.

"Welcome! I hope your journey wasn't too taxing. Travelling through town can be tiresome on the best of days," she exclaimed kindly. "Once you are settled, I think a rest may be in order. Dinner is served at 7:00, ample time to relax. I'll come fetch you. Aunt Caroline is eager to meet you."

"So, here? This cottage? This is where I'll stay then?" Edwina watched distractedly as a group of servants appeared from parts unknown and began to unload her belongings and move them inside. Hanna joined in striving to keep up. They reminded her of ants scurrying about as fast as they could, almost on the verge of colliding but somehow managing to avoid it at the last moment.

A shadow of concern flickered across Mary's face.

"Is this all right then? Aunt Caroline was hesitant, but Mr. Holmes suggested this would be more to your liking than the main house. He can be very persuasive. If not, we can move..."

"Oh, no, it's perfect," assured Edwina quickly, "not that the main house wouldn't also be fine but no, this is lovely... so lovely," she sighed as they stepped over the threshold and into the small parlor. A warm smile of remembrance touched her lips as she surveyed the inside. It reminded her of the small farmhouse near Salzburg where Aunt Liesel lived. She and her mother had spent many a happy hour there while visiting from Vienna. She ambled around the room, taking in everything, exploring every crook and cubbyhole.

"I'm glad you like it. Used to belong the gamekeeper when they kept deer on the estate. Aunt Caroline was going to take it down and put up another folly, but Mr. Holmes... well, he convinced her to leave it as is. He used to come here when he needed an escape... some place quiet, away from Baker Street, when the madness and the clients became too much. He'd sit and read – think for hours on end, work on his experiments. Often, when John accompanied him, I'd join them. The three of us would play cards, late into the night. He's a wicked player Mr. Holmes," she laughed with a shake of her head. "He seemed content... happy even... more social. There was even talk of putting in beehives and..." Mary suddenly stopped a look of dismay clouding her features. "Well, that was all before..." she murmured and then paused again, wondering if she had said too much.

"Before what?" pressed Edwina, her curiosity thoroughly piqued. Her mind returned to those shadows she thought she had detected.

Mary flushed, embarrassed and looked away for a moment. She was torn wanting desperately to share what she knew about Holmes' episodes of melancholy with this young woman who so obviously cared for him and the knowledge that she shouldn't. She had promised not only John, but also Holmes, and it was a vow she took very seriously. "I'm sorry. I shouldn't have said. It is a confidence I cannot share," she sighed sadly. Seeing Edwina's look of alarm, she reached out and pressed her hand reassuringly. "Oh no, you mustn't worry. Mr. Holmes is well. The Doctor tells me he has at least two cases at hand and Mr. Holmes is always happiest when he's fully engaged. Now I must return, so I'll leave you to unpack. Rest up. I'll come around at half five."

Edwina frowned a bit, her mind still on Mary's explanation or lack of one but thanked her nonetheless as she followed her to the door. As Mary began to leave, she abruptly reached out and grabbed her forearm, making her pause.

"Mary, before you leave, I was wondering, what exactly is Mr. Holmes' situation?"

Mary frowned and repeated the words silently, puzzled by the question and the earnest expression of interest on Edwina's face. Then as comprehension filtered through, she began to smile. It wasn't a question she was used to hearing – certainly not from the women in her family; no one was ever that bold.

"Well, as far as we can tell… that is… the Doctor and I... he doesn't have one." She frowned a bit, seeking to clarify. "An attachment I mean to say if that is what you are inquiring about." It was a complicated situation but again she hesitated to disclose anything further.

"Ahh, well I was just curious," remarked Edwina with deliberate nonchalance. Mary peered thoughtfully at her and then began to smile. To her, it seemed the sparkle in the Edwina's eyes hinted at more than a passing interest.

"One more thing – a favor..." began Edwina, her eyes warming, the previous air of detachment evaporating. "Thank him for me, for all he has done, his great generosity. Words cannot express my gratitude."

A sly little smile lit Mary's face and reaching out, she pressed Edwina's hand encouragingly.

"Ahh, best done in person. I suggest at Tea this Sunday. He and the Doctor will both be attending. Now, I must be off. Aunt Caroline is reviewing the sweets with Cook for Sunday and she requires my opinion. Take time to rest. I'll return at half five." Having nothing further to add, she smiled warmly at Edwina and then vanished out the door. A few moments later, the Clarence carriage headed off down the lane towards the main house. Edwina waved, watching it until it disappeared around the edge of the pond. Then, with a jubilant smile, she rubbed her hands together in anticipation and headed back in to unpack, all the while humming a whimsical little tune.

»»«

TEA
Sunday afternoon

"Holmes..."

There was silence...

"Holmes!!" This time the voice was more insistent and irritated.

Still no answer, the only the sound was of the clock on the mantle chiming half past four. Watson frowned, grunting softly to himself as he stepped to the window and glanced out. Down below, a hansom cab, fresh from the barn and thus far mostly free of mud and dung (Holmes had been specific) waited at the curb. He glanced at his pocket watch checking the time again and then frowned impatiently at the closed bedchamber door.

"Holmes...What the devil are you about man?" he cried, his voice rising in volume and exasperation. "The hansom is here at the time you specified and..." He sputtered to a stop as the door banged open and Holmes emerged, looking dapper in dark grey striped trousers, a black waistcoat and freshly starched shirt and collar. In his hands, he carried his top hat which contained light grey gloves; a new grey frock coat was draped over his arm.

"I thought you said you were ready," Holmes remarked with an arch of his brow and frown of disapproval. He turned his attention to the mantle where he began to gather up his cigarette case, keys, wallet, a fresh pocket square.

Watson scowled and glanced down at his own neatly pressed but more informal navy suit.

"It's only tea," he grumbled. After all, he'd been to tea at Lady Montague's with Mary almost every Sunday for the past six months and the suit had always served him well enough.

"The first formal tea of season is never 'just tea,'" sighed Holmes. "You look like a tradesman."

"I am a tradesman... as are you."

"Perhaps, but do you always have to look like one?" retorted Holmes. "Now, off you go. Change and quickly, the hansom is here," he growled and then turned back to fastening his black silk cravat.

Watson pursed his lips, ready to protest and then gave up. With a shrug of resignation, he headed off down the hall to change. A few moments later, he re-entered the room, this time suitably attired in a black cutaway coat with matching trousers and a burgundy vest. While waiting for Holmes (who had once more vanished into his room), he examined his reflection in the mirror. Frowning in concentration, he removed a small, fine comb from his pocket and carefully groomed his moustache, dressing the very tips with a bit of wax.

"Ahhh, much better," chuckled a voice from behind.

Watson turned to find Holmes back in the parlour and now diligently searching the roll top desk for items unknown. He pursed his lips, ready to comment on the lateness of the hour when Holmes uttered a satisfied grunt, his search apparently at an end.

"Why the blazes are you bringing that?" Watson exclaimed. He watched, utterly bewildered as Holmes withdrew a small black velvet pouch from the top drawer and began to fold it over into neat sections, taking care not to dislodge the contents. The pouch contained a set of fine lock picks, files of varying sizes, a set of master keys, a long-handled tweezer, and a small stethoscope; in essence, the tools of a burglar.

"Clear night; new moon; perfect opportunity," he said with a grin as he pulled on his coat and then tucked the pouch neatly into the inside pocket.

"For what?!" exclaimed Watson.

"The second shop of course." Holmes frowned a bit, a shadow darkening his face as he explained. "Lestrade stopped by earlier whining about a 'lack of progress'." Man practically accused me of procrastinating," he muttered with some bitterness as he gathered up his walking stick, hat, and gloves. He headed quickly out the door and down the stairs, Watson scrambled to keep pace.

"And are you?" puffed Watson, catching up to him as he was reaching for the door to the hansom. Holmes froze, fingers on the handle and glanced back sharply over his shoulder.

"What? Why would I?"

The intensity of Holmes' reaction took Watson by surprise. He turned a little pale, shifting uneasily on his feet. "Well, I don't know. Out of kindness... compassion. Perhaps you're waiting for the right moment... a way to soften the blow. He is her father after all. There's little left of her family now. I know you realize that when he's arrested, it will be devastating."

Holmes said nothing and remained stationary, his hand still grasping the handle of the cab door. After a pause, he shrugged and then without a word, climbed inside taking his seat and leaning far back into the shadows. He kept his eyes averted, fixed on some point outside the cab, watching absently as the hansom pulled away from the curb. Watson remained silent also, waiting, sensing that he had more to say. Following what seemed like an eternity, Holmes spoke; his voice firm, cold, almost callous.

"I solve the case Watson, that is my mission. The aftermath is none of my concern."

Watson furrowed his brow and leaned forward a bit, a look of doubt in his eyes.

"You say that, yet I find it difficult to believe that the case is all that is on your mind when you have gone to such great lengths."

Holmes cut him off with a warning glance.

"Everything I do, Doctor, is for a reason -- logical and calculated."

"I didn't say that it wasn't Holmes. But as you well know, the mind is incredibly complex. I believe we are not always aware of, or want to admit, the true reasons behind our actions."

Amusement flickered in Holmes' eyes and he began to chuckle. He sighed heavily after a moment and then shook his head, advising: "I think Doctor, that you best content yourself with Freud's lesser monographs. The one on Cocaine perhaps, a personal favourite," he suggested with a wry smile. Watson bristled, determined to have his say on the matter. "Mock me if you must Holmes, but to me it seems that..."

Holmes groaned aloud, interrupting him with a weary smile and dismissive wave.

"My intention is not to offend Watson but allow me to remind you of the dangers of ascribing sentiment where none exists. I am not you Watson. One can hardly compare the workings of our minds. It is an unequal comparison as chalk is to cheese."

Ignoring the slight, Watson compressed his lips, his face taking on an expression of resolve. He smiled at Holmes through clenched teeth.

"Yes, in many ways we are most certainly 'chalk and cheese' as you say, but there is one thing that we have in common that cannot be disputed."

Holmes lifted his gaze to the ceiling and rolled his eyes, his patience wearing thin. "What's that then? Do enlighten me," he sighed.

Watson laughed, a triumphant little smirk curling his lips. "You are flesh and blood, my friend. Human as am I. Not a machine despite your best efforts. And that condition Holmes, comes with all sorts of attributes including sentiment and emotions, regardless whether you care to acknowledge them."

Holmes stared at him, momentarily at a loss for words and then began to laugh. When he had finished, he drew a deep sigh and then shrugged in resignation, a melancholy smile playing on his lips.

"A discussion best left for another time. Look, we've arrived."

Watson turned to gaze out the window into the deepening twilight, as the hansom cab pulled through the gates of Bexley Manor. It fell in behind a parade of other carriages, all heading for the main house, which now glowed softly with a mixture of gas and candlelight.

»»««

Edwina lingered under the canopy of the great oak, hovering at the edge of the lawn. She gazed skeptically at the long table, draped in white linen and dressed in fine crystal and china. In the center of the table were several ornate flower arrangements, including one that contained a small fountain, which bubbled and splashed softly. Pleasant enough for the moment though she secretly hoped she wouldn't be seated too close. She expected it would grow annoying after the novelty wore off. The table was illuminated by numerous paper lanterns, some fashioned in the shape of cranes and pagodas, which were strung overhead. They dangled from the tree canopy and from poles that lined the paths; everything glowed – it was wondrous and quite surreal. Nearby, an army of servants stood by waiting patiently for the guests who were milling about chatting to take their proper places (assigned of course) at the table. Dear God, if this was only tea, what was a formal dinner like? As she reviewed the scene, her fingers strayed nervously first to her lapel watch and then to her neck. She toyed with the cloisonné bead and green crystal necklace and smiled, somewhat comforted by the familiar feel. It had been a gift from her mother many years ago, created by one of her mother's artisan friends. Costume jewelry, hardly worth anything but rich in sentimental value. Even so, she rarely wore it as she seldom wore any jewelry other than the lapel watch. In fact, it was only by chance that she had come across it, buried in the bottom of her mother's trunk of costumes under an old cloak, when she

180

was unpacking. Hanna had noticed it first and remarked that the color would complement her hair and that she needed something to wear to tea. All the other ladies would be wearing their finest. She grinned, chuckling to herself; she didn't have the heart to tell Hanna that this simple piece of costume jewelry certainly couldn't compare to what the other ladies would be wearing. The truth was, she didn't care what they thought; her mother had given it out of love and in her eyes, that was all that mattered.

As more guests arrived, her uneasiness increased; she wet her lips, which were now suddenly dry. Her eyes scanned the crowd for a friendly face. There was one, Mary Morstan. Unfortunately, she was at the far end of the table talking with Lady Montague and her rather unpleasant cousin, Clara, if she remembered correctly. They had been briefly introduced earlier in the week and Edwina, despite her best intentions not to make hasty judgments, had taken an instant disliking to her. A pretty enough girl – the problem being that she was fully aware of it. That arrogance along with her insipid conversation and constant fluttering of eyelashes and coy little smiles, left Edwina seething inside. In fact, the mere sight of those bobbing ringlets made her grit her teeth; she looked to the table, eyes settling on the cutlery. She fervently hoped that she would not be seated next to Clara. If that were to occur, she prayed the knives were sharp.

"Psst... go on now Miss. What are you waiting for?" urged Hanna's voice from behind. She gently nudged her mistress forward.

Edwina smoothed the silk folds of her dark green tea gown, resisting the urge to hide her hands in the pockets of the over jacket. It was a lovely gown, if still a bit snug. Mary had lent it to her and graciously permitted Hanna to alter it slightly as the two girls, though similar in weight, differed greatly in build. Mary's petite frame didn't allow much room for Edwina's taller, curvaceous frame. If not for Hanna's skill with a needle, it would have been futile. The end result was a stunning creation of green silk edged with lace that accentuated her curves and de-emphasized her height. Even so, it was more snug than she was accustomed to, though the discomfort she experienced was most likely due to the corset which she had reluctantly agreed to wear.

"Hanna, I'm not sure how long I can bear this," she whispered to the shadows beneath the oak. She stood erectly, one hand pressed to her side, taking careful breaths. She wanted to look behind her but was finding it difficult to pivot and turn. "I can scarcely breathe, I can't imagine how I will manage to sit."

There was silence for a moment and she frowned. She cocked her head and turned slightly until a sharp pain in her side made her stop. She could see only out to the side but not directly in back. "Hanna?" The girl seemed to have vanished.

Leaves and grass rustled behind her as a soft low chuckle filled her ears.

"My dear Miss Schraeder, it seems you are now entirely the correct shape. How can this possibly be?"

Overcome with delight at the sound of his voice, she forgot to take care and whirled around to greet him. Her reward was a spasm in her ribs so fierce that she gasped out loud and turned pale. Astonished, Holmes moved forward to steady her, his fingers lightly holding onto her forearm. She forced a weak smile and waved him off, concentrating on suppressing the pain. It gradually subsided and after a moment, she smiled again, though her cheeks were flushed with embarrassment.

"I would gladly join you in mocking my appearance Mr. Holmes, if laughter wasn't so painful," she wheezed. "Breathing and having the correct shape seem to be at odds."

"Slow shallow breaths," he advised as he took her hand gently in his, "inhale when I squeeze your hand and only then... exhale on the next squeeze."

She nodded that she understood and after a few moments of following his guidance, her breathing returned to almost normal.

"Thank you," she whispered. "I must look ridiculous... and you are very kind not to mention it."

Holmes chuckled a bit and smiled, his eyes unexpectedly compassionate.

"On the contrary Eddy, it seems to me you have never looked lovelier despite your change in shape."

The words cheered her and she gazed up, a flush of warmth coloring her cheeks. *Dear God, he looked even more handsome than usual. How was that possible? The word debonair came to mind.* She smiled, searching for a clever way to return the compliment without sounding like a fawning schoolgirl; the tinkle of a crystal bell from the table interrupted her.

Holmes nodded towards the table, and smiled, offering her his arm. "Put your gloves on Eddy, time to show us what you've learned from Mrs. Beeton."

She paused and cocked her head to the side, a slight frown clouding her face.

"I didn't actually read the book Holmes... only your comments, the rest was... drivel," she murmured, holding onto his arm as he led her towards the table.

The sound of his laughter warmed her. "Ah, well perhaps it's best not to voice that opinion just yet. Mrs. Beeton was a good friend of Lady Montague. I'd hate to see you end up at St. Mary's after all."

Edwina smiled, suppressing her laughter for fear of aggravating her breathing. As they approached the table, she hesitated, a momentary look of alarm on her face.

"Holmes... I haven't quite figured out how to sit down," she whispered.

"Think of it as lowering Eddy, not sitting," he chuckled, carefully observing as the other guests began to take their seats. There were a few faces that he did not recognize.

She nodded that she understood and then paused again, a mischievous smile lighting her face. "And if I faint?"

"You won't," he reassured.

"But if I do?" she persisted.

He began to laugh and shook his head. "Then I promise that I shall catch you before you fall into the sweets." He pulled out her chair and waited as she carefully lowered herself into it.

Elated at the successful completion of the task, Edwina sighed in relief and gazed around the table, watching as guests drifted around the table, checking the place holders for their assignments. She frowned – a thought suddenly occurring.

"How fortunate that we are seated next to each other," she whispered, her eyes sparkling with suspicion. She noted that Dr. Watson and Miss Morstan were also next to them.

"Never rely on luck Eddy," he murmured, "she can be a fickle mistress. Now, gloves off and in your lap. Prepare to be bored for the next few hours. Not so bad really once you've accepted it. Listen carefully and observe, you never know when what you hear tonight may be of use."

She nodded that she understood and glanced around the table listening to all the little snippets of conversation, carefully observing the little gestures and interactions between the guests. Concentrating, she tried to see the world as he did; it was utterly fascinating and exhausting. She turned back to him and smiled, filled with a renewed sense of respect and appreciation for the genius of the man.

"Thank you, Holmes," she whispered. Impulsively, she reached out and grasped his hand.

Startled, he glanced down at her hand holding so gently onto his. Once again, he was struck by the feeling of warmth and comfort her touch aroused within him. He lifted his gaze and managed a tentative smile. "Whatever for?" he asked quietly, searching her eyes for the usual signs of deception or artifice he had come to associate with the fairer sex. He found none; only sincerity, gratitude and undeniable affection. It was troubling and flattering simultaneously. Not quite certain how he should respond, he squeezed her hand in response and then quickly released it.

Edwina began to laugh. How odd that he could see everything else but not this.

"Everything," was all she said and with a smile, turned back to watching the rest of the guests.

Holmes studied her quietly for a moment, realizing that a speedy resolution to the case was probably best for all concerned.

»»««

THE COLONEL

A hush fell over the room, as all with a few exceptions, leaned forward eagerly to hear the conclusion to the Colonel's tale.

"My dear sir," whispered Clara Barclay, eyes wide with horror, "whatever did you do? I would have fallen dead from fear." She shook her head for emphasis, ringlets bobbing wildly as she gazed adoringly at the Colonel. With his golden hair, rugged face and broad shoulders, she thought him the second most handsome man in the room... perhaps even first.

"Schwachsinn, mumbled Edwina, "will this ever end?" She glanced sideways at Holmes who rewarded her with a sly grin of concurrence. Bollocks did seem the appropriate word.

Colonel Sebastian Moran, a little less than three weeks home from distinguished service in Kabul, straightened the medals on his dress uniform. He flashed a wide, if somewhat patronizing smile, in Clara's direction. Holmes noted however, with some disquiet, that his eyes never strayed far from Edwina.

The Colonel cleared his throat and continued with the story. "With two of my men wounded by the savage beast, I knew I must finish the deed. He'd tasted blood and would not rest until he had torn us all to shreds. So, I bid farewell to my comrades and taking up my rifle, I crawled down into the ditch after the man eater. I soon caught up with him and after a fierce struggle, I bested the monster with a single shot between the eyes." A collective gasp echoed through the room; fans blossomed, creating a small breeze at the table. "As you can see," he began with a twisted smile, "he left me with a memento to remember him by..." He ran his finger along a jagged scar that ran from the bottom of his right ear lobe down along his chin, ending just near the center. "Still, I have the better trophy – his head on my wall."

The room erupted with applause, the men clapping vigorously, many of the ladies still fanning themselves over the excitement of the story. Holmes joined in with a polite though lackluster, clap. The only exception was Edwina, who sat rigidly in her chair, a look of unabashed revulsion clouding her face. She kept her hands folded in front of her, refusing to join in.

Colonel Moran took note and compressed his lips. "You disapprove of hunting Miss Schraeder?"

"I disapprove of cowards."

An uneasy titter rippled across the table. Most of the guests stared at her unable to believe their ears. Lady Montague turned a little pale, uncertain how she should react.

"Steady," murmured Holmes in an attempt to subdue her. It wouldn't do for her to be thrown out within the first week after he had worked so diligently to secure her a place.

The Colonel chuckled. "You think it is cowardly to hunt down the beast that wounded your men?"

Edwina fixed her eyes on him, unable or unwilling to contain her growing irritation.

"I believe it's cowardly to bait the creature into a trap, wound it and then end its life. That tiger didn't seek you out, you tracked it. It attacked your men in self-defense and attempted to flee – you said as much in your story. But you couldn't leave well enough alone, so you followed it, cornered it and slaughtered it. There is nothing noble in assassination Colonel – nor in those who practice it."

The uneasy murmur, which had been increasing steadily as Edwina spoke, stopped abruptly. All eyes focused on the Colonel waiting on his response. He was quiet for a moment and then smiled, nodding briefly in her direction.

"Well, one could never accuse you of being less than forthright Miss Schraeder, or demure."

"Would you say that if I were a man?" she retorted, ignoring the gentle nudging under the table as Holmes tried to get her attention. She realized that she was letting her emotions get the better of her but at the moment, it didn't matter.

"But you are obviously not a man," chuckled the Colonel. He flashed a condescending smile as laughter once more rippled across the table.

"So, my opinion is invalid then. because I am a woman," she hissed, practically vibrating with anger.

The Colonel shrugged. "Because you are a woman, you shouldn't concern yourself with things beyond your scope of understanding."

The color drained from Edwina's face. As she sprang from her seat, Holmes caught her hand under the table and gently pulled her back. A moment later, she slowly sank back down into her chair, as if directed by an unseen force.

"You are mistaken in your analysis sir," Holmes voice was calm and controlled, though there was no mistaking the undercurrent of warning in it.

All eyes turned to the detective. They waited on the Colonel's response.

"How so Mr. Holmes? Will you argue science with me? It is well established that the male brain is larger than the female."

"Agreed. Physically larger. However, recent studies show no conclusive correlation of brain size to intelligence."

The Colonel's grey eyes registered first astonishment and then annoyance. "Are you saying Mr. Holmes, that women are as intelligent as men?" His mouth twisted with scorn and disbelief.

"In most cases, more," muttered Edwina, her words just loud enough to be heard.

There was a grumble of indignation, followed by laughter from the men at the table. Holmes pressed her hand sharply and cast a stern look in her direction. The ladies at the table continued to fan themselves and looked at each other, not quite sure how they should feel.

Holmes arched his brow and then smiled coolly.

"What I am saying sir, is that intelligence is not based on gender. Women, given the same opportunity, are more than capable. Any limitations are due solely to the restrictions that we as a society impose on them, not on any inherent deficiency."

There was a moment of silence at the table and several of the ladies stopped fanning themselves. They looked up entirely bewildered by what they were hearing. On the opposite side of Dr. Watson, Mary Morstan leaned forward in her seat and nodded warmly at the Detective.

"Well said," she mouthed with a smile while Watson, who had long since tired of the discussion, uttered a deep groan of resignation.

Edwina, perched on the edge of her seat, slowly began to relax. She turned slightly in her seat to gaze at Holmes, her eyes brimming with profound admiration.

The Colonel's mouth twisted into a grin; he erupted with laughter and shook his head. As he spoke, he lightly slapped the table for emphasis.

"Dear God man, for a moment I thought you were serious. What next? Give them the vote?"

Edwina leapt to her feet, her smile and all traces of calm gone in an instant. As she pursed her lips to speak, Lady Montague — perhaps sensing an imminent crisis — stood abruptly, reached for the small crystal bell on the table and rang it forcefully. The spell was broken. The Colonel's mouth twisted into a peculiar smile, his gaze once more fixed on Edwina, who remained standing by her seat, struggling to maintain control. After a moment, he shrugged, allowing the discussion to end, presumably bored with the matter. Edwina compressed her lips angry still. but once more took her seat.

"Well, wasn't that lively?" remarked Lady Montague with forced cheerfulness and a nervous chuckle, mindful of the undercurrent of tension at the table. "I suggest we all take a moment to clear our heads while the table is reset. As our French friends would say, it's time for Le dessert ... sweets and champagne."

Wildly enthusiastic applause sounded all around. Relieved by the lessening of tension at the table, she smiled, with greater confidence. "And perhaps, if I ask very nicely, " she continued with a mischievous twinkle, "upon our return, Mr. Holmes will honor us with one of his many excellent adventures. Preferably, one without tigers."

A titter of polite laughter sounded at the remark and even Edwina managed a weak if somewhat sheepish smile.

"I believe I can accommodate your request, as long as no one objects to a little murder. No tigers involved, Holmes assured with a chuckle.

"Splendid! Now everyone go off and socialize. Gentlemen, I remind you of your manners and ladies, you as well. This is your opportunity to mingle with each other but properly. I'll have no scandal at Bexley Manor - particularly if I'm not involved. Let us all agree to meet back here in thirty minutes." So with that caution, Lady Montague once more rang the bell and the guests slowly dispersed.

Edwina, her nerves still raw and on edge from the altercation with the Colonel, heaved a sigh of relief as she watched the guests move on to socialize. Now was her chance to regain her composure and make amends for her lapse of control. She turned to speak to Holmes and was met with an empty chair. He and the Doctor had vanished. Trying to mask her disappointment, she rose from the table and crossed to the edge of the lawn, peering out into the deepening twilight. She could discern nothing at first but as her eyes adjusted to the darkness, she thought she glimpsed moving shadows - two men near the follies - Holmes and Dr. Watson perhaps. With a cautious glance, she took as deep a breath as she could and set out after them. The very least she could do was offer an apology, not so much for the words she had expressed for she didn't regret them at all, but for having made a scene. She'd lost control of her emotions; she only hoped he wasn't too disappointed in her.

>>«<

"Quite a spectacle," grunted Watson with a shake of his head. "I've never heard such rubbish. To question the character of a man so distinguished. Shameful I tell you. That girl is out of control Holmes. Why do you encourage it?"

Holmes, who was seated on the small stone bench that sat in the center of the temple looked up from behind a haze of cigarette smoke.

"Distinguished?" His eyes flickered with skepticism.

"Did you not see?" exclaimed Watson with some exasperation, "honors from Kabul and Jalalabad. He's been mentioned in dispatches at least twice, perhaps more."

Holmes chuckled, always amused at Watson's quick and unswerving admiration for veterans of the wars.

"Of course I saw. How could I not? The man's a peacock. He must spend hours polishing those honors. Distracting... all that rattling."

Watson drew a deep breath, resolved to remain calm. Of all the disagreements he and Holmes had, this one irritated him the most. He reminded himself that it must be difficult for Holmes to understand the bond of honor that all men of the campaigns felt, having no military background of his own.

"Even so, for a man so distinguished to have his character questioned by..."

"Need I remind you Doctor," interrupted Holmes with some sharpness, "Her Majesty's prisons are full of men with honors. I've put a few there myself. Sent one or two to the gallows as well."

Watson chewed the edge of his mustache greatly vexed. He struggled to quash his first inclination which was to fiercely rebut Holmes' assertion. Upon further reflection however, infuriating as it was, he concluded that Holmes had a valid point.

Holmes grinned, realizing he had won the skirmish but decided to refrain from reveling in his victory too much. Watson was proud and protective of his military past; it would serve no purpose to turn the knife. He paused for a moment, eyes focused out across the pond, watching the reflections cast by the Chinese lanterns; he chose his words with the utmost care.

"I mean no disrespect, Watson – to you or those who have served so valiantly. I offer a word of caution, however, to remember that outward appearances may easily deceive. It seems to me the Colonel was fixed on

Edwina from the moment he saw her. I believe he purposefully provoked her. To what end I am not sure. I need to know more about this man. His intent."

Watson grew thoughtful, not entirely convinced that the explanation wasn't a simple one.

"Holmes, have you considered that he may have provoked her because he has an interest in her?"

Holmes glanced up sharply. "Interest? How do you mean?"

A slight smile curled the Doctor's mouth under his moustache. Beneath that look of annoyance on Holmes' face, he thought he perceived something else. He wasn't altogether sure what, but it certainly warranted further probing.

"Men often act oddly when taken by the charms of a woman Holmes. You have remarked on it yourself. Perhaps it's just that, a deep attraction; that spark between two people of which you often speak so disdainfully. Which begs the question, if that is the case, of what concern is it to you? As you've said many times, you have no time or disposition for such useless sentiment or…"

Holmes snort of indignation interrupted him before he could continue.

"Tread lightly Watson…" growled the Detective as he stabbed out his cigarette and rose from the bench. He was about to elaborate on his warning when a soft rustle on the path caught their attention. Both men turned, surprised to find Edwina standing at the base of the temple stairs. She blushed, looking uncomfortable at having been discovered and then managed a weak smile.

"Gentlemen, hello. Sorry, I don't mean to intrude, but I was wondering if I could have a word Mr. Holmes? When you and the Doctor have finished of course." She smiled sheepishly and took a step back, nodding towards the pond. "Perhaps I shall wait down by the pond until you are finished."

"No need," advised Holmes with a quick smile, "our business is completed. Dr. Watson was just leaving."

Watson frowned.

"I was?"

"Oh yes. Off you go." Holmes waved his hand dismissively in the general direction of the house.

But Watson lingered, watching curiously as Holmes offered his hand to her as she carefully climbed the stairs. She nodded to the Doctor with a sweet but distracted smile; he noted that her eyes never strayed from Holmes. For his part, Holmes' expression was now openly warm and genial. It left Watson wondering where the truth lay. Was this genuine or just one of the many masks Watson had witnessed the Detective adopt during the course of a case? Holmes was a master at manipulation. He had fallen prey to it many times himself. That sly, inviting smile could easily be a mask, a clever ruse to draw one in and gain confidence. All these years in and still he wondered what really churned in the recesses of his friend's mind. It was a mystery that eluded him.

"And still you remain," remarked Holmes with a frown, noting that Watson had yet to leave.

"Well, I'll be off then. I shall see you both shortly," he mumbled. With a slight nod, he backed up, turned, and headed down the path. He paused only once to glance back over his shoulder. They were seated on the bench now, their backs to him as they faced the pond, side by side, shoulders almost touching. His brow wrinkled with intense reflection. Very curious indeed.

Edwina waited until Watson could no longer be seen and then turned to Holmes with a bittersweet smile. "He shall never approve of me. I'm afraid my debate with the Colonel did little to change his mind. I offended him. I could tell by his expression. I will apologize to him and Lady Montague but first, I wanted to apologize to you."

"Apologize? Whatever for?" A look of mild surprise crossed his face. "You spoke honestly. I applaud that. It is a rare trait, particularly in the fairer sex, I'm sorry to say."

Edwina's eyes sparked a bit at these words. Strange, they were the first openly critical words she could recall him voicing with regard to women. She frowned wondering but pushed the thought from her mind for the moment. She was there to apologize ... to redeem herself in his eyes.

"Not for my words. I don't regret those," she added swiftly, "but I lost control of my emotions." She paused for a moment, her cheeks coloring slightly as her shame rose to the surface. "His words made me furious. So pompous. I just... well... I wanted to throttle him. I made a fool of myself Holmes, and after all you have done for me. Lady Montague as well. When you disappeared, you and Dr. Watson, I... well I feared..." She broke off and averted her eyes; her lips were pulled into a tight little smile of regret.

"What did you fear Eddy?" he prodded with a gentle smile. He had been silent all this time, listening, absorbing every word, nuance in tone, watching the shifting emotions play across her face. It was a sight to behold... so open... vulnerable... and in its own way, incredibly beautiful.

Eddy uttered a little sigh and then winced, a sharp stab of pain reminding her that she best not breathe too deeply. Her shoulders sagged forward a little more and she kept her eyes fixed on the reflection of the lanterns in the pond.

"I was afraid that I had disappointed you. More than that, made you angry. You would have every right to be angry after all the consideration you've shown me. I owe you so much. It is only through your great and kind efforts that I am not languishing at St. Mary's. You must think me horribly ungrateful." Her voice dropped off into a murmur and as she spoke, she winced and pressed a hand to her side in an attempt to massage away the pain.

Holmes' eyes crinkled warmly. "What nonsense," he chuckled with a shake of his head. His voice grew more serious as he noted her discomfort. "Clearly your restrictive garment has muddled your thought process – lack of oxygen will do that. I disappeared, as you say, to indulge in one of my lesser vices." He nodded towards the silver cigarette case which lay on the end of the bench, a mischievous gleam in his eyes. "If the Colonel insists on telling more "stirring" tales from the campaigns, I expect I will require more along with some exceptionally strong spirits... perhaps something even stronger."

Cheered by his words, she lifted her gaze to his and began to laugh. It was short-lived however as a sharp jab across her ribcage turned her joy into a gasp of pain; she had once again forgotten the dangers of unrestrained laughter. Edwina leaned forward, head nearly on her knees - her face devoid of all color as she struggled to regain her breath.

"Bloody hell Eddy! This won't do," he said, a look of mild alarm on his face. His hand rested gently on the back of her shoulder, fingers squeezing lightly, comfortingly. "If you are incapacitated, I will be forced to endure this nonsense on my own with no one of intelligence to share my misery. Would you be so heartless as to abandon me to such a fate - of braggart's tales of man-eating tigers and Miss Barclay's ridiculous ringlets?"

She managed a smile, suppressing her laughter as best she could.

"Please, if you could refrain from making me laugh."

A flicker of mischief curled his mouth.

"Impossible," he declared and then with utter resolution, reached out and grasped her shoulders, gently lifting her up. "Come along then, time to remedy this situation once and for all." As he raised her up, his eyes scanned the area of the temple, particularly the darkened corners by the far columns.

With scarcely any time for thought, Edwina found herself on her feet, ushered into the shadows of the furthermost column of the temple. She looked up at him, her eyes inquisitive but also with a hint of unease.

Sensing her hesitation, Holmes met her gaze levelly.

"It's imperative that I have your trust. You do trust me don't you Eddy?"

She gazed into infinite blue eyes and then smiled, a little flutter of warm anxiety, not an altogether unpleasant sensation, in the pit of her stomach. She nodded that she did and gave him her hand. If she was going to follow any man into a darkened corner, this man was her only choice.

"Splendid! Now do as I say. Remove your wrap and turn to face the column. In fact, I would suggest you lean against the column. Wrap your arms around it and hold on securely. Stay absolutely still," he whispered.

Mystified, Edwina nonetheless complied and handed the tea jacket to him. She wrapped her arms tightly around the smooth marble column, staring out towards the pond and waited - for what she wasn't sure. She had no experience other than a furtive kiss she had stolen from her university professor before her mother had claimed him as her own; she hoped it didn't matter. He was so close now. She could feel the brush of his clothing against her ...the gentle pressure of his leg pressed against hers... the warm tickle of his breath on the nape of her neck. Exotic notes of Persian tobacco, lime, sandalwood, pine and leather assailed her nostrils. She breathed it in as best she could and let it carry her off - floating in a sea of surging warmth and giddiness. The night breeze picked up, blowing in across the pond. Edwina shivered as it drifted over her bare arms and shoulders. When she had managed to stop shivering, she became aware of an increase in the pressure on her back. More cool air flowed over her skin and she gasped in surprise; the back of her gown was loosening and falling open. She compressed her lips but said nothing, only tightening her grip around the column as she closed her eyes. The flutter in her stomach intensified as she felt his fingers softly but firmly, moving across her back seeming to caress the satin of her corset. Her heart quickened ... pounding with feverish anticipation and a trace of apprehension. Should she protest? At least on principal? She had no clue. A second thought also occurred. Wasn't it odd... their positioning? Perhaps she should try to turn around? Wouldn't that be more convenient for both of them? She supposed this would work. No reason it wouldn't from a biological standpoint. In fact, in one of her mother's books she remembered seeing something similar...though considerably less clothing was involved. She couldn't swear it was exactly the same... she'd only caught a brief glimpse. Still, it seemed to her it would be better if she could turn around and loose herself in those eyes ... bury herself in those strong, wiry arms. She decided then and lifted her head, attempting to turn towards him.

"Stay still," he scolded, in a low voice that rumbled in her ear.

Edwina sighed in resignation and pressed her cheek against the smooth cold marble. She supposed it really didn't matter... she wasn't going to stop him.

Both of his hands were on her now ... one resting lightly on the space between the curve of her hip and back, the other lay on the small of her back. He was working loose the laces of her corset. Cool fingertips slid over her bare skin leaving little trails of goosebumps in their wake. Edwina smiled blissfully, her heart beating so fast she feared it would burst. A thousand delicious thoughts swirling in her head including the realization of the potential danger and awkwardness of the situation should they be caught. It mattered not, this daydream had never been far from her mind. Not since they had met and now...

A sharp click sounded; cold and metallic. She froze at the sound, her eyes flying open and craned her neck, trying to peer over her shoulder. Christ, it sounded exactly like the blade of a jack-knife springing open. She released the column and jerked upright, twisting slightly away from him, that tingle of unease surging forth.

"What are you doing?" she cried, pushing futilely against him. But it was no use as he used the weight of his body to pin her fast against the column; his left hand gently but firmly grasped the back of her neck, preventing her from turning around.

"You trust me... remember..." he chided. "Almost finished..."

"But...but wait... I..." Edwina continued to push against his hand trying to look over her shoulder again. The firmness of his grip only increased on her back and she froze as she felt what could only be the point of a knife blade pressing into the fabric over the right side of her ribcage.   "You   must... remain... absolutely still," he warned, "if you move... I'll hurt you and neither one of us wants that Eddy."

She stopped struggling and held her breath.

191

There was a muted pop; the sound of a seam being pried open. A few more pops, a few more precise slits with the tip of the jackknife along the seam on the right side; the process was immediately repeated on the left. Edwina felt the corset begin to loosen... soften. Miraculously, the rigidity was vanishing from the sides of the garment. His fingers slipped briefly, lightly under the bottom edge of the corset, as if to check the distance and tightness between flesh and fabric. She trembled at his touch though a smile, albeit a rather embarrassed one, returned to her face. She took breath - a deep one. Her smile widened in relief as she filled her lungs with the cool night air. Dear God, she could breathe freely again.

"Well, now that wasn't so bad was it?" Holmes murmured as his fingers, quick and nimble, re-laced her corset and fastened the back of her gown. As he stepped back, she found she could once more turn and move about. She took her wrap which he held out to her and slowly pulled it on, feeling extremely foolish and more than a little disappointed.

"No," she admitted, painfully aware that her cheeks were burning, "not so bad. Thank you." She kept her eyes fixed on the ground - not wanting him to see her shame.

Holmes was quiet for a moment and then shrugged. He reached out and took her hand, gently pressing several whalebone stays into her palm. There was an odd light in his eyes... more than a little kind... sympathetic even.

"Your girl can easily sew these back in if necessary."

He paused a moment, as if searching for something else to say. She wouldn't look at him and he wondered why it bothered him so much.

"I'm sorry Eddy, I seem to have disappointed you," he added simply.

Although acutely mortified, she forced herself to look up and meet his gaze.

"No... I'm so grateful," she said quickly as she pocketed the stays, "it's just..."

The words died in her throat. How on earth could she possibly explain without appearing a complete fool? She bit her lip and then forced a smile, peering up at him. Perhaps a bit of humor would help smooth over the awkwardness of the situation.

"That's the second time Holmes, that you've had your hands on my corset." She said it with as much confidence and levity as she could muster.

Surprise flickered in his eyes and then he began to laugh. He shook his head and grinned, eyes dark with reflection.

"Well my dear Miss Schraeder, you know what they say?" he remarked with a sly grin and arch of his brow. He studied her expression; she really did have a lovely smile.

Edwina shook her head not sure where he was going but her smile remained.

"Third time's lucky," he announced. "Come along then. We'd best return before tongues start to wag." He held out his arm and nodded back towards the house, where the other guests had started to gather.

Edwina smiled secretly up at him and permitted herself to laugh, the tension of the moment broken. She took his offered arm and allowed him to lead her back towards the table thinking, one could only hope.

»»««

THE LOCKED ROOM - MURDER OR MISADVENTURE?

The small bell rang once more summoning them all back to the table. Lady Montague stood by her seat, beaming happily, watching as her guests drifted back in to reclaim their seats. All the while the serving staff slipped in and out amongst them ghostlike, serving champagne and sweets. As she watched, her heart swelled with pride. Another success to be sure... somewhat livelier than she had expected, but a success all the same. Her dear Mrs. Beeton would have approved. For one last time, she rang the bell and as everyone finally settled in, the assemblage lapsed into silence.

"And now as promised, Mr. Holmes will share one of his splendid adventures with us... perhaps one not yet published by the good Doctor ... though I thoroughly enjoyed the one about the lynx."

The table erupted with vigorous applause. Edwina choked back a laugh as she detected the briefest flash of exasperation on the Detective's face. It lasted only a moment as Holmes nodded briefly in acknowledgment at the accolade and smiled though his gaze seemed to fix briefly but pointedly, on the Doctor. Leaning back in his chair, he cleared his throat and began, steepling his fingers under his chin as he spoke.

"Tonight, instead of one of my esteemed colleague's yarns, I shall relay to you the curious facts of an incident that occurred some eight years past – prior to our acquaintance. It so happened that one summer I was down in the area of Eastbourne, near Beachy Head on the Downs, inspecting some property that would be suitable for bees, when the local constabulary sought my counsel. At the time, I was not so fully engaged in the profession, a few minor cases here and there. My predilection was still focused towards academia. I freely admit I was disinclined at first to accept their petition for assistance until I heard the odd particulars of the case. With her Ladyship's kind permission, I will lay them before you and let you decide."

All leaned forward eagerly, except for the Colonel, whose attention once more seemed focused on Edwina.

"A young couple, Mr. and Mrs. X we shall call them, newlyweds on their honeymoon in fact, had travelled to Brighton seeking the pleasures of the seaside and of course each other's company." A small titter of laughter rippled around the table - a few of the ladies lifted their fans to hide their flushed cheeks. Holmes smiled as patiently as he could, waiting for their full attention and then continued.

"Mr. X was a practical man. A bank clerk by trade, therefore not particularly wealthy. Still, he desired to give his bride a lovely trip -- the best he could provide. To that end, he booked their accommodations at Wickham Shore, a small hotel that had, to be quite frank, seen better days. To call it "shabby" would not be an exaggeration. Still, one could say it had a certain charm about it. The proprietor was a hospitable fellow. It sat directly on the beach quite near the bathing machines and most importantly, was within Mr. X's means. A large portion of the property's charm was a result of the thick evening and morning fog which blanketed the coast daily. When the fog rolled in, the hotel virtually vanished. Mrs. X, several years younger than her husband and of a more excitable nature, was by all accounts caught up in the "romance" of the fog. To that end she insisted, when they were initially given landside rooms, they be exchanged for ones that faced out to the ocean. The proprietor, though initially welcoming, balked and attempted to dissuade his guests without elaborating on the details. Mr. X, wed for less than two days, had already learned a valuable lesson and persisted lest he incur the displeasure of his lovely but histrionic wife. The proprietor finally agreed with a fair amount of trepidation. The oceanside rooms were considerably damp, the floors warped by the ocean mists, the steam heating notoriously unreliable. Still, if the guests insist."

At this point, Holmes paused in his narrative noting that most of the guests were thoroughly engrossed, including Edwina, who was diligently scribbling cryptic notes on the back of the place cards. Holmes took a leisurely sip of champagne and continued.

"The only saving grace was the windows had been repaired and were now tight; the drafts were eliminated; the damp was not. There was also the question of the rats who seemed to enjoy the oceanside ambiance and the romance of the fog almost as much as Mrs. X. The rats were a problem; a very visible one. The proprietor was a practical man and not wanting to risk losing his only customers of the season, he did what a practical man would do, he called in the local exterminator. The exterminator was a serious young man, dedicated in his work. He kept up with the latest inventions in the field of rodenticide and, in fact, had just returned from America, but, I digress. He made his inspection and discovered that the rats had taken a fancy to assembling in the space between the floorboards. They had a particular liking to the area just over the pantry which was on the ocean side of the hotel. Arriving past midnight so as not to disturb the guests, he plied his trade and set out the bait. Two days later, the proprietor received an irate visit from Mr. X whose wife was in hysterics after having seen two rats on the ledge just outside their window. The rats were clearly sick, but not dead; a common fault of rodenticides. Increasingly exasperated by his guests (the wife had in one way or another managed to antagonize the small staff), the proprietor once more called in the exterminator. He revisited the site once again under cover of darkness, determined not to fail.

The next day, Mr. and Mrs. X failed to come down for breakfast. Not unusual for a newlywed couple to sleep in ... they had in fact done just that the previous day; the kitchen and dining room staff were greatly relieved. The chamber maid avoided the room as the Do Not Disturb sign remained in place, hanging from the doorknob. The circumstance was repeated again at dinner - the Do Not Disturb sign still swung from the door. They all rejoiced at their good fortune. The next day, when the chambermaid once more approached the room with the intention of changing the bed linen, she was again greeted by the Do Not Disturb sign. It irritated her greatly, but it didn't strike her as peculiar until she noticed Mr. X's black wingtips still sitting just outside the door exactly where she had returned them two days earlier after polishing. Alarmed, she went around to the French doors that faced the ocean and tried to peer in but the heavy curtains were drawn. She fetched the proprietor, who was unable to open the door, being locked from the inside as were all the windows. Fearing the worst, he broke a pane out with a rock and pulled open the door. The air that wafted out was foul, cold and damp. He entered, stepping gingerly over several dead rats. One look was all it took - he reemerged white as a sheet and immediately called the constabulary who then contacted me. Upon entering, I found that the rats were not the only ones who had met their demise. Mr. and Mrs. X lay on their marriage bed, locked together in an embrace, clearly in the midst of one last night of wedded bliss. There were no obvious signs of trauma."

A murmur of bewildered horror rippled across the table as the guests began to whisper to each other. Holmes allowed them to chat for a moment or two and then cleared his throat. He took out his pocket watch and noted the time.

"I have laid out the details I was first presented with, so I leave it for you to decide: Murder or Death by Misadventure and the means by which death occurred. Time allotted is thirty minutes; only logical queries will be entertained. Off you go."

The table erupted in a cacophony of noise as small groups of men broke off, arguing vehemently in favour of murder or murder-suicide. The favourite theories by far were: murder by strangulation (Mr. X on Mrs. X), Mr. X's subsequent suicide by rat poison, double suicide by rat poison or the astonishingly improbable, simultaneous throttling. This one elicited a hearty chuckle from Holmes. The ladies, for the most part, observed looking perplexed, horrified or equal parts thereof; the exception was Edwina who by now had filled several of the place cards with notes and questions. At the thirty-minute mark, Holmes announced the time and sat back waiting. He listened with as much good humour as he could feign as the guests put forth their often ridiculous theories; the one where the entire hotel staff had crept in and suffocated the couple in their sleep was particularly amusing, especially considering the bed chamber door was still locked from the inside, key firmly in the lock. One by one he listened to them all until only Edwina was left (the Doctor and Miss Morstan had decided not to participate already having some knowledge of the outcome). She studied her notes briefly and then smiled up at him with great assurance and a twinkle in her eyes.

"I don't believe it was murder at all... Death by Misadventure..."

Holmes arched his brow and smiled slyly. "Explain..."

She paused, an intense look of concentration clouding her face and then instead of explaining proceeded to ask several questions:

"Were the dead rats inside or outside?"

"Both."

The answer seemed to puzzle her for a moment but after scanning her notes, she continued.

"Was the room warm or cold on the inside?"

"Bitterly cold... and damp."

Again, she seemed perplexed. "You mentioned that the steam heater was unreliable - was it warm or cold upon entering the room?"

"Ice cold to the touch."

Again, it seemed not to be the answer she had expected. Holmes expression grew somewhat sympathetic and as an afterthought he added: "But there was a small puddle of condensation at the base of the heater - and the radiator itself was damp to the touch."

"So, the heater must have come on sometime during the two days," she mused.

"Undoubtedly."

Edwina narrowed her eyes in suspicion. "You described the floor as warped; how large were the cracks between the floorboards?"

"Some large enough to insert a guinea others with no gap at all."

Once again, she lapsed into silence, her head bowed slightly, lips drawn tightly with concentration as she reviewed her notes. The silence was longer this time and for a moment, a look of disappointment flickered across Holmes' face. Had she lost the thread? When she'd been so close? It would be most unfortunate...

"Tell me," she asked, her voice wavering with uncertainty, "when the bodies were examined, what was the condition of the stomach? Was it inflamed. Any signs of poison?"

"No inflammation and no foreign substances either."

The response did little to lift her spirits – she looked crestfallen, and a low murmur of disappointment went around the table. Several of the guests shook their heads in commiseration for though they hadn't a clue as to the answer themselves, it seemed obvious that she had made a wrong turn somewhere. But Edwina was undaunted, in fact, the Detective's answer seemed to re-vitalize her spirit. She lifted her head, an expression of gleeful cunning lighting her eyes as she leaned forward, elbows now propped on the table in a most unladylike manner.

"And what was the condition of the lungs?"

Holmes' lips curled into a slow smile of approval.

"Red and greatly inflamed."

"And the poison used on the rats - two types?" Her questions were coming faster now, increasing in speed along with her confidence. She was half out of her chair, hovering at the edge of the table as she had been before when she had confronted the Colonel. But there was no anger this time, only the thrill and excitement of discovery. She had regained the scent. Holmes nodded encouragingly, it was a feeling he well understood; the sight of her untangling the skein, following the thread to its point of origin was exhilarating ... captivating.

"Yes, two kinds. Two attempts. The first rather unsuccessful, arsenic pellets, the dosage was too small. The second, well as I said, the exterminator was always looking to improve his skills. He tried out a new rodenticide, hydrocyanic acid, which he pumped into the pantry...which was oceanside and..."

"...under Mr. & Mrs. X's room..." Edwina exclaimed, finishing his sentence, suddenly on her feet, her face feverish with a mixture of delight, horror, and elation. "Dear God, the cracks in the floorboards! They were tight and closed when it was cold but the moment the steam heat came on, they expanded drawing the gas up into the room. And the new windows, they were tight also; no drafts so none of the gas could dissipate. But why didn't they get up Holmes? It would have taken some time. There would have been an odour. There would have been headaches, perhaps dizziness. I don't understand, why didn't they leave?"

Her words, which had initially tumbled out at lightning speed, slowly trailed off. She now appeared exhausted ... almost drained... a feeling with which he was also well acquainted.

Holmes remained silent for a moment, eyes brooding and veiled as he chose his words.

"I've often said that all emotions are dangerous, love being the most dangerous of all. I put forth this case as a prime example. The room was bitterly cold; once again - the heater was unreliable. The windows, newly repaired, were shut tight against the damp and cold of the fog which Mrs. X so loved. The seal was tight. No air could enter, nor could it escape. As to why Mr. and Mrs. X made no attempt to escape, one only has to look at the details for an explanation. Married for less than three days, they were clearly still in the full bloom of their passion for each other. They were found locked in each other's arms. They had complained of the heating before, they knew full well the heater was unreliable. I propose that they decided to make the best of the situation and attempted to raise their bodily temperatures in a way that would also give them pleasure. By the time they noticed, if they noticed, it would have been too late. Love is a distraction, in their case, a lethal one."

The thrill and excitement the guests experienced at having the case solved right before their very eyes faded quickly; Holmes' words cast a pall over the gathering. Lady Montague, not overly fond of focusing on such serious matters such as one's mortality, found herself in the uncomfortable position of having her sprightly little soiree transformed into a sullen, morose wake. She had in fact seen happier faces at a requiem, corpse included. Dear Holmes, it was always a risk when she gave him a platform. She was quite fond of the man - all his quirks included but sometimes she wondered why she even invited him. Of course, she knew she always would because ultimately, it was his eccentricity, acerbic wit and the controversy he often provoked that made her gatherings so memorable. Nevertheless, it was time to reclaim the evening and end it on the right note. So, rising to her feet once more, she put on her brightest smile, instructed her staff to serve one more round of champagne and sweets and led them all in a closing toast.

"To my honoured guests... gracious friends old and new..."

"To friends old and new... hear hear..."

»»««

The carriage door swung open and with a slight grunt, Watson climbed inside. He settled onto the seat and glanced to the sleeping man across from him; he frowned and cleared his throat to announce his presence. The carriage slowly moved off, falling in line behind a long queue of carriages as they wound their way down the lane heading for the street. Behind them, the lights of Bexley Manor began to fade, winking out one by one. Watson cleared his throat again.

"I heard you the first time," Holmes said with some weariness from the darkened corner of the cab.

"Well, I did as you asked, delivered it. I have an answer."

Holmes' eyes opened and he nodded, eyes opaque with reflection.

"I trust you were discreet." Reaching out, he took the note which was folded over in tight thirds. He held onto it but did not open it, his fingers moving slowly over the creases.

"Of course," said John with a hint of exasperation, "but I don't really see how it matters. You two were thick as thieves all evening. I don't think anyone would be surprised if ..."

"Surprised?" Holmes frowned slightly, an odd light in his eyes. "Once again Doctor, you've made a leap without the data. Discretion is necessary when one is being observed, especially when the intentions of the observer are unclear."

"Observed?" Watson seemed puzzled at first but as comprehension sank in, he rolled his eyes unconvinced. "Oh, I presume you are talking about the Colonel. Well, no mystery there. Interesting fellow though," continued Watson. "While I was waiting for her response, I took the liberty of sniffing about... discreetly of course. He is a graduate of Oxford and Eton and was decorated for bravery on the battlefield. He comes from fine stock Holmes. His father served as Minister to Persia some years back. Additionally, he is a member in good standing of the East India United Service Club. No small feat. It took several attempts before my application was accepted."

Holmes shrugged, barely able to contain his disdain.

"And this has bearing on what exactly?"

"With all due respect Holmes, I think you have misjudged his character, allowed personal prejudices to color your perception. You are quite correct that the Colonel is interested in Miss Schraeder, but his intentions appear honourable. I overheard him speaking with Lady Montague. He presented her with letters of introduction for Edwina. He has the blessing of her father. It appears Pennington is preparing to marry her off. Nothing sinister in that, just

198

a man looking to provide for his daughter. After all, she is fast approaching the age where these things become more difficult to achieve. Presumably the thought of having another unmarried woman in the house has spurred him to action. She could do far worse"

Holmes was quiet for a moment and then shook his head, his mouth curling contemptuously.

"It is unconscionable Watson, to be denied the freedom to choose one's path."

"According to the law Holmes, she cannot choose ... she hasn't the right by law."

"Then the law is wrong," growled Holmes, interrupting him, his face tight with aggravation.

Watson was taken aback. He and Holmes had often debated the conventions of society including the question of women's suffrage, but it had always been an academic argument. This however struck him as personal; the intensity of his reaction in itself was cause enough to give him pause.

Perhaps regretting his momentary lapse of control, Holmes attempted to rectify the situation. The icy mask of logic that Watson was accustomed to, once more lowered into place.

"You say you see nothing sinister... perhaps. But I say to you Doctor, consider how did this come about? As you mentioned earlier, the Colonel is a man of exceptional quality and breeding, a family of exceptional standing, certainly he would be no stranger to these circles. Pennington has some wealth, but his family never had the status to lift him out of what he is and always will be, a tradesman. A successful one, but a tradesman all the same. Their circles should never have intersected, but how did they? How is it that he knows Pennington - a man who has no military background... an entirely different social class? What or who is their connection? There must be one...for by all rights, they should never have breathed the same air."

A look of astonishment clouded Watson's face.

"By God Holmes, I never thought of it that way," he conceded. He sat back in his seat, staring absently out the window as the carriage pulled to a stop in front of Baker Street. "But how will we find out? What shall we do?"

Holmes began to laugh. "We, that is you, my dear fellow, will collect as much data as you can on the Colonel. Shouldn't be too difficult. Do what you do best Watson – socialize, mingle, play cards."

"I don't understand."

"You said it yourself, the Colonel is a member in good standing of the East India United Service Club as you are, so that is where you are going. Take the cab, I shall get another when I am ready," he announced as he quickly climbed down from the carriage.

"Tonight? Now? I hadn't planned on it," Watson protested, his brow furrowed in irritation.

"Splendid! Nothing to interfere with it then. Off you go."

Watson leaned out of the window, a look of bewilderment on his face. "But, I assumed you had made some kind of arrangement to meet..."

Holmes flashed a smile and paused, glancing up at the night sky. Up above, the moon was still a bright sliver in the sky. "I have, but not just yet. Too much light at present. Perhaps another hour... new moon is on the way."

"But you didn't even look at the note," argued Watson, "it is possible you haven't received the answer you expect." He glanced at his pocket watch, nearly half past 12:00. How much longer would he wait then?

Holmes began to laugh and with a shake of his head, withdrew the note from his pocket. Without a word, he carefully unfolded it and held it up for Watson to see. The message was succinct and perfectly clear.

"Delighted," was all it said.

"This may not be wise Holmes," warned Watson, still leaning out the window as the carriage began to roll away. Holmes only shrugged and lifted his hand in farewell.

"Good hunting, Watson," was all he said and then vanished up the stairs to Baker Street.

CHAPTER 6

An Adventure Under The Stars

Edwina lay in the darkness, staring out through the small gap in the curtains on the French doors that looked out onto the terrace. She waited, fingers curled around the edge of the quilt, listening as Hanna's footsteps receded down the hall. She thought the girl would never leave, prattling on endlessly about how lovely the ladies and gentlemen had looked, the elegant table settings and the grand array of refreshments offered. And if that wasn't annoying enough, she continued chattering about how fortunate Edwina was and how she must be happy as a lark that the Colonel had taken an interest in her. Edwina almost, almost told her how she really felt about the Colonel but thought better of it. It wouldn't be prudent to risk offending her benefactress Lady Montague, and though she trusted Hanna, she had some misgivings about how private her conversations with the girl would remain. Servant quarters were rife with rumours and gossip. All it would take would be one careless slip and she might end up at St. Mary's after all despite Mr. Holmes kind intervention. So, she held her tongue and managed a feeble smile, saying only that it was best not to plan too far ahead as things often had a way of turning out exactly the opposite of what one expected. That is what she said, not what she thought, for she would sooner throw herself into the Thames than be attached to the Colonel; or better yet, throw him in the Thames. Finally, when it seemed she could bear it no more, Hanna seemed to run out of energy and small talk. After turning out the lamps and checking that all was secure, she bid her mistress good night, quietly exiting the room. To Edwina, it seemed to take forever for the girl to reach her quarters just a few doors down. Finally, the sound of the latch being drawn could be heard followed by the soft click of the door closing. Edwina threw back the covers and sprang from the bed. Fearing someone would see, she left the lamps turned off and pulled open the curtains to allow what little moonlight remained to filter in. Once her eyes had adjusted to the gloom, she quickly began to gather her clothes, reminding herself that his note had urged her to dress comfortably and for warmth. No problem there she thought, grinning as she tossed the loathsome corset to the side. She was slightly disappointed to find that her favourite pair of jodhpurs were still out for mending. Deciding to make the best of the situation, she pulled on grey wool stockings, black lace-up ankle boots, her grey walking skirt (opting for only three of the customary seven petticoats). She topped it off with a sensible white blouse and her black riding jacket. Once she had finished dressing, she glanced briefly in the mirror and started to unpin the French braid that Hanna had worked so diligently on. It was lovely, and she'd received many compliments on it, including an unexpected one from Holmes, but it was now giving her a headache. Besides, he had stressed dressing for warmth and she could think of no easier way to keep her neck warm from the damp night than to loosen her hair. She reached for her cloak, ready to head out the door, and then paused, her eyes settling on the cloisonné necklace that she had worn earlier. Edwina picked it up, her brow furrowed in thought. She didn't consider herself particularly vain and she was well aware that it wasn't very practical, but she felt drawn, almost compelled to wear it. He'd noticed it earlier – remarked on how unusual it was, complimenting her quietly when they were away from prying eyes. She put it on fastening it around her throat and smiled, remember the warm glow that filled her when he praised her. Holmes was often generous with his praise, quick to laud her cleverness or sharp wit. But this had been different, this time he had noticed her not so much for her intellect but as a woman and that was a very lovely feeling indeed. But she had no time to daydream for in the distance, she could hear the bell of the Great Clock in Westminster tolling the hour of one. If she didn't hurry she would be late. She fastened her cloak and hurried out the door, heading quickly and quietly across the lawn. She skirted the edge of the pond, her sights set on the ivy-covered wall that lay behind the follies. Pausing briefly to get her bearings, she withdrew his note, peering at the directions in the dim light. As wisps of mist wafted up from the pond, she tightened her cloak and adjusted her course, hurrying quickly past the crumbling tower folly towards the wall. Her eyes scanned the expanse of the overgrown wall searching for the hidden moon gate.

»»«««

Archibald Dolan blew on his hands, stamping his feet against the cold as he waited by the hansom, his cheeks reddened by the brisk night air. Damnation he should have worn his heavier coat. But in truth, neither man had expected to be out so late.

"Bloody hell, it's a right cold one tonight. A cup of me gran's broth would set me right."

Jenkins his partner, an older man with large muttonchop whiskers, laughed a bit and withdrew a whiskey flask from inside of his overcoat. He took a large swig and then offered it to him.

"Well, I can't help you with broth, but this will do the trick."

The younger man hesitated and glanced uncertainly across the street and down the block towards the light in 221B. He shook his head, didn't seem right to him, not while they were on the job.

"Go on, don't be such a prat," grumbled the older man as he took another swig from the flask. "He ain't about to leave without us seeing him."

"I don't know," hedged the younger man. He scratched the back of his neck where his freshly shorn hair was itching. "Doesn't seem we should, what if the Inspector..."

Jenkins snorted out loud once more taking a draught from the flask, his cheeks also ruddy but for different reasons.

"Well, he ain't here is he? Warm in his bed while we're out here freezin our arse following this toff." He held out the flask once more. "Come on, get your blood jumpin."

"Well, maybe just a nip," he sighed and with a guilty smile, took the flask and took a deep gulp. His veins flooded with liquid fire.

Abruptly, the light in 221B went out; both men were instantly on alert. The outer door swung open and much to their surprise, Holmes emerged and stood at the curb hailing a hansom. Gone were the formal clothes he had arrived in, replaced by dark, sensible clothing.

"Now where's he off to now? Right busy bee he is tonight." Jenkins narrowed his eyes, watching suspiciously.

Moments later, a hansom pulled to the curb and Holmes vanished inside. Both men seemed caught off guard for a moment. Jenkins was the first to recover. He reached out and quickly took back his flask and then after a quick nip, climbed into the hansom. He looked quizzically at his young partner, who remained on the sidewalk seemingly frozen. Irritated, he reached out and smacked Dolan only once but soundly on the side of the head.

"Come on man, look lively. Ain't going to wait for us to catch up. We lose him, Lestrade, he'll have our hides."

Shaken from his daze, the younger man watched the hansom disappear up the street in the swirling mists and then scrambled inside. Moments later they headed off after the hansom, disappearing into the thickening fog as well.

»»«««

"Careful, one misstep and you'll break your neck and all our plans will have been for naught," Holmes' voice, nonchalant and slightly amused, drifted up from the darkness.

Edwina froze mere inches from the top of the wall and twisted her neck, peering back and down over her shoulder. She'd given up on waiting for him. On finding the moon gate locked, she decided to climb the wall, thinking surely, he was waiting on the other side.

"Holmes!" she exclaimed, clinging tightly to the vines, "What the devil! How long have you been here?"

"Long enough."

"I called out to you several times."

"Yes, I heard."

She readjusted her grip and compressed her lips, a slow flush of irritation spreading across her face.

"What? And you said nothing! Why?"

He grinned up at her and shrugged. He looked marginally apologetic.

203

"I suppose I was curious to see what you would do."

She was momentarily speechless and then uttered a low growl of expletives in Russian.   He began to laugh. Perhaps she had forgotten he spoke Russian ... maybe not.

"You have a cruel streak Holmes. It's quite unbecoming." She clung to the wall, her cheeks crimson, eyes fiery and accusing.

"So I've been told," he agreed with a smile. "Coming down?"

"No," she snorted and then continued to climb up towards the top of the wall.

Remarkable; such defiance and obstinacy from any other woman would seem disrespectful even spiteful.   In Edwina, it only spoke of her fierce independence and strength of character. It was utterly endearing. Whatever lay ahead for her, Holmes hoped fervently, it would not alter her spirit.

She had reached the top of the wall now where she perched somewhat like Humpty Dumpty, legs dangling over the side.

"How did you get in?" she asked, her voice a little less sharp than before. "The gate is locked." She peered closely at him. Perhaps he had climbed over as well though there was not a speck of soil on him.

A slight smile curled his mouth as he reached into his frock coat. He withdrew a large skeleton key and dangled it for her to see.

"Bloody hell!" she swore under her breath and then swiveled around on top of the wall to where she could look out towards the street. Giving up, Holmes unlocked the gate and moved through to the other side, relocking it behind him.

"Well, come along then, we're losing time," he chided, arms folded, impatient grin - eyes fixed on her. "Do you require assistance?"

Edwina gave no response other than a scowl. Repositioning her hands, she surveyed the wall looking for handholds. The flutter of unease in her stomach continued to grow.   The vines were sparse on this side and much farther apart. She glanced back down at Holmes. He had lit a cigarette now, a smug little smile on his face as he waited and watched. Her irritation surged once more.   She'd be damned if she was going to ask him for help now; she already looked like a fool.   Pushing back her anxiety, she abruptly climbed down onto the face of the wall, stretching to grasp onto the vines. She began to descend slowly. Damned petticoats...with every movement she made, her boots caught in the fabric of the hem. She paused for a moment clinging to the vines, eyes fixed forward on the wall as she planned her next move.

"Well?"

"A moment," she snapped, trying to conceal the anxiety in her voice. She looked down; she was still a good distance away from the ground. Too far to jump down without risking possible injury. Christ, she had made a mess of it for sure. It was not exactly how she had imagined the start to their adventure.

Holmes stepped back to assess the situation and nodded sagely.

"Stuck then? Common problem. Easier to climb up than down. Has to do with perception. Just like Mrs. Hudson's tabby, climbed to the top of the Oak at Baker and then couldn't climb down. Yowled incessantly for days...bloody nuisance."

Edwina bristled, setting her jaw squarely.

"I'm not stuck... just..." Her words trailed off. She wasn't fooling anyone least of all herself.

"And did I not say sensible clothing.? Seems to me if you had followed my counsel you would not..."

"Damn it Holmes, you're not helping," she cried, venting her frustration. Now was not the time for a lecture.

There was a moment of silence. Edwina closed her eyes focusing on the problem at hand. Perhaps if she tried to turn around and climb down facing forward... At least if she lost her footing and fell, she could at least see where she was heading and hopefully adjust her landing.

Vines rustled and scraped against the wall beneath her, breaking her concentration. She glanced down, startled to discover that Holmes, having shed his coat and jacket, was climbing steadily up the wall underneath her.

"What are you doing?" she cried. This time, there was no mistaking the alarm in her voice. If she fell now she'd take him down as well.

"Be still Eddy," he advised calmly. Moments later, he was behind her, reaching around, holding securely onto the vines, his body pressing tightly against hers. His breath was a warm tickle on the nape of her neck and she allowed herself to smile for a moment enjoying his closeness despite the awkwardness of her predicament.

"Do exactly as I say... lean back against me but continue to hold on... only move when I do."

She nodded that she understood and followed suit, leaning back her cheeks flushing with a mixture of embarrassment and excitement. Dear God, he must think her a complete idiot.

"I almost had it Holmes. Another moment is all I needed. I... I... don't really need you to rescue me," she muttered in protest, but her voice lacked conviction.

His left arm wrapped tightly around her waist, his chin lightly brushing against the back of her head.

"Of course not," he soothed, "just think of it as speeding up the process."

As they began their descent, Edwina felt her tension begin to fade. His arm remained secure around her waist, his grip never once slackening. It was the safest she had felt in a long time. It was obvious he was no stranger to climbing. This was a man she could trust implicitly.

In no time at all they were down on the ground. Edwina breathed a sigh of relief, watching as he brushed off his sleeves and then pulled on his jacket.

"Thank you, Holmes." She handed him his coat, her smile awkward and embarrassed but grateful nonetheless. Holmes shrugged, a playful twinkle in his eyes.

"Well, unlike the cat, I could scarcely leave you there."

Dismay flickered across her face.

"What happened to the tabby?" she asked suspiciously.

He began to laugh and shook his head. "She came down on her own eventually. Mrs. Hudson rewarded her stupidity with a large bowl of cream and sardines. Feline wiles never cease to amaze me."

Edwina laughed and moved a little closer. "I don't like sardines."

"Definitely in your favour," he replied with a quick grin and then with a nod towards the waiting hansom, he offered his arm. "Come along Eddy, we've delayed long enough."

Only too happy to oblige, she took his arm and fell into step beside him as they carefully made their way through the thickening fog.

She glanced up at him as they walked along, her eyes full of curiosity. There was so much she didn't know about this man.

"Have you climbed much then? It seems to me you have experience; with tandem in particular."

He arched his brow, a little surprised at the question and the knowledge it hinted at.

"You are familiar with tandem rappelling techniques?"

She smiled and shook her head. "Not personally, but several of mother's friends climbed. I used to marvel at all their gear; the ropes and pulleys, the cleats for the ice. It was all so very exciting. They offered to teach me and I was eager to learn, but Mother wouldn't allow it. She was usually so agreeable, but I suppose because of what happened with Julian she was afraid. She didn't like for me to venture too far. So off they went to climb the Weisshorn without me." A shadow flickered across her face momentarily and then she continued, her eyes growing more solemn. "Two of the men didn't return. They were tethered to each other and one fell into a crevasse and took his partner with him. The others, well there was nothing they could do. I suppose they are still up there somewhere. Mother was sad for a very long time after that – couldn't bear to look at the mountains. We started spending more time in Vienna then and Paris." Her eyes clouded at the memory and as she spoke, her hand crept to the necklace about her neck, fingers sliding absently along the beads.

Holmes remained silent, eyes dark with reflection as they followed the movement of her hand. The more he learned of her childhood, the more he understood the need for her to always have something of her mother's near. First the lapel watch and now the cloisonné necklace. That necklace. What a curious thing it was. Clearly a piece of costume jewelry, not particularly striking, common, and yet something about it made him want to take a closer look.

They had reached the hansom cab that waited at the curb. Edwina had fallen silent as he helped her in, speaking only to instruct the driver to head for the West India Docks. Holmes arched his brow, his interest piqued. She hadn't given an exact address, just the West India Docks. The Docks, being very near to Limehouse, seemed to him an odd choice for the warehouse of a respected tradesman; especially a supposedly legitimate one.

"No address then?" he queried, leaning back in his seat studying her expression to see what he could glean from it.

206

Edwina blushed a bit, a little embarrassed at her carelessness.

"I'm afraid I didn't take note of it. Last time I was here with father, he was less than pleased that I had come along. Not to worry, I'll know it when I see it Holmes. There was a tavern not far from it. An odd, ramshackle little place. Remarkably seedy. I kept teasing Father that we should go in and have a dram. He was appalled at the suggestion."

"The Folly?" Holmes' face settled into a frown. "This was during the day I presume." His contempt for Pennington increased with this revelation. No doubt she had badgered him into allowing her to tag along. She was headstrong to be sure, but the man was spineless. The Docks and the surrounding areas of Whitechapel and Limehouse were a maze of cheap warehouses and decrepit tenements. It was figuratively and literally, in times of high rains, the conduit through which London's effluent flowed on its way to the Thames. The inhabitants didn't care much for strangers; you were barely tolerated if you were there to do business. Anything and everything could be bought and sold there; if they didn't have it, it could be procured at the right price. No place for an honest man; certainly no place for a woman, even a resilient one, especially when in the company of a man who was sure to tuck his tail and run at the first hint of trouble.

"Was he embarrassed then, the Doctor, when you came to his rescue?"

The words, the first she had spoken in quite some time, surprised him. It took a moment for him to realize that she was referring to their previous conversation about climbing. She had turned away from the window, perhaps bored with not being able to see very much in the fog. Her attention was fixed on him - her tone was inquisitive...searching.

Holmes met her gaze soberly, choosing his words. This was not a subject he cared to discuss at any great length.

"Watson has more sense. At times, he can barely climb the stairs let alone anything else." His voice was clipped, a clear signal that he wished to discuss the matter no further.

Edwina's face registered surprise for even though she had her suspicions from the beginning that it was someone else other than the Doctor, the bitterness with which he delivered the words caught her off guard.

"Oh, I see," she murmured, her brow furrowed in thought. She looked up, a curious but empathetic expression in her eyes.

"A woman then? A.... sweetheart?" she offered tentatively. Her mind drifted back to their earlier meeting at Baker Street and her eyes sparked to life with realization. "The one who gave you the dressing gown," she exclaimed, triumphant that she had pieced it together, ignoring the signs this was not a topic to be discussed.

For a moment, he said nothing at all. His eyes narrowed and fixed on hers with an abrupt iciness that made her flinch.

"A woman, yes," he hissed, "as for the other word, I contend there is nothing in that word that is applicable. She is neither the first and lacks the second."

The disdain and vitriol in his voice were almost as unsettling as the words themselves. Edwina sank back against the seat mortified, unable to meet his gaze. She had gone too far.

"Forgive me," she whispered after a moment. "I just assumed... I... it seems such an intimate gift... I..." Her voice trailed off, the explanation unfinished. She turned away sick with remorse, unable to meet his gaze. Perhaps it was best to say no more.

Whether it was the sincerity of her words or that he could see she was truly distressed, Holmes' demeanour began to thaw. Losing his temper was a mistake, there was too much at stake to allow himself to be sidetracked. Perhaps a direct approach would close the issue.

"Apology unnecessary and yes, you are correct, it was a gift."

"You need not explain... please," she whispered, mortified at having raised such an obviously loathsome and perhaps painful subject.

"We were lovers on occasion," he continued, his voice detached - expression impassive as if he were reciting from a scientific text. "It was mere convenience for both us, nothing more. It ran its course. Now, seeing as how I've answered your questions, I expect there will be no more." With a slight shrug, he then took out his pocket watch and noted the time, the discussion closed. "Tell me about this warehouse then ... the particulars. I'd very much like to hear," he broke off, his face settling into a frown. He leaned forward to look more closely into her face. She was distressed, her eyes, what he could see of them, moist and threatening tears. She kept her eyes averted. He compressed his lips, lost in thought for a moment and then reached out gently pressing her hand.

"I know my words seem harsh - cold even, but as a man of logic and science Eddy, I cannot allow myself the luxury of anything else, especially sentiment."

Edwina lifted her gaze to his and as he spoke, she felt herself overcome with a such a surge of tenderness and compassion that it took every ounce of willpower for her not to throw her arms around him. If only she could make him see, convince him, that it didn't have to be this way. Sentiment, the love and affection he so maligned and distrusted, could co-exist with logic and reason, thrive even, with the right partner. But she held her tongue and only managed a feeble nod of her head, struggling to contain her emotions which threatened to spill over at any moment.

She inhaled, gathering her ragged nerves and forced a smile though the waver in her voice betrayed her anguish.

"And, what of friendship Holmes? Is there room in your world for that?"

His expression grew reflective, somber at the question and then he smiled with unexpected warmth and some resignation.

"Ahh, that is a battle I lost long ago I'm afraid. The good Doctor taught me the value of it, or more precisely, corrupted my beliefs. It is a weakness I have learned to accept and allow with a select few. And yes Eddy, you are among the few that I permit myself to call friend."

In that moment, her resolve to be restrained utterly failed. She threw her arms around his neck, her lips on his cheek (she still had some control after all it seemed) tender and sweet.

"You honour me sir... more than I deserve," she whispered. The kiss she bestowed on his cheek itself was swift, more like the flutter of a moth's wing on his skin. Nevertheless, it produced a genuine smile of joy on Holmes' face, despite the hint of unease that stirred in the core of his being. He held her at arm's length and shook his head. She was luminous, and he couldn't deny that he had grown fond of her company.

"Steady, we've an entire night before us. Best to pace ourselves. Who knows what the night will bring," he cautioned, the solemnity of his voice betrayed by a playful wink.

"Bollocks," she sighed with a grin and a roll of her eyes. She settled back in her seat, her anxiety fading, spirits raised by the admission that he did have affection for her after all.

"How will we know when we are close Holmes? I can't make anything out at all." She gazed out the window again trying to discern the shapes of the buildings as they passed by. It was futile; the fog had settled in blanketing the buildings like a shroud.

"We'll be stopping before then. Hansoms won't go all the way to the Docks, especially on a night like this. We'll travel the rest of the way on foot – it'll be easier then. I've brought a lantern. Not to worry. I have some familiarity with the Folly. Once we reach it, I'm sure you'll find your bearings. Now, as we still have a ways to go, tell me about this charming necklace. Delightfully unusual. It caught my eye earlier, but I didn't get a chance to really look at it. Would you be so kind?" He held out his hand, palm open and waited.

"Of course," she said brightly and without a moment's hesitation unhooked it from about her neck, depositing it into his open palm. While Holmes examined it, running his fingers carefully over each bead, she began to relate the tale of how her mother had left it to her – hidden in the trunk of old clothes.

As Holmes listened, his curiosity only increased. Unlike most cloisonné, the beads were rough and uneven in size. A glint of suspicion kindled within. Most unusual. The lack of uniformity, the roughness of the surface which felt almost chalky. Unexpected, even for a cheap necklace. He said nothing however and after a moment, smiled and thanked her having finished his inspection for the time being.

Edwina smiled and held out her hand, expectantly. She was pleasantly surprised when he leaned forward and instead of handing back the necklace, gently draped it about her neck. The sensation of his fingers on her skin as he secured the clasp elicited a contented smile and a shiver of warmth and it seemed to her that they lingered a bit longer than necessary. She cast a quick, furtive glance in his direction, searching his expression for any clues and then continued with her tale.

Shrouded in the fog, a careful distance behind, a second hansom cab continued its stealthy pursuit. Further back, the brass lamps of an elegant brougham gleamed as it also joined the hunt.

»»««

THE DOCKS

Faces and shapes seemed to emerge from within the fog, rising like some hellish vision from one of Blake's paintings. The area bustled with activity; rough looking men delivered and offloaded goods and wares. Those with no work, loitered in the shadows smoking, playing cards and drinking. The air was foul; heavy with smoke from the burning barrels of rubbish that lined the quay and cast a disquieting orange glow. Underneath it all was a rotting stench that hung over the river. Edwina gagged a bit and looked towards Holmes for an explanation.

"Slaughterhouses and other pleasantries."

With a grim fascination, Edwina edged closer to Holmes as they made their way towards the noise and din of The Folly. As they passed, the door flew open; a few drunken sailors stumbled out followed by a gnarled old woman, her grimy face pock-marked and worn. She staggered towards them, reeking of sweat, filth and whiskey. Most of the sailors dispersed, shuffling off down the alley save for one who hovered near the old woman, swaying slightly on his feet as he watched. The crone fixed her watery eyes on Holmes and grinned, revealing rotting teeth and blackened gums. She stuck out her filthy palm. Edwina tried vainly not to show her revulsion reminding herself the world was full of those less fortunate.

"Cor...ain't you a fine un," she cackled gleefully as she sized him up. "Nip round back guv... three penney upright...bring a right smile quicker'n young miss here can member her name."

Holmes choked back a laugh and shook his head as he reached into his pocket for a few coins. Edwina looked on in bewilderment. She didn't quite understand the old woman's words and she had the distinct impression that Holmes would be reluctant to explain.

"I must decline Madame. Here are two shillings for your trouble... buy yourself a meal." He reached out to drop the coins in her palm and then stopped as the drunken sailor, who seemed not so very drunk anymore, straightened up and lurched forward. The man was barrel-chested, thick-necked and slightly less squalid than his companion. He also towered over Holmes by at least three inches.

"I say seven mate, only fair with the time Gran is wasting when she could be earnin. Pay up. then you an your miss, she's right cherry, can be on your way. Not a hair on her pretty head I'll muss... swear. If not, well as I see it, she'd fetch more than Gran here wouldn't she? Once she was trained up

210

proper." The seaman left off, the threat unfinished. He grinned crookedly and spit into his filthy palm which he then offered to Holmes to shake.

Holmes smiled tightly, bitterly and with a brief nod of his head, reached into his pocket and withdrew more coins.

"Fair enough," he said as he dropped them into the man's palm, declining the handshake.

"Good evening," he muttered darkly and then took Edwina by the arm, moving her along quickly - steadily.

The sailor and old woman burst into laughter. They stumbled back inside, eager to celebrate their good fortune and gloat over their victory.

"Keep close... quiet... cover your hair," Holmes urged. They moved swiftly down along the dock, past more burning barrels of rubbish and scraps, where ragged figures gathered and warmed themselves.

"I don't understand ... what just happened?" she whispered, ignoring his counsel. "Why did you pay him?"

Holmes cast a sideways glance at her and chuckled.

"Did you not see his size?"

"I saw he was drunk and not very smart," she protested.

He continued to move her along, all the while keeping a wary eye on the streets. They were getting further away from the commercial area now, the streets dimly lit, lined with weathered warehouses and decrepit tenements. It was nearly deserted save for a single horse drawn cart, manned by four Chinamen in coolie hats who followed along, picking through the rags and scraps that had been discarded on the curb. They chucked what they salvaged into the back of the cart.

"Not as drunk as you think."

"But you're so much more clever."

"Clever enough to know my limits."

Holmes quickened his pace and opened the shutter on the lantern slightly, allowing a thin shaft to illuminate the path before them. They hurried by the Chinamen who barely gave them a glance.

"We could have outsmarted them," Edwina sighed with a shake of her head.

He stopped in the street and turned to face her, his eyes sober and dark.

"We? A risk not worth taking. The stakes were too high."

Edwina gazed up at him, her eyes just as firm, earnest and devoted.

"I wasn't afraid. I have faith in you... in us."

Her words gave him pause and he set the lantern down, his eyes turning to hers. With a hesitant smile, he reached out and gently pushed back a few errant strands of auburn hair that tumbled out from beneath her hood.

"Fear is important Eddy... essential for survival. Always, always believe in yourself first   before all others." His fingers moved to the hood, pulling it closer over her hair, then drifting down to the ribbons which he tied securely into a neat bow.

Edwina's eyes grew soft and with a radiant smile, she reached out and caught his hand, pressing it tenderly.

"There is no one in this world Holmes that I trust more than you."

Their eyes met and for a moment he found himself unable to look away. There was no pretense in her words, no artifice in her eyes; she spoke from her heart. He compressed his lips and pushed back the swell of what felt like guilt rising from the pit of his abdomen.

"Time to move on and find the shop Eddy, it's growing late." He managed a smile and tightened his hand around hers. With a shrug of resignation, Edwina acquiesced, moving on as he urged her forward. She scanned the surrounding area, looking for something familiar and stopped abruptly. A look of excitement lit her face as she pointed down a narrow passage between the buildings.

"Down there, the third door, the green one. I'm sure of it," she cried and darted off, forgetting his counsel. Holmes had to scramble to catch up. As he reached the doorway, she reached out and grabbed his hands, laughing in delight.

"I told you I'd find it."

"And so you have." Her exuberance made him smile, it was contagious. He set the lantern down, opening the slide a little more, studying the lock.

A sudden frown crossed her face.

"Bollocks., I haven't a key." She chewed her lower lip and looked at him cagily.

"Not a problem," he replied with a quick laugh and removed a velvet pouch from the interior of his coat. He knelt, directed the small beam of light at the lock and unfurled the pouch. A variety of probes, pick-locks, skeleton keys, an auger and a crow bar glittered in the dim light.

"Bloody Hell Holmes! Are you going to burgle my father's shop?" she exclaimed a look of sheer admiration lighting her face.

He shrugged, a sly grin curling his mouth. "Well, not exactly. As your father's daughter, I expect I have your permission." Adjusting the light, he began to sift through the picks, searching for just the right one.

"Will you teach me? Is it difficult?" She crouched down next to him, her cheeks flushed with excitement at the prospect.

"A clever girl like you... shouldn't be a problem. The real question is... should I?"

Her lips settled into a pout and she sat back on her heels, looking crestfallen.

"Why not?" she grumbled, "it's not like I'm going to turn to a life of crime. Look at you... you're picking a lock...burgling my father's shop and I wouldn't call you a criminal. An unlawful act does not necessarily make one a criminal Holmes."

He paused, reflecting on her words and then turned back to working on the lock.

"What if there's a pattern?"

"What pattern?"

"Well, there was the incident with the trolley."

She rolled her eyes at him and sniffed dismissively. Her attention was unwavering - focused on his every movement as he worked the lock with the pick.

Holmes paused for a moment, checked his pocket watch and then glanced out to the street. Still deserted; good news indeed. He returned to his work.

"Mind the time Eddy... keep alert... the watchman circles around on the half hour... we're about 10 minutes in."

She nodded that she understood and then frowned, not ready to let the argument go.

"You said a pattern... one misunderstanding does not make a pattern."

He arched his brow at the use of the word "misunderstanding" and glanced sideways at her, a crafty glint in his eyes.

"Ahhh, but there is the question of the dosing."

By the sharp gasp she made and the silence that followed, Holmes knew the revelation had caught her completely unaware. He paused once more and glanced up to see her face devoid of all color, eyes wide with alarm. His expression softened.

"Of course, I knew right from the beginning. Grendel is hardly the type to suffer from the vapours. Convallaria majalis... am I correct? In her tea. It would have been my choice."

She was silent for a few moments more and then lowered her eyes, unable to meet his gaze. "It was only to make her sleep to let me have some peace. I would never hurt her. I swear it Holmes, never. I just wanted her to let me be," she stammered. She raised her hands to cover her face, thoroughly shamed.

He caught her hands and carefully lowered them, his eyes were unexpectedly compassionate.

"I understand Eddy, and I believe you. But take care... little transgressions have a way of escalating. The thrill of it... the danger... I understand the appeal. One could easily get carried away and I would find it most disturbing should we ever end up on opposite sides."

She was quiet a little longer and then grinned, a mischievous gleam in her eye as she extended her hands, palms down, wrists close together for ease of shackling.

"I'm not quite so sure Holmes... I would mind all that much."

He looked at her and then began to laugh. "Mind the time Eddy," was all he said and then turned back to the lock. The pin in the tumbler clicked and the lock released. Holmes looked triumphant and a little smug as he gathered up his tools and pushed the door open. They ducked inside quickly, and Holmes locked the door after them. He pulled her forward into warehouse and then abruptly shut the lantern, coming to a dead stop as he listened. Edwina stumbled into him, swearing softly as the meagre light suddenly vanished, leaving only a faint glow from the transom windows near the roofline.

"Bloody Hell, can we not have a little..."

He clamped his hand over her mouth, cutting off her words and then held his finger up to his lips. When he was sure that he had her full attention and that she understood, he slowly removed his hand and motioned towards the front door. Outside the click of hobnail boots echoed across the cobble stones accompanied by the jangling of keys. There was a flash of light outside as the watchman opened his lantern and then the doorknob rattled, turning ever so slightly. But it never opened as the watchman, apparently satisfied by the locked door and quiet, replaced his keys and moved off, the glow of his lantern slowly receding.

Edwina, who had been holding her breath, heaved a sigh of relief. It was short-lived however as a moment later, Holmes opened his lantern.

"What are you doing? Are you mad!"

He laughed slightly and looked at his pocket watch. "Not to worry... that was the last round before the changeover. We've at least two hours before the next man comes on... if he does at all. The late guards are notoriously slack."

He moved further into the warehouse, shining the light around surveying the machinery that was scattered around the vast open space. Edwina followed him and then abruptly stopped - a look of surprise and confusion on her face as she slowly pivoted to survey the interior.

"Something wrong?" he queried, puzzled by her expression.

"Well, they're mostly gone. I don't understand. They were here not more than a month ago. The presses, the new ones that father has been working on."

"New ones?"

"Yes. they were smaller, more compact; the plates easily removed and changed out. Quite ingenious really."

And as she spoke, Holmes took a closer look at the warehouse floor, noting the impressions on the floor where the machinery had once stood. The floor was also marked with deep scratches where something heavy had been dragged across. He also noted something else: a large metal ring in the center of the floor, the outlines of a trap door nearly obscured by a heavy layer of dust and debris.

"Perhaps that's what he meant about needing space in Calais. Very strange indeed," she murmured.

"Calais?" Holmes was instantly alert. It was a well-known haunt for underground connections.

Edwina continued to circle the floor, talking more to herself than anyone in particular.

"But why didn't he mention it?" She sighed deeply and then shook her head, a frown settling across her face. "No doubt the Professor's idea. Blasted meddler."

"The Professor?" he pressed, "who is he? Your father's partner?" That was the second time he remembered hearing that name with little explanation given.

Edwina looked uncertain and shrugged. "Well, I'm not really sure. I don't think so. Father doesn't have a partner, at least not officially. His counsel perhaps. He is always around. They're great friends... known each other since I was a little girl. Odd duck though... bit creepy."

"Name?"

214

She shrugged once again. "Not sure. Never heard him called anything else. Might be John or James. I don't know about the last name. Mother didn't care for him. I don't either."

For a moment, he stood there silently processing this information, a feeling welling within that he was onto something. But he said nothing more about it only nodding in agreement that he also though it peculiar - nothing more.

"Well then... how about the samples? Must not forget why we are here," he reminded.

She looked at him blankly for a moment and then flashed a smile, slowly coming out of her daze.

"Of course," she murmured and then carefully made her way towards the back. She disappeared into a small office and Holmes could hear her opening what sounded to be a large cupboard, rummaging about. He knew it would not be long before she returned so he moved quickly, following the scratches to the trap door. He lifted it as quietly as he could and peered down into the darkness. A draft of fetid, damp air wafted up and as his eyes adjusted to the gloom, he could just make out a stone staircase leading down to an underground cavern. Judging by the smell and sounds of water slapping against stone, it was obviously an underground tributary of the Thames. He hadn't a doubt that it traversed the length of the building and led all the way out to the River and who knew where else. Perhaps even Fleet Street where Perkins and Bacon, the crown's plate makers, were located. Now that would be bloody convenient. He smiled and quietly closed the trapdoor, moving away.

"Something wrong?" she asked. Edwina stopped in the center of the room, a look of unease flickering across her face. He was inspecting a press in the corner of the room though she couldn't shake the feeling that he had been elsewhere seconds before. She readjusted her grip on the large packet of papers she carried and then held them out to him after a brief hesitation.

Holmes glanced towards her and shook his head. "Not at all," he replied soothingly, flashing that familiar grin. He reached out and took the papers from her.

"Holmes, you would tell me wouldn't you? If something was wrong?" she asked softly, her eyes searching his for reassurance. Doubt fluttered in the pit of her stomach.

For a moment, he looked away and then quickly smiled.

"Of course," he said and then extended his hand to her. "Now come along... time to get you home."

She managed a slight smile and willingly took his hand, following him out into the street. But a tinge of doubt gnawed at her and for perhaps the first time she wondered if he was being completely truthful.

»»««

Dolan sputtered in disbelief.

"Blind me if that isn't Pennington's daughter!" He struggled to keep his voice low as he craned his neck around the corner of the tenement, eyes fixed on the darkened warehouse. His youthful face contorted with disbelief as he watched the figures emerge and fade into the shadows. They had been following Holmes since he had left Baker Street. Followed him to Bexley Manor where he had met a mysterious, cloaked woman and now finally to a warehouse in one of the worst sections of the West India Docks. But never would he have imagined, when the cowl fell away from her face, that the woman was the daughter of their prime suspect, Wilfred Pennington.

Jenkins chuckled a bit and scratched his whiskers thoughtfully.

"Bit chummy ain't they?"

"But what's it mean? You think he's mixed up in it then?"

Jenkins snorted. "Holmes? Naw, e's too slick. If e' set this up, we'd ave never gotten this far," He shook his head, a thoughtful look on his face as he weighed the possibilities. "I seen him coax the truth out of the most miserable curs you ever set eyes on. An the whole time they not realizin they givin it up. Got a gift that way; silver tongue. My guess, e just sweet talked young miss into rattin on the old man."

A look of displeasure crossed the young man's face. He didn't much care for trickery - even when it was in the pursuit of justice.

"So, the girl, does she know?"

Jenkins shrugged. "Maybe. Hard to say. Don't much care. Ain't no business of mine. At least not till Inspector says it is. All I know is my feet are achin. I'm bone cold and could surely use a drop. Duty done boy... duty done. Inspector'll be pleased as punch. Now, what say let's head back to the Folly for a warm up before we head home."

"But, shouldn't we follow them still?" Dolan continued to watch, with some apprehension, as the figures receded and eventually disappeared around a corner.

A look of annoyance crossed Jenkin's face. He reached out and thumped his young partner soundly on the forehead.

"Work day's done lad. Ain't gettin paid to think past our shift. Besides, ain't gonna see anythin differn than what you expect at this hour 'tween man and woman on their own in the dark." With a crude wink and a nudge to Dolan's ribs, he began to cackle so lewdly that the young constable's cheeks turned crimson at the insinuation. With a heavy sigh, Dolan pulled his cap on and then nodded in surrender. He tightened his jacket against the wind that was now coming up off the river and followed the older man back down towards the Folly. What did he know? Jenkins had been on the force a long time.

>>«

The brougham waited at the curb, a few blocks down from the Folly, where it clung to the shadows of a towering tenement. Tempted by the unusual sight of such a fine carriage amongst the squalor, a few of the bolder unfortunates shuffled closer for a better look and perhaps the chance to score something of value. As they approached however, they seemed to lose courage and quickly moved off, thinking the better of it. There were no guards, just the stone-face driver in the box. He said not a word - watching them impassively. Still, there was something about the glistening carriage with its horses who were preternaturally calm; an undeniable sense of power that was tinged with an undercurrent of malice.

A tall shadow emerged from the darkness of an alley and quickly made its way towards the carriage. As the man climbed inside, a match flared inside the carriage. The Professor lit a cigar and inhaled deeply, leaning back against the luxurious cushions.

"Well, what news then?"

The man leaned forward, the glow of the Professor's cigar illuminating the jagged scar that marred his otherwise handsome face. Sebastian Moran scowled, his aggravation evident as he delivered the news.

"That bloody vixen led him right to the warehouse!"

"Mind your manners dear fellow. I find it in poor taste to malign this young woman. There is no malice in her actions," replied the Professor with calm detachment.

"She's a fool. Holmes is manipulating her," snarled the Colonel, his feelings of anger only exacerbated by the Professor's seeming lack of concern.

"I quite agree. He's a master at it. He wasted no time in finding her weakness. She's young, impulsive –blinded by feelings of affection."

"Ridiculous woman. And now because of her, we may be discovered. Perhaps ruined."

The Professor smiled oddly and then shrugged, taking a long draw on his cigar. He wondered perhaps if the Colonel's wrath was fueled more by Edwina's fascination with and apparent affection for Holmes than the possibility of their ruin at the hands of the detective. Having spent the greater part of the night listening to Moran recount the evening's events at Lady Montague's, one fact was abundantly clear – Edwina had been less than impressed with the Colonel and had made no secret of it. She had in fact either treated him with contempt or worse, ignored him all together. There was one thing that he knew about the Colonel; like all true egotists, he despised being ignored – especially by a woman.

"If anyone is to be ruined, it will be Pennington. Calm yourself. Even as we speak, wheels are in motion. The operation will relocate before long."

"But surely if Pennington is arrested..." protested the Colonel, his face contorted with anger and concern. It was one thing to be involved in a little skullduggery, quite another to be caught in it. He had his reputation to consider, his military honor and that of the family name.

"If he is, then so be it," announced the Professor with a dismissive wave of his hand. "Sometimes sacrifices must be made."

"And if he talks?"

"He won't, too much at stake and of course, there are ways of ensuring silence."

Moran nodded and then lapsed into silence as he reflected upon all he had heard. The Professor seemingly had no qualms about sacrificing an old friend should the need arise, a fact which offered some comfort, yet also served as a warning. Leaning forward, he raised his hand to rap on the ceiling to instruct the coachman to drive on until the tip of the Professor's walking stick caught his palm holding him back.

"Not yet. You're not finished."

Moran looked on in surprise.

"I need you to go back out there. Continue to follow them; discreetly of course. Shouldn't be difficult to locate them again, given your tracking skills. I want to know their every move but do not interfere."

Moran frowned, ready to protest but then thought better of it. Moments later he slipped from the carriage into the shadows.

»«

"So, how will we celebrate?"

"Celebrate?" Holmes glanced sideways at her. She was walking slightly ahead of him, a spring in her step, eyes turned upwards to the sky. Looking at the stars it seemed. The lack of moon had made them quite bright. The low-lying haze enshrouding the streets dissipated above the rooftops, leaving the night sky largely unobscured.

"Celebrate. Yes, the case. Why it must be nearly finished." Edwina's hood had slid down once more and the flickering light from the gas lamps reflected occasional flashes of burnished copper.

"Ahhh. Yes, nearly," he replied with some caution.

She stopped and turned, waiting for him to catch up.

"You mustn't be so gloomy Holmes," she chided, eyes sparkling with mischief. "You'll soon have another case to puzzle over. I'm certain of it. I believe your time would be better served by planning my reward."

"Reward?" He choked back a laugh though the irony of her words struck a chord of disquiet within him.

"Of course, it's only proper. Where would you be without my help? Perhaps Dr. Watson can include me in his next chronicle in the Strand? Nothing too flashy mind you, a brief nod will suffice. I can see the banner now: Esteemed Detective cracks another baffling case with the able assistance of his new colleague, the brilliant and beguiling young adventuress, late of Paris and Vienna."

"Adventuress?" he chuckled.

"No?"

"And beguiling?"

"Too much then?"

"Not at all," he replied with great fondness.

218

"Hmm, maybe, I wouldn't want Dr. Watson to take offense or think I was trying to steal his thunder. It might alienate him even more."

"I rather doubt that's possible."

Edwina arched her brow, the sarcasm not lost on her, but ignored the remark. She fell into step beside him, brow furrowed in thought.

"Well, Lady Montague is throwing a ball at the end of the month. Some extravaganza," she ventured after a long silence.

"First ball of the season – always a grand event," he remarked, "for those who like that sort of thing." As he spoke, he surveyed the passage ahead. Deserted save for another group of Chinamen collecting scraps. This time no horse, just four men and a pushcart trudging along, focused on their menial task.

"I only mention it as she has been carrying on about it for days now." Edwina rolled her eyes, signifying her true feelings on the matter of the ball. "Frankly, I dread the thought of it. I have been informed that my attendance is required – some nonsense about being properly presented ... whatever that means. Apparently, father has sent letters of permission for me to attend along with other instructions I have not yet been made privy to. I certainly don't wish to offend Lady Montague, nor my father, so I suppose there's no getting out of it." She paused briefly, her face darkening upon consideration.

"It would be lovely to see a familiar face there." She stopped once more and turned to face him - her eyes bright with hope.

Holmes remained quiet, his expression guarded.

A breeze lifted off the river and a faint trace of lilies of the valley filled the air, momentarily lessening the stench from the Thames. With a pensive expression, Holmes reached out and once more lifted her hood, covering her hair. Her eyes were luminous, radiant with unwavering affection. It was unsettling for more reasons than he wished to ponder.

"You do dance Holmes, don't you?" she prodded, a sly smile curling her lips.

For a moment, neither spoke, the only sounds that of the increasing clatter of horse hooves behind them as the first group of Chinamen grew near, continuing their hunt for rags and scraps.

"As little as possible," he said, finally breaking the silence. With a reluctant smile, he grasped a few errant strands of silken hair and tucked them behind her ear.

Edwina laughed heartily and shrugged, leaning in to confide.

"I'm rubbish at it... avoid it as much as possible."

"Two left feet?"

"Hooves. Mother tried to teach me. Gave up. Said she's seen oxen with more grace."

He began to laugh. "Come along," he urged, lightly taking her by the arm, "it's really quite late." The Great Clock of Westminster chimed half past two as if to emphasize the point.

"But you still haven't answered my question about the ball," she reminded as she linked her arm through his. They walked easily side by side.

There was another silence. "It may not be possible," he said somberly, his eyes focused on the path ahead.

"Oh," she sputtered awkwardly, surprised and disappointed. She peered at him, her frown increasing; he would not make eye contact.

"I may not be available," he offered. He met her gaze with a solemn expression hoping the statement would satisfy her.

The shadow of discouragement clouding her face told him it had not.

He pressed her hand in reassurance. "I have no doubt Eddy that your dance card will be full in spite of your hooves."

The attempt to cheer her failed miserably; her face continued to cloud with doubt and bewilderment.

"I don't care about the dancing or the blasted dance card."

She stopped and turned to him, that vague feeling of unease once more settling in.

"Have I offended you?"

"No. Not at all," he sighed, weary of the questioning but reluctant to offer further explanation.

He tightened his hold on her arm as they continued to make their way from the docks. The street had narrowed considerably becoming one long stretch unbroken by any side alleys. The tenements that lined the streets crowded up against each other with little room between their walls; the few gaps that existed were hardly wide enough for a cat. Up above, a series of ramshackle balconies ranged across the crumbling facade of the buildings, their wooden boards warped and twisted with rot. It all filled him with a sense of unease though he could detect nothing amiss.

"Dr. Bell then?"

Her voice jarred him back to the present. She hadn't spoken in some time of which he had been admittedly grateful. He had taken it as a sign that she had decided to let the matter rest. Clearly, he was mistaken.

"Dr. Bell?"

"Dr. Joseph Bell... the physician from Scotland."

"I'm quite aware who he is," he snapped. His patience was almost at an end.

Edwina compressed her lips, her concern over what she could have possibly done to annoy him gave way to growing irritation. She had developed a tolerance, even empathy, for his mercurial moods, more so than most of his acquaintances. She fully accepted that one had to make allowances for the eccentricities of a brilliant mind. Even so, she was finding it difficult to remain patient. He seemed particularly contrary and petulant since they had left the warehouse despite her numerous attempts to cheer him. Still, she counted to ten and smiled with as much patience as she could muster.

"He's giving a lecture next Saturday at the Royal Academy of Physicians. I overheard Dr. Watson discussing it. I'd love to attend ... he's going to perform a dissection and analysis. It's open to the public."

"The public Eddy, at this time does not include the fairer sex."

"But also to members of the Academy," she added impatiently. She didn't need to be reminded that women were routinely excluded from events that were termed public.

"Not an Academy member," he stated.

"But Dr. Watson is," she argued, "surely he would add you to the guest list. And then, you could add my name as your guest."

"We shall see," he murmured, interrupting her.

"But surely..."

"Enough!"

The word rang out with surprising ire, echoing off the cobblestones.

Edwina stood transfixed, stunned, lips pursed to continue the argument, but no sound came forth. A shadow darkened her eyes, her expression alternating between incredulous anger and hurt. She said nothing for a moment and then compressed her lips, her eyes fierce and wounded.

"You are unbearably hateful at times," she announced and then strode off down the passage without him, pulling her cloak tightly around her.

He nearly laughed and then groaned aloud as he watched her disappear down the dim street. "Eddy... Bloody Hell! You don't even know the way... wait!"

She ignored him and continued on.

Surrendering, he quickened his pace and sprinted after her, increasingly aware of the growing silence around them. Even the sounds of the horse cart that had trailed along behind them had stopped. There was only the sound of their own footsteps and the distant clang of a ship's bell in the harbour.

"Stop! Wait!" he called out. This time it wasn't a request but a command. She turned around and waited, disturbed by the look of unease on his face as he hurried forward.

"Give me your hand... come close... quickly!"

"What? Why are you so acting so stra..." The words died in her throat as her eyes fixed on the empty street behind him. Except it wasn't empty... the horse cart remained. It was no longer moving, now pulled across the narrow street blocking the passage. The Chinamen, however, had vanished.

"Where have they gone?" she whispered, trying to control the slight tremor in her voice. She took his hand and moved closer.

Holmes tightened his hand about hers and shook his head, his eyes scanning the darkened passage.

"Not sure, but the others are gone as well."

"The others?" she murmured, puzzled at first until she remembered the second cart. She turned and stared down the passage. The pushcart was there as well blocking the passage in front. Again, the Chinamen had disappeared. She struggled to suppress the icy fear that gripped her.

"Do they mean to rob us?"

Holmes shook his head. "We've got to run."

"What? Where? Each way is blocked..."

"Doesn't matter... we have to go ... now... over it... under it..." he insisted, pushing her forward. She hesitated, moving reluctantly until he grabbed her arm tightly and began to pull her along the street in the direction of the cart.

"But..."

"Keep moving... don't stop Eddy... no matter what."

"We'll pay them... like before..." she gasped, trying to catch her breath. She struggled to keep from tripping as he increased his speed; he was practically dragging her. And then she stumbled, her heel catching in the hem of her skirt. She pitched forward towards the wall until he caught her, pulling her back, steadying her.

"For Christ's sake.... the money doesn't matter... I'll give it gladly...." she panted. Her face had gone white with fear; a slight sheen of perspiration on her forehead.

Holmes squeezed her shoulders, his expression bleak and remorseful.

"I'm so sorry Eddy... if money was only what they were after."

She gaped at him - dumbfounded.

"But... I don't under..." She froze, her words trailing off.

A rustle followed by the rasping creek and groan of rotting wood under pressure sounded from above. They both glanced up and then stumbled back as seven black clothed figures seemed to materialize from the mist, dropping down from the balcony; they landed with feline grace. The Chinamen, coolie hats pulled low over their emotionless eyes, silently advanced surrounding them.

Holmes pulled her close and slowly turned, scrutinizing their faces. His hand grasped the lantern, his face calm though inwardly he castigated himself for not bringing a pistol. He fixed his gaze on the tallest of the men.

"I would speak to your leader."

The Chinamen stared at him wordlessly.

He repeated the command again this time in impeccable Mandarin.

A flicker of surprise registered on a few of the coolies' faces and after a moment, the circle parted slightly to allow a young man through. He was slight of build, perhaps in his mid-twenties and unlike the others, wore the fine black silk robes of a Mandarin. His glossy jet hair was shaved back from his temples in the traditional manner and then woven into a long braid. On his head, he wore a simple black silk skull cap, embellished by a single red tassel that hung from the back. Perched on his nose were a pair of gold-rimmed pince-nez.

"Your Mandarin is commendable Mr. Holmes. I congratulate you. Limehouse has provided you with many things including our language."

Holmes narrowed his eyes at the youth... for that is what he was despite the elegant garb. Still, there was an air of authority about him that advocated caution.

"Who are you?" he asked sharply, his hand tightening around Edwina. She stood silently by his side, waiting anxiously. She had not understood one word though the tension in Holmes' voice was clear.

"I am called Tai Quon." He bowed slightly and then smiled. "A name unfamiliar I expect..."

"Please... if it's money you want..." she blurted.

The sound of her voice surprised both of them. Holmes shook his head, giving her hand a sharp squeeze in warning to remain silent.

Tai Quon smiled in amusement and turned his attention to Edwina.

"She's charming Mr. Holmes. A pretty price she'll fetch. To be honest, I had almost given up hope. My client has very particular tastes and has been growing impatient. She meets the criteria of the contract quite nicely," he explained, but this time in concise English. "I have been searching for some time now. You can only imagine my delight when she walked past us earlier this evening. For that, I thank you." He flashed a mocking grin and then bowed.

Edwina stared at him in horror; there was no mistaking the true meaning of the threat.

"I will double your contract," offered Holmes. "Let her go..." His fingers flexed and then tightened around the lantern.

The young man burst into laughter and shook his head.

"I sincerely doubt you can fulfill that promise, despite your success Mr. Holmes."

"My personal means are limited true enough, but my access and motivation are infinite."

The Mandarin shook his head. "So noble," he sighed with a scornful smile, "and yet, I cannot, I am a man of my word." The Mandarin began to advance, followed by the others; they quickly spread out and tightened the circle.

"As am I. Double the contract. No repercussions. No one need ever know. Believe me sir, I am doing you a great service. If you do not take my offer, I guarantee that within a very short time you will discover that the trouble she brings is hardly worth the fee."

Tai Quon paused for a moment and then burst into laughter. After a moment, he uttered a deep sigh and then smiled.

"Respectfully, I must decline. You are free to leave Mr. Holmes, I have no quarrel with you," he added softly though his eyes were full of menace. "Now, if you please," he said and motioned with his hand for Edwina to step forward.

For a brief moment, there was only silence, and all remained in place - seemingly frozen. It was short-lived however as Tai Quon, his face now red with indignation, abruptly barked a command. The Chinamen surged towards them as one.

"Run!" shouted Holmes as he shoved her to the side and then swung the lantern in a circle with all his might. Edwina staggered and then fell to her knees, tumbling almost under the Chinamen, wincing at the sound of the lantern as it connected with facial tissue and bone. She struggled to her feet and cried out in horror as Holmes disappeared under a sea of black robes.

"Get off him you bastards!" she shrieked and threw herself into the fray, striking out with her fists. She managed to land a punch or two before she was wrenched back by a pair of powerful arms.

"Holmes!" she cried out, yanking frantically at the arms that held her, kicking out as she was dragged back. It was futile; a rag reeking of a cloying sweetness was clamped over her mouth and nose. She struggled for a few moments trying not to inhale but eventually gave in, unable to hold out any longer. Her head swam dizzily and as her knees buckled under her, the last thing she saw was Holmes struggling to his feet.

Swiping at a trickle of blood that oozed from a gash on his forehead, he looked up just in time to see her being carried off. The very sight of it, burlap sack wrapped around her head, seemed to energize him filling him with rage; he lunged forward again. This time, his attackers did not beat him back but only held him. Tai Quon, who had not participated in the melee, approached, his face cold and full of contempt.

"I warned you, Mr. Holmes..."

"Free her... now!" snarled Holmes, "or you will rue this day." He lunged at the Mandarin, despite the hands that held him.

A look of sheer incredulity flickered across Tai Quon's face.

"No Mr. Holmes... I beg to differ," he hissed, his eyes cruel and disdainful behind the spectacles. He paused for a moment and then lurched forward - a flash of silver in his hand. Holmes saw it too late. As the blade ripped through his coat and into his flesh, he dropped to his knees, unable to breathe, crippled by searing pain that radiated across his chest and right shoulder.

The Chinaman stood above him while the others held him fast. Tai Quon grabbed a handful of his hair, yanking his head up so he could look into the eyes of this foolish Englishman and shoved the blade in once more. This time he stopped only when the tip grated against bone.

"I warned you," he growled, this time in Mandarin. Stepping back, he twisted the dagger so severely the blade snapped, separating from the hilt. He glanced at the broken dagger in his blood-smeared hand and then sighed. With an expression of mild disgust, he threw it down next to Holmes, wiped his hands on the sleeve of the nearest coolie and then turned, heading off down the passage. His men waited for a few moments and then released Holmes, silently disappearing after their master.

Holmes remained on his knees, gasping for breath and strained to extend his left hand and examine the wound. As his fingers encountered the oozing and ragged edges, he grimaced but willed himself to his feet. Leaning heavily against the wall for support, he staggered forward trying to convince himself that perhaps it wasn't so bad. His fingers continued to probe the injury and then stopped on meeting cold, jagged steel; the haft of the blade was buried deep in his shoulder. *Perhaps worse than originally thought.* Bracing himself against the wall, he gripped the slippery edge of the blade and attempted to remove it. It wouldn't budge. He readjusted his grip and tugged again with as much strength as he could muster. The surge of pain was intense and

224

immediate. He staggered forward a few feet, sliding along the wall and then collapsed the world descending into darkness.

When he came to, he was lying on his back near the wall. His eyes focused on the night sky as he listened to the faint gurgling of water in the gutter. He lifted his hand to his face, it was damp, his clothes as well but only slightly. *Must have rained - but no more than a brief shower.* He looked at the stars - their positions were virtually the same as earlier. Not much time had passed, perhaps no more than 30 minutes at the most. *Encouraging... he could do with a little good news.* With the utmost care, he pushed himself up to a sitting position and leaned against the wall, trying to move his shoulder as little as possible. The bleeding seemed to have stopped, the broken blade acting as a cork, at least for the moment. The pain, however, remained, surging with every movement he made no matter how careful or minute. Gritting his teeth, he fastened his coat and struggled to his feet ignoring the pain as best he could. After a brief rest against the wall to catch his breath and get his bearings, he started off down the passage. All was quiet, deserted, no trace of the Chinamen or their rag carts save for a sparse trail of horse droppings. He followed it. It soon became obvious the trail was heading back towards the river. *Of course - they would head back to the docks...where more likely than not she'd be smuggled onto a steamship along with the cargo. But which one and where?* There were dozens of steamers in port – many bound for the Orient or the Americas. A brief wave of dread enveloped him – time was of the essence. If he didn't find her before the transfer, he suspected he never would. Moving forward with a renewed sense of purpose, he followed the trail until it vanished, lost among the debris of the well-travelled street as it wound back down to the river. He paused on the slight rise that overlooked the river, scanning the docks, uncertain where to begin. So many slips – filled with small skiffs and wherries that shuttled cargo to the larger ships in port. They were mostly deserted. It was late, close to four he guessed and no sign of the Chinamen. For lack of a better plan, he decided to start at the furthest slip. As he made his way towards it, his eyes detected a shadow moving along the dock near a skiff just off to the left. He paused straining to see but the shape soon vanished amongst the boats tied up at the dock. With a renewed sense of urgency, he moved forward again quickening his pace until his foot made contact with something that crunched underneath. He froze and lifted his foot. Looking down, he was bewildered by a whitish fragmented substance. A sharp stab of pain radiated out from his shoulder as he crouched down for a closer look; he ignored it, reaching out to grab the object. As his fingers touched it, he realized it was the remains of a cloisonné bead. *A bead from her necklace ... the strand must have broken during her struggles. At least he was heading in the right direction.* Holmes scrutinized the bead closely, carefully working off the powdery coating. There was something intact beneath the debris. Little by little a shape began to emerge, oval and dull green in color. Holmes' eyes widened in disbelief. *Bloody Hell! Could it be?* He wouldn't know for sure until it was analyzed. He stood up and once more moved forward with great care, inspecting the path. There, a few more beads scattered amongst the gaps between the cobblestones. A few were crushed - most whole; finally, he found the necklace, the strand snapped, but the beads mostly intact. As he tucked it into his pocket, he was nearly overcome with a sense of jubilation at the discovery. Holmes could scarcely believe his good fortune until he remembered. if he didn't find her, it would be a hollow victory. With a grim expression, he moved forward once more.

»»«<

Upon waking the second time, the odor is what she noticed; it may very well have been what woke her. Oppressive and putrid, the smell of rotting fish permeated the air. It was all she could do to keep from retching. The dull throb in her head from the chloroform and the dryness of her throat didn't help. Edwina ignored it as best she could and carefully twisted her head to see where she was, but there was nothing but darkness. A brief wave of panic swept over her until she realized there was something pulled over her head. It was scratchy and coarse – a sack of some kind. She slowly exhaled, marginally relieved. At least she wasn't blind. She forced herself to focus; in her mind, she could almost hear Holmes' voice, composed and cool, offering counsel. Holmes... Christ... where was he? Was he well? Where was she for that matter? A flutter of anxiety resurfaced, but she took a deep breath and forced it back; losing control of her emotions wouldn't help either of them. So, she lay there motionless and following the voice in her head, listened to see what she could discover.

At first, she was struck by the quiet except on closer listen, it wasn't really silent - there were still sounds, but they had changed. No longer the sounds of the street, no grating of the wheels on the cobblestones, no creaking of the axles as they turned and most importantly, no voices jabbering in a language she didn't understand. They were replaced by the soft clanging of a bell, a distant fog horn and, underneath it all, the barely perceptible, rhythmic splash of water against wood. She pressed her ear more tightly against the hard wooden surface beneath her and listened. Yes...most definitely - the sounds of water. Reaching out with her hands, which were still bound at the wrist, she felt along the bottom and then up along the side. There were ridges, almost like ribs. A boat of some sort ... no doubt about it and judging by the fact that she could reach out with her bound feet and touch either side, not a very large one. Cautiously, she began to push herself up a little unnerved by the fact that every movement resulted in a disconcerting sway of the boat. It subsided after a moment and she continued to lift herself up until her head met with resistance and she could go no further. Over her, stretching across the boat, was some sort of material ... canvas or tarp. Damn! Discouraged, she slowly sank back down. Not only could she not see, no one could see her and no doubt her voice would be muffled as well.

She was planning her next course of action when footsteps sounded, approaching along what she concluded must be the dock. She froze... waiting ... her body tensing. The skiff began to sway as someone stepped down into it;

226

overhead she could hear a faint rustling... fabric - they... whoever they were... was fiddling with the tarp. The boat swayed a little more and then a waft of damp air flowed over her as the canvas was pulled back. Clenching her bound hands together, she drew them tightly against her and waited. He was over her now ... most likely leaning... reaching down. There was a sound... he was speaking... really more of a labored breath... she couldn't make it out. It didn't matter by God, she'd had enough of being manhandled – she was not going quietly. Hands grasped her shoulders. She uttered a savage cry and lashed out with all her strength. Fueled by a wave of anger induced adrenaline, she punched her assailant fiercely in the chest, her feet kicking out at the same time. The boat rocked violently for a moment, there was the sound of feet staggering back... followed by a low grunt of anguish.

"Stop! it's me."

She froze at the sound of his voice, her anger turning to incredulity.

"Holmes?" She struggled to sit up. This time, she was successful with his help.

"Shh... not so loud," he groaned. Kneeling in the bottom of the skiff, Holmes quickly untied her wrists and ankles. As he removed the sack from her head, he was nearly knocked off balance again as she lunged forward. This time, however, she threw her arms around him in tender welcome and buried her face against his chest - holding on tightly.

"Bloody Hell. Sorry."

As her head made contact with his shoulder, he winced but said nothing. He eased her head further down onto his chest away from his shoulder and held her close until her trembling subsided.

"It's all right," he soothed, ignoring the throbbing pain in his shoulder as best he could. He helped her to her feet.

Edwina wiped quickly at her eyes, striving to regain control of her emotions.

"I thought the bastards had come back," she said indignantly. "I wasn't going to make it easy for them."

"I would expect nothing less," he remarked with a slight grin. "Are you all right then?" With the utmost care, his fingers lightly grasped her chin and he turned her head from side to side for inspection. Fortunately, only a few scrapes here and there, smudges of dirt on her cheeks. Her hair was disheveled as were her clothes though he did not believe she had been interfered with. Tai Quon was first and foremost a businessman; damaging the client's goods would lessen their value perhaps even negate the contract. The most notable of her wounds were the abrasions on her knuckles; no doubt there was a Chinaman or two that had bruises to match.

Edwina took a deep breath and nodded that she was fine. It was her turn now; she studied him with dark and somber eyes.

"Christ... you're a bit of a mess," she sighed, gently wiping a smear of dried blood from his forehead with the edge of her sleeve. His jaw was bruised, bottom lip split and his left eye showed signs of swelling.

"I've seen more color in a corpse... are you hurt?" Not only was he pale, but his face had taken on a disturbing greyish cast. More unsettling, the shoulder of his coat was ripped open, the fabric around darkening with a moist stain that was steadily growing. Edwina drew a sharp breath and leaned in for a closer look. It was the wrong color to be from the rain. Her fingers reached out to examine it, but he drew back abruptly, turning away from her.

"Come along Eddy... quickly." He stepped up from the boat onto the wharf and grabbed her hand, lifting her up as well. He hurried her along, keeping his body turned slightly away - aware that his wound was once more beginning to bleed.

Edwina scrambled to keep pace, fear clouding her face.

"Wait... your coat..."

"No time to wait," he interrupted, "Best keep moving." He tightened his grip on her hand and pulled her along.

They had left the pier and were now heading down the lane away from the shadowy docks, their goal the more populated area just across the Ratcliffe Highway. The lights of the commercial street loomed in the distance, beckoning. If they were to find a hansom, it would be there. As they trudged along, Holmes continually scanned the area but there was hardly a soul to be seen. Most significantly, not a trace of the Chinamen. He quickened his pace despite the wave of pain it produced. Tai Quon and his men had vanished inexplicably abandoning their trophy. It didn't make sense. Had something or someone spooked them? Perhaps ... it was best not to find out.

"Stop!"

The word rang out sharp - piercing the silence with utter frustration as Edwina abruptly stopped; still holding onto his hand, she forced him to pause as well. Holmes turned around and tried to move her forward; she refused planting her feet firmly. She grabbed his coat sleeve and yanked so fiercely and with such force he had no choice but to face her. They had stopped under the flickering light of a street lamp. Her eyes fixed on his coat, settling on the ragged tear over the shoulder. Horrified, she watched a large, reddish stain began to seep through the fabric.

"Blood... that's blood."

"It's nothing," he grunted though he sounded less than convinced.

"You're bleeding. How can it be nothing?"

He shook his head and tried to get her moving again, tugging on her hand.

"Nothing a return to Baker Street won't mend," he groaned, "please Eddy... we have to keep moving."

"Not until I get a better look," she protested and before he could prevent her, she had pulled open his coat to reveal the injury. The sight of it — his white shirt now crimson — ripped open at the shoulder made her recoil, but what horrified her the most was the dull glint of metal protruding from the wound.

"Is that?" was all she managed to gasp, unable to complete the question.

"Part of a knife... yes," he wheezed. "Can we move on now?" The vexation in his voice was overshadowed by a growing fatigue. Unexpectedly, he leaned against the lamppost, breathing unevenly - small beads of perspiration dotting his forehead. Clearly, he was in distress - his strength fading with each passing moment.

"Tell me what to do. How to help?" she implored, struggling to keep calm. She stared at the bloody wound, the jagged metal and compressed her lips grimly.

"Should I... I... try to... remove it?" She lifted her trembling hand and tentatively reached out towards him.

He grasped her hand and held it fast, shaking his head.

"No, exactly what you must not do."

"But the bleeding..."

"Will be worse if you remove it."

For a moment, she seemed frozen in place, her face almost as pale as his, eyes wide with fear. Easing her hand from his, she tenderly wiped the perspiration from his brow and took a deep breath, nodding that she understood. He needed her to be strong and she would be damned if she failed him.

"Tell me..." she said once again, this time with contrived calmness, though her eyes threatened tears.

He managed a smile - heartened by her resolve.

"Get me to Baker Street..."

"Surely a hospital."

"Only if you want to put me in the ground. Baker Street... quickly." His voice trailed off and then he grew quiet, sliding down the pole a little further to where he was nearly sitting on the cobblestones.

Edwina grasped his shoulders, holding him upright trying to contain the panic within that threatened to break free.

"It's all right Eddy, if you can't." he mumbled after a moment, "Leave me – go on to Baker... send someone back."

The permission to abandon him jolted her back to the present helping to focus her mind. First and foremost, she needed to staunch the bleeding or Baker Street wouldn't be much use but how and with what? A flicker of cognition lit her face and without hesitation, Edwina reached under her skirt and yanked off her petticoats, quickly tearing them into long strips.

Holmes managed a feeble smile, watching her with great admiration.

"This problem with your undergarments... getting to be quite a habit...Tongues will wag..." His words faded off into a spasm of coughing.

With an expression of grim resolve, she pushed back his coat and carefully wrapped the fabric around his shoulder, bandaging the wound tightly but taking care not to dislodge the broken blade. For the first time, she wished she had worn the conventional seven petticoats though she was grateful for the three.

"Let them," she said with a shake of her head, as she finished tying off the bandages. "Fortunately for you Holmes, I am not as liberated as the French or as I attempt to be. Most French ladies forego them entirely now...

only knickers or bloomers. In this case, I fear my knickers would be of little use."

He managed a feeble laugh. "A noble sacrifice all the same… if only to bring a smile of delight."

She repaid his attempt at humor with a tender smile of encouragement. When she was satisfied that the bandages were as tight as she dared make them, she refastened his coat and drew a deep breath.

"Can you stand?" She gazed into his eyes trying to gauge his strength; there was great pain but also incredible resolve.

Holmes nodded that he could and with her assistance struggled to his feet, leaning heavily against her for support. Moments later, they wobbled off down the street like two drunk lovers - holding each other up as best they could.

In the distance, Edwina could hear the clatter of horse hooves and wheels grating on the pavement. Encouraged by the sound, she tightened her grip on him and increased her pace. As her spirits rose, she could also feel his strength dwindling; time was now their greatest adversary.

»»«««

RETURN TO BAKER STREET

The pain was unlike any he could recall: white hot, relentless, searing every nerve–every cell. His body stiffened, rebelling against it; his lips parted, but he found he could not cry out, his tongue was useless. The anguish increased until he thought he could stand no more; then, with the slightest prick on his arm, it all began to fade. The stiffness in his limbs gradually gave way, loosening. As he slid into sensuous pool of alternating warmth and cool, the darkness lifted from his mind replaced by a hazy feeling of general well-being. Sweet euphoria. Holmes sank down further vaguely aware, for the first time, of voices above and around him. He considered opening his eyes but decided against it, content to let them float above in anonymity. There was a pleasing coolness on his forehead and soft but indistinct words of comfort in his ear. The voice was feminine and familiar; he smiled faintly as a gentle warmth caressed his cheek and a hint of lilies of the valley tickled his nose. With eyes still closed, he pursed his lips to say her name but found he hadn't the strength. Comforted, he surrendered to the siren song of sleep and allowed his mind to slip further away.

»»«««

"Pleasant dreams then?"

The words were terse – full of reproach and followed by the harsh clang of metal on porcelain. Holmes groggily opened his eyes and raised up slightly

230

to find Watson, crimson streaked shirt sleeves rolled up to his elbows, examining an object in the basin. His face was haggard—the face of a man who had been up all night—engaged in a task of the most serious and taxing nature.

"I never dream," groaned Holmes, managing a feeble smile through clenched teeth. With great effort, he forced himself up and sat on the edge of the bed, gingerly exploring the new bandages — proper ones now — that covered his shoulder. Early morning sunlight dappled the floorboards as it poked through the partially drawn shade; he looked to the window and exhaled heavily, relieved to see the familiar oak.

Watson dropped the broken blade back into the basin, which was filled with crimson water and the stained remnants of petticoats.

"Humph... Well, what was it then? That caused you to call her name? Three times... twice as Eddy and the last as Edwina."

Holmes glanced up and then quickly looked away, but in that brief instant, Watson was certain he detected an expression of disquiet. After a moment, the Detective smiled on noting the fresh needle prick on his forearm. On the table next to the bed lay his Moroccan case, the syringe lying next to it – the vial of morphine half empty.

"Ahh, well that explains it," he said as he inspected his forearm. "The sweet relief from pain you provided obviously clouded my mind. As you well know Watson, what a man says when in the grip of morphine dreams is not to be trusted. Still, I am exceedingly grateful for your kindness, and I trust that you will replace what you have used."

Watson scowled in response. It was well-known that he was averse to keeping narcotics, other than a bottle of laudanum, in his medical bag. For Holmes to remind him to replace what he had used of his personal supply of morphine was insufferable.

"For a brilliant man, you're quite the idiot," he growled. "And you should be more than grateful, especially to that girl who somehow got you home. How she and Mrs. Hudson managed to get you up the stairs is confounding. Even more so considering that despite all the chaos, she still had the presence of mind to send the Irregulars out to find me. By the time I arrived back from the club, you were unconscious – half dead. For Christ's sake man, what were you thinking? You could have both been killed. And what's this nonsense about Chinamen? She was babbling something about a boat and dustmen. What in the blazes is this all about?" he pressed as he wiped his hands on a towel and set the basin down on a side table.

Holmes expression grew quite solemn. He leaned over and retrieved the blade from the basin – inspecting the inscription in Mandarin. The blade was of fine quality – not the weapon of a common coolie.

"They tried to take her. I could not let that happen," he murmured, his expression deeply troubled. He dropped the broken blade back into the basin and then grimaced a bit as he began to push himself up off the bed.

"They? The Chinamen?" Watson gaped at him – bewildered. "Why on earth would they..." He paused, thinking and then as comprehension sank in, horror clouded his face. "Great Scott man... do you mean white slavers? But how on earth did you escape them?"

"Good question. For reasons unknown, they abandoned their prize and vanished," said Holmes. He gingerly lifted his shoulder and winced, testing the strength of the muscle. Satisfied that there seemed to be no permanent damage, he took a few steps away from the bed and turned around, scanning the room. "My coat – where is it then?"

Watson frowned. After all the troubles of the night, Holmes' main concern was for the whereabouts of his coat. He shook his head and pointed wordlessly to the crumpled and stained garment which lay on the floor in a heap near the bedpost.

Holmes pivoted and headed back towards the bed. As he drew near, a flash of silver and green caught his attention. It was pinned to the edge of the pillow where he had lain. He drew to a halt and knit his brow, surprised that he hadn't noticed it earlier. The lapel watch.... He sat on the edge of the bed and carefully unpinned it, eyes dark and unsettled as he turned it over in his fingers. He couldn't recall a time when he had seen her without it... why now? He looked to Watson for an explanation, the watch now cradled in his palm.

Watson's expression softened. "I don't expect you remember... you were delirious with pain. The blade was deep... close to the bone. It took longer than expected to extract. It seemed the morphine would never take effect. To her great credit Holmes, Edwina did whatever I asked without hesitation, though I could tell she was horrified by the serious nature of your injury. I have no doubt that it was her swift action to bind your wound that prevented you from bleeding out. I fear I have grievously misjudged her. She never left your side ... kept watch along with me   bathing your brow, tending your dressings. It was only when she nearly collapsed from exhaustion that Mrs. Hudson and I were able to convince her that the danger had passed and that she must rest. Before she retired, she pinned that watch to your pillow. She said it had always brought her comfort – she hoped it would bring the same to you.

Holmes grew quiet. His fingers closed gently around the watch as he rose from the bed.

"Where is she?"

Watson nodded towards the door. "In the parlour... Mrs. Hudson offered her a bed downstairs in her flat, but she refused... she would not leave this flat."

Holmes nodded soberly and without a word left the room, his hand still cradling the watch. On entering the parlor, the sight of her made him pause. She was curled up on the divan, her face partially obscured by a cascade of disheveled locks and wrapped in one of Mrs. Hudson's hideous flowered housecoats. Her own clothes were too stained with blood — his blood — to continue wearing. The housecoat was enormous and dwarfed her slender frame, drawing attention to a fragility in her that he had not previously noticed. Taking great pains to be quiet, he settled on the edge of the ottoman that faced the divan and leaned over, carefully easing the chintz throw back up

232

over her shoulders. As he reached out to pin the watch onto her pillow, her eyes abruptly opened. Edwina stared at him dazedly for a moment and then sat up quickly, blinking rapidly as she attempted to rub the sleep from eyes.

"Holmes... Bloody Hell... you're awake."

"Indeed I am. Watson tells me you were invaluable. You have my sincere gratitude...you and your petticoats," he added with a grin.

Despite his attempt to make light of the matter, her face turned a little pale, her eyes suddenly anxious as the memory of the previous night revisited her.

"You bled so much... were so weak... unresponsive," she murmured, her face growing pale, eyes beginning to moisten. "I was... I was..." Her words faltered and then died out. She bit her lip and wiped quickly at her eyes, struggling to maintain her composure. "I was so afraid that I was going to lose you," she whispered and then abruptly threw her arms around him, holding on tight, hiding her face against his neck.

The intensity of the moment caught him off guard and as her moist cheek brushed against his, he felt his own emotions stir despite his best efforts. His arms drew her closer as if on their own.

Edwina lifted her face from his neck and met his gaze, her eyes rimmed with red, brimming with tears. "In all my life Holmes -- I've never been so frightened."

He said nothing but nodded that he understood, allowing her the comfort of his embrace for a few moments more. Eventually, when he sensed that she was more in control, he gently grasped her shoulders and moved her away holding her at arm's length. There was no denying the raw candor and fervor of her words had touched him. He took her hands in his and pressed them, offering reassurance.

"No need to fret so," he soothed, a wry smile tugging at his lips. "Your fears are groundless. Haven't you heard? I am known to be indestructible. It says so in the Strand. Watson wrote it, so we know it must be true."

Edwina stared at him for a moment and then began to laugh, her anxiety beginning to face.

"Christ... you are an arrogant toff..." She sighed deeply and managed a feeble smile as she wiped at the last traces of her tears with the back of her hand.

"Yes, also in the Strand thanks to Watson." Holmes flashed a quick grin and handed her an immaculate pocket square. Edwina took it gratefully and dried her eyes, a look of relief on her face – her spirits lifted by his attempt at humor. She had no doubt that he was still feeling the effects of his injury and that his lightheartedness was for her benefit.

"Shouldn't you be resting?"

"I'll be fine," he assured. "I've had a lovely narcotic nap and I do have the benefit of a doctor for a flatmate. You, however, must rest. Dr. Watson tells me that Lady Montague will send a carriage for you in a few hours. I suggest you try to get as much sleep as possible." As he spoke, he withdrew the lapel watch from his pocket and placed it into her palm, carefully closing her fingers around it. "Thank you Eddy, but I won't be needing this now. All the same, it was a lovely gesture. Oh, and you needn't worry. Miss Morstan has promised to bring some fresh clothes for you. It would be an abomination to send you home in that garish circus tent." He gave her hand one last squeeze and then began to rise, releasing her hand. However, instead of letting go Edwina unexpectedly tightened her hold on his hand and pulled him back. He paused, a curious expression on his face as he glanced down at the hand that still grasped his with tender firmness. He settled back onto the ottoman once more waiting for her to explain.

"Holmes, words cannot express how grateful I am that you are on the mend, but... but..." Edwina paused for a moment and then after gathering her thoughts, flashed a peculiar little smile. "Forgive me, this may sound strange, but don't you think that except for the Chinamen and... well of course the knife, that it was a rather glorious adventure?"

A look of surprise flickered across his face and then he chuckled nodding his head in agreement.

"An adventure sure to remain sharply fixed in my mind for quite some time – of that I am certain." With a slight smile, Holmes rose to his feet. He pressed her hand once more warmly and then released it. "Now, the time for talk is past... rest." Moments later, he lowered the shade on the parlor window and then disappeared down the hall. As the room descended into darkness, Edwina yawned wearily and lay her head back down on the pillow. She pinned the watch to the pillow and closed her eyes, a faint smile on her lips as she listened to the faint tick. *A very grand adventure indeed.*

»»«««

He stood at the window peering out into the fading light of early evening, pensive eyes fixed on the street below. As the carriage pulled away from the curb, he lifted his hand motioning slightly.

Watson, sitting in his armchair, arched his brow, taking in the scene. By God, had the man just waved? It was almost imperceptible, but he was certain of it. His lips pulled into a slight grin.

Abruptly, Holmes turned back around from the window. He narrowed his eyes noting Watson's look of amusement.

"What the devil are you smiling at? No time for it... we've work to do!"

"Work?"

"Yes, Work. Now, where the blazes is my coat? Ahh!" he cried on spying it laying crumpled in the corner. With a gleeful expression, he scooped it up and began to rummage through the interior pockets. After a few moments, he uttered a cry of satisfaction and withdrew the packet of paper samples. He placed them on the laboratory table and returned to searching the coat pockets.

"So, you have your samples," grunted Watson. He rose from his chair and crossed to the lab table, watching him with mild curiousity, "you can complete your analysis – wrap this up; Lestrade will be ecstatic."

"Yes, purely a formality. We already know the results – still best to follow procedure," he replied, a look of mild exasperation on his face as he continued to search the pockets.

"What on earth are you looking for? You have your samples."

"Something even more valuable."

"What are you talking about? What could possibly be more valuable?" Watson watched in bewilderment as Holmes uttered a triumphant cry and withdrew the broken necklace. He held it aloft for Watson to see.

"But that necklace, isn't that Edwina's? The one she wore at tea? I don't understand, simple costume jewelry... 10 a penney..." he protested.

Holmes arched his brow and picked up one of the loose beads – one he had worked most of the coating off of. He studied it for a moment and then tossed it to Watson.

"I wouldn't be so certain. Look again Watson and tell me what you see."

Watson held the bead up to the light. As he studied it, a look of bewilderment clouded his features. Under the remnants of the coating, he could barely discern a dull green shape.

"Dear God, are you telling me that this is an emerald? But how... and why? It makes no sense. Why would someone go to such great lengths to conceal it?"

"Not just one, old fellow," said Holmes as he picked up the strand and then handed it over to Watson for a better look, "but I expect that once I finish cleaning off the rest of the coating, we will find twelve. Twelve extraordinary cabochon emeralds. Just as described in the documents our Austrian friends provided."

Suspicion flickered in Watson's eyes. "The Austrians? How could this be? Bloody Hell Holmes, how does Edwina come to have them? What does this mean?"

Holmes fell silent for a moment – his expression grew troubled. "It means, that the solution to both cases is well at hand. It means there exists an unfortunate link."

Watson looked at him dully – the full meaning of the situation still eluding him.

"You remarked on it yourself earlier Watson," continued Holmes. If you recall, the documents provided by the Austrians listed the Emperor's known and suspected indiscretions, many of them in the arts and theatre. And in that list, amongst all the names, you noted one in particular – Katerina Schraeder."

Watson grunted, chewing the edge of his mustache as he considered the information.

"The girl's mother... a gift then – from the Emperor to a favored mistress?"

Holmes shook his head, a cynical smile on his lips. "Gift? I think not. Why be so foolish as to expose your indiscretion by giving such a gift and then expose yourself again by claiming it was not. As for Katerina, if it was a gift, why take such great pains to conceal them? I don't believe it was a gift

Watson. Furthermore, I suspect that the Emperor wasn't the only one Katerina Schraeder was concealing the jewels from."

A shadow of unease crossed Watson's face. "Who then? Pennington?"

"Pennington can't even control his own daughter. It seems unlikely that he could strike such fear in his wife that she'd go to such great lengths. No Watson, there are players in the game that we have yet to meet."

A look of some concern clouded Watson's face. "What will you do Holmes? What next?"   Holmes shrugged. "Do? Well, what I always do – I'll solve the case man."

"No, that's not what I mean. What will you do. about Edwina? When will you tell her?"

An uncomfortable silence descended on the room and Holmes paused in the middle of his examination of the beads. His expression was a mixture of regret and bitter resolve. He avoided Watson's glance, focused on preparing a solution to dissolve the rest of the enamel coating that cloaked the emeralds.

"I cannot. The risk is too great. It would compromise the case. And you must not say a word either Watson – not even to Miss Morstan."

Watson stared at him dumbfounded. After a few moments, he sighed and rose from the table, a look of deep recrimination on his face.

"Have you no inkling of the devastation you'll wreak? First the father and now the mother? For God's sake Holmes, how can you be so callous? What are you playing at? You offer her friendship, lure her in by hinting at the possibility of something more and..."

Bitter resentment flashed across Holmes face as he cut him off.

"Tread lightly Watson – you speak rashly, and I am tired and not in the frame of mind for it. My commission is to solve the case or more correctly – cases. I am bound to fulfill my obligation to the client. I will do all that is in my power to not inflict harm if it can be avoided. I have no desire to cause her distress... but in the end, it may be unavoidable."

There was an uneasy silence and then Watson spoke, his voice grave and disillusioned.

"I have known you all these years and we have disagreed on many things, but I have always known you to be an honorable man. You are correct, you do have an obligation to fulfill your contract to the client, but at what cost Holmes?" His queries were met with stony silence as Holmes continued with his lab preparations. Watson uttered a deep groan of exasperation.

"If you can ignore the potential harm that will ensue, then I must surely have been mistaken, for I could have sworn that when I tended your injury, it was blood that flowed from your veins and not ice water. This girl is more than fond of you... a fact of which you are well aware and have used to advantage. She risked her life for you Holmes... does that mean nothing to you? Can you betray her trust so easily?"

Holmes, who up to this point, had continued with his work impervious to the Doctor's argument. But something in the doctor's last words seemed to land home. He suddenly froze and looked up from this work, his face white as a sheet though his eyes burned fiercely.

"You know nothing," he hissed. "of what's in my mind... or in..."

A sharp rap on the door cut him off and before he could finish his thought, it creaked open as Mrs. Hudson cautiously poked her head in.

"Beg pardon Mr. Holmes, two gentlemen are here for you." She wrung her hands nervously, sensing the tension in the room.

"Send them away."

A look close to panic darkened her face. "But I cannot sir, they say they must see you."

"What do you mean you cannot? Send them away," he snarled.

"I cannot sir," she protested, "they're from the Yard. They say you are to come down."

"Bloody Hell!" Cursing darkly under his breath, Holmes pulled on an inverness coat and began to follow Mrs. Hudson out the door. As he passed Watson, he shrugged - the anger having now drained from his face.

"Coming?" he asked with a hint of a smile.

Watson stared at him for a moment and then uttered a soft groan of resignation as he took up his coat and followed him down.

»»«««

The carriage rattled along at a fast clip, weaving its way in and out of the early evening traffic as it headed towards Whitehall street. Inside, Watson attempted to contain his growing irritation by making notations in his pocket notebook while Holmes sat next to him, regarding the two detectives opposite them with disdain.

"Well gentlemen, any chance you'll be enlightening us? Mrs. Hudson is very particular about her dinner hours. I know Dr. Watson would hate to miss his evening supper."

Dolan smiled somewhat apologetically and removed his hat. It was apparent he was still somewhat in awe of the Detective. But before he could utter a word, the older man elbowed him in the ribs.

Jenkins smiled crookedly and scratched his muttonchop whiskers. "Ain't for us to say... Inspector sent us round to fetch you. I expect you'll find out soon enough."

Resigned to the notion that the yarders would not be giving out any information, Holmes settled back in his seat and glanced idly out the window. He soon became aware however of the older detective's searching gaze.

"Something you wish to ask me Detective?"

The older man narrowed his eyes shrewdly.

"Looks to me like you've been in a bit of a dust up Mr. Holmes... recently too."

Holmes arched his brow. "Your point being?"

But there was to be no further discussion on the matter as they carriage pulled through the back entrance of the Met headquarters. As they stepped from the carriage, Lestrade came striding up, a serious expression on his face. Without a word, he motioned for them to follow him as he hurried across the great yard, passing the horse stables and carriage barns, the assembly yard, the equipment room until finally he came to a low squat building made out of large whitewashed blocks of stone. It was long, narrow and nearly windowless having only small panes of glass at the very top near the roofline to allow light in. Holmes and Watson looked to each other; they had visited here before many times – the morgue. On entering, they were greeted by the stench of death; they ignored it as best they could as they followed Lestrade down past covered stretchers - most occupied. A harried looking man of about 50 in a stained leather apron came scurrying up. On seeing that it was Lestrade, he shrugged and retreated to the corner of the room where he continued his work on what appeared to be a child of about 7. As they made their way toward the center of the room, Lestrade came to a halt in front of a group of stretchers. He cast a wary eye on Holmes and then threw back the sheet on the first stretcher to reveal the ghastly grey face of a Chinamen — slightly bloated — eyes open. He moved quickly to the second and then to the third, and each time the sight was the same – another Chinamen. If Holmes was surprised, he didn't show it. Instead he moved closer, inspecting each corpse noting with interest the long, clean slice that stretched across each man's throat.

"Well, what do you know of this?" Lestrade's question was accusatory.

"What makes you think I have knowledge of this?"

"I heard you were down on the docks."

Holmes smiled slyly. "Rather a large area Inspector. Where did you find them? "

"Floated in on the tide early today. Listen to me Holmes, if you know something."

Holmes ignored him and glanced up – an odd expression on his face.

"Any more?"

Frustrated at being discounted, Lestrade strode to the last stretcher and threw off the sheet. From behind a pair of broken pince nez glasses, the lifeless eyes of Tai Quon gazed up at the ceiling. Holmes studied the body carefully. Manner of death was the same - one long, very clean slash across the throat, most likely with one stroke. There was however one important difference - Tai Quon's long braid had been severed at the hairline and stuffed into his mouth. It brought a slight smile to his face.

"Well?" Lestrade looked to him expectantly.

"Well what? I am not sure what you are looking for Inspector. They were all killed in the same manner, most likely minutes apart and dumped in the river. Other than that, I cannot tell you anything else. So, if there is nothing else you require... come along Watson."

Holmes strode from the room without waiting for Lestrade to reply and ignored his protestations as he hurried after them. "Quickly Watson... if you please... "he urged as they crossed the Yard Square and headed out onto the main street in search of a hansom.

Red faced and puffing with exertion, Lestrade caught up with them just as they were climbing into a hansom. "Dammit Holmes, if you are withholding information... "

"Yes, yes, noted Inspector."

And before Lestrade could object, the hansom moved off leaving the Inspector standing on the curb his face a mixture of anger and bewilderment.

"Well that was diverting." Holmes lit a cigarette and leaned back, lost in thought.

Watson stared at him silently, a troubled look on his face as he considered what he had just observed. He wanted to ask him to be direct but just couldn't bring himself to voice the words that formed in his mind.

As if sensing his suspicions, Holmes arched his brow and chuckled.

"The answer to your unvoiced question is no, though I must admit I am pleased with the outcome. Let's examine this though. What kind of knife would make such a clean wound? To cut so deeply with one stroke?"

Watson thought for a moment and then looked up in surprise.

"A hunting knife."

Holmes nodded in agreement. "My thoughts precisely. A hunting knife... wielded by an accomplished sportsman."

Watson's eyes widened. "But what are you saying Holmes... why?"

"Excellent question so, let's begin by you telling me everything you learned about our dear Colonel at the Club... and I mean everything. Ahhh, this case Watson... this deliciously twisted case," he murmured with an expression of sheer delight.

»»««

AN UNEXPECTED VISIT

A faint noise drifted over the pond on the afternoon breeze. Edwina yawned and set her reading aside as she sat up and listened. Shielding her eyes against the water's reflection, she peered out across the rushes at the water's edge. The sun was strong and warm; the air held the promise of Spring.

Again, the sound. This time there was no mistaking it. Someone was calling her name. Moments later, Hanna came hurrying up the path that ran along the water's edge, face flushed from the warmth of the day and her exertion. On seeing her mistress, she came to a halt and exhaled in relief.

"There you are Miss, I wasn't quite sure where'd you gone off to. I've been looking for you near quarter of an hour."

Edwina frowned, looking somewhat sheepish. "If it's about missing the morning etiquette exercise, please convey my apologies to Lady Montague. I woke with such a headache, I thought the fresh air would help." It wasn't a total lie; she was thoroughly enjoying the fresh air - much more than she would have enjoyed practicing the art of flirtation with fans.

"Oh no, Miss, that's not why I've come. Miss Mary sent me to fetch you. You have a visitor. She and Lady Montague are with the gentleman now and..."

"A gentleman," she cried out, "why didn't you say so in the first place?" She scrambled to her feet, quickly brushing leaves and grass from her skirt. "Come along Hanna, mustn't keep Holmes waiting." And before Hanna could utter a word, she gathered up her reading materials and darted off down the path towards the house. Hanna stared after her in bewilderment... if only she had let her finish. With a shake of her head, she trudged after her mistress.

Edwina flew through the front door, past the astonished footman barely avoiding a collision with the front parlour maid. As she rounded the corner of the grand staircase, her smile widened as she glimpsed the silhouette of a tall figure elegantly attired in a dark grey cutaway suit. He was chatting quietly with Miss Morstan and Lady Montague in the shadow of the grand staircase.

Forgetting all manners, she bounded towards them, exclaiming, "Bloody Hell man! Not a word from you in three days. I've been worried you were feeling poorly and . . ."

The words died on her lips as the figure turned around. Colonel Sebastian Moran flashed a darkly charming smile - the white of his scar quite noticeable as the skin stretched along the curve of his chin. He bowed slightly to her in greeting.

"My dear Miss Schraeder, I see you have mistaken me for someone else. I hope you are not too disappointed."

Edwina paled, mortified at her error and then looked away. "Colonel Moran, I scarcely recognized you without your uniform and all those medals," she added with some sarcasm.

The Colonel seemed taken aback by the thinly veiled insult - his lips compressed underneath his moustache. Lady Montague fluttered her hands, looking mildly embarrassed.

"Edwina dearest, your manners," she whispered. Turning back to the Colonel, she smiled apologetically.

"You must forgive her Colonel. Poor dear was feeling a bit out of sorts earlier but seems to have recovered now."

"And apparently decided to take a roll in the grass – or were you gardening perhaps?"

A slow flush of color rose to her cheeks. She bit her lip, determined not to let him goad her into losing her temper.

"Reading by the pond." She smiled, albeit through clenched teeth.

"Reading? Ahhh, a pleasant diversion. Poetry or perhaps the latest gothic serial?" Without waiting for her answer, the Colonel grasped the monograph and slipped it from her fingers. As he surveyed the title, he began to chuckle.

"The Use of Disguise in Crime Detection - S. Holmes..." His voice dripped with disdain as he read the title aloud.

"Dear God, what drivel. No doubt as tedious and mundane as the author himself."

"On the contrary," she retorted, "I find it every bit as brilliant and exhilarating as the gentleman who penned it. Perhaps Colonel," she added, her mouth curling into a sly smile, "it is simply beyond your scope."

Moran's smile tightened as his eyes flickered over her.

"My dear Miss Schraeder, it seems that the "Great Detective" is ever present in your thoughts. Given our circumstances, I think more than is prudent – certainly more than is courteous."

"Our circumstances?" A frown darkened Edwina's face - anxiety stirring in the pit of her stomach. Lady Montague turned a little more pale and smiled placatingly at the Colonel. She reached out and touched his arm lightly in reassurance.

"Dear Mr. Holmes, he has the most wondrous adventures, though I often find myself at a loss as to how he solves them. He has been a good and loyal friend to our family, and now he has been gracious enough to extend the kindness of his friendship to Edwina. Rest assured Colonel, there is nothing untoward in his attentions. He is a consummate gentleman and has been a stalwart advocate on her behalf. You may be unaware, but it is solely due to Mr. Holmes that Edwina is here with us at Bexley Manor."

An odd smile flickered across Moran's face as he fixed his gaze on Edwina.

"And how is that my dear lady? Has our esteemed Detective branched out into social affairs now as well? Surely there is more than enough crime in our fair city to keep him engaged."

"The wit of you gentlemen!" laughed Lady Montague. "I look forward to another event where you and Mr. Holmes may 'cross swords' - figuratively of course." She fixed him with her most alluring smile and swatted his arm playfully with her fan. Edwina groaned inwardly but said nothing uncertain as to whether she could speak civilly.

Moran managed a slight smile - the white of his scar taut across his chin. He bowed politely and replied, "For your amusement dear Lady, I stand ready for either. It has been a while since I have 'crossed swords'. I have heard that Mr. Holmes is a skilled opponent when he finds the courage to engage."

"An intelligent man uses his wits first and his fists only when necessary but I suspect Colonel, that this also may be beyond your scope."

The smile on Moran's face faded a bit.

"Edwina, enough child. Such sharpness is unbecoming," cried Lady Montague. She fanned herself rapidly, a look of sheer mortification on her face. "To be playful is one thing but you go too far. We wouldn't want the Colonel to think you are disinclined to his visit," she advised forcefully, though she continued to smile. With a last warning glance at Edwina, she then turned her attention back to Moran.

"You must forgive her Colonel, she is a "diamond in the rough" so to speak. Indeed, it is the very reason she is here. My niece, Miss Morstan, had made her acquaintance and was charmed by her spirit. She, my niece that is, just so happens to be the fiancée of Dr. John Watson, Mr. Holmes' assistant. Miss Schraeder's father is a tradesman... printing profession I believe – quite lovely cards he makes. Nevertheless, still a tradesman. Mr. Holmes, after having made her acquaintance was quick to realize that despite her father's success as a printer, he would never be able to provide her with the opportunities to progress into society. He was aware of my involvement in advancing the proper social graces of young ladies and requested my assistance. So you see Colonel, it was only the kind act of a true gentleman – nothing you should be concerned over."

"How very chivalrous of Mr. Holmes to take such an interest in your welfare, Miss Schraeder. I shall be certain to thank him properly when next we meet. And my gratitude to you also Lady Montague for your graciousness. I am more than certain that Miss Schraeder is truly a rare gem hidden amongst the baubles. I am honoured that her father has given permission to make her better acquaintance. I trust that in time she will come to regard my acquaintance as favorable as that of Mr. Holmes and one day not far off, even more so."

Edwina pursed her lips to object, a look of revulsion on her face at the mere thought of any connection with the Colonel. It was useless, however, as Lady Montague silenced any further protests by sending her off to change. With Mary to accompany her, she returned to her room and settled at the dressing table, a distressed look on her face as she watched in the mirror as Mary wove her hair into a French braid and pinned it. Mary smiled sympathetically and gave her shoulders a reassuring squeeze.

"You mustn't be so harsh Edwina. There are many types of men in this world and..."

"I think the term "man" is generous in his case," muttered Edwina, tugging at the braid to loosen the pins a little.

Mary sighed patiently and helped her loosen the pins.

"I think you are hasty in your judgement. You have scarcely given him a chance. "

"A chance? He's arrogant, rude, condescending... he treats us..."

"Us?"

"Women, like we're feeble minded children who need to be taken care of."

"And you provoke him at every opportunity."

Edwina stared at her in disbelief. "Why are you defending him? Did you not hear the way he talked about Mr. Holmes and Dr. Watson? He is disrespectful not only to me, but to Mr. Holmes as well."

Mary's face suffused with understanding. "I know you are very fond of Mr. Holmes Edwina, but rest assured, he doesn't need you to defend him."

Edwina bit her lip and stared pensively into the mirror.

"He would do the same for me... he has – on more than one occasion."

Mary frowned not quite sure she understood but decided not to question her further. She smiled placatingly and straightened the girl's gown.

"You must practice patience and tolerance. The Colonel is here appropriately with your father's permission. His pedigree seems impeccable. The Moran's are a family of status and some wealth. John tells me his father was minister to Persia and now sits in the House of Lords. All this will pass from father to son."

"You know I care little about these things," sighed Edwina with a frown, "I don't know why you even mention them. What of your Doctor? He has no title, little money and that doesn't seem to concern you."

"Like you, I have little concern for these things," agreed Mary with a conciliatory smile. "All I am saying is that you should not discount him so quickly. Sometimes it's the luck of the draw. Mother used to say it is as easy to love a rich man as a poor man. The Colonel has had a distinguished military career and is well situated. All very respectable Edwina. Your father has your best interests at heart. He seems a suitable choice and he is not unpleasant to look at, even with the scar."

"I don't bloody well care. It isn't my choice and it should be," she exclaimed, her eyes angry and indignant.

The door opened interrupting them as Hanna entered smiling from ear to ear. She carried a large vase of red roses which she set on the edge of the dressing table.

"For you Miss! Aren't they lovely? Such a thoughtful man the Colonel. I wish my Tom were a little more like him though he could scarcely afford the likes of these. I'd settle for some posies though."

Edwina stared at them, her eyes brimming slightly. "Take them away Hanna, please, I don't want them in my sight."

The girl stared at her in disbelief. "But Miss, I can't."

"Yes, you must! Please, if you don't take them from my sight, I will pitch them out the window." The girl, a little more than disturbed by her mistress's agitation, took up the vase and hurried from the room.

Edwina wiped at her eyes and then smiled fiercely as she turned to Mary.

"If he is the only choice then I will not choose. I would rather be alone than join with a man who respects me so little and for whom I have no respect. I will appeal to my father once more. In the meantime, I will participate in this charade only as much as to be polite. Now, let us return downstairs. We'll have our tea and visit. But let's be done with this as quickly as possible as I am fast losing my resolve to be pleasant."

»»««

The first stone hit the window frame just above the glass. It made a rattling sound as it bounced off and rolled down onto the small ledge that ran under the window. Holmes ignored it and readjusted the magnification on the microscope as he examined the emerald. The second stone hit the glass – thankfully not hard enough to break it. He sighed in annoyance but still did not look up.

"Watson take a look," muttered Holmes, "see if it's one of the Irregulars. If he breaks the window, I'll have his hide. Mrs. Hudson has been particularly ill tempered as of late."

There was only silence until another stone skipped off the balcony rail and rattled into the gutter. Holmes groaned aloud in frustration.

"Bloody Hell man, must I do everyth..." He looked up from the microscope and stopped in mid-sentence astonished to find he was alone. Watson's chair was empty, the newspaper he had been reading carefully folded onto the side table. On the mantle, the clock ticked softly and then began to chime – half past six. Long shadows stretched across the room as evening began to set it. The curtains billowed slightly as the breeze picked up. The warmth of the day had faded replaced by a cool and growing damp as the fog began to set in. Outside, a faint glow could be seen as the street lamps were lit. He remembered then - Watson had mentioned at tea that he was to meet Stamford at the club; he had scarcely paid attention. That had been around four. Had two and a half hours passed already? He ran a hand through his rumpled hair and stretched cautiously, wincing a bit at the stiffness of his shoulder. *Damned nuisance... the damp wasn't helping either.* His eyes drifted to the Moroccan case on the desk. He considered and then decided against it. He had work to finish and besides, Watson had yet to replenish the supply. Holmes sighed a bit and picked up one of the beakers swirling it slightly, watching the solution turn milky as a dull green stone began to emerge from beneath the enamel. It had been a bit tedious — vexing — requiring a fair amount of tinkering with the solution before he found just the right balance of acid; one strong enough to dissolve the coating but not etch the stone. But his perseverance had garnered results and now only six stones remained to be stripped of their coating. The cleaned stones lay in a glass dish. A few cloisonné beads and green glass from the broken necklace strand scattered nearby on the table, the only remnants of the original necklace. Very soon he would be able to contact the Austrians and conclude this case. He should have felt elated but instead there was a dull sense of misgiving. As the conclusion to both cases loomed, he realized that he would not only be destroying the reputation of her father, but also the memory of her mother. Holmes grit his teeth, a slow surge of resentment rising from within. Damned sentiment, he'd been listening to Watson too much as of late. There was no reason for him to feel any culpability in what may come; after all, his commission had been to solve the case, nothing more.

A sharp thwack rang out as another stone, this one much larger, hit squarely in the center of the frame nearly cracking the glass. Cursing under his breath, he sprang to his feet, crossed to the window and threw up the sash.

"Listen you little gutter rat, if you break this glass I'll drag..." The words died on his lips as a figure, wrapped in a light green wrap, looked up, ghostly pale and shivering in the gloom beneath the oak tree.

"Eddy... bloody hell, have you taken leave of your senses?" He looked up and down Baker Street; it was deserted due to the damp miserable conditions. There was no sign of a carriage.

"The door is locked... I knocked several times, but no one answered. May I come up?" Her voice was apologetic and tremulous, so much so that the words had barely been spoken before he was down the stairs and throwing back the bolt on the door. The first cracks began in his resolution to remain stoic.

"Come in quickly," he urged. A look of alarm flickered across his face as he reached out and gently pulled her inside. "Your hands are like ice. How have you come here? Has something happened?" As he ushered her up the stairs, he noted that instead of her usual woolen walking skirt, she was dressed in a pale green tea gown and carried only a light satin wrap of the same color. His unease increased as he looked down. On her feet, she wore light green satin slippers which were now stained and soaked from the damp. Formal dress – as if she'd been entertaining. He settled her into the wingchair by the fire and took a throw from the divan wrapping it around her shoulders.

"Did you walk here?" he pressed, and then as he settled on the ottoman in front of her, he once more repeated "Has something happened?"

Edwina didn't answer at first, she seemed as if in a daze and the concern in Holmes' eyes increased. He peered more closely into her face; her teeth were chattering. He took another throw, this time from Watson's chair, and tucked it around her legs. As he did so, he eased off her sodden slippers and set them on the hearth to dry.

"You're damned near frozen, your stockings soaked. Remove them or you'll never warm up. I'll give you some privacy while I fetch something to warm you."

When he returned moments later with a steaming cup of mulled wine, she had moved from the chair to the ottoman; her stockings now neatly laid out by her shoes on the hearth. She sat facing the fire, hands extended towards the flames, bare feet on the hearth stone, silent, brooding.

Holmes settled on the edge of the hearth and handed her the drink. "Now tell me, what's happened?"

Edwina remained silent for a few moments more and then let out a dismal sigh.

"I had a visitor today," she began in a slow, distracted voice, "At first I thought it might be you. I hoped it would. Well, it's been three days and I was worried that you were unwell." She paused for a moment and took a sip of the wine, lifting her eyes to his. "I'm so sorry... it is rude of me to disturb you and your work and I haven't even asked about your shoulder. How is it? How are you Holmes? Better I hope."

Holmes looked down at her hand which she had rested lightly on top of his. Much to his disquiet, it was trembling slightly. He covered it with his hand offering comfort.

"I'm fine Eddy but no more delays. You must tell me," he insisted. "For surely something has happened. By your dress, I can tell that you were entertaining this afternoon and the very fact that you didn't change your shoes before setting out in the damp tells me that something has disturbed you greatly."

She took a long breath and finally when she was ready to explain, turned back to face him her eyes threatening tears.

"My visitor was Moran. He came for tea ... brought me bloody roses. They are as vulgar and disingenuous as he is." She pulled the throw more tightly around her as if suddenly chilled. "I'm sorry," she murmured, "I

245

realize it's unfair of me to show up unexpectedly and bother you with such a trifle, especially when you are in the midst of your cases, but you are my greatest and truest friend Holmes. There is not a day that passes when I am not grateful for the friendship and consideration you have shown me. That being said, I am afraid that I must ask your assistance once more."

His hand tightened around hers and he nodded for her to continue.

"I should like to hire you"

"Hire me?" Astonishment flickered across his face and he might have chuckled if she had not been so obviously distressed.

"I shall pay you of course... eventually," she added with a rueful sigh.

"Nonsense! Now tell me," he demanded, suspicion darkening his face, "What has he done Eddy?" He leaned in closer, his jaw tightening as he scrutinized her for any signs of maltreatment. "Has he hurt you? Been inappropriate in any way?" A small knot of anger and dread tightened in the pit of his stomach as his mind turned to thoughts he'd rather not entertain.

She realized instantly where his mind had turned and shook her head, squeezing his hand tightly.

"No... No... not that. I think he would not dare, at least not yet, but he has started calling and he's made his intentions quite clear. Come the end of December, when my formal period of mourning has ended, he will ask my father for my hand. Unfortunately, by all accounts, it is a foregone conclusion that my father will give permission. Everyone Holmes, Lady Montague, Hanna, even Mary, are full of congratulations at my "good fortune" but my heart is sick ... and full of loathing. They tell me that I am unreasonable, that I have not given him a chance. But I know Holmes, I can feel it deep in my heart that there is something untrue in this man, perhaps even sinister. I have tried to talk to my father, but he will not listen. He truly believes that this is the best possible opportunity for my happiness in life. How little he knows me. So, I wish to hire you to find out anything about this man that I can use to discredit him in the eyes of my father. Surely then he will listen to reason. I know that you are in the midst of wrapping up two cases, but please, will you consider taking on one more?"

"Yes, of course," he assured. "As for my fees, they are generally fixed save when I choose to forgo them altogether as I would on your account."

Edwina looked up and for the first time that evening, a smile tugged at the corners of her mouth. "I knew I could count on you," she said, the relief evident in her voice. She glanced down into her empty cup and then looked up, a mischievous twinkle in her eyes as she held it forth.

"I'm still feeling a bit of a chill... would it be possible to have another?"

"Only one more," he advised with a smile as he took the cup and rose to his feet. It was a great relief to see the first hint of a return to her normal demeanor. "It's quite potent and although Mrs. Hudson will be elated that you enjoy her concoction, she would be less than pleased if I send you home in a less than sober state."

"If we both drink enough, perhaps you won't send me home."

Holmes paused at the door and turned back to look at her. Despite her playful tone, there was a deep sincerity behind the words. "Only a little more then – for both us," he advised with a bittersweet smile. "You need to rest and I have work."

"Of course... work," she sighed but he had already left the room.

When he returned moments later, the sight that greeted him nearly caused him to drop the mulled wine. She was standing by the microscope, brow knit in concentration as she inspected the beakers filled with the remnants of her mother's necklace. His mind raced furiously for a plausible explanation.

Edwina looked up, eyes wide with astonishment. "My God Holmes, Mother's necklace - you found it. I thought it was gone forever. But... I don't understand... what are you doing? This is acid, are you dissolving it?"

Holmes handed over her cup and then took a sip of wine as he chose his words carefully.

"Eddy, what can you tell me... of this necklace and the circumstances of how your mother came to it?"

"Well, I don't exactly know. She's always had it; as far back as I can remember. I assume it was a gift from one of her patrons." A shadow of irritation darkened her face. "But you haven't answered my question... what are you doing? It's not that valuable but very dear to me and..." She broke off abruptly, catching sight of the dull green stones in the specimen dishes. She picked one of the stones up and studied it. Her hand began to tremble a bit as she held it up for closer inspection.

"Is... Is this what it appears to be Holmes? Is this?"

"An emerald, yes, a rather exquisite one. Needs a bit of polishing. In fact, unless I am greatly mistaken, there are eleven others just like it."

Edwina fixed her gaze on the remaining stones and turned deathly pale. Holmes grew alarmed fearing she might faint as her fingers grasped the edge of the table. But as he moved forward to offer assistance, a look of sheer jubilation lit her face and he found himself tightly encircled by her arms.

"By God Holmes," she murmured, her cheek nestled against the lapels of his dressing gown, "Fortune surely smiled upon me the day I nearly trampled you and the Good Doctor."

The memory of that meeting brought a smile to his face, but he soon grew troubled as his fingers gently brushed at the wetness on her cheek.

"Why are you crying then?"

Edwina began to laugh and beamed up at him, eyes still glistening. "Because I am overcome with happiness...."

"I don't understand."

Her laughter increased. "It's silly sentiment, of course you don't understand. Tears are not only for sadness Holmes, also joy and you bring me such great joy." She wiped at her eyes and then took a deep breath as she regained her composure. After a moment, she once more looked up and this time there were no more tears, only fervent, unwavering devotion.

"Once again, you have saved me and I am forever in your debt. These stones, my mother's gift, will buy my freedom. Don't you see, with these it doesn't matter what my father chooses for me. I will have financial independence. I will have the power to choose; to strike out on my own if I wish, to seek and fulfill my own destiny."

A look of discomfort darkened Holmes' face. "The stones need to be tested Eddy. I've only begun the examination," he cautioned, suddenly uncomfortable with how the conversation was progressing.

Edwina shrugged nodding in acknowledgment. "Whatever the outcome," she began, her fingers lightly smoothing back the lapels of his dressing gown, "I know that you will do everything in your power to restore my freedom to choose."

Her words left him momentarily speechless and feeling more than a little guilty. Even more unsettling was the awareness of her closeness. The warmth of her skin seemed to seep through the thin fabric of her dress – through the dressing gown onto his skin. Every breath, every small movement she made, stirred feelings within him he knew he must suppress. So, as she smiled up at him, as her hand rested lightly on this chest, his mind drifted to what it would be like to abandon all constraint and loose himself in the warmth of her affection. Against his better judgement, he allowed himself to relax. His arms tightened around her, hands resting on the curve of her waist. He leaned his head forward to where it rested on the crown of her head. He inhaled deeply and smiled - lilies of the valley.

Edwina, sensing the shift in his mood, smiled up at him. Now was the time, finally, when she could divulge the true nature of her feelings.

"Holmes, that night when I thought I was going to lose you... I was so afraid, and I wanted to tell you the words that are in my heart. Doctor Watson told me that whatever it is that I would say, I must not. I don't understand why, but I will say it now... that I... with all my..."

The door to the flat banged open. The spell broken, Holmes drew back a step and quickly released her. He stepped aside, flashing a tentative smile while Edwina looked up crestfallen.

Watson stormed in shaking the rain from his coat, cursing the weather under his breath.

"A night fit for neither man or beast. Bloody Hell Holmes, I..."

On seeing them, he drew to a halt, a slow frown clouding his face.

"Miss Schraeder, I wasn't expecting to find you here... again... at such a late hour," he announced, his voice betraying more than a trace of disapproval. His frown deepened on glancing down and discovering that she was not only barefoot but also devoid of stockings.

"I beg your pardon for my interruption," he murmured. His eyes drifted questioningly to Holmes who seemed to him more than a little ill at ease.

"No need," Holmes announced. "Eddy was just leaving," His voice had taken on a deliberate air of detachment.

"I was? But..." She sputtered to a stop, speechless at how quickly the atmosphere had changed.

"Watson's correct, it's quite late. I shall call you a cab. Quickly now, go and put on your stockings. Time to see you home. Lady Montague will be furious if she discovers you are out alone again."

And yet she still hesitated, bewildered by the abrupt shift in his manner.

"Now Eddy, please," he repeated firmly.

Edwina compressed her lips, a slow surge of irritation rising. She paused ready to protest but realized it would be futile. With a sigh of resignation and a baleful glance in the Doctor's direction, she gathered up her stockings and disappeared into Holmes' room, slamming the door soundly after her. She was gone only a few moments, not even long enough for Watson to light his pipe and mull over the questions he wanted to ask Holmes. She emerged from the room, stockings pulled on carelessly, the seams crooked, hands holding the wrap tightly around her. Most telling of all, her face was flushed, her eyes dark with embarrassment and indignation.

"Good night gentlemen," she muttered and with scarcely a glance towards either of them, strode from the room. The sound of her steps as she headed down the stairs seemed to stir Holmes to action; he hurried after her, grabbing his greatcoat on the way. Intrigued, Watson crossed to the window and peered out, a thoughtful expression on his face as he watched taking long slow draws on his pipe.

Holmes caught up with her just as she reached the curb. A light drizzle had begun to fall as she lifted her arm and tried to hail a hansom. It clattered on by without even slowing. She shook her fists, cursing the disappearing cab. The drizzle began to increase.

"Come back into the doorway," he coaxed and before she could protest, had wrapped his coat around her and moved her back inside the entryway. Stepping out into the drizzle, he withdrew a small silver whistle from his pocket and gave a short blast. Moments later, a hansom pulled to the curb. As he helped her up into it, he paused – a rueful expression on his face.

"I know my actions have caused you distress... it wasn't my intention... it's just..." He paused for a moment finding himself uncomfortably at a loss for words. He gazed up into her face – her eyes were moist again and rimmed with red.

"You...You are very dear to me," he murmured as he tucked a strand of hair behind her ear, "but my nature... my vocation prevents...demands a dedication which may seem unnatural."

Edwina choked back a laugh, understatement to be sure and then sighed. "I understand your dedication Holmes. I would never dream of interfering, but I cannot, will not, deny what I feel any longer."

At this he looked away for a moment and then turned back to face her - his eyes wistful and troubled.

"Dearest Eddy, somethings are best left unsaid."

Edwina met his gaze and after a moment nodded that she understood. With a melancholy smile, she leaned forward and tenderly kissed his cheek. "Perhaps, but not speaking them Mr. Holmes, doesn't mean they don't exist."

she whispered. "I'll leave you to your work for now after all, you do have my emeralds to look after. One more thing, don't forget about Dr. Bell."

"Dr. Bell?"

"Yes, Dr. Bell... remember? You promised to try to secure permission for me to attend." A sly look entered her eyes and she smiled. "Or perhaps you've changed your mind and have settled on the ball instead."

Alarm briefly flashed across his face and then he shook his head surrendering.

"Dr. Bell then. I shall do my best."

"I expect nothing less Holmes." She began to laugh and reaching out squeezed his hands, her eyes warm and hopeful. "Till Saturday then."

He nodded, it was futile to continue the debate.

Moments later, the hansom rattled off. Holmes watched it until it disappeared around the bend in the street and then slowly climbed the stairs back to the flat. It only took one look at his face for Watson to realize that Holmes was less than pleased at the current situation.

"A fine mess you've created eh Holmes?"

Holmes narrowed his eyes at him as he crossed back over to the worktable.

"Leave me be Doctor."

Watson grunted softly to himself and followed him over, watching as he continued to work with the stones. He stared at the stones for a moment and then lifted his head, surprise lighting his face. "So, she knows then... about the necklace. Great Scott!"

"She knows they are emeralds, yes.," affirmed Holmes in a weary voice.

"But not that they are stolen. Not about the Austrians."

"Correct."

Watson's frown deepened. "And you will not tell her?"

"Astute as ever," muttered Holmes sharply. He began to move the beakers and equipment about noisily, his aggravation growing with Watson's continued badgering. Watson grew quiet for a moment and then scratched his head - a new thought occurring.

"Why was she here then?"

Holmes paused and compressed his lips struggling to control his rising anger.

"Not that it's any of your concern, but she was concerned for my health and also to ask for my assistance. She wants to engage my services."

Watson stared at him. "To hire you?" He choked back a laugh. "For what purpose?"

Holmes ignored the reaction. "To investigate Moran. She hopes I will find sufficient information to discredit him so her father will rescind his permission for courtship. When she saw the emeralds... if you could have seen her... so ecstatic at the prospect that she would be financially free - no longer dependent on her father. Free to choose...." He paused briefly, a shadow darkening his face. "I tell you Watson, the end of this case shall not come soon enough."

Watson grew quiet, deep in thought. "You'll break her heart then," he announced with great solemnity.

Holmes stopped in his work and then began to tidy the equipment. He averted his eyes, his expression pained.

"Yes, I fear it must be so. Now, if you forgive me, my shoulder and the damp remind me that it has been a long day. I shall retire early. Good night Doctor." He crossed to his room and then paused before the door, turning back to face Watson. "And remember, I am counting on your discretion."

CHAPTER 7

Deception

Saturday - midafternoon - Bexley Manor

"It was kind of you to allow her that small victory," said Mary with a grateful smile. The two girls, croquet mallets swung over their shoulders, strolled back down the path towards the cottage.

"Anything to silence her incessant fussing," Edwina glanced back towards the lawn and shook her head. Clara Barclay was still capering about, regaling the spectators with the details of her triumph. Ridiculous ringlets bobbing.

Mary laughed and looked at her sideways, her blue eyes crinkling warmly. "Well to be fair, you did take one or two shortcuts that were not exactly sanctioned. Holmes showed you those didn't he?"

Edwina grinned slyly and moved towards the door. "I've been sworn to secrecy."

The bright jingle of a bicycle bell rang out as she opened the door. Both girls paused on the threshold as a mail courier rode up. The lad, smooth-faced, just on the brink of manhood, braked to a stop, sending up a small spray of gravel from the path. As he hopped off, he proudly flicked the dust from his royal blue uniform and after straightening his hat, removed a small white envelope from his mailbag. "Miss Edwina Schraeder?" he inquired courteously as he extended the envelope toward both women.

"I am, thank you." She quickly took the envelope, her lips pulling into a smile of delight as she recognized the precise script. While Mary gave the boy a few coins, she eagerly tore open the envelope and removed the note. As she read however, the smile began to fade from her face. Moments later, without a word, she pushed open the door to the cottage and disappeared inside.

Curious, Mary followed her in and found her seated on the old trunk that sat near the hearth, staring into the fireplace. "Bad news then?" she asked sympathetically as she settled next to her on the trunk.

Edwina only sighed and with a bleak expression handed her the note. A frown creased Mary's brow as she began to read.

Dearest Eddy,

Unforeseen matters necessitate a cancellation of this evening. My deepest apology. I realize you were very much looking forward to Dr. Bell's presentation. I shall endeavour to right this shortcoming at some future date.
With Kind Regards,
H.

"I am so sorry," Mary said quietly as she refolded the note and returned it to Edwina. "I cannot tell you the times I have spent waiting on the Doctor only to find out that *unforeseen events* required a change in plans. Unforeseen events usually meaning Mr. Holmes. I thought I should strangle them both in the beginning," she added with a wry smile. "Eventually, I learned to live with it and little by little, the Doctor has come around."

Despite her gloom, Edwina chuckled a bit. "Well, as you are to be married soon, I would hope so."

Mary smiled compassionately. With a kind but serious expression, she reached out and took her hand. "For Holmes, his work is everything Edwina, it will always come first. It is far more demanding than any wife or mistress could be. It does not mean, however, that he has no regard for you. On the contrary. I suspect he has more than he would care to admit. This choice will always be a struggle for him, so that is why I caution you. Do not pin your hopes on something that may never come to fruition. A friendship with Holmes may be the best you can hope for; that in itself is an exceptional achievement. As for something deeper or constant, you would be wise to consider more sensible opportunities."

A flicker of irritation crossed Edwina's face. She had no doubt that Mary spoke with only the kindest of intentions, but the idea that a more sensible opportunity awaited her in the form of Colonel Sebastian Moran set her teeth on edge. Still, she managed to hold her tongue and only smiled, replying, "Then I shall content myself with the favor of his friendship until such time he comes to his senses."

Mary stared at her for a moment and then burst into laughter. *Dear God, she was just as obstinate as the man himself. If anyone were to succeed, surely she stood the best chance.* Realizing further discussion was futile, she gave Edwina a warm hug and then rose to her feet. "I'm sorry you will miss Dr. Bell's lecture. What will you do now? You are welcome to join us for dinner. Afterwards, Clara is giving a short recital in the drawing room. Her singing voice is quite lovely, not grating at all... surprising really."

Edwina managed a smile but shook her head. "Thank you, but no. I think I shall catch up on my sketching. And perhaps use the time to sort through mother's trunk. I never really have given it my full attention."

"Very well," sighed Mary, "have a lovely evening then," she said and then quietly exited the cottage. Alone once more, Edwina settled down at the wooden table by the window. She began to sketch, doodle really as she couldn't seem to focus, absently listening to Hanna humming in the small kitchen as she prepared supper. Her eyes drifted to the handbill for Dr. Bell's lecture.

NOT TO BE MISSED - MYSTERIES OF THE HUMAN FORM AN EDUCATIONAL EXPLORATION

SATURDAY - 8:00 IN THE EVENING -

MEDICAL AMPHITHEATRE - ST. BARTHOLOMEWS

PRESENTED BY DR. JOSEPH BELL, Doctor of Medicine from Edinburgh - Fellow of the Royal College of Surgeons of Edinburgh (RSCEd) with the kind sponsorship of the Royal Academy of Physicians LONDON

GALLERY VIEWING BY MEMBER INVITATION ONLY

Limited Floor admission and viewing. 2 shillings for well-behaved members of the public

You will be astounded, shocked and enlightened!

Edwina sighed in resignation and began to crumple it fully intending to throw it into the fire. Instead, she changed her mind and after carefully smoothing it out, folded it and slid it into her skirt pocket. She turned her attention to the trunk that sat in the corner. *Well, she did have free time now, so no time like the present. Besides, the cloisonné necklace, which everyone had discounted as mere costume jewelry, had lain buried under her mother's theatre costumes and clothing for years and it had turned out to be precious stones. So perhaps something even more valuable awaited discovery.* Resolute, she crossed the room and sank to her knees in front of the trunk and threw open the lid. She began to sift through her mother's possessions and the memories that accompanied them.

»»««

Baker Street - Late afternoon – Saturday

"I picked up your mail while at the post office."

The words, delivered casually by Watson, effected a sudden burst of activity from Holmes, who, up to this point, had been inert in his wing chair, reading old case notes. Rising abruptly, he crossed the room and snatched the mail. He sorted rapidly through it, his eyes dark and somber.

"You posted my note then? Saw to it that it went out with the first courier run." His voice was low, the tone tense, on edge.

"Yes, I posted the revocation of your invitation. Late cancellations are in poor taste old man," Watson chided.

Holmes compressed his lips and looked away. "Unavoidable," he murmured as he found the letter he was searching for and tore it open, scanning the contents.

254

Watson peered over his shoulder at the letter trying to discern who it was from but soon gave up; it was in German. "Well, it was folly to invite her in the first place. Why you encourage..."

"Yes, yes, I stand corrected," growled Holmes cutting him off. He glanced at the letter in his hand once more and then dropped it onto the side table with a deep sigh. After a moment, he crossed to the mantle where he stood with one hand resting on the shelf, eyes focused somewhere beyond the flames of the fire. His demeanour spoke of weary disappointment.

Intrigued, Watson grunted to himself and picked up the letter. He unfolded it and despite the fact that he didn't read German, attempted once more to glean some information from it. He frowned a bit as his eyes settled on the one thing he could understand - a name.

"Liesel Baecker? Who is she?"

"Katerina's Schraeder's sister — Edwina's aunt — they have a small farm not far from Salzburg."

"Why are you inquiring about her aunt? I don't understand."

Holmes didn't answer immediately and instead, picked up the sketch which Edwina had given to him. His eyes grew distant, his lips pulling into a melancholy smile as he studied it and then carefully replaced it to its' position of honor on the mantle between the clock and the bust of Goethe.

"Did I tell you, Watson," he began in a low, joyless voice as he stood with his back to Watson, eyes fixed on the hearth, "it's finished now. Well, perhaps one or two minor loose ends. But, in essence, solved. I worked it out, the missing piece, while you were on your errands this afternoon. I was reviewing the case notes trying to piece together how Pennington could have produced such fine work. Yes, the paper is key but also the printing. The quality of it is in large part due to the plates. The paper is nothing without the plates. How did he come by the plates? Especially when no theft had been reported. And then it struck me. I remembered there was something in the notes that seemed a bit odd, out of place, just a brief comment about something found at the scene."

"Scene? Scene of what?" grumbled Watson in exasperation. He frowned and picked up the case notes from the table. It was the file on the break-in at Perkins, Bacon & Co. of 69 Fleet Street some eighteen months earlier.

"Scene of the crime," murmured Holmes as he finally turned back to face Watson.

Watson's frown increased. "Hardly a crime as I remember. A break in but nothing was taken. Lestrade dismissed it as minor vandalism – most likely the result of drunken vagrants. You did not disagree at the time," he added pointedly.

"Yes. Nothing was taken. Not a plate was missing but something was left behind. It's just a small comment right here in the margins, easy to miss, which of course I did," Holmes admitted with a rueful expression as he picked up the notes and pointed to the comment in question.

Watson focused intently on the note scribbled in the margin, reading aloud: "Traces of oily residue found on plates - floor also contains spatters of paraffin." He shrugged still not understanding and looked to Holmes for further explanation. "Paraffin... candle wax, isn't it?"

Holmes began to laugh and shook his head. "Among other things, but so much more. It's also used in machine shops to make precise casts and moulds of machinery. The wax reproduces all the fine details needed for delicate cogs and gears. So you see Watson, the thieves didn't need to take the original plates - only make an impression of them to cast at a later date. I'm quite certain that once the warehouse is thoroughly searched, they will find the equipment to cast the moulds; perhaps even a few of the moulds themselves. The plates are most likely locked away at Fern Hall in the vault just beyond Pennington's library."

A look of jubilation lit Watson's face and grinning broadly, he clapped the Detective on the back in congratulations. "Great Scott man, you truly have solved it. Well done."

Holmes for his part looked less than triumphant managing only a grim smile. "Well... now... all that's left to do is turn the analysis over to Lestrade. The rest is up to him and the Yard."

"And when will you do that?" asked Watson, once again sensing reluctance on Holmes' part to hand over the case to Lestrade for disposition.

"I had hoped to have better news before doing so," confessed the Detective, nodding towards the note on the table. "But I can scarcely put Lestrade off much longer. I will meet with him tomorrow afternoon and turn over the case," he said with great resignation.

"So then you do have concerns about the girl," concluded Watson, a little surprised by such an open display of fondness. "That's why you are inquiring about the Aunt. But why are you so certain that she will not remain in London once her father is arrested? She seems content at Lady Montague's and she will still have family here and an estate... an Aunt."

"How can she?" said Holmes with some bitterness. "Lady Montague, kind as she may be, will almost certainly not keep her on. As much as she pretends to delight in scandal, she will not risk the damage to her standing or family name by such an association. Edwina's only recourse will be to return to Fern Hall under the care of her father's sister. Can you imagine how that will go? Gretchen Pennington already resents her presence. How much will that increase once her brother is arrested?"

"So, to her Aunt then in Salzburg?"

"Unfortunately, the news is discouraging. My contacts inform me that Liesel Baecker and her husband have fallen on hard times. The husband has been ill, and the farm has been leased out to tenants. They have moved in with his relatives on a smaller farm to conserve their few pitiful resources. I doubt they could sustain another mouth to feed and one who, for all practical purposes, could contribute little." He paused for a moment and then managed a wry smile, adding, "Well, she's hardly a farm girl, isn't she? Now I have one more avenue to explore. We will stop on the way to send a telegram... a letter will be too slow. Go and change. Your better tweeds will do. It's half-past 5:00 and the post closes at 6:30. If we hurry, we may even have the opportunity for a glass of brandy at Simpson's, something I would dearly welcome. It will be a long evening."

Watson looked up in bewilderment.

"On the way... to?"

Holmes glanced over his shoulder as he headed towards his room to freshen up and change. "St. Bartholomew's of course. Dr. Bell's lecture."

Watson stared at him dumbfounded. "But you cancelled."

"I rescinded her invitation. I had always intended to go," he said with a rueful smile. "I need a diversion this evening Watson, not a distraction."

"Ahhh, and you do not find me distracting?"

Holmes looked up and for the first time that evening, there was a hint of his former good humor and wit. He managed a slight smile.

"Distracting? No Watson. At best, you are simply irksome."

>>«<

RECRUIT

The boy hurried along the cobbled streets as fast as his ill-fitting boots allowed, pausing only long enough to readjust the rags he had stuffed into the toes to make them fit better. They would have to do, the others had not been right; the buckles far too out of fashion. He reluctantly discarded them in the alleyway and "borrowed" the worn-out boots from a back doorstep. Along the way, he also "acquired" a patched woolen jacket which had been dangling from a clothesline and a pair of knitted fingerless gloves that had seen better days. The jacket was coarse and made his neck itch. It was far too big, hanging down to his knees, looking more like a frock coat. The gloves were full of holes, but it didn't matter, the evening damp was beginning to set in and the simple shirt and breeches he had set out in offered little protection from the cool night air. Along with warmth, the oversized jacket and gloves provided him with a sense of security.

As the clock in Westminster struck the hour of half past six, he tightened the flat cap on his head, tucking in a few unruly strands of hair and increased his pace. His destination loomed ahead – the broad courtyard that fronted St. Bartholomew's Hospital. Already the cobbled drive in front of the Henry VIII gate was filling with hansom cabs and carriages. Throngs of well-dressed gentlemen milled about under the statue of Henry VIII, smoking and socializing as they waited for the gate to open and allow them entrance. He kept moving, the front gate was not his destination. He skirted the edge of the crowd, slipping between the hansoms, keeping his cap low and tight. As he approached the small alleyway off the quadrangle, his heart fluttered with excitement. They were already there, waiting at the back entrance for the general public, an unruly, ragtag group of a half-dozen or so boys of various ages. He recognized them immediately –The Baker Street Irregulars. The boy paused once more to catch his breath, his mouth suddenly dry; once again he checked the fit of his shirt and jacket. Adjusting his cap, he took a deep breath and headed for the back of the queue, checking his pockets once more for the few shillings he had managed to scrape together.

>>«<

ST. BARTHOLOMEW'S SURGICAL AMPHITHEATRE

"Well, it's increasingly clear that you have no concept of discretion." The Professor lit a cigar and leaned back in his gallery seat. He glanced briefly at the London Times and then set it aside, fixing his gaze on his companion. His manner was one of icy disdain.

Sebastian Moran settled uneasily into his seat, a swell of irritation rising within. He did not appreciate the lecture but tempered his anger knowing full well it was best not to trifle with this man.

"An unforeseen complication arose, I handled it," he said simply, matching the Professor's manner in nonchalance.

The Professor arched his brow, incredulous, and rolled the smoke of the Partagas over his tongue. He was quiet for a moment; his gaze wandered to the floor of the amphitheater below, watching as the standing area began to fill with all manner of tradesmen and those lower. A slight smile formed on his lips; the common man ... they reminded him of cattle as they jostled and vied for position to get ahead in the chute, utterly oblivious of the fate awaiting them at the end.

"You acted rashly," he said, eyes still fixed on the floor below. "Fortunately, there seems to be little interest in dead Chinamen... no mention until page three. I caution you, this is not a tiger hunt, theatrics are ill-advised."

Moran bristled. "I had no choice but to act. That sniveling little rat Tai Quon, he was only supposed to scare the girl, take the necklace and incapacitate Holmes. Damned fool. He actually believed he was going to get away with selling her; had a client lined up. He forced my hand."

Scorn curled the Professor's mouth as he turned back to meet his gaze. "Yes, well as the saying goes, no honour among thieves."

"Surely you didn't expect me to just leave her there?" protested Moran with great indignation. "After all, she is your partner's daughter. Cold-blooded, even for you."

The Professor took a long draw on his cigar and studied the Colonel through the haze of smoke. "Well as it turns out, you did just that. Holmes is the one who came to her aid. Freed her despite his injury. And the necklace, where is it now? Lost? In Holmes' possession? Have you any inkling what you have done? Other than further attract that meddler's attention and strengthen her attachment to him, what exactly is it you have achieved Sebastian?"

Moran sputtered but held his tongue. After a brief pause, he compressed his lips and bitterly declared, "She'll come around. After all, what choice does she have? As for the necklace, mark my words, it will be recovered in due course."

To this, the Professor said nothing for quite some time and turned his attention to the rest of the upper-level gallery, which was quickly filling up with gentlemen on both sides. As he peered across to the other side, he suddenly began to smile. "Well, my dear Colonel, if all else fails, perhaps you can just ask him for it. Unless I am mistaken, your rival has just arrived."

Moran glanced up and looked across the empty space between the galleries; resentment darkened his face on seeing it was indeed so.

»»«

"Oh...you there! Where in the bleedin' hell are you going?" The shout was accompanied by a small stone which smacked the boy soundly on the back of the neck. He froze and lifted his hand to his neck. His fingers came away with a splotch of blood. Still he did not turn to face his assailant. Instead, he stood motionless, heart pounding, eyes fixed straight ahead, racking his brain for what next to do.

"Deaf are ya? Turn around runt."

The boy took a deep breath and slowly turned to find himself surrounded by a group of a half dozen of the Irregulars. He kept his eyes fixed on the ground. A rotund, baby-faced boy of about thirteen approached, his cheeks flushed and dotted with perspiration. He moved closer, panting with every step.

"Back of the line ... ain't no cuts."

The boy who was a little taller than his accuser, but half the size nodded that he understood. He hadn't intended to move ahead of them but had only moved with the flow of the crowd. The Irregulars had been too busy roughhousing to pay attention and fallen behind. Nevertheless, the last thing he wanted was an altercation and began to step back. As he did, one of the others stuck out their foot; he went down hard, sprawling into the dirt. It was only by sheer luck that he managed to keep his cap on. Laughter erupted all around and as he scrambled to his feet, he clenched his fists by his side. He took a deep breath, willing himself to remain calm though his cheeks burned brightly. He had come this far, he wasn't going to let a group of unruly brats ruin his evening. Brushing off his clothes, he averted his eyes and began to move past them towards the back of the line.

"Oi! Not till you say sorry," warned his stout aggressor. "Say it then..."

The boy remained silent and then bobbed his head in acknowledgement. The heavyset boy moved closer, studying him curiously. "Somethin' wrong wit you? Cat got your tongue then?" Another chorus of laughter and jeers erupted.

"Maybe e's sick in the head like old man Chadwick ...'cept he jabbers all the time... even when no one's there," laughed a thin slip of a boy wearing a battered top hat.

"Naw," countered a sickly-looking boy of about twelve with only three front teeth, "I bet e's one of them deaf mutants. I saw one once, on the corner of Piccadilly... beggin' he was... had a bitty monkey."

The boy with the top hat smacked the boy with only three teeth in his arm. "Git off you idiot, tweren't no mutant only a midget, and I 'eard 'im chattering plenty of times...'specially when the dollymops are about."

The heavyset youth waved his arms in annoyance and shushed them, turning his attention back to the boy. "Well then, what kind of freak are ya then? You tell me or..."

"Leave him be Dobber, he ain't doing you no harm," warned a sharp, clear voice. The boys, who had been gathering in a semi-circle, abruptly parted and grew silent as a tall, lanky youth of about seventeen dressed in a patched waistcoat and trousers, stepped forward. His face was long and angular, the eyes bright and shrewd. On a good day, he might have been considered moderately handsome if it were not for the misshapen nose which overshadowed his other features. It had been broken numerous times and sat crookedly in the center of his face. Still, it did not diminish the glimmer of intelligence in his eyes.

"Wot's your name boy?" he asked calmly as he advanced.

For the first time that evening, the boy experienced genuine unease. He took a step back and pulled his cap even lower, keeping his eyes on the ground; he said not a word.

"Ain't said word one Bill, e's a freak, or lunatic... mebbe from Bethnal House," suggested Dobber in an attempt to regain respect.

"Shaddup," growled the lanky youth. "Ain't no lunatic. Ain't no crime not to talk. Me gran can't talk an she's got more sense 'en the lot of ya." Once he had shamed the rest of the Irregulars into silence, he once more turned back to the boy. He paused for a moment and then grinned amiably. Wiping the grime from his hand onto his trousers, he stuck out his hand.

"Bill Wiggins the name but most just call me Wiggins."

The boy hesitated and then tentatively extended his hand.

Wiggins grinned and took his hand, pumping it in welcome as he tried to get a better look at the boy. He was about average size for his age which he judged to be about fifteen or so. Bit of meat on his bones still, pale but no yellow tinge to the skin like the others yet and his hands, what he could see and feel of them under the gloves, lacked calluses and were clean. So, using the skills he had observed his mentor use so often, he concluded: not on the street long - perhaps just hours. "That's it... got a name then?"

With a shrug, the boy slid his hands in his pockets. He nodded and then using the toe of his boot, scrawled "NED" in the dirt.

The grin on Wiggin's face widened. "Ned, it is then. Welcome Ned," he said and clapped the boy soundly on the shoulder. "Say 'ello to Ned boys, e'll be joinin us today... mebbe longer?"

260

The others responded with a greeting, though some a little less warmly than others. By this time, the line had started to move forward again. Wiggins, still holding him by the shoulder, steered Ned towards the front of the standing area which was already beginning to fill up. "Not such a bad lot once you git to know em. You'll see, they won't worry you no more."

Ned nodded absently, his attention elsewhere as he surveyed the amphitheatre taking in all the sights and sounds. In the center of the room was a dais on which stood a podium and a gurney – empty at the moment. The gas on the lamps was still up high and he shaded his eyes with his hand as he looked up at the galleries, casually watching the gentlemen take their seats. As the lamps began to dim, he began to shift his gaze back towards the stage and then suddenly froze, uttering a small gasp - the first sound he had uttered all evening.

Wiggins looked at him curiously. "You all right Ned?" He followed the boy's gaze, curious as to what had startled him and then began to smile in understanding. Lots of the newcomers had that same reaction when they first laid eyes upon him in person. "Right, the man himself." He leaned in a little closer to the boy, a proud smile on his face. "E's a great man...e is. We work together sometimes. Me and the boys 'elp him. Tell u wot', - you stick wit me an' I'll introduce you. Mr. Holmes, e's quite a gent...bet e'd be happy to take you on... clever boy like you."

The lamps faded save for the dais, which was now brightly lit. Ned remained silent. A frown darkened his face, a scarlet flush colouring his cheeks as he shifted his attention back to the dais. Moments later, the theatre erupted with thunderous applause as Dr. Bell took to the stage. Ned barely gave him a glance - his thoughts elsewhere...

"Bravo! Bravo!"

A rousing cheer of delight and applause thundered throughout the amphitheatre, patrons rising to their feet to signal their amazement as Dr. Bell and his assistants carefully unwound and then displayed the twenty feet of the cadaver's small intestine. Watson paused in mid-clap and peered back over his shoulder. A slight frown creased his face. Holmes had barely moved all evening – still seated in his chair, his attention focused on scribbling notes in his small leather book. The lamps slowly brightened, signaling the beginning of intermission. Watson settled back into his chair watching idly while down below, Dr. Bell disappeared back behind the curtains while his assistants soon followed. They wheeled the cadaver off the dais, his intestines now neatly laid out on his chest. After the intermission, they would soon return with a fresh specimen. He was quiet for a few moments and then lightly cleared his throat as he turned his attention back to Holmes.

"You have barely lifted your head all evening. I thought you enjoyed Dr. Bell's lectures?"

Holmes paused in his writing and glanced up, a petulant expression curling his mouth.

"Hardly a lecture," he sighed. "If I want to see a man's bowels on display, I'll visit the morgue. This is theatre Watson, not science. It seems Dr. Bell has lost his way."

"The public want to be entertained Holmes. Besides, it was your suggestion. You said you required a diversion."

To this, Holmes only shrugged and went back to his notes. Watson's expression grew more solemn disquieted by the Detective's marked descent into melancholy. He reached out and carefully eased the notebook from Holmes, his frown deepening as he scanned the notes that were more a series of words and fragments of thoughts than a cohesive passage.

Moran's attentions... why Eddy? Lovely - charming but there are more alluring. Negligible dowry - too independent for his tastes. Pennington lower status - the necklace? How would he know? Eddy doesn't know. Katerina - conceal emeralds from whom - not Moran - too young. Pennington - too weak... another player? Moran...accomplice? Competencies - marksman - tracker - soldier - skilled with a knife...brute - marginal intellect? Who is he? How is he here? Who is mastermind?

Watson returned the notebook with a sigh. "Being a hunter and soldier hardly makes him a criminal or a brute. As for intelligence, well he does not strike me as an idiot."

Holmes chuckled slightly, detecting a trace of indignation in the Doctor's manner.

"Idiot, no. I would not call him that, but it seems to me he lacks the finesse or vision to craft such a scheme. He's a follower Watson, not a leader."

Watson compressed his lips and shrugged in resignation. "Well, need I remind you, at this point, it's all just conjecture, isn't it? Unless you have some proof I am not aware of. And, according to Mary, he has been quite courteous and proper in his attentions to Edwina. Just the other day, he brought her roses."

"Roses..." Holmes snickered. "It is this very 'courtesy' that troubles me."

"Perhaps you are letting your prejudice color."

"Prejudice?" interrupted Holmes, a flash of irritation in his eyes.

Watson began to chuckle and leaned back in his seat, a knowing smile on his lips.

"I find it odd how your antipathy towards the man has increased exponentially concurrent with his interest in Edwina. Admit it, Holmes, she has gotten under your skin. It's obvious to everyone else but you."

The pronouncement was met with a half-smile and sigh of exasperation. "This conversation is tedious," announced Holmes as he rose abruptly from his seat.

Watson hesitated, gathering his thoughts before speaking, not quite ready to let the matter go. "There is no disgrace in allowing yourself to be human," he counseled soothingly. "It's a welcome change. I have seen more genuine joy and cheer in you these past months Holmes, than I have seen in years. It's apparent you enjoy her company and she has made no secret of her affection for you."

There was a moment of awkward silence. Gradually Holmes' expression softened, his brow furrowed in reflection. "I will admit to a certain fondness... her intelligence – spirit are endearing, but anything more, I..." His words abruptly stopped, a look of disbelief and bewilderment clouding his face as he peered across to the opposite gallery. "Bloody Hell, he's here," he murmured, his mouth tightening with ill-concealed displeasure.

"What? Who?" asked Watson, confused by the sudden shift in topic. He followed his gaze, trying to see what or whom had diverted the Detective's attention.

"Moran," muttered Holmes. "But why? Hardly his element and who the devil is that with him? Strange, an odd pairing for sure. Watson, your theatre glasses, do you have them?"

"Yes, of course," Watson replied and quickly handed over a pair of small binoculars which he kept in his breast pocket. Holmes peered through the glasses and then shrugged, a look of consternation clouding his face.

"The unknown player, perhaps," he mused and then with a sigh, handed the glasses back to Watson. "I don't suppose you know this man."

Watson peered through the glasses and then much to Holmes' surprise nodded. Actually, I have seen him come to think of it, at the club the other night. He was there with Moran. Yes, that is definitely him. Older gentleman – tall, gaunt...distinguished, smokes cigars, very expensive. Stamford mentioned his name... let me see... he's an academic... retired Professor, mathematics I believe."

"Professor?" exclaimed Holmes keenly, his eyes intense and alert. *Again, that designation.* Watson continued to ramble as he searched back through his memory of the previous evening. "...and his name was... Professor James... or was it John... Ahh... Damn... it escapes me now. As for the last name, I haven't a clue, something with an M. Perhaps Irish if I recall. Sorry Holmes, a few too many brandies. I'm afraid I wasn't listening all that closely." But his apology didn't seem to matter for Holmes was once more in motion, hastily pulling on his gloves and coat.

"Are we leaving then? The second half is about to start," Watson began to rise, reaching for his coat as the gas lamps began to flicker and dim signaling the end of the intermission.

Holmes smiled bleakly and shook his head. "I'm afraid I've no taste for it, but you stay. In fact, I insist. As for me, a thought has occurred... an avenue of inquiry I've neglected... avoided."

A tinge of unease clouded Watson's face. "What avenue? Where are you going Holmes? I think I should come with you."

The Detective paused, top hat in hand, fingers travelling lightly along the brim, his eyes veiled and sober. At first, he remained silent. Then with the most resolute and forbidding of expressions, he shook his head, announcing, "No Watson, I insist, you must not. Do not wait for me. I expect to be quite late," he advised with great solemnity and turned on heel, heading swiftly down the aisle. Moments later, he had vanished, blending in amongst those who were hurrying back to retake their seats. Watson reluctantly sank back into his seat, his mind ill-at-ease unable to shake a vague sense of foreboding.

>>«<

"2 farthings says e cracks the noggin and prys out 'is brain," sniggered Dobber as he slapped his coins down on the small rail that separated the common area from the dais.

A chorus of whistles and jeers erupted from the Irregulars as they occupied themselves with dice while Dr. Bell's assistants moved about the dimly lit dais in preparation for the next presentation.

"Mebbe so," snorted the boy with three teeth, "best take a good look then Dobbers, closest you'll ever come to one." Dobbers stared at him - momentarily perplexed while the rest of the Irregulars burst into laughter. Slowly as comprehension sank in, his plump cheeks burned bright crimson.

"All right you lot... settle now," advised Wiggins in a benevolent growl. He cracked a grin and gave the plump boy a good-natured clap on the back. "Don't pay 'im no mind Dobbs... my money says brains it is. Wot 'bout you Ned?" He swiveled his head, looking around for their newest recruit. "Brains or more innar..." He stopped in mid-sentence, the boy was nowhere to be seen. Bloody 'ell! Where's e got to?" He looked to the rest of the Irregulars for an explanation, a concern creasing his face. "Ned... Neddie?"

A few of the boys shook their heads, they hadn't really been paying attention, no one had seen him slip off. Dobbers grinned a little smugly. "I tole you, e's a queer one alight."

A frown darkened Wiggin's face as he thought back to his own first days on the street. It was hard enough for a young one to be out on the street alone with no voice or experience to rely on. If you were lucky enough to survive the weather, lack of shelter or food or the various maladies, there were the low-lifes and hooligans to contend with. As for the law, they were often indistinguishable from the ruffians. Fortune indeed had smiled upon him that day when he and a few of his mates had tried to pick Mr. Holmes' pocket as he stood chatting with the newsagent on the corner of Baker and Marylebone Road. They'd failed – miserably. Despite the protests of the newsagent, Holmes had refused to call the constable. Instead, he'd led them to Baker Street where after much wrangling, he convinced a reluctant Mrs. Hudson who had filled their bellies and let them sleep in the coal cellar. The very next day Holmes put them to work doing what they did best, freely roaming the streets where no one paid them any mind. They had become his eyes and ears on the streets of London.

Wiggins had hoped to help Ned in the way that Holmes had helped him. He was convinced that the boy had what it took to join the network; a special blend of unflagging determination and a quick wit. But it was all for naught, the boy had simply vanished before he could act.

"E'll be all right Wiggins. Tweren't no fool, never mind what Dobbs says," said the boy with three teeth in an attempt to lighten his mood.

Wiggins shrugged and then nodded at the boy. Maybe, maybe not, the plain truth was it was out of his hands now.

>>«<

DARK REVELATIONS

Ned paused at the edge of the alley, hugging the shadow of the tenement, grateful for the opportunity to catch his breath as he peered out across the dimly lit street. He was utterly bewildered by the sight that lay before him. It was inexplicable, a stately Georgian manor house fronted by spreading chestnut trees. Eight granite steps led up to a bright crimson door; above the lintel was the bas-relief of a lotus flower.

For nearly an hour, he had scrambled to keep up with the Detective, blindly hurrying after him down increasingly narrowing lanes and streets. He'd been thankful at first when Holmes had decided not to avail himself of the hansoms that had queued in front of St Bart's, knowing full well that once inside a hansom, he would never be able to keep pace with him. Instead, Holmes had set out on foot, heading down Giltspur Lane at a leisurely pace. He seemed a man out for an evening stroll, meandering casually through the city streets – past St. Paul's, St. Mary LeBow, even past the stately Mansion

House where the Lord Mayor of London resided. Ned wondered briefly if perhaps Holmes had business there, but the Detective continued without breaking stride. So he followed, down Leadenhall towards Aldgate, the streets narrowing the shops becoming less refined and more suited to the common Londoner. Still, this border area was crowded with hansoms, peddler carts and a generous mix of classes. As they moved away from the market district, Holmes quickened his pace, causing Ned to increase his as well. On crossing Commercial Street, Holmes abruptly paused and glanced behind him. Ned ducked behind a vegetable cart, his mouth suddenly dry, unsure as to whether he'd been seen. The Detective stood motionless for a moment as if considering his route and then set off again. He veered sharply south towards the river. For the first time that evening, as the foul miasma from the Thames assaulted his nostrils, Ned felt a twinge of anxiety. The crowds had thinned, now mainly composed of seamen, tradesman and an occasional woman of questionable repute. No one, however, gave him a second glance. The discomfort caused by the coarseness of his "borrowed" clothes now seemed a small price to pay for his anonymity.

By the time they skirted the edge of Whitechapel and entered Limehouse, the light bands of magenta in the evening sky had given way to deepening shades of royal blue and purple. The streets were now little more than dingy alleys shrouded in rising fog, dimly lit and filled with all manner of debris. Voices and sounds echoed eerily off the walls of the buildings and with his heart in his throat, Ned wondered what possible reason the Detective could have for being in such a squalid area. Still he followed, increasingly mindful of his surroundings and his pace. Then, just as unexpectedly as it had begun, the journey came to an end as the alley emptied out onto the wide avenue lined with graceful chestnut trees which fronted the impressive manor house.

He struggled to make sense of it as he watched Holmes cross the street and ascend the steps without the slightest hesitation. The Detective had barely knocked when a footman in formal livery emerged and greeted him cordially; he ushered him inside without hesitation. Unsure as to whether he should continue, Ned lingered in the shadows studying the white stucco front of the building and the windows all shuttered with heavy drapes. The building was scrupulously maintained, but its' very presence troubled him; it didn't fit the surroundings. Perhaps he should wait until the Detective re-emerged. As he turned the matter over in his mind, an elegant Clarence carriage rolled up to the curb and four dapper gentlemen, attired in top hats and cutaways climbed out. Chatting with great excitement, they mounted the stairs and rapped on the crimson door. The footman reappeared and took their cards, scrutinizing them. He spoke to each man briefly in quiet tones and then apparently satisfied, stood back and allowed them entrance. Ned's curiosity and unease increased. Holmes had not presented a card but was granted entrance nonetheless, so he was apparently known to the footman. The gentlemen, however, had only been allowed entrance after scrutiny and presentation of their credentials. What manner of place was this that would allow both the known and unknown entrance equally at the sole discretion of a footman? Why were all the curtains drawn so tightly that not a sliver of light peeked through? Ned racked his brain, considering how he would gain entrance fairly certain the answer to his questions lay inside and that said footman would not give him a pass.

The sound of a door opening off to the side caught his attention, interrupting his rumination. Shifting his gaze, he noted a small courtyard just around the edge of the house. A pool of light spilled out as the door opened illuminating a small fountain flanked by a few stone benches. It was close to the edge of the property and backed up next to a small cobbled alley that ran down the long side of the building before winding its' way back to the main street. He inched closer to the edge of the wall where he lingered in the shadows, trying to get a better look. There, on a few of the benches, sat a small group of boys, ragtag like the Irregulars only quieter. They waited near the fountain, holding onto small wooden boxes or balancing trays filled with matches and novelties that hung by leather straps from their necks. Every so often, the side door would open and a small Chinese woman, white-haired and stooped with age, would appear. After inspecting the boys, she would point a long bony finger at one or two, and they would disappear with her through the door. Ned drew a deep breath and once more checked the fit of his cap and jacket; the way in was clear – now all he needed was the courage to act.

»»««

LOTUS HOUSE

The odor, pungent and sensual, hung in the air like a velvet drape. Holmes' eyes grew languid for a moment as he drew the sweet aroma deep into his lungs and followed the footman down the plush, carpeted hallway. He glanced casually to the side as they passed several parlours, all rapidly filling with gentlemen who were settling in at the gaming tables or on settees to socialize and smoke. Silently and with effortless grace in the midst of all these men, glided several raven-haired Chinese beauties. Each was wrapped in an exquisite silk mandarin robe, the color chosen to complement their delicacy. Carrying fine silver trays, they offered tea, fine spirits and long elegant pipes for those who wished to partake of the house specialty. And for those who had been approved by Madam Xiu Li Chang and could pay the fee, there were additional pleasures offered. A slight smile curled Holmes' lips - The Contagious Diseases Act seemed far from anyone's mind - business was brisk.

Further back, several of the parlours were closed off with heavy velvet drapes drawn across the openings, muffling sounds and providing anonymity for the occupants. Holmes barely gave them a glance; he had little interest in what politicians or gentry may be concealed behind them or what engaged their interests. The only evidence of their inhabitation was the sweet aroma of the pipe that wafted out into the hall and the shoes neatly set outside the

267

curtains. Every so often a scruffy youth would dart past him in the hall and collect them, heading back down towards the servants' kitchen to polish them. Madam employed a small army of street urchins on an ad hoc basis. They silently roamed the halls and parlours selling their matches and offering shines to the gentlemen as they socialized and smoked. Depending on the length of your visit, it was even possible to have your collars and waistcoats steamed and pressed while you indulged. Madam Chang was an enterprising woman, utilizing employees from her family's other thriving business empire in Limehouse, the laundry. He continued to follow the footman down the long hallway until they reached a small library. The footman knocked once and then waited; moments later the door was opened open by a petite Chinese woman also clothed in traditional Mandarin robes only hers was ebony in color. Her skin was unblemished and free of wrinkles, her grey eyes clear and bright and although her dark hair showed small traces of gray, it was difficult to pinpoint her age. On seeing Holmes, her face lit up with genuine warmth and she took his hands in hers, pressing them in welcome as she drew him inside the room.

"My dearest Holmes, how pleased I am that you have returned. It has been too long... many months now." She looked behind him expectantly and then sighed heavily.

"Again, no Dr. Watson? My girls will be disappointed."

Holmes chuckled. Watson had long been a favorite of the ladies, a distinction he seemed to prefer to forget as of late. He bowed his head in respect and pressed her hands in return. "My dear Madam, there are certain things the good Doctor has relinquished since his engagement. He intends no slight and sends only warm greetings and deep respect for you and your lovely ladies. He is, however, a man who takes his betrothal vow quite seriously. I do not expect you will see him here again."

To this Madame Chang only shrugged and with a sly grin replied, "Well, we shall see then once he has married. As they say, the rose fades fast once plucked. Lotus House is filled with many gentlemen who have taken such a vow... my best clients. Fortunately, my dear Holmes, we still have you. I will send word to Mei Lien. She will be most pleased – she has oft asked after you."

Holmes hesitated knowing full well his response must be crafted with great care. Madam Chang's insight into the workings of Limehouse and the Docks had proven to be invaluable; he would loathe to lose it. "With humble apologies to your daughter Madam, I must admit the purpose of my visit is of a professional nature," he said with a slight nod and smile of regret.

Disappointed, but pacified by the tone of his answer, Madam Chang shrugged and lightly clasped his arm. She arched her brow, regarding him with shrewd curiosity and led him over to the sofa. "Well, to deny yourself so, it must be of great importance. You must tell me every detail Holmes and leave nothing out."

As they settled on the divan, she clapped her hands once and an elderly man bent with age, stepped out from behind a red and gold satin screen. He bowed deeply, his long white beard flowing in wisps to his waist as he brought forth an ebony tray inlaid with mother of pearl. He set it on the table in front of them and then bowed, taking his leave. Holmes' eyes grew veiled, his mouth suddenly dry. *A fine line to tread indeed.* On this tray sat two long pipes of jade and ivory fitted with silver bowls. The remainder of the tray was filled with the paraphernalia required to prepare and smoke the Chandu. Madam Chang smiled contentedly as she selected a pipe and then held it out to him. "Some stories are best told with the aid of smoke. I sense perhaps this is one of them."

Holmes was silent for a moment, his eyes fixed on the pipe. He had already declined her hospitality once, to do so again might prove unwise. He sighed and then with a smile of resignation, nodded in acceptance.

"Excellent!" cried Madam in delight as she busied herself with the preparations. Lifting the glass chimney of the lamp, she lit the wick and then replaced the glass when satisfied with the flame. She selected a small brown pill of raw opium about the size of a pea from the porcelain jar. Holmes watched intently. Although he had more than a passing acquaintance with the process himself, he was still fascinated by the ritual. With an expression of utmost gravity, Madam Chang placed the opium in the bowl of the pipe, added a few drops of water and began to heat the metal. The water began to boil and soon the pill liquefied, leaving a brown fluid behind. *Only a weakness if allowed to be so...* He compressed his lips, mentally reminding himself. The metal was now sufficiently heated, and the liquid opium began to vaporize. Holmes took the pipe and inhaled, drawing the smoke deep into his lungs. The sensation was immediate and euphoric, the tension from his body and mind dissipating along with the vapors. As he lifted the pipe to capture the remaining fumes, his eyes drifted to the soft glow of the ancestor shrine on the mantle. He had seen it before of course, the small votive candle in the lotus shaped holder which was always lit in front of the framed tintype of Madam's long deceased husband. He focused on the soft glow of the flame and then suddenly paused, lowering the pipe. Alongside the photograph of Madam's husband stood another, with its own votive candle and offerings. Holmes laid the pipe on the table and rose to his feet, his attention now focused on the second shrine.

"My dear Madam," he began in soft apology as he crossed the room to investigate, "I fear I have been remiss. You are grieving, and I have not offered my condolences. My deepest apology." As he drew closer to the mantle and the features on the tintype became sharper, he abruptly stopped, an unexpected twinge in his shoulder. The last remnants of his euphoria vanished when his eyes settled on the image of a slim faced young man with a long dark braid, a pair of gold pince-nez perched on his nose. Tai Quon, looking considerably better then when last he had seen him, gazed out serenely from behind the glow of the ancestor shrine. Holmes turned to Madam Chang, choosing his words with great care. "Your nephew Madam?"

A look of mild sadness darkened the woman's face and she forced a bleak smile as she also set aside her pipe. "Not by blood Mr. Holmes but we are close in Limehouse. My brother's ward – an orphan. He and his late wife, the blessings of our ancestors upon her sweet soul, took him in as a child, raised him as if their own. A bright boy but troubled, full of envy and anger despite their best efforts. My brother employed him to assist with the ledgers; he had a natural ability for numbers. It was not enough, however, to keep him from misfortune; he was greedy – hungry for wealth. Lately, we had come to fear that he was involved in trade that was less than honorable with men who could not be trusted."

Holmes knit his brow at the irony of the statement but remained silent. Upon reflection, the operation of a brothel and opium house was marginally better than trading in white slavery. At least the former involved some form of free choice on the part of the participants. He nodded for her to continue though he already knew the ending to the story.

"He came to a violent end, fished from the river a few days past. I pray to the ancestors to forgive his transgressions and grant his spirit peace." She bowed her head reverentially.

"I am sorry for your loss Madam. And the police, any news?"

Madam Chang smiled bitterly and shook her head. "No news Mr. Holmes. I expect none. What is one more dead Chinaman to them?" She gazed up at the shrine, her eyes far away for a moment and then sighed, turning back to face him. "But enough of such talk, the past cannot be undone. You have come here for my help Mr. Holmes, so please, tell me what can I do?"

Holmes nodded and then reached inside his coat, withdrawing a small photograph he had clipped from the Illustrated London News. He had found it buried on the society pages; it showed Colonel Sebastian Moran receiving a medal for valor along with some of his men upon their return from Kabul.

"Do know this man Madam? Have you seen him here?"

She studied the picture carefully and then slowly nodded. "Yes, I believe so Mr. Holmes, but he did not stay long."

"And why is that Madam?" he asked with a frown.

Madam Chang hesitated for a moment, choosing her words carefully. It was ill advised to speak too freely about a customer's proclivities even if you were unable to accommodate; her business was based on discretion and word travelled quickly in the community. If the question had been asked by the Yard or any other detective, she would have declined to answer, but she had known Holmes for several years and realized that if he asked, it was of great importance.

"I do not know the particulars. It occurred while I was visiting my brother's family. I understand that he was asked to leave, which he did willingly and with no ill temper. Mei Lien was in charge. If you require details then you must ask her. She will be most happy to help you Mr. Holmes. Shall I send word to her that you wish to see her?"

With an air of resignation, Holmes nodded his assent. Madam Chang's eyes sparkled with glee and clapping her hands together, she once more called the old gentleman forth from behind the screen. She barked out instructions in Mandarin and sent him off upstairs to alert her eldest daughter.

"It will not be long. So tell me, what is your pleasure then? Will you share another pipe Mr. Holmes? It would please me greatly. Or perhaps, there are the gaming tables?"

Holmes arched his brow, it was tempting, but shook his head. "You are most gracious Madam and your hospitality is most appreciated but as I need a clear mind, I think the gaming tables are better suited."

A look of disappointment clouded Madam's face, but she nodded that she understood. Taking him by the arm, she led him over to the gaming parlour and settled him at one of the tables. After ensuring that he was well supplied with a bottle of the finest Claret, she wished him good health and then bowed, taking her leave. Holmes lit a cigarette and poured a glass of claret deciding to make the best of it as he waited. A few other gentlemen settled at the table — one of two he knew casually — perhaps a game or two of cards to pass the time. As they waited for another player, a slight smile tugged at his mouth. He and Watson had spent many an evening pleasantly engaged, it was a fond memory. That was all past now.

"By God, the prodigal has returned."

The voice, slightly slurred and dripping with disdain, sounded from behind him. It grated on his nerves interrupting his reverie. Holmes sighed, he did not even need to look up. He recognized it instantly as the voice of Percy Gilchrist.

"Percy, I take it your "Aunt" has reinstated your allowance. Have you something for me then?"

Percival Gilchrist's face turned bright scarlet as the other gentlemen at the table sniggered. It was common knowledge that Percy's Aunt wasn't related to him at all but rather a lonely old dowager with very deep pockets who liked her men young and easily bought. It was also common knowledge that Gilchrist still owed the Detective a fair amount from their last card game. He forced an embarrassed smile and sank into a seat opposite Holmes, nervously smoothing the ends of his mustache. A phantom pain coursed through his jaw reminding him of their last encounter at the tables.

"I don't suppose old man, you could extend me the courtesy of a bit more time? Things have been a little rough ... run of bad luck."

"Ahh, that is unfortunate," chuckled Holmes wryly, "but how bad can it be Percy? You seemingly have enough to waste at the tables or on Madam's ladies."

Laughter once more erupted at the table. Percy cleared his throat and smiled weakly. He seemed at a loss for words for a moment and then blurted, "I don't have your money Holmes. That's the truth of it." He turned a little pale and then leaned forward, lowering his voice, "To be honest old man, I'm in a bit of a jam. I lost everything at the tables this morning... and... well... I don't even have the money to pay my bill. Madam... uh... doesn't know yet. It would be much appreciated if you could see your way to keeping this between us."

Holmes almost laughed, the man was truly pathetic. Maybe it was due to the mellowing effect of the pipe or maybe he was just weary of the situation – it didn't matter. After a moment, he shrugged and reached for the card deck. "Consider it done Percy, not a word. In fact, I forgive you your debt."

"What? Bloody Hell," gasped Percy in astonishment.

Holmes fixed him with a sober look and leaned forward. He paused for a moment and then took the newspaper clipping from his pocket and set it on the table. "I need you to keep an eye out for this man," he said, his finger tapping the photograph of Sebastian Moran, "not only here, but any of the other places you inhabit."

"Just like Watson then?" chuckled Gilchrist in utter delight. "What's he done then?"

"Discreetly Percy," warned Holmes, hoping that he wasn't making a mistake. "At the moment, nothing I am aware of. Can you do this then?"

Gilchrist nodded that he could. The two men shook hands to seal the bargain and then settled back. Holmes slid the bottle of claret across the table to Gilchrist and picked up the deck of cards. He glanced at his pocket watch wondering how long he would have to wait on Madam's daughter, Mei Lien.

"Well, I've a bit of time it seems, what say you? Double our last game?"

Gilchrist started to reach for the cards and then hesitated. "As I mentioned earlier, I am a little short on cash."

Holmes sighed heavily and shrugged. "I'll stake you Percy, once again," he said as he dealt the cards.

"Capital," cried the man in delight. Rubbing his hands together, he picked up his cards and took a sip of Claret.

"Well Holmes, I must say, you've certainly become more reasonable considering our last encounter."

"Just play Percy," sighed the Detective with as much patience as he could muster.

"Granted, there was that girl... they're always trouble. Little minx. What do you suppose ever happened to her?"

Holmes paused, but kept his eyes focused on his cards.

"I'm sure she's fine Percy."

"I'll say. Fine bit of muslin - though I wager I could teach her a thing or two."

At this Holmes lowered his cards a bit, an odd light in his eyes. He smiled wryly and shook his head, thinking back to that day on the road to Fern Hall.

"Well, judging by past events Percy, I rather think she wouldn't let you."

»»«««

UNMASKED

She was the most beautiful and exotic creature Ned had ever seen. He had been collecting shoes in the hallway, loitering, eyes fixed on the gaming parlour when she glided past in a whisper of red silk embroidered with golden thread. Delicate and willowy, the smooth fabric of her robe clung to her like a second skin. She left a trace of sandalwood, musk, and nutmeg in her wake. This scent combined with the heavy sweetness of the opium laced air left him feeling lightheaded and unsettled. As she entered the gaming parlour, long jet-black hair streaming down her back to her hips, scarlet lips curved with absolute confidence; there wasn't a gentleman that failed to notice her, no matter how engrossed in their cards or the pipe. It was obvious, however, as she gracefully maneuvered around the crowded tables and settees, that her sights were set on one gentleman in particular. Ned watched mesmerized as she approached the table where Holmes played cards. All it took was one smile and a simple crook of her slender finger, long red nail beckoning, and Holmes was on his feet. With the briefest nod to his companions, accompanied by a sly smile, he took up his winnings and followed her. They ascended the stairs, chatting softly in an unknown language, walking side by side so closely that her shapely hip brushed periodically against his. Holmes didn't seem to mind. It was a revelation that left Ned with an odd tightness in his chest as he crept up the stairs after them. He still held onto the boots he had collected, dangling them by the laces. As he followed them down the long hallway, he kept his head low, eyes fixed on the oriental carpet that assisted in muffling the sounds of laughter and pleasure that drifted out from behind the doors. Off to his right, a door opened and he froze for a moment as a red-faced man with greying hair, shirt open to his waist, leaned unsteadily against the door frame and peered out into the hall with dull eyes. A woman in blue silk, who could easily have been the younger twin of the creature with Holmes, stood behind the man laughing softly. With one hand, she held a pipe while the other gently grasped the belt loops of the man's trousers. They both saw him, Ned was sure of it, but paid him no mind. Why should they? To them, he was just another guttersnipe, no one of importance. Moments later, the woman gently reeled the man back inside and shut the door. Ned breathed a little easier and then refocused his attention. He looked up and caught a glimpse of Holmes and the creature disappearing into a room at the end of the hall. He hesitated, wracked with uncertainty as to whether he should continue. The evening had been filled with many surprises, most of them unpleasant, a few darkly disturbing. The Detective's very presence in this place troubled him. As he watched Holmes in the gaming parlour, he had almost convinced himself that surely the Detective was on the trail of something – engaged in a case. The doubt truly began when Holmes took up the pipe. It increased exponentially when the creature appeared and with nary a word spirited him away.

The door closed after them. He stared down the hall for a moment, undecided and then found himself following them, his legs moving on their own. By the time he reached the creature's room, his mouth was as dry as sandpaper, his heart throbbing wretchedly in his chest. Ned sank to his knees by the door and made a few half-hearted swipes at the boots with a brush he had lifted from one of the shoe shine kits. He had taken it on the odd chance that someone might happen by, but the hall was quiet and deserted. The moments ticked by, the need to know burning inside with increasing ferocity. So with a queasy feeling in the pit of his stomach, Ned gathered his courage and reluctantly pressed his eye to the keyhole.

»»«

"Been long time Holmes, you no come so long. I think maybe you no like anymore." Mei Lien Chang closed the door firmly and moved to the center of the room where she stood with her hands on her hips, a shrewd glint in her hazel eyes as she appraised the Detective.

"It has been a long time Holmes," he corrected with a grin. "Full sentences Mei Lien are the very cornerstone of..."

"You no correct my English I no correct your Mandarin!" she interrupted crossly. After a moment, her expression began to soften. "We speak Mandarin then, no English. You need practice!" She paused a moment and then flashed a mischievous smile. "I hope that all that rusty."

Holmes began to laugh and bowed his head slightly. "I always welcome the opportunity to improve my Mandarin Mei Lien. As for the other, well my visit today is of a professional nature. I require your assistance – some information." As he spoke, he moved further into the room, smiling as he surveyed it. Unlike the rest of Lotus House, Mei Lien's room was mostly devoid of Oriental furnishings, instead being an almost perfect replica of a proper English drawing room, burgundy velvet chaise included. She was determined to enter English society by any means necessary and had on more than one occasion expressed the desire to marry an Earl or at the least, a wealthy landowner.

Mei Lien shrugged her delicate shoulders and shook her head. "Professional? Hah! So you say always… we see. But tell me Holmes, Mother say you no come around; just like Dr. Watson, now you have pasty English sweetheart."

Holmes arched his brow in surprise. "I do not have a sweetheart Mei Lien, nor is she pasty or English." He paused for a moment, his expression growing serious. "How do you know of her?"

She shrugged once more and set about preparing a pipe. When it was ready, she set it on the tray that sat on the small side table next to the chaise. She looked up, meeting his gaze, her eyes serious – grave. "Limehouse close community ... we see everything. You English no see us except when you need clothes cleaned or dustbins emptied or itch scratched."

The edge of bitterness in her voice took him by surprise and he wondered how much of her temperament had been affected by the death of her adopted cousin. "I didn't come here for that Mei Lien," he soothed, "but I do need information." He slid his hand into his breast pocket to take out the photograph of Moran. She reached out and gently grasped his wrist, holding on tightly for a moment. Her eyes were dark and warm, and as she moved

274

closer to him, a provocative smile played on her lips, all traces of bitterness vanished.

"I no mad at you Holmes, you gentleman always, not like others." She released his hand, her slender fingers sliding under his lapels and latching onto the ends of his black silk cross tie. "I very happy scratch your itch," she said and with a firm tug, popped the center button. The ends of the tie now dangled loose and with an impish pout, she grabbed hold of them, using them to turn him around. She edged him backwards until he could go no further, the back of his legs pressed up against the burgundy chaise. "I think English girl no good please you Holmes. Your eyes very sad ... tired... I make better... all pain go way... promise," she whispered, her hands sliding over his chest, simultaneously sliding his jacket off and then moving to the buttons of his waistcoat.

Holmes closed his eyes for a moment, unable to deny the sense of pleasure that filled him at her touch but also cognizant of a twinge of unease just beneath it. Determined to remain focused, he grabbed her hand gently, staying it for a moment. He held forth the picture of Moran. "Mei Lien, this man, your mother says he was here and that you asked him to leave. Why is that? Tell me. I need to know. It's important."

A look of frustration clouded her face. She sighed, her fingers still poised on his chest but motionless. "He here. I remember. Pretty blonde hair, nice face, ugly scar. He seem like gentleman - speak nicely at first but I no like him. Still, he pay good money - I give him chance. No stay long. Act big, boss girls around, very rough. What he want, we no can help him. Not here, not in this house. I give him money back ... give him name of house he can go; say goodbye. He take address. they leave, end of story."

"What do you mean they?" prodded Holmes, suddenly alert, his concern growing. "Who was he with? Tell me, what did he want?"

But Mei Lien's patience was beginning to wear thin and with a defiant frown, she shook her head.

"No more talk - finished now. Maybe later if you nice," she advised and then with a mischievous grin and a surprising show of strength, she tapped him firmly on the chest with her fingertips and knocked him off balance. Holmes fell backward awkwardly onto the chaise with a grunt. He struggled to sit up but found himself hindered as Mei Lien scrambled up onto the chaise and straddled him, sliding forward - the silk of her robe riding up to reveal exquisite calves of porcelain. Her fingers slid over his chest, caressing him, deftly unbuttoning his shirt.

Holmes groaned aloud and shifted, trying to ease her off him. "Mei Lien, I've no time for games I...."

She cut him off, clamping one hand over his mouth. "No, no games Holmes, business." She took the pipe in her free hand and took a long draw, inhaling the vapours, her eyes growing wide and languid as she held the smoke in her mouth. Then, with a blissful smile she leaned forward and exhaled, quickly moving her hand from his lips, parting them slightly with her thumb as she blew the smoke into his mouth. Holmes inhaled involuntarily, his eyes beginning to droop slightly as the Chandu seeped in and gradually eroded his resistance. He closed his eyes and sank back down onto the chaise, inhaling deeply as she placed the pipe under his nose. He knew he should resist, that he was losing focus... but time itself seemed lost to him along with his will, slipping quietly into the shadows.

"Much better," she purred as she took his hands in hers and placed them on her hips, holding them there until they began to move on their own, caressing - exploring. As her fingers slid under the waistband of his trousers, Holmes abruptly opened his eyes. He stared in bewilderment at the woman hovering over him and blinked hard, for the eyes he was gazing into were not hazel anymore but bright emerald, her nose pale and lightly sun freckled. He shut his eyes tightly, feeling muddled – aware that it was the Chandu but powerless to control the effects. He turned away trying to will the vision away; her name on his lips, a twinge of what felt like remorse nagging at him. It was not enough however to derail the inevitable.

»»«««

Outside the chamber, Ned fell back on his heels away from the door, pale - heart pounding. He raised his trembling hands to his face not wanting to believe what he had seen, too afraid to look through the keyhole again for confirmation or what else he might witness. It couldn't be true, it just couldn't. What had she done to him? Beautiful vile temptress.

"You there... stop! What are you about?!!!"

Ned froze, scarcely daring to breathe. Turning his head in the direction of the angry voice, he found himself face to face with the man Holmes had been playing cards with and another of Madam's daughters. Swallowing hard, he struggled to remain calm and kept his head down, cap pulled low and tight. He recognized this man, they'd met briefly once before, the circumstances had been most unpleasant. Realizing he dared not make a sound, he kept his eyes on the floor and held up the boots and brush to explain his presence by the door. The man was unconvinced and lunged forward grabbing him roughly by the back of the coat, dragging him towards the staircase. Ned uttered a guttural squawk and held onto his cap with one hand, kicking out and grabbing at the door frame with the other, but it was to no avail. The woman accompanying him shrieked in fear, covering her eyes with her hands while up and down the hall, doors sprang open. A few patrons stumbled out and listlessly watched the man drag the struggling boy down the hall and down the stairs.

Mei Lien cried out in surprise as Holmes, at the sound of the commotion outside the door, shoved her aside unceremoniously and sprang to his feet.

"Where you go? It's nothing." she protested. She climbed to her feet, fastening her robe, face flushed with irritation. Fortunately, all that was injured was her pride. She pouted at him, shaking her head. "Most likely boy... they sometimes trouble ... steal... peep... no worry... you stay."

276

Holmes, however, seemed rattled by the disturbance and despite still being held in the grip of the Chandu, stumbled towards the door, pulling on his shoes and clothes as quickly as he could. He bowed his head slightly and reached for the door. "Apologies Mei Lien... truly," then he was gone, vanishing down the hallway after them. Mei Lien's frown deepened as she brushed off her robe and smoothed her hair. Honourable mother was right - Chinese... English... no matter, all men same... big start but no good finish anything. Noting he had left his coat and hat behind, she sighed in resignation and carefully gathered them up from the table, setting out after him.

Ned put on an extra burst of speed as he scrambled away from the man, his ill-fitting boots flapping as he darted across the courtyard, heading full-steam towards the fountain and the alley entrance that lay just behind it. As he rounded the fountain, he cried out in pain as his knee caught the edge of a stone bench. The fabric of his breeches ripped along with his skin, but he kept going, hobbling slightly as a warm sticky ooze began to flow down his leg; he ignored it as best he could. The darkened entrance to the alley loomed ahead; further on, beyond the end of the passage, the dim glow of the lamps of the main street beckoned. He bent his head forward, panting raggedly   still holding onto his cap and made for the alley. Just a little more speed... not far now... almost there.

The jolt was so abrupt and fierce that it lifted him off his feet for a moment. Struggling to regain his footing, Ned found himself being yanked back by the scruff of his jacket and then thrust towards the brick wall. He slammed into it, holding up his hands at the last moment to lessen the blow. It helped... some. Dazed, he slid down onto the slimy cobbles of the alley, the man's curses ringing in his ears.

"Miserable cur! I'll teach you to spy."

Ned curled up defensively, shielding his head with his bleeding hands as the man struck him across the shoulders with what felt like a cane.

"Percy... Stop! Bloody Hell! Have you gone mad?"

Holmes' voice thundered across the courtyard echoing off the walls. Ned froze and curled up even tighter, scarcely daring to breathe. He peered warily from between his fingers, trying to control his trembling as he waited for an opportunity to escape.

Percy Gilchrist spun around, his face flushed with indignation, the walking stick in one hand while the other still grasped the boy's jacket.

"You should be thanking me Holmes... wretched mongrel was spying on you."

"He's just a boy Percy, leave him be," ordered Holmes as he moved forward a bit unsteadily, still trying to shake off the effects of the pipe. He fixed his eyes on the boy who had yet to lift his head or utter a word. Poor little wretch, reminded him of his Irregulars only more pitiful. His frame was decidedly frail for a boy of his age though he supposed a few of Mrs. Hudson's meat pies would fix that along with a good scrub up. She would be furious, she always was... at least at first.

"A good beating, that's what's needed," argued Percy, turning to the patrons who were slowly drifting out from Lotus House to see the cause of the disturbance. An angry murmur of consensus drifted across the courtyard. Holmes looked around uneasily, their faces were most uncharitable; many had no doubt been stolen from or spied upon themselves.

Encouraged by their response, Gilchrist jerked the boy up from the ground, lifting him by the scruff of his jacket. "Look at him... all bandaged. Looks like someone's had a go at him already." Indeed, as the jacket rode up, it revealed a worn and patched shirt from beneath which dangled the edges of what appeared to be bandages. Percy uttered a snort of disgust and released the jacket. The boy fell to the ground and remained there, head turned to the wall. Holmes tensed, anger slowly washing away the lethargy caused by the Chandu.

Snarling, Holmes grabbed the cane from Percy's hand.

"This is not your business. If anyone is to deliver a thrashing..." His words abruptly died out and a shiver of dread coursed through him as he leaned over to take a closer look at the boy. Ned's cap had finally been knocked askew and a few tangles of auburn hair dangled down from beneath it, covering his face. Holmes crouched down, tensing. What Percy had called bandages were not bandages at all but looked very much like the linen strips that were used in the theatre for binding. *Binding... what the devil?*

"Boy, look at me," he growled, his face growing pale, a queer feeling in the pit of his stomach. The boy wouldn't budge however, still pressed to the wall, hands covering his face.

Exhaling sharply in frustration, he reached out to turn the boy around.

"I said... look at me." As his hand grasped the boy's shoulder, he drew back in surprise as what felt like a current of electricity shot through him. The boy must have felt it too and flinched, making a small whimpering noise. Astonished, Holmes drew a sharp breath and reached out once more, grasping the boy's chin and turning him around. A pair of terrified emerald eyes peered up at him. Holmes felt his senses temporarily desert him as he found himself looking into the pale face of Edwina Schraeder. The growing anger of the crowd called him back to the present. With his breath coming in ragged bursts, he pulled Edwina to her feet, hissing, "Not a word... hear me... not one!" Moments later, Holmes, still clutching the cane in one hand, disappeared down the alley dragging the "boy" with him. A round of applause and cheers of approvals went up from the crowd. Satisfied that punishment would be meted out accordingly, they began to slowly drift back towards their evening's diversion.

By the time they reached the street, Edwina had recovered some of her courage and began to struggle, tugging futilely at his iron grip as he dragged her out of the alley and onto the street.

"What are you doing? It's me Holmes. Let me go."

Several rough looking men on the street paused watching them with interest. A few began to cross the street.

Still holding onto her, Holmes waved the cane and flagged down a carriage. It had barely rolled to a stop before he opened the door and shoved her inside down onto the floor.

"Quiet you little fool. Stay down before you get us both killed!" he hissed. Before she could protest, he slammed the door shut and tossed a few guineas to the driver, ordering him to lock the carriage and open it for no one save himself. He was to wait for his return unless there was trouble, at which point he was to make with all due haste to Baker Street. He then turned and disappeared down the alley, heading back in the general direction of Lotus House.

Edwina lifted her head and peered cautiously out the carriage window. Moments later, he reappeared carrying his coat and hat. She backed away from the window, allowing the flap to fall back into place. The door flew open and as Holmes climbed in, the carriage jolted off, the horses setting a brisk pace as they made their way out of Limehouse.

"I can explain," she ventured tentatively, struggling to regain her balance against the rocking of the carriage as she climbed onto the seat.

Holmes was looking out the window, as if he were expecting trouble. At the sound of her voice, his head snapped round and with an expression of icy rage, he flung his coat at her.

"Cover yourself and stay down till I say so."

Stunned by the sheer wrath in his voice, Edwina caught her breath and then shrank back against the seat. Moments later, she laid down on the seat and fighting back tears, slowly drew his coat over her.

»»««

FALL FROM GRACE

"Murder!!!"

The shriek of that single word jolted Watson up from his pillow. He stared into the darkness of his room, breathing hard ... listening. *Nothing* .... just the faint, comforting tick of his pocket watch on the night stand; he breathed a little easier. *Dreaming ...worries of the day and perhaps one too many brandies. God knows there was plenty of both lately.* Suppressing a yawn, he slowly lowered his head towards the pillow, staring absently towards the door. The faintest glow of light seeped in under the crack from the hallway. *Home at last... about damn time.* He'd given up waiting for Holmes and in a fit of peevishness, nearly finished his "precious" Armagnac before retiring for the night. *The man was insufferable at times - no regard for the concerns of others. No telling what he had gotten up to...bugger.* Watson's eyelids began to droop...

"God save us. Doctor, please stop him!"

His eyes flew open. The anguished wail was now directly outside his room and followed by fierce pounding on his door. *Definitely not a dream.*

Watson stumbled up from the bed, fully awake now on recognizing the terrified voice of Mrs. Hudson. Pulling on his robe, he flung open the door and found her, white faced and trembling, so agitated that she could do little more than babble and point down the hall. No further explanation needed, he flew past her and burst through the door to 221B.

"Holmes! Let him go! Have you lost your mind?"

Watson lurched to a halt, dumbfounded by the sight before him. Holmes appeared to have one of the Irregulars backed up against the wall, shaking him firmly by the shoulders as he berated him. The boy's clothes were muddy and torn, the fabric of one knee ripped out and hanging down, the skin underneath abraded and bleeding.

"Quite possibly," snarled the Detective, "and not your affair!" Holmes never once turned away from his prey and continued to pin the poor wretch to the wall, one hand on each shoulder.

Watson advanced quickly but with great caution. The room reeked of opium which emanated from the clothes of Holmes and the boy. He had seen his friend in many states, some of them altered, ranging from unbridled mania to fathomless depression, but this exhibition of outright rage alarmed him; particularly as it didn't fit. Opium was a depressant - Holmes' mood should have been one of deep languor and relaxation not agitation.

"Whatever he's done?" soothed the Doctor, "He's just a boy."

Holmes abruptly released the boy and pivoted to face the Doctor, his face drawn and tight. The boy's legs gave way and he slid down the wall onto the floor where he remained seated, back against the wall, trembling hands over his face.

"He's done nothing," he snorted, "She however..." He seemed unable to finish the thought and strode towards the fireplace, hands laced tightly behind his neck.

"She? What the Devil are you about?" Watson was confounded, but Holmes refused to answer and instead pulled a poker from its stand on the hearth. He began to jab at the kindling in the fireplace sending sparks into the air.

Watson groaned in exasperation. He'd get no explanation from Holmes. He never could when he was in such a state. He turned his attention to the boy and moved closer, his face one of compassion as he extended his hand to help him to his feet.

"It'll be all right boy, his bark is worse than his bite. Give me your hand. Let me take a look at your knee."

The boy uttered a muted whimper and gave a slight nod though he kept his eyes focused on the ground. After a moment, he seemed to gather himself and reached out, grasping firmly onto Watson's hand as he pulled himself up. Using the back of his sleeve, he made a few swipes at his smudged face and then lifted his head.

Watson's eyes widened in astonishment as he found himself staring into a muddied but familiar face.

"Edwina," he gasped. It was all he could manage.

"Hello Doctor. So sorry to disturb you," she murmured quietly.

"Great Scott! What's the meaning of this?!" he sputtered, pivoting towards Holmes.

The poker clanged loudly as it was flung down onto the hearthstone.

"Yes, by all means, enlighten us," snarled Holmes. "Explain why you followed me - spying ... invading my privacy."

Edwina turned ashen, her eyes blurring with angry tears. "I didn't follow you," she retorted, "at least not at first. I meant no disrespect. But when I saw you at Dr. Bell's, I couldn't believe my eyes." She clenched her fists at her side so tightly the knuckles turned white.

"Dr. Bell's; you were there?" interjected Watson in astonishment. "Ahh, that would explain the boy's clothes."

"Spot on Watson, as always," snickered Holmes. He turned to Edwina, his face drawn, eyes burning with indignation. "You stalked me; lurking in the shadows like a common prowler."

Something in his words or tone struck a note of discord. Edwina drew herself up a little straighter and compressed her lips. "I went to see Dr. Bell," she repeated pointedly. "Imagine my surprise to discover you lied to me! Why did you lie Holmes?"

For the first time, her directness seemed to unsettle him.

"I had my reasons," he replied, his tone much subdued.

"Yes, as I soon discovered...." she hissed acidly, her eyes moist but defiant.

Holmes looked up and then shook his head, lips curled into a bleak smile. This was more than simple anger at being lied to; this was bitterness laced with jealousy. The misery in her eyes was more than he could bear at the moment. He looked away, uneasy at his own increasing sense of culpability.

"So, now you would judge me."

Her face contorted with dismay, but she offered no reply. Her struggle to rein in her emotions was evident to all.

Holmes took a deep breath, running his hands restlessly through his hair.

"Have you any idea of the danger you put yourself in? If you had been discovered in that place Eddy... amongst those men. Men in such a condition as they were, debauched, addled with narcotics, no moral constraints. Are you so blind not to see what might have occurred had I not been there?" he asked tersely, his voice controlled but vehement all the same.

She lifted her head, a cynical smile darkening her face.

"You were there Holmes. Amongst them and also in such a condition. What am I to make of that? Should I fear you as well?"

Her words, though spoken softly, exhibited an acrimony he had not believed her capable of. After a long pause, he shook his head and turned away. "Perhaps. God knows Eddy, at this moment it seems Percy was right and a good thrashing is what's needed."

"You go too far Holmes. Enough!" protested Watson, his face grey with alarm.

Holmes held up his hand and uttered a short laugh.

"Be at ease Watson. I have no doubt any such attempt would be returned in kind." He turned his attention back to Edwina once more and managed a grim smile.

"My patience is at an end and there is nothing more to be said."

Edwina's eyes widened and then sparked with indignation as she lurched forward.

How dare you dismiss me? If you had not lied... if you... How could I imagine you would go to such a place?" The words choked in her throat. She bit her bottom lip until she drew blood, determined not to let tears overwhelm her.

Holmes met her gaze levelly though deep inside, compassion began to rear its ugly head.

"Watson take her downstairs to Mrs. Hudson where she can rest but ensure she is locked in. In the morning, you will see her home. Instruct Mrs. Hudson to draw her a steaming bath. By God, she reeks of the alley and Limehouse."

All color drained from Edwina's face. "And you of Opium and whores!" she spat, her voice raw and strained.

Holmes winced – it was brief but noticeable; the room descended into an uneasy silence. Edwina regretted her words the moment they left her lips. She had wounded him, but it brought her no joy. She fumbled to find words to amend the situation without sacrificing her dignity; it was futile. In the end, Holmes broke the silence, his expression grave, the mask lifting to reveal a hint of guilt.

"Well," he said, mouth curled with a sad smile, "it seems we are both full of disappointments today. I would never expect such sanctimonious virulence from you. It doesn't suit you Eddy. Perhaps, you are not as liberated as you would like to believe."

Her face grew hot, her eyes blurring as her mind drifted back to every time she had sparred with Grendel and accused her of being judgmental.

"Holmes, this serves no purpose," murmured Watson. He wound his arm gently around Edwina in an attempt to comfort her.

Holmes nodded, his eyes growing cold and veiled; he gestured towards the door.

"Quite right Watson, so I bid you both Good Night."

"Someone's been at the Armagnac; almost gone," noted Holmes with a glum expression as he stood in front of the sideboard and held the decanter up to the light. "No matter, there's always cognac." He removed two snifters from the cabinet and divided the precious contents between them. "Come Watson, sit. Tell me, is she settled now? And the wound on her knee, nothing serious I assume?" He turned and extended the glass to the Doctor who stood on the threshold, door still open.

Watson closed the door and slowly crossed the room. A crisp breeze lifted the curtains from the open window; the air was considerably fresher, only a faint trace of Opium lingered which he was immensely grateful. Holmes had also freshened and changed; his rumpled evening clothes exchanged for pressed trousers and shirt covered by his burgundy dressing gown. His face, however, remained pale, eyes hollow and dull. Watson settled into his chair and took the glass, wondering how much of Holmes' worn appearance was the result of residual narcotics and how much general fatigue.

"Nothing serious – cleaned and bandaged. As for settled, as well as can be expected given the circumstances. Holmes, that was cruel even for you. What's this all about?"

Holmes stared into his glass. "She put herself in great danger Watson. Needlessly... such foolishness."

"Not the first time," interrupted the Doctor brusquely, "almost certainly won't be the last. God knows, you do nothing to discourage it."

"What do you mean?"

Watson snickered beneath his moustache. "Little more than a week ago, down on the docks. Need I remind you? Your little Chinese adventure."

"That was different," murmured Holmes, his shoulder twitching involuntarily.

"How?" snorted Watson. "You created this Holmes. Banging on about how clever she is, praising her skills, her independence. Encouraging her to always follow the trail, never stray from the scent until the logical conclusion was at hand. She acted exactly as you instructed, she followed the clues to find the answer."

Holmes drained his glass and abruptly rose. He turned to the sideboard and uncorked a bottle of cognac.

"She invaded my privacy... stalked me."

As Holmes poured a glass for each of them, Watson noticed a faint tremor in his hand. "Only because you lied to her," the Doctor muttered. He took the newly filled glass but paused as he raised it to his lips, a sage glint in his eyes. "... for whatsoever a man soweth, that shall he also reap."

Holmes stared at him and grunted in disdain. "Galatians 6:7; predictable."

Watson arched his brow, his expression somber. "No? Well then, perhaps 'Pride goeth before destruction, and a haughty spirit before a fall.' Better?"

Holmes paused in mid sip and lowered the glass from his lips. "Your little game is beginning to bore me. Are you quite through?"

Watson leaned forward and sighed. The air in the room had taken on a definite chill.

"She's discovered your dark little secrets. That's what this is really about isn't it?"

"She put herself in danger."

"Yes, yes, in danger, so you've said." Watson cut him off with a wave of his hand dismissing him as he had been dismissed so many times in the past. He paused a moment, carefully choosing his words, his expression softening. "I have no doubt your concern for her safety is genuine, but this anger... this is about your fall from grace, your tumble from the pedestal she placed you on."

"I never asked for that."

Watson shrugged. "Not in so many words, but you did nothing to discourage it."

Holmes frowned but said nothing. Watson could be uncomfortably perceptive at times; it was a rather vexing trait. With drink still in hand, he crossed to the hearth where he stood quietly, his back to Watson, eyes fixed on the sketch on the mantle. He lifted it carefully, studying it in the glow of the hearth. *Such a lovely sketch... just enough detail to capture the essence of the room and the moment. She had potential - the talent was raw... but abundant... and such a fine eye for detail... those eyes... they really were quite...* He shook himself, derailing the thought and replaced the sketch on the mantle; he took up his glass, swirling the remnants of the cognac.

"If I could alter the course I'd chosen this evening Watson..."

Watson leaned forward, concern growing in his eyes. Holmes had yet to fully explain what had occurred and such an open admission of regret only increased his apprehension. Thus far, all he knew for certain was that Edwina had followed him from St. Bart's to Limehouse. Edwina's bitter words just before Holmes banished her downstairs came to mind; his eyes widened in dread. Opium and whores were words he suspected were foreign to her usual vocabulary.

"She followed you to Lotus House..."

"Yes."

"Bloody Hell! How far?"

His query was met with silence.

Watson cautioned himself that perhaps it wasn't as grave as it appeared. It was possible that she had remained outside and had only deduced the true nature of the establishment by observation – she was a clever girl. That did not however explain the strong reek of opium on her clothes; for that she would have had to have gone inside. Still, inside was vague encompassing many things: gambling parlours, smoking rooms, a most excellent spirit bar and of course...He compressed his lips tightly.

"How far?" he demanded.

Holmes sank back down into his chair, the near empty glass still in his hand and leaned back, his attention focused on some indeterminate point on the ceiling. He drained the contents of the glass and began to explain although not directly.

"It occurred to me Watson, while at Dr. Bell's, that Moran, a soldier just returned from the campaigns, would have the inclination to visit certain... establishments. So, I set off – my sole intention to explore this line of enquiry. After exchanging pleasantries with Madame Chang..."

"Pleasantries...?" grunted Watson, interrupting him. He knew precisely what that entailed. *Clever old shrew, the first pipe. Regrettably, it seemed that lately, it was rarely the only pipe.*

Holmes ignored the remark and continued. "She confirmed my suspicions. Moran had indeed visited Lotus House but she could offer little in the way of details advising that it would be best to speak to her daughter Mei Lien."

Watson groaned aloud but offered no remark, waiting for Holmes to continue.

"So, I passed the time in the gaming parlor playing cards with Gilchrist and smoking." Holmes paused for a moment. "I'm afraid Watson, that I became distracted, may have overindulged, and when Mei Lien arrived I..." He hesitated and then shrugged, shifting his gaze back to the hearth. "Well, I presume I need not explain further."

Watson was silent for a moment and then sat forward in his chair, his face somber.

"How much did she see?"

The Detective's face darkened, his mouth twisting bitterly.

"I cannot say for certain but undoubtedly more than enough. Gilchrist discovered her crouched down by the door. By the time I reached the hall, he had already dragged her off. At the time, neither one of us realized the true nature of the situation. I'd only caught a glimpse. Just some bedraggled little wretch spying as boys that age often do. I found them outside near the alley. He was moments away from beating her Watson, in which case the truth surely would have been discovered. It was the binding; the edges had come loose. I noticed them dangling from beneath the jacket. Percy thought they were bandages, but I understood their significance immediately. And then Watson, I looked into those eyes and I knew. I convinced him that any punishment to be administered was my prerogative as I was the one who had been wronged. I dragged her off much as he had. The hour was late, and I concede that my own condition was less than ideal and would have only alarmed Lady Montague. So, I brought her here. I must admit Watson, I have never been so furious, and the thought did cross my mind that what was needed most was a good thrashing. It took every ounce of willpower to resist."

Watson said nothing for quite some time and then sighed. "Well Holmes, quite the fall indeed. Really more of a plummet, but then you never were content with halfway measures were you? And the information you sought?"

Holmes smiled blackly. "Still unknown. And, given the unfortunate nature of my exit, I expect it will remain." He suddenly stopped, a frown darkening his face as he held up his hand instructing Watson to remain silent. With a growl of exasperation, he strode across the room and yanked open the door.

"Twice? In one night!"

Edwina stood just outside the door, wrapped in one of Mrs. Hudson's hideous robes, her hair still damp from her bath.

"I was about to knock," she said her expression earnest if somewhat defensive.

Holmes sighed. Her hand was indeed raised as if she had intended to do just that. He turned away from the door and moved back inside.

"What a novelty that would be," he muttered.

Embarrassment darkened her face. "Holmes, a word... please." She hesitated on the threshold, waiting for his permission to enter.

"More words... still?" he scoffed, "what more is there to say? And how are you here? Or did the Good Doctor fail to lock you in as instructed!" He narrowed his eyes at Watson.

"It's not his fault, he did exactly as you requested," she replied, quickly coming to Watson's defense. "The lock was really quite simple given your previous instruction."

Watson began to chuckle and glanced at Holmes. "As I said, your creature." A trace of a smirk lurked underneath his moustache.

Holmes sighed in exasperation and motioned for her to enter. "Speak your piece then."

Edwina compressed her lips and glanced hesitantly at the Doctor. "I would have a word in private."

"There is nothing you need say to me that Watson cannot hear."

Her cheeks turned scarlet but after a moment, she took a deep breath and entered, quietly closing the door behind her.

"Very well. I... I am here to say how very sorry I am. Following you was wrong no matter how angry I was. I know that. You have every right to your privacy and I have no right to judge you."

"Quite so," agreed Holmes, "well, apology accepted. Now if you please, it's late and..."

"Please, I'm not quite finished," she interrupted, and then with a plea in her eyes, turned once more to Watson. "Doctor, please, may I prevail upon your kindness? What I have to say to Mr. Holmes is for his ears only."

Watson arched his brow in surprise and then looked to Holmes for direction. Holmes frowned, it was apparent she was determined to be heard. After a moment, he sighed in resignation and then nodded to Watson.

"As the lady wishes Watson. It seems she will be heard. Get some rest, in the morning, you will see her home."

Watson hesitated. The air was fraught with tension and barely restrained emotion, and despite Holmes' chilly demeanour, not just from Edwina.

"Are you certain Holmes?"

A hint of a smile curled the Detective's lips and he nodded.

"Good night Doctor," was all he said.

Edwina waited until the door had closed and then moved further into the room. Her fingers clutched the sash of the robe, fiddling with the ends. She seemed to be weighing her words and seemed not to know where to look or begin.

"So, you forgive me then?" she murmured, her gaze fixed on the floor.

Holmes knit his brow, a look of unease in his eyes. Her complexion had gone nearly grey, lips almost colorless. "As I said, apology accepted," he replied cautiously. This fragility in her was uncharacteristic and worrisome.

A look of anguish clouded her eyes. "It's not the same though, as forgiveness," she stammered. "I need to know... that you..." She faltered, her words trailing off as she was wracked with a tremor so violent that Holmes feared she might collapse. Astonished, he lunged forward and took hold of her shoulders with gentle firmness, steadying her. He guided her to his wingchair and once she had settled, poured a large cognac and pressed it into her hands. His hands covered hers in an attempt to ease their trembling and reinforce her grip on the glass.

"Drink this..." he soothed, lifting the glass to her lips.

Edwina took a large gulp and immediately began to sputter and cough as the cognac coated her throat with liquid heat.

"Small sips are best," he advised with a kind smile as he poured her a tumbler of water.

She nodded and drank the water, clearing her throat. When she had recovered her breath, she took a few sips of the cognac, this time slower and smaller, following his advice. With her emotions more firmly in check, she took a deep breath and lifted her eyes.

"My words were hateful... repugnant... I am sorry... you must believe..."

He poured a cognac for himself and sat down on the ottoman opposite her chair.

"I do believe you," he assured softly. "I know you regretted them the moment you spoke Eddy. And truth be told, they were not wholly undeserved," he admitted.

She lifted her head. She was calmer now, her eyes less frantic but still pained.

"So, it was all a lie from the beginning? You never intended to take me?"

His eyes grew dark and he didn't answer at first. After a moment, he took a sip of cognac and nodded that it was so.

"Why?" A look of pure disappointment contorted her face.

"I had a thought, regarding a line of inquiry. I realized it would entail a visit to a less than reputable establishment. I could scarcely abandon you at Dr. Bell's. I decided it was the logical choice given the circumstances."

Edwina stared at him in disbelief. "You could have told me the truth from the very start."

"And you would have argued then as you are now. I couldn't risk being diverted from my line of inquiry."

"Inquiry! And what part of the inquiry required the use of Opium?" she countered acidly. Then in a much softer voice, she leaned forward and gently laid her hand on top of his.

"Why would you take such risks? You know the dangers. How it affects the chemistry of the brain. Are you an addict Holmes? Tell me truthfully, I'll understand. You take on so much. The pressure must be unbearable at times. My anger was misdirected, it was just such a shock. You must know, my true concern is for your welfare."

A bittersweet smile touched his lips. He set his glass down on the side table and leaned forward, pressing her hand tenderly in his.

"I'm not an addict Eddy... a controlled user. And yes, I am quite aware of the risks."

Her eyes fixed on his, mirroring disbelief and grief. "My mother said the same, about the Laudanum, right up to the day she drowned. I always deferred to her; after all, she was my mother. Certainly, she knew more than I did. But

I was wrong, wasn't I? Maybe if I had challenged her Holmes, if I had been more vigilant." Her voice faltered and then trailed off as her eyes drifted off towards the hearth. Her hand slipped from his and lay lifeless on the arm of the chair. "I wasn't there for her when she needed me most ... just like Julian. I failed them." She grew quiet for a moment and then turned to face him, her eyes fervent. "But I cannot ... will not fail you Holmes. There is nothing I would not do if you need my help."

Her sincerity effected a strong surge of affection within him and he took both of her hands in his. "I'm fine Eddy, be at ease. It was a simple error in judgement. I became distracted and overindulged a bit that's all."

She shook her head still not convinced but realized the argument was useless. She fell into silence. Holmes waited with a growing sense of disquiet – it was apparent that she had not yet finished her questions.

"And what of," she paused, her cheeks turning crimson as she struggled to find the appropriate words, "your Chinese girl? Have... Have you... known her long?"

It was such an awkwardly phrased question. Her embarrassment with the subject matter was obvious and he almost smiled but refrained for there was misery underneath her chagrin.

"Mei Lien? Yes, it's several years now, though I wouldn't call her my girl. She is exactly what you deduced Eddy, though I am certain she would prefer the term concubine over prostitute."

"She's ... she's beautiful," she murmured after a pause, her voice barely above a whisper.

"Well, given the nature of her trade, surely an asset," he laughed. She didn't join in however and remained silent with her head tilted down, avoiding his gaze. The smile faded from Holmes' face. With the utmost gentleness, he reached out and lifted her chin up with his fingertips. "There are many forms of beauty Eddy. Some more pure ... transcendent. They will remain long after the physical fades, that is what makes them sublime. Such is yours. There is no reason to be envious."

A shadow of a smile tugged at her lips at his words of comfort though her unease and bewilderment at his actions remained.

"Why then Holmes?"

Surprise flickered across his face followed by mild amusement.

"As a student of the sciences Eddy, surely you don't need me to explain the birds and the bees."

Her face turned crimson. "I know *why*," she stammered, "but why that way Holmes?"

He sighed, a sober expression replacing the smile. "It's a logical solution to a vexing problem. A fee is paid, services are provided," he said simply.

"It sounds so cold for something so intimate," she murmured, her fingers nervously picking at a seam on her robe.

Holmes' expression softened. Despite her intellect and adventurous spirit, there was a naiveté about her when it came to such matters. He shook his head; it was endearing and dispiriting all at once. "You know my views. I abhor emotional entanglements. Simply put, it was nothing more than physical gratification Eddy. An itch to be scratched if you will. There was nothing intimate about it."

She grew quiet and he could tell by the expression on her face that she was still processing the information trying to make sense of it.

"Is that why you wouldn't kiss her?" she asked after a moment.

The question took him by surprise. He arched his brow and met her gaze steadily, comprehending fully just how much she had seen.

"Logically speaking Eddy, the question should be, why would I? A kiss is the most intimate act two can share - even more so than the physical act of copulation. It's sentiment in its highest form and to be avoided at all costs." He would have continued, reiterating his disdain for all things sentimental when he became aware that she was no longer looking at him. She had turned away and judging by the quivering of her shoulders, he deduced she was weeping though doing her best to disguise it. Her hands were raised partially shading her face as if she had a headache, but he was not fooled. Reaching out, he gently grasped her shoulder and turned her back around to face him. He sighed heavily, his expression one of weary regret as he reached out and gently moved her hands away from her face. Her cheeks were damp, her eyes rimmed with red.

"Dry your eyes Eddy. One day, you will meet someone who is truly worthy of your affection. You must save your tears for him."

Edwina drew a deep breath and gazed deep into his eyes.

"I've already met him only he doesn't need me, or even want me for that matter."

A flicker of pain darkened his eyes. With a melancholy smile, he reached out with his fingertips and gently brushed at her tears.

"I assure you, that is not the case at all. The truth is what we desire in life is rarely what is best or needed. Often, to be at our best, we have to make sacrifices. This is the path I've chosen. It is the one that makes sense for my work and my nature."

At these words, her expression became somewhat bitter and she wiped quickly at her eyes as if she were embarrassed that she had lost her composure. She compressed her lips - a fierce look of determination on her face.

"Then I shall do the same... harden my heart and eschew all sentiment. I shall follow your cue and be the brain without a heart...a thinking machine."

"Impossible," he sighed with a fond smile. "Not in your nature and thankfully so. The loss of your kind and affectionate heart Eddy would leave a void in the lives of many. Now, the hour is inexcusably late. Time you returned downstairs to rest. Watson will see you home in a few short hours."

"May I not stay here... on your divan? Mrs. Hudson snores something terrible," she asked with a plea in her eyes.

For a brief moment, he hesitated but upon further consideration, shook his head. He took her by the hand and gently lifted her up from the chair, speaking softly as he escorted her towards the door.

"I fear that would be an unwise choice – for both of us. And one more thing Eddy, from now on I think it best you contain your visits to daylight hours with the appropriate chaperone."

His words left her speechless and she could only stare at him too overwhelmed to protest. With an expression of misery, she managed a slight nod and then disappeared down the stairs, her words of farewell a mere whisper.

Holmes waited until she had vanished from view and then slowly closed the door. Alone once more, he retreated to his chair to reflect on all that had transpired; he poured another cognac.

CHAPTER 8

The Skein Unravels

Watson stood in front of the mirror, a slight frown creasing his brow as he held the white cravat up in front of his black cutaway. On the table next to the mirror lay another cravat, this one in black silk along with two bow ties - one black, one white.

"Cravat or bow tie?" he murmured in the direction of the mirror. He detested having to make these choices, preferring to leave such things to Mary's capable hands. She was, however, unavailable, engaged in preparing the young ladies for the evening's festivities. He would do his best to meet her expectations.

"First ball of the season - always the most formal. White is the proper choice. Bow tie, no cravat," murmured a jaded voice from the corner of the room.

Watson glanced towards the wing chair where Holmes had been lounging most of the afternoon, eyes closed, feet propped on the ottoman, case notes scattered. Sleeping, or so he had assumed. "You could come," he suggested, "ample time to dress. Lady Montague would be delighted, as no doubt others." He selected the white bow tie and fastened it under his collar, smiling at his reflection in the mirror. *Not bad... still liable to catch an eye or two....*

Holmes opened his eyes and watched Watson go about his preparations, a hint of a smile tugging at his lips. "Thank you... no. I'm rather looking forward to the peace and quiet."

"Nothing but peace and quiet since the banishment of your disciple," Watson muttered, "even Mrs. Hudson has noticed."

Irritation flickered across Holmes' face. "Hardly a banishment. I merely advised it would be best if..."

Watson cut him off with a snort and wave of his hand. "No matter, seems she isn't much troubled by the exile. Afternoon tea three times this week and riding twice in Regent's with the Colonel. He's quite an accomplished equestrian by all accounts and as I recall, she is quite fond of horses, something you are not."

A frown darkened Holmes' face as he lowered his legs to the floor and sat up rigidly in the chair. "All properly chaperoned and arranged by Lady Montague. What is your point?" Watson shrugged. "Only that perhaps she isn't missing your presence all that much. Riding twice..." he needled. "I hear the bridle paths are lovely... secluded..."

Holmes abruptly rose and began to rummage for his tobacco. "Nonsense, she converses primarily with the horse and I daresay, with more intelligent results."

Watson made a clucking sound and smiled. "Now how would you know that?"

Holmes paused for a moment as he rolled his cigarette. "I have my sources," he admitted, avoiding Watson's gaze.

"Interesting that you would be keeping tabs on her activities and the company she keeps, considering how you *abhor sentiment* in all its forms."

Holmes' head snapped up, his eyes narrowing as he placed the cigarette between his lips and lit it. "Best hurry Watson," he growled, "lest you be late." And, as if to reinforce the farewell, he tossed him his top hat and gloves.

With a sigh of resignation, Watson took up his coat and headed for the door. On reaching the threshold, he paused and turned back to Holmes. "Time is running out Holmes," he reminded soberly.

"For what?"

"To make things right. You must warn her about her father. As you've said, the arrest is imminent."

"We've had this discussion before, you know I am bound not to speak."

"A pledge you have broken before when it was warranted. Surely this is such a case. Holmes, the potential for lasting harm is great as you have made note of yourself. I know this weighs on your mind more than you care to admit. Why else would you have exerted so much energy in the attempt to locate family that could take her in when events come to pass?"

Holmes leaned forward in his chair, fingers steepled under his chin, eyes dark and pensive. "An exercise that has proved futile," he admitted dispiritedly. "Her mother's sister and family are barely able to care for themselves."

"And what of the Russians? Did you not say there was a great aunt... somewhat wealthy?"

Holmes sighed in exasperation. "Yes, Madame Ludmila Olegovna Petrovna - apparently wintering in Odessa. Attempts at contact have been unsuccessful. A few minor cousins scattered about... no success there either. Katerina Schraeder's choice of profession seems to have alienated quite a bit of the family. A solution eludes me still Watson. Edwina has no means of securing her independence, so as distasteful as it is, it seems she will have to remain with Pennington's sister – at least until I can find an alternative."

Watson shook his head as he pulled on his gloves. "Well, family at least and perhaps a bit of discipline would..."

The look Holmes fixed him with, halted his words in mid-sentence. Watson paused a moment and then sighed. "By any account, bad luck about the necklace. It would have surely offered some financial relief. How did this all come about Holmes? Was this active thievery on the part of her mother or some unfortunate misunderstanding? It's difficult for me to envision a woman being so devious."

Watson's words elicited an ironic smile from the Detective. How quickly Watson had forgotten the duplicitous nature of some members of the fairer sex, but he had not forgotten. He said nothing on the matter however and only shrugged, his face etched with somber reflection. "The very fact that Katerina Schraeder took such great pains to conceal the true value of the necklace Watson, does not speak to some accident. It was a conscious act. It's quite obvious that she knew the value and also knew that she must hide her good fortune."

"But why and from whom? Her husband...?"

At this, Holmes only shook his head. "Judging by her daughter, I daresay Katerina Schraeder was more than a match for Pennington and had little to fear from him. You saw him, quaking in his boots at our first interview and clearly still mourning the loss of his estranged wife even after all the years of separation. His distress so great that he went to the expense of bringing her remains back with their daughter. He may have abandoned Katerina all those years ago, but he never forgot her. No Watson, there's someone else in the mix that I have yet to uncover. Someone who has a connection to both. I believe that this unknown party orchestrated the theft and Katerina strayed from the plan. He's the one she feared. I also believe that this same party, this puppet master, is behind Pennington's counterfeit scheme as Pennington has neither the creativity or intelligence to craft such a plan. I have tried to impress this upon Lestrade, but he is impatient and will not listen. He has settled on the most obvious choice and is content to go no further."

"Well, you have tried your best Holmes. If such a mastermind does exist, surely Pennington will reveal all once his head is on the block. You will have your man then."

"I'm not so sure," murmured Holmes, "I fear the stakes may be too high."

Watson knit his brow in consternation. Riddles again. He sighed heavily. "Well, one more misfortune Holmes, that she is unaware of. It does seem that in light of all these circumstances, a well-appointed marriage may be the best solution."

Holmes, who by now had taken up his usual post by the window, stiffened. "If you are referring to Moran, I take issue with the use of 'well appointed'. Such a pairing could only bring misfortune. Her happiness would best be served if she were allowed to set her own course. She is a most singular woman. Given the opportunity, she will go far."

"Singular does not equate to financial security. How will she provide for herself? Seems to me," mused Watson, "a husband is what is needed. And as far as Moran, need I remind you that other than some anecdotal information regarding a visit to a brothel, which I'm sure I do not have to remind you is not a crime, and some conjecture on your part, thus far, you have no evidence to the contrary."

There was an awkward moment of silence until Holmes, gaze still fixed out the window, announced, "Your hansom is here Watson. I trust you'll convey my regards."

Watson pursed his lips, hat in hand ready to make one last entreaty but in the end, changed his mind. These battles were exhausting and useless at best. Murmuring farewell, he pulled on his coat and hat and headed out the door.

From the upstairs window, Holmes watched the hansom pull away from the curb into the gathering twilight. He remained at the window motionless long after it had vanished from view, his face drawn with melancholy reflection. Watson was correct, time was running out. As the lamps below were lit, he stirred from his reverie and returned to his case notes with a renewed determination. *There must be something he had missed...*

»»««

FERN HALL
Twilight

Cook shook her head in bewilderment as she peeped out the small kitchen window that overlooked the small yard between the back of the house and the stable.

"Lord bless us. Are they still at it then? What are they about?" whispered Brigit, the parlour maid. She hovered behind cook too afraid to look outside for herself. On the job for less than two months and already Fern Hall was proving to be a very strange place indeed.

Outside in the gathering dusk, sparks danced up from the flames of the pit as George McTavish and young Tom, faces streaked with soot, reached into the garden cart which brimmed with green covered ledgers. Grabbing a handful, they continued to throw them onto the fire while Wilfred Pennington watched at the edge of the pit, wiping his brow nervously.

The older woman surveyed the scene anxiously from behind the curtain and shook her head. "Stoking the very fires of hell, it seems," she muttered. "Good thing Mrs. is still at evening prayers. She'd have the Father over here casting out demons for certain." The young maid crossed herself quickly, an uneasy look on her face.

Pennington stared into the flames with anguished eyes, his attention fixed on the mound of smouldering ledgers. Every now and then, he would remove his pocket watch to check the time and watch the progress of the two men as they continued to feed the ledgers into the fire. Catching sight of a black ledger in the hands of young Tom, he turned a deathly pallor and darted forward, snatching the book from the astonished boy's hands at the last minute.

"No!!No!! Only the green! God's sake man, only the green." He cradled the black ledger to his chest, his hands shaking as he held onto it. *All his precious work... the planning and careful maneuvering... his security... and it was now all for nought. It couldn't be helped...he had no choice.* McTavish and his nephew exchanged troubled looks. They had seen Pennington agitated before, but never quite so unhinged as now. He had been in such a state since returning from London earlier in the day, and now the man was almost in tears as he watched the flames devour the books. They nodded that they understood even though they truly didn't, and carefully sifted through the cart, making sure there were no more black ledgers mixed in amongst the green. They had spent the better portion of the afternoon helping Pennington separate and haul his precious ledgers from the strong room behind the library out to the fire pit. And now he was burning them; it made no sense...but little did it seemed these days.

»»«««

**A Georgian Townhouse in Mayfair, overlooking Berkeley Square
Twilight**

Moran pulled out his pocket watch once more to check the time as he moved restlessly along the rows of odd looking plants. The air was uncomfortably warm and moist, the glass walls and ceiling of the conservatory were beaded with fine droplets as they captured and contained the last rays of the meager winter sun. Grunting in irritation, he removed his silk handkerchief and wiped the perspiration from his forehead. *A poor excuse for a joke...making him wait in the conservatory. He hadn't felt humidity this hellish since the forests of Jeypore in Assam. At least then, his choice of clothing had been more suitable. Well, he would give the man just a few moments more... after all, he had an event to attend.* His plan of action decided, he began to head back towards the entrance to the main house. Movement along the leaves of a strange looking specimen caught his eye making him pause. It stood about 1 and 1/2 meters in height and consisted of a large bulbous pitcher, orange in color. Glossy green leaves and tendrils along with a lid dangled over the pitcher. The lid itself was a lighter green and fanged. Droplets of a sticky, sweet smelling liquid collected on the tip of the fangs and occasionally dripped down into the pitcher. He leaned closer watching in fascination as a small line of black ants marched along the pendulous leaves and tendrils, carefully climbing along the edge of the pitcher but avoiding the falling drops. Inside the pitcher itself were the remains of something but he couldn't tell what exactly. It was a muddy brown and somewhat shapeless – almost liquid but not quite. *Disgusting but fascinating all the same.* He reached out with his gloved hand to give the pitcher a poke.

"Careful! Bloody fool!"

The words rang out sharply and with such authority that Moran yanked his hand back from the plant. "Is it dangerous?"

295

The Professor began to chuckle. "Only if you're an insect or a small animal, say a rat. Are you a rat Moran?"

Moran compressed his lips tightly, the scar along his chin bulging noticeably but didn't respond to the insult. The Professor arched his brow in amusement. With the utmost care, he took up an atomizer and gently misted the plant. "Nepenthes Bicalcarata - fanged pitcher plant. This lovely came all the way from Borneo. Despite her ferocious appearance, her digestion is quite delicate, easily disrupted. She must be nurtured and tended to with diligence and patience."

"Absolutely vile," snorted Moran as he stared at the unrecognizable mess in the base of the plant, "... and all those bloody ants crawling about."

"Ahh, the ants. Little soldiers marching along; quite a unique partnership. The ants burrow into the leaves and nest deterring other insects from digging in. They also clean the lip of the pitcher, keeping our friend here free of excess debris ensuring that putrefaction doesn't set in. In exchange, she gifts them with nectar so they don't stray too far."

"What if they overrun, become too numerous, burrow too many nests? Wouldn't that weaken your precious lovely?"

The Professor paused, an odd gleam in his eye as he set down the atomizer. "Oh, not to worry. If they get out of hand, she merely secretes an excess of nectar along the lip of the pitcher and washes them into the trap where she digests them quite slowly. Amazing how quickly they learn to take care and not upset the balance. Remembering one's place Moran, is the foundation to a mutually beneficial relationship."

An awkward silence ensued for a few moments. Unable to conceal his discomfort and annoyance, Moran smiled tightly and tugged a bit at the collar of his dress shirt. "Well, as requested Professor, I am here. I came as soon as I received your message. As you know, I have a social engagement ... an important one... one you specifically instructed I attend."

A wry grin curled The Professor's lips on noting the slight sheen of perspiration on the Colonel's face. "Ahh, yes of course, first ball of the season. And look at you, the dashing officer certain to set the ladies' hearts aflutter. Let's retire to the library. I suspect you'll find it more comfortable there. I wouldn't want to inconvenience you." Then, without waiting for Moran to respond, the Professor exited the conservatory and headed down the long, dark paneled hall towards the library. He settled in behind an ornately carved gothic desk and poured two glasses of sherry while Moran remained on his feet, hovering impatiently. With a sigh of exasperation, the Professor slid a glass towards Moran, his expression one of the utmost gravity. "Sit down Moran. I've called you here to impart a few words of wisdom and to remind you to mind your manners this evening. It is imperative that you not antagonize Edwina or cause her undue stress. Leave off about the necklace ... it's..."

"I don't understand," interrupted Moran as he sank into a chair obediently. "I thought that was the goal - to discover the whereabouts of the necklace."

The Professor waved his hand dismissively. "One of the goals, but no longer needed. I know exactly where it is. Holmes has it. He's had it all along. Ever since your little escapade on the docks."

"Has he now?" sputtered Moran, his face flushing with anger as he sprang to his feet. "Well then I can assure you it won't be for long. I'll round up a few of the men and we'll make short work of..."

"You'll do nothing of the sort," hissed The Professor with undisguised menace. His hand shot out suddenly and grabbed onto the Colonel's wrist, holding on so tightly that Moran winced in pain. "Sit down and listen! If we play our cards wisely, the necklace will be handed back to us. At the moment, however, we've more important matters to discuss."

Rubbing his wrist, Moran frowned in bewilderment but complied, once more retaking his seat. Once he was satisfied that he had the Colonel's undivided attention, the Professor folded his hands together on the desk and leaned forward, his eyes fierce and resolute.

"Pennington will be arrested tonight, and it is imperative that you be on your best behaviour. Edwina will need someone to turn to in her hour of need. That someone should be you."

Moran gaped at him in astonishment. "And you know this how?"

The Professor began to laugh and shook his head, a glint of derision in his eyes.

"Please, don't insult my intelligence. It's my business to know these things. Right now as we speak, that idiot Lestrade is gathering his men and preparing to set out for Fern Hall."

Moran stood up so abruptly that the chair nearly toppled over. "Bloody Hell! How can you sit there so calmly? We must warn Pennington. Ensure that he doesn't talk."

"When you have finished panicking like a school girl Moran, do take your seat. Pennington is quite aware of his impending fate. Where do you think I spent the afternoon? I have impressed upon him the gravity of the situation and the role he must play. He understands what is to come. He is prepared to fall on his sword."

Moran's expression signaled great doubt tinged with fear. "How can you be certain? If he talks... if he..."

"He won't. He dare not," insisted the Professor with a peculiar smile.

"But how can you be certain?" repeated Moran. "He stands to lose everything. His estate, his business..."

The Professor sighed deeply and didn't answer at first as he opened a delicately carved humidor made of Spanish cedar and removed a Partagas. He clipped the end with great precision and then lit it, drawing the smoke deep into his lungs; a smile of intense pleasure lit his face as he rolled the smoke over his tongue.

"Because dear fellow, the stakes are too high. He knows that while he is away I will have unlimited access to that which he values most – his daughter. No need to worry about Pennington, he understands his situation completely.

Now shouldn't you be off? I wouldn't want you to be late," he advised and with a wave of his hand sent Moran, still brooding, on his way.

»»«««

Baker Street – Dusk

A light drizzle was falling as Holmes stepped outside and shut the door to Baker Street behind him. He glanced up into the yellow haze created by the gas lamps and the rising mist; not much moon tonight despite the thin veil of clouds in the sky. Already the temperature was beginning to drop. He pulled up the collar of his overcoat as he moved to the small iron fence that surrounded the entrance. Leaning against the fence, he began to rummage through his pockets for his cigarette case, his mind very much elsewhere as he lit a cigarette. His eyes absently watched the curl of smoke drift up into the darkening sky. He needed to clear his head... re-evaluate. Hopefully, the crisp night air would do the trick.

The sound of running footsteps and panting interrupted his reverie and on glancing up, he was surprised to see one of the Irregulars tearing up the sidewalk towards him. The boy was a thin little wretch of about twelve with sharp, weasel-like features and the appropriate moniker of Ferret. Holmes waited impatiently as the boy grabbed onto the fence to steady himself and bent over slightly, taking in large gulps of air as he tried to catch his breath. When he had recovered sufficiently enough to speak, he raised his head and took off his cap, nodding respectfully.

"Beg pardon Mr. Olmes, I run all the way... afraid I'd not find ya...but Wiggins said I'd best try... it being so important."

A frown darkened Holmes' face. "Well boy, out with it then."

Ferret took a few deeper breaths and then scrunched up his face as he concentrated on remembering the message he was to relate. "Wiggins says, I'd best tell the Yarders are on the move. Lestrade and his like got themselves the Black Maria all fitted up and was heading out up towards Golder's Hill - regular Peelers with im too.... about a dozen or so..."

On hearing these words, Holmes drained of all color. Fern Hall was up Golder's Hill. He compressed his lips grimly and fixed his gaze on the boy. "How long ago?" he pressed curtly. It was still a good two-hours ride - at least, there was that.

The boy thought for a moment. "Not more'n 20 minutes or so..."

The words had barely left the boy's lips before Holmes tossed him a few coins and then darted towards the curb to hail a hansom. Moments later, the hansom clattered off down the street in the direction of Bexley Manor. If he were lucky, he'd still have time to soften the blow.

298

BETRAYAL
Bexley Manor - Half past nine

By the time Edwina reached the folly, the drizzle had turned into a light but steady shower. Grasping the folds of her gray taffeta gown, she lifted her skirt and quickly climbed the steps to the Temple. With a quick glance over her shoulder towards the main house, she headed further into the shadows of the folly and then settled onto the marble bench in the center. She arranged her skirt over the bench, gloved hands absently smoothing the folds of her skirt as she stared solemnly out across the lake. Its surface shimmered with reflected light from the house; disembodied voices, snatches of music and laughter drifted out across the dark water to the accompaniment of a light patter of rain. She sighed and rested her chin in the palm of her hand. They were all so easy and light-hearted and from what she could ascertain, mostly without purpose. She supposed it was the money, though it was widely rumoured that several in attendance only had the appearance of money and traded on the good will of their wealthy connections... charlatans. A slight frown darkened her face. Who was she to judge? She was as much an interloper as they... living in a world she clearly didn't belong. She had promised Mary that she would try to enjoy the festive nature of the event, but it was proving difficult. She found herself haunted by memories and thoughts – some quite dark. It used to be that she thought of him mostly on sleepless nights but lately, he was ever present, lurking just below the surface along with the spectre of her mother. A melancholy smile touched her lips. He would have been twenty this very day if he had lived. Poor little Julian. What would he be like? No doubt quite handsome ... sure to turn a few ladies' heads. What would he have thought of this spectacle? More likely than not, he would have reveled in it. He always sought to be the center of attention... the apple of father's eye. Edwina grew troubled...sullen. Julian would have charmed everyone and unlike her, would have embraced society's expectations. He would not be in hiding. As for her, the evening could not end soon enough; she longed for the sanctuary of her room and the solace of her books. Perhaps mother had been right to warn her of the perils of thinking too much but what was she to do? It was her nature. A fact which very few seemed to understand, except for Holmes. Holmes, what would Julian have made of Holmes or, for that matter, what would Holmes make of him? Her expression clouded. No word from him for nearly a week; not since the disastrous events of Lotus House and her subsequent exile. She bit her lower lip, hands curling tightly into fists as they rested on her lap. It served no good purpose to dwell on past events, she knew that. But if she could go back in time, not that she had been wrong, but she would have reined in her emotions. She had allowed her emotions to take control; a cardinal sin, at least in his eyes. She had disappointed him and in the process, disappointed herself as well.

The breeze shifted, and she wrinkled her nose as she caught a whiff of cigarette smoke drifting out from the shadows behind her ... shag tobacco ... Turkish blend to be exact. Excitement fluttered in the pit of her stomach as she turned around on the bench and stared into the gloom near the far columns. To the right of the furthest column, could be seen the faint cherry glow of a cigarette.

"Holmes...?" She sprang to her feet and took a few tentative steps toward the darkness.

The cigarette flared briefly and then went out as he stepped from the shadows.

"Hello Eddy. How lovely you look. Grey suits you."

She smiled, her cheeks suddenly warm.

"You're very kind. It is a lovely gown but...well... it's all a bit over the top isn't it? I feel like the farmer's prize cow on display at the local village fair. Look, I even have a judging sheet of sorts," she quipped and held up the dance card that dangled from her wrist.

"Well, I'd vote blue ribbon," he replied with a laugh.

Edwina shrugged and gazed off towards the lights of the manor house.

"Not much difference it makes. Eventually, we all end up in the abattoir," she replied with a bleak smile. She gazed up at him, her expression settling into a slight frown.

"What are you doing here Holmes? Lady Montague relayed your regrets."

He arched his brow, amused. "Curious question from one who is clearly hiding," he replied, ignoring the question which he was not prepared to answer just yet. "The ball has scarcely begun, I doubt your shoes are even properly broken in."

"A little of this nonsense goes a long way."

"Still, not much of a hello," he chided with a slight grin. "Are you not happy to see me Eddy?"

"Of course I am... always," she asserted quickly, "but, after what happened, this is the last place I would expect you." A trace of sadness darkened her eyes.

He moved closer, eyes dark and brooding. As expected, Watson's ridiculous assertion that she was untroubled by the 'exile' from Baker Street was entirely incorrect. This knowledge filled him with both a deep sense of satisfaction and a modicum of remorse. If she had indeed turned her affection towards another as Watson had suggested, the coming task would be so much easier. Yet, the very prospect of the loss or reduction of her affection left him feeling strangely cold and hollow.

"As Watson will attest, I am a difficult man. Interactions are more often than not contentious; friendships are rare... but the ones that prevail Eddy, are forged through adversity and become tempered like steel. I will not let them go easily. Watson and Miss Morstan's is such... yours as well. Dwelling on past squabbles is senseless and best avoided."

Edwina's heart surged with love. Overcome, she reached out and grabbed his hand, pressing it tightly. "You honour me with your friendship," she whispered, her eyes blurring. She wiped quickly at her eyes and then peered up at him, her expression growing solemn. "But you still have not told me why have you come?"

A melancholy smile curled his mouth as he glanced down at her hands wrapped so tenderly around his. He squeezed her hand in fond acknowledgement and then cast a quick glance at his pocket watch. There should still be time. Once again, he ignored the question and instead, reached down and lifted the dance card that dangled from a cord looped around her wrist.

"Full dance card, despite your 'oxen hooves' ... well done," he remarked, a tease in his voice. As he scanned the list of names, a look of disdain clouded his face. "I see Moran is making an absolute hog of himself. Certainly signed up for more than his fair share of dances. Poor taste. We will have to remedy that," he declared and took up the small pencil that dangled from the card and proceeded to scratch through a few of the dances assigned to Moran. Upon completion, in the margin next to each scratch out, he neatly inscribed S Holmes – a sly smile of satisfaction on his lips.

Edwina smiled hesitantly equally amused as she was alarmed, her unease growing along with her exasperation. "Holmes, you must tell me...." she pressed with greater firmness.

"I fancied a dance," was all he said with a laugh and gently tucked the dance card into the palm of her gloved hand, folding his fingers over hers.

She stared at him astonished. "With me?" she sputtered, choking back a laugh, "Are you mad?"

His eyes crinkled warmly as he tightened his hold on her hand, strong fingers gliding along the satin of her gloves. The pressure of his fingers on her palm brought another bright flush of color to her cheeks. Edwina averted her eyes, embarrassed at her inability to mask the extent of her feelings for him and momentarily forgetting her unease at his reluctance to answer her question.

"I am really quite hopeless," she murmured, "just ask any of the poor gentlemen I've danced with tonight... they're quite easy to find...just look for the limp."

Holmes' expression grew bittersweet. Releasing her hand, he grasped her chin and gently turned her face back to his. "The truth Eddy is that you are the only one I wish to dance with, and now, at this very moment, it is the thought that consumes me entirely."

The words, spoken with such uncharacteristic sentiment, rendered her temporarily mute; she raised her eyes to his, lips pursed but unable to make a sound.

His eyes softened with compassion. "Will you favour me with your hand for this next dance?" he asked with a smile so genteel and a bow so perfect, Lady Montague would have applauded.

Edwina sighed in resignation and then nodded, placing her hands in his, but forgetting to curtsey – an error Lady Montague would have also noticed, though not favourably.

"Yes, of course, only I must warn you, the dance lessons did little good."

"Not to worry. With the right partner, I promise you'll fare much better," he soothed. He cocked his head, listening. The strains of a lively mazurka drifted across the lake.

"Not this," he advised with a shake of his head, "tempo is unpredictable besides, it's nearly finished. I suggest the next one which if I recall from your dance card, is a waltz."

He offered her his arm, waiting for the waltz to begin.

She balked, a look of panic on her face. "Not the waltz."

Holmes couldn't help but smile as her fingers nervously tightened around his.

"Simple three step. All you have to do is count and follow my lead."

"My second dance this evening was a waltz... a fiasco," she blurted in desperation.

"I stomped on Moran's toes, which I freely admit I am not sorry for, but also managed to collide with the lead couple. I nearly knocked them into the musicians. I was mortified as was Lady Montague, and most everyone else present."

Holmes burst into hearty laughter and pulled her very close; Lilies of the Valley wafted up tickling his nose. "Fortunately, we have an entire floor to ourselves with only the columns to avoid, and the good news is, they will not be moving. You will not trod on my toes Eddy, I insist. Now, gloves off."

"What?" She stared at him perplexed; she had no objection, but it seemed an odd request.

"Off please... you'll find it much easier to follow my lead if you can feel the signals. Slight pressure in the right palm, move to the right, increased pressure on your back, move to the left. Remember to count, silently of course, and most important of all, do allow me to lead. Only one of us should lead, I suggest it be the one who knows the steps."

"But, perhaps it would be best to wait for..."

Her protests fell on deaf ears however, as the opening measures of a Viennese waltz sounded, and Holmes pulled her into position. Realizing the battle was lost, she slipped off her gloves and handed them to him. He tucked them into his pocket for safekeeping and moved her into the center of the folly, drawing her close - much closer than would have been permitted on the dance floor under the watchful eye of Lady Montague. His right arm slid securely around her waist until his palm lightly rested on the small of her back. The music swelled and as he stepped forward to the beat. Edwina took a deep breath and smiled bravely up at him, concentrating on following his lead, ignoring the growing flutter in the pit of her stomach as best she could. Much to her relief and delight, they were moving with surprising ease, in harmony with each other and the music, by the middle of the first dance. Her confidence restored and filled with the radiant glow of contentment, she rested her head on his shoulder and closed her eyes.

"Sherlock Holmes... Master Detective and now Dance Master," she mused, "I would not have thought dance was a skill necessary in the pursuit of justice."

"A skilled detective has an array of weapons at his disposal ... some more pleasurable than others..." Holmes chuckled, savouring the moment, his arm tightening around her waist.

She began to laugh and then suddenly drew to a halt, reaching up on tiptoes, her hands holding onto the lapels of his frock coat.

"You captured my heart long before this dance Holmes, though it is an unexpected and most delightful bonus," she whispered as she leaned forward and pressed her lips to his cheek.

The sweetness of her kiss made him pause in the midst of the waltz. There was a purity in her affection that made him hesitate once again in the carrying out of his task. He pressed her closer, his eyes fixed on hers and carefully tucked a loose strand of hair behind her ear.

"You are so very dear to me Eddy, you must always remember that..." he murmured. With the utmost gentleness, he took her hands in his and pressed them to his chest. He held them there for a moment as he met her gaze. He wanted to remember the look of devotion in her eyes - he doubted he'd see it again. "Come sit with me ... I have something to tell you..." he said after a moment of silence. He nodded in the direction of the bench, his hand tightening around hers.

The noticeable shift in his demeanour and the gravity in his voice sent a shiver along her spine.

"Of course, but I'd rather stand," she replied with some trepidation.

He shook his head, his eyes growing guarded as he led her over to the bench.

"You should sit... we shall both sit."

She complied, her unease growing as she settled onto the bench next to him. She took a deep breath, focused on suppressing the slight quiver in her hand as she held onto his. Whatever it was he had to tell her, it weighed heavily on him. Her thoughts raced. Perhaps he was going to tell her the analysis of her mother's necklace was complete, and it was mostly paste after all. Disappointing news to be sure, but nothing she could not overcome. Edwina peered up at him, eyes full of compassion and squeezed his hand in reassurance.

"You are my truest friend Holmes... there is nothing you cannot tell me. Go on then."

A twinge of regret caused another moment of hesitation, but he knew there was no choice. He compressed his lips and met her gaze with deliberate detachment.

"Eddy, I have some unfortunate news...with regard to your..."

A chorus of shouts and calls interrupted him, drifting out across the lake, growing louder with each passing moment. Startled, they both stood. Edwina watched in bewilderment as a small group of men in what appeared to be dark blue uniforms made their way down the gravel path that ran alongside the lake. Behind them, rolled two carriages at a slow and steady pace. Their torches flickered in the growing dusk, lighting up the grassy expanse that stretched from the manor house to the folly. A small group of men broke off and headed across the field, they seemed to be searching for something or someone. Silence descended, broken only by the sounds of the men as they continued their advance. The music from the house had died out and groups of guests had begun to congregate on the outside terrace to watch the spectacle. As the men grew closer, she could see that they were indeed in uniform- the uniform of the Metropolitan police. Edwina swallowed dryly and clasped her hands together anxiously on realizing that the name they were calling out was her own.

The procession was led by Lady Montague who was clearly distressed, and an unknown man in a bold patterned plaid suit. Dr. Watson and Mary Morstan followed not far behind looking solemn and grim; a few others trailed behind not content to watch from a distance. As the carriages grew closer, Edwina grew paler, the knot of anxiety in her stomach tightening. The first in line was an official looking hansom bearing the somber colours of Scotland Yard but the one that struck fear within her was the sight of her father's brougham following close behind. "Something's happened..." she murmured as she took a faltering step away from the bench.

Dread flickered across Holmes' face. "Eddy, wait," he said, reaching out to restrain her but it was too late. She was gone, moving with surprising speed down the steps and out across the damp grass towards the men waiting on the gravel lane. He sprang after her.

On reaching the small assemblage, Edwina drew to a halt, panting - her shoes slipping on the gravel. "What's happened? Is it my aunt?" she cried, holding onto her sides as she fought to regain control of her breathing.

Lady Montague stepped forward, her face drawn with distress and shame.

"You must go with these men child. Now, quickly. I will send your things on in the morning." Her voice was a desperate plea as she glanced back over her shoulder towards the ever-growing crowd gathering on the terrace.

Edwina stared at Lady Montague dumbfounded. It was at this point that she became aware of the strangest of sounds coming from inside her father's carriage. It was heart-rending, alternating between soft weeping and unintelligible cries. She paled and whirled to face the man in the plaid suit as he seemed to be in charge.

"Go... Go where? Who are you? What's happened?" she pressed, struggling to contain her rising anxiety.

"Inspector Lestrade - Scotland Yard," he announced proudly. "Miss Edwina Pennington, I presume..."

"Yes ...," she acknowledged hesitantly, "but I prefer Schraeder. What's this about Inspector?" she repeated with some sharpness. There was something about him she didn't trust ... besides his suit and his over slicked hair. She studied his face with the eyes set too closely together and his exaggerated mutton chops; it came to her - his eyes squinted when he moved his mouth and it made her think of a wharf rat with very large, unkempt whiskers.

"I've come to collect you. You must come at once," Lestrade instructed in his most officious tone.

"Collect me! I'm not going anywhere, Scotland Yard or not, until you tell me what this is about!"

Lestrade sputtered a bit, flabbergasted and scratched his whiskers, unsure of how to proceed. The Devil, these women and their nonsense. He drew himself up and cleared his throat, preparing to take control of the situation. "Now look here Miss... I..." His words died abruptly as he stared into the shadows baffled as Holmes stepped forward. "Holmes! Bloody Hell ...did not expect to find you here."

"A moment Lestrade," he said brusquely and motioned for the Inspector to remain silent; it was an order not a request. Without waiting for the Inspector to respond, Holmes shifted his attention to Edwina. His expression softened and reaching out, he gently took her hand in his. "Please Eddy, I must speak to you." He gave her hand a gentle tug, attempting to move her off to the side.

Edwina grasped his hand tightly - unsettled by his expression. There was something in his eyes... something more than just unease at the situation. All the while the weeping continued from inside the carriage, growing progressively louder and more wretched. Distracted by the sound, Edwina turned and stared at her father's carriage, her face devoid of all color.

"Who's in there? Tell me... for God's sake. Won't someone tell me what's happened?" she pleaded. She looked to Holmes for an answer, but before he could utter a word, the sobbing from inside the carriage suddenly ceased and the carriage door flew open. Dolan and Jenkins, who had been posted as guards, were knocked aside and went reeling. An unearthly shriek pierced the air as Gretchen Pennington, bonnet askew, her usually tidy chignon undone and in disarray and with eyes like some crazed beast, launched herself from the carriage.

"Ruined! Ruined! All of us. Ungrateful harlot... cursed seed!" she screeched as she fell upon the stunned girl and began to pummel her with her fists.

"Christ Lestrade! Have you no control?" shouted Holmes as he sprang forward and snatched the hapless girl from the woman's grasp. He pulled Edwina close, using his body to shield her from further attack while Dolan and Jenkins, finally recovered from their stupor, grabbed the hysterical woman and held her back. All the while Gretchen Pennington continued to fill the air with a barrage of incoherent shrieks and curses as she kicked and flailed about.

Humiliated, Lestrade took hold of the woman and shook her roughly.

"That's enough out of you. Another outburst and I'll clap you in irons."

Instead of calming the situation, the threat only served to send the woman into an even more frenzied state. She sobbed inconsolably and leaned heavily on Dolan and Jenkins as they dragged her back to the carriage.

"What's the meaning of this... tell me!" demanded Edwina, pale and shaken from the assault. She held onto Holmes' arm tightly as if to draw strength from it.

Lestrade's patience was at end. "Your father's been arrested. I am to return you to Fern Hall and the care of your Aunt at once," he said bluntly.

The words took her breath. Edwina stared at him dumbfounded.

"Arrested? On what grounds!"

"Crimes against the Crown - counterfeiting. He's been taken to Newgate pending trial."

"You're mad. You've made a horrible mistake."

"No mistake Miss... the evidence..."

"Your evidence is flawed!" she interrupted, desperate to make him see his error.

At this Lestrade smirked somewhat and shook his head. "Not likely Miss, the evidence..."

"What evidence!!"

"The paper Miss, ironclad, irrefutable as well as the source."

"Paper...!! What pap..." Her words trailed off as realization slowly sank in. She turned to Holmes incredulous - aghast. "You....you did this!"

Holmes had stood by silently all this time dreading moment but knowing there was nothing to be done now but face it. He met her gaze and nodded, steeling himself.

"The evidence is clear Eddy - although I do not believe your father acted alone," he remarked and cast a withering glance in Lestrade's direction. He paused briefly and then turned back to her, his eyes earnest and clouded with remorse. "I am truly sorry, but I could not jeopardize the investigation - I was bound to silence." As he spoke, he slowly reached out to take her hand in his and offer some comfort.

Edwina seemed unable to speak at first and stared numbly at her hand which lay in his. Slowly, she slipped her hand free and began to step back, her eyes full of anguished disbelief. There was a long awkward silence and then she squared her shoulders, narrowing her eyes, her expression growing dark and bitter. Her hands began to curl into tight little fists at her side.

"How long?" she rasped, her breath coming in short staccato bursts.

Holmes hesitated – revealing the answer to that query would only exacerbate the situation.

Anger sparked in her eyes as she lurched forward, her cheeks crimson.

"Tell me! How long have you known?" she hissed.

He met her gaze unflinchingly. "Known, not long. Suspected, well... since the very first interview," he admitted.

"The first..." The words caught in her throat leaving her struggling for air. She remembered that day. The meeting on the road with the man with the whip, the Old Russian peddler and horse and later, Holmes' scaling the trellis. A cherished memory... until now. The color drained from her face and her knees began to buckle. Alarmed, Holmes sprang forward to steady her. It was a mistake. As his fingers grasped her arm, she abruptly raised up and twisted free. She lunged at him, eyes ablaze, her right hand raised. The sound of the slap echoed in the night air along with a gasp of shock that rippled through the onlookers. Holmes swayed slightly from the force of the blow but made no attempt to either move out of reach or ward off another blow. He stood his ground, waiting ...

"I bared my soul to you... shared things I've told no one... you know my heart. How could you? Do I mean so little to you?" she cried with great bitterness, struggling to control the tears that blurred her eyes and threatened to overflow.

It was at this point that Lestrade seemed to recover his senses and moved forward to restrain her, but Holmes waved him off. Although unwelcome, it wasn't unexpected and he conceded .... long overdue. With an expression of remorse, he stepped forward again and attempted to take her by the hand; once more, she stepped away.

"It was never my intention to hurt you Eddy, you must believe that. You mean more to me... more than I ever exp..." He abruptly broke off unable to finish, uncomfortable with the thoughts and feelings that stirred within. He stiffened, his fingers gingerly exploring his cheek where already a red welt was beginning to appear; his eyes grew guarded as he sought to recover a modicum of detachment. "I have an obligation Eddy... to my profession," he continued, his voice calm and steady, "to ensuring that sentiment does not overshadow the pursuit of the facts or justice..."

Icy resentment hardened her expression and she took a deep breath, wiping away the remaining traces of her tears.

"Thank you, Mr. Holmes... for reminding me in no uncertain terms of the folly of *sentiment*. My deepest apologies for having been so slow and dull to comprehend. Rest assured I understand now and will not make the same error in the future."

Having no more to say to him, she turned away and focused her attention on Lady Montague and Mary Morstan who had stood by watching in uncomfortable silence. Edwina drew herself up, gathering her composure.

"Lady Montague, my humblest apologies... You've shown me only kindness. I hope that one day you'll find it in your heart to forgive my bringing this shame upon your household. I will not darken your door any longer. I'll send for Hanna and my things in the morning. And you, my dearest Mary," she added with a sad smile, "you've been a gracious and steadfast friend. I wish you only happiness." The two women embraced for a moment and then Edwina pulled away. She turned to Lestrade, her eyes resolute and unnaturally bright, her demeanour unnervingly calm. "Now Inspector, if you please, I'm quite ready to leave now," she announced and then moved off towards the carriage. She brushed past Holmes without a second glance. As she approached the carriage, Moran emerged from the back of the crowd. He stepped forward and offered her his arm, affecting his most sympathetic smile. Edwina stopped for a moment and stared at him lips curling in disdain.

"Get away from me," she snarled and then took Lestrade's arm as he helped her into his carriage. Lestrade, after vehement urging from Holmes, had finally acquiesced to his suggestion that it would be best if she rode with him instead of her aunt, who still filled the air with occasional wretched sobs. Moran faded back into the crowd with a look of petulant indignation. As Lestrade helped her into the carriage, Holmes started forward as if to have one last word. Watson caught him by the arm and held him back.

"Let her be Holmes, no good will come of it now," he counselled. Holmes reluctantly complied and they both stood silently, watching the carriages roll down the lane towards the gates of Bexley Manor.

Lady Montague who had been silent for some time now, seemed to remember her guests. She shook her head, watching the carriages disappear from view and then turned back to them, her expression agitated but also tinged with sadness.

"I want you to leave Mr. Holmes, now... as you sorely test the bounds of my hospitality. As for you Dr. Watson, as you are my niece's fiancé, you may remain but truthfully, I would not be displeased to see you depart as well. Goodbye gentlemen, I have guests to attend to and my good name to salvage. Come along Mary, I require your assistance," and then she was gone, striding purposefully across the lawn towards the manor house - practicing her most apologetic smile. Mary hesitated, her expression a mixture of mounting anger, shock and grief. She looked to the men and then shook her head, her eyes fixed angrily on Holmes.

"This was despicable, even for you. I would not have believed you capable of such cruelty. If it had been me, I would have slapped you twice and much harder. As for you John Watson, it is increasingly clear that you knew of this charade all along and said not a word. You are no better!! I suggest you both leave... quickly, before I advise my aunt to set the dogs loose..." And then she was gone as well... hurrying after her aunt.

They remained in place for a few moments more, standing side by side in silence on the gravel drive watching as the gala slowly returned to life. Music once more floated out across towards them; in the distance, a couple of dogs barked restlessly.

Holmes sighed a bit and cast a sidelong glance at Watson. "Well, that could have gone better I suppose," he remarked and began to trudge up the lane toward the gates.

Watson stopped in the middle of the lane. "Better! For God's sake man."

Holmes shrugged and then turned away, continuing to make his way towards the street.

"I'm sorry about Mary, John," he said quietly after a few moments of silence. "If you'd like, I shall try to talk to her – explain when the dust has settled. Your loyalty to me has caused you undue grief."

Some of the anger began to fade from Watson's face. He hurried to catch up with Holmes. "Oh, she'll come around ... eventually," he sighed in resignation. Not the first time I've made her angry. I suspect it won't be the last. At least the dogs are still penned."

Holmes managed a slight grin. "Well, for the moment ... perhaps we should increase our pace."

And although it was said in jest, both men moved a little faster. As they reached the gates and headed out to the street, Watson fell in step beside him. He raised his brow, a faint smile on his lips on noting the redness that continued to deepen along his friend's cheek.

"You'd best let me have a look at that... she's marked you. I bet you'll have a bruise."

"Don't sound so pleased Watson, I concede it wasn't undeserved. I must admit, the intensity caught me by surprise. She has quite the wicked right hook. Still, could have been worse...at least, no weapons were involved," he added dryly as he stepped to the curb to hail a hansom.

Watson stared at him, taken aback at his making light of all that had just occurred and then realized Holmes was deflecting – his way of dealing with feelings he'd rather not acknowledge.

"Well, at least it's finished now," he said with a shake of his head. "I for one would welcome a return to our normal routine."

"Finished! No, not by any means," exclaimed Holmes with a sharp glance as a hansom pulled to the curb. He opened the door and quickly climbed in, waiting for Watson to join.

"But surely the case is closed," protested Watson wearily as he sank into the seat across from Holmes. "Lestrade has made an arrest...and..."

"Lestrade is an idiot," he growled curtly. "I will not let him close the books on this. It is inconceivable that Pennington is behind this. Any fool can see. I will not let this settle until I have ferreted out the answer. Now - tonight we rest. Tomorrow, we start anew."

"Anew?"

"Oh yes. From the beginning. I shall review every aspect of this case and you my friend, I shall need you to once again conduct interviews at your club and..."

Watson let out a loud groan and leaned forward in disbelief.

"For the love of God man, what more can be done? Why?"

A look of anger flickered in Holmes' eyes.

"What more can be done?" he repeated, "Justice Watson. Justice can and will be done."

Watson grew silent then nodded as he searched his friend's face.

"Justice? Is that what this is about? Truly? Or maybe, is it absolution?"

The insinuation caught Holmes by surprise. He fell silent, his eyes pensive as he stared into the darkness. Avoiding Watson's glance, he lit a cigarette and closed his eyes, remaining motionless for so long that Watson became convinced he had fallen asleep. With a heavy sigh, Watson leaned forward to remove the still burning cigarette from between Holmes' fingers. At the first tug, the Detective's eyes flew open. He smiled with more than a trace of melancholy, admitting, "The truth Watson is both."

»»««

REGRETS

"Well, that's one more nail in the coffin." Watson closed the London Times and laid it on the seat next to him.

Holmes, who for all purposes appeared to be napping, shifted slightly in his seat and opened his eyes. His gaze drifted to the paper, eyes narrowing as he scanned the headline. With a snort, he sat upright and grabbed the newspaper; his voice dripped with disdain as he began to read aloud.

COUNTERFEIT SCHEME SMASHED - SCOTLAND YARD TRIUMPHS

The cunning mastermind of a dangerous forgery scheme has been taken into custody and is held at her majesty's pleasure pending trial thanks to the brave and swift action of Scotland Yard. "It was only a matter of time. I had the miscreant pegged from the very beginning.," said the ever diligent and intrepid Inspector G. Lestrade - the man responsible for uncovering the ..."

Holmes sputtered to a stop and threw the paper down in disgust. "Intrepid!! Pennington all but served them tea upon their arrival to arrest him. His sister poses more of a threat. The woman is unhinged... and to call him a cunning mastermind..." He seemed to run out of steam for a moment and compressed his lips tightly. With a shake of his head, he muttered, "Idiot..." and glanced absently out the window of the carriage. Already, the late morning sunlight was giving way as thick clouds began to roll in from the east. Ladies and gentlemen alike on the avenue took a firm hold of their hats as an occasional gust of wind sent tiny swirls of dust and debris across the road. Another storm on the horizon.

Watson nodded in commiseration and took up the newspaper once again, neatly folding it into thirds. He cleared his throat. "Well, to be fair, given the evidence, it does seem a logical progression."

"Pennington expected his arrest ... any fool can see that," growled Holmes impatiently. "He's taking the fall, but for whom? Lestrade is too eager."

Watson shrugged in resignation. "Be that as it may, we haven't been able to provide him with anything to the contrary Holmes, despite our continued efforts. Perhaps, it is time to accept that this case is closed and..."

"Driver!! Stop!"

The carriage lurched to a halt with such force that Watson was nearly thrown from his seat. "Bloody Hell! Can you not do that!"

"Did you see her?" cried Holmes. He was agitated, on his feet, hand on the door latch poised to spring from the carriage.

"What? Who?" grumbled Watson, still in the process of righting himself.

"The girl," he rasped, pointing down the street as he flung open the door and scrambled out.

"What girl?" called Watson as he leaned out the door, watching in bewilderment as Holmes darted down the sidewalk.

"Hold the cab Watson, I shan't be long!" was the only response and then Holmes disappeared into the market-day crowds that milled about along the High Street. Watson peered down the street for a few moments more, trying to see who had caught his attention but it was no use, they had already vanished. With a sigh, he sank back down into his seat and once more took up the newspaper, there being nothing more to do but wait.

It wasn't a long wait; less than thirty minutes had passed when the door to the carriage opened, and Holmes climbed back in. He was greatly subdued as he took his seat, all previous excitement evaporated.

"No joy then?" asked Watson, puzzled by his noticeable lack of energy.

Holmes hesitated a moment and then shrugged. "Not entirely. She wouldn't stop to speak though I could swear she saw me. To be expected I suppose given the circumstances."

"Who?" pressed the Doctor impatiently, his curiosity piqued on noting the small grey satin pouch that Holmes cradled in his hands. *A woman's perhaps... Mary had one similar...*

"Hanna... did you not see her?"

"Edwina's maid? No, I did not... she gave that to you then?"

Holmes smiled bleakly and glanced down at the bag, his long fingers curled around it.

"If she would not even acknowledge me, is it likely she would hand this over? No, I followed her. She went into Pearsons. I waited until she had left and then I retrieved it. They were eager to sell, convinced it would never be reclaimed. A pretty sum it cost me."

Concern clouded Watson's face. E.A. Pearsons was a well-known pawnbroker with a reputation of asking few questions of those who sold their goods or those who bought them.

"Retrieved what Holmes?" he asked gently, "What's in the bag then?"

Holmes carefully placed the bag in Watson's hands. "An item Watson, which I would never expect to find at a pawnbroker."

Watson frowned at the dismal tone of his friend's voice. Loosening the drawstring, he tilted the pouch and shook the contents into his palm. Surprise flickered across his face. "Her mother's watch," he murmured. He stared at it for a few moments and then tucked it back inside. "Could the girl have stolen it?" he asked as he handed the bag back to Holmes. He didn't really believe it, but then again desperate times could tempt the most trustworthy of servants.

Holmes shook his head and removed a note from his pocket. "She delivered the watch with this note."

Watson took the note, studying the graceful, flowing script. It was an authorization from Edwina for the girl to pawn the watch. He returned it with a heavy sigh. "I'm afraid I have knowledge that I perhaps should have relayed to you earlier. Mary called upon Fern Hall earlier in the week. She was concerned - not a word from Edwina since her departure from Bexley Manor. When Edwina greeted her, she was courteous but aloof - as if reluctant to see

311

her. Eventually, she relented and invited Mary inside. Holmes most of the staff have been let go ... the stables emptied - animals sold off. Some of the furnishings, the finer antiques and paintings, have vanished as well. It seems Pennington has substantial debt, and his creditors are beginning to call in their loans. With Pennington awaiting trial and his shop shuttered, there is no income. The Crown has frozen his accounts; the household has only what had been set aside prior to his arrest. Whatever friends he had seem to have vanished as well."

Holmes' eyes grew dark - sullen. "The vultures are circling ... they want their pound of flesh before the Crown takes it all." With an expression tinged with bitterness and more than a smattering of guilt, he ran a hand through his hair. "All I wanted Watson, was to solve the case, not ruin a family."

Watson leaned forward. "Not the first time a family has suffered because of the misdeeds of a member Holmes, certainly will not be the last. You have said as much yourself in the past. Your commission was to solve the case, present the evidence and leave the doling out of justice to the Courts. That is what you have done. I agree, Pennington may not be the mastermind, but he is certainly not without guilt. So then, what makes this case so different? Is it perhaps that you care about..."

"I care about justice," he interrupted sharply, "that the truth be known - the entire truth. Not what is expedient or convenient for Scotland Yard."

Watson suppressed a chuckle and shrugged. "Of course, justice...what else could it be?"

Holmes' smiled tightly though he offered no rebuttal. He lapsed into silence, his attention focused out the window as the carriage rolled on towards Baker Street. As the carriage stopped in front of 221B, Watson glanced at his watch and climbed out. "Good... time enough then... bit of lunch before the Austrians arrive and..." He suddenly stopped and stared up into the carriage. Holmes hadn't moved an inch and had in fact, sunk further back into the cushions of the carriage. "Come along then ... mustn't tarry..." he urged firmly.

Holmes said nothing for a moment and then glanced down at the pouch in his hands. He tucked it into the pocket of his coat, his brow knit in reflection. "I'm afraid I won't be attending," he announced with great solemnity.

"What! What do you mean?"

"A thought has occurred. I must attend to other matters." It was a simple statement offered with a marginally apologetic smile.

"Are you mad? Damn your thoughts. You can't do this Holmes," sputtered Watson. "The Austrians are on their way to collect the necklace – at your invitation, need I remind you. You cannot put them off again."

"No, I cannot ... but you must. Hear me, Watson, under no circumstances are you to return the necklace."

"Chance'd be a fine thing. I haven't a clue as to where you've hidden the blasted thing."

Holmes began to laugh. "Yes, best keep it that way and lest you be getting any ideas to root around for it, I would strongly advise against it. I have taken precautions," he advised with a sly smile and then turned to rap lightly on the ceiling to give instructions to the cabman.

"But what shall I say?" groaned Watson.

Holmes was quiet for a moment and then leaned out the window. "You're the wordsmith Watson," he said with a wry grin, "the writer of epic tales. I am confident you'll think of something..." And then he was gone - the carriage clattering off at a brisk pace.

Watson watched until it was no longer visible and then with a sigh put his key in the door of 221B. As he entered, the clock on the mantle struck 12:00. He gave the air a sniff. The delicious aroma of Mrs. Hudson's meat pies scented the hall, making his mouth water, lifting his spirits. He shrugged in surrender and headed upstairs to await lunch and construct his fiction for the Austrian delegation. After all, his muse was always strongest after a hearty meal.

»»«««

NEWGATE

Edwina set her jaw and stood, a surge of anger slowly welling within. She looked around the dismal room, with its grimy walls and cracked floors, the benches worn and pitted from the untold women and children who had occupied them as they waited. The room was now empty, save for herself, and had been for nearly an hour. Reminding herself to remain calm, she made her way towards the long table at the front of the room, cradling a small, wrapped parcel that contained fresh clothes, a few tins of salmon, condensed milk, and whatever else she could scrounge from the larder. As she approached, the Chief Warder, a stout man with a cheerless expression and bright red whiskers, looked up briefly and then returned to his ledger; he continued to make notations as if she didn't exist. Her irritation surged again.

"How much longer must I wait?" She stood as straight as she could keeping her expression calm but resolute as she stepped up to the table. The Warder's pencil stopped moving and with a weary sigh, he raised his head. "As long as it takes. There is a process. You will be called in order - there are others before ..."

"There is no one left but me!" she exploded, all resolve to remain calm forgotten. Her fingers tightened around the bundle and she took a deep breath, exhaling slowly.

"You have my paperwork and my fee...what more could you possibly need?" she murmured, moderating her tone.

Annoyance knit his brow. *Damned impertinent women - what was the world coming to?* Reluctantly, he glanced to the stack of forms on the table; his vexation increased on discovering that he did indeed have the forms. With a grudging nod, he began to shuffle through albeit with painstaking slowness. When finished, he shrugged as if in resignation and looked up at her. "Well...

313

all in order it does seem. Now if you please, your parcel - let's have a look then... there wouldn't be any tools in here would there?"

Edwina sighed in exasperation and shook her head as she surrendered the package. *What did he think, that she was going to smuggle a pick axe or spade for her father to tunnel his way out?* She watched him warily as he unwrapped the bundle and inspected the cans of salmon.

"Lovely, salmon...what a thoughtful girl you are... any more of these then?"

"Those are the very last! I brought them for my father. Mr. Saunders, my father's solicitor, said there would not be a problem bringing in a few tins."

The Chief Warder sighed and then reluctantly replaced the tins and retied the bundle. "No, not a problem Miss," he assured with some disappointment as he handed the parcel back to her. "Now, onto to more pressing matters...your escort and his fee - when will he be along then?"

"What?" Edwina gaped at him in surprise.

The Chief Warder nodded solemnly and motioned towards the sign on the wall just above the archway that marked the entrance to the holding cellblock.

WOMEN AND CHILDREN MUST BE PROPERLY ESCORTED AT ALL TIMES

A slight flush of color reddened her cheeks. "I am here to see my father sir, I do not need an escort. I am more than capable of taking care..."

"This is a prison Miss," he grumbled through his whiskers, "not the market or gardens at Regents. You cannot just stroll through. There are men here, vulgar, hardened criminals, who..."

"Ahh, good! Ready to begin are we...sorry for the lateness."

Several coins dropped down onto the table. Both the Chief Warder and Edwina started and turned to find Sherlock Holmes standing behind her.

"Mr. Holmes," exclaimed the Chief Warder, "I don't quite understand..."

Holmes smiled genially and leaned forward, speaking in a casual but firm voice. "Ahhh ... Good! You know my name sir and now you have your fee - surely that is sufficient. Be so kind as to mark my name as escort and let us be on our way. Miss Schraeder is eager to see her father and judging by her look of irritation, you have kept her waiting long enough."

The Chief Warder grew flustered. "But Mr. Holmes, this is most irregular. Are you not part of the Crown's case against Pennington?"

"Irregular it may be... but there is no law against it, is there?" reminded Holmes. "Will you deny this dutiful daughter the right to see her father?"

The man's face grew pale at the mere suggestion of such uncharitable behavior. He was a Christian man with a wife and five children - family was sacred, but the rules were not to be taken lightly. "Of course not, but Inspector Lestrade sir," he sputtered, "I think he would find this most unsuitable..."

Holmes began to laugh. "Well then perhaps it is my mistake," he remarked with some sarcasm, "for I was under the impression that as Chief Warder, Newgate was under your control sir, not Scotland Yard. Of course, if it is not within your power to make such a decision..."

314

The Warder's face took on the appearance of a tomato too long on the vine - overripe, ready to burst. He rose to his feet, fingers fumbling at the large keyring which dangled from his belt and made his way towards the massive wooden door that secured the entrance to the cellblock. "It is entirely my decision, and I have decided... come along then," he proclaimed. With no further hesitation, he unlocked the door and pushed it open, the iron hinges groaning in protest. Edwina, however, made no movement towards the door at all and instead turned to the Warder, her eyes fierce, expression agitated.

"Is there no other way? Cannot one of your guards escort me?"

He gaped at her in astonishment. "I don't understand... are you refusing Mr. Holmes' kind offer?"

Her lips pulled into a tight smile as she cast a skeptical glance in Holmes' direction. "Kind? I am well acquainted with Mr. Holmes' "kindness". It is his "Kindness" and my foolish belief in it, which has brought this about."

The man was too stunned to reply and looked to Holmes, who also appeared unsettled by the bitterness in her tone.

"Eddy, my intentions..." he murmured as he reached out to take her hand.

"Your intentions can no more be trusted than your words," she hissed and pulled away. "and do not address me so...you have lost that right."

The color drained from Holmes' face as he sought to suppress a ripple of anger. Ignoring her protests, he grasped her elbow firmly and moved her off to the side - all the while, the Chief Warder looked on in bewilderment. "Could you be so angry... so full of resentment... that you refuse my help out of sheer spite?" he growled. "I extend my hand to you in friendship - and you strike at that hand! Are you so flush with friends that you do not need my assistance? Where are they? Where is Moran - your Colonel? Should he not be here now - at your side? I thought he would champ at the bit to ingratiate himself in your favour. Or is he only suitable for afternoon carriage rides in Regents? Is your Colonel put off by the whiff of taint Newgate conjures?"

The acrimony of his words along with the insinuation, left her speechless - stricken. Edwina averted her eyes withdrawing inside herself.

It was a mistake... a total lapse of reason and logic he realized it too late. "I'm sorry," he mumbled, "I lost my wits...spoke out of turn." The guilt that nagged at him was disquieting; his words had been needlessly cruel and more than that - untrue. What strange, twisted paths his mind had veered down as of late. Logic and his ability to remain detached seemed rare commodities these days - too often derailed by emotion; it was a truth that tormented him. Even now, as he looked on her, he found himself suppressing the urge to once more take her hand. "These events that have occurred ... you must believe Eddy - there was no malice. It was never my intention to hurt you - cause distress. I never lied to you - directly."

She lifted her head, her eyes still defiant but also moist. "No, you never lied... directly. You were very careful. But the omission was just as deceitful. You used my trust... my belief in you to secure information for the purposes of your investigation. You manipulated my friendship Holmes, so forgive me if I am hesitant to accept your offer, I am certain there is another motive behind it other than "kindness".

The words stung - mostly for the truth behind them, and his first impulse was to deflect her accusation, but as he looked into her eyes, he hesitated. Despite the deep hurt and lingering doubt, he could see that she still desperately wanted to believe in him - trust him. Armed with that knowledge, he took the only logical path, he told the truth. "There is some truth to it," he admitted with a resigned smile, "my motivation is not altogether altruistic. I have petitioned to interview your father, but my requests have been rebuffed, not only by Lestrade but by your father as well. As I have no official standing, he has that right. Lestrade for his part fears that any further investigation will diminish his limelight and bring to the case new information that might weaken the case again your father. Most of all, he fears the Yard will look incompetent. Make no mistake Eddy, your father is guilty of this offense, but he is not the mastermind. I know you realize that. He is shielding someone. Talk to him, urge him to speak with me. Help me unravel this tangled skein once and for all; it can only help his cause with the Crown."

Edwina grew quiet - contemplative. Her father had confessed upon his arrest. Any illusions she originally held regarding his innocence had long since faded. She had come to accept his guilt in taking part in the counterfeiting scheme but steadfastly refused to believe he could have originated the plan. He was a follower - a lackey, nothing more, possessing neither the cunning, acumen, or creativity such a scheme required. Holmes was right; he was taking the fall but for whom? She had her suspicions - yet the mere thought of offering the name left her feeling cold and uneasy.

"Well then, what will it be Miss? Not much time left ..." reminded the Chief Warder with some impatience.

She looked first to the Chief Warder, who stood in the open doorway, waiting on her answer and then to Holmes. He had not spoken since his appeal and watched her with a solemn expression that was difficult to decipher. With a sigh of resignation, she managed a faint smile and stepped towards him. "Thank you for your honesty. I accept your offer and I will urge my father to speak with you. However, I cannot promise he will agree. If he doesn't, I ask you not to badger him. Will you agree to this?" she asked and extended her hand to him.

A smile slowly curled his mouth and he nodded as he reached out and gently grasped her hand. "Agreed. I await your instruction." He pulled her close and took her by the arm, holding on with gentle firmness as he led her through the portal. As they followed the Chief Warder into the damp and fetid corridor and began to move past the adjacent cells, a chorus of jeers and lewd taunts erupted. Unsurprisingly, many of the occupants seemed to recognize Holmes. Edwina did not break stride and continued forward, but Holmes could sense her tension as her fingers tightened on his arm. "Pay these idiots no mind," he whispered with a flash of a smile, "most of their suggestions are physically impossible..."

Edwina paused to look up at him and then began to laugh, her expression one of relief and gratitude.

Warmed by her laughter, he gave her hand a reassuring squeeze. "There... that's better... no reason to be afraid."

She met his gaze - her eyes pensive but resolute. "I know, I'm not," she declared and stood a little straighter as she walked at his side.

He nodded in approval and gazed into her face. *An exceptional woman, so full of determination - even when she was more than likely wracked with fear inside. To have such a daughter - the mother must have been truly extraordinary.*

"More "friends" of yours?" she asked with some slyness as the catcalls continued from the adjacent cells.

It was his turn to chuckle. "Friends? An oversimplification perhaps ... it is a complicated bond."

Edwina arched her brow and then uttered a little sigh. "With you Holmes, is there any other kind?"

His eyes twinkled at the question, but he offered no reply. It had always been so - it seemed the only way. With a smile that was rather apologetic, he shrugged and gently increased his hold on her arm, drawing her closer as they moved on down the hall.

Damn...there it was again....

Pennington paused and lifted his pen from the journal, his eyes squinting uneasily towards the far corner of the cell. Nothing – at least that he could see. The chamber was long and narrow, the only natural illumination provided by a barred opening located high up, almost to the ceiling on the wall. The light was paltry, even on sun-blessed days, a candle was needed; it was certainly not enough to penetrate the gloom of the far recesses of his cell. Although he had been a "guest" of Newgate only a short while, already he was finding it difficult to track the passage of time - the hours seemed to stretch from twilight to twilight. Blowing on his hands to warm them, he took up the candle and angled it towards the corner wondering if perhaps he should go closer to investigate. The very thought made his insides crawl. He remained in his seat - perhaps it was best to leave things as they stood. The "visitors" had first come to his attention earlier in the week as he lay on his cot, staring up into the shadows of the ceiling; a few squeaks followed by tiny claws scrabbling around in the corners of the room. He had barely slept. In the morning, he could see the evidence of their activity - the gnawing on the bottom of the small table that stood in the center of the cell and the massive wooden cell door. Thus far, they had chosen to remain on their side of the room, at least as far as he knew. Determined to keep it that way, he broke off a corner of stale bread and tossed it into the shadows. That seemed to satisfy them and after a few moments, the sounds faded off. Pennington experienced a brief surge of relief which rapidly devolved into a profound sense of despair as he considered his situation. Removing his glasses, he let his head slump into his hands and began to rock slightly in his chair - to and fro. *Dear God, what had he done? How could things have gone so wrong? All he had wanted was to provide a better life for his daughter and his dear sister. Was that such a crime?* Wiping the moisture from his eyes, he slowly raised his head and replaced the glasses on his nose. He supposed it could be worse. There were two types of guests at Newgate; the first, such as himself, were merely awaiting trial. They had the better accommodations, luxurious even, or so he had been advised by his jailers. He had nearly laughed in the face of the Chief Warder until he had caught a glimpse of the other cells. With no furnishings other than a pallet of straw on the floor and two buckets, one for water and one for waste, his rickety cot and three-legged stool and table did seem almost palatial. What had his life come to when he was grateful just for a bucket of clean water every day so he could wash? And for a pretty price, he could purchase the right to fresh clothes and additional food. There were no such amenities available for the second lot who were also temporary residents of Newgate but in a much different way. For the unfortunates convicted of capital crimes against the Crown, the gloomy corridors of Newgate were the last sight they would see on their way to the gallows. Still, he found his current state of affairs a bitter pill to swallow; to have come so close to greatness and then fallen so far. But he mustn't lose faith he reminded himself - he would only be inconvenienced a moderate period of time as coining, though a serious crime, was no longer considered a capital crime. Edwina, and his sister would be well looked after; the Professor had assured him that in the end - all would be well-taken care of.

The sound of keys rattling in the door lock cut short his rumination. Pennington looked up in surprise as the Chief Warder's voice called out advising him to step well back from the door. Although he wasn't exactly sure of the time, having traded his pocket watch earlier in the week to a guard for an extra blanket, he thought it was late afternoon. He wasn't expecting any visitors having instructed his solicitor he wished not to receive any. There was too much shame involved for him and his loved ones. As the heavy door swung open, his face contorted in a contradictory mixture of dismay and delight as Edwina pushed past the Chief Warder into the cell. Ignoring the Warder's shouts for her to wait, she ran to the little man and threw her arms around him, holding on tightly. After a few moments of warm welcome, Pennington slowly untangled himself from his daughter's embrace and gently brushed at her damp cheeks.

"Edwina, dearest, is my sister with you? You should not have come... this is no place for you..." he protested.

She deposited a gentle kiss on his cheek. "Nonsense father... now take this," she said firmly and pressed the bundle into his hands. "It's not much... some fresh clothes and a few tins to hold you over for a bit until I get you out of this dreadful place. Aunt Gretchen is still unwell... but sends her love," she added with a reassuring smile. *Unwell was a bit of an understatement. The woman rarely ventured from her room and then only for chapel or to roam the halls of the manor, Bible in hand, offering up prayers for the swift punishment of the sinners who had brought her to this misery. No doubt her name along with Holmes', occupied the top slot of that list.*

Pennington's heart swelled with love and shame. So much like her mother - strong yet tender. What a fool he was to have abandoned them both so long ago. "How are you here my dear?" he asked quietly and cast a nervous look towards the still open door. The Chief Warder blocked the doorway with his back to him, engaged in serious conversation with a tall gentleman he could not quite see. "Has the Colonel brought you here then?" He licked his lips, his eyes like a frightened rabbit. The Colonel made him almost as nervous as the Professor... almost....

Edwina's lips curled with contempt. "Please, can we not speak of that man? You know I find his company distasteful."

"Then who has..." the words died on his lips and Pennington turned deathly pale as the Chief Warder stepped aside to reveal Sherlock Holmes. "What are you thinking child?" he gasped, as he leaned on the table for the support, "that you would bring this man here? Surely you realize..." He once more sputtered to a halt as Holmes stepped into the room and flashed a slight smile in his direction, though he maintained a discreet distance.

Edwina grasped her father's arm in an effort to steady and comfort him. "There was no other way father," she explained, "they would not let me in without an escort. Mr. Holmes recognized my dilemma and was kind to offer..."

"Kind!" Pennington turned beet red and nearly choked on the word. He clutched his daughter's arm for strength and averted his eyes from Holmes' penetrating gaze. "That demons would be so kind..." he muttered, in a voice that was not as quiet as he would have liked.

Holmes arched his brow and chuckled a bit as he took a few steps closer. "I think you'll find I am kinder than most and certainly more trustworthy than your Master..."

Pennington's head snapped up and he stared at the Detective with such an expression of utter dread that Edwina feared he might collapse. "You are mistaken Mr. Holmes. I do not know of what you speak..." he rasped, his voice raw with emotion. His eyes darted towards the closed door at the sound of footsteps in the corridor and he only began to relax as the guard continued on past the cell without pause. With a shake of his head, he squeezed Edwina's hand, keeping his eyes fixed on the table. "If you have come to question me Mr. Holmes, you have wasted your time... I will not bargain with the Devil."

There was a short silence followed by Holmes' sudden burst of laughter.

"Ahh, if only that were the case Mr. Pennington, then you would not be in your current predicament."

Pennington flinched, swaying slightly on his feet and refused to meet his gaze. Edwina tightened her hold on him and gently eased him down onto the cot. Once he was seated, she settled onto the stool in front of him and leaned forward, taking his hands in hers. "It's all right father," she soothed. "Mr. Holmes has promised me he will not persist if you decline to speak with him - he promised me," she repeated forcefully, turning to look in Holmes' direction, "and I am counting on him to keep his word."

Pennington swallowed hard and shook his head. "I thank you for escorting my daughter Mr. Holmes... but I assure you, you have wasted your time," he murmured, his eyes still fixed on the floor.

At this, Holmes gave a small nod of resignation. "I shall wait by the door then," was all he said. With a reluctant smile of surrender, he took the small chair from the table, lit a cigarette and withdrew to wait by the cell door.

Edwina exhaled slowly, expelling the noxious odors of Newgate from her nostrils and lungs as they exited the massive iron gate. With a small smile, she turned to Holmes, who walked silently beside her. "Thank you," she murmured and reached out to press his arm, "for not insisting on trying to speak to Father. I know... you are disappointed."

Holmes chuckled wryly and stepped up to the curb, his arm still entwined with hers as he scanned the street for a hansom. "I promised you I would not persist. With all that has occurred, it seems the least I can do." A shadow clouded his eyes. "Misleading you Eddy, has brought no joy."

Such an unexpected admission of remorse touched her very core, eating away at her resolve to remain a modicum of detachment. Her lips pulled into a smile of compassion and abruptly, she reached up on tiptoes and brushed her lips to his cheek.

"Then I strongly suggest Holmes, that in the future such behaviour be avoided."

His eyes crinkled with warmth and with a quick laugh, he nodded. "Dinner? I know of place not far from Regents. Thereafter, I shall see you home," he advised as the hansom pulled to the curb. He opened the door and extended his hand to help her in.

Edwina hesitated, her eyes mildly suspicious. "Dinner? I thought digestion interfered with your process - slowed you down." It wasn't that she found his company disagreeable, quite the contrary but given their current circumstances, she couldn't help but wonder at his motivation.

He met her gaze reading the doubt in her eyes. "It usually does but I am feeling a bit peckish," he admitted as he drew closer, his hand closing around hers. His eyes grew pensive - shaded with concern. "Quite frankly Eddy, by the fit of your jacket and skirt, I estimate you've lost at least half a stone - if not more. A substantial meal is in order..."

She looked away, suddenly quite conscious of the intensity of his scrutiny and the ill fit of her clothes. There was also the uncomfortable sensation of her palm beginning to moisten. "I think you are mistaken," she demurred, concentrating on trying to keep her palm from perspiring.

Holmes' eyes flickered in amusement. "No, not at all. I remember this jacket - it fit you exceptionally well, but now the shoulder seams have slid forward and the waist gaps where it is now too loose. You are not eating sufficiently - either by design or circumstance ... perhaps an unhappy combination of both..." he added somberly.

"Why would you notice such a thing?" she murmured, her cheeks slightly pink as she self-consciously smoothed her jacket.

Holmes gave her hand a gentle squeeze. "Why wouldn't I?" he replied quietly and then pulled open the carriage door, nudging her towards it. "Come along Eddy, if we delay any longer it will be supper instead of dinner. Besides, there are matters we must discuss."

Ahh, there it was...the reason...more questions. She narrowed her eyes, her embarrassment fading, replaced by wariness. "About my father?"

"Among others," he admitted. The contents of his pocket along with the truth he had long withheld regarding her mother's emeralds weighed on him like the proverbial albatross. The time to shed his burden had come.

Edwina paused, her eyes grave with reflection and then took his hand. "Dinner then," she agreed and climbed into the hansom.

SIMPSON'S GRAND DIVAN TAVERN

"When you said dinner, I did not expect..." Edwina's words trailed off, her eyes scanning the gold lettering on the canopy, the gleaming brass plaques bearing the proud name of Simpsons Grand Divan Tavern. Hesitant, she stepped underneath the canopy, her eyes drifting first to the red and white marble chess board squares that decorated the facade above the entrance and then finally to the polished wood and leaded glass doors themselves; the stately entrance to the once unassailable sanctuary of London male society. "Are you certain?"

Holmes grinned and took her arm. "Change has come even here, although we shall have to dine on the ground floor. The terrace and main dining hall are still restricted. At present only one dining room is mixed, and I am afraid it is located by the galley."

Edwina stared at him in disbelief and then burst into laughter. "How gracious of these gentlemen to now allow ladies to dine in their fine establishment by the kitchen. A word in advance Holmes, I do not scrub pots."

"Well noted," he chuckled and entwining his arm with hers, he pushed open the door and led her into the vestibule. Immediately, a tall, lean man with a striking van dyke that perfectly matched his elegant grey hair, materialized in the reception area and held out his hand in fond greeting to Holmes. He was impeccably attired in full evening dress and had Edwina met him on the street instead of the vestibule of Simpson's, she would have taken him for a gentleman on his way to the Royal Opera rather than the maître d' of a fine dining establishment.

"My dear Mr. Holmes... always a pleasure. Your usual table? Will the Doctor be along shortly?"

"Ahh Bernard, a pleasant evening to you as well. Dr. Watson will not be joining us this evening, as he is otherwise engaged. As you can see, however, I do not lack for charming company. Your best table please – quiet and suitable for serious discourse."

Dismay clouded the maître d's face as he seemed to notice Edwina for the first time. He hesitated, his smile anxious as he appraised Holmes' unexpected companion. "Good evening Madame, I trust you are well." He gave her a brief nod of welcome and then turned to Holmes, a smile of apology on his lips as he leaned in, lowering his voice to a whisper.

"Mr. Holmes, you must forgive me, but I am afraid I cannot seat you, the mixed salon will not be open for another hour. If you and Madame would care to return then."

"But we are here now Bernard. My usual table will serve quite well," persisted Holmes, a hint of amusement in his eyes as he noticed the first sheen of perspiration begin to appear on the man's brow.

The maître d' turned pale and forced a smile in obvious discomfort. "Mr. Holmes, it is with great regret that I must inform you it is quite impossible. It will simply not be allowed. The gentlemen in the main salon will be greatly disturbed by her presence."

Edwina snorted in disdain. "God forbid I disturb *the gentlemen...*" Then, in a softer almost resigned voice, she turned to Holmes. "We should leave Holmes," she sighed, "surely there are other places. Besides, I've little appetite."

"Absolutely not," he proclaimed, "I promised you dinner and I intend to keep my word." He then turned the maître d' and fixed him with a look of steely shrewdness.

"Tell me Bernard, does Miss Adler still keep a private dining salon here? I believe it was in the back just off the terrace, with a private courtyard."

For a moment, the maître d' seemed baffled by the question. Gradually, relief flickered across his face as he remembered. Miss Adler had entertained extensively at Simpson's in the past and Mr. Holmes, for a short period of time, had been a frequent guest. "Of course Mr. Holmes, Madame has not used them for quite some time as I believe she is still abroad, but they are kept ready for her arrival. An excellent idea! As a close friend, I am certain Madame will not mind. If you please, come this way."

Moments later and with her thoughts much distracted by this curious information, Edwina found herself following the two men down a narrow, carpeted hall, enclosed by rich mahogany paneling on one side and a wall of stained glass on the other. She paused for a moment to peer through the glass. The images were somewhat blurred though she could make out a large dining hall aglow with magnificent crystal chandeliers, round tables dressed in the finest linen and cutlery. Amidst all this splendor sat small groups of men, dining or smoking cigars and drinking brandy while they played chess and socialized. There was not a woman anywhere to be seen. Contempt curled her lips and she wondered for a moment how they would react if she could somehow break through the glass and invade their little sanctuary.

"It's really not as grand nor pleasant as it seems... the smoke can be particularly foul."

Edwina turned to find Holmes at her elbow, watching her with uncanny perception. She frowned and then shrugged, a look of bitterness marring her expression. "How lovely it would be to have the opportunity to make that discovery on my own rather than have it relayed to me by some gentleman."

"One day you will," he soothed, "patience...we are on the cusp of a new era."

"It cannot come soon enough," she remarked dourly but once more accompanied him down the hall. Soon they came upon an unmarked door – almost indistinguishable from the paneling in the wall. Upon entering, Edwina found herself in an ornate salon decorated with rococo ceilings, elaborate wall sconces and a selection of oil paintings so sensual it brought a faint blush of color to her cheeks despite her best efforts. "My god, this is over the top," she remarked as she explored the room, "even for that woman." It wasn't unusual for an actress to keep private rooms for entertaining. Her mother had also had salons in both Paris and Vienna, but nothing on this scale nor as decadent. Tucked away in the corner of the room near the fireplace, was a velvet chaise of gold trimmed crimson. A small dining table sat near a set of French doors which overlooked the private garden where the soft murmur of a fountain could just be heard. It reminded her of the elaborate rooms at Versailles.

Holmes chuckled with more than a trace of disdain. "You are familiar with Miss Adler then?"

Edwina made a face as she ran her hand along the velvet of the chaise. "Horrid creature. I met her once when I was thirteen. But tell me, how is it you know her?" she probed, her curiousity piqued. "Client? I can only imagine the nightmares she could be involved in."

Holmes paused a moment choosing his words with the utmost care. "We have conducted business," he admitted warily.

"Business," she murmured, not entirely satisfied with his answer as she considered the possible meanings of "business". The nagging suspicion that *business* had less to do with his services as a consulting detective but more in the sense of his Chinese girl at Lotus House plagued her. But there was something in his demeanor that signaled the topic was a source of discomfort for him and she decided not to pursue the matter. With a sigh, she settled onto the edge of the chaise, watching absently as the maître d' and a few waiters bustled about preparing the dining table.

"I heard she had married – is that not the case?" she remarked after a moment. She wracked her brain for small talk and that was unfortunately the best she could do.

Holmes laughed once more, this time with more than a trace of contempt.

"Several times over if I'm not mistaken. Marriage for Miss Adler appears a temporary condition at best...like a snake who sheds one skin and takes on another...it is a process that is continued on ad infinitum."

"Sounds exhausting."

"Quite," he agreed with a flash of a smile as he sat down next to her. "Now tell me, how is it you are acquainted? Through your mother?"

Edwina nodded, her expression growing peevish. "I had the misfortune of encountering her when I was thirteen. We were living in Paris then. Miss Adler had been an understudy to mother in several plays, so when Mother took ill during the previews, she assumed the lead. Nothing unusual in that however, when Mother recovered her health, the Artistic Director decided to keep Miss Adler in the lead role. Mother was devastated but bore it graciously – much more so than I would have. She took me the opening night and afterward, backstage to congratulate Miss Adler. I was so excited. I had heard so much about her. She was much younger than I expected. Striking, elegant. I must admit I was rather awestruck, especially by her confidence and the way everyone seemed to defer to her. Most of mother's other retinue   generally paid me no mind so I thought maybe this would be a woman I could learn from and..." Edwina paused, disillusionment darkening her eyes. "Well... she took one look at me and then turned to my mother and shook her head as if she was overcome with inconceivable sorrow at my mother's misfortune. She pinched my cheeks until they turned red and then in the most mocking, insincere voice I have ever heard, announced to all in the room that it was fortunate that I was such a clever girl as it was obvious I had little chance of making a good marriage. Some ducklings she said, always remain awkward and never transform into swans - such was my lot, and I must content myself with being a shop girl or governess. I admit, I was too stunned to fully comprehend the insult and just stood there staring at her no doubt with my mouth agape. Mother was utterly mortified. We left without speaking one more word to that dreadful creature. As far as I know, mother never spoke to her again. I tell you this Holmes, if I were to encounter her again, I would not be so silent."

"Nor should you," advised Holmes with frown. "The capacity of some women for cruelty never ceases to amaze me – they seem to revel in it." His expression softened and his hand gently enveloped hers. "Fortunately, they are few and far between, offset by those of a kinder and more noble heart."

Edwina lifted her eyes to his and managed a smile, though it was tinged with sadness.

"Kinder," she sighed, "but perhaps not wiser. Anyway, it's such a trivial matter – especially in light of current events. I don't even know why I mentioned it."

"We shall speak of it no more," he agreed, giving her hand a squeeze. "Ahh, the table is set; dinner first and then," he added, his tone growing somber, "we shall talk."

She nodded in agreement and then took his arm as he led her over to the table.

After one or two more cursory pokes, Edwina laid her fork down on the plate and carefully dabbed at her lips with the napkin.

"Madame, did you not enjoy the medallions? Shall I bring you something else?" The maître d's voice was full of dismay as he hovered at her elbow, staring down at the half-full plate of beef and mushrooms.

Chagrin colored her cheeks. "Oh no, it was lovely," she said quickly, "But I'm afraid I haven't had much appetite lately." The man seemed unconvinced however and continued to linger until Holmes also removed his napkin. His plate was also half full but that was to be expected.

"It's all right Bernard, please clear this away and bring us a decanter of Armagnac."

With a slight bow of acknowledgement, the man quickly gathered up the plates and then vanished. Edwina watched him disappear and then turned back to Holmes, her expression apologetic and hesitant. "It really was quite lovely. It just doesn't seem right somehow, to enjoy such a meal when father is imprisoned."

Holmes studied her over the candlelight and then slowly nodded. "No need to apologize," he advised with a comforting smile. "Half a meal is better than none. You must take care Eddy, you'll be of little help to your father if you fall ill." As if on cue, Bernard reappeared bearing the requested Armagnac and two snifters. When he had once more vanished out the door, Holmes took up the decanter and carefully poured out two generous portions. "Take this and remember, sip it slowly."

She took the snifter gratefully and sipped it carefully, allowing the warmth of the liquid to drizzle down her throat and envelop her. When she felt her strength and confidence returning, she set the glass down and fixed her gaze on Holmes. "Thank you for keeping your word this afternoon. I know you were disappointed."

He met her gaze with eyes dark and sober. "I will speak plainly Eddy, your father will be convicted. Fortunately, it is no longer a capital crime. What is at stake now is the length of his incarceration. His cooperation in uncovering the head of this scheme is the only thing that will curry favor with the Crown. You must persuade him to speak with me Eddy – it is his only hope."

The bluntness of his words took her by surprise though she did her best to conceal it. "I will do my best to convince him," she pledged, her eyes resolute though Holmes noticed a slight tremor in her hand as she set the snifter down. "My father is not a wicked man Holmes. I don't know why he..." Her words trailed off and she took another long sip of cognac, eyes fixed on the tablecloth.

"I never said he was," said Holmes, suppressing the urge to reach out and offer comfort. Now was not the time to be distracted or weak. With a sober expression, he reached into his breast pocket and withdrew the newspaper clipping. He set it on the table in front of her, his eyes watching for her reaction. "Until that time, I need you to tell me what you know of this man."

Edwina started in surprise as she looked at the clipping and then gazed up at Holmes. "I don't understand," she hedged, a tingle of unease creeping over her as she gazed at the grainy image of Professor James Moriarity.

"Yes, I believe you do," he prodded, "Tell me Eddy, everything you know about him." He was leaning forward now, his eyes piercing and unwavering as he waited for her response.

She hesitated, the words catching in her throat at first, aware that her hands were trembling again. She took a deep breath, not quite sure how much she could bring herself to tell, and then began to speak. "His name is James Moriarity — Professor — he... he's an academic of mathematics ... a friend... acquaintance of father's."

"Business partner, associate?"

She shook her head and looked away for a moment. "No, I don't believe so ... at least that I know of. He may have invested in some of father's business ventures, but I don't believe he is a partner."

"How does he know him?"

Edwina shrugged, her fingers picking restlessly at the edge of the tablecloth. She still avoided his gaze. "I'm not sure really. University perhaps. He always seems to have been there... with us... even when I was a little girl. It was always the three of them... together... even on holiday."

"Your mother knew him as well," exclaimed Holmes in surprise. It was a fact he had failed to consider. He cocked his head and studied her face. "Was she also afraid of him?"

"I am not afraid!" she cried out, her eyes suddenly fierce as she met his gaze. After a moment, she began to waver and then compressed her lips. "Mother did not like him and nor do I. It's not that I'm afraid, but I do not trust him. He..." She faltered and then lapsed into silence.

"He...?"

Edwina licked her lips which were suddenly dry and interlaced her hands on the table, each hand clasping the other so tightly that Holmes could see indentations on the skin forming under her fingertips. "He has a way of looking at a person," she began in a quiet voice, "reading them... as you do. It's as if he can read every thought – anticipate them even. But where you and he differ is that you perceive all, the light and the dark. The Professor, it seems, focuses only on the dark. He sees what we struggle to keep hidden, Holmes."

Unease clouded his face and forgetting his resolve to remain detached, he reached out and covered her hand with his. "Stop! You mustn't brood on this. The man is manipulating you Eddy, trying to make you believe things of yourself that are not true."

"I'm not so sure anymore. He sees the darkness in us Holmes. Not only what we've done, but also what we are capable of."

Holmes shook his head and tightened his hold on her hand, disturbed by the self-doubt in her eyes. "I know your heart Eddy," he insisted, "it is entirely without malice."

Her eyes misted with gratitude. "I pray you are right." She grew quiet for a moment and sat back in her chair, eyes distant. "That's all I know of him Holmes... not much really. My father will be able to tell you more. I will urge him to speak with you, but I can make no promises."

"It is all I ask."

Edwina nodded and lapsed into silence. She glanced down at their hands which were still entwined; it brought a smile to her lips for despite all that had happened between them. His touch still offered her comfort. She hoped it would always be so. Perhaps now was the moment to solicit his help.

"I've a favor to ask with regard to my mother's emeralds."

The smile faded from Holmes' face; his expression grew solemn as he waited for her to continue.

"I know that I had asked you to keep them for me, and I do appreciate it, but I must ask for them back. The Crown has blocked access to father's accounts and the household expenses are becoming difficult. Father's solicitor has been of little help, he's incompetent at best. If I could sell them Holmes, it would help us greatly. Perhaps you can suggest a reputable jeweler. Someone who would be interested in purchasing them."

He didn't answer at first unsettled that she had raised the very subject that weighed on him. With a melancholy smile, he gently slid his hand from hers. "Regretfully, I cannot."

"What?" she gasped utterly astonished.

"They are no longer in my possession." It was a lie provided that Watson had followed his instructions.

"Dear God, they've been stolen?" Her expression was divided between indignation and despair.

Holmes shook his head and prepared himself to deliver the news. "They have been returned to their rightful owner."

"You're making no sense," she murmured, a knot of anxiety beginning to rise from within. "Rightful owner? I'm the owner. Mother left them to me."

"They were never hers to give Eddy. I'm sorry."

His words left her speechless. She stared at him unable to grasp what he was saying at first. But then as comprehension began to filter in, a look of disbelief mixed with smouldering anger contorted her face. Grasping the edge of the table, she slowly rose holding on for support. "What are you saying?" she rasped. "That my mother was a thief?"

"Not my words," he replied quietly, disturbed by the pain in her eyes. But he could not change the truth of the matter and steeled himself to deliver the blow. "I have no knowledge if she actually took them Eddy, but the facts cannot be ignored. She was in possession of jewels that were not hers. A fact she was surely aware of as she took great pains to disguise them. If she had no knowledge of the crime, why would she do this?"

Holmes braced himself waiting for the explosion of anger, but it never came. Instead, her anger seemed to fold inwards. She averted her eyes and tightened her grip on the table, swaying slightly as if disoriented. Alarmed, he reached out to steady her, but she pulled away wiping at her eyes.

"Bravo Mr. Holmes," she said bitterly, "how clever of you. Two cases solved, one family of criminals: the coiner and his thief wife. You must be very proud." And then she was gone, fleeing across the room and through the doors, oblivious to those in her path, her only goal to escape. By the time he caught up with her, she had already passed through the outer doors and was standing on the curb in the queue for the trolley. She was shivering having forgotten her coat which he now carried draped over his arm.

Edwina caught sight of him just as she was about to board the trolley. Flustered, she tried to urge the woman in front of her to hurry. She grabbed onto the rail to pull herself up into the carriage and then uttered a squawk of indignation as his arm encircled her waist and gently but firmly, pulled her down.

"Let go," she cried, trying to wriggle free as he pulled her further down the pavement as he searched for a hansom.

"Stop making a fuss," he growled, his patience wearing thin. "I promised you dinner and to see you home. I will keep that promise." The hansom pulled to the curb and he reached for the door with one hand while keeping a firm hold on her arm with the other.

"I do not need or want your help," she snarled fiercely. "Why won't you leave me be?"

Holmes paused and then released her arm. He said nothing for a moment and then turned to face her, his eyes dark and pensive. "Because I can't."

The admission took her by surprise and she stared at him speechless for a moment. Her anger began to fade, though the hurt still lingered below the surface. "Is... that my coat?" she asked, not knowing what else to say.

Holmes nodded and gently wrapped it around her shoulders. He opened the carriage door and waited. "Will you get in now please? It'll be dark soon."

With a sigh of resignation, Edwina took his offered hand and climbed in. She settled onto the seat, pulling her coat tightly around her, avoiding his gaze. As the carriage pulled out onto the street, she finally spoke.

"My mother was a good woman Holmes, not some villain." This time she met his gaze directly, her eyes resolute and fierce.

His expression softened. "I never said she was. Good people sometimes choose the wrong path Eddy. Perhaps your mother felt she had no choice but that doesn't change the facts. I cannot return to you what does not belong to you as much as I would like to."

Edwina nodded that she understood and gazed out the window, watching absently as the streets of London began to gradually recede as they began to make the climb up Golder's Hill. She wiped quickly at her eyes, struggling to suppress the tears that threatened to overwhelm her.

With a slight smile, Holmes began to reach into his pocket for his handkerchief and then paused as his fingertips brushed against the satin pouch. He'd almost forgotten. He withdrew them both offering her the handkerchief first, the pouch balanced on his knee.

"Thank you," she murmured gratefully as she took it from him. She dabbed at her eyes and then suddenly froze, catching her breath as she spied the pouch in his hands.

"How did you get that? What have you done? Did you bully her?" she cried, her anger threatening to rise up again.

Holmes began to laugh and carefully opened the pouch, removing the watch. He held it up studying it carefully. "Hanna is not to blame. She doesn't even know I have it. I retrieved it from Pearson's. No need to worry, the debt is paid in full."

"I don't understand...why?" she murmured, her eyes mirroring her confusion.

He smiled and leaning forward, gently placed the watch in her palm, folding her fingers around it. "Because this, I can return. Your mother left this to you Eddy. It is yours without a doubt and you should never be without it."

Edwina looked down at the watch in her palm and then burst into tears. Still clutching the watch, she threw her arms around his neck and hugged him thanking him. He pulled her close, letting her cry for a few moments more and then released her, easing her back onto the seat.

As the hansom pulled to a stop at the entrance of the drive to Fern Hall, Edwina wiped away the last traces of her tears and composed herself. She glanced out the window at the faint glow of lights from the house.

"I'd best get out here. Aunt Gretchen is less fond of you than ever."

"Give the dear my best," he chuckled as he held open the door for her.

She uttered a quick laugh and then paused, her expression growing serious as she looked back up into the carriage.

"Thank you, Holmes... for this. I'll do my best to convince Father, I promise."

"I know you will," he replied with a warm smile. He reached out and for a moment, caught her hand and squeezed it tenderly. "If you need anything, if I can help, do not hesitate." And then he was gone, disappearing back inside the cab as the hansom quickly headed back down the hill towards London. Edwina watched until she could she could see it no longer and then turned and began to head up the drive, her emotions swirling as she made her way towards Fern Hall.

»»««

MAYFAIR - BERKELY SQUARE

Archibald Dolan leaned forward in the hansom as it pulled to a stop in front of Berkely Square and peered out the window in bewilderment. Darkness was beginning to settle in, and only a few people lingered on the tree-shaded paths that traversed the park square which sat across from the row of fine Georgian terrace houses. It was a quarter of London he had little experience with. He used to policing the docks or the alleys of the East End though he supposed crime existed everywhere – even here. He knit his brow and looked to his partner for an explanation. "I don't understand sir. Are we not heading back to the Yard to report our findings to the Inspector?"

As per Lestrade's instructions, they had spent the day shadowing Holmes and consequently Pennington's daughter, from Newgate to Simpson's and finally out to Fern Hall where Holmes had delivered the girl just outside of the front gate. Afterward, Holmes had returned to Baker Street, and Dolan had fully expected that they would return to the Yard to deliver their findings. Instead, Jenkins had diverted the hansom, and now they were sitting in front of an unfamiliar residence in a part of town they rarely frequented. It made him uneasy... something seemed not quite right. They had received no summons to investigate; had no reason to be here, at least that he was aware of.

Jenkins grinned crookedly at his young partner and took a long swig from his flask, wiping his mouth with his sleeve. "Aye... and we will... first things first!" He offered the flask to the lad - a sly look in his eyes. "You be in the game as long as me boyo, you learn to hedge your bets."

Dolan's unease increased. He wasn't quite sure what was going on, but he had the feeling that it was not something the Yard would look kindly on. He had a lot to learn from Jenkins and he was beginning to suspect that not all of it was on the up and up. Still, he felt a sense of loyalty – the man was his mentor. He took the flask with some reluctance and took a long drink in an attempt to numb his conscience. "Should I come along then?" he suggested tentatively.

330

Jenkins looked him up and down and then shook his head. "Not today," he said, clapping the lad on the shoulder, "best you wait...keep a look out... won't be long..." He took one more deep pull from the flask and then climbed out.

Secretly relieved, Dolan watched the elder detective walk quickly through the iron gate and up the granite stairs. As Jenkins disappeared into the house accompanied by a liveried butler, Dolan leaned back in his seat and glanced uneasily at his watch. Emily would be waiting dinner for him and would be most displeased as he was bound to be late again. No doubt she had put the little ones to bed already. His apprehension growing, he began to wonder if perhaps he should have not been so eager to sign on as a detective.

»»««

BAKER STREET - SUNRISE

"There you are, Dr. Watson. I was just about to lay the tea. Scones and jam to start?" Mrs. Hudson stood at the top of the stairs, beaming at him, holding out a tray laden with tea and a light repast. "Could you take it then? Do you think he'll be wanting more than this?" Her face was drawn with maternal concern.

Watson paused in the dim hall outside his room and blinked wearily as he tightened the sash on his dressing gown. "Is he up then?" he asked with a nod towards the flat. He took the tray from her and began to make his way down the hall. Not a trace of light shone from under the door.

"Not certain. Haven't heard a peep," she admitted with a shrug and descended the stairs. "You be letting me know. I'd be happy to make him a fry up," she chirped from the landing, and then added seemingly as an afterthought, "you as well of course." Moments later she vanished into the sanctuary of her kitchen.

With a sigh of exasperation (it was maddening to perpetually be the afterthought), Watson balanced the tray with one hand and unlocked the door. On entering, he was struck by the complete absence of light and warmth in the room. The hearth was stone cold; not one glowing ember amongst the ashes. It had not been lit since the previous evening when he had sat up waiting with growing apprehension for Holmes to return. He gave up just past midnight and after extinguishing the fire, retired to his own room to brood and worry. Holmes' bedroom door was still closed. Perhaps he was asleep or perhaps he hadn't returned. Struggling to contain a surge of irritation and anxiety, he crossed to the windows and threw up the shade; bright morning light flooded the room.

"Bloody Hell, Watson! Must you blind me so! Do adjust the shade, it's like a knife in my corneas."

Watson froze and then whirled to face the chair in the shadows. A chair which he could have sworn was empty. Holmes was tucked away against the cushions, legs folded beneath him, arms draped listlessly over the sides of the chair. As Watson drew closer, he noticed the faint stubble on his chin and the redness of his eyes. His frown deepened. Holmes appeared to be clad in the clothes he had last seen him in when he had bolted from the carriage in front of Pearson's.

"Great Scott man! Have you been in that chair all night?"

"It's possible," Holmes admitted with a wan smile. "Now, if you please, the blind."

Grumbling, Watson lowered the shade, reducing the light to a soft glow and then returned to the console; he moved the tea to the table. "Mrs. Hudson has laid out tea... shall I pour for you?" He poured himself a cup, his irritation beginning to wane. Holmes didn't answer at first. Watson's frown returned. Taking a sip, he peered across the room, first at Holmes and then towards the rolltop desk. Suspicion began to stir. "Are you.... well?" he asked cautiously.

Catching his gaze, a wry smile spread across Holmes' face. He sighed heavily and propping his elbow on the arm of the chair, rested his chin in his palm. "Would you say I am a clever man Watson?" As he spoke, his eyes also drifted to the rolltop desk.

Watson wrinkled his brow, bewildered by the question. "Why yes... of course...the cleverest."

Holmes turned back to Watson, a derisive smile curling his lips. "Then has it never occurred to you, that being such a clever man, should I care to indulge, that I would take pains to replenish and adjust the levels, anticipating your inclination to monitor?"

Watson set the cup down and stared at him, appalled. It had not occurred. "Is that what you've done Holmes?"

Holmes chuckled and brushed off the question with a wave as he launched himself from the chair. He poured a cup of tea and absently poked at a scone, breaking off a small portion to nibble. "Just making conversation Doctor," he said, as he hovered restlessly over the table, moving a few items about.

"Something has kept you up all night then," persisted Watson, "it's obvious you haven't slept."

Again, Holmes waved him off. "I was reflecting... lost track of time."

"Reflecting... on what? The case? Or..." Watson paused noting for the first time the black satin ribbon wound around the cuff of Holmes' sleeve. He grinned knowingly and finished the question. "Or whom?"

For a brief moment, Holmes averted his eyes. "Your affinity for the sentimental never ceases to amaze."

"Says the man with a hair ribbon wrapped around his sleeve."

Holmes glanced down and then paled almost as if he had forgotten or was unaware of its presence. He stared at it for a moment and then sighed. "Point well taken," he murmured in a melancholy voice. Gently, he unwound the ribbon from his sleeve and laid in on the mantle, placing it carefully next to the sketch. He lingered for a few moments by the mantle, fingers rearranging the items on the shelf, keeping his back to Watson. "When this case is finally at an end Watson," he began in a weary voice, "I think a rest will be in order. Sussex Downs or perhaps... further." As he spoke, he removed his coat and tossed it towards the divan.

Watson's face suffused with kindness. "Rest would benefit you greatly Holmes," he agreed, "as well as the company of a caring friend."

"The journey may be further than Miss Morstan would care for you to travel," Holmes said. "Given your engagement, she has been most generous with your time."

"To be honest, it wasn't me I was thinking of," admitted Watson with a slightly guilty smile. "There is another who cares for you greatly, whose company I feel would be of great solace, even curative, for both of you."

Holmes glanced back at Watson and then nodded in acknowledgment. "Although I admit, there is much appeal in your suggestion, it can never be," he said somberly.

Watson frowned, exasperated. "Why? Why this infernal insistence on detachment? It makes no..."

"It is entirely rational!" insisted Holmes with sudden sharpness, cutting him off. His annoyance lessened, and he shook his head, his expression growing dark. "It is how I must be... and must always remain." He glanced back towards the mantle with a bitter smile. "Even at times if I wish it were not so"

"Blast it Holmes... this..."

"Matter is finished... enough!"

The words, sharp and curt, sliced through the air silencing the Doctor. There was an awkward pause and then, when the tension had eased, Holmes gave a nod towards the table. "Hand me that fruit bowl Watson, if you please," he requested, his demeanor subdued.

Watson scowled sullenly but complied. "You never explained where you went yesterday."

Holmes took the basket and began to remove the fruit, piece by piece. "No, I did not," he replied, offering no further information. "Did you follow my instructions? Put the Austrians off?"

"You know I did," growled Watson, watching in growing frustration as Holmes neatly lined up each piece of fruit on the table. "Bloody hell man, what the devil are you do..." He sputtered to a stop, nearly choking on his words, his eyes widening in amazement as Holmes abruptly grasped the cloth that lined the bottom of the basket and pulled it back. In the bottom lay the emeralds. "Are you mad?" he gasped. "Have they been there all this time?"

Holmes grinned and gave a little shrug as he lifted them from their nest. "Safe a place as any. I knew you'd never find them seeing as how you avoid most anything nutritious. Though I suppose I shall need to find a new hiding place now."

Watson threw up his hands in frustration. "I just don't see the point of it... for the life of me. Why don't you just return the blasted things? At the very least, lock them in a vault."

"Because old friend, a trap is useless without bait," he said and tucked the emeralds into the pocket of his jacket.

"A trap? Trap for whom? Who is it you're expecting Holmes, and when?"

"At present unknown on both accounts, though I have my suspicions. One thing is for certain, they will come after them and when they do, it will be in a most unexpected way. Now forgive me but I feel the need to rest for a while. Please inform Mrs. Hudson that I will not see any clients today." As he spoke, Holmes moved across the room towards his room, but paused in front of the door. "Will I see you at supper then? Half past 6? Unless you have plans with Miss Morstan..."

"No, none today," Watson replied. "She's on the ward this afternoon at the Royal and after, she has made plans to dine with Lady Montague." A slight frown creased his brow. "I, however, was not invited."

Holmes began to laugh. "Ahh, no doubt you will be the topic of discussion!" And then, perhaps noting Watson's look of unease, added, "No need to worry old man, from my viewpoint, there is little fault they can find."

Perhaps heartened by the unexpected kindness of Holmes' words or perhaps because he was no longer able to contain his curiousity about Holmes' whereabouts the prior day, Watson called out to him. "You saw her yesterday didn't you?"

Holmes paused, his fingers on the doorknob. He didn't reply at first and then shrugged, though he kept his back to Watson.

"At Newgate," he confirmed, his tone deliberately cool, "she had gone to visit Pennington."

"Ahh, I knew it," cackled the Doctor, unable to conceal his glee for having worked it out.

Holmes turned to him with a bleak smile. "Congratulations Doctor. Now if we're..."

"Not so fast," protested Watson, eager to prolong his moment of glory. "You could not have been at Newgate all that time. Visiting hours end at 4:00. Now, where did you go for that many hours with a young lady that would not seem untoward? You must have dined then, at..." He paused for a moment, his face contorted with concentration.

Holmes uttered a groan and pursed his lips as if to supply the answer – anything to end the agony of Watson's drawn out deductions. But it wasn't needed as Watson's face erupted with joy as enlightenment struck. "Simpsons!" he cried. "Simpsons by God. They have a mixed dining salon and it is not too far from Newgate."

"Bravo! You will make a fine detective one day." Holmes clapped half-heartedly and turned once more to leave.

Undaunted by his sarcasm, Watson persisted. "And then you..."

"What now?!" snarled Holmes.

Watson recoiled at the sudden eruption of rancor. He peered closely at the Detective and experienced a surge of guilty compassion. "You told her. You finally told her everything," he murmured. "How did she receive the news?"

Holmes glanced up, his eyes fierce and bitter. "How would you take it Doctor, if the man who put your father in prison now informs you that the legacy left to you by your mother, quite possibly all you will have left after the Crown is finished with your father, is unlawful as your mother was a thief. Your father will be imprisoned, his assets seized, and now the mother that you revered has been besmirched. Your future is uncertain at best and all because you placed your trust in the very instrument of your downfall."

Watson bowed his head, briefly cowed and then looked up. "And yet," he began, a shrewd look in his eyes as he scrutinized Holmes, "you are unmarked unlike last time. She did not strike you. She forgave you Holmes... again."

A look of anguish contorted Holmes' face; he averted his eyes. "Her nature... her... heart Watson, is most generous. Undoubtedly, more so than I deserve." Holmes shrugged after a moment, explaining, "I returned her mother's watch. She was so grateful for such a small kindness." He paused and then shook his head, declaring with a sigh, "Sentiment..."

Watson was silent for a moment and then nodded. "Yes, sentiment. But I say, it's more than that Holmes. More than you returning the watch. She forgave you even this and we both know why."

Holmes slowly lifted his head, a look of disquiet on his face. He forced a grim smile. "That my dear Watson, is one more deduction than I care to make," he asserted and then disappeared into his room, shutting the door firmly behind him.

CHAPTER 9

Judgement

A murmur rippled through the gallery, gradually increasing in volume until it became a continuous low-level drone. The spectators, out for a cheap day of entertainment, had grown bored and restless. Many had arrived early to the Court expecting a ghastly murder trial or at the very least, a rousing tale of assault. They soon found themselves disappointed on many accounts; from the unimpressive defendant, a drab little man in spectacles, who cowered in his shackles as he sat on a stool in the dock, to the very fact there would be no trial at all, only a pronouncement of sentence. The pitiful man had pled guilty to coining. A crime that epitomized the word humdrum. As they waited for Lord Wareham, the High Court Judge, to return from Chambers to make his pronouncement, packs of cards and dice appeared. They needed a way to pass the time until the next hopefully, more exciting proceeding. Despite the best efforts of the clerks who roamed the gallery attempting to keep order, the atmosphere was closer to an evening spent in Vauxhall Pleasure Gardens than the High Court of the Old Bailey.

Watson scowled in displeasure at the general lack of civility around him and glanced at his pocket watch. Where the devil was Holmes? He had already missed the reading of the charges. On such an important day, he had fully expected him to be on time. His eyes drifted up to the second tier of the gallery where Edwina and her Aunt were seated. To her great credit, Edwina was fully composed, hands folded neatly in her lap, unlike Gretchen Pennington, who huddled in her seat, muttering as she read from her prayer book. Watson nodded in the girl's direction, to offer encouragement. She flashed a hopeful smile in return, though it seemed to him as her eyes settled on the empty seat beside him, the corners of her mouth began to droop. She looked away after a moment, turning her attention back to her father, her disappointment evident. As he was digesting this, a light pressure touched his elbow.

"What have I missed?"

Watson shifted around to find Holmes sliding onto the bench beside him. "The Devil take you," he exclaimed, "where have you been man?"

"Discussing lodging... apologies. What have I missed?" Holmes repeated, his eyes scanning the courtroom as he spoke.

Watson stared at him in astonishment. "Lodging... what?" he blurted. "On today of all days."

Holmes wrinkled his brow and then uttered a weary groan. "Not for us Watson."

There was silence as Watson pondered the answer. As comprehension sunk in, a sheepish expression darkened his face. "So, you think it will go badly then?"

"I think there can be no other outcome. With regard to lodging, Mrs. Hudson's sister..."

"All rise... The Honorable Lord Wareham," boomed the Chief Clerk as the doors to the Court swung open. The courtroom grew quiet as Lord Wareham adjusted his wig and with the soberest of expressions, entered the court. As he took his seat under the carved mahogany canopy that overhung the dais, a murmur once more drifted around the room – this time of anticipation. He waited for the room to settle and then fixed his gaze on the prisoner.

"The prisoner will stand to accept sentence..."

A look of sheer terror washed over Pennington's face but at his barrister's urging, he struggled to his feet, his chains rattling. Up above in the gallery, Edwina's face reflected her apprehension though she said nothing. She compressed her lips steeling herself and gently grasped her Aunt's hand to offer comfort and quiet her murmurings.

Lord Wareham leaned forward, his expression grim and reproachful.

"I have reviewed the facts of your case with the greatest disappointment Mr. Pennington. It is inexcusable that a man of your class and education, who has had every advantage to lead an honest and reputable life, profitable trade, a loving family, should throw that all away in a moment of sheer greed. Your utter lack of regard for the law greatly offends me, much more so than if you were a common thief who garners some sympathy due to their ignorance and poor breeding. Be that as it may, I will tell you that today you are in some ways fortunate for in my father's time coining was a capital offense, and your sentence would have been the gallows guilty plea or not. The Crown, for better or worse, has put those days behind us. I have reviewed with great care and consideration, the petitions for mercy on your behalf submitted by your family and by parties unexpected." The judge paused for a moment, his eyes drifting briefly to Holmes and then returned once more to the prisoner. "I have taken all of this into account. However, nothing can change the fact of what you have done. Your particular offense, although no longer punishable by death, is still a crime of treason and you persist in maintaining silence with regard to any assistance you may have had in its commission. Therefore, due to the severity of the offense, coupled with your obstinate refusal to cooperate, your sentence will be equally severe." He paused once more and then continued in a grave tone.

"Wilfred Pennington, you are sentenced to 25 years hard labour to be served at Pentonville Prison in Barnsbury. Your sentence will commence upon your arrival. The Court grants you one day of visitation tomorrow with your family prior to your transportation."

A gasp rose from the crowd. Holmes glanced quickly up to the gallery. Edwina was still seated but leaning forward in her seat now her face impassive but deadly pale. Lord Wareham however, was not finished by any means and banged his gavel commanding silence. He cleared his throat and continued. "Furthermore, all property, furnishings, your estate, your business holdings are now forfeit to the Crown. Your family must quit Fern Hall within a fortnight – only their personal belongings may go with them."

"Thieves! Impious Heathens all!!! Who are you to sit in Judgement! It is not your right!"

The unearthly shriek sounded from the upper gallery shattering the silence that had befallen the dumbstruck courtroom. Gretchen Pennington had lurched to her feet. She waved her prayer book threateningly at Lord Wareham and those below, her eyes ablaze with righteous indignation. An undercurrent of excitement snaked through the courtroom. Perhaps not such a boring case after all.

"Madame, control yourself!" Lord Wareham banged his gavel in warning and peered up into the gallery in astonishment.

"Auntie... please..." begged Edwina. Grasping the woman's arm, she attempted to ease her back into her seat. Gretchen Pennington whipped around to face her belligerent.

"Get away from me cursed abomination! This is your doing. You and that godless meddler!" She jerked away and directed her attention to her brother below, who seemed dumbfounded at best, quaking as he stood in the dock. Her face suffused with sheer misery.

"Oh, my poor brother...Why...? Why?" she wailed. "I tried to warn you, but you went ahead and married that French whore. And now, we all pay the price. God have mercy on my soul, but he should have struck her down while that demon seed was still in her belly. Instead, he allowed that Jezebel life and took that poor sweet boy instead."

The courtroom erupted with jeers and raucous taunts. Edwina stood at the rail pallid, silent and seemingly immobilized by guilt.

"Madame, if you cannot be silent I will have you removed!!" The gavel rang down repeatedly as Lord Wareham sought to regain control.

Gretchen Pennington fixed him with the wild eyes of a religious zealot and motioned upwards with her prayer book. "You are not the Judge of me! Only He can judge..."

Lord Wareham gaped at her incredulous and slammed the gavel down on the block, splintering the handle. "Out!" he bellowed. Immediately, two officers of the court scrambled up the stairs to the gallery and took hold of the woman. As they dragged her from the court, she turned to look over her shoulder, her eyes venomous and wild.

"You spout empty lies and half-truths," she spat bitterly. "I answer to a higher authority. Mark my words, you will not take my home for surely as I stand here before God and the heavens, I will see it in ashes and you in Hell before that unhappy circumstance." The door to the courtroom slammed soundly behind her, and a pall of gloom descended on the room. Lord Wareham took a moment to regain his composure and then looked to Edwina, who had begun to make her way down from the gallery.

"My sympathies Miss. I fear you have not only lost your father but your aunt as well. She has surely taken leave of her senses. I strongly advise that you do your best to calm her. If she is still unfit in the morning, you must leave her at home and visit your father alone."

Edwina paused in the aisle and stared at him too stunned to react as he departed the room, his words an incoherent buzz in her ears. As the bailiff escorted her father from the dock towards the prisoner's exit, she seemed to crumple a bit and then slipped out the doors into the vestibule.

Holmes stood abruptly, his attention now focused on Pennington. "Watson, look to the ladies," he instructed and then scrambled after the bailiff. He caught up to them just as they were entering the corridor that led back to Newgate.

"Pennington, consider your daughter!" he cried out. The officers of the court moved quickly to block his entry. The little man looked up, his eyes blurred and rimmed with red. As they led him away, he managed a barely imperceptible nod. Holmes stood alone for a moment in the now empty courtroom, watching and then headed out into the vestibule.

"Where are they?" he exclaimed, a trace of irritation seeping through as he found Watson sitting alone on a bench. Edwina and her aunt were nowhere to be found.

"I tried Holmes, but the old woman was still ranting. Edwina thought it best to get her home. I suggested a sprinkling of laudanum and cinnamon in her tea. Bad business this. Inconceivable. Not an ounce of mercy from the Crown. Why Holmes? Why? The man is a coiner, not a murderer. I've seen far worse get lighter treatment... and to punish the family..."

Holmes shrugged, a troubled look in his eyes as he crossed the wide hall, heading towards the outer door. "They are making an example of him. What happens to the family only serves to reinforce the warning. Perhaps this will do the trick Watson, and Pennington will reconsider his silence." He pushed open the door and stepped out. They were immediately assailed by a sudden gust of cold wind which sent leaves and dirt swirling.

"Is there still time then?" asked Watson, drawing up his collar, grimacing against the biting air.

Holmes glanced up at the ominous thunderclouds overhead and shook his head.

"Uncertain," was all he said and then headed off down the street to hail a hansom.

>>«<

Pennington sat motionless on the cot staring at the puddle beginning to form in the corner under the window grate. The rain was relentless, rivulets streaming down the wall as thunder rumbled overhead, rattling the brackets that held the gas light above. The puddle increased, tendrils of wetness creeping towards him. A foul stench wafted up from the flooded drains; he gagged in revulsion.

"Oi... Pennington... mind the water... mustn't drown... tomorrow's the big day!"

The taunt was followed by a cackle of glee from the neighboring cell. Pennington didn't answer, his mind still overwhelmed by the rulings handed down by the Court – both the length of his incarceration and the punishment meted out to his family.

"'ear the law come down 'ard on you 'n yours. Bad luck. They put my missus sister in the debtor's house. Do the same for yourn' suppose. Packed it in not long afer. As fer the lass, well, I 'ear she's right cherry. Best stay clear of the workhouse. She'll do right better down Brick Lane ...long as she steers clear of 'ol Jack."

Horror and disgust contorted Pennington's face at the advice. Goaded to action, he sprang from his cot and cursing, flung his tin cup at the wooden door. It hit the small barred opening and bounced off clattering across the floor. A burst of laughter drifted across from the neighboring cell. Clutching his head in misery, he sank onto the rickety chair by the table. After a moment, he took up pen and paper, his face worn with defeat. Folding the note over carefully, he gathered the few precious items he had left that might be enticing and crossed to the door calling out for the night guard. The time had come, he was out of options.

»»««

RED LION
Commercial Street, Whitechapel - Quarter past 9:00

Jenkins swayed a bit and leaned on his elbow. He frowned at the boy who stood shivering at the table's edge - a scraggly, drowned rat dripping on the floor of the Red Lion. His mouth curled into a smirk - the water had left a clean patch. He drained his glass of ale and set it down on the table, reaching for the bottle of rye that waited on his attention. One of these days, he'd be able to afford a better drinking hole.

"Well, you gonna speak boy or am I supposed to guess why you're here?"

The boy sneezed loudly and then wiped his nose with the ragged cuff of his jacket.

"I ain't sayin...till' I get what I was promised...'e said you'd pay ... two shillings..."

Jenkins snorted. "'ou said...?" He downed the rye and poured another.

"Ol' Barton..."

"Barton? Tom Barton from Newgate?" Jenkins leaned forward, his curiosity piqued. Barton was a night guard at Newgate. A well-known snitch who traded in information he overhead on the cell block. He wasn't above taking a bribe from the inmates, their family or the police.

"That's 'im...'e said you know parties intrested... an' you'd pay..."

"Pay fer what?"

The boy grinned crookedly and removed a folded note from his pocket. "'Dis 'ere...'" He dangled the note in front of the detective's face.

Jenkins eyes widened as he read the name scrawled on the outside of the note. He reached out to grab it, but the boy was quick and pulled it back.

"Not so fast... two shillings... or mebbe... I just take it meself to Mr..."

"Aw right - misrable cur! Give it.!!" The coins rang down onto the table. As the boy scooped them up, Jenkins snatched the note. He began to chuckle as he scanned the contents. He glanced up and then snorted on noticing the boy was still there. "Go on... beat it... afore I run you in." The boy needed no further urging and disappeared out into the deluge.

Jenkins checked the time, quarter past nine, and then looked at the bottle. Half full; he poured another tumbler and then slid the bottle inside his jacket. Miserable night out, best to have a warmer upper. Carefully pocketing the note, he pulled up his collar and made his way to the door.

»»«

BERKELEY SQUARE - MAYFAIR - 11:00 pm

"May I offer you a libation Constable? A little something to take away the chill? I've an excellent Cognac. Colonel, would you be so kind to bring the decanter."

Moran paused in mid-sip and stared at the Professor in bewilderment. He did as told however, and after setting the tray with the decanter and snifters down on the desk, took up his drink and stepped back into the shadows to observe. The man was already in his cups, the Professor was playing.

"Don't mind if I do," announced Jenkins, "but it's Detective." He took the snifter and after a brief sniff downed the liquid in one gulp. "Not bad. I'm a whiskey man meself, but this'll do. Now, on to business..."

"Yes. Business. I was told you have something that might interest me."

Jenkins chuckled and withdrew the note from his pocket with a flourish. The Professor extended his hand to take it but the Detective pulled it back. "Not so fast guvnor... what I have 'ere... bein' that it's addressed to a certain gentleman on Baker Street, must be worth somethin' other than a glass of spirits...Time's 'r bit rough...Yard don't pay much."

"Ahh, how much do you require then Constable? What do you feel would be an appropriate *contribution?*"

"Detective," growled Jenkins, "an I was thinkin' somethin' like this well, must be worth at least two months wages given the risk...125 shillings."

Moran choked on his drink. "Are you mad?" he sputtered.

Jenkins smiled slyly. "Mad? Naw, jes underpaid."

342

The Professor waved his hand in dismissal, his lips curling slightly as he reached into the pocket of his smoking jacket for his wallet. "Pay him no mind Constable. A fair enough price to keep the guardians of our fair city on the job. Now, 125 shillings... that would be a little over 6 pounds... let's make it an even 7," he offered and began to count out 1-pound notes until Jenkins interrupted him.

Jenkins eyes glistened with greed. "That's all well 'n fine. but if it's jes the same, I'll take it in coins; crowns or sovereigns 'ill do nicely. Can't be too careful now'days wat wit' all the counterfittin 'n such goin' 'roun."

There was an awkward silence and then the Professor burst into hearty laughter. He gave a little nod towards Jenkins, his eyes fixed on Moran. "Words to live by indeed. Colonel, please pour Constable... ahh, a thousand pardons... **Detective** Jenkins another drink. I have a very fine Islay Single Malt in the library I believe he'll find to his liking. Detective, if you'll accompany Colonel Moran to the library and wait, I will retrieve your fee from the safe. I will meet you there presently."

And so they separated, the Professor heading off down the hall and Moran and Jenkins to the library. Moran stationed himself on the divan, waiting with growing impatience for the Professor to return, listening to Jenkins' tedious and increasingly drunken blathering. After some 15 minutes had passed, the Professor returned and entered the room, a smile on his face and a small leather pouch in his hands. He crossed the room and offered the pouch to the man. "Detective Jenkins, it has been truly enlightening. Your service is most appreciated," he announced and extended his hand to shake.

Jenkins ignored the hand and quickly opened the pouch. A gleam of gold caught his attention. Uttering a cackle of delight, he drew the bag shut and pumped the professor's hand energetically. "Pleasure, it's been..."

"Capital! Now, I must bid you farewell as I have pressing business in the morning. Please tarry a while and enjoy the hearth Detective and when you are ready, Colonel Moran will see you home in the Clarence. Tempestuous weather seems to bring out the worst sorts in the city. We mustn't provide them the opportunity. Now if I may borrow the Colonel a moment for a few reminders. Please enjoy my hospitality... perhaps another scotch. And once again, thank you for your service. Farewell."

Basking in the warmth of the fire and the Professor's geniality, Jenkins once more took up the decanter and filled his glass while Moran and the Professor stepped out into the hall. As the door shut behind them, Moran turned to the Professor - his eyes incredulous.

"This is lunacy! You gave that weasel 7 pounds and your finest scotch for a piece of paper. Have you even read it?"

"Careful Sebastian. I find your tone most disagreeable. It was a very short note. The length is not important, the content, however, speaks volumes." As he spoke, he took the note from his pocket and handed it to Moran. It was very short indeed. The outside bearing the name of Mr. Sherlock Holmes - 221B Baker Street. The inside consisted of two short lines scrawled in the tremulous script of a man who was overwrought.

I have reconsidered. Please come tomorrow morning.
W.Pennington

Moran read the note and then handed it back. "What are you going to do?"

The Professor chuckled. "All arranged. While you were entertaining our guest, I sent a message to our friends at Newgate. No need to worry. They are skilled at taking care of loose ends. As for our friend, I leave that loose end to you, Moran. I have the utmost confidence you will take care of it. Only, a word of advice – a little more discretion this time. The Chinamen were rather ostentatious." He paused for a moment, listening to the sound of the rain beating on the roof. "The night is ghastly, isn't it? Use it to your advantage. Anything can befall a careless man on a night such as this... anything at all," he suggested and then he was gone, humming an odd little folk tune as he made his way down the hall.

>»«<

NEWGATE PRISON - 8:00 AM.

"No time for your nonsense Holmes," grumbled Inspector Lestrade, narrowing his eyes in warning as Holmes and Watson approached. "I'm a man down this morning." He increased his pace as he passed through the iron gates of Newgate prison and began to make his way across the outer courtyard.

Holmes caught up to him easily, "A man down?"

Lestrade smiled tightly. "On a bender more than likely... not the first time. Look, I've lots to do and a short time to do it. The Crown asked me to oversee the visitation, so here I am to play nanny." He puffed out his cheeks in annoyance as they arrived at the massive wooden door, a relic from the prison's medieval origin as part of the city gate and dungeon.

"I know why I'm here but why the blazes are you? The case is closed Holmes, in case you've forgotten." With a scowl, he turned and banged on the door until a guard appeared; the door slowly creaked open.

Ahh, but is it?" Holmes countered as he slipped through the door behind him.

Lestrade stopped abruptly and turned on heel. "Bollocks! don't start that again." He shook his head and then continued on his way, a scowl darkening his face as he noted that Watson had also fallen in step. "Bloody parade..." he muttered, ignoring them as best he could, as they marched along the dingy outer corridor towards the main reception hall.

"Lestrade's in a pleasant mood," remarked Watson in a quiet voice. "Admittedly, he does have a point. What are we doing here? The sentence has been passed, the case is finished."

Holmes compressed his lips. "In light of what occurred in court, the severity of the sentence, I was certain Pennington would reconsider."

"But he has not."

There was silence and then Holmes shrugged. "No, he has not," he admitted grudgingly. He ran a hand through his hair, his eyes troubled. "I cannot fathom how he can allow his own daughter to suffer so and..." He broke off abruptly as they entered the reception where the Chief Warder presided over the entrance of visitors to the prison. Lestrade was already on the bench deep in conference with the Chief Warder. Holmes smiled, no doubt complaining. His eyes continued to scan the room. "Watson, the ladies have arrived."

"The Aunt as well I see," Watson noted with a grunt. "Pray God she is lucid today. In light of the uncertainty of her disposition, perhaps we best not..." His words were in vain however as they had scarcely left his lips before Holmes was half way across the room heading directly towards Edwina and her aunt. Groaning in dismay, Watson hurried after him.

Edwina closed her eyes and concentrated on trying to block out the buzz of her Aunt's incoherent mutterings as she sat next to her on the bench. She clasped her hands together in her lap as tightly as she could, intent on suppressing the sense of resentment and despair welling within.

"Good morning Ladies. I trust you are well."

Her eyes flew open in surprise. "Holmes, you're here. I didn't expect..."

"I'm sorry Eddy, I didn't intend to startle you," he soothed. "I missed the opportunity to speak with you after Court. Are you well? How is your Aunt?" And then in a louder but still gentle voice, he turned to address Gretchen Pennington. "How are you today Madam? Better I trust..."

The muttering stopped, and the older woman looked up from her prayer book; her eyes which had previously been dull and listless pinpoints, now smouldered with malice. "The righteous will rejoice when he sees the vengeance. He will bathe his feet in the blood of the wicked." She said nothing more and then returned to her prayers.

Holmes arched his brow, a faint smile tugging at his lips. "Still the same I see"

Edwina cast a nervous glance at her Aunt and then stood. "Perhaps we should speak in private..." she suggested in a low voice. As they stepped a few paces away, Holmes looked back at the old woman. "This concerns me Eddy, she is not in her right mind. It is unwise for you to remain at Fern Hall. Mrs. Hudson's sister has rooms to let not far from Baker Street. I have spoken with her and..."

"You want me to abandon her? When we are on the brink of losing all..."

"She won't be abandoned," he soothed, "there are still a handful of staff to look after her. Eddy, she is unstable and her animosity toward you is alarming. Watson and I will do what we can to find her lodging. There are places that..."

Edwina drew herself up. "An asylum you mean..."

Holmes let out a deep sigh and nodded. "She is unbalanced. Perhaps after she receives treatment she can return."

"Return? Return to what? Or have you forgotten that we shall be homeless in two weeks!" The sharpness of her words took him by surprise and perhaps sensing this, Edwina's expression softened. She reached out and laid her hand on his arm in apology. "Forgive me Holmes. I believe you mean well... but I cannot, will not, leave her. It's true, there is bad blood between us, but she is my father's sister and I owe it to him to look after her. The very least I can do is ensure that she finds appropriate lodging and I do not mean an institution. I will not shirk my responsibility. After all, I am the one who brought this about. If it hadn't been for me, she wouldn't be losing her brother and her home."

A look of anguish darkened his eyes. "The only thing you are guilty of is a trusting heart. It was never my intention to cause such distress. I must confess, I did not anticipate your father's refusal to cooperate or the severity of the Crown's verdict. That you should lose your home, fills me with deep regret but..." Holmes faltered as if unsure whether he should continue.

"But you would do it again wouldn't you, to solve the case?" she murmured, finishing the thought for him.

A look of discomfort flickered across Holmes' face. "My profession demands that my actions be guided by logic Eddy, not sentiment." He was silent for a moment and then his hand tightened around hers. "Lately, it is a choice I do not make easily."

Her eyes grew melancholy and she laid her hand warmly on top of his. "And yet you continue to make that choice..."

Dismay furrowed his brow. "Eddy, I..."

"Come along then, the time to socialize has passed," barked Lestrade, jangling the keys to the cell block door as he returned from the Chief Warder's bench. "If you please Ladies, we've delayed long enough." As they approached the door to the cellblock, Lestrade let out a groan of exasperation as the doorway was now partially blocked by a wizened old man dressed in prison issue who labored to maneuver a wooden cart laden with battered tin trays. They were smeared with what looked to be the remains of breakfast.

"Keep moving father," growled the Inspector as he gave the cart a shove to the side and then squeezed past, pulling the ladies along with him. Holmes once more fell in behind, but this time found the door to the corridor quickly shut in his face.

"Not this time," cackled the Inspector as he ducked through the doorway, urging the ladies on ahead. The sound of the key turning in the lock behind him ended the matter.

Thwarted, Holmes turned his attention to the old man, scanning the contents of his cart, a curious light in his eyes. Most trays were empty. A few showed traces of what appeared to be a thin gruel - scraps of dubious meat clinging to the metal.

"You deliver all meals to the inmates?"

"Twice daily guv... mornin' and eve... porridge this morn' - bit of bangers."

"Is that what that is?" muttered Watson, unable to hide his revulsion.

The old man flashed a toothless grin. "Mos' don't complain... ain't the Savoy...but betterin' mos... specially up the road at Pentonville."

346

"But not all agree – this tray is untouched..." said Holmes, indicating the tray near the top.

"Guess 'e tweren't hungry...wat wit' the move 'n all...'appens at 'times... Ate' las night...nary a peep this morn...didn't even take 'is tray...'ill be sorry when 'is bellys growlin..."

A look of apprehension crept across Holmes' face. "Whose tray is this?"

"Pennyton' - forger bloke..."

"And he didn't take the tray from you?" exclaimed Holmes, his brow knit in reflection. "When did you last see him?" His tone had become somber.

"Didn't...'taint no nanny," replied the old man with a shrug, "open the hatch an'set the tray on the ledge...up to 'im to git it...ate las' night...not this morn..."

"Not this morn..." repeated Holmes. His words trailed off, his face growing pale and taut with unease. "Give me your keys," he demanded abruptly, reaching to take them.

"Wot? Why?" The old man shrank back in surprise.

"Quickly now, give them," insisted Holmes, growing more agitated.

"What the Devil man," sputtered Watson in astonishment, "so he missed a meal. I don't see why you are..."

"Something's wrong... something," muttered Holmes, ignoring Watson. With a cry of exasperation, he snatched the keys from the old man and pushed past him, frantically inserting each key in the lock, searching for the correct one.

"Which one? Which one, show me!" he shouted but before the old man could react, he found the right key and the lock clicked open. Without further explanation, he shoved open the door and darted through, nearly toppling a guard coming around the corner. He swerved around him, oblivious to the cries to halt and increased his speed as he neared the cell block. In the distance, he caught a glimpse of Lestrade and the ladies nearing the cell.

"Lestrade, wait.,. don't open the door!" he shouted.

Thoroughly alarmed now, Watson raced after him.

But the warning came too late as a blood curdling shriek split the air, echoing off the stone floors and walls. Both men reached the cell at the same time and drew to a halt. Other than that single cry, the room was silent. They approached cautiously, the door stood wide open. Inside they found Lestrade, Edwina and her Aunt motionless, staring transfixed by the same gruesome sight.

"Oh Dear God..." Watson crossed himself as he entered behind Holmes.

Wilfred Pennington, his face the color of ripe eggplant, dangled from the gas pipe above, twirling slowly as the rope around his neck wound and unwound.

Lestrade shook himself and scratched his head bewildered. "Now if that don't beat all..."

"Quiet you fool... the ladies," growled Holmes. "Watson, please take them from here."

"Of course," the Doctor murmured.

As he turned to Gretchen Pennington, the woman suddenly awoke from her stupor. With a snarl, she lunged forward towards Edwina and Holmes, hands extended like claws, eyes wild with rage. "Murderers! Assassins! As God is my witness. I...!" But as Watson gently restrained her, her rage seemed to lessen, replaced by heart rending sobs. She leaned against him weeping, holding on for support as he led her away. Lestrade hesitated a moment and then hurried after him to inform the Chief Warder and gather some men to secure the cell.

As the door shut behind him, Holmes turned to Edwina. She hadn't moved nor uttered a sound, even when her Aunt had threatened her. He approached her cautiously. He had never seen her so pale or so still as she stood rigidly in the center of the room staring up at her father, scarcely breathing, cheeks streaked with tears. He positioned himself in front of her attempting to block her view of the corpse.

"Come away Eddy, there's nothing more we can do..." he urged gently. As his hand grasped hers, she seemed to notice him for the first time and fixed her gaze on him, eyes wide – dazed. "What have I done? She's right...been right all along," she whimpered, her voice raw and wavering.

A prickle of alarm ran along his neck. He tightened his hold on her hand which was beginning to tremble. "No, listen to me...you're not to blame."

She pulled free and turned away, pulling at her hair in agitation. "But I am... she's right... I'm cursed... and they paid the price. First Julian, then Mother and now... Fath..." The words caught in her throat and with a sob, she suddenly wobbled as her knees began to buckle under her.

Holmes caught her quickly, cradling her head against his chest.

"It's all right. I have you."

She sagged against him, burying her face in his coat, fingers gripping his sleeves.

"I won't faint. I cannot be weak..." she sobbed, trying to will herself back into an upright position.

He hugged her tightly, his fingers gently smoothing back her tangled hair.

"You could never be weak," he soothed, his eyes locked on hers.

Edwina wiped at her eyes, calmer now and then slowly straightened up. She took a deep breath, holding it until she was sure she would tremble no longer and then looked at her father's corpse.

"Why Holmes? It makes no sense, to leave us in such straits."

"I agree, it makes no sense. Things are not as they appear."

Edwina looked around the room as dispassionately as she could, focused on remaining composed. He was right, something was off, but she couldn't quite figure it out at the moment.

The door to the cell opened and Watson entered once more, his face drawn and grim. On seeing her, he smiled kindly and extended his hand. "Come with me now my dear. I have a carriage waiting."

She hesitated and looked to Holmes. "And my Aunt?"

Watson took her by the arm, gently urging her forward. "Calm... sedated. You need to rest... both of you. Inspector Lestrade has agreed to post a man at the house. And I have sent word for a nurse to check in on your Aunt later this evening."

She glanced uneasily towards the body still dangling from the gas pipe. "And what of father? What will happen now?"

Holmes' expression was grim but kind. "Leave it to me. I'll see to it," he reassured, gently pressing her arm. "Now, go with Watson... he'll see you home."

He walked them to the door where they were met by the Chief Warder who quickly took her by the arm and led her away. As Watson was about to step out, Holmes grabbed his arm making him pause.

"See to it Watson, but come back quickly," he whispered, "and try to keep Lestrade occupied and away from here for a while."

"What do you mean? The man hung himself. What are you about?" he exclaimed, a frown creasing his face.

Holmes suddenly grinned his eyes bright and lively. "Doubtful," he announced crisply as he withdrew a tape measure and a small notebook from his pocket.

Watson eyed him suspiciously. "Lestrade won't like it," he muttered under his breath.

Holmes snapped the tape measure, his eyes already calculating the distance from the gas pipe to the floor.

"He never does... off you go then."

CHAPTER 10

The Reckoning

Baker Street - Saturday Afternoon

Watson paused in the hall just outside the door to the flat listening. A slow frown began to spread across his face, and his fingers paused in fiddling with his black cravat. He could make out the voices of Holmes, Mrs. Hudson and a male guest whose voice though unknown, had a ring of familiarity about it. As he was about to enter, the door suddenly opened, and Mrs. Hudson stepped out. She stepped back in surprise on seeing him and uttered a nervous squawk.

"Oh, Doctor, it's you. My you gave me quite a fright."

"Apologies dear lady. Can you tell me, is he ready?"

Mrs. Hudson looked anxiously over her shoulder back into the flat. "Well... no, I don't believe so Dr. Watson. You see, there seems to be a client..." she hesitated, wondering how much she should reveal.

"A client? Today? But it cannot be Mrs. Hudson. Mr. Holmes and I will be attending a memorial service today."

She shook her head in commiseration. "I believe the plans may have changed, but you had best have that discussion with Mr. Holmes yourself." And then she was gone, retreating quickly down the stairs.

On entering the flat, Watson was astonished to find that Mrs. Hudson was correct. Holmes seemed indeed to be interviewing a client. A tall, thin young man dressed in a cheap dark suit with red hair who looked vaguely familiar to him. Not wanting to appear rude, Watson nodded briefly in his direction in acknowledgment but then turned his attention to Holmes who was only half dressed, still wearing his dressing gown over the top of his black suit trousers. A cigarette dangled precariously from his lips.

"Holmes, what is the meaning of this? Mary will be here shortly with the Brougham and then we are to proceed to the chapel on Golder's Hill. You did not forget?"

Holmes hesitated a moment, his face solemn. "No, I did not forget. I believe it would be best if you and Miss Morstan attended the service while I remain behind. My presence does seem to agitate Mrs. Pennington. I believe Edwina could do with less strife. Please, you and Miss Morstan extend my condolences. I shall remain behind," he announced and quickly knocked the dangling ash into a pewter tray on the sideboard. He finished the cigarette and stubbed it out. He took out his cigarette case and opened it but hesitated and did not remove a cigarette.

Watson's face darkened in disapproval. "Holmes, you promised you would be there. This is unconscionable."

Holmes averted his eyes. "Yes, I suppose it is, but it is for the best. Please, Watson, extend my apologies. Something has come up that I must attend to." He gave a brief nod in the direction of the young man sitting in the parlor. "Dr. Watson, this is Constable Dolan, one of Inspector Lestrade's men. Perhaps you remember him from Lady Montague's." Holmes was tempted to add, "*and having followed us on several occasions...*" but didn't.

Recognition flickered over Watson's face as he recalled the two men that had accompanied Lestrade to Lady Montague's to assist in the arrest of Pennington. Nodding, he extended his hand to the Constable. Archibald Dolan rose from his seat and genially extended his hand. "An honour Dr. Watson, I assure you. I have the greatest admiration for your and Mr. Holmes' endeavours."

Pleasure drifted over Watson's face at the compliment. "Thank you, Constable. Now, is there something we can assist you with?"

A look of dismay clouded the young man's face. "My partner, mentor, he had gone missing..."

"Lestrade's man down if you recall?" reminded Holmes.

Watson nodded recalling Lestrade's lament of "a man down" at Newgate. Had? So, he is found then?" Apprehension darkened Watson's face.

The young Constable nodded. "Yes. Found."

He did not elaborate though by his expression, Watson surmised it was not a happy ending. He turned to Holmes for an explanation.

"As you have most likely assumed, the ending is not a happy one. Constable Dolan's partner, Constable Jenkins, washed up yesterday morning near the Isle of Dogs... not far from the docks. Purportedly the victim of a vicious robbery."

"Purportedly?"

Holmes arched his brow, an undeniable twinkle in his eyes. "There is some doubt. I will know more once I have examined the body. I would ask you to accompany me, but one of us should attend the memorial out of respect for Miss Schraeder."

Watson nodded. "So, would it not be better if a medical man were to examine the body? Perhaps I should go, Holmes? That would leave you free to attend the service. I shall, of course, take extensive notes."

Holmes compressed his lips as he considered the suggestion. After a moment, he shook his head. "I think it best if we leave it as is Watson... you attend to the living whilst I attend to the departed. It is an arrangement that has in the past proved most effective."

Watson nodded but reached out and took a firm hold of Holmes' sleeve, nudging him to one side out of earshot of the constable. "I ask that you reconsider Holmes, in light of the circumstances of this case. Do you not see that it is you who should extend your condolences and offer comfort?"

"Comfort, my dear Watson, empathy, is something that does not come easily to me as you are well aware. You and Miss Morstan are more suited to it. You have the temperament," Holmes protested.

Watson's face grew stern. "There is a level of comfort Holmes, that only you can offer Edwina. She looks to you. Your heart cannot be so callous that you do not see this."

The words seemed to surprise Holmes. He looked up, his brow drawn in irritation and dismay. "Times like these call for a level head... the heart has no place... and yes, I do see... and I will tell you this... what Eddy looks for is something I cannot offer Watson, ever. The head must always rule the heart."

"Even in times such as these? My God, surely there is ice water in your veins. And tell me then, if the roles were reversed, do you think she would be so heartless?"

Holmes averted his eyes and after a moment, only shrugged murmuring, "No, she would not. Her nature is too sentimental though she would deny it. Her heart too open and tender. Make no mistake Watson, I wish her only happiness and good fortune. My intention is not to be cruel."

Watson scanned his face searching his expression and then let out a long, deep sigh. "No, I suppose you do not intend, but can you not see that is what you are? Not only to her, but to yourself as well."

"I have decided," declared Holmes, his expression firm, "further debate is useless. Please relay my good wishes and sympathies to Edwina and her Aunt. We shall regroup later this evening when you return and recount the day's events." And the matter being closed, at least as far as he was concerned, Holmes removed his dressing gown and reached into the armoire for his tweed jacket. "I shall see you then this evening Doctor, please extend my regrets and condolence."

Realizing it truly was futile, Watson nodded in resignation and took up his outer coat. After adjusting his cravat one more time, he nodded in the direction of both men and then took his leave heading down the stairs to wait at the curb for the brougham which would be arriving shortly with Miss Morstan.

Holmes and Constable Dolan soon followed though they remained inside the vestibule of 221 and did not go outside until Watson and Miss Morstan had departed. Afterward, they set out in a hansom for St. Bartholomew's morgue where the unfortunate Constable Jenkins lay in repose.

»»««

Parish Churchyard of All Saints - Adjacent Golder's Green - Child's Hill Near Dusk - @ 8:22 pm.

It was just after sunset, the deepening sky already painted with soft streaks of red and orange as the hansom pulled to a stop alongside the churchyard of All Saints.

Holmes quickly got out and glanced up at the sky. The old proverb flashed in his mind as he pushed open the iron gate that marked the entrance to the churchyard. *Red sky at night - sailor's delight - red sky in morning, sailor's warning.* Well, the sky wasn't red strictly speaking though he supposed an argument for it could be made and it wasn't morning, not for a few hours at least. In any event, it was of no consequence, he took no stock in superstition or folklore. Still the evening was pleasant, a light breeze stirred the leaves of the overhanging tree canopy as he picked his way carefully in the dim light across the ancient markers – many unreadable. He set a course directly towards the back edge of the plot, the furthest away from the church itself. That's where he needed to be — the unconsecrated plot — a small area that the church had set up in concession to those unfortunates who died in what was deemed a lack of grace, which included non-believers, unwed women who perished in childbirth, papists who had been married to parishioners, anyone who had taken their own life or those convicted of criminal activity. That's where Pennington would be along with his estranged wife. The two of them separated in life now once more together in death.

As he reached the back gate that offered transit from consecrated to unconsecrated ground, he paused momentarily and glanced off to his right. Just beyond the trees he could see the dim glow of lights from Fern Hall. His hand rested on the gate as he debated whether he should go to the house first and make his presence known. He hadn't really expected to be there at all, even in the cemetery. But as he had left the morgue, he had been overcome, haunted one might say, by the feeling that he was doing a disservice to Edwina if he did not at least pay his respects in person. So here he was trekking through the ancient churchyard as the sun disappeared in the sky, on his way to pay his respects to a man he had not only brought to justice, but perhaps inadvertently caused the death of. It was a feeling he was not used to experiencing; a feeling that caused discomfort. Watson would call it guilt. He preferred to think of it as self-doubt or self-castigation for errors made in the investigation of the case. Either way, it was a feeling that did not set well with him.

On approaching the back gate, he caught sight of the massive yew tree that shaded the far side of the unconsecrated lot and realized that he was on the correct heading. Now all he needed was to find the weeping angel monument where Katia Schraeder Pennington rested and he would find her husband next to her. Still he had a ways to go; it did seem the consecrated lot was larger than he had expected. Apparently, the good parishioners of All Saints placed a high value on dying in a state of grace.

At last he reached the back gate and as he gently pushed open the gate, he caught sight of a soft white glow towards the back directly under the yew. It could only be the angel monument. He quickened his pace and pushed on through, eyes focused on the monument. As he approached, his nostrils flared a bit catching the scent of freshly dug earth and cut flowers. He smelled the new grave before he actually came upon it. A fresh mound of soil piled high, strewn with flowers that lay directly beneath the yew and adjacent to the angel monument which hovered over both the graves. He approached slowly, eyes fixed on the fresh soil and then suddenly drew to a stop, startled by sudden movement just off to the left of the mound of fresh soil in the empty space between the fresh grave and the fence that marked the edge of the lot. Something was stirring, a shape moving about on the ground. He couldn't quite make out what it was due to the low light. The breeze picked up and something black and lacey fluttered in the breeze over the soil. He inhaled once more and this time the faint scent of lilies of the valley tickled his nose. Holmes froze, staring at the ground in disbelief.

"Edwina?" he called out, moving closer trying to make sense of what he was seeing.

The shape beneath the veil suddenly sat up and then a soft laugh sounded from a mass of what seemed to be black crepe, velvet and lace.

"What the devil? Holmes, what are you doing here? Watson said you could not come."

He moved closer, his face clouding darkly as he could see that the moving shape between the graves was indeed Edwina Schraeder, shrouded in black mourning crepe and lace, her face obscured by a heavy black veil. He crouched down in front of the form.

"I finished what I needed early. I thought I'd pay my respects. By God Eddy, what are you doing? You're covered in leaves and soil."

Edwina leaned forward, her elbows resting on her knees and brushed at the dirt on her gown. "Not to worry, it's all dry, it'll brush off easily. It couldn't be helped. I was measuring..." Her face was a soft pale glow beneath a net of black, a flash of green eyes and red lips.

He almost laughed but couldn't quite manage it. "Measuring... measuring what?" he pressed and leaning forward, gently grasped her veil lifting it. "You don't mind, do you? I find veils quite distracting. You're quite a mess."

Edwina blushed, her cheeks suddenly warm as his fingertips lightly brushed away a bit of dirt on her forehead.

"Measuring the space left," she explained with the utmost seriousness. Her hand gently rested on his as he continued to straighten her tangled hair beneath the veil. She lifted her eyes to his and held his gaze. "Mr. Appleton the sexton assures me there is plenty of room left. It does seem he is right though truthfully, it is a bit tight." She spread her arms across to demonstrate the space left between her father's grave and the fence. "Though I suppose it won't really matter at all, will it? It's not like I'll notice then," she added with an odd smile.

Her eyes were focused on him. He had taken a seat on the marble bench in front of the grave. She waited for him to smile which much to her surprise, he didn't. Instead, his face settled into a dark frown, lips pulled tight in disapproval as he reached down and grasped her forearm firmly and began to lift her up onto the marble bench next to him.

"Stop it," he commanded as she uttered a soft squawk of astonishment. She settled on the bench and stared at him. "Stop what?"

"This talk... sheer nonsense... stop it now Eddy."

She drew herself up and set about arranging her skirt, brushing off the dirt and leaves, trying to suppress the indignation she felt rising within. "Why? What makes it nonsense? We all die someday. You of all people, a man of science, are aware of that."

"Yes, we do, but you are a healthy young woman with a full life ahead of her and ..."

"How do you know?" she interjected with great solemnity, "I could drop from a heart ailment or some unknown fever tomorrow. Our time is limited... the length unknown."

"Yes, true, but this is needlessly morbid... this preoccupation with death."

"Morbid!" she cried out, her eyes bright and more than a little amused. She tightened her hold on his hand and pressed it to her cheek as she began to chuckle softly. "Morbid!" she repeated with a shake of her head. "Strange accusation from a man who prefers to spend his time at the morgue amongst the dead than with the living. I'm not morbid Holmes, just realistic," she sighed, leaning in and resting her cheek against his shoulder. "If I don't plan ahead, who will plan for me? Grendel will more than likely put me out for the dustman to collect if allowed. Besides, I will soon be out of a home. I must plan ahead. Now that Mother and father are together again, something I never thought would happen, I was thinking it would be nice to be with them when the time comes. I've contacted our solicitor, he is researching the idea of relocating Julian from Pere Lachaise. We would all be together again... a family."

And though he knew it was overly sentimental, Holmes couldn't help but admit that her words touched him more than he was comfortable with. As her head rested against his shoulder, his arm wound around her waist and he drew her closer. His eyes met hers, his hand holding tightly onto hers. "I would look out for you even then," he pledged, "if that is your wish. I would see to it..."

She glanced up at him, her eyes luminous and grateful. "Careful Holmes," she teased, "your humanity is showing. That was, dare I say, almost sentimental."

He suppressed a smile and smoothed the veil back once more from her face. "Your fault... completely," he murmured, his eyes locked on hers. "In all seriousness... please, no more talk of this."

She nodded solemnly in agreement and crossed her fingers over her heart. "Promise...no more... you needn't worry... I assure you, I have no intention of throwing myself into the Thames or any other body of water for that matter."

He nodded in acceptance but as he continued to study her face, his eyes locked on the slight red smudge on her lips. He reached out and tentatively touched the corner of her mouth with this index finger. A smear of red transferred onto his skin. Lip color... scarlet...

"What has happened here?" he asked abruptly, the frown returning.

Edwina glanced down at his fingertip and on seeing a slight smudge of color, blushed intensely and averted her eyes.

"Mary., Miss Morstan, she gave me some lip color... she said I was too pale... and... and... after the service I..." Her words began to falter and then died out, her cheeks suddenly devoid of all color.

Holmes arched his brow, studying the smudge on her mouth. "I think you would not be so incompetent in the application of some lip color. I've seen your sketches...you've a steady hand. What happened Eddy?"

And still she remained silent, her eyes cast down avoiding his gaze.

"It was nothing... really," she murmured at last, never lifting her head, "a misunderstanding."

But he wasn't convinced and gently cupped her chin, lifting her face to his. "Misunderstanding? What kind of misunderstanding? Who did this?" he pressed, his dark eyes lit with a spark of smouldering anger and suspicion."

She didn't answer, not directly and just hung her head. "It was just a kiss Holmes... nothing more. He said I looked so sad... that I needed comforting..."

"A kiss... but one against your will or else you would not be smudged like this," he sputtered, the anger in his voice surprising even himself.

Edwina hid her face against his shoulder. "Nothing happened," she repeated, her voice muffled by the fabric of his coat. "I let him know the error of his ways."

"It was Moran wasn't it?" He spat the words out as if he had bitten into something vile. "Wretched low-life. I shall have a word... I..."

Edwina's face jerked up in alarm, her eyes suddenly wide with fear. "No, please... it's over. I beg you... nothing happened... please..."

He met her gaze and tenderly brushed back her bangs. "No one has the right to treat you so Eddy... no one, especially not the man your father selected for you as a suitor. It seems to me a lesson in manners is warranted and..."

The sound of her laughter broke his train of thought and he gazed down at her bewildered by the sheer amusement on her face. "Are you laughing at me? Have I missed the joke?"

Edwina wiped at her eyes and beamed up at him sweetly. "No. No joke Holmes. I am not laughing at you, just the situation. Careful, I fear you are on the very precipice... your words are so noble... so gallant... and it seems to me that for a man who professes to abhor all that is sentimental, that is exactly what this is... sentiment. It is what makes you feel you have to defend me. It is also what prompted you to your noble actions on my behalf. I had an interesting conversation with the vicar just before the service Holmes, and he told me that it was only through your intervention and insistence that somehow you managed to convince the parish council to allow my father to be buried here, and that you had also expedited the release of his body from Newgate and paid the fees. That is kindness and sentiment beyond the pale, and I cannot express to you how grateful I am."

He averted his eyes for a moment, embarrassed and then turned to meet her gaze.

"Yes. Perhaps it was sentiment... but considering all I have put you through, I feel it was the least I could do. Eddy, it was never my intention to cause you any harm or distress ...you must believe that."

"I do.," she acknowledged as she gazed up at him with eyes warm and full of love. "You have a most noble and gracious heart Holmes, you just need to be reminded of it every now and then."

He rolled his eyes a bit and looked to the side, quipping, "And you think you're the girl for it then, to remind me as needed?"

Her hand tightened firmly around his and she moved her face to where he couldn't avoid her gaze. "Yes, I do," she replied with utter confidence.

"Why?" Holmes sighed in resignation wondering how he had lost control and the conversation had suddenly veered onto this troublesome topic.

"Because Sherlock Holmes," she began, sitting up a little straighter, her eyes clear and bright with certainty, "I love you...completely... without reserve... with every fiber of my being. Whether you choose to accept or acknowledge it doesn't change how I feel. I know this is something you do not want to hear, so I have been advised by those who know you best. But I can no longer hide my true feelings from you. I will not pretend that I do not love you. I have loved you I think from the moment I met you and I will always love you whether you feel the same or not. To deny this, to hide it, is lying not only to you but also to myself, and I will no longer do that. If I have learned anything from my father's death, it is that life is too short to waste on not taking risks and that one should never delay saying what is in their heart lest the opportunity be lost. So, yes, I will gladly be the one who reminds you of your humanity whether you want me to or not."

Holmes stared at her in silence for a moment, his face an odd mixture of joy and apprehension. His long fingers cradled her face and he drew her closer. "Dearest Eddy, you will always have a special place in my heart and I will always do my utmost to help you in whatever way that I can. That being said, I must tell you that it truly pains me that I cannot be the man you so rightly deserve."

A sly smile curled her lips. "And what about the man I need or desire?"

He chuckled a bit, she was persistent, no doubt about it. "Nor those. But be advised, I will be watching and when you finally meet him, should he ever mistreat you, I will set him straight and remind him that you deserve better."

That was all it took, those few simple words of his, not even a return declaration of love, to cause her to abandon all caution and decorum. With a fervent exclamation of devotion, Edwina threw her arms around him so fiercely that had it not been for his firmly planted foot, they would have both toppled from the bench onto the gravesite. As her lips locked fervently on his, she felt him shudder. It was not the response she had hoped for but it was a response and therefore encouraging. Her hopes were soon dashed however as moments later he gently pushed her away and disengaged his lips from hers.

And even though it did seem to her that he moved away with some reluctance, he nevertheless moved away.

Despite her best efforts to remain composed, a small sob escaped from her.

"I'm sorry," she murmured as her head sank slowly down onto his chest. "I meant no offense. I thought maybe... if I... well... if I could express to you in no uncertain terms... the depth of my feelings that you would... you would..." Her words died off seemingly stuck in her throat as they dissolved into a muffled sob in the folds of his coat.

Holmes tightened his arms around her disturbed by not only her anguish, but also by the realization that she had ignited something in him (perhaps long ago) that he still could not come to terms with or accept.

"You did not offend me Eddy," he soothed, as his fingers gently stroked her hair. "If anyone has caused offense, it is me. And for that, I am deeply sorry."

Another sob escaped from her as she burrowed deeper into folds of his coat. "I just don't understand. Why it is that you don't want me? I know I am not as beautiful as your Chinese girl, but I do not believe I am hideous. And, as evidenced by the events of that night, you are certainly capable of feeling. You are not the machine that you present to the world."

The words cut him to the quick and filled him with remorse and irritation – irritation at being reminded of the incident of Lotus House. "Enough," he growled with some sharpness and then his tone gentled as his fingers gently grasped her chin and lifted her face to his. "You think that I feel nothing for you," he rasped, his voice gentle but somewhat hoarse, "but you are mistaken. You know I care Eddy."

She bit her lip until she drew blood. "Care?" she muttered, "such an ambiguous word."

His fingertips firmly raised her chin up even higher until their eyes met. "And for the record, you are certainly far from hideous. As for my Chinese girl as you call her, you are comparing apples to oranges. What you offer me. What you have professed to me is deeper than that isn't it? There is more than desire in your kiss, there is passion, and passion and lust are not the same are they? Passion is something deeper, but as I've explained time and again, there was nothing deeper at Lotus House than desire... lust if you will... purely physical, a biological drive which I could no longer sublimate. Other than physical desire, Mei Lin and I have no connection. I know that what you feel - want from me is deeper than that... but I cannot return those feelings."

"Why?" she pressed, her eyes clouded and miserable. "I would never come between you and your work Holmes. I have the utmost respect for your endeavours."

His eyes grew sad and with a wistful expression, he used his thumb to gently brush at the wetness on her cheeks.

"Because, I must always remain detached and to remain detached, I must be free to walk away. But if I were to engage more deeply with you Eddy, I could not bring myself to walk away and my work would be affected. In truth, it has already been affected as I have allowed my judgement and actions to be swayed as of late by sentiment rather than by the facts of the case.

Edwina hung her head and uttered a heavy sigh. "The grit on the lens," she murmured in a mournful voice, "that's what I've become."

Holmes nodded, his hands tightening on her shoulders. "yes... I'm afraid so."

She leaned her face against his arm. "And now it's time to flick me away lest I cause permanent damage."

He managed a small chuckle and pulled her closer. "No, not a flick... perhaps a gentle brush... never a flick."

Edwina took a deep breath and composed herself. "Well, either way the result is the same isn't it?" She gently untangled herself from his arms and stepped away, her eyes fixed on his. "It won't change anything you understand – how I feel. Unlike you Holmes, my heart has the final say in this matter despite what my head tells me. But be that as it may, brush away as you must. I'll still love you... that is a constant."

He nodded that he understood and offered his arm to her, his face drawn in resignation. The parish clock began to chime half past nine. "It's really quite late now... you should return, they will be worried about you. Allow me to escort you. I wouldn't want anyone to think anything improper has occurred."

Edwina wiped at her eyes and sighed a bit as she interlaced her arm with his. "Well, it certainly seems nothing improper will ever occur between us will it? Speaking of improper, did I ever tell you about my grandmother's grave in Pere Lachaise," she asked as they began to make their way down the path towards Fern Hall.

Holmes suppressed a laugh and shook his head. "Grandmother's grave... sounds intriguing... proceed."

With a wicked grin, she leaned in closer, tightening her hold on his arm as they made their way down the drive towards the front of the house. "Several years ago, when mother and I were travelling, we were in the midst of sharing a bottle of ouzo in a taverna in Athens, and she began to relay this tale to me. She was thoroughly convinced, due to the closeness in dates, that I was conceived at my grandmother's funeral. In fact, after the service on the very steps of grandmother's mausoleum."

Holmes paused to stare at her and then burst into laughter. "Dear God... what an extraordinary tale."

"So perhaps that explains my proclivity for all things dark and macabre."

"Well, that's one explanation. Or perhaps you are just twisted," he chuckled. As they neared the front entrance, he once more drew to a halt, his eyes drawn to the upper floor where he had seen a vague shape in an unlit window and a curtain falling back into place.

Noting his gaze, Edwina looked up as well. "What is it?"

"We're being watched," he announced.

"Most likely Grendel," sighed Edwina, "she retired much earlier, not long after the service. I believe Dr. Watson may have given her something to calm her nerves."

"If she's up and about now, obviously not enough."

Edwina's face suffused with sympathy and she shook her head. "You mustn't be so unkind... she's had a terrible blow. Father seemed to truly be the only person she cared about in this world. She feels as if she has lost everything, especially now that we are losing the house as well. It's been in the family for generations... she has never known anything else. "

Holmes fell into silence his eyes still locked on the house. After a few moments, he turned to face her. "Eddy, I think it would be wise if you returned to London with me tonight... Mrs. Hudson will fix a bed for you downstairs."

"What? Why?" she gasped. "But I'm needed here... I cannot just disappear."

Holmes shook his head and turned to her, his hands resting gently on her shoulders.

"I can't explain why for certain other than I am not comfortable with the situation as it stands. Your Aunt is unstable..."

"Of course she is... she has just lost her brother and will soon be homeless. She is distraught Holmes, a perfectly normal reaction."

"But she blames you for this misfortune."

"And not without reason,' sighed Edwina with a shake of her head. "I will be fine Holmes, you mustn't worry. Besides, It's not as if I'm alone here. Cook, Hanna and a few others..."

"Promise me you'll lock your door and if you feel unsafe at any time, you'll leave. You are welcome at Baker Street anytime."

"I promise," she sighed and gently hugged him, resting her head on his chest. "You know, for a man who is supposed to be brushing away the grit, you're not doing a very good job of it," she chided.

His arms pulled her closer and then he gently lifted her chin up, his eyes locked on hers.

"I agree... the problem is... it seems I've grown rather fond of the grit." With a tender smile, he leaned down and pressed his lips to her forehead. "Good night Eddy... promise me you'll take care."

She promised that she would and after depositing a warm kiss on his cheek, she bid him good night and disappeared into the house. Holmes looked up again towards the upper windows, but all was dark and quiet. Still, the feeling of unease lingered. He waited until the light came on in Edwina's room and then slowly turned and walked back down the drive to where the hansom waited. Moments later, he was heading back down Golder's Hill towards London.

»»««

Fern Hall - Just after Midnight

Edwina awoke with a start and sat up in bed, her head throbbing and her mouth feeling like it was filled with cotton. The room was quiet and dark, the only light being a faint glow from the last embers of the fire in the hearth. She didn't understand why she felt so groggy, she felt like she had barely slept. She had been feeling restless, unable to sleep, too many things on her mind, from grief over her father's passing and the unsettling fact that she and her aunt would soon be homeless, to the bewildering nature of her relationship (if she could even use that word) with Holmes. She had thought that maybe declaring her feelings to him in no uncertain terms would force the issue and perhaps move him to clarify his stance once and for all. Well, if anything, she felt even more confused – even though he had restated his need to be free from any sort of commitment (needing the freedom to "walk away" as he so eloquently termed it), when she had kissed him, it seemed to her that he had almost responded. In fact, if anything, on top of the reluctance he exhibited to "brush her off", she thought she had detected a desire within him to respond. To her, it seemed his reluctance stemmed perhaps not from lack of attraction but more from fear; fear of what might happen if he let his heart rule his head. In the end, she had given up on trying to comprehend it and had asked Cook for a cup of herbal tea hoping it would ease her mind so she could rest. And so it had, considerably more than she had expected. A nagging suspicion crept upon her as she reached for the cup on the nightstand. She gave the few remaining drops of reddish brown liquid a quick sniff... nothing unusual. It smelled of the usual cinnamon, cardamom, clove and nutmeg... her favorites. Cook knew her well though she had thought it tasted sweeter than usual. She gave it another sniff detecting, or so she thought, a faint whiff of bitterness. She leaned back against the headboard a look of annoyance on her face. *Laudanum? Could it be? It was known to be bitter. Her mother had often infused her own tea and wine with it to disguise the bitter taste.* That would explain the sudden sleepiness and also the cotton mouth and headache She compressed her lips in irritation, she abhorred the use of most narcotics, particularly laudanum, it had after all taken her mother's life. Still, it had helped her fall asleep and she was certain that Cook had meant no harm - only trying to be helpful.

Rubbing her eyes wearily, she forced herself to sit on the edge of the bed and slid her feet into a pair of slippers. Her hands searched on the bed next to her for her wrap. The room was beginning to get a chill, the fire in the hearth had been out for a few hours now and as she forced herself up from the bed, she drew the green velvet shawl securely around her cotton nightgown. As expected at this time of early morning, the house was silent but as she stared at the faint light peeking in under the door from the hallway, she had the uneasy feeling that something was wrong.

First, the color of the light itself was odd .... it was orange and more of a glow than anything else. Definitely not coming from the hall sconces, and there was also the smell. It was faint... she could barely smell it... at least by the bed... but as she rose and approached the door... it grew stronger. So, she

361

deduced the smell was emanating from the hall... and it was really two smells... one pungent and oily, reminding her of paraffin wax and the other acrid, sharp, the smell of something... fabric perhaps... burning...

Burning ... Fire... the very idea sent a wave of terror through her but knowing that she needed to remain calm, she took up the lamp from her bedside table and walked quickly to the door. She touched it tentatively; it felt cool and after adjusting the wick in the lamp to give off more light, she carefully opened the door to look out in the hallway. The moment she stepped out into the hall she was nearly overcome by the pungent smell of paraffin. She looked down towards the far end of the hall and started in horror ... the drapes were on fire... the flames licking upwards towards the ceiling. She ran towards them at first and then froze ... her shoes were making odd squelching noises and she realized that her slippers were soaked from the carpet. The hallway reeked of paraffin and it was then that she realized that the carpets had been doused with lamp oil. She stood transfixed... staring at the heavy drapes as they continued to burn and then realized that there was no way she was going to be able to pull them down. Flames were already beginning to spread out across the wall paper and now the carpet was beginning to catch... popping, crackling and sizzling as the flames made contact with the paraffin trail. It began to advance. As the hallway began to fill with smoke, Edwina realized there was nothing she could do to put the fire out and did the only thing she could think of, she ran down the hall pounding on each door shouting "Fire! Get out! Fire!"

Finished with her floor, she ran down to the next floor... banging on each door. Cook and Hanna, both clad in only their nightclothes, struggled from their rooms and they each took up the cry - continuing the alarm. Fortunately, there were very few staff left in the house. They roused Old McTavish and his nephew from the ground floor; they immediately ran out to begin filling buckets of water, lining them up outside the house. When finished, Tom the nephew ran down the lane towards the village to summon the local fire brigade. For a short while, Edwina remained with cook outside the house, looking up in disbelief at the house as the glow of the fire could be seen spreading from floor to floor. Hanna and Cook hugged each other with tears in their eyes. It was while Edwina was watching the fire spread from one floor to the next that she realized that her Aunt was nowhere to be found. Dread filled her; she must still be inside the house. Despite the protests of Hanna and Cook, she ran back inside. She couldn't just abandon her, leave her there. She owed it to her father's memory to at least try to help her.

She paused in front of the staircase and stared up in horror... the upper floors were already engulfed and she knew that if her Aunt was indeed upstairs still, it was already too late. She was about to turn and head back outside when out of the corner of her eye, she caught a shadow crossing in front of her father's library. She wasn't certain, but she thought it might be her Aunt. "Aunt Gretchen... you have to come out now... quickly!" she called out, running after the shadowy figure as it moved down the hallway. Still there was no response. The shadow hurried away from her and slipped inside the

362

library. The lower hallway was now beginning to fill with thick smoke and Edwina focused on trying to keep calm as she followed the shadow into the library. As she paused in the middle of the room, waiting for her eyes to adjust to the minimal light, the door slammed shut behind her. It made her jump but what truly froze her heart was the unmistakable sound of a key turning in the lock. She whipped around to where the sound was coming from and came face to face with Gretchen Pennington, still dressed in her mourning clothes, an oil lamp in each hand. Edwina's heart quickened as she noted that the key from the library dangled from a ribbon looped around her wrist. She stared at her Aunt uneasily, only one of the lamps was lit. Gretchen Pennington had removed the chimney from the other lamp and unscrewed the top from the reservoir and was now splashing oil all around her onto the carpet and furniture... an expression of glee on her face as she set about her task.

"Auntie... please...stop... We have to leave now... quickly," pleaded Edwina, struggling to disguise the fear in her voice. The woman had lost her mind - there could be no other explanation.

Gretchen Pennington stared at her and then burst into laughter.

"I am not going anywhere... and neither are you miserable child. This is your doing ... this is what you have wrought. You and that Godless meddler! You brought this on us... deprived my brother of his life... deprived me of his company... this house... my future. Cursed abomination! You will burn in hell. I will see to it even though it will be the last thing I do!"

Edwina started to advance and then froze upon realizing that the woman was serious.

"No - Stop - Please!" she shrieked in desperation, but Gretchen Pennington seemed not to hear her and in one quick motion flung oil from the lamp in her direction. Edwina jumped back as the liquid spattered onto the carpet in front of her, some of it splashing up onto her nightclothes.

"Burn in hell vile creature - at least I know I shall go to my reward!" shrieked the old woman as she made the sign of the cross and then turned the lamp on herself, pouring the oil over her head and down the front of her clothes. Moments later, she touched the lit wick to her dress; her body exploded in a burst of orange flame as her maniacal laughter mixed with cries of agony and filled the air.

Edwina stumbled back in horror, watching helplessly in disbelief as her Aunt crumpled to the ground, curling up into what resembled a grotesque charred mannequin. There was nothing she could do. It was too late and gagging on the odor of burning flesh, she covered her mouth and ran to the door. She tugged on it frantically to no avail - it was locked from the inside and she didn't have the key. She began to pound on the door, calling out for someone to help her but even if they heard her, the door was locked from the inside. She glanced back at the smouldering charred remains of what had once been her Aunt. Somewhere in that scorched and blackened mess of fabric, flesh and bone was the key to the door. She needed that key. Horrified, she glanced around the room looking for something she could smother the flames with as there were still some flames on and around the body. Nothing, nothing that wasn't already burning. The heavy drapes that covered the French Doors to the Terrace were already in flames, wisps of fire greedily climbing across the surrounding walls and up across the ceiling. Pieces of blackened plaster and wood were beginning to crumble and splinter and then rain down upon the room as the ceiling began to give way. There only a few pockets in the library that were untouched by fire near the heavy mahogany bookcases. Using her shawl to cover her mouth, Edwina once more looked toward the terrace doors realizing in an instant that it was the most logical escape route. As she sprinted past the smoldering remains of her Aunt and neared the bookcases, she was startled by a sharp cracking and splintering sound. She skidded to a stop and looked up - transfixed by the horrific sight of the main support timber cracking and beginning to bulge outward. Large chunks of burning plaster and wood showered down upon the room, dropping down onto everything in its path. Edwina drew the wrap over her head and raced towards the terrace doors. As she was passing the last mahogany book case, she heard a loud crack and then a heavy thud as the end of the timber pulled loose from the brace and swung free, sending burning embers and sparks down into the room. The timber crashed into the top of the bookcase and toppled it. Edwina tried to jump out of its path, but she realized too late exactly what was happening. Moments later, she was falling to the ground amidst a shower of smoldering books and plaster, pinned to the carpet by the massive bookcase. As her head swam and she began to lose consciousness, her only consolation was that she expected that she would more than likely asphyxiate from the thickening smoke in the room before burning to death. If that were the result, at least, Holmes would have something to bury.

»»««

Baker Street - Half past 11:00 pm

"Dear God man... could you open the window at least a crack?" grumbled Watson as he pushed open the door to the flat. He was immediately enveloped in a thick cloud of cigarette smoke.

"As you like...." muttered Holmes - scarcely bothering to glance up as Watson, overcome with a fit of coughing, entered and quickly crossed to the windows. He flung open the sash and leaned his head out, taking deep breaths as he attempted to clear his lungs of the noxious fumes.

Holmes set aside his notes and uttered a deep sigh. "And now you know how I feel when you fire up that foul pipe of yours."

"Yes, well at least I have the decency to open the window."

Holmes rolled his eyes and returned to his case notes as Watson hovered nearby. Watson stripped off his black silk gloves and removed his cravat which he laid on the table and draped his coat over the sofa, his lips pulling into a frown beneath his mustache. "Are you not even going to inquire how the Memorial Service went?" He grabbed Holmes slightly damp coat which was balled up in his chair and draped it over the back of the sofa next to his coat.

"I assume all went well... everyone in their proper place. I take it the deceased was on time."

Watson's frown increased as he settled into his armchair. "That is not even remotely amusing."

Holmes shrugged, a slight smirk played on his lips. "No, I suppose not."

"It was a lovely service," began Watson, "beautiful flowers... nice procession... must have cost a pretty penny... I don't know how on earth they were able to pay for it."

"Who?"

"Edwina and her aunt of course... the house is practically bare... anything that the Crown is not taking has been sold off. I fear they are in desperate straits."

"Well, it stands to reason that they didn't pay then doesn't it?" muttered Holmes crossly.

Watson gazed at him and narrowed his eyes, his fingertips lightly brushing over his moustache as he considered the possibilities.

"Was it you then? I know that you expedited and paid for the release of the body."

Holmes looked up and then shook his head. "No... when I enquired at the Funeral Home - I was informed that all the arrangements had been taken care of by an anonymous donor."

"Anonymous?"

Holmes set down his pen and nodded. "It's not hard to surmise who that might be."

Watson shrugged. "Enlighten me!" He leaned forward in his chair, waiting for Holmes to continue. As he did so, his eyes scanned the detective's face and then drifted down to his shirt collar. There was something odd there... small red smudges on the starched band... not blood... but it did remind him of something... but he couldn't quite work it out at the moment.

"Well, the most logical choice is the Professor, and of course, I am sure that Moran has also played a part, which would explain his reprehensible sense of entitlement where Eddy is concerned."

Watson arched his brow quizzically. "Why anonymous Holmes? They were known to be long-time friends."

Holmes steepled his fingers under his chin. "He is a man who prefers to remain in the background – a puppet master if you will."

Watson grunted in assent. "Well, in any case, he was not at the service, only Moran."

Holmes muttered something he couldn't quite catch. Watson frowned, his curiousity piqued. "And what do you mean by Moran's sense of entitlement?"

"He is no gentleman," growled Holmes with disdain. "He seeks to use the confusion and sorrow of the situation to take liberties with Edwina."

Watson sat up rigidly, a look of bewilderment on his face. "And how would you know that?"

"He tried to force himself on her..."

"There was a kiss, but how would you know that?" repeated Watson sharply, his expression one of astonishment. He thought back to when he had moved Holmes' coat from his chair – it had been quite damp to the touch. If Holmes had been in all evening since returning from the morgue, surely it would have been drier. "You were there, at the service!" he exclaimed, "why did you not come forward man?"

Holmes frowned in irritation and shook his head. "I was not at the service."

"Your coat tells another story, it is still damp!" protested Watson.

"Oh Watson, once again you have made a leap too far. My coat only tells you that I was out later than expected."

Watson compressed his lips in irritation and leaned forward. With a snort, he reached out and snatched the collar from Holmes' shirt. "But this... this tells me that you were there... that you saw Edwina... and do not tell me that this is blood from a shaving nick... I am a medical man who has seen more than his fair share of blood. I know what this is... it's lip color. Mary's lip color. She gave it to Edwina before the service. Poor girl looked like a wraith. So, do not lie to me and tell me that you were not there and that you did not see her," he cried out, waving the collar in front of Holmes' face.

Holmes was silent for a moment and then managed a bleak smile of resignation as his eyes also rested on the stained collar. *It must have happened when she had rested her head on his shoulder. How could he have not noticed? Losing his edge...could it be?* "I did not lie... I merely said I wasn't at the service, which I was not. I arrived after."

"But you did see Edwina," prodded Watson with an air of satisfaction that his deductions were not that far off the mark.

Again, Holmes let out a heavy sigh. "Yes. I finished early at the morgue and decided to pay my respects. She was still at the churchyard when I arrived. She was distraught, lying in the earth next to the grave... talking nonsense about death and measuring the space left in the plot to see if there would be room for her alongside her mother and father. I have never seen her so... I tried to... reassure her. She told me about Moran then said it was only a kiss and that she had set him straight... but I wonder... she was evasive... embarrassed. She's frightened of him Watson, and I think perhaps not without reason."

"And so you kissed her?"

At this Holmes glanced up and outwardly flinched; he shook his head firmly.

"For the record, she kissed me. There is a difference Doctor."

Watson chuckled a bit and shook his head, shifting the stained collar in his fingers as he studied it.

"Hmmm... well... obviously, you did not push her away, at least not right away. That is the story this tells."

Holmes nodded in resignation. "It caught me by surprise. I... well... her words were so dark... her mind in such a fragile state Watson, I was afraid for her and... and then when she kissed me... and told me..." His words faltered and much to Watson's surprise, Holmes lapsed into silence his eyes fixed on the flames in the hearth.

"What did she tell you Holmes?" The words were a gentle but firm nudge for him to continue, though Watson had a good idea of what the answer would be.

Holmes didn't answer straight away. When he finally replied, he could not bring himself to meet Watson's knowing gaze. "That she loves me Watson ... still... even after all of this. And that she will always love me, even though I do not feel the same."

Watson nodded and remained silent for a moment. "And tell me then, how does that make you feel?"

Holmes averted his eyes and said nothing for quite a long time. Just when Watson thought he would not answer, he shook his head and in a low melancholy voice replied: "Honoured, that such an exceptional creature should feel such devotion towards me but mostly... mostly wretched, as I cannot respond in kind."

"That is an obstacle of your own making Holmes."

"It must always be so Watson. My work..."

Watson snorted cynically and shook his head. "Your work... your work will do little to keep you warm or care for you in your senior years Holmes. Don't you think it's time to stop hiding behind this tired excuse? This is a woman Holmes, who loves you for who you are - accepts you as you are. Take my word, as a man who is well acquainted with your demons, that willingness, patience in itself, shows great courage and character. She could be a great help to you in your professional as well as your personal life. She has already proven her intelligence and resilience and it's obvious to all that you are quite fond of her – more so than you care to admit."

Holmes once more averted his eyes. "I wish her only good fortune Watson. Nothing would please me more than to see her happy and settled properly."

Watson arched his brow at this and then chuckled softly. "So you say, but I wonder... Well, I suppose time will tell won't it? Though it certainly does seem that Colonel Moran is at the head of the line."

A look of intense displeasure contorted Holmes' face. "That must never happen... certainly not to such a brute as Moran..."

"It may happen sooner than originally expected. Now that Pennington is gone and the Crown has seized the estate, Edwina may have no choice but to marry. She has no income, no way of providing for herself. Would you rather see her in the workhouse or perhaps working Brick Lane? Without a guardian, a father or husband to provide for her, those are her options Holmes, she doesn't even have the credentials to be a domestic."

"She is intelligent, determined...there is nothing she couldn't achieve Watson."

"She is also a woman in a world that still has limited resources for an unmarried woman no matter how intelligent or clever."

Holmes lapsed into silence and looked down at his case notes. "I think this discussion is best tabled Watson, as we will never see eye to eye."

A flash of anger darkened Watson's face for a moment and then he shrugged. "As you wish. After all, as you say, it really is none of your concern," he replied with great sarcasm. "Your commission was to solve the case, which you did – at least to Lestrade's satisfaction if not your own. Pennington is dead ... punished for his crime some would say, even if by his own hand."

"Pennington didn't take his life, he was murdered."

"What?! That man hung himself in his cell. We both saw... even you cannot dispute that!"

Holmes withdrew his notes and sketches from a folder and spread them out on the table.

"Yes, I do not dispute that he died by hanging, but I tell you this, he did not hang himself... it was not his doing."

Watson stared at him in disbelief. "The man was in a locked prison cell."

"And there are many at Newgate who could have had access. It would not be the first time a prisoner died under mysterious circumstances."

"But we found him hanging from the gas pipe... dangling. There were no signs of a struggle... nothing moved in the cell," protested Watson.

"Yes, exactly," exclaimed Holmes. "Nothing moved, nothing at all. The chair and table were still in place by the wall, as was the cot, still by the wall. Tell me Watson, what is the most common way a person hangs himself?"

Watson was silent for a moment and then frowned. "By climbing up onto a chair or table or even a bed, placing their neck in the noose and then jumping off."

"Precisely. And tell me, what usually happens to the table or chair?" A look of realization clouded Watson' face. "It usually remains near or under the body... sometimes it kicks out a little but usually not too far."

"Precisely. But if you look at this sketch of Pennington's cell that was made upon the discovery of his body... what do you see?"

Watson stared at the sketch. "The table and chair are nowhere near the body, neither is the cot."

"So it stands to reason that..." prompted Holmes.

Watson turned pale. "Pennington didn't use them to climb up on. But maybe... have you considered maybe he tied the noose, placed it around his own neck and threw it up over the pipe and hoisted himself up... if he was determined."

Holmes began to laugh and shook his head. "Not a chance as short as Pennington was. I doubt he could have gotten the rope that high up over the pipe and even if he did, how could he hoist himself up? It wouldn't have worked even if he did."

"How so? Explain yourself."

Holmes smiled darkly and removed a noose and a length of rope from the drawer of the roll top desk.

"I performed a little experiment while you were out and about to test my theory. I placed the noose around my neck and tried to hoist myself up over the ceiling beam."

Watson stared at him horrified. "Are you mad? You could have..."

Holmes began to laugh and waved him off. "Not to worry, I had Mrs. Hudson standing by to cut me down should something go amiss. But as I was saying, I slipped the noose around my neck. and attempted to hoist myself up, which is extremely difficult I assure you. Now granted, Pennington was much smaller in height, but not exactly a light man so I would say he would have had some degree of difficulty as well. So, good Doctor, you're a medical man, you are well aware of the mechanics of hanging. What do you suppose I discovered?"

Watson shook his head still too stunned to think further on the matter. "I... I don't know... what did you discover?"

Holmes looked disappointed that Watson had nothing to offer. "I was only able to achieve a few inches. before I passed out. As you are well aware, hanging that occurs from a low height, that is not from a gallows or high tree limb where one drops from a considerable height, the cause of death is by strangulation, asphyxia, the noose cuts off the carotid arteries and sometimes even crushes the windpipe. It is a rather slow process which is why a drop from a gallows, if done correctly, is more merciful and quick as the cause of death is from separation of the spine not asphyxia. However, by hoisting oneself up, you encounter a particular problem in that you will never achieve any sort of height. Death would occur from the weight of your body in the noose compressing the windpipe and the arteries; death by strangulation, asphyxia, not spinal separation. If you jump from a chair or table, you will also more than likely die by asphyxia (unless it is from a height great enough to cause spinal separation). The problem with trying to hoist yourself up is that by the time you have even achieved any sort of lifting, you are already beginning to cut off your oxygen supply. The process is simply too slow. I tried three times Watson, and all three times I passed out before I could achieve any considerable height and in doing so, my grip relaxed and I released the rope and dropped to the floor. This of course resulted in a lessening in the pressure on my neck. I regained consciousness within a few moments and with Mrs. Hudson's help, was able to try once more after a brief rest. And then... there were the bruises on Pennington's body..."

"Bruises," repeated Watson dully, still numbed by the revelation that Holmes had tried to hang himself as an experiment not once but three times.

"Yes... bruises... deep bruises. Clear fingermarks. They were mostly spread over his shoulders and arms - forearms specifically."

Understanding flickered in Watson's eyes. "As if someone had held him or lifted him."

"Precisely," confirmed Holmes.

Watson sighed heavily and looked through the case notes. "But... why Holmes? Why now?"

"Ahh, well I believe because of this," Holmes explained and removed a blank sheet of paper from the file.

Watson took it from him and held it up to the light. In doing so he could see that it wasn't really blank. Holmes had smeared it with what looked like ash, and as he moved it closer to the light he could just make out from the indentation:

I have reconsidered. Please come tomorrow morning. W.Pennington

"This was addressed to you, but you never received it," exclaimed Watson in astonishment.

"Yes, it was intercepted."

Watson knit his brow. "How do you know that?"

"I made some inquiries. The Irregulars proved themselves invaluable once again. They pointed me in the direction of a young lad – not an irregular but someone known to them. He frequents the area around Newgate and has been known to pass notes and other items to and from the inmates. All for a fee of course. There is quite a thriving black market Watson, in and out of Newgate in case you weren't aware. In any event, I spoke with him and after an assurance that the Yard would not be informed, he confirmed that he did not deliver the note to me as he had heard that there were certain parties interested in any flow of information going from Newgate in my direction. Of course, a payment for this information was involved. Would you care to guess to whom that note was ultimately delivered?"

Watson nodded his curiousity thoroughly piqued.

"He delivered it to the Red Lion in Whitechapel."

"The Red Lion! Why does that sound familiar?" muttered Watson, racking his brain as to why that struck him as important.

Holmes began to laugh. "Because dear fellow, the Red Lion is the last place Constable Jenkins was seen drinking the night of his death... and according to the boy, the Constable is the man the note was delivered to and who paid the fee."

"What? Why?" exclaimed Watson incredulously.

"Ahh, therein lies the crux of the matter. It seems Constable Jenkins was collecting information on any dealings I might have at Newgate. This information was routed to a certain gentleman who lives just off Berkely Square in Mayfair."

"What? Dear God man, you can't just go throwing around such serious accusations. These are powerful people"

Holmes began to laugh and shook his head. "Oh yes, powerful indeed. I have it confirmed though, the note was intercepted and delivered to Jenkins who in turn delivered it to The Professor's townhouse."

"What! Who confirmed this information?'

"Archibald Dolan."

Watson stared at him, thoroughly astonished. "Jenkin's partner? Dear God."

"Yes, according to Dolan, although he was never invited inside to attend any of these meetings, they happened on a fairly frequent basis. It seems that

370

the Professor has had quite an interest in our comings and goings, especially with relation to Pennington's case."

Watson shook his head. "And now Jenkins is dead as well. Do you suppose it's related?"

"How can it not be?" replied Holmes confidently. "Especially after examining the Constable's body this morning."

"But... he was robbed. The murder happened during a violent robbery," protested Watson.

Holmes scowled. "No, it's the reverse. The robbery was incidental, the constable was robbed to cover up the murder."

"And you can tell this how?" Watson was skeptical. "According to Lestrade, the proprietor of the Red Lion confirms that Jenkins was drunk off his mind when he was forced to leave the bar. He was on his way home when he was attacked, viciously beaten during the robbery and then pushed into the Thames. He drowned being too injured and drunk to climb out of the river."

Holmes began to laugh and thrust a series of detailed sketches of the victim into his hands. "Primarily because of certain wounds on the body. Jenkins died of exsanguination before he drowned...very little water in the lungs. Take a look at these sketches I made this morning Watson and tell me what you see."

Watson stared down at the detailed sketches of the Constable's injuries. He looked up after a few moments. "There is a mark on the back of his head unlike the crush marks on his forehead. It is different in size and shape. The forehead marks are crude like they were made with a brick or stone. The one on the back of the head is round and left a cylindrical impression like he was struck with a... a..."

"A cane... or walking stick... "prompted Holmes.

"Yes, exactly. A very fine one. There is a pattern on it - some decoration."

"Capital. Please continue... what else?"

Watson once more focused on the sketches this time his attention was drawn to the large gash that ran across the constable's throat.

"The knife wound... his throat... it was cut... with a large blade... a very clean cut. I've seen this before... I know it... I..." Watson abruptly stopped and then looked up. "The knife... a hunting knife... just like the Chinaman... Moran? Surely you don't think?"

Holmes shrugged. "It stands to reason that if Moran is acting as the Professor's lieutenant..."

"But... but you have no proof."

"No, currently I do not, but that does not mean it is not so."

Watson set the sketches down, a look of bewilderment on his face. "But... but why... why kill a policeman Holmes... and one attached to Scotland Yard at that? Why take such a chance?"

"Because, Jenkins was a link... a link between Pennington and the Professor. I only know this because Pennington's murderers failed to take this scrap of paper which contained an indentation of the note and they failed to consider that the boy would be found at all."

Watson sighed heavily and rose from the table, rubbing his head. "Well... what good is it though... with no proof? Lestrade will certainly not act on this." Needing to clear his head, he crossed to the window, leaned out and inhaled deeply.

"Dear God man, the longer this case goes on the more convoluted it becomes."

Holmes nodded in agreement but remained silent staring down at the case notes on the table. "The stakes are much higher than originally thought... so much to consider. I tell you Watson, I shall welcome the end of it. I look forward to a trip to the Downs."

Watson nodded in agreement. The case had taken a toll on them all, particularly Holmes.

"A well-earned rest, that's definitely in order. Well, I think I... Dear God... what the blazes is that? Cannot be the sunset... the sun set hours ago."

Holmes glanced up to find Watson staring out the window, a look of bewilderment on his face. "What are you talking about?"

Watson turned to him and raised his arm pointing out the window across the rooftops to a bright orange glow that lit the sky just outside the city.

On seeing it Holmes turned deathly pale. He ran to the window and leaned out, sniffing the air. On the night breeze there was a strong odor of smoke but not the smoke from the factory coal fires or even the smoke from chimneys. This was the acrid, biting smell of wood burning. Wood not from a forest but wood mixed with other articles such as fabric, plaster, wallpaper - all those things that comprised a house.

"Golders Hill... it's up on Golders Hill... Fern Hall Watson... Fern Hall is burning!" Holmes cried out in alarm and without waiting for Watson to respond, he was gone. Watson caught up to him at the curb just as the hansom pulled up and climbed in next to him.

"It might not be... it could be the church or any other of the homes in that area," suggested Watson in an attempt to offer reassurance. He had surely never seen such a look of utter fear on Holmes' face before.

Holmes shook his head. "It's too large to be anything else.... and the old woman. Don't you remember? At Court she vowed that she would see it in ashes before the Crown got their hands on it." Unable to continue, Holmes turned his attention to the driver and began rapping on the roof of the cab, exhorting him to go faster.

All along the road out of London towards Golder's Hill, the hansom not only had to dodge a stream of carriages also heading in the same direction but also had to move out of the way for the local fire brigade as they screamed past in their horse drawn steam powered fire engine. By the time they crested the hill and made their way around the gawkers who had taken cabs or their own carriages up onto the rise to view the fire, the house seemed fully engulfed. As the hansom drew to a stop at the end of the drive, Holmes scrambled out and without waiting for Watson, ran towards a small crowd that he recognized as domestic staff that had gathered near the gate watching as the flames shot up from the roof and windows, painting the sky a garish orange glow. At the front of the house, the members of the fire brigade were unfurling their hoses and running them out to the pond. Already the loud clank of the steam engine could be heard as it began to draw water out of the pond into the hoses. Holmes ignored the commotion and ran straight to the staff. He looked from face to face, searching but did not find the one he most hoped to find.

"Where is she?" he demanded. "Where's Eddy?"

No one answered. In fact, a few of them looked away. Spying the small little blond girl, the one he recognized as Hanna her maid, Holmes ran to her and grabbed her.

"Where is she... where's your mistress Hanna?" he cried as he shook her trying to rouse her out of her stupor.

The girl, who was already in great distress, began to weep so pitifully that Watson intervened pulling Holmes off her. At this, the girl began to cry even more uncontrollably. After a moment, she wiped at her eyes and managed to blurt, "I'm sorry... I tried... but she wouldn't listen... she was here... but then she left... she went back in... when she realized Mrs. Pennington was still inside... to try to find her."

A look of horror crossed Holmes face as he gazed at the house. And then much to Watson's surprise, he took up a bucket of water, poured it over himself and then pulled on his gloves and wrapped his scarf around his mouth and nose and ran towards the house.

Watson caught up with him just as he was turning back from the front door which was impassable.

"Stop... you're mad... it's too late Holmes..."

Holmes kept moving, surveying the lower half of the house searching for a way in. "I will not leave her... I have to try...She's clever - she'll find a place."

Watson's grabbed his arm trying to hold him back. "You'll never find her Holmes... it's too late... I'm... I'm sorry but you can't help her now. Stop... please..." he pleaded.

Holmes pulled free and shook his head.

"I will not just leave her, not without trying. You wouldn't say that John if it were Mary." And then he was gone, heading towards the terrace just off the library which was in flames but not as much as the front of the house.

Something exploded on the second floor sending down a shower of glass and sparks and as Watson moved back towards the staff who had gathered, he realized Holmes was right. For Mary he would not hesitate.

The house emitted a loud groan and shuddered violently as the second-floor hallway gave way with a loud crack and collapsed smothering the first floor with charred furnishings, plaster, burning timbers and debris. As a shaft of orange flame mixed with dust shot up into the night sky through a breach in the roof, Hanna emitted a horrified shriek and clung onto Cook for comfort, burying her head in her apron. Another shower of sparks and embers rained down outside, this one much closer and the fire chief signaled for his men to abandon the house. The structure was lost; there was nothing more to do other than try to contain the fire to the property as best they could. They had to consider the church now and the surrounding properties.

As the men began to move back dragging their equipment and hoses, Watson approached the Chief of the Brigade - his face drawn with worry and fear. "Captain wait! My friend, Mr. Holmes, he went inside to search. There are two women believed to still be inside."

The man stared at him in horrified disbelief and then removed his blackened leather helmet to wipe at the sweat collecting beneath the brim; he shook his head. "My dear sir, I am sorry, the house is beyond saving and unstable. If your friend is still inside as are these women, I am afraid they are on their own. I will not risk my men on such foolishness. If you are a praying man, you might want to give that a try...you might have a better result. The sad truth of the matter is they are most likely lost." He turned back to his men to supervise the packing up of the equipment.

Watson stared numbly at the fire ravaged house and turned away, overcome with a sense of absolute helplessness and despair. *Holmes had often joked he was indestructible and he had skirted death so many times, that he had almost begun to believe it.* Watson slowly began to make his way towards the back terrace where he had last seen Holmes as he was searching for an entry point. He settled on the low brick wall that ran along the far edge, separating the small flower garden from the terrace. The heat from the fire had blasted and withered most of the blooms and thick clouds of dark smoke were billowing out of the shattered French doors. He lowered his head and moved a little further away on the wall to avoid the suffocating smoke as he debated whether he should venture in himself. *Surely it couldn't end this way....* but as he looked up at the shell of what had once been a modest manor house, it was hard for him not to think the worst and that maybe Holmes' luck had finally run out. How ironic would it be that the thing that Holmes abhorred most, sentiment, would be the cause of his demise. Watson had no doubt that it was sentiment pure and simple that had driven him into the inferno in a desperate bid to save a woman he could not bring himself to admit he had feelings for. And so it was while he sat on the wall with his head in his hands, powerless to do anything more than listen to the house disintegrating and reflecting on how it had all gone so wrong, when he heard a rasping cough drifting out across the terrace. Startled, he lifted his head and stared in astonishment as a familiar figure loomed in the shattered terrace doorway and stumbled through a curtain of billowing black smoke. In his arms, he carried a bundle of what looked like fabric.

Watson leaped to his feet straining to see. "Holmes?"

The figure stumbled forward a few more feet. "Bit of help Watson, if you can manage..." came the hoarse reply, interrupted by a harsh fit of coughing.

Watson leaped up, his face lit with relief and joy and ran forward. As he grew closer, he noticed that Holmes was in his shirtsleeves, covered with soot and cinders, some of which were still smoldering. His expression became even more incredulous when he realized that the bundle Holmes carried was Edwina Schraeder, wrapped in Holmes overcoat.

"Dear God man... you found her... how on earth?" exclaimed Watson as he ran forward and extended his arms to help.

But Holmes refused to hand her over and instead continued across the terrace until he reached the tree line where he gently laid her down beneath the shade of a towering oak.

"You must help her Watson... she is not responding... and I cannot hear any breath in her..." And though Holmes' voice was calm, Watson thought he detected a note of despair.

Watson knelt next to Holmes and carefully unwrapped the coat, his eyes scanning her injuries. She was clad only in her nightgown and a wrap. Remarkably, her torso, upper body and abdomen, were mostly unscathed despite the soot and cinders that blackened her clothing. Her arms and legs however were a different story; the skin was charred and peeling to reveal raw flesh...the same for the left side of her face - which was blackened and beginning to blister. The right side of her face fared much better - mostly untouched as she had fallen on her right side. Her eyebrows were singed and there were entire sections of her hair which were scorched and brittle to the touch where they hadn't been burnt off.

"Dear God, where did you find her?" murmured the Doctor aghast at her condition. He pressed his ear to her chest - listening.

Holmes wiped futilely at the soot on his face with the cuff of his shirt and held her up - taking care to avoid her blistered skin.

"In the library – she was pinned beneath a bookcase which had toppled over..."

Watson nodded. That explained why the burns to her extremities were more serious as well as one side of her face instead of both. After a few moments, he sat back up - a grave expression on his face as he wrapped the coat back around her.

"I won't lie to you, her burns are very serious. We must keep her warm to prevent shock. She is breathing... though it is faint and labored. In addition to her burns, I fear she may have lung damage due to the heat and smoke of the fire. She needs to be in hospital Holmes... time is of the essence. But I caution you, it may not be enough."

Holmes nodded that he understood and quickly stood, taking her back up into his arms.

"Hospital it is..." he declared and began to hurry as quickly as he could down the drive towards the lane where several carriages and hansoms were still parked, their occupants standing on the opposite side of the lane watching the house fall into ruin as if they were taking in the races at Ascot on a Sunday afternoon.

As they approached the lane, Watson caught up to him. "A hansom will be too cramped... a Clarence would be better," he advised, and then shrugged in dismay, "but I do not see any for hire."

Holmes continued to stride determinedly towards the vehicles. "Not a problem... tell me Watson, did you bring your revolver by any chance?"

Watson stopped for a moment bewildered.

"Revolver? Why? What on earth for?" he exclaimed. On searching his coat pockets, Watson discovered that he did indeed have it with him. He extended it to Holmes with a wary expression waiting for his explanation. But Holmes didn't offer any and continued to move towards the vehicles studying each carefully. After a moment, he abruptly turned to Watson and held forth the unconscious woman. "Take her Watson, please... can you carry her for a moment?"

"Yes, of course," replied Watson, quickly taking the limp form into his arms. Holmes thanked him and then with the most somber of expressions, urged him to follow. He strode purposefully towards a newer model Clarence led by a team of two healthy looking mixed breed horses. The liveried driver sat atop the carriage while the owners, a fashionable young man in new tweeds stood on the small rise opposite the carriage with his elegant wife; they were watching the house burn with utter fascination. As Holmes approached, his hand slid into his pocket resting lightly on the revolver.

"I require the immediate use of your carriage... this woman is severely injured... we need to get her to hospital without delay..."

The gentleman's wife, an elegant woman in rose colored silks with matching parasol, wrinkled her nose distastefully at the acrid odor of smoke that clung to both Holmes and Edwina and on seeing the injured woman, uttered a startled cry and covered her mouth in horror.

The gentleman glared at Holmes. "Away with you sir! Can you not see you are distressing my wife?"

Holmes eyes grew fierce. "And can you not see we need your assistance? This woman is severely injured... I need your Clarence."

The man stared at him and then shook his head. "You must look elsewhere... this carriage is new — a wedding gift from our family — I will not have you foul it with soot and ashes."

Watson stared at the couple in disbelief, he was always astounded by the lack of empathy some people exhibited for those less fortunate. But he wasn't one to force the issue and he began to back away, already looking down the line of carriages for another. But Holmes called him back with one terse phrase. "Watson stay!" And then Watson heard a sound that chilled him to the very core; the sound of the hammer being cocked on his Webley revolver. He froze and glanced up to find Holmes pointing the revolver at the head of the reluctant Clarence owner.

"Holmes... for God's sake man. What are you doing?" he gasped.

Holmes nodded towards the carriage, his eyes still locked on the couple. "I have found a suitable carriage Watson – please do get inside."

"You're mad!" protested the man as his wife grabbed onto his arm, hiding her face against him. "You can't do this..."

Holmes smiled darkly. "But I already have. Please do not make the mistake of thinking that I will not pull this trigger. I have no time or patience

376

for the likes of your kind. I am taking this carriage one way or another. Now, there are plenty of hansoms here. I'm sure you have the funds to hire one to take you home."

"But... my driver..." sputtered the man.

"Will stay with us," declared Holmes, "and when he has delivered us to the hospital, he will return to you with the carriage. Now, I suggest you look to hire a hansom and do tend to your wife sir, as she looks ready to faint at any moment."

The man raised his eyes to look at the revolver which was pointed at the exact center of his forehead. He slowly nodded and backed away. "Of course... as you wish."

"Watson, do get in," urged Holmes once more and then he slowly climbed in after him, still pointing the gun out the carriage window. Moments later, the carriage pulled away moving at a fast clip down Golder's Hill heading towards London. After instructing the driver to head directly to the Royal London, Holmes leaned back in the seat and carefully un-cocked the gun, pulling back the hammer until he could safely clear the trigger and then put it back into his pocket. He looked to Watson who was cradling the still unconscious woman.

"I shall hold onto this for a little while longer in case we meet others who need convincing..." he commented, indicating the revolver.

"Surely you were bluffing," murmured Watson, though his own voice lacked conviction as he uttered the words.

Holmes met his gaze -a look of anguish darkening his face as he looked on the motionless form of Edwina Schraeder. "I will do what it takes Watson. How is she?"

Watson uttered a heavy sigh and with the utmost care, shifted her position, gently laying her head on Holmes knee, taking care to keep her on her back and her injured side away from direct contact. "Her injuries are very grave," he replied after a long pause. "The London has the best doctors... but even so... you must be prepared... it may not be enough... Even if she survives she will be scarred... perhaps even maimed."

Holmes looked away, his eyes fixed on the darkness outside the window. "We must do everything we can Watson. She must recover." As he spoke, his hands gently smoothed the collar of the coat wrapped about her though he was careful not to touch her injured face.

Watson was quiet for a moment and then nodded. "Before, while you were persuading the owners of their need to cooperate, Edwina murmured something. She may have thought I was you... her eyes were closed...."

Holmes nodded for him to continue. "What did she say?

"Not much... only... remember your promise... something to that effect."

Holmes turned deathly pale and averted his eyes.

Noting his distress, Watson leaned forward, curious. "What did she mean Holmes? What promise?"

Again, there was a long pause, the only sound was that of the wheels clattering on the rutted lane as they sped on towards London. Finally, Holmes answered, a look of anguish on his face. "When I saw her after her father's funeral, as I said, she was distraught. She was lying on the ground Watson, next to the fresh grave, measuring the space left in the plot. To see her in such a state... so distressed. She asked me... she asked me to promise should anything happen to her, that I would ensure she was laid to rest with her parents. I gave her my word Watson, but it must not come to that."

"Some things are out of our hands Holmes. You must have faith."

"Faith," snorted the detective, "I have faith... in science and medicine."

"That is not what I meant."

Holmes' expression hardened. "I know... but I tell you, there is nothing else."

Watson's eyes grew sad and with the utmost care, he carefully checked the motionless woman's pulse one more time. "I hope for her sake you are wrong."

As the Clarence pulled up in front of the Royal London, Watson opened the door and climbed down. He disappeared up the stairs and into the entryway of the hospital and moments later re-emerged with several attendants who wheeled out a patient trolley. After helping to load Edwina onto the trolley, he grabbed Holmes' arm and both men made their way into the hospital.

As Edwina disappeared beyond the double doors of the treatment room, Holmes started to follow until Watson gently pulled him back. "These are good men here Holmes...they will do everything they can for her, but you must not interfere."

It seemed at first that Holmes would protest but ultimately, he allowed Watson to pull him away. He settled onto a bench not far from the treatment room, staring at the double doors with a troubled expression while Watson took a seat next to him.

"Good... now... let's have a look at you," began Watson as he reached for the Detective's hands, which were clad in leather gloves that were cracked and burnt from the fire. "Dear God man, what have you done to yourself?" he exclaimed as he gently examined them. Although the gloves had offered some protection from the fire, there were places on his palms where Holmes had obviously picked up something that was either still burning or incredibly hot as the leather had split open and burnt away to reveal skin that was raw and beginning to blister. Watson disappeared for a moment down the hall and then moments later returned. This time Mary Morstan followed him rolling a small cart which contained a basin of water, bandages, scissors and ointments. He spoke to her quietly for a moment and then disappeared back into the treatment room to check on Edwina.

Mary Morstan watched him go with unmistakable affection and then readjusted her hair under her crisp nurse's cap. She turned to Holmes with a reassuring smile. "I hear you have gone and banged yourself up again - let me see then..."

"Please, it is nothing... no fuss," protested Holmes. He rested his hands on either side of him on the bench.

Her smile began to fade replaced by a look of obstinance.

"I am the nurse here Holmes. My cap tells the story. You are in my place of business now. I don't tell you how to solve crimes, please don't tell me how to treat patients." She fixed her gentle but firm gaze on him until he relented and with a sigh of resignation slowly extended his hands.

With the utmost care, she removed his gloves cutting away some portions that seemed stuck to the skin. When she had removed almost all the leather, she carefully submerged his hands in a basin of cool water. After a few minutes, she lifted his hands out and removed the remaining pieces of leather. She dried his hands and applied a cooling salve that smelled of mint and then began to lightly wrap his hands with gauze.

"John told me what you did. How you did not hesitate to go in after Edwina. That was extraordinarily brave and noble."

Holmes averted his eyes, unable to meet her gaze any longer as if ashamed. "I am a man who is not prone to regret Miss Morstan, but if there is one case I regret having solved, it is this one. Not for the solution to the crime you understand, but for the aftermath. Edwina had no blame in the crime. Her only failing was placing her trust in me. For her to be so cruelly punished... I..." His voice faltered the words dying out.

Mary Morstan pressed his forearm comfortingly. "You could not have known what would happen."

His head sank a little lower. "I could see the old woman was unbalanced – even before the trial. I should have insisted... found some way to convince her, prevent her return to Fern Hall. She felt obligated because of her father. I don't understand; to feel this... even for someone you know has nothing but malice in their heart for you, it is incomprehensible. Her heart is too kind, too forgiving. One need look no further than the fact that she forgave me. If she had not, she would not be suffering so."

"Ah, there you have it Mr. Holmes. Unconditional acceptance — forgiveness — the hallmark of love."

"And much underserved," murmured Holmes.

Mary Morstan smiled. "I am not so sure. I think perhaps she is a better judge of character than us all."

Holmes looked unconvinced. He thanked her for bandaging his hands and the kind words and then lapsed into silence.

Sensing that he needed to be alone, Mary rose and began to gather the bandages and ointments, replacing everything onto the cart.

As she was about to leave, Holmes suddenly rose. "I would like to see her..."

Mary shook her head. "Not tonight, it is too soon. I expect she will be in an oxygen tent most of the night, under close watch. You must let us care for her. She is still unconscious Holmes. They are giving her morphine to ease the pain. She needs rest and quiet."

"But if her condition should change... if..." He didn't finish and looked away. "I... I wouldn't want her to be alone..." he murmured.

She paused for a moment. She had known Sherlock Holmes almost as long as she had known John Watson and the changes he had undergone in the last year astounded her. This man that stood before her, attempting to conceal the raw emotion that rattled him, was a far cry from the aloof, imperious man she had been introduced to some five years previously.

"I promise you, we will take good care of her. I will be on the ward with her all night," she reassured. "And if…" Mary hesitated, choosing her words carefully. She took a breath, forcing herself to say the words her profession demanded; it was difficult for this was her friend as well.

"Should her condition worsen, I will send word immediately. She will not be alone Holmes. You have my word."

"When… when do you think I will be able to see her?"

"Perhaps tomorrow. Come back then – in the afternoon. But first, I want you to go home and get some rest. Try to use your hands as little as possible. Listen to John, he is a Doctor after all."

"True, though I must say I find his bedside manner somewhat lacking. Fortunately for him, your graciousness helps to fill the void."

Mary blushed at the compliment but smiled nonetheless. "But I am only a nurse, not a doctor."

Holmes shrugged. "A shame really, perhaps you should re-consider. I hear the Blackwell sisters have established a school on Hunter Street — The Royal Free Hospital School of Medicine — specifically for the training of female physicians. With your solid nursing skills, I have no doubts with regard to your success."

Mary smiled somewhat wistfully and nodded. She had heard the news as well. Emily and Elizabeth Blackwell were a major topic of discussion among the nurses lately; both women had trained and received their medical degrees in the United States and now had returned to try and promote the training of female physicians in England. They had been warmly embraced by the suffrage movement that was sweeping the country.

"Perhaps one day," she sighed, "it is a consideration. However, there is a wedding in the near future and as you well know, Dr. Watson is not too keen on my continuing on with my full-time nursing practice once we are married. He feels it will keep me from devoting my time to the marriage and household duties. I doubt he would look kindly upon my enrolling in medical school."

At this Holmes rolled his eyes a bit. "Perhaps he fears you might outshine him," he remarked dryly. But he let the matter rest. Watson's reluctance to accept the changing role of women was well-known and often a sore point of discussion. "Well, perhaps in time Miss Morstan, you can change his mind. I have no doubt that you are eminently capable of navigating a marriage, family and profession simultaneously. It would be a shame to waste such talent."

Deeply moved by such unexpectedly kind words of confidence in her abilities, Mary reached out and gently pressed his forearm.

"Thank you, Holmes. Your belief in my abilities is most gratifying. Now, seeing as how you have such confidence, take my advice, get some rest, avoid using your hands and listen to Dr. Watson. Come back tomorrow afternoon and rest easy, we will take good care of Edwina." Then she was gone, rolling the small cart down the corridor. She paused momentarily as the door to the treatment room swung open and Watson emerged, deep in conversation with another doctor. On seeing her, he ended his conversation and approached her. After a quiet conversation and a fond kiss to her forehead, he slowly approached Holmes. A smile crossed his lips on seeing the bandages. "I see Mary was able to convince you of the need for aid."

Holmes chuckled. "Well, it's all in the manner of approach or so I've been told. You would do well to emulate her Watson. She has an innate sense of empathy. A welcome trait in a physician."

Watson stared at him in disbelief. "I agree, though forgive me if I am reluctant to take counsel from a man who professes a disdain for all sentiment." The words slipped out before he could stop them. They seemed to visibly affect Holmes; his head jerked up though he offered no rebuttal. He looked away after a moment. It was this lack of response that caused Watson to regret his words. He shook his head, disgusted at his own lack of compassion. "I'm sorry Holmes, that was uncalled for. It's been a long day."

Holmes met his gaze steadily. "Yes, it has," he agreed, a decided chill in his voice.

Thoroughly chastened, Watson managed a conciliatory smile. "There's nothing more to be done here. They'll take good care of her... the very best. Time for us to leave Holmes. A bit of Mrs. Hudson's supper and a good brandy is what we need. I'd like to recheck your hands before you retire."

To this Holmes only arched his brow and without a word, turned on heel and strode out the door. Watson caught up to him at the curb as he was hailing a hansom. The ride back to Baker Street was passed in uncomfortable silence.

»»««

BAKER STREET - Next morning

Watson slid into his chair at the empty breakfast table and frowned; there was only one place setting on it – his. As he reached to remove the silver dome from the breakfast tray, his eyes drifted toward Holmes' bedroom door. It was closed. An empty bottle of brandy and a glass sat on the table next his armchair, the ashtray was overflowing. The black velvet ribbon was looped over the arm of the chair. A slight frown creased Watson's brow – *he must have finished it after I changed the dressing on his hands and retired for the night.* He looked up at Mrs. Hudson who was bustling about clearing empty glasses.

"Is he up yet? Have you heard him?"

She paused in her straightening and smiled. "Up? Why he's been up for hours now... out and about... said I was to tell you not to wait on him for breakfast."

"Out?" "But where?"

But before she could answer, a familiar step sounded in the hall and as the door opened, Holmes entered accompanied by a whiff of acrid smoke that clung to his clothes. Watson half-rose from his chair, more than a little alarmed while Mrs. Hudson crossed to the window and opened it.

"Where on earth have you been at this hour?"

"Fern Hall... or what remains of it." Holmes fumbled with his overcoat and after a few moments of fumbling, as he was hindered by his bandages, managed to shrug out of it. He dropped it on the floor where Mrs. Hudson quickly retrieved it and wrinkling her nose at the smell, carried it over and laid in on the sill of the open window.

"What? Why?" Watson's frown increased when he noticed that the dressing on Holmes hands were blackened with what appeared to be soot and ash.

Holmes ignored the question for the moment and settled at the table where he attempted to pour a cup of tea until Watson came to his aid. He took a sip and then carefully reached into his pocket where he withdrew a silk handkerchief. "For this," he replied quietly as he unwrapped the parcel, "Fortunately, Lestrade was smart enough to post a guard at the site to prevent looting."

Watson looked down, his eyes mirroring disbelief as they came to rest on Edwina's lapel watch. "Dear God, how on earth did you find it?" The emeralds were covered in soot as was the silver case of the watch, the ribbons had burned away, but it was mostly intact.

Holmes carefully picked up the watch and began to gently clean off the soot and ash with one of Mrs. Hudson's good linen napkins. "I knew that she is almost never without it. I thought perhaps she may have pinned it to her wrap, but it wasn't there when I found her. It most likely dropped off during the fire. I searched the library area near the bookcase where I found her and there it was, buried in the soot and ashes. Coincidentally, not too far from where they found Gretchen Pennington, or what was left of her."

A look of compassion clouded Watson's face. "Poor woman... horrible way to die."

Holmes eyes grew cold - hard. "I would not waste any sympathy on her. Miserable witch, she set the fire Watson. The staff heard them arguing earlier in the evening... the signs were unmistakable... she intended to destroy Fern Hall Watson and Edwina with it."

Watson shook his head. "But why Holmes?"

Holmes shook his head, his eyes focused on the watch. "I find the machinations of most women unfathomable Watson. Who can say for sure what lurks in their hearts or mind at any given moment." He paused for moment, staring down at the watch as he opened it. Part of the photograph on the inside had burned away, only Katerina Schraeder remained, her dress slightly scorched and blackened. Little Julian fared far worse; mostly burned away, only his face remained. "Jealousy perhaps," he murmured as he cleaned the soot from the photograph.

"Jealousy... why?"

Holmes shrugged. "Again, the mind of a woman... but I suspect the aunt felt threatened. She had her brother all to herself all these years and then suddenly she had to share him with a daughter... and one she found willful and troublesome. She resented the wife. It stands to reason she would resent the daughter. And then to add fuel to the fire, she blamed Edwina for Pennington's arrest and the loss of the family home. Add a good dose of religious zealotry and it was a tragedy waiting to happen. Only I was too shortsighted to realize the danger." He lowered his head for a moment. "I will take this to her this afternoon. She shouldn't be without it," he murmured and then lapsed into silence. After a moment, he crossed over to his library and began rummaging through the books.

Watson watched him with a curious expression. "What... what are you doing?"

"Selecting reading material."

"Reading material? Holmes, she is unconscious. The drugs they are giving her for pain are keeping her in a stupor. I think you are overestimating her recuperative powers."

"And I think you are underestimating the power of the mind Watson. The Viennese have been doing numerous studies on the ability of the unconscious - subconscious mind to grasp and hear. It has been shown that the reading of mentally stimulating material as well as calm conversation, has a positive effect on the patient. It may even help them regain their awareness." He paused in his rummaging and pulled a short hand-bound volume from the shelf. "Ahh, here we go. Should do nicely... stimulating but light enough."

Watson stared at the slim book and couldn't help but smile on noting the title. *Practical Handbook to Bee Culture with some Observations upon the Segregation of the Queen. S Holmes.* "A book you've written on bees."

"Well, a first draft really... have not submitted for publication yet. A bit rough still but the foundation is solid... and... and... Why are you smiling? You find this amusing?"

Watson shook his head. "No, no. I'm sure it's a wonderful book...but... well... it's about bees and..."

"Yes, of course it's about bees. Why does that surprise you? What would you read if it were Miss Morstan?"

Watson frowned. "Well, it wouldn't be about bees. Perhaps a bit of poetry or more likely letters I had written to her... but mostly, I would talk to her and tell her how I felt. How much I loved her. How much I needed her to fight because I needed her in my life. That's what I would do."

Holmes was quiet for a moment, his eyes focused on the book in his hand. "Well, I am not you and Eddy has a very scientific mind, she will appreciate this."

Watson sighed heavily. "Perhaps, but she's also a woman. A woman who has professed a deep love for you. What I am saying to you is that if ever there was a time for you to lower your guard and say what is truly in your heart, it is now. You may not have another chance Holmes."

Holmes looked up, his face suddenly pale. "What are you saying Watson? Is there something you are not telling me?"

Watson shook his head. "No, no. I am not saying this to alarm you but you must face the facts. She is gravely injured Holmes. Her burns severe, and if she..." he paused and then quickly amended his words as disapproval clouded Holmes' face. "When she recovers, she will be forever changed... perhaps maimed...her extremities... her feet were terribly burned... there will undoubtedly be tissue necrosis... and her face was damaged as well. She will bear those scars for the rest of her life... both the physical and the emotional. So, in light of that, I am not convinced on how much comfort a book about bees will provide."

"You see no value in a book about incredibly resourceful and valiant creatures?" Holmes voice was sharp.

Watson uttered a heavy sigh and ran a hand through his hair. "All I am suggesting is that maybe something more personal would be of greater comfort." His words were met with icy silence and in the end, he threw up his hands in surrender. "Do as you wish – you always do." He picked up his coat and pulled it on, reaching for his hat. "We should get a move on then if you're coming. Mary will be getting off shift soon. I'll call for a hansom."

Holmes lingered a few moments in front of the bookcase. His eyes drifted down to the book in his hands. To him, it seemed the best of the lot. With a sigh, he slowly pocketed it and then followed Watson outside to where a hansom waited.

»»««

LONDON HOSPITAL - Half past 2

Mary Morstan leaned down and gently straightened the gauze drape over the sleeping woman's face. At the rustle in the doorway, she raised up and turned in the direction of the sound.

"Are you going to come in then or just loiter in the doorway?" she scolded with a smile.

"If it's all right..." Holmes murmured; still he hesitated in the doorway moving to the side allowing another nurse to enter.

"Well, either in or out but we can't leave the door open all day. She needs quiet. The noises from the hall are distracting. So then make your choice."

He nodded and then stepped inside, shutting the door behind him. He took a few tentative steps forward and then stopped his face ashen as he stared at the motionless figure in the bed.

"You can come closer... come sit... it will be all right," she reassured kindly. "She's just had another dose of morphine so I'm afraid she's drifted off again. But if you'd like to come and sit..." she suggested as she pulled over a chair and set it next to the bed. "You can read to her or even just talk... she may not respond... but I've heard it can be very therapeutic.... and..."

Holmes arched his brow and slowly approached. "You've been reading the Viennese," he remarked with a sly smile.

Mary blushed and managed a nod. "John's medical journals. I sneak a look every now and then but don't you tell him... please...." She paused for a moment as she smoothed the blankets on the bed. "It is a bit of a sore point," she admitted and then added, somewhat bitterly, "he thinks they are beyond my comprehension."

Holmes approached quietly and shook his head. "It's not that at all. He is fully aware of your capabilities. If you ask me, I believe he's afraid."

"Afraid?" Of what?" exclaimed Watson's voice from the door.

Mary froze, a look of dismay on her face as she fumbled for words.

"That you will be late again for tea. My fault of course... as usual," interjected Holmes with a wry grin.

"Well, we might come to think of it. Are you nearly finished then?" pressed Watson as he took out his pocket watch and checked the time.

Mary flashed a look of gratitude in Holmes' direction. "I will finish much sooner if you gentlemen leave me to my duties. Now Holmes, take a seat and let me take a look at your hands before I leave."

Holmes chuckled a bit and settled into the chair she had pulled out for him but shook his head. "Dr. Watson changed the dressing this morning, but if you're unsure of his handiwork..."

Her eyes flashed warningly. "No. I am sure it's quite fine," she replied quickly.

Holmes suppressed a laugh but said nothing and turned his attention back to the sleeping girl. He leaned in closer, his expression grim. "The gauze on her face?"

Mary compressed her lips wondering how long it would be before he noticed. "Her left side was badly burned...the drape is necessary to keep the skin protected."

Holmes eyes studied the gauze drape. He could just make out the burnt and blistered skin of her cheek beneath the cloth. The mere sight of it rattled him. But what shook him even more was when he noticed it was all gone. His eyes widened in shock. "What have you done?" he cried, his face a mixture of horror and dismay. It was gone — her hair — cropped raggedly to where nothing remained below her ears. And then he remembered, the shears on the tray of the nurse who had passed him.

Mary shook her head, her eyes full of sorrow. "It had to be done to properly dress her burns. So much of it was damaged as well... burnt... and the hair that wasn't burnt, well, we couldn't just leave it so uneven in patches. So, we cut it off as well so when it begins to grow back, it will all be even."

Her words died out after a moment however for it seemed to her that Holmes seemed not to be listening any longer and was instead staring at a cigar box that sat on the bedside table. "Was she awake then... when you... Does she know?" he murmured.

"I don't know," Mary admitted quietly, "it was just after we gave her a second dose of morphine."

Watson drew closer and reaching out, lightly pressed Holmes' shoulder. "It's only hair," he soothed. It will heal — grow again — much faster than her skin will recover."

Holmes nodded and forced a bleak smile, his eyes drifting over to the sleeping woman's face. "Yes, I know... but... well... it's not that she is vain... never vain, but she is proud of her hair. She... she hates to pin it at all... drives her Aunt mad. She has the loveliest hair, Eddy does... long locks... auburn... ties it back with a black ribbon... also has this sharp little homburg as well, a satin band, green feather... her fathers'... she..." His words abruptly died out and he took a deep breath, his eyes now focused on the cigar box. "Is that it then?" he asked with a nod towards the box. "May I see?"

Mary nodded and retrieved the box which she gently placed in his bandaged hands. Holmes carefully opened the box and stared down at the two luxuriant locks of hair. "May... may I take these then, to keep them for her until she is well enough?" His bandaged fingers hovered momentarily over the locks and then he quickly closed the lid.

Mary smiled. "I know she would insist on it."

Satisfied, he made sure the lid was closed tightly and then slipped the box into his inner pocket. Once more, he took out his book and as he slowly opened the cover, Mary looked to John Watson and smiled inquiringly, "I believe you were taking me to tea then?"

Watson seemed a bit startled. "Tea... yes of course but..."

She shook her head. "No buts... it's time that we leave." And after a final fluff of the pillows, she smiled in Holmes direction. "Good afternoon Holmes, enjoy your visit and should you need anything, there are nurses in the corridors just ring the bell on the table, they will come quickly. There's a small glass with water as well, and a sponge should she wake and be thirsty," instructed Mary, as she took Dr. Watson firmly by the arm and left the room.

As the door shut behind them, Holmes turned back to Edwina, surprised to see a glint of emerald from bleary, half-opened eyes.

"Eddy... are you awake then?" He slid his chair closer, peering into her face.

There was silence for a moment and then he saw her lips begin to purse. "H... Holmes..." was all she could manage.

He leaned over her and gently adjusted the blanket across her shoulders. "Yes, the very same. Don't strain your voice... it's fine not to speak... if it's too difficult..."

Her eyes followed the movement of his hands. "H...Hurt..." she gasped.

He could see that she was staring at his bandaged hands. "A bit... it's nothing. I've done worse...with chemicals..." And then he froze - alarmed as he noticed tears welling in the corner of her eyes. "Please don't cry," he whispered and quickly took out his silk pocket square. As his hand reached for the gauze drape, a look of sheer panic crossed her face and her bandaged hands reached out and grabbed hold of his with surprising strength.

"No... don't...look..." she begged as she tried to turn her face away from him. She was only partially successful and as she felt the silk fabric gently dabbing at the tears, she closed her eyes in concentration and forced out the words... "H...H...horrible... monstrous..."

The words left him dumbfounded on realizing that she was referring to herself and for a moment he couldn't speak. "No... never," he rasped after a moment and then added, "I don't ever want to hear that again, do you understand me? You will heal... it will take time... but it will happen."

She didn't reply and only managed a weak nod of her head. As he lifted more of the gauze off her face, she turned her face away once more. "Better to have left behind. I think...why... why not?" she murmured with great effort after a moment.

And this time the words left him filled with horror – her meaning all too clear. Once again, he couldn't find the words at first but then after a moment managed a smile and with the utmost gentleness, smoothed back what remained of her hair.

"Because the world would be so much more ordinary without you..."

Her head slowly turned back towards him and for the first time, she managed a faint smile. Her eyes drifted to the slim book that was sitting on the table.

"Book? About?"

He visibly relaxed and returned her smile. "Bees..."

She seemed puzzled at first. "Bees....Bumble...?" she asked after a moment.

"And honey... mostly honeybees...the particulars... about the social order - the structure of the hive and..." He paused, a look of alarm on his face as she had started to make an odd little choking noise until he realized that she was laughing. "Are you all right?"

Edwina managed a nod... "Sorry..." she managed with a cough.

Relief swept over him and he sighed. "No, it is quite all right. I was going to read to you about the bees but perhaps I can find something else."

Her hand reached out and gently grasped his. "No, no please... I want to hear... about the bees... on the Downs is it?... Your property... where you went to raise them."

A look of surprise crossed his face for he couldn't recall having told her about the farm in Sussex Downs. "Yes, how did you know?"

She looked a little embarrassed. "I... I overhead Dr. Watson talking to Lestrade not long ago. He was complaining that you were going to retreat to the country one day; abandon everyone and everything to go and build your blasted aviary... but... I don't think that is the right word... is it?"

Holmes made a face and shook his head. "Apiary... he never does get the word right... and who is he to complain when he very soon will abandon us all to go off and marry?"

Edwina managed a smile again though he could tell it caused her some discomfort. "Well, to be fair, I don't think the comparison is proportionate..."

Holmes rolled his eyes looking unconvinced. "Well, in any case, that is the plan. When the time comes ... off to the Downs and build the apiary."

"Sounds lovely... so peaceful," she murmured wistfully and then reaching out once more, nudged his hand. "Do you suppose that maybe one day... could come and visit you... and the bees?"

And as he looked on this woman, swathed in bandages, her hair chopped off raggedly, blistering cheek hidden by gauze, he felt a lump rise in his throat. She had never before seemed so fragile to him or transcendent. His bandaged hand clumsily grasped hers. "I would be disappointed if you did not." He lapsed into silence unsure of what else to say, suddenly uncomfortable with the emotions welling within. It was then he remembered the watch in his pocket wrapped in Mrs. Hudson's linen. He reached into his pocket and while she looked on in disbelief, unwrapped it and then pinned it on her pillow. "I thought you might like this back... "

Her eyes widened with disbelief.

"How did you find it?"

He shrugged as if it was nothing at all. "It's all in the search - if one is methodical... I was bound to find it sooner or later."

"Thank you... thank... I... you are a most extraordinary man..." she blubbered, her eyes filling with tears once more.

Holmes offered her his handkerchief and then gently dabbed at her eyes on realizing that she found it difficult to make such delicate hand movements due to the bandages.

"Should I still read then?" he asked when her tears had finally subsided.

She managed a nod and a smile. "A very good idea..." she murmured and then took a deep breath and closed her eyes, allowing herself to drift off on the sound of his voice.

»»««

ONE WEEK LATER

The afternoon sun was warm on her face and Edwina breathed in the sweet smell of meadow grass as they climbed the rise towards the cluster of hives which sat behind the tidy cotswold stone cottage. Holmes was speaking. The words were indistinct, but it didn't matter, the sound of his voice filled her with warmth as did the pressure of his hand gently holding onto hers.

"Bees..." she murmured shifting on her pillow with eyes still closed, turning her face to the late afternoon sun as it peeked in through the open hospital window.

"Bees? Is that the drivel he has been reading to you?"

The voice jolted her awake. It was not a voice she had expected to hear nor one that she welcomed. She forced her eyes open only to find the Professor seated in the chair next to her bed. He was leafing through the book on bee culture that Holmes had left on the bedside table.

She moved her lips to call out but her throat was dry and managed only a slight croak. Her eyes darted to the table to where the small bell to call the nurses should have been; it was gone.

"Are you looking for this? Shall I ring for tea then?" he taunted. "Pity, I'm afraid it won't garner much attention, seems the clapper has gone missing." As he spoke, he turned the bell over to show her that indeed the clapper was missing. With a grin and a flourish of his other hand, he uncurled his palm to reveal the missing clapper.

Her eyes flashed. "What do you want?" she managed to wheeze after a few moments.

The Professor shrugged his shoulders and set the bell back on the table. He leaned in closer for a better look.

"Poor dear... quite the mess you are.," he remarked with a shake of his head. His words had more a ring of disapproval than pity or compassion.

"Why are you here?" she croaked once more, her fingers beginning to tremble as they clutched onto the blanket. She did her best to conceal her fear.

"Ahh, what do I want? Well, I am here to tell you a tale as it were. One I think you will find much more interesting than some nonsense about bees. But first, would you like some water? You look thirsty dearest. You should drink. You must keep your fluid level up, it is vital for cell regeneration," and before she could protest, he had taken a glass, filled it with water and lifted the gauze from her face. As he pressed the glass to her lips, she sputtered a bit... choking at first and clumsily pushed the glass away spilling water onto the bedclothes. She hadn't tried to drink from a glass in quite some time; the nurses had mostly used a moist sponge or a small glass pipette when she required more than a few drops of water. The Professor however was insistent and with unexpected gentleness, grasped her shoulders and raised her up until she could lean against the headboard. He refilled the glass and held it to her lips until she began to drink. It took her a few moments but soon she was able to nearly drain the glass.

"I knew you could do it... mustn't let them coddle you... it'll make you weak," he commented as he set the glass down on the table.

Edwina didn't reply and watched him uneasily as he withdrew a bundle of what appeared to be letters from his inner pocket. She glanced towards the closed door knowing her voice was too weak for them to hear if she cried out. "What do you want from me? Why can you not leave me be?"

An odd light entered his eyes as he fixed his gaze on hers; he settled back in the chair.

"I am here because it's time my dear..."

"Time... time for what?" she murmured as she cast a desperate glance towards the door. *Any other day the nurses were in and out so many times she could hardly sleep... not today...*

The Professor said nothing for a moment and then smiled. "The time has come for you to know the truth..."

"Truth!" she sputtered, "Truth about what? And why should I believe anything you say?"

Again, there was silence. He arched his brow and ran a hand through the fringe of silver hair that ringed the high dome of his forehead. "The truth Edwina about your legacy. And you will believe me, because we share a

389

secret you and I, about that day on the lake and poor weak little Julian. A secret that I do not believe you want known."

The words took her breath away, and she began to cough as she struggled to regain her composure. "What do you want from me?" she gasped after a moment, trying to blot the memory of that day from her mind. *Julian's pale little face, his expression of utter confusion and fear, staring up at her as he sank beneath the surface of the lake.*

The Professor leaned forward and adjusted the pillows beneath her. "Only that you listen and after you have heard, we shall discuss the next step."

She looked towards the still closed door and nodded her head in resignation. Her eyes settled on the letters in his hand and as she studied the script on the envelope, she turned ashen. "You are going to read from those?"

"No doubt you recognize the hand that wrote them."

Her mouth was suddenly dry and for a few moments, she could not find her voice. She did recognize the writing instantly upon seeing it, as that of her mothers. She took a deep breath and tried to push down the fear that she felt welling within. "How do you have these?"

The Professor, looking somewhat smug, held one of the envelopes closer so she could read the address. "Because they were sent to me."

Disbelief mingled with contempt clouded her face. "Why... why would mother correspond with you? And... how do I know that what you are reading is what is in the letters?"

The Professor smiled and this time, it was almost benevolent. "Because my dear, when I have finished reading from them I will give them to you and you can read them for yourself. I have no reason to lie to you. All will be revealed, and then you will understand that I have only come here with your best interests at heart. So tell me then, shall I proceed?"

Edwina was silent for a moment and then nodded. And though she had the distinct feeling that she would not enjoy what he had to say, it seemed the only reasonable course of action. She slid back down onto the pillow and pulled the covers up higher around her for reassurance.

Holmes stared at the nurse in astonishment as he stood in the corridor outside the room, awkwardly clutching a large spray of white lilies of the valley in his bandaged hands. "What do you mean she won't see me...? Is she ill? Has her condition declined?" There was an edge of apprehension beneath the indignation in his voice.

The young woman took a deep breath and smoothed her apron nervously but held her ground against the tall, lean man with piercing eyes as he towered over her. "I cannot say sir... all I know is that Miss Morstan sent me out to advise...."

"Miss Morstan... Mary is she in with her? I will speak to her then... immediately..." he demanded, his voice rising sufficiently to cause several of the staff passing in the hall to pause and look to see what was going on.

The young nurse became flustered, struggling to regain control of the situation; the door abruptly opened and out strode Mary Morstan a stern look replacing her usual gracious smile. She narrowed her eyes and pointed

390

towards the bench in the anteroom, where John Watson sat on a bench, watching the events unfold, a smile of amusement on his face.

"Mr. Holmes, if you do not lower your voice and go and sit down, I will have you ejected from this hospital."

He stepped back, surprised at the formality of the address as well as the fierceness of her response. He pursed his lips to object but then seemed to reconsider. Apprehension clouded his face and his chin sunk down a bit.

"Tell me please, has she taken a turn for the worse?"

Mary's face suffused with compassion and she reached out, gently pressing his forearm. "Physically she is much stronger, but her mood has turned black, morose. You know about the loss of a few of her toes."

He compressed his lips tightly and nodded. "Watson had mentioned there was some necrosis...that there might be a need for amputation."

"Two of the minor appendages on each foot... early this morning. The good news is once she gets acclimated it should not significantly affect her balance, though she may require the use of a cane in the beginning."

The corner of his mouth twitched at the news. "The source of her depression then?" he pressed.

Mary shrugged, her face drawn with concern. "I... I am not sure. She has borne so much at this point it may be cumulative. The night duty nurse informed me that she was very restless last night, tossing and turning, whimpering in her sleep. Something is troubling her. There was a name, Julian I believe. Was that not her brother? The one who drowned?"

Holmes nodded, his expression tinged with worry. "Yes. They were both very young. She has expressed a sense of guilt over the event before but not in quite some time," he replied somberly. "The morphine, the dosage, you must be careful... too much can..."

"Yes, I know Holmes, too much can deepen depression. We are being very cautious. I assure you, it is not the morphine. Something else is weighing heavily on her mind. Something she cannot bring herself to speak of."

For a few moments, neither one spoke. Mary finally broke the silence.

"You must let us care for her Holmes. It will be a long journey and not an easy one. We will take good care of her."

He said nothing at first and then managed a slight nod. "I understand. I... You will tell her then that I was here and that I enquired after her?"

A knowing smile tugged at her lips. "Yes, of course. Shall I take these then?" Mary asked as she reached out and took the flowers. As she studied the flowers, her expression continued to soften. "These are lovely Holmes, certain to lift her spirits. They will look splendid on the bureau next to the others."

He had begun to turn away perhaps uncomfortable at having been caught in the midst of what could be seen a purely sentimental action and then paused in mid-step. "Others?" he repeated, his expression suddenly tense. There had been no flowers in the room the previous day when he had visited.

"Yes, a lovely bunch of roses and purple orchids... quite exotic looking."

"Did you see who brought them? Was it Moran?" he pressed sharply. *That in itself could account for the downturn in Edwina's mood.*

Mary shook her head, a frown creasing her brow. "No, I do not know. It was after my shift had ended."

"The visitor's log?"

Mary shook her head. "You may check at the duty station, but I fear it may not be of any use. Signing the visitor's log is not a requirement as you know yourself having never signed in."

"Bad news indeed," murmured Holmes. His expression became determined. "From this point on, I insist on being apprised of all visitors other than myself and Dr. Watson. In fact, visitation should be limited only to myself, Dr. Watson and medical staff as necessary. Anyone outside those parameters would need approval."

"Approval? By whom?" she exclaimed though she already knew the answer before she asked. She took a deep breath, tempering her indignation. "Surely you are over reacting. This is a public institution, we have an open visitation policy. We cannot just bar visitors without a basis for doing so."

"I have grave concerns with regard to her state of mind and her safety. What more of a reason do you need?"

A flush of color shaded her cheeks, and Mary drew herself up proudly, straightening her apron and cap. "I sincerely hope you are not insinuating that we do not take our responsibilities seriously Mr. Holmes. This hospital... our staff are committed to the well-being of every patient. The wards are staffed day and night. Edwina is checked on frequently. What could possibly happen?"

Holmes compressed his lips tightly preparing to rebut but was interrupted by a light touch on his arm. He glanced to the side to see Watson standing next to him.

"You will not win this argument, my friend," warned the Doctor in a hushed voice, with a wisdom born of many lost battles.

Mary stood firm, hands planted on her hips and nodded. "As I said before, you are in my place of business now. Please allow us to do our jobs without interference." And then perhaps regretting the harshness of her words, her tone softened. She reached out and gently pressed his forearm. "We will take the very best care of her Holmes... nothing will happen," she promised. "Now if you will pardon me, I have patients to attend to," she finished then strode away down the corridor.

"Well, seeing as how we've been dismissed, we should leave. Shall I call for a hansom?" suggested Watson after a few moments of unbearable silence during which time Holmes remained standing in the corridor staring at the closed door. Finally, after what seemed like an eternity to Watson, he heaved a sigh of resignation and nodded, striding out the exit and down the steps to the curb. As they climbed into a hansom, Watson studied his friend's face.

"What is it Holmes? I don't understand. Something has you spooked. Why are you so worried? As Mary said, she's growing stronger with each passing day... she's healing."

"She refused to see me Watson. That has never happened before. Even when she was upset or angry, she always faced me, she never withdrew..."

392

Watson frowned considering the information. "Well, perhaps she's feeling self-conscious about her burns or perhaps she just was not feeling well enough for a visit. She has been through a lot in a short period of time not to mention the fact that once she is well enough to leave the hospital, she has no place to go. The truth of having no home, no relatives, must weigh heavily on her mind. The workhouse looms as an option – perhaps a viable one. At least she will have a roof over head, regular meals and the opportunity to learn a trade. I know you find this disturbing... but isn't it preferable to her begging on the streets or working Brick Lane to survive? Of course, there is also the possibility that Moran will make good on his offer of marriage after her period of mourning has ended."

"Hardly a favorable alternative," muttered Holmes as he leaned back against the seat, lips drawn in apparent disdain.

Watson couldn't help but smile. "Yes well, I wonder if perhaps you are letting your personal dislike of the Colonel color your opinion on what's best for Edwina. Thus far, he seems to be the only one who is offering a feasible solution to her predicament. Unless of course you know of anyone else?"

Holmes frowned darkly and turned his head to gaze out the window. "She doesn't need a husband Watson. She is an intelligent woman extremely capable of navigating her own path in life. What she needs is the opportunity to provide for herself not some egotistical martinet to tell her what to think and do, to manipulate her."

Watson couldn't help but suppress a laugh and shook his head. "Ahh, manipulation. Interesting choice of word... and you, of course, would not have any experience in that area."

Holmes' face contorted with anger. Watson leaned back in his seat bracing for the sharp rebuke that was sure to come but instead there was only the sound of the clatter of the horses' hooves and creak of the cab as it made its way down Marylebone. Holmes turned his head away, eyes focused on the dim streets of London as they passed by. As the hansom pulled to the curb, Holmes leaned forward and grasped the handle. He climbed from the carriage and then paused a moment, glancing back over his shoulder, his face pale and worn.

"I have made grave errors in this case Watson. Errors that have caused considerable harm. If you think I am unaware of this, you are quite mistaken," he advised, and then vanished through the entrance to 221 leaving Watson at the curb.

When Watson entered the flat, Holmes had already retreated to the sanctuary of his armchair - glass of amontillado in hand. Watson crossed to the sideboard and took up the decanter, pouring himself a glass. With a sigh, he pulled up his chair and settled across from Holmes, his expression full of regret.

"My words were unduly harsh, for that I am sorry. I know you care. That the affection you feel for her is greater than you will ever admit. You demonstrated that by risking your life, however, the fact remains the workhouse is a solution, as is marriage to Moran. Thus far, I have not heard you offer an alternative. What will you do Holmes? What is your solution?"

Holmes only response was to lean back in his armchair his bandaged fingers resting lightly on the black velvet ribbon which dangled from the arm of the chair. After a few moments of silence, he shook his head and gazed off into the flames of the hearth. "It is with great difficulty that I confess I have nothing concrete to offer. I shall reach out once more to Lady Montague — perhaps enough time has passed — and through her connections a position as governess could be secured. Or perhaps my contacts abroad could find her a position at University as an assistant or researcher. It does seem the French and Viennese have progressed further in their acceptance of women in academia than we have. She would be an asset to any institution that took her on."

Watson nodded in agreement reflecting on his words. But after a moment, he sighed a bit and leaned forward in his chair. "All well and good... opportunities for her to make a living and put a roof over her head... but there is more needed than that Holmes. What of her emotional well-being?"

"I don't understand."

Watson uttered a short laugh and shook his head. "Yes, I believe you do. Why else would you be so troubled by her decline in mood. You know perfectly well what I am speaking of. Now more than ever, she needs someone to offer encouragement, reassurance, stability. She needs a protector, a guardian, a role traditionally fulfilled by a husband."

"Moran is an idiotic brute. He would be a far greater hindrance to her than a boon," growled Holmes peevishly, reaching for the decanter to refresh his drink.

Watson smiled and held forth his glass for Holmes to refill. "I wasn't thinking of Moran..."

The sherry splashed into his glass and then abruptly ceased in mid-stream as Holmes stopped pouring staring at Watson in disbelief.

"If you are suggesting..." Holmes words trailed off and unable to finish the thought, he sank back in his chair and drained his glass. "You should retire for the night Doctor," he advised coolly. "I fear the turmoil of the day has muddled your mind. You know my thoughts on this subject – my views on marriage."

Watson grunted in exasperation. "Yes, yes I know... that you shall never marry... for fear of biasing your judgement. That marriage, romantic entanglement, is in direct opposition to all that is logical. And yet, against all reason and logic, you ran into a burning building on the verge of collapse, knowingly placing yourself in mortal danger, to rescue a woman you will only admit to being... 'fond of'."

Holmes was silent for a moment and then shrugged, peering into the depths of his glass. "She is a most extraordinary woman," he admitted.

"I agree and to her great credit or detriment, which, I have not completely decided, she finds you extraordinary as well. Two like-minded souls... non-conformists... surely together you could find contentment."

Holmes choked back a bitter laugh and drained his glass. "Is that the goal then? Contentment? A slow descent into dullness and mediocrity?"

"It does not have to be that way," protested Watson, "My God, that woman... what did she do to you to make you so bitter, so cynical?"

Holmes flinched but would not meet Watson's gaze. "If you are referring to Irene Adler, I would caution you that a comparison between the two is erroneous. The only similarity they share is their sex."

"Yes, exactly my point," exclaimed Watson. "So, what is it you fear? Edwina has shown you nothing but love and devotion. I believe she understands you better than most."

Holmes grew quiet and then after a moment shrugged. He rose from the chair and crossed to the mantle, where he placed the ribbon, arranging it carefully next to the sketch and the small box containing the locks of her hair. "Perhaps... perhaps... the fear is more that I would fail her, be a disappointing companion at best. She deserves better."

The revelation left Watson astonished and for a few moments – he couldn't think of a suitable response. With a nod of commiseration, he drained his glass and rose, crossing to the mantle to join Holmes. "A fear we all share. A fear that is mostly unfounded. But you will never know unless you try Holmes." Watson's eyes drifted to the objects that Holmes had arranged so painstakingly. A shrine... that is what it called to mind.

Holmes smiled firmly. "Then it shall always remain a mystery. But this I do know Watson, this conversation has run its course. Now, should you care to discuss another topic, I shall entertain it. If not, I bid you good night. Tomorrow I will contact Lady Montague. You are welcome to join me if you care to, if not, I shall meet up with you at the hospital in the late afternoon."

There was no mistaking the dismissal in his voice. With a sigh, Watson nodded and taking his sherry, retreated to his own rooms. As the door closed after him, Holmes once more retreated to his chair to reflect on all that had been said and plan his entreaty to Lady Montague.

»»««

The following day - London Hospital - Late afternoon

Watson waited at the top of the granite stairs that fronted the hospital entrance, pacing restlessly, shading his eyes from the late afternoon sun as he peered down the road. As a hansom pulled to the curb, he took a deep breath and adjusted his cuffs watching as Holmes, clad in formal dress, top hat in hand, climbed out and surmounted the stairs. As he grew closer, Watson's anxiety increased. He surmised by the Detective's grim expression that the meeting with Lady Montague had not gone well. He prepared himself, gathering his thoughts for the news he had to share was troubling as well.

"Ahh, Watson. 4:00 pm precisely. Your promptness is appreciated. I trust your afternoon has gone well... hopefully better than mine," announced the Detective as he reached the top of the stairs. Watson, at a loss for words, managed a non-committal grunt and fell in step with Holmes as he strode down the corridor towards Edwina's room. As they rounded the corner and the door loomed up ahead, Watson seemed to find his voice.

"Wait!" he cried, reaching out to grasp Holmes' forearm. "There is something I must tell you before you go in."

Holmes however did not pause. "Well, what is it then?" he muttered impatiently, increasing his pace as he caught sight of the door – it was partially open. Watson scrambled to keep up. Once more he reached out and grabbed Holmes' arm, this time much more firmly.

"Please, before you go in..."

"What? What is it Watson? Cannot it not wait until after?" His words abruptly died out for as he pushed open the door the sight before him made him stop in his tracks. A young nurse - the one who had forbidden his entry the previous day, was changing the sheets on the bed. An empty bed. Edwina Schraeder was nowhere in sight. As Holmes surveyed the room, his face drained of all color. He moved in quickly, a look of disbelief on his face.

"What is the meaning of this? Where is she?"

The nurse jumped at the sound of his voice and clutched the pillow in front of her, eyes wide with fear...

"Answer me," he demanded, moving further into the room.

"Holmes, you must stay calm," urged Watson, moving to stand next to the young woman, who was clearly frightened.

"Calm... I am calm... I just want my question answered. Where is she?"

As Watson began to explain, the door opened once more and Mary Morstan entered looking weary and apprehensive. Holmes moved forward, his face raw with anguish and disbelief.

"You told me she was healing, getting stronger. What's happened? Tell me!"

She looked to Watson in bewilderment. "Have you not told him?"

"I hadn't the chance."

Holmes glanced up sharply. "Will you not just tell me what has happened! Where's Eddy?"

Mary took a deep breath. "She's gone..." and then seeing the look of horror on Holmes' face, quickly stepped forward and grabbed his arm gently. "No, no, not in that sense," she added quickly. "She is healing, getting physically stronger. But she is gone Holmes and I'm afraid we do not know exactly where."

He stepped back, his expression tense. "How could you let this happen? How could you let her be taken away?"

A flush of color rose to Mary's cheeks and she drew herself up proudly. "No one let her be taken away. As I said, despite her injuries and needing the occasional use of a wheelchair or cane, she is quite on the mend. She signed herself out Holmes, and according to the night staff, although she seemed tired, was quite lucid. She left in the company of an elderly gentlemen, quite distinguished looking, who coincidentally paid her hospital charges in full."

Comprehension darkened Holmes' face. "The Professor," he muttered, and then in an exasperation exclaimed, "And you just let him carry her away! Where is this night duty nurse? I shall have a word."

"You will lower your voice Mr. Holmes. I remind you that this is a hospital we have the health of the patients to consider."

"Fine thing to remember that now," he snorted.

The color drained from Mary's face and she compressed her lips. "I understand that you are disturbed by this as am I, but need I remind you Mr. Holmes, this isn't a prison. If a patient feels well enough and the duty staff concurs, there is nothing to keep them here – particularly when no threat is perceived."

"And the hospital charges are paid." spat Holmes bitterly.

Mary Morstan stiffened visibly and as she pursed her lips to reply, Watson quickly stepped forward and placed himself in between them.

"Please, need I remind both of you that this... this bickering accomplishes nothing. Should we not just speak to the night duty nurse Holmes?"

Holmes said nothing for a few moments. He seemed disoriented and most of all, chastened. He avoided their gaze. Finally, he turned to face them, his expression apologetic.

"Thank you Watson, for being the voice of reason. Miss Morstan, I am at a loss to explain my lack of restraint. I have been unduly harsh with you and for that I... I..."

Before he could finish, Mary had crossed the room and without hesitation, wrapped her arms around him offering comfort while Watson looked on in astonishment. As she drew away, she smiled and gave his arm a reassuring squeeze, "One should never apologize for being human Holmes. I do understand. We are all concerned but I am sure that all will be well. Now, if you feel composed enough, I will take you to speak with the night duty nurse as she has just come on shift for this evening."

»»««

"Mayfair - Berkeley Square driver - with all due speed!" Holmes had barely opened the door to the hansom before he called out instructions.

As the hansom clattered off towards Mayfair, Watson leaned forward, a look of doubt on his face. "So, we are just going to show up at the Professor's? Is that the plan?"

Holmes leaned back against the cushions looking worn and uneasy. "Not much of a plan I admit."

"What about Lestrade? Should we not at least enlist his assistance?"

Holmes shook his head. "He has not put any stock in my suspicions regarding the Professor thus far. I doubt he will start now. Especially on hearing from the night duty nurse that Eddy left with him of her own volition and seemed lucid."

Watson frowned beneath his moustache. "Hardly a compelling cause for action," he agreed and then fell silent. After a moment, he ventured a look in

Holmes direction. "Have you considered," he began with great caution, "that perhaps you are mistaken and the Professor is merely reaching out to offer aid to the daughter of his former friend? There may be nothing sinister in this at all. The man is a respected academic Holmes – a Mathematics Professor; he has known the family for a long time."

Holmes stared at him, astonished. "You cannot seriously be suggesting that this is a mere act of charity? Have you forgotten Pennington's death? His so-called suicide and the death of Constable Jenkins? Have you forgotten that the link between them is the Professor?"

"I understand that you feel it is a link, but you have no proof Holmes."

"Feel!" sputtered Holmes with great indignation. "Mind your words Watson. I am making a logical..."

At this, Watson began to laugh and with a shake of his head, leaned forward. "My dear Holmes, whether you care to admit it or not, as of late, feeling, not logic has been the order of the day with you. It is the very reason why your hands are bandaged."

Holmes' lips moved as if to protest but he offered no response and merely turned his attention to the window. After a considerable silence had elapsed, he shrugged. "I concede that my actions of these past few days are as puzzling to me as to you. All I know is that I had no choice Watson. When I saw the house in flames and I knew she was inside, I could not just stand by. Inaction was not an option. I am at a loss as to what is happening to me Watson. What the devil is wrong with me?"

Watson smiled compassionately as he leaned forward. "Wrong? Some would say Holmes, that in this case, it is not a case of what is wrong but what is right."

His words however were not met with a smile of agreement. "This discussion has become tedious. We have reached our destination, are you coming along Dr. Watson?"

He had barely uttered the terse words as the hansom pulled to a stop across from the Georgian Townhouses that lined Berkeley Square. Without waiting for a response, Holmes flung open the door and climbed out from the carriage. He stood on the curb, eyes focused keenly on the row of elegant, nearly identical cream coloured townhouses that lined the block.

Watson scrambled from the hansom, catching up to him in the middle of the street as he was crossing, heading directly towards the third residence in from the corner.

"Wait... you just can't... but we don't even have a house number Holmes. How do you know which one?" panted Watson. He paused to catch his breath. "Dolan said he never saw the house number as they were always here at night. Should we not reconsider? They all look alike."

Holmes stopped abruptly as he reached the small iron gate of #3 Berkeley Street.

"Do they? As always Watson, you see but you do not observe. Look again."

Watson stared up at #3; it looked identical still in the fading light, until he caught the glint of a reflection from the roof of a free-standing structure in the side yard. He frowned and rubbed his eyes and then realized that the reflection was coming from panes of glass.

"A conservatory - #3 has a conservatory!" he exclaimed but then once more settled into a frown of bewilderment. "And, that is important why?

"The orchids in the room did you not see them?" The exasperation in Holmes' voice was unmistakable.

"I saw many flowers in the room... lilies..."

"Which I brought..."

"Yes... there were violets, from Mary & I... and roses..."

"From Moran; she hates those," grumbled Holmes.

"And yes, there were orchids - so? Oh, you believe the orchids are from the Professor?"

"Of course, they are from the Professor - who else is left? Besides, the orchids in her room were fresh. They were cultivated here but they are not a species native to England. China – Japan, that is where they originate. Exotics are difficult, requiring extraordinary care including a carefully controlled climate."

"Such as one might find in a conservatory!" exclaimed Watson joyfully as comprehension sunk in.

"Precisely."

As Watson studied the townhomes, his look of elation began to fade. "Wait, how do you know that the other buildings do not also have a conservatory? Perhaps located toward the back of the property hidden from our view?"

Holmes sighed heavily. "They very well might but not set up to cultivate Orchids."

"What? I don't understand..."

"Because of the positioning of the structure Watson. The best location is a north-south axis so that the sun travels the entire length of the structure as it moves from east to west, allowing for maximum sunlight. Also, the other plots have numerous shade trees. #3 does not. Shade trees would reduce the amount of sunlight, a necessary component for the cultivation of fragile orchids."

"Oh... yes... of course... makes sense," murmured Watson, somewhat embarrassed as it made perfect sense once it had been laid out for him.

"Delighted you finally agree. Now, are you coming?"

Watson stared at him, still uneasy. "So, you are really just going to go knock on the door?"

Holmes burst into laughter, his mouth curling with sarcasm. "The lights are on Watson, there is no need to be uncivilized, or would you prefer I just toss a brick through the window and climb in?" A this he strode through the gate and up the granite steps where he grabbed the gleaming brass Lion Head and knocked firmly on the door.

At the knock, several lights flared to life inside streaming down from th windows. Moments later, the door swung open and they were greeted by a mountain of a man with the battered face of a boxer; he was clad in the uniform of a butler. As Holmes nodded in greeting and reached into his breas pocket for his calling card, the man shook his head. "Your card is unnecessary Mr. Holmes, I know who you are. I was told to expect you and Dr. Watson." He moved to the side with surprising grace for his size and allowed them to enter the vestibule.

Holmes was momentarily surprised but recovered quickly. He cast a knowing glance in Watson's direction. "I wish to see the Professor. Please advise him of our arrival."

The butler smiled oddly. "The Professor had business to attend to and is not presently available Mr. Holmes. He did advise that you would be calling and that I should reassure you that all is well and the situation will become quite clear to you in due course."

"In due course... I see..." murmured Holmes. He glanced around the elegant vestibule, noting the marble statuary and old-world masters adorning the walls. The furnishings spoke of a refined taste, yet there was also a coldness to it that unsettled him. It spoke of a collector. It reminded him of a mausoleum.

"As the Professor is unavailable, I wish to see Miss Schraeder. Please advise her of my request."

The butler's smile began to fade. "You must be mistaken Mr. Holmes, there is no one here by that name."

A flush of color darkened Holmes face but he managed to suppress his irritation. "Edwina Schraeder, or perhaps she is known to you as Edwina Pennington. The young woman who was taken from the Royal London..."

The butler paused a moment and then shook his head. "I am sorry sir, again, there is no one here by that name."

Holmes stared at him. "Do you deny that she is here?" he cried, his voice beginning to rise in volume.

The butler, who had been stooping slightly, stood up to his full height, which Watson estimated to be somewhere near six feet seven inches. In any event, he towered over Holmes by at least 5 inches. He gave his vest a quick brush with his massive white gloved hand and fixed his gaze on the Detective. "I do not deny anything Mr. Holmes. I am merely stating that there is no lady here by either of those sur names."

To Watson, the matter was finished, at least for the moment but much to his astonishment, Holmes apparently did not agree as he made a sudden move towards the staircase.

"Mr. Holmes, that is ill-advised," growled the behemoth. "Now, I must insist both of you gentlemen leave as you are dangerously close to trespassing. If you do not, I shall be forced to call the authorities."

"If you must, you might ask for Inspector Lestrade," snorted Holmes already three stairs up. He did not progress much further however as the butler reached out and took a firm hold of his shoulder, dragging him back down the stairs. Watson, not having brought his pistol on this occasion, did the only thing he could think of and head-butted the giant in the side. He staggered back, the man was unmoved. It had been like hitting an ancient elm. But before the melee could progress any further, a door on the second-floor landing swung open.

"What is the meaning of this commotion? Have you no sense? Brawling like common thugs..." cried out a stern voice from the railing above.

Holmes and Watson looked up to discover a stout, middle-aged woman in a nurse's cap and smock glaring down at them. The butler released them and stepped away though he hovered in the shadows. Holmes ran a hand through his hair and winced a bit as he checked his shoulder. Nothing was dislocated however, and he straightened his clothes and struggled to his feet, attempting to regain his dignity. Cautiously, he moved to the top of the stairs and stood on the edge of the landing trying to peer past the woman into the room. She had partially left the door open but all he could see was the vague outline of someone underneath a duvet on the bed.

He moderated his tone and nodded towards the room. "I apologize Madam for the disturbance. My only concern is for your patient's well-being. May I see her?"

The woman folded her arms and fixed him with an icy stare. "I am a professional Mr. Holmes. I assure you, she is well-cared for."

"Then you have no objections to my seeing her," he persisted, flashing his most charming smile.

She didn't return his smile and without a word, turned on heel and disappeared into the room, shutting the door behind her. A few moments later, she re-emerged - once more shutting the door behind her and made her way towards them. She was carrying a small object in her hands.

She smiled - a cruel little smile - and held out the object to him which on closer inspection was a book. Holmes looked down and turned ashen. It was the book on bee culture he had left it in the hospital room. It had disappeared along with Edwina.

"She doesn't want to see you Mr. Holmes. She asked me to tell you and to return your book. She has no need of it anymore nor you," she announced with great contempt.

"I don't believe you," said Holmes after a pause. He took the book reluctantly as she thrust it towards him. With a grim expression, he began to move forward. The woman moved into his path and remained there, her eyes hard and baleful as she fished a folded note from her pocket. "She thought you might say that. Here, this is for you. Take it, read it and then be gone. You are not wanted here."

Holmes yanked the note from her fingers and unfolded it. And as he scanned it, his expression changed from disbelief to anger. "What have you done to her?"

"I don't know what you mean."

Holmes waved the note in the air. "She would not write this."

"Is this not her hand?"

401

He did not respond directly to the question, snarling in response, "You coerced her... tricked her."

"If anyone is guilty of trickery and deceit, I think we need look no further than you Mr. Holmes. Now, if you refuse to leave, I shall have no choice but to send for the authorities. But it seems to me that if you are as concerned for her welfare as you claim, you will respect her wishes and leave her in peace. Peace and quiet is exactly what is needed for her recovery. Now, what shall it be then?"

Holmes remained silent and indeed seemed frozen on the stair until Watson gently nudged him. "Holmes, nothing is to be gained by this."

Holmes eyes drifted up towards the closed door once more and then after a long pause, he slowly nodded. He started to turn as if to head back down, hand on the bannister and then paused. He swiveled back around and fixed his gaze on the nurse. His eyes burned with a ferocity that surprised even Watson.

"You take care to perform your duties well Madam and tend to your patient. If I hear otherwise, I shall give you no peace." And with that, he turned abruptly and headed down the stairs and out the door. His sudden exit caught all by surprise. Watson caught up with him as he was climbing into the hansom.

"Where are we going then? What next?" ventured Watson after a long silence had passed between them.

"Baker Street," came the weary response from the opposite corner. "I need to think."

Watson nodded and then also lapsed into silence unable to think of a suitable response. As he sat there reflecting on all that had transpired, his eyes drifted across to Holmes who seemed to him more exhausted and downhearted than he had ever seen him – even considering the events of the fire at Fern Hall. At least then, the cause of his turmoil had been apparent.

"Well, at least we can take comfort in the fact that she is being cared for."

"Physically, yes," came the muted response.

A slight frown curled Watson's mouth as he observed the note was still held tightly in Holmes right hand. "May I?" he asked overcome with curiosity as to what words could have produced such a profound depression in the Detective.

Holmes offered no resistance or response. With the greatest of care, Watson slipped the note from between his fingers. He unfolded the note and sat back to read it, a sense of unease settling in as he scanned the words that had caused the detective so much distress. The handwriting was unmistakably that of Edwina Schraeder and stated:

"I will not - cannot see you. Everyone has a destiny - mine has now been made clear. Our paths must and will diverge - for the well-being of all concerned. No good will come of a further association. You once said to me that you must be free to walk away - grant me that same freedom. Goodbye."

Watson read the note over once more and on a second reading, was struck by how dissimilar it was to any other correspondence he had seen from Edwina Schrader. There was a deliberate coldness to the note; a calculated attempt to be unsentimental, logical. It was a note he would have expected from the hand of Sherlock Holmes. Perhaps not as of late but certainly not from the woman who had professed unconditional devotion to the detective. As he continued to study the note, his brow creased deeply. "Most uncharacteristic...I grant you," he murmured, "and yet there seems to be no signs of duress in the script... no wavering, no smudge marks. The wording is odd, yet the hand is firm and resolute... no signs of coercion."

Holmes snatched the note from his hand and narrowed his eyes - barely able to contain his anger. "Physical coercion no, I agree. But the signs are clear, he is poisoning her mind."

"But why Holmes? Why all this bother? If he intended harm to her, why hire a nurse to look after her?"

"I don't know Watson. There is something I have missed... some connection. I am at a loss."

Watson shrugged in resignation. "Well, the butler did say that in due course all would become clear. Though I must admit, I don't care for the sound of that."

"Neither do I," agreed Holmes, "but it does seem to me that the next move is not ours."

CHAPTER 11

The Cuckoo in the Nest

"There you are Mr. Holmes. Bless us, a night not fit for man or beast! I was on my way up with tea for the client but seeing as how you are back..." Mrs. Hudson's chipper voice drifted down from the stairs where she stood on the landing balancing a tea tray.

"Client?" Holmes exclaimed, utterly incredulous. He scowled at his landlady and hung his dripping overcoat on a peg in the foyer of Baker Street. "I left specific instructions this morning that I would not be seeing clients until further notice."

"I know sir, and I am sorry," she murmured; there was no mistaking the annoyance in his voice, "but you see, I had to run out earlier in the day, the cream had gone off. Mrs. Turner was over visiting from next door and while I was gone..."

"I know who she is Mrs. Hudson... do get to the point."

Mrs. Hudson blushed, deeply embarrassed. "I am afraid Mr. Holmes in my haste, I must have forgotten to mention it to her. By the time I returned, she had already let the young widow in."

"Widow?"

"Well, that is what Mrs. Turner said. I haven't seen the lady myself. Mrs. Turner showed her upstairs before I returned. Poor dear... it really is not her fault."

"No... indeed it is not," scolded Holmes. He glanced up towards the flat where he could see the faint glow of light shining out from under the door and then shrugged in resignation. He made his way to the stairs and then paused at the bottom glancing back towards the empty coat peg next to his. "Is Doctor Watson in?"

Mrs. Hudson shook her head, a shadow of unease clouding her face. "No, he left not long after you this morning. In quite a hurry too. "

"Something wrong? Where to?"

"He didn't say Mr. Holmes. All I know is that he received a message by courier about quarter past 11 this morning and then he was gone in a flash. Haven't seen or heard from him since."

404

Holmes' frown deepened as he slowly began to make his way up the stairs. He abruptly paused four steps from the landing. "Mrs. Hudson, you said a widow?"

"Yes Mr. Holmes...well... according to Mrs. Turner," she corrected, shifting the heavy tea tray in her hands. She held it out towards him as he approached but he seemed not to notice.

"Why does she say that?"

Mrs. Hudson shrugged. "Well... as I said, I have yet to lay eyes on the lady myself, but Mrs. Turner said she's in the finest widow's weeds... and the poor dear's a bit lame... has a walking stick and all."

Holmes froze on the stair and glanced up towards the door to the flat. It was then he became aware of it, the delicate scent of lilies of the valley lingering in the air near the landing.

Without another word, he bounded up the stairs past Mrs. Hudson.

"Mr. Holmes, what about the tea?" she called out in frustration.

He paused long enough to glance down over the railing, his expression of mixture of excitement and apprehension.

"Never mind the tea Mrs. Hudson. I believe something stronger may be warranted," he announced, shutting the door firmly behind him.

»»««

As Watson scrambled out of the hansom, a gust of wind-driven rain propelled him towards the door of Baker Street or perhaps it was a combination of the weather and his increasing despair and rage. He burst through the front door and raced up the stairs without pause, his Macintosh leaving a trail of water on the stairs and bannister. On reaching the door to the flat, he flung it open crying out, "Holmes! Holmes! It's Mary... she's disa..." As he stumbled inside, the words died in his throat, and he uttered a gasp at the sight before him. He staggered to a stop, seized with dread. "God in heaven! What is the meaning of this?"

Sherlock Holmes was seated in his favorite chair facing the door, a glass of sherry in his hand; a common enough sight. What was uncommon however was the shadowy figure standing behind his chair – a woman shrouded in black lace and crepe, a mourning veil masking her features. Watson didn't need to see her face to know it was Edwina Schraeder. Her hands, covered in black lace gloves, were what concerned Watson the most and left him motionless in the open doorway. Her left hand was nestled gently in Holmes' hair, fingers caressing softly, entwined in the locks of his hair, stroking along his forehead and temples. The right, however, chilled him to the bone - as it held a silver, double-barreled derringer. The hammer was cocked, the barrel pressed firmly against Holmes' head, resting just above his right eyebrow.

Edwina smiled at him through the veil. "Do step inside Dr. Watson. Best take off your wet overcoat. Please, close the door." Her voice was soft, cordial but terrifying all the same.

Watson looked nervously to Holmes. "I... I don't understand."

Holmes let out a heavy sigh. "I think it best you follow instruction Watson and come inside or Mrs. Hudson will soon be complaining abou another mess to clean up. Pour yourself a drink. And while you are at it, think I may need another myself if I am allowed. What about you Eddy Something to calm your nerves? I wouldn't want you to pull that trigge before you fully intend." As he spoke, he tilted his head back slightly an shifted his eyes up towards the woman who held his life in her hands.

Her response was a deep frown and a sharp tug on his hair – so much s that he winced. "Only you would taunt the woman holding a gun to you head... behave..." she whispered in reproach, her lips brushing the top of his ear. And then just as quickly, her fingers tenderly smoothed the locks that she had just tugged, her expression softening.

"Madwoman!! What have you done? Where's Mary?" cried Watson, bewildered and overcome with emotion as he took a step forward. He stopped just short of the threshold, the door to the flat still open behind him.

Holmes felt Edwina's hand stiffen once more against the nape of his neck. "Watson, please, do as she says," he urged with deliberate calmness. "This is not the time to let emotions run rampant."

"Rest assured, my emotions are firmly in check," remarked Edwina in a voice as cold as the grave. "Now Dr. Watson, step inside, close the door and do keep your hands at all times where I can see them. I recall that you often carry an Adam's revolver in the right pocket of your jacket. Listen carefully. I want you to remove your outercoat, hang it on the coatrack but under no circumstances are you to turn your back to me. Then step forward with both hands still in front of you, walk to the fireplace and then very slowly remove the gun from your pocket and lay it on the mantle next to the clock. Once you have done that, step away, very far away in fact. Do pour yourself a drink and give the decanter to Holmes. You should sit down in your chair and remain there. Most important of all, remember to keep your hands where I can see them at all times...."

Watson stood rooted in place, his eyes studying the situation before him. He remained silent though his gaze shifted to Holmes as if waiting for instruction. A flush of color shaded Edwina's face and her grip tightened as she pressed the derringer more firmly against Holmes' brow.

"I know what you are thinking Doctor," she began, her voice hoarse and terse. "You see this gun... and you say to yourself... it's only a derringer... not much firepower. Besides, she's only a woman. I could rush her or make a grab for my revolver... and even if she fired at me, the bullet would probably miss or not do much damage. True, Dr. Watson, if I fired at you the distance would be too great for such a low powered weapon but I assure you that if you attempt anything so foolish, I will fire this gun into Holmes' head and being that it is resting on his supraorbital ridge and that it is a .41 caliber bullet, it will penetrate his skull and unfortunately will destroy a large portion of his beautiful brain if not kill him outright." Edwina paused to steady her hand which had begun to tremble once more. For a moment, she said nothing and then took a deep breath. "Please Dr. Watson, do not force me to take such a reprehensible action."

"An action, I would very much like to avoid," interjected Holmes with a faint smile. "Need I remind you Watson, Mrs. Hudson just replaced the rug. I doubt she'll be pleased about another mess."

Watson nodded in resignation and then with the utmost care, removed his revolver, placed it on the mantle and then slowly sank into his chair, his eyes fixed on Holmes and the gun. "Why? Why are you doing this Edwina? What have you done to my Mary? She has always been a good friend to you."

"Mary?" exclaimed Holmes in disbelief. "Eddy, what have you done?"

"Nothing has happened to her, she'll be all right, I promise," swore Edwina, a slight tremor in her voice. "She is only being held as additional incentive. It was not my idea I swear to you ... but... I've been given a task... and I must not fail."

Holmes sighed heavily, his face even more ashen. "If you are here about the emeralds, as I have already explained, I cannot return them, they are not yours – they never were. Besides, they have been returned."

Anxiety flickered across Watson's face at the obvious lie. He recalled the last time he had seen the jewels; they had been hidden under the fruit basket. But he kept silent, there was no mistaking the warning glance that Holmes cast in his direction.

Her anger was immediate, and Holmes uttered a sharp yelp as her fingers once more yanked his locks. "Liar!" she cried and as the hand holding the gun trembled once more. Watson shrank back against his chair, tensing as he waited in dread for the sharp report of the gun. It didn't happen however, as she regained control once more and steadied her hand.

"Please, no more lies... please," she implored. "He has associates you see, everywhere, even the Austrian embassy... so I know that you have not returned them. I must get them back. I have no choice. Listen to me, I'm begging you. He is a dangerous man – more dangerous than you could imagine... please if you val..."

The door abruptly swung open, interrupting her mid-sentence as Colonel Moran, his face flushed with anger and impatience, swaggered into the room. "What the Devil is taking you so long? A simple task..."

And for a moment, as Edwina's face hardened at the sight of him, the gun lifted slightly from Holmes' forehead, the barrel now pointed at the Colonel.

"I am handling this. I do not need your help. Get out!"

"You stupid little fool. You think I am afraid of you and that pea shooter? I'll wring your neck before..."

"Mind your words Sebastian, remember who it is you are speaking to," growled a low voice as a tall, gaunt shadow loomed in the open doorway. Sebastian Moran bristled at the remark though wisely kept his tongue.

Holmes looked up and managed a faint smile. "Ahh, Professor Moriarity I presume. We meet at last. Forgive me for not standing to greet you properly... for the moment it seems wise to remain seated. "

The professor chuckled a bit and nodded as he stepped into the room, his eyes taking in every detail. "A prudent course of action Mr. Holmes. If I may take a moment to express that I have looked forward to this day for quite some time. Your reputation precedes you. I have long admired your work. Yours as well Doctor Watson."

Holmes nodded, his mouth curling into a slight smirk. "Your reputation precedes you as well Professor. Though I would not say I have "admired" your work... your ingenuity perhaps... but never the results."

The Professor shrugged feigning disappointment. "Ah... well, we all have our parts to play Mr. Holmes before we shuffle off this mortal coil..." He crossed the room and then stopped at the mantle, an amused expression on his face as he picked up and examined the sketch, the hair ribbon and finally the box containing Edwina's shorn locks. His eyes drifted to Edwina and then back to Holmes, his lips drawing into a knowing smile. "Rather an unusual collection... unexpected... for a man who proclaims to eschew sentimentality."

Holmes remained silent though the tension in his brow betrayed his irritation at the remark.

"What have you done to Mary? Where is she? How dare you... kidnap her," burst Watson, unable to contain his growing anger.

The Professor chuckled. "A bit of an overstatement my dear Dr. Watson. Miss Morstan happened to see a friend in a carriage, one she had not seen in a while and went off with her."

Watson stared at Edwina, dumbfounded. "It was you! You... You did this?"

Edwina looked away unable to meet his gaze. Overwrought, Watson abruptly moved forward in his chair as if to rise. As he did, Moran was suddenly behind him holding him back down in the chair, a flash of steel in his hand, a blade held to his throat.

"No!" Edwina cried out in desperation and then she turned to the Professor, her voice calmer although none the less imploring. "You promised... promised to let me handle this... that no one would be hurt... please...please..."

There was silence for a moment and then the Professor nodded. "And so I did... Moran, put away your blade... we are not savages."

The Colonel stared at him dumbfounded, his face flushed with indignation. "This is nonsense... all this talk," he sputtered. "You let me convince them...I'll get to the emeralds soon enough."

The Professor arched his brow, his lips drawn into a tight smile as he leaned against the mantle. "You would be wise to remember your place Sebastian and what happens to those who forget..."

The words, spoken quietly and with considerable coolness, were apparently enough to persuade the Colonel for the next moment, he looked down at the floor and silently sheathed his knife, slipping it back into his pocket.

"Splendid!" chuckled the Professor. "As a matter of fact, I suggest you go down and wait at the carriage. Take Edwina as well...these gentlemen and I have business to conduct. Now, as I was saying..."

"No... I will remain," she said defiantly.

There was a short silence and then the Professor burst into hearty laughter. "The obstinance of women..." he mused with a shake of his head. His expression grew cold as he met Holmes' gaze. "She fears for your safety gentlemen. It seems she distrusts me almost as much as the Colonel." His expression soured as he turned toward the Colonel who still lingered by the door. "Off you go then Moran," he announced and with a wave of his hand, dismissed the man who fixed them all with one last sullen scowl before he vanished out the door.

"Why would she trust you at all?" spat Watson venomously, "the man who murdered her father..."

The Professor smiled. "I assure you Dr. Watson, her father is quite alive..."

"What! Are you mad?" "We saw him - saw your handiwork... the poor devil strung up- dangling in his cell..." sputtered Watson. At his words, Edwina uttered a small sob and for a brief moment, swayed a bit on her feet until she grabbed onto the back of Holmes' chair and steadied herself.

"Watson, there is no need for this..." admonished Holmes quietly, the first words he had spoken in quite some time. He looked at the Professor and then without taking his eyes off him, reached up slowly with his right hand and gently laid his hand on Edwina's as it rested on the edge of the chair. "It will be all right Eddy," he soothed though he made no attempt to take the derringer from her. As their hands made contact, she made a little whimpering noise.

The Professor narrowed his eyes and then extended his hand towards her. "I think you had best come stand by me dear... you look exhausted... shall I take that from you?"

She remained in place for a few moments, her eyes moving uneasily from man to man in the room. Pale as a ghost, she took a few faltering steps out from behind Holmes' chair leaning heavily on a slender silver handled cane. She came to stand a few steps away from the Professor but tightened her grip on the derringer which she fixed on Holmes once more.

"I'll be fine," she murmured in a hollow voice, "though if it's all the same, I shall keep this... I have a task to finish..."

The Professor nodded in approval. "Yes... you do... as you wish my dear."

"The emeralds... where are they?" she asked sharply, turning back to Watson and Holmes, "and do not lie to me... if you value Miss Morstan's life, you will not play games. No harm will come to her as long as you cooperate."

Watson's face turned crimson. "If you harm one hair on..." he rasped.

"Enough!" Holmes reprimanded sharply, silencing him. He turned back to the Professor "Do you think me so foolish that I would keep them here? I will get them Professor, but you must allow me time to do so. Will you give me time?"

The Professor furrowed his brow in consideration. "What do you think Edwina? Should we trust him not to play tricks?"

She was quiet, her eyes fixed on Holmes. After a moment, she nodded "He would not gamble with Miss Morstan's life... she is too dear to Dr Watson," she murmured from beneath the veil.

"Agreed. Well then, you have 24 hours Mr. Holmes," advised the Professor. "We will see you tomorrow then at 9:00 pm. Charing Cross Station – the entrance at the Victoria Embankment. You know it?"

"I know it," Holmes confirmed, his gaze moving first from the Professor then to Edwina.

"Splendid... well gentlemen- until tomorrow then," announced the Professor as he moved towards the door. He paused for a moment in the doorway. "If you are thinking Dr. Watson, that Lestrade and his idiot yarders may be of assistance tomorrow, I would suggest you reconsider exactly what is at stake." And then he disappeared out the door, his firm footfalls sounding on the stairs as he descended. Edwina seemed frozen in the doorway – listening.

She turned to both men, a look of deep agitation and remorse on her face beneath the veil. "I promise you Dr. Watson, she will be safe tonight... I will see to it... ease your mind."

"God in Heaven, why are you doing this?" pleaded Watson.

"Edwina, come along then!" The Professor's voice, stern and commanding, echoed up the stairs through the hall.

Edwina's head drooped forward, and her shoulders quivered slightly as a soft sobbing sound could be heard for a few moments. As Holmes moved towards her, she raised her hand to dissuade him though the derringer had been pocketed. He drew to a stop as instructed but extended his hand offering her his pocket square.

Edwina took it gratefully and wiped at her eyes. "Always the gentleman, even now," she sighed with a bleak smile. She gazed from man to man and then fixed her gaze on Holmes, nodding in Watson's direction. "Explain it to him, won't you? I see that you understand now."

Holmes nodded never taking his eyes off her as she moved towards the door.

"Explain... explain what?" exclaimed Watson, overcome with frustration and fear.

Edwina paused at the door, one hand on the handle and glanced over her shoulder, her face devoid of all color beneath the veil. She shrugged in defeat, her slender shoulders slumped as if overcome with a vile burden. "I'm the cuckoo in the nest..." was all she said and then disappeared out the door, closing it softly behind her.

Watson stared after her, dumbfounded. "Great Scott! Can no one just say what they mean instead of speaking in riddles?" he exclaimed in frustration as he turned to find Holmes standing at the window peering out at the street below. He poured himself a large sherry and collapsed into his chair. "We have a madman who's taken my fiancé - who claims the man he killed is still alive, and she is going on about bloody birds."

"It would be a mistake to call the Professor a madman... he is anything but that. Everything he has done thus far has been calculated and well-planned... an orderly mind – disciplined... logical... but completely immoral." Holmes turned away from the window and settled into his chair, his face drawn and weary.

Watson grunted in protest. "He had Pennington murdered and now claims he is alive... if that isn't mad..."

Holmes shook his head. "But that's not what he said is it? His exact words if you recall were: 'her father is quite alive'..."

"But it's all semantics, isn't it? Pennington is dead. we saw him. So... I don't see how..." Watson faltered, a look of doubt coming over him as cognition seeped in. "Dear God, if Pennington is dead... but her father is alive... then it must follow that... that..."

"Pennington isn't her father..." finished Holmes. "It was there all along... right in front of me... but I missed it... missed the connection."

Watson stared at him still not fully comprehending the situation. "But if Pennington isn't her father then who is?"

Holmes didn't answer, not directly, seemingly lost in his own reflection. "I didn't see it... not until I saw them together. And then it all came together... there was no mistaking it... the strong jawline, fierce determination, the intelligence... everything that Pennington was not."

A look of horror crossed Watson's face. "What are you saying... that ... that the Professor is her father? My God, how could that be?"

Holmes shook his head. "The forest for the trees... Edwina had mentioned it herself... even as a little girl she remembered him as the family friend who was always there somehow in the background. Pennington's confidante, business associate, and then when she mentioned the cuckoo..."

"I don't understand..."

Holmes smiled grimly. "Many species of cuckoo are brood parasites... the female cuckoo will lay her egg in the nest of another bird, a host nest, the unsuspecting host parents will hatch the cuckoo's egg and rear it's offspring often to the detriment of its own brood. The cuckoo hatchling has been known to throw the host parents offspring out of the nest to ensure its own survival..."

Watson stared at him horrified. "Dear God, her brother... the lake... do you mean she...?"

"No... no I do not," Holmes cut him off abruptly, almost vehemently. "But that is what he wants her to believe... to maintain control."

Watson fell into silence and then shook his head. "So... Pennington didn't know that she wasn't his daughter."

"If he did... he was wise enough not to say anything."

"All these years she grew up believing her father was Pennington ..." Watson rubbed his brow wearily. "And now her world is in pieces...

everything she thought she knew about her mother and her father, a lie. devastating. Is that why she's doing this?"

Holmes was silent for a moment and then shrugged. "Perhaps she feel this is her destiny and she's afraid. Perhaps both."

Watson sighed heavily and held the coolness of the glass to his head "What now? What of my Mary?"

Holmes smiled reassuringly and then rose, quickly crossing to the coa scuttle. "She is safe enough for now. I believe Eddy... she will look out fo her. You mustn't worry." And while he spoke, he dug down to the very bottom of the coal scuttle and withdrew a battered tea canister. Using one o Mrs. Hudson's linen napkins, he wiped off the coal dust and unscrewed the lid withdrawing a small velvet pouch. He tossed it Watson. "Guard them well..."

Watson eagerly pulled open the bag and poured out the emeralds. "They were here all the time."

Holmes looked away. "I just couldn't bring myself to return them. I don't even know why."

Watson nodded – he knew but thought it best not to say.

"So, tomorrow then?"

Holmes nodded. "Best get some rest... we will need all our wits about us."

Watson had almost made it to the door and then paused. "What about Lestrade? Should we not alert him?"

"We already know that Jenkins was in his network. There are surely to be others in the Yard as well. Is that a risk you want to take – knowing what is at stake?"

Watson grew silent and then shook his head. Quickly draining his drink, he pocketed the emeralds and then rose. After bidding Holmes good night, he began to leave and then paused momentarily by the mantle. He retrieved his revolver which was still lying next to the clock and pocketed it. He wasn't certain he would need it the following night but he did not want to risk being without it.

As the door closed after him, Holmes retreated to his chair lost in reflection on all that had occurred and what was possibly to come. And as he brooded, his fingers rested on the black satin ribbon which once more dangled from the arm of his chair.

CHAPTER 12

Farewell

"Damn this bloody fog ... tonight of all nights." Watson sank back from the window of the hansom into his seat, fidgeting. The lights of 221B were little more than a feeble suggestion as the hansom headed out at a slow trot from Baker Street; the night was a thickening soup of grey mist and industrial grit.

Holmes lifted his chin though his eyes remained closed as he reclined against the seat. "No doubt you've brought your revolver." It was an observation made with great weariness.

Watson rankled at the tone. "Of course, I have. Have you forgotten what is at stake? My Mary."

"Precisely, your Mary and others." Holmes opened his eyes at last and fixed his gaze on his companion. "I am well aware of what is at stake Doctor, I merely remind you that a show of force may gain us nothing and indeed exacerbate the situation. This is a time for cool heads Watson, you must rein in your emotions."

Watson's mouth twitched as he struggled to contain his agitation.

"Forgive me if my blood runs warmer than yours," he said with some indignation. "I find it difficult to remain nonchalant when my fiancé's life is at risk. Of course, what would you know of these matters? It's all just sentimental nonsense to you. All you have at stake is the disappointment of losing... having to admit that you were bested by Moriarity."

Holmes remained silent, his furrowed brow the only evidence of a reaction to Watson's bitter words. Perhaps fearing he had gone too far, Watson rubbed his forehead in discomfort and shook his head. "Forgive me... I... losing Mary... losing her would be unbearable Holmes... I..." The words caught in his throat, and as his head began to sag forward in despair, gentle pressure on his arm startled him. He looked up to find Holmes leaning forward his expression uncharacteristically compassionate.

"Then we must act wisely and do everything in our power to ensure she is returned to you safely." The hansom lurched to a stop in front of the entrance to Charing Cross, and as Holmes reached for the door, Watson withdrew the revolver from his pocket and held it forth, his hand trembling slightly. "Perhaps... perhaps it's best if you take this then... I fear I..."

Holmes' gaze rested on the gun and then with a shake of his head, he pushed it back towards him. "You will make the right choice Watson. You always do when it matters most," he said climbing out into the thickening fog. Watson stared past him into the fog for a moment then quickly pocketed the gun and scrambled out of the hansom. He caught up with Holmes as he was passing the Eleanor Cross which stood just outside the archway that graced the main entrance to the station. He hesitated, his hand grasping Holmes' elbow. "But... but where to? We have no idea where they will be," he fretted, staring at the multitude of arched passages; each one leading to a different platform for a train heading to various destinations; all dimly lit and uninviting.

Holmes paused staring at the choices before him. He smiled after a moment and pointed to a series of passages at the far end. "One of those... I'm certain of it."

"What? But... how could you be?" Watson stared at him flabbergasted, then hurried to keep pace as Holmes headed towards the furthest passageway.

"Simple logic my dear fellow. This group of passages leads to the platforms for the Southeastern Line – specifically the boat trains. According to Bradshaw's, there is a train leaving in 45 minutes to Folkstone."

"Cross-Channel? So, you think they'll head abroad then? To Boulogne?"

"Of course, wouldn't you? Moriarty needs time to regroup... away from prying eyes."

Watson thought for a moment then shrugged. "But he could also just as easily go Dover to Calais and then to Paris..."

"True. Paris may be the final destination," admitted Holmes with a nod. "But as for the route, the volume of service is far greater from Folkestone. There are more ferries to Boulogne than Calais... higher passenger volume... easier for him to disappear should he fear being followed."

Watson frowned, still not convinced. "But ultimately - conjecture at this point."

"True again," Holmes laughed, "but look, we shall have our answer soon enough." As Watson turned to look in the direction Holmes was pointing, a ragged boy of no more than 12, reed thin and gawky, stepped out from the shadows of the furthest archway and approached. He paused briefly on seeing the two men and wiped his nose using his cap. After a few moments of careful study and still holding the cap in hand, he stepped forward to address them.

"You Mr. Holmes?" he ventured tentatively, peering up at Holmes but not without first glancing uneasily over his shoulder towards the darkened archway.

"I am. Have you a message for me?" queried Holmes, noting the boy's nervousness.

The boy nodded. "That I 'ave... the gentleman..."

"Professor Moriarty," snorted Watson shifting his weight anxiously as he glanced towards the shadowy passage.

The boy looked at him blankly and then shrugged. "Didn't give no name but e's a fine ol' gent...give me two shillins ta give you a message."

Holmes nodded. "Well then, let's have it."

The boy twisted the cap in his grimy hands and closed his eyes tightly as he concentrated on the message. After a brief pause, he blurted in one breath, "Says meet 'im on Platform 10 - there's a waitin room... door'll be open...... Take that furthest passage... you an'the Doctor only...don' bring no peelers - package might get roughed up."

Watson's face reddened at the veiled threat, his hand sliding into the pocket of his greatcoat which held the Adams revolver. Noting the movement, Holmes shook his head in warning and then turned back to the boy.

"Anything else?"

The boy shook his head. "Not a peep guv..."

"Right. Off you go then!" growled Holmes, dismissing the boy with a curt nod. But as the boy shuffled off, he seemed to reconsider and motioned him back. "Take these then...for your troubles," he murmured and tossed the boy three shillings. The boy's face brightened in amazement as he caught the coins then scrambled up the embankment and disappeared. Holmes once more began to move towards the darkened passage.

"Is this wise? Might be a trap," cautioned Watson, panting a bit as he struggled to keep pace. Holmes shrugged and paused at the mouth of the passage, peering into the dim tunnel.

"Yes, it very well might, but it seems to me that we have no choice. We'll know soon enough, won't we? Keep the Adams close Watson, but I urge all due caution. As you said earlier, there is much at stake," he cautioned.

Upon emerging, they found themselves inside the station and on the correct platform –#10 but on the opposite side. At the far end of the platform on the opposite track idled the train, its smokestack sending thick billows of black towards the vents in the skylights that lined the glass and steel framed roof. Despite the open vents, a haze of steam and gritty smoke fouled the air dimming the meagre lights of the platform lamps.

"Over there... we need to cross," advised Holmes pointing towards a set of stairs that led to a high, narrow walkway that traversed the tracks. Upon crossing, they found themselves on a platform that was deserted save for a few porters loading the last of the luggage. Most of the passengers had already boarded. In the middle of the platform stood a small passenger waiting room and lingering by the doorway was Colonel Moran. As they approached, he greeted them with a contemptuous smile and a revolver sporting a menacingly long barrel.

"Well, you decided to show. Step forward. I would ask that you hold your arms away from your body as I will need to search you."

Holmes stepped forward quickly holding his arms out to the side. "I don't need a firearm Colonel. I have my wits," he assured as the Colonel carefully patted him down.

Moran stared at him levelly and then burst into laughter as he proudly brandished the revolver. "Wits!!! Hardly a match for the firepower of my Enfield Mr. Holmes. That I can guarantee. I should be happy to demonstrate."

Holmes smiled slyly as he met Moran's gaze and arched his brow conspiratorially at Watson. "And yet I have heard Colonel, that it isn't really the size of the weapon that matters." He looked past the Colonel into the room, his gaze settling on Edwina and Mary Morstan. They were seated on a bench in the far corner of the room. Mary was bound by the wrists, her head covered by a dark canvas sack. Despite this, she did not cower but sat erectly feet planted firmly. Edwina looked in Holmes' direction and then quickly looked away, her face obscured by her dark veil of lace. Her hand, which held onto Miss Morstan's bound wrists, began to tremble slightly.

Moran's anger was delayed but upon processing the remark, visible. With a snort, he leaned forward, his eyes full of spite and indignation as he followed Holmes' gaze. And then just as suddenly he smiled smugly, as if a thought had occurred.

"Well Mr. Holmes, another of your absurd theories. Pity you'll never have a chance to prove or disprove it," he chuckled and then turned to Watson, quickly searching him. On finding the Adams revolver, he removed it and after pocketing the weapon, wagged a disapproving finger in the Doctor's direction. With a mocking half-bow, he stepped back away from the doorway and motioned for them to enter. On stepping through the door, Holmes slowed his pace and turned back to face Moran as he followed them.

"Her heart will never be yours Moran, nor her respect."

The words, though spoken in a low tone, conveyed such conviction and intensity that Watson paused a moment, surprised.

Moran's face contorted as if he didn't know how to process the remark. He drew to a stop. With a florid face and nasty smile, he leaned forward. "Perhaps," he hissed, "but what does it matter when all else will be mine? Besides, what concern of this is yours?"

Watson tensed, noting the sudden contraction of Holmes' right hand into a fist and the tightness of his jaw. He'd seen this reaction in Holmes before on those rare occasions when the Detective forgot his own advice regarding the reining in of emotions; a strong right cross inevitably followed. "Holmes... the problem at hand..." he reminded quietly as he cast a worried glance in his fiancé's direction.

Holmes' jaw tightened and then he nodded, his fist slowly uncurling, a strained smile upon his lips.

"As much as I would love to continue our discussion Colonel, the good Doctor has reminded me of the business at hand. Perhaps another time. But for now, do please let your *Master* know we are here as requested."

Moran uttered a foul curse and abruptly raised the Enfield, pressing it squarely into the center of Holmes' forehead.

The detective's eyes registered momentary surprise and then he managed a slight smile. "Ahh, again... seems I've been here before. I do hope this is not becoming a trend."

Edwina sprang up from the bench in alarm, deserting her charge for the moment.

"Stop... this serves no purpose!" she cried out. She lurched forward and it seemed as if she would grab onto Moran's arm until he cocked the weapon and pressed it even more firmly into Holmes' forehead, pinning him to the wall.

"Sit down girl!" he snarled. "Unless you want me to paint the walls with the contents of Mr. Holmes' skull. Are you paying attention Dr. Watson? You mind your manners as well as unlike Edwina, I have no qualms on pulling this trigger. I am in charge, no one, certainly no girl, is going to tell me what to do."

Edwina froze, swaying slightly as she leaned on her cane for support. Keeping her eyes focused on Moran and Holmes, she slowly backed away until she reached the small office. She whirled around to the door and raised her fist as if to knock, but before she could land one blow, the door swung open. The Professor, a faint smile on his lips, looked out from the doorway, a lit Partagas between his fingers.

"Ahh, gentlemen, right on time!" he exclaimed affably. Upon noting the gun in Moran's hand, his expression turned dark and disdainful.

"Do put that ridiculous thing away Moran," he sighed. "We are all gentlemen ... all quite aware of what is at stake."

Moran balked, his expression baleful. "I say we dispense with all this nonsense and just take back what we are promised."

"Well... where's the satisfaction in that? You disappoint me Moran. The game is almost as important as the prize... and the game must be played well," scolded the Professor.

"I don't like games," hissed Moran.

"Ahh, but perhaps if you weren't so dull," needled Holmes.

Moran blanched and increased the pressure of the barrel on his forehead. "I am going to end you Holmes," he rasped.

"Father please, call him off," interjected a plaintive voice, "you promised me..."

The Professor frowned in irritation, noticing his daughter had abandoned her post and hovered at his elbow.

"Mind your charge Edwina, I shall handle this," he instructed then turned his attention back to the Colonel. Edwina hesitated and then with great reluctance, made her way back to the bench where she settled next to Mary Morstan. Her eyes wide with fear, remained focused on Moran and Holmes.

"Moran!" The Professor's voice sliced through the air like a knife and the Colonel flinched glancing back over his shoulder to find him directly behind him, his usually impassive expression tight with controlled fury.

"If you pull that trigger Moran, you will regret it. You will wish you were on the barrel end of the gun instead of Mr. Holmes as you will no longer have my protection... and you very well know what that means. Two weeks at the most... if you are fortunate. I advise you to stop and consider. Do you want to take that chance?"

The Colonel blanched then slowly lifted the gun from Holmes' forehead. His arm fell to his side, his face a study in absolute defeat. As he stepped back into the shadows of the room without a word, the defeat transformed into mask of bitter enmity.

Holmes managed a grin and raised his fingers to the indentation from th barrel in the center of the forehead. "Well... that was decidedly unpleasant."

The Professor shrugged. "You must accept my apologies Mr. Holmes The Colonel is quite dedicated but can be over zealous."

"A sense of humour along with manners would be of benefit... and a shorter leash."

There was a moment of uneasy silence before the Professor burst int laughter. He shook his head in utter delight. "My dear Mr. Holmes, I do se enjoy our banter. I shall miss it." He paused a moment, the smile beginning to fade, "but onto the business at hand. I trust you have the emeralds."

Holmes patted the breast pocket of his coat. "I do... but first if you please a word... in private."

The Professor arched his brows an expression of mild surprise at the request. Nevertheless, he nodded towards the inner office. As the two men made their way towards the office, Edwina turned pale once more, her face tense, and half rose from the bench again leaning on her walking stick.

"Father... I..." she paused a moment to catch her breath and steady her nerve. "Miss Morstan..." she began, her eyes darting from the Professor and then to Holmes. She took a deep breath. "May I release Miss Morstan... a show of good faith... after all, as Mr. Holmes has the emeralds and he will be in with you, what harm could there be?" She drew herself up and in as unemotional a voice as she could muster, stated, "We still have control. Colonel Moran still stands at watch. A reasonable action, logical. As you stated earlier, we are not savages."

The Professor grew silent. After a moment, he nodded and favoured her with a smile. Moran watched in disbelief from the far reaches of the room as Edwina murmured heartfelt thanks and returned to Mary, quickly freeing her wrists and removing the hood. Without hesitation, the young woman raced across the room seeking the relative safety and comfort of Dr. Watson's embrace.

The Professor took a deep draw on his cigar and then exhaled, his face still lit with amusement as he watched the proceedings. "Mr. Holmes and I have business to discuss. I trust all of you will behave. I need not remind you of potential consequences. Moran, stand watch but at a distance and Edwina, please try to not aggravate the Colonel. As long as we all act accordingly, we shall soon part ways... civilly." With the utmost geniality, he opened the door to the small room turned to Holmes and motioned him for him to enter.

"I see you've taken over the communications office (the room had served as the telegraph office), convenient," noted Holmes as he stepped inside, his eyes scanning the deserted room. A series of small tables stood in the corner, each one equipped with a telegraph key but all was silent, and there was not an operator to be seen.

"A necessary precaution should you or the good Doctor decide to attempt to wire the authorities."

"And the operators?"

The Professor rolled the cigar between his fingers shrugged. "Nothing sinister I assure you. An extended break... amazing what a few extra shillings will purchase these days... a bit of peace and quiet. Come morning time, when we are well and away, all will return to normal."

"Relatively speaking," remarked Holmes dryly.

"Well said Mr. Holmes," chuckled the Professor as he sank into a leather chair behind the main desk. "Now, do please take a seat and tell me what is it that compels you to seek a private conference? I gather it is something more than to return the emeralds." The Professor paused, a shrewd twinkle in his eyes as Holmes settled opposite him. "You wish to discuss my daughter," he announced.

Holmes' eyes flickered, he paused a moment, choosing his words. "To intercede...yes... on Edwina's behalf."

"Intercede? A curious choice of words Mr. Holmes," replied the Professor with a sly grin, "but please, do explain."

Again, there was a pause and Holmes shifted in his chair as if uncomfortable with the topic in general. He set his jaw after a moment and fixed his gaze upon the Professor.

"What are your intentions Professor?"

"My... intentions?" Surprise flickered across the Professor's face and then he burst into hearty laughter. With a shake of his head, he lightly slapped the desk with his hand and after taking a deep draw on his cigar, once more grew calm. "Even more curious Mr. Holmes, and dare I say, quite uncharacteristic. I am well aware of my daughter's fondness for you... she wears her heart on her sleeve... but this..."

Holmes' face grew taut, lips compressed. "I have concern for her as I do for the welfare of Miss Morstan, as I would for anyone who found themselves in such circumstance as this."

"Circumstance... Hmm... so you say. Notwithstanding Mr. Holmes, this question would more commonly be directed at you as to intentions. It is within my purview as her father."

"Holmes was silent for a moment and then set his jaw, his eyes firm and cautionary.   "She is fragile... has been through a great ordeal... suffered."

"I am well aware of my obligations. I do not need you to remind me of them," interrupted the Professor icily, "nor remind me of what she has endured. Need I remind you Mr. Holmes, that her misfortune was in large measure brought about by your actions. She is my daughter, my charge... my responsibility... and I will care for her – choose for her as I deem in her best interests."

Anger sparked in Holmes' eyes. "And Moran, do you consider him in her best interests?"

"You astonish me Holmes!" the Professor cried out. "Can this be the true reason for your concern... the green-eyed monster rears his head? I thought your tastes ran more to opium whores and fickle contraltos."

A momentary twitch in the corner of Holmes' mouth was the only evidence of a reaction. He met the Professor's gaze coldly. "I speak out of concern for her well-being. Moran is a brute...you have said as much yourself."

The Professor leaned back, studying Holmes through a haze of cigar smoke. "Agreed... a brute... albeit a loyal one. Also, not one of the brightest I admit - but his lineage is strong - he is healthy... sturdy."

"She is your daughter... not breeding stock," growled Holmes, his disgust barely contained. He paused to draw a deep breath and regain control. "A most extraordinary woman, surely she deserves the right to self-determine."

The Professor arched his brow and nodded, his eyes contemplative. "I am aging Mr. Holmes and I am a pragmatist. I have no male heir. As much as I agree that my daughter is extraordinary and capable in many ways, the world, our society, does not yet recognize such abilities in women... or value them. So, until that time, I will choose for her. Moran has the ambition, the ruthless drive to continue in my place when the day arises that I am no longer capable. He is however lacking in the ability to reason and see beyond the immediate gain. That is where Edwina comes in. Together they will be a formidable duo – he the figurehead to be feared, the enforcer at the helm, she the rational force, the strategist that steers the course. And in time, they will produce an heir and my empire will live on. Surely you cannot fault the logic of this plan?"

Holmes was quiet and then leaned forward, his eyes filled with loathing. "Do you not see that this is not in her heart... her character? Would you twist, corrupt her so? Your own daughter?"

The Professor took a long draw on the Partagas and then firmly stubbed it out on the side of the desk. He leaned back in the chair, a sly smile on his lips as he scrutinized Holmes.

"I find it curious that a man who professes to disdain all sentiment continues to concern himself with the state of my daughter's "heart". As for corruption, you are mistaken. One cannot corrupt or twist that which is already well along the path. Or did you forget her sweet little brother and what happened at the lake?"

Holmes paled, his face uneasy. "She was nine... a child."

"Yes, a child chronologically. Indeed, the authorities saw it that way. My dear Holmes, I simply relate what I saw. Like you, I am also a firm believer in facts over sentiment. I was there – on the shore. Let us leave it at there is a darkness in Edwina that surprises even me – something she keeps hidden away. My daughter is not the innocent you believe her to be."

Holmes rose abruptly, his chair scraping on the worn boards as it kicked back. "I will never believe that," he rasped, his face ashen. "Let us finish our business and be done with it."

The Professor shrugged and extended his hand. "So be it... the emeralds then."

Holmes reached into his pocket and withdrew the velvet pouch but then hesitated, a peculiar light in his eyes. "You said before that these were to be hers then..."

"Yes," continued the Professor wearily, "her legacy..."

Holmes looked down at the pouch for a moment and then smiled, pocketing them once more. "Then I shall return them to the rightful owner. I trust you have no objection Professor."

There was an uneasy silence which was broken moments later once more by the sound of the Professor's laughter. He shook his head at Holmes and then rose from his chair.

"Of course, Mr. Holmes, you may return them to her and say your goodbyes. The Colonel and I shall await Edwina on the train, but do not keep us waiting too long." He paused to glance at his pocket watch. "The train leaves in 30 minutes, it would displease me greatly to miss it. Also, please consider that although I have every confidence that you will behave as the gentleman I believe you to be, I assure you, Colonel Moran lacks such conviction. In light of his irritable nature and fondness for firearms, it would be best not to give him cause for aggravation. I advise you to say your farewell on the outside platform to avoid any appearance of impropriety. I shall send Edwina along." The Professor rose from behind the desk and quickly crossed the room, an oddly satisfied expression on his face. As he reached the door, he paused and turned to face the Detective.

"Mr. Holmes, should you ever care to throw your hat in the ring, I would not be averse to consider it. You would be an undeniable asset to our organization – much more so than Moran. And, I am confident I would not be the only one to welcome your presence."

Holmes' face suffused with anger. "There is nothing you could offer in exchange for my principles!"

The Professor arched his brow, incredulous. "Astonishing... nothing? So be it. It seems I was mistaken then."

As the gravity of his words seemed to settle upon Holmes subduing him, the Professor smiled and pushed open the door. "30 minutes Mr. Holmes," he advised as he exited the room.

Holmes paused standing in the doorway watching as the Professor confer quietly with Moran and Edwina. They moved off after a few moments, all three stepping out onto the dimly lit platform, tendrils of noxious smoke creeping in through the still open door. As Holmes headed for the door, Watson leapt to his feet. "Is that it then?" he pressed, his arm wound protectively around Mary Morstan. "Finished?"

"Not quite ... but soon..."

Watson's expression grew uneasy as he looked out the open door towards the fog enshrouded platform. "I don't understand... what's left?"

Holmes followed his gaze out the door. "Farewell..." he murmured as he began to head outside. He paused briefly in the doorway and turned to face them, his face drawn, pallid. "You should take Miss Morstan home Watson, she must be exhausted from her ordeal."

421

Watson gaped at him in surprise. "I don't understand... what of Lestrade Surely we should..."

"You must not!" Holmes rebuked sharply. His manner softened after a moment and with a shake of his head advised, "There are times Watson, when even I must admit defeat."

"What?! You? You're going to just give up then? Allow them to walk away?" Watson stared at him in disbelief.

Holmes didn't answer directly. "Take Miss Morstan home Watson, I shall see you back at Baker Street."

Mary, who had been silent all this time, found her voice. She reached out and grabbed Holmes' sleeve, her face gray, eyes distressed. "But what are you saying? What of Edwina? You cannot just abandon her!"

Holmes looked down at the delicate hand on his sleeve and with the utmost gentleness removed it, placing it on Watson's arm. "I have every confidence Miss Morstan, that she will be all right. She is strong, resilient, as you are," he soothed. "Now, go with the good Doctor... he will look after you, you need to rest," he counseled and then headed through the door, moving purposefully down the platform to where Edwina sat on a small bench not far from the idling train.

"Come along dearest," urged Watson with a melancholy air of resignation, "there's nothing to be done for it ... when he has set his mind..." And before she could offer further protest, he took her by the arm and quickly led her out of the room heading toward the walkway that traversed the tracks. As they reached the other side, she made him pause just outside the entrance to the passageway that led outside to look back across the tracks.

At the sound of his footsteps, Edwina rose to her feet, leaving her cane behind laid out across the worn surface of the bench. She swayed a little unsteadily at first but quickly corrected, her hands clasped tightly before her, her mouth drawn tight with grim resolve beneath the veil.

"Father said you wished to see me," she murmured, struggling to keep her voice neutral.

Holmes arched his brow and drew to a stop studying her. "Lift up your veil," he instructed his voice firm though gentle.

"What? Why?" she gasped in surprise. Then clutching her hands even more tightly, she turned her head to look past him towards the train. "Look... if this is a trick...Please Holmes, I implore you... do not cross him... do not..." The words died on her lips and with a shake of her head, she continued, her head bowed slightly, "he is not a man to be trifled with... please..."

"No tricks Eddy, I promise. I have the emeralds... right here," he soothed as he produced the pouch from his pocket.

She lifted her head at the use of her pet name and managed a small, although tentative smile. Her eyes remained focused on the pouch in his hand. After a moment, she reached into the pocket of her coat. "I have something for you as well. Moran is furious, said it was utterly foolhardy, but father said I could return it to you to give back to Doctor Watson, he said he knows your character and that you would not take advantage."

Holmes arched his brow in surprise as he looked down. She held out the Adams revolver to him. He took it carefully, his smile broadening as he opened the cylinder. "Still loaded I see... now that is trusting."

Edwina lips grew taut, her eyes anxious. "Moran is convinced you'll use this weapon to take back the emeralds... perhaps even hold me hostage until the authorities arrive."

"Well... it is a logical step ... surprising that the Colonel thought of it..." remarked Holmes with a chuckle.

"So, you had thought of it then..."

"Briefly," he admitted with an apologetic sigh.

"So, what is there to stop you? One could hardly blame you – a bit of turnabout is fair play," she murmured.

Holmes knit his brow and pocketed the revolver. "I have no animosity towards you Eddy..."

She choked back a laugh and lifted her head. "I held a gun to your head. I might have even pulled the trigger," she cried in disbelief. "How could you not?"

He said nothing for a moment and then nodded. "True... you did," he said soberly. "But I am also aware of the great duress you are under, that you are not wholly in control of your actions. I know you Eddy, your character, your heart."

Her head sank forward again. "How could you know for certain?" she mumbled despondently, "I don't know who I am any longer. Grendel was right. I'm cursed - an abomination." As she spoke, a shudder overtook her and she raised her hands beneath the veil and covered her eyes for a moment. She drew a deep breath and then lowered her hands, drawing herself up. "Please. Please, just give me the emeralds and you can be done with us all," she pleaded, swaying unsteadily.

Holmes reached out quickly and grasped her shoulders to steady her. "I have them yes, and I shall return them to you. But first you will lift up your veil."

She stifled a sob. "Why?"

His fingers gently pressed into the flesh of her shoulders. "Because I want to see you Eddy, the real you, not your father's agent."

A sad smile touched her lips. "What if she doesn't exist anymore?"

"I don't believe that's the case but let's find out, shall we?" he said, and before she could offer further protest he grabbed the lace and gently lifted it, folding it back over her head. Her head drooped downwards a bit but he arrested the progress, his fingers gently sliding beneath her chin, lifting it so that her eyes met his.

"Well, what do you see?" she murmured, a tremor in her voice as her eyes began to glisten.

He was quiet for a moment and then smiled. "Just as I thought... still there ... maybe somewhat hidden but still there ...the extraordinary woman who nearly trampled me, who faced down an angry crowd to protect an unfortunate old man. A courageous woman who saved my life, but mostly I see your

423

mother's daughter... that is who I see, and that is who I return these to," h
asserted quietly and gently placed the pouch in her palm curling her finger
around the bag.

Edwina looked down at the pouch. She was quiet for a moment and the
slid it into her coat pocket shaking her head. "I'm... I'm so sorry... s
ashamed... I never... I never wanted this to ..." Her voice faded off for
moment but after a gentle pressure on her arm to continue, she drew a deep
breath and pressed on, lifting her eyes now brimming with tears to meet hi
gaze. "You were my best friend... my truest friend. I made no secret of my
feelings for you and, I always held out hope that one day, you would conside
me more than a friend. But even if that was never to happen, I never expected
that we would become... become..." She faltered once more, her lips pursed
but no sound came out.

"Become?" he prodded gently with a deep frown and used his gloved
index finger to wipe away a tear that welled at the corner of her eye.

Edwina seemed unable to answer at first and then pushed it out with a
ragged breath.

"Enemies..."

The word seemed to take him by surprise and his eyes widened in
astonishment.

"Enemies!" he exclaimed, his expression torn between disbelief and
disquiet.

Edwina's head sagged forward, no longer able to meet his gaze.

Holmes' expression softened, his face drawn with concern. "How can you
even think that? It will never be," he soothed, his hands once more holding
her by the shoulders.

She offered no reply, the only sound that of her soft weeping.

Holmes' face contorted with anguish and he drew her closer, gently
lifting her chin up.

"Stop! Enough with this nonsense! Listen to me. You are not, will never.
There is nothing you could possibly do to become my enemy! Do you
understand?"

Again, there was silence. He once more lifted up her chin - a look close to
desperation in his eyes. "Say you understand Eddy," he prodded, giving her
shoulders a firm shake.

She looked up at last and then nodded. It seemed as if she would speak
but the shrill whistle of the train split the air silencing her. A large cloud of
steam vented from between the wheels, filling the platform with mist and as a
cry of 'All Aboard' rang out from the porter, she turned back to the train for a
moment.

"I... I must go..." she stammered. She hesitated a moment and then turned
to him her eyes wild with dread, "Should I run Holmes... at the next station... I
could excuse myself... when they are not expecting. I'm ashamed to say...
I'm... I'm afraid"

"No! Absolutely not! You must not run Eddy, he will expect it," he
warned. "There is no shame in being afraid. Only a fool has no fear in the

face of danger, but you must be shrewd and logical. He will come after you. He will not let you go so easily. Listen to me. I truly believe you are in no immediate danger. Moriarity will care for you, provide for you. You must bide your time... use it to your advantage... play the game Eddy... play it well... but never forget who you are."

Her eyes welled with tears once more. "How could I forget ... his daughter," she said bitterly.

Holmes expression warmed, and he took her hands in his, offering comfort. "An unhappy accident of birth, but more importantly, you are your mother's daughter. Never forget."

The whistle sounded once more. Edwina looked back at the train with dread and then turned to him holding fiercely onto his hands. "There is so much I want to say to you... so much in my heart," she whispered and reached up, kissing his cheek tenderly. "But I am certain you already know that," she sighed, managing a faint smile as she drew away. "Goodbye Holmes...I hope you'll think of me sometimes... with kindness."

She wiped at her eyes quickly pulling the veil back over her face as she hurried towards the first-class car.

Holmes stared after her vanishing figure - seemingly disoriented by her departure. His eyes scanned the platform and then he unexpectedly lunged towards the bench.

"Wait!" came the sudden cry and Edwina felt strong but gentle hands pulling her to a stop. She turned unsteadily to face him - bewildered.

"Something you've forgotten?" she asked, hope awakening in her eyes.

"No... you" he replied with a mischievous grin as he pressed the handle of the cane into her palm.

Her expression crumbled at the appearance of the cane. " Ohhh, I see... well... thank you," she murmured her disappointment obvious. "I must be going then..." she announced in a dull voice and then turned once more heading towards the car where the porter waited to help her onboard. She made it no further than three steps forward when once again she felt herself being pulled back. This time she turned around with an expression of some impatience and hurt.

"What now? I can't have forgotten anything else. I've nothing left to leave," she protested, her cheeks blushing slightly with annoyance. "I really must go... they are waiting... watching our every move."

Holmes seemed ill at ease and glanced once more towards the train car but drew closer nonetheless. "Yes, I'm well aware, but this time, it is me," he admitted with some trepidation, "something I've overlooked."

There was something in his voice, a resonance she could not recall hearing previously, that gave her pause and transformed her irritation to concern. Forgetting the train for the moment, she threw her veil back so she could get a clearer look at his face. "Tell me," she whispered, her voice tinged with apprehension but controlled, "Is it important? How can I help?"

He paused and seemed to be considering his response. A few moments passed and then he smiled an odd little smile. "You already have," he sighed with an air of resignation.

Edwina gazed up at him utterly bewildered, her confusion only increasing as his hands gently grasped her shoulders and drew her close. "I... I don't understand..." she began but never had the chance to finish as his lips abruptly smothered hers, silencing all words yet demanding her response. The intensity of the kiss left her breathless at first but after a few moments, his ardor seemed to lessen. He slid his lips from hers, tenderly pressing them to her forehead.

"Remember who you are Eddy, guard your heart... and remember, I'll be watching... never too far..." he advised, gently releasing her and giving her a nudge towards the train.

She stared up at him her fingers touching her lips which still tingled from the warmth of his kiss. "I... I..." was all she could manage at first and then took a deep breath, struggling for control as her eyes welled with tears. "Auf Wiedersehen Herr Holmes," she breathed, slowly stepping away - forcing a smile. (Good by Mr. Holmes)

"Bis wir uns wieder treffen Fräulein," he replied. She waited until she could see him no longer and then slowly climbed onboard the train. (Until we meet again Miss).

»»««

BAKER STREET - Early morning hours

The clock was just beginning to chime the hour of 4 am when Watson wearily climbed the stairs, pausing to once more brush the water from his Mackintosh, the miserable weather having resumed outside. He paused at the landing staring at the soft glow coming from under the door to the flat wondering whether he should enter or just go on to his own quarters. It had been a long and trying night, the culmination to an equally trying week. He was exhausted and yet in light of all that had passed, he hesitated unable to shake the feeling of nagging concern. He unlocked the door and entered pausing in the dim firelight for his eyes to adjust.

The room appeared empty, absolutely still and at first, he thought Holmes had retired for the night until he caught sight of the glow of his cigarette from shadow of his wingchair.

"Do shut the door Watson, you're allowing the heat to escape."

Watson fumbled for an answer staring into the shadows... "I thought you had retired..."

There was silence at first followed by a stream of smoke blown in his direction.

426

"As you can see I have not... now... the door," came the eventual reminder.

Watson quickly complied shutting the door. His action was met with a grunt of satisfaction from the wingchair. Brimming with questions, Watson settled into the chair opposite Holmes. He noted that once again the black velvet ribbon dangled from the arm of the chair beneath Holmes' fingers.

Holmes studied him lazily, his face impassive behind the haze of cigarette smoke.

"I trust Miss Morstan is well... no ill effects from the ordeal."

"Tired, but she will be fine... with rest," assured Watson. He knit his brow - concentrating and then finally blurted, "And what of you Holmes? Are you well?"

Holmes narrowed his eyes in suspicion. "What do you mean? Of course, I'm well. Why wouldn't I be?"

Watson grew flustered no longer sure of the wiseness of his queries but unable to derail his thought process. He hedged, stammering, "I only wondered... in light of..."

"In light of what?"

"You know..."

"If I did, I wouldn't ask you," growled Holmes.

Watson took a deep breath and then smiled. "We were on the platform - just across... Mary and I ... and... and we saw... well... you know..."

Holmes stared at him his face suddenly pale, indignation barely concealed. "Spying on me? You disappoint me Watson. I expected better from you... and certainly Miss Morstan."

Watson reddened in embarrassment. "It wasn't intentional," he offered in apology, "but... but we did see."

"What?"

Watson stared at him. "The kiss... you kissed her Holmes."

Holmes was silent at first and only stared at him icily. "I've kissed her before... a buss to the cheek or forehead. What are you going on about? Do you not kiss Mrs. Hudson in greeting or your Aunt or..."?

Watson stared at him in disbelief and then burst into laughter. "No... not like that Holmes. That... that was a kiss... a proper one." He shook his head and grinned in glee at Holmes obvious discomfort.

Holmes compressed his lips and it seemed at first as if he would continue the argument but much to Watson's surprise, he let out a deep sigh and then shrugged, taking a deep draw on his cigarette. "Hmmm... yes... well... I suppose it was," he admitted, his eyes focused on the hearth.

The unexpected admission left Watson speechless for a moment. He leaned closer scanning the detective's face for further clues. "So, so how did you find it then?" he prodded unable to stop himself. He braced himself for the angry rebuttal but instead was met with stony silence.

And then Holmes leaned back in his chair, his eyes focused on some point beyond the flames of the hearth and exhaled deeply. "It was... it was everything I expected Watson, and much more than I deserved..."

Watson sat up a little straighter surprised at the frankness of the answer. But he had one more question to ask. Perhaps the most important one of all. "So... how could you then... how could you walk away? If it had been me... if it had been Mary... I cannot imagine letting..."

"But it was not you," came the fierce reply, "nor was it Mary! It was me Watson, and it was the logical choice ... the rational choice." With a cry of exasperation, Holmes launched himself from the wingchair and crossed to the mantle, the ribbon still dangling, looped around his wrist. "You know my methods Watson, you know my work ethic."

The ferocity of the rebuke left Watson at a loss for words and after a moment, he uttered a deep sigh. "I'm sorry Holmes... I... I meant no disrespect." He reached for his journal which lay on the side table and in an attempt to distract himself from the tension of the moment, began to leaf through the accounts of their adventures. He paused at a fresh page staring at it and then reached for his pen.

Holmes remained at the mantle his back still to Watson. "It wasn't an easy choice Watson, if that is any consolation to you."

An awkward silence fell broken only by the faint scratching of Watson's pen as he began to write. He paused for a moment and glanced over his shoulder towards Holmes.

"So, do you think you'll see her again?"

Holmes was quiet for a moment and then shrugged as he carefully straightened the objects on the mantle. He slipped the ribbon into the pocket of his dressing gown. "Perhaps - seems inevitable... given the Professor's penchant for lawlessness."

Watson looked up, one more question on his lips but decided not to ask and continued to write in his journal. Holmes seemed suddenly aware of the noise of the pen. He frowned and quickly crossed the room. "What the devil are you writing?" he growled and abruptly snatched the journal from Watson's hand. He stared at the page - his face intensifying in color as he read.

Daughter of Evil... The Case of the Missing Emeralds
The Adventure of the Counterfeiter's Daughter

He compressed his lips tightly and then slowly handed the journal back to Watson, his face slowly returning to a normal color though his eyes remained troubled.

"A favour Watson..." he began his voice tightly controlled.

Watson looked up, still a bit shaken from having the journal snatched away.

"Yes Holmes..."

The detective managed a smile. "I do not think this is a suitable tale for your readers. I would ask that you not make an account of it. In fact, I insist."

"Insist?" Watson stared at him in surprise. It wasn't the first time Holmes had asked him to refrain from writing an account but to insist?

Holmes flashed an apologetic smile. "Strongly request then..."

Watson nodded unconvinced. "Why is that?"

Holmes considered the question for a moment. "Because it is an unsatisfactory tale... with no definitive conclusion. A rather distressing trend in current literature. Surely another tale will come along, one more rousing, more suitable to the tastes of your current readership."

"No clear ending..." he repeated. He put his pen down and closed the journal. He was quiet for a few moments and then sighed. "Well, surely there will be an ending Holmes...there has to be."

Holmes paused for a moment, his hands in the pockets of his dressing gown and smiled cryptically.

"Perhaps Watson, but as to when and how, well that remains to be seen."

Made in the USA
Coppell, TX
04 January 2025

43915757R00256